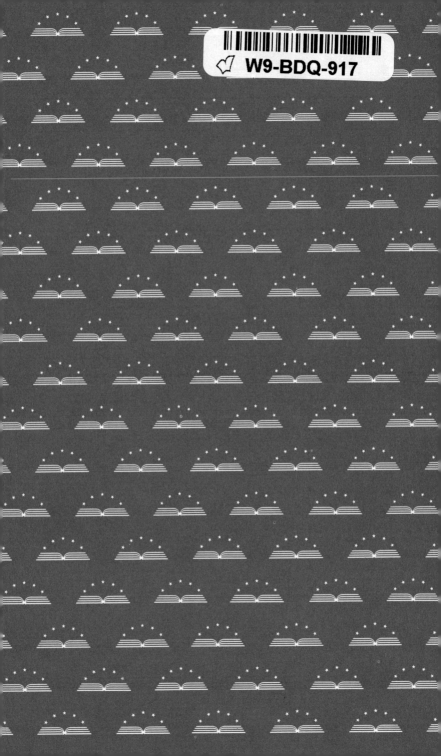

ZORA NEALE HURSTON

ZORA NEALE HURSTON

FOLKLORE, MEMOIRS, AND OTHER WRITINGS

Mules and Men
Tell My Horse
Dust Tracks on a Road
Selected Articles

The paper used in this publication meets the
minimum requirements of the American National Standard
for Information Sciences—Permanence of Paper for Printed
Library Materials, ANSI Z39.48—1984.

Distributed to the trade in the United States
by Penguin Books USA Inc
and in Canada by Penguin Books Canada Ltd.

Library of Congress Catalog Number: 94–21384
For cataloging information, see end of Notes.
ISBN 0–940450–84–4

First Printing
The Library of America—75

Manufactured in the United States of America

CHERYL A. WALL
SELECTED THE CONTENTS AND WROTE
THE NOTES FOR THIS VOLUME

*The restored text of Dust Tracks on a Road,
published here for the first time,
has been established by The Library of America.
Special thanks to Henry Louis Gates, Jr.,
for consultation on this new text.*

*The publishers express their appreciation to
the Beinecke Library at Yale University for the use of
Zora Neale Hurston material.*

Contents

MULES AND MEN

Illustrations by
Miguel Covarrubias

Forward

Ever since the time of Uncle Remus, Negro folk-lore has exerted a strong attraction upon the imagination of the American public. Negro tales, songs and sayings without end, as well as descriptions of Negro magic and voodoo, have appeared; but in all of them the intimate setting in the social life of the Negro has been given very inadequately.

It is the great merit of Miss Hurston's work that she entered into the homely life of the southern Negro as one of them and was fully accepted as such by the companions of her childhood. Thus she has been able to penetrate through that affected demeanor by which the Negro excludes the White observer effectively from participating in his true inner life. Miss Hurston has been equally successful in gaining the confidence of the voodoo doctors and she gives us much that throws a new light upon the much discussed voodoo beliefs and practices. Added to all this is the charm of a loveable personality and of a revealing style which makes Miss Hurston's work an unusual contribution to our knowledge of the true inner life of the Negro.

To the student of cultural history the material presented is valuable not only by giving the Negro's reaction to every day events, to his emotional life, his humor and passions, but it throws into relief also the peculiar amalgamation of African and European tradition which is so important for understanding historically the character of American Negro life, with its strong African background in the West Indies, the importance of which diminishes with increasing distance from the south.

FRANZ BOAS

TO
MY DEAR FRIEND
MRS. ANNIE NATHAN MEYER
WHO HAULED THE MUD TO MAKE ME
BUT LOVES ME JUST THE SAME
— ZORA NEALE HURSTON

Contents

Part II

HOODOO

I

II

III

IV

Introduction

I WAS GLAD when somebody told me, "You may go and collect Negro folk-lore."

In a way it would not be a new experience for me. When I pitched headforemost into the world I landed in the crib of negroism. From the earliest rocking of my cradle, I had known about the capers Brer Rabbit is apt to cut and what the Squinch Owl says from the house top. But it was fitting me like a tight chemise. I couldn't see it for wearing it. It was only when I was off in college, away from my native surroundings, that I could see myself like somebody else and stand off and look at my garment. Then I had to have the spy-glass of Anthropology to look through at that.

Dr. Boas asked me where I wanted to work and I said, "Florida," and gave, as my big reason, that "Florida is a place that draws people—white people from all over the world, and Negroes from every Southern state surely and some from the North and West." So I knew that it was possible for me to get a cross section of the Negro South in the one state. And then I realized that I was new myself, so it looked sensible for me to choose familiar ground.

First place I aimed to stop to collect material was Eatonville, Florida.

And now, I'm going to tell you why I decided to go to my native village first. I didn't go back there so that the home folks could make admiration over me because I had been up North to college and come back with a diploma and a Chevrolet. I knew they were not going to pay either one of these items too much mind. I was just Lucy Hurston's daughter, Zora, and even if I had—to use one of our down-home expressions—had a Kaiser baby,[1] and that's something that hasn't been done in this Country yet, I'd still be just Zora to the neighbors. If I had exalted myself to impress the town, somebody would have sent me word in a match-box that I

[1] Have a child by the Kaiser.

9

had been up North there and had rubbed the hair off of my
head against some college wall, and then come back there
with a lot of form and fashion and outside show to the world.
But they'd stand flat-footed and tell me that they didn't have
me, neither my sham-polish, to study 'bout. And that would
have been that.

I hurried back to Eatonville because I knew that the town
was full of material and that I could get it without hurt, harm
or danger. As early as I could remember it was the habit of
the men folks particularly to gather on the store porch of eve-
nings and swap stories. Even the women folks would stop and
break a breath with them at times. As a child when I was sent
down to Joe Clarke's store, I'd drag out my leaving as long as
possible in order to hear more.

Folk-lore is not as easy to collect as it sounds. The best
source is where there are the least outside influences and these
people, being usually under-privileged, are the shyest. They
are most reluctant at times to reveal that which the soul lives
by. And the Negro, in spite of his open-faced laughter, his
seeming acquiescence, is particularly evasive. You see we are a
polite people and we do not say to our questioner, "Get out
of here!" We smile and tell him or her something that satisfies
the white person because, knowing so little about us, he
doesn't know what he is missing. The Indian resists curiosity
by a stony silence. The Negro offers a feather-bed resistance.
That is, we let the probe enter, but it never comes out. It gets
smothered under a lot of laughter and pleasantries.

The theory behind our tactics: "The white man is always
trying to know into somebody else's business. All right, I'll
set something outside the door of my mind for him to play
with and handle. He can read my writing but he sho' can't
read my mind. I'll put this play toy in his hand, and he will
seize it and go away. Then I'll say my say and sing my song."

I knew that even *I* was going to have some hindrance
among strangers. But here in Eatonville I knew everybody
was going to help me. So below Palatka I began to feel eager
to be there and I kicked the little Chevrolet right along.

I thought about the tales I had heard as a child. How even
the Bible was made over to suit our vivid imagination. How
the devil always outsmarted God and how that over-noble

hero Jack or John—not *John Henry*, who occupies the same place in Negro folk-lore that Casey Jones does in white lore and if anything is more recent—outsmarted the devil. Brer Fox, Brer Deer, Brer 'Gator, Brer Dawg, Brer Rabbit, Ole Massa and his wife were walking the earth like natural men way back in the days when God himself was on the ground and men could talk with him. Way back there before God weighed up the dirt to make the mountains. When I was rounding Lily Lake I was remembering how God had made the world and the elements and people. He made souls for people, but he didn't give them out because he said:

"Folks ain't ready for souls yet. De clay ain't dry. It's de strongest thing Ah ever made. Don't aim to waste none thru loose cracks. And then men got to grow strong enough to stand it. De way things is now, if Ah give it out it would tear them shackly bodies to pieces. Bimeby, Ah give it out."

So folks went round thousands of years without no souls. All de time de soul-piece, it was setting 'round covered up wid God's loose raiment. Every now and then de wind would blow and hist up de cover and then de elements would be full of lightning and de winds would talk. So people told one 'nother that God was talking in de mountains.

De white man passed by it way off and he looked but he wouldn't go close enough to touch. De Indian and de Negro, they tipped by cautious too, and all of 'em seen de light of diamonds when de winds shook de cover, and de wind dat passed over it sung songs. De Jew come past and heard de song from de soul-piece then he kept on passin' and all of a sudden he grabbed up de soul-piece and hid it under his clothes, and run off down de road. It burnt him and tore him and throwed him down and lifted him up and toted him across de mountain and he tried to break loose but he couldn't do it. He kept on hollerin' for help but de rest of 'em run hid 'way from him. Way after while they come out of holes and corners and picked up little chips and pieces that fell back on de ground. So God mixed it up wid feelings and give it out to 'em. 'Way after while when He ketch dat Jew, He's goin' to 'vide things up more ekal'.

So I rounded Park Lake and came speeding down the straight stretch into Eatonville, the city of five lakes, three croquet courts, three hundred brown skins, three hundred good swimmers, plenty guavas, two schools, and no jail-house.

Before I enter the township, I wish to make acknowledgments to Mrs. R. Osgood Mason of New York City. She backed my falling in a hearty way, in a spiritual way, and in addition, financed the whole expedition in the manner of the Great Soul that she is. The world's most gallant woman.

PART ONE

FOLK TALES

I

As I CROSSED the Maitland-Eatonville township line I could see a group on the store porch. I was delighted. The town had not changed. Same love of talk and song. So I drove on down there before I stopped. Yes, there was George Thomas, Calvin Daniels, Jack and Charlie Jones, Gene Brazzle, B. Moseley and "Seaboard." Deep in a game of Florida-flip. All of those who were not actually playing were giving advice—"bet straightening" they call it.

"Hello, boys," I hailed them as I went into neutral.

They looked up from the game and for a moment it looked as if they had forgotten me. Then B. Moseley said, "Well, if it ain't Zora Hurston!" Then everybody crowded around the car to help greet me.

"You gointer stay awhile, Zora?"

"Yep. Several months."

"Where you gointer stay, Zora?"

"With Mett and Ellis, I reckon."

"Mett" was Mrs. Armetta Jones, an intimate friend of mine since childhood and Ellis was her husband. Their house stands under the huge camphor tree on the front street.

"Hello, heart-string," Mayor Hiram Lester yelled as he hurried up the street. "We heard all about you up North. You back home for good, I hope."

"Nope, Ah come to collect some old stories and tales and Ah know y'all know a plenty of 'em and that's why Ah headed straight for home."

"What you mean, Zora, them big old lies we tell when we're jus' sittin' around here on the store porch doin' nothin'?" asked B. Moseley.

"Yeah, those same ones about Ole Massa, and colored folks in heaven, and—oh, y'all know the kind I mean."

"Aw shucks," exclaimed George Thomas doubtfully. "Zora, don't you come here and tell de biggest lie first thing.

Who you reckon want to read all them old-time tales about Brer Rabbit and Brer Bear?"

"Plenty of people, George. They are a lot more valuable than you might think. We want to set them down before it's too late."

"Too late for what?"

"Before everybody forgets all of 'em."

"No danger of that. That's all some people is good for— set 'round and lie and murder groceries."

"Ah know one right now," Calvin Daniels announced cheerfully. "It's a tale 'bout John and de frog."

"Wait till she get out her car, Calvin. Let her get settled at 'Met's' and cook a pan of ginger bread then we'll all go down and tell lies and eat ginger bread. Dat's de way to do. She's tired now from all dat drivin'."

"All right, boys," I agreed. "But Ah'll be rested by night. Be lookin' for everybody."

So I unloaded the car and crowded it into Ellis' garage and got settled. Armetta made me lie down and rest while she cooked a big pan of ginger bread for the company we expected.

Calvin Daniels and James Moseley were the first to show up.

"Calvin, Ah sure am glad that you got here. Ah'm crazy to hear about John and dat frog," I said.

"That's why Ah come so early so Ah could tell it to you and go. Ah got to go over to Wood Bridge a little later on."

"Ah'm glad you remembered me first, Calvin."

"Ah always like to be good as my word, and Ah just heard about a toe-party over to Wood Bridge tonight and Ah decided to make it."

"A toe-party! What on earth is that?"

"Come go with me and James and you'll see!"

"But, everybody will be here lookin' for me. They'll think Ah'm crazy—tellin' them to come and then gettin' out and goin' to Wood Bridge myself. But Ah certainly would like to go to that toe-party."

"Aw, come on. They kin come back another night. You gointer like this party."

"Well, you tell me the story first, and by that time, Ah'll
know what to do."

"Ah, come on, Zora," James urged. "Git de car out. Calvin
kin tell you dat one while we're on de way. Come on, let's go
to de toe-party."

"No, let 'im tell me this one first, then, if Ah go he can tell
me some more on de way over."

James motioned to his friend. "Hurry up and tell it, Calvin,
so we kin go before somebody else come."

"Aw, most of 'em ain't comin' nohow. They all 'bout goin'
to Wood Bridge, too. Lemme tell you 'bout John and dis
frog:

It was night and Ole Massa sent John,[1] his favorite
slave, down to the spring to get him a cool drink of
water. He called John to him.

"John!"

"What you want, Massa?"

"John, I'm thirsty. Ah wants a cool drink of water,
and Ah wants you to go down to de spring and dip me
up a nice cool pitcher of water."

John didn't like to be sent nowhere at night, but he
always tried to do everything Ole Massa told him to do,
so he said, "Yessuh, Massa, Ah'll go git you some!"

Ole Massa said: "Hurry up, John. Ah'm mighty
thirsty."

John took de pitcher and went on down to de spring.
There was a great big ole bull frog settin' right on de
edge of de spring, and when John dipped up de water
de noise skeered de frog and he hollered and jumped
over in de spring.

John dropped de water pitcher and tore out for de big
house, hollerin' "Massa! Massa! A big ole booger[2] done
got after me!"

Ole Massa told him, "Why, John, there's no such
thing as a booger."

"Oh, yes it is, Massa. He down at dat Spring."

[1] Negro story-hero name. See glossary.
[2] A bogey man.

"Don't tell me, John. Youse just excited. Further-more, you go git me dat water Ah sent you after."

"No, indeed, Massa, you and nobody else can't send me back there so dat booger kin git me."

Ole Massa begin to figger dat John musta seen some-thin' sho nuff because John never had disobeyed him before, so he ast: "John, you say you seen a booger. What did it look like?"

John tole him, "Massa, he had two great big eyes lak balls of fire, and when he was standin' up he was sittin' down and when he moved, he moved by jerks, and he had most no tail."

Long before Calvin had ended his story James had lost his air of impatience.

"Now, Ah'll tell one," he said. "That is, if you so desire."

"Sure, Ah want to hear you tell 'em till daybreak if you will," I said eagerly.

"But where's the ginger bread?" James stopped to ask.

"It's out in the kitchen," I said. "Ah'm waiting for de others to come."

"Aw, naw, give us ours now. Them others may not get here before forty o'clock and Ah'll be done et mine and be in Wood Bridge. Anyhow Ah want a corner piece and some of them others will beat me to it."

So I served them with ginger bread and buttermilk.

"You sure going to Wood Bridge with us after Ah git thru tellin' this one?" James asked.

"Yeah, if the others don't show up by then," I conceded.

So James told the story about the man who went to Heaven from Johnstown.

You know, when it lightnings, de angels is peepin' in de lookin' glass; when it thunders, they's rollin' out de rain-barrels; and when it rains, somebody done dropped a barrel or two and bust it.

One time, you know, there was going to be big doin's in Glory and all de angels had brand new clothes to wear and so they was all peepin' in the lookin' glasses, and therefore it got to lightning all over de sky. God tole some of de angels to roll in all de full rain barrels and they was in such a hurry that it was thunderin' from the east to the west and the zigzag lightning went to join the mutterin' thunder and, next thing you know, some of them angels got careless and dropped a whole heap of them rain barrels, and didn't it rain!

In one place they call Johnstown they had a great flood. And so many folks got drownded that it looked jus' like Judgment day.

So some of de folks that got drownded in that flood went one place and some went another. You know, everything that happen, they got to be a nigger in it— and so one of de brothers in black went up to Heben from de flood.

When he got to the gate, Ole Peter let 'im in and made 'im welcome. De colored man was named John, so John ast Peter, says, "Is it dry in dere?"

Ole Peter tole 'im, "Why, yes it's dry in here. How come you ast that?"

"Well, you know Ah jus' come out of one flood, and Ah don't want to run into no mo'. Ooh, man! You ain't *seen* no water. You just oughter seen dat flood we had at Johnstown."

Peter says, "Yeah, we know all about it. Jus' go wid Gabriel and let him give you some new clothes."

So John went on off wid Gabriel and come back all dressed up in brand new clothes and all de time he was changin' his clothes he was tellin' Ole Gabriel all about dat flood, jus' like he didn't know already.

So when he come back from changin' his clothes, they give him a brand new gold harp and handed him to a gold bench and made him welcome. They was so tired of hearing about dat flood they was glad to see him wid his harp 'cause they figgered he'd get to playin' and forget all about it. So Peter tole him, "Now you jus' make yo'self at home and play all de music you please."

John went and took a seat on de bench and commenced to tune up his harp. By dat time, two angels come walkin' by where John was settin' so he throwed down his harp and tackled 'em.

"Say," he hollered, "Y'all want to hear 'bout de big flood Ah was in down on earth? Lawd, Lawd! It sho rained, and talkin' 'bout water!"

Dem two angels hurried on off from 'im jus' as quick as they could. He started to tellin' another one and he took to flyin'. Gab'ull went over to 'im and tried to get 'im to take it easy, but John kept right on stoppin' every angel dat he could find to tell 'im about dat flood of water.

Way after while he went over to Ole Peter and said: "Thought you said everybody would be nice and polite?"

Peter said, "Yeah, Ah said it. Ain't everybody treatin' you right?"

John said, "Naw. Ah jus' walked up to a man as nice and friendly as Ah could be and started to tell 'im 'bout all dat water Ah left back there in Johnstown and instead of him turnin' me a friendly answer he said, 'Shucks! You ain't seen no water!' and walked off and left me standin' by myself."

"Was he a *ole* man wid a crooked walkin' stick?" Peter ast John.

"Yeah."

"Did he have whiskers down to here?" Peter measured down to his waist.

"He sho did," John tol' 'im.

"Aw shucks," Peter tol' 'im. "Dat was Ole Nora.[3] You can't tell *him* nothin' 'bout no flood."

There was a lot of horn-honking outside and I went to the door. The crowd drew up under the mothering camphor tree in four old cars. Everybody in boisterous spirits.

"Come on, Zora! Le's go to Wood Bridge. Great toe-party goin' on. All kinds of 'freshments. We kin tell you some lies most any ole time. We never run outer lies and lovin'. Tell 'em tomorrow night. Come on if you comin'—le's go if you gwine."

[3] Noah.

So I loaded up my car with neighbors and we all went to Wood Bridge. It is a Negro community joining Maitland on the north as Eatonville does on the west, but no enterprising souls have ever organized it. They have no schoolhouse, no post office, no mayor. It is lacking in Eatonville's feeling of unity. In fact, a white woman lives there.

While we rolled along Florida No. 3, I asked Armetta where was the shindig going to be in Wood Bridge. "At Edna Pitts' house," she told me. "But she ain't givin' it by herself; it's for the lodge."

"Think it's gointer be lively?"

"Oh, yeah. Ah heard that a lot of folks from Altamonte and Longwood is comin'. Maybe from Winter Park too."

We were the tail end of the line and as we turned off the highway we could hear the boys in the first car doing what Ellis Jones called bookooing[4] before they even hit the ground. Charlie Jones was woofing[5] louder than anybody else. "Don't y'all sell off all dem pretty li'l pink toes befo' Ah git dere."

Peter Stagg: "Save me de best one!"

Soddy Sewell: "Hey, you mullet heads! Get out de way there and let a real man smoke them toes over."

Gene Brazzle: "Come to my pick, gimme a vaseline brown!"

Big Willie Sewell: "Gimme any kind so long as you gimme more'n one."

Babe Brown, riding a running-board, guitar in hand, said, "Ah want a toe, but if it ain't got a good looking face on to it, don't bring de mess up."

When we got there the party was young. The house was swept and garnished, the refreshments on display, several people sitting around; but the spot needed some social juices to mix the ingredients. In other words, they had the carcass of a party lying around up until the minute Eatonville burst in on it. Then it woke up.

"Y'all done sold off any toes yet?" George Brown wanted to know.

[4]Loud talking, bullying, woofing. From French *beaucoup*.
[5]Aimless talking. See glossary.

Willie Mae Clarke gave him a certain look and asked him, "What's dat got to do with you, George Brown?" And he shut up. Everybody knows that Willie Mae's got the business with George Brown.

"Nope. We ain't had enough crowd, but I reckon we kin start now," Edna said. Edna and a sort of committee went inside and hung up a sheet across one end of the room. Then she came outside and called all of the young women inside. She had to coax and drag some of the girls.

"Oh, Ah'm shame-face-ted!" some of them said.

"Nobody don't want to buy *mah* ole rusty toe." Others fished around for denials from the male side.

I went on in with the rest and was herded behind the curtain.

"Say, what *is* this toe-party business?" I asked one of the girls.

"Good gracious, Zora! Ain't you never been to a toe-party before?"

"Nope. They don't have 'em up North where Ah been and Ah just got back today."

"Well, they hides all de girls behind a curtain and you stick out yo' toe. Some places you take off yo' shoes and some places you keep 'em on, but most all de time you keep 'em on. When all de toes is in a line, sticking out from behind de sheet they let de men folks in and they looks over all de toes and buys de ones they want for a dime. Then they got to treat de lady dat owns dat toe to everything she want. Sometime they play it so's you keep de same partner for de whole thing and sometime they fix it so they put de girls back every hour or so and sell de toes agin."

Well, my toe went on the line with the rest and it was sold five times during the party. Everytime a toe was sold there was a great flurry before the curtain. Each man eager to see what he had got, and whether the other men would envy him or ridicule him. One or two fellows ungallantly ran out of the door rather than treat the girls whose toe they had bought sight unseen.

Babe Brown got off on his guitar and the dancing was hilarious. There was plenty of chicken perleau and baked chicken and fried chicken and rabbit. Pig feet and chitterlings[6] and hot peanuts and drinkables. Everybody was treating wildly.

"Come on, Zora, and have a treat on me!" Charlie Jones insisted. "You done et chicken-ham and chicken-bosom wid every shag-leg in Orange County *but* me. Come on and spend some of *my* money."

"Thanks, Charlie, but Ah got five helpin's of chicken inside already. Ah either got to get another stomach or quit eatin'."

"Quit eatin' then and go to thinking. Quit thinkin' and start to drinkin'. What you want?"

"Coca-Cola right off de ice, Charlie, and put some salt in it. Ah got a slight headache."

"Aw naw, my money don't buy no sweet slop. Choose some coon dick."

"What is coon dick?"

"Aw, Zora, jus' somethin' to make de drunk come. Made out uh grape fruit juice, corn meal mash, beef bones and a few mo' things. Come on le's git some together. It might make our love come down."

As soon as we started over into the next yard where coon dick was to be had, Charlie yelled to the barkeep, "Hey, Seymore! fix up another quart of dat low wine—here come de boom!"

It was handed to us in a quart fruit jar and we went outside to try it.

The raw likker known locally as coon dick was too much. The minute it touched my lips, the top of my head flew off. I spat it out and "choosed" some peanuts. Big Willie Sewell said, "Come on, heart-string, and have some gospel-bird[7] on me. My money spends too." His Honor, Hiram Lester, the Mayor, heard him and said, "There's no mo' chicken left, Willie. Why don't you offer her something she can get?"

"Well there *was* some chicken there when Ah passed the table a little while ago."

"Oh, so you offerin' her some chicken *was*. She can't eat that. What she want is some chicken *is*."

"Aw shut up, Hiram. Come on, Zora, le's go inside and

---

[6] Hog intestines.
[7] Chicken. Preachers are supposed to be fond of them.

make out we dancin'." We went on inside but it wasn't a party any more. Just some people herded together. The high spirits were simmering down and nobody had a dime left to cry so the toe-business suffered a slump. The heaped-up tables of refreshments had become shambles of chicken bones and empty platters anyway so that there was no longer any point in getting your toe sold, so when Columbus Montgomery said, "Le's go to Eatonville," Soddy Sewell jumped up and grabbed his hat and said, "I heard you, buddy."

Eatonville began to move back home right then. Nearly everybody was packed in one of the five cars when the delegation from Altamonte arrived. Johnny Barton and Georgia Burke. Everybody piled out again.

"Got yo' guitar wid you, Johnnie?"

"Man, you know Ah don't go nowhere unless Ah take my box wid me," said Johnnie in his starched blue shirt, collar pin with heart bangles hanging on each end and his cream pants with the black stripe. "And what make it so cool, Ah don't go nowhere unless I play it."

"And when you git to strowin' yo' mess and Georgy gits to singin' her alto, man it's hot as seven hells. Man, play dat 'Palm Beach'."

Babe Brown took the guitar and Johnnie Barton grabbed the piano stool. He sung. Georgia Burke and George Thomas singing about Polk County where the water taste like wine.

My heart struck sorrow, tears come running down.

At about the thirty-seventh verse, something about:

Ah'd ruther be in Tampa with the Whip-poor-will,
Ruther be in Tampa with the Whip-poor-will
Than to be 'round here—
Honey with a hundred dollar bill,

I staggered sleepily forth to the little Chevrolet for Eatonville. The car was overflowing with passengers but I was so dull from lack of sleep that I didn't know who they were. All I knew is they belonged in Eatonville.

Somebody was woofing in my car about love and I asked him about his buddy—I don't know why now. He said, "Ah ain't got no buddy. They kilt my buddy so they could raise me. Jus' so Ah be yo' man Ah don't want no damn buddy. Ah hope they kill every man dat ever cried, 'titty-mamma' but me. Lemme be yo' kid."

Some voice from somewhere else in the car commented, "You sho' Lawd is gointer have a lot of hindrance."

Then somehow I got home and to bed and Armetta had Georgia syrup and waffles for breakfast.

II

THE VERY next afternoon, as usual, the gregarious part of the town's population gathered on the store porch. All the Florida-flip players, all the eleven-card layers.[1] But they yelled over to me they'd be over that night in full. And they were.

"Zora," George Thomas informed me, "you come to de right place if lies is what you want. Ah'm gointer lie up a nation."

Charlie Jones said, "Yeah, man. Me and my sworn buddy Gene Brazzle is here. Big Moose done come down from de mountain."[2]

"Now, you gointer hear lies above suspicion," Gene added.

It was a hilarious night with a pinch of everything social mixed with the story-telling. Everybody ate ginger bread; some drank the buttermilk provided and some provided coon dick for themselves. Nobody guzzled it—just took it in social sips.

But they told stories enough for a volume by itself. Some of the stories were the familiar drummer-type of tale about two Irishmen, Pat and Mike, or two Jews as the case might be. Some were the European folk-tales undiluted, like Jack and the Beanstalk. Others had slight local variations, but Negro imagination is so facile that there was little need for outside help. A'nt Hagar's son, like Joseph, put on his many-colored coat and paraded before his brethren and every man there was a Joseph.

Steve Nixon was holding class meeting across the way at St. Lawrence Church and we could hear the testimony and the songs.[3] So we began to talk about church and preachers.

"Aw, Ah don't pay all dese ole preachers no rabbit-foot,"[4] said Ellis Jones. "Some of 'em is all right but everybody dats up in de pulpit whoopin' and hollerin' ain't called to preach."

[1]Coon-can players. A two-handed card game popular among Southern Negroes.
[2]Important things are about to happen.
[3]See glossary.
[4]I ignore these preachers.

"They ain't no different from nobody else," added B. Moseley. "They mouth is cut cross ways, ain't it? Well, long as you don't see no man wid they mouth cut up and down, you know they'll all lie jus' like de rest of us."

"Yeah; and hard work in de hot sun done called a many a man to preach," said a woman called Gold, for no evident reason. "Ah heard about one man out clearin' off some new ground. De sun was so hot till a grindstone melted and run off in de shade to cool off. De man was so tired till he went and sit down on a log. 'Work, work, work! Everywhere Ah go de boss say hurry, de cap' say run. Ah got a durn good notion not to do nary one. Wisht Ah was one of dese preachers wid a whole lot of folks makin' my support for me.' He looked back over his shoulder and seen a narrer li'l strip of shade along side of de log, so he got over dere and laid down right close up to de log in de shade and said, 'Now, Lawd, if you don't pick me up and chunk me on de other side of dis log, Ah know you done called me to preach.'

"You know God never picked 'im up, so he went off and tol' everybody dat he was called to preach."

"There's many a one been called just lak dat," Ellis corroborated. "Ah knowed a man dat was called by a mule."

"A mule, Ellis? All dem b'lieve dat, stand on they head," said Little Ida.

"Yeah, a mule did call a man to preach. Ah'll show you how it was done, if you'll stand a straightenin'."

"Now, Ellis, don't mislay de truth. Sense us into dis mule-callin' business."

Ellis: These was two brothers and one of 'em was a big preacher and had good collections every Sunday. He didn't pastor nothin' but big charges. De other brother decided he wanted to preach so he went way down in de swamp behind a big plantation to de place they call de prayin' ground, and got down on his knees.

"O Lawd, Ah wants to preach. Ah feel lak Ah got a message. If you done called me to preach, gimme a sign."

Just 'bout dat time he heard a voice, "Wanh, uh wanh! Go preach, go preach, go preach!"

He went and tol' everybody, but look lak he never could git no big charge. All he ever got called was on some saw-mill, half-pint church or some turpentine still. He knocked around lak dat for ten years and then he seen his brother. De big preacher says, "Brother, you don't look like you gittin' holt of much."

"You tellin' dat right, brother. Groceries is scarce. Ah ain't dirtied a plate today."

"Whut's de matter? Don't you git no support from your church?"

"Yeah, Ah gits it such as it is, but Ah ain't never pastored no big church. Ah don't git called to nothin' but saw-mill camps and turpentine stills."

De big preacher reared back and thought a while, then he ast de other one, "Is you sure you was called to preach? Maybe you ain't cut out for no preacher."

"Oh, yeah," he told him. "Ah *know* Ah been called to de ministry. A voice spoke and tol' me so."

"Well, seem lak if God called you He is mighty slow in puttin' yo' foot on de ladder. If Ah was you Ah'd go back and ast 'im agin."

So de po' man went on back to de prayin' ground agin and got down on his knees. But there wasn't no big woods like it used to be. It has been all cleared off. He prayed and said, "Oh, Lawd, right here on dis spot ten years ago Ah ast you if Ah was called to preach and a voice tole me to go preach. Since dat time Ah been strugglin' in Yo' moral vineyard, but Ah ain't gathered no grapes. Now, if you really called me to preach Christ and Him crucified, please gimme another sign."

Sho nuff, jus' as soon as he said dat, de voice said "Wanh-uh! Go preach! Go preach! Go preach!"

De man jumped up and says, "Ah knowed Ah been called. Dat's de same voice. Dis time Ah'm goin ter ast Him where *must* Ah go preach."

By dat time de voice come agin and he looked 'way off and seen a mule in de plantation lot wid his head all stuck out to bray agin, and he said, "Unh hunh, youse de very son of a gun dat called me to preach befo'."

So he went on off and got a job plowin'. Dat's whut he was called to do in de first place.

Armetta said, "A many one been called to de plough and they run off and got up in de pulpit. Ah wish dese mules knowed how to take a pair of plow-lines and go to de church and ketch some of 'em like they go to de lot with a bridle and ketch mules."

Ellis: Ah knowed one preacher dat was called to preach at one of dese split-off churches. De members had done split off from a big church because they was all mean and couldn't git along wid nobody.

Dis preacher was a good man, but de congregation was so tough he couldn't make a convert in a whole year. So he sent and invited another preacher to come and conduct a revival meeting for him. De man he ast to come was a powerful hard preacher wid a good strainin' voice. He was known to get converts.

Well, he come and preached at dis split-off for two whole weeks. De people would all turn out to church and jus' set dere and look at de man up dere strainin' his lungs out and nobody would give de man no encouragement by sayin' "Amen," and not a soul bowed down.

It was a narrer church wid one winder and dat was in de pulpit and de door was in de front end. Dey had a mean ole sexton wid a wooden leg. So de last night of de protracted meetin' de preacher come to church wid his grip-sack in his hand and went on up in de pulpit. When he got up to preach he says, "Brother Sexton, dis bein' de last night of de meetin' Ah wants you to lock de do' and bring me de key. Ah want everybody to stay and hear whut Ah got to say."

De sexton brought him de key and he took his tex and went to preachin'. He preached and he reared and pitched, but nobody said "Amen" and nobody bowed down. So 'way after while he stooped down and opened his suit-satchel and out wid his .44 Special. "Now," he said, "you rounders and brick-bats—yeah, you women,

Ah'm talkin' to you. If you ain't a whole brick, den you must be a bat—and gamblers and 'leven-card layers. Ah done preached to you for two whole weeks and not one of you has said 'Amen,' and nobody has bowed down."

He thowed de gun on 'em. "And now Ah say bow down!" And they beginned to bow all over dat church.

De sexton looked at his wooden leg and figgered he couldn't bow because his leg was cut off above de knee. So he ast, "Me too, Elder?"

"Yeah, you too, you peg-leg son of a gun. You bow down too."

Therefo' dat sexton bent dat wooden leg and bowed down. De preacher fired a couple of shots over they heads and stepped out de window and went on 'bout his business. But he skeered dem people so bad till they all rushed to one side of de church tryin' to git out and carried dat church buildin' twenty-eight miles befo' they thought to turn it loose.

"Now Ellis," chided Gold when she was thru her laughter, "You know dat's a lie. Folks over there in St. Lawrence holdin' class meetin' and you over here lyin' like de crossties from Jacksonville to Key West."

"Naw, dat ain't no lie!" Ellis contended, still laughing himself.

"Aw, yes it 'tis," Gold said. "Dat's all you men is good for—settin' 'round and lyin'. Some of you done quit lyin' and gone to flyin'."

Gene Brazzle said, "Get off of us mens now. We *is* some good. Plenty good too if you git de right one. De trouble is you women ain't good for nothin' exceptin' readin' Sears and Roebuck's bible and hollerin' 'bout, 'gimme dis and gimme dat' as soon as we draw our pay."

Shug[5] said, "Well, we don't git it by astin' you mens for it. If we work for it we kin git it. You mens don't draw no pay. You don't do nothin' but stand around and draw lightnin'."

"Ah don't say Ah'm detrimental," Gene said dryly, "but if Gold and Shug don't stop crackin' us, Ah'm gointer get 'em to go."

[5]Short for sugar.

Gold: Man, if you want me any, some or none, do whut you gointer do and stop cryin'."

Gene: "You ain't seen me cryin'. See me cryin', it's sign of a funeral. If Ah even look cross somebody gointer bleed."

Gold: "Aw, shut up, Gene, you ain't no big hen's biddy if you do lay gobbler eggs. You tryin' to talk like big wood when you ain't nothin' but brush."

Armetta sensed a hard anger creepin' into the teasing so she laughed to make Gene and Gold laugh and asked, "Did y'all have any words before you fell out?"

"We ain't mad wid one 'nother," Gene defended. "We jus' jokin'."

"Well, stop blowin' it and let de lyin' go on," said Charlie Jones. "Zora's gittin' restless. She think she ain't gointer hear no more."

"Oh, no Ah ain't," I lied. After a short spell of quiet, good humor was restored to the porch. In the pause we could hear Pa Henry over in the church house sending up a prayer:

　　. . . You have been with me from the earliest rocking
　　　　of my cradle up until this present moment.
　　You know our hearts, our Father,
　　And all de range of our deceitful minds,
　　And if you find anything like sin lurking
　　In and around our hearts,
　　Ah ast you, My Father, and my Wonder-workin' God
　　To pluck it out

And cast it into de sea of Fuhgitfulness
Where it will never rise to harm us in dis world
Nor condemn us in de judgment.
You heard me when Ah laid at hell's dark door
With no weapon in my hand
And no God in my heart,
And cried for three long days and nights.
You heard me, Lawd,
And stooped so low
And snatched me from the hell
Of eternal death and damnation.
You cut loose my stammerin' tongue;
You established my feet on de rock of Salvation
And yo' voice was heard in rumblin' judgment.
I thank Thee that my last night's sleepin' couch
Was not my coolin' board
And my cover
Was not my windin' sheet.
Speak to de sinner-man and bless 'im.
Touch all those
Who have been down to de doors of degradation.
Ketch de man dat's layin' in danger of consumin' fire;
And Lawd,
When Ah kin pray no mo';
When Ah done drunk down de last cup of sorrow
Look on me, yo' weak servant who feels de least of all;
'Point my soul a restin' place
Where Ah kin set down and praise yo' name forever
Is my prayer for Jesus sake
Amen and thank God.

As the prayer ended the bell of Macedonia, the Baptist church, began to ring.

"Prayer meetin' night at Macedony," George Thomas said.

"It's too bad that it must be two churches in Eatonville," I commented. "De town's too little. Everybody ought to go to one."

"Dey wouldn't do dat, Zora, and you know better. Fack is, de Christian churches nowhere don't stick together," this from Charlie.

Everybody agreed that this was true. So Charlie went on. "Look at all de kind of denominations we got. But de people can't help dat 'cause de church wasn't built on no solid foundation to start wid."

"Oh yes, it 'twas!" Johnnie Mae disputed him. "It was built on solid rock. Didn't Jesus say 'On dis rock Ah build my church?'"

"Yeah," chimed in Antie Hoyt. "And de songs says, 'On Christ de solid rock I stand' and 'Rock of Ages.'"

Charlie was calm and patient. "Yeah, he built it on a rock, but it wasn't solid. It was a pieced-up rock and that's how come de church split up now. Here's de very way it was:

Christ was walkin' long one day wid all his disciples and he said, "We're goin' for a walk today. Everybody pick up a rock and come along." So everybody got their selves a nice big rock 'ceptin' Peter. He was lazy so he picked up a li'l bit of a pebble and dropped it in his side pocket and come along.

Well, they walked all day long and de other 'leven disciples changed them rocks from one arm to de other but they kept on totin' 'em. Long towards sundown they come 'long by de Sea of Galilee and Jesus tole 'em, "Well, le's fish awhile. Cast in yo' nets right here." They done like he tole 'em and caught a great big mess of fish. Then they cooked 'em and Christ said, "Now, all y'all bring up yo' rocks." So they all brought they rocks and Christ turned 'em into bread and they all had a plenty to eat wid they fish exceptin' Peter. He couldn't hardly make a moufful offa de li'l bread he had and he didn't like dat a bit.

Two or three days after dat Christ went out doors and looked up at de sky and says, "Well, we're goin' for another walk today. Everybody git yo'self a rock and come along."

They all picked up a rock apiece and was ready to go. All but Peter. He went and tore down half a mountain. It was so big he couldn't move it wid his hands. He had to take a pinch-bar to move it. All day long Christ walked and talked to his disciples and Peter sweated and strained wid dat rock of his'n.

Way long in de evenin' Christ went up under a great big ole tree and set down and called all of his disciples around 'im and said, "Now everybody bring up yo' rocks."

So everybody brought theirs but Peter. Peter was about a mile down de road punchin' dat half a mountain he was bringin'. So Christ waited till he got dere. He looked at de rocks dat de other 'leven disciples had, den he seen dis great big mountain dat Peter had and so he got up and walked over to it and put one foot up on it and said, "Why Peter, dis is a fine rock you got here! It's a noble rock! And Peter, on dis rock Ah'm gointer build my church."

Peter says, "Naw you ain't neither. You won't build no church house on *dis* rock. You gointer turn dis rock into bread."

Christ knowed dat Peter meant dat thing so he turnt de hillside into bread and dat mountain is de bread he fed de 5,000 wid. Den he took dem 'leven other rocks and glued 'em together and built his church on it.

And that's how come de Christian churches is split up into so many different kinds—cause it's built on pieced-up rock.

There was a storm of laughter following Charlie's tale. "Zora, you come talkin' bout puttin' de two churches together and not havin' but one in dis town," Armetta said chidingly. "You know better'n dat. Baptis' and Methdis' always got a pick out at one 'nother. One time two preachers— one Methdis' an de other one Baptis' wuz on uh train and de engine blowed up and bein' in de colored coach right back of de engine they got blowed up too. When they saw theyself startin' up in de air de Baptis' preacher hollered, 'Ah bet Ah go higher than you!' "

Then Gold spoke up and said, "Now, lemme tell one. Ah know one about a man as black as Gene."

"Whut you always crackin' me for?" Gene wanted to know. "Ah ain't a bit blacker than you."

"Oh, yes you is, Gene. Youse a whole heap blacker than Ah is."

"Aw, go head on, Gold. Youse blacker than me. You jus' look my color cause youse fat. If you wasn't no fatter than me you'd be so black till lightnin' bugs would follow you at twelve o'clock in de day, thinkin' it's midnight."

"Dat's a lie, youse blacker than Ah ever dared to be. Youse lam' black. Youse so black till they have to throw a sheet over yo' head so de sun kin rise every mornin'. Ah know yo' ma cried when she seen *you*."

"Well, anyhow, Gold, youse blacker than me. If Ah was as fat as you Ah'd be a yaller man."

"Youse a liar. Youse as yaller as you ever gointer git. When a person is poor he look bright and de fatter you git de darker you look."

"Is dat yo' excuse for being so black, Gold?"

Armetta soothed Gold's feelings and stopped the war. When the air cleared Gold asked, "Do y'all know how come we are black?"

"Yeah," said Ellis. "It's because two black niggers got together."

"Aw, naw," Gold disputed petulantly. "Well, since you so smart, tell me where dem two black niggers come from in de first beginnin'."

"They musta come from Zar, and dat's on de other side of far."

"Uh, hunh!" Gold gloated. "Ah knowed you didn't know whut you was talkin' about. Now Ah'm goin' ter tell you how come we so black:

Long before they got thru makin' de Atlantic Ocean and haulin' de rocks for de mountains, God was makin' up de people.[6] But He didn't finish 'em all at one time. Ah'm compelled to say dat some folks is walkin' 'round dis town right now ain't finished yet and never will be.

Well, He give out eyes one day. All de nations come up and got they eyes. Then He give out teeth and so on. Then He set a day to give out color. So seven o'clock dat mornin' everybody was due to git they color

[6]See glossary.

except de niggers. So God give everybody they color and they went on off. Then He set there for three hours and one-half and no niggers. It was gettin' hot and God wanted to git His work done and go set in de cool. So He sent de angels. Rayfield and Gab'ull[7] to go git 'em so He could 'tend some mo' business.

They hunted all over Heben till dey found de colored folks. All stretched out sleep on de grass under de tree of life. So Rayfield woke 'em up and tole 'em God wanted 'em.

They all jumped up and run on up to de th'one and they was so skeered they might miss sumpin' they begin to push and shove one 'nother, bumpin' against all de angels and turnin' over foot-stools. They even had de th'one all pushed one-sided.

So God hollered "Git back! Git back!" And they misunderstood Him and thought He said, "Git black," and they been black ever since.

Gene rolled his eyeballs into one corner of his head.

"Now Gold call herself gettin' even wid me—tellin' dat lie. 'Tain't no such a story nowhere. She jus' made dat one up herself."

"Naw, she didn't," Armetta defended. "Ah *been* knowin' dat ole tale."

"Me too," said Shoo-pie.

"Don't you know you can't git de best of no woman in de talkin' game? Her tongue is all de weapon a woman got," George Thomas chided Gene. "She could have had mo' sense, but she told God no, she'd ruther take it out in hips. So God give her her ruthers. She got plenty hips, plenty mouf and no brains."

"Oh, yes, womens is got sense too," Mathilda Moseley jumped in. "But they got too much sense to go 'round braggin' about it like y'all do. De lady people always got de advantage of mens because God fixed it dat way."

"Whut ole black advantage is y'all got?" B. Moseley asked indignantly. "We got all de strength and all de law and all de

[7] The angels Raphael and Gabriel.

money and you can't git a thing but whut we jes' take pity on you and give you."

"And dat's jus' de point," said Mathilda triumphantly. "You *do* give it to us, but how come you do it?" And without waiting for an answer Mathilda began to tell why women always take advantage of men.

You see in de very first days, God made a man and a woman and put 'em in a house together to live. 'Way back in them days de woman was just as strong as de man and both of 'em did de same things. They useter get to fussin' 'bout who gointer do this and that and sometime they'd fight, but they was even balanced and neither one could whip de other one.

One day de man said to hisself, "B'lieve Ah'm gointer go see God and ast Him for a li'l mo' strength so Ah kin whip dis 'oman and make her mind. Ah'm tired of de way things is." So he went on up to God.

"Good mawnin', Ole Father."

"Howdy man. Whut you doin' 'round my throne so soon dis mawnin'?"

"Ah'm troubled in mind, and nobody can't ease mah spirit 'ceptin' you."

God said: "Put yo' plea in de right form and Ah'll hear and answer."

"Ole Maker, wid de mawnin' stars glitterin' in yo' shinin' crown, wid de dust from yo' footsteps makin' worlds upon worlds, wid de blazin' bird we call de sun flyin' out of yo' right hand in de mawnin' and consumin' all day de flesh and blood of stump-black darkness, and comes flyin' home every evenin' to rest on yo' left hand, and never once in all yo' eternal years, mistood de left hand for de right, Ah ast you *please* to give me mo' strength than dat woman you give me, so Ah kin make her mind. Ah know you don't want to be always comin' down way past de moon and stars to be straightenin' her out and it's got to be done. So give me a li'l mo' strength, Ole Maker and Ah'll do it."

"All right, Man, you got mo' strength than woman."

So de man run all de way down de stairs from Heben till he got home. He was so anxious to try his strength on de woman dat he couldn't take his time. Soon's he got in de house he hollered "Woman! Here's yo' boss. God done tole me to handle you in which ever way Ah please. Ah'm yo' boss."

De woman flew to fightin' 'im right off. She fought 'im frightenin' but he beat her. She got her wind and tried 'im agin but he whipped her agin. She got herself together and made de third try on him vigorous but he beat her every time. He was so proud he could whip 'er at last, dat he just crowed over her and made her do a lot of things she didn't like. He told her, "Long as you obey me, Ah'll be good to yuh, but every time yuh rear up Ah'm gointer put plenty wood on yo' back and plenty water in yo' eyes."

De woman was so mad she went straight up to Heben and stood befo' de Lawd. She didn't waste no words. She said, "Lawd, Ah come befo' you mighty mad t'day. Ah want back my strength and power Ah useter have."

"Woman, you got de same power you had since de beginnin'."

"Why is it then, dat de man kin beat me now and he useter couldn't do it?"

"He got mo' strength than he useter have. He come and ast me for it and Ah give it to 'im. Ah gives to them that ast, and you ain't never ast me for no mo' power."

"Please suh, God, Ah'm astin' you for it now. Jus' gimme de same as you give him."

God shook his head. "It's too late now, woman. Whut Ah give, Ah never take back. Ah give him mo' strength than you and no matter how much Ah give you, he'll have mo'."

De woman was so mad she wheeled around and went on off. She went straight to de devil and told him what had happened.

He said, "Don't be dis-incouraged, woman. You listen to me and you'll come out mo' than conqueror. Take dem frowns out yo' face and turn round and go

right on back to Heben and ast God to give you dat
bunch of keys hangin' by de mantel-piece. Then you
bring 'em to me and Ah'll show you what to do wid
'em."

So de woman climbed back up to Heben agin. She
was mighty tired but she was more out-done than she
was tired so she climbed all night long and got back up
to Heben agin. When she got befo' de throne, butter
wouldn't melt in her mouf.

"O Lawd and Master of de rainbow, Ah know yo'
power. You never make two mountains without you put
a valley in between. Ah know you kin hit a straight lick
wid a crooked stick."

"Ast for whut you want, woman."

"God, gimme dat bunch of keys hangin' by yo'
mantel-piece."

"Take 'em."

So de woman took de keys and hurried on back to de
devil wid 'em. There was three keys on de bunch. Devil
say, "See dese three keys? They got mo' power in 'em
than all de strength de man kin ever git if you handle
'em right. Now dis first big key is to de do' of de
kitchen, and you know a man always favors his stomach.
Dis second one is de key to de bedroom and he don't
like to be shut out from dat neither and dis last key is de
key to de cradle and he don't want to be cut off from
his generations at all. So now you take dese keys and go
lock up everything and wait till he come to you. Then
don't you unlock nothin' until he use his strength for
yo' benefit and yo' desires."

De woman thanked 'im and tole 'im, "If it wasn't for
you, Lawd knows whut us po' women folks would do."

She started off but de devil halted her. "Jus' one mo'
thing: don't go home braggin' 'bout yo' keys. Jus' lock
up everything and say nothin' until you git asked. And
then don't talk too much."

De woman went on home and did like de devil tole
her. When de man come home from work she was
settin' on de porch singin' some song 'bout "Peck on de
wood make de bed go good."

When de man found de three doors fastened what useter stand wide open he swelled up like pine lumber after a rain. First thing he tried to break in cause he figgered his strength would overcome all obstacles. When he saw he couldn't do it, he ast de woman, "Who locked dis do'?"

She tole 'im, "Me."

"Where did you git de key from?"

"God give it to me."

He run up to God and said, "God, woman got me locked 'way from my vittles, my bed and my generations, and she say you give her the keys."

God said, "I did, Man, Ah give her de keys, but de devil showed her how to use 'em!"

"Well, Ole Maker, please gimme some keys jus' lak 'em so she can't git de full control."

"No, Man, what Ah give Ah give. Woman got de key."

"How kin Ah know 'bout my generations?"

"Ast de woman."

So de man come on back and submitted hisself to de woman and she opened de doors.

He wasn't satisfied but he had to give in. 'Way after while he said to de woman, "Le's us divide up. Ah'll give you half of my strength if you lemme hold de keys in my hands."

De woman thought dat over so de devil popped and tol her, "Tell 'im, naw. Let 'im keep his strength and you keep yo' keys."

So de woman wouldn't trade wid 'im and de man had to mortgage his strength to her to live. And dat's why de man makes and de woman takes. You men is still braggin' 'bout yo' strength and de women is sittin' on de keys and lettin' you blow off till she git ready to put de bridle on you.

B. Moseley looked over at Mathilda and said, "You just like a hen in de barnyard. You cackle so much you give de rooster de blues."

Mathilda looked over at him archly and quoted:

> Stepped on a pin, de pin bent
> And dat's de way de story went.

"Y'all lady people ain't smarter *than* all men folks. You got plow lines on some of us, but some of us is too smart for you. We go past you jus' like lightnin' thru de trees," Willie Sewell boasted. "And what make it so cool, we close enough to you to have a scronchous time, but never no halter on our necks. Ah know they won't git none on dis last neck of mine."

"Oh, you kin be had," Gold retorted. "Ah mean dat abstifically."

"Yeah? But not wid de trace chains. Never no shack up. Ah want dis tip-in love and tip yo' hat and walk out. Ah don't want nobody to have dis dyin' love for me."

Richard Jones said: "Yeah, man. Love is a funny thing; love is a blossom. If you want yo' finger bit poke it at a possum."

Jack Oscar Jones, who had been quiet for some time, slumped way down in his chair, straightened up and said, "Ah know a speech about love."

Ruth Marshall laughed doubtfully. "Now, Jack, you can't make me b'lieve you know de first thing about no love."

"Yeah he do, too," Clara, Jack's wife defended.

"Whut do he know, then?" Ruth persisted.

"Aw, Lawd," Clara wagged her head knowingly. "You ain't got no business knowing dat. Dat's *us* business. But he know jus' as much about love as de nex' man."

"You don't say!" Johnnie Mae twitted her sister-in-law. "Blow it out, then, Jack, and tell a blind man somethin'."

"Ah'm gointer say it, then me and Zora's goin' out to Montgomery and git up a cool watermelon, ain't we, Zora?"

"If you got de price," I came back. "Ah got de car so all we need is a strong determination and we'll have melon."

"No, Zora ain't goin' nowhere wid my husband," Clara announced. "If he got anything to tell her—it's gointer be right here in front of me."

Jack laughed at Clara's feigned jealousy and recited:

Song Poem

When the clock struck one I had just begun. Begun with Sue, begun with Sal, begun with that pretty Johnson gal.

When the clock struck two, I was through, I was through with Sue, through with Sal, through with that pretty Johnson gal.

When the clock struck three I was free, free with Sue, free with Sal, free with that pretty Johnson gal.

When the clock struck four I was at the door, at the door with Sue, at the door with Sal, at the door with that pretty Johnson gal.

When the clock struck five I was alive, alive with Sue, alive with Sal, alive with that pretty Johnson gal.

When the clock struck six I was fixed, fixed with Sue, fixed with Sal, fixed with that pretty Johnson gal.

When the clock struck seven I was even, even with Sue, even with Sal, even with that pretty Johnson gal.

When the clock struck eight I was at your gate, gate with Sue, gate with Sal, gate with that pretty Johnson gal.

When the clock struck nine I was behind, behind with Sue, behind with Sal, behind with that pretty Johnson gal.

When the clock struck ten I was in the bin, in the bin with Sue, in the bin with Sal, in the bin with that pretty Johnson gal.

When the clock struck eleven, I was in heaven, in heaven with Sue, in heaven with Sal, in heaven with that pretty Johnson gal.

When the clock struck twelve I was in hell, in hell with Sue, in hell with Sal, in hell with that pretty Johnson gal.

"Who was all dis Sue and dis Sal and dat pretty Johnson gal?" Clara demanded of Jack.

"Dat ain't for you to know. My name is West, and Ah'm so different from de rest."

"You sound like one man courtin' three gals, but Ah know a story 'bout three mens courtin' one gal," Shug commented.

"Dat's bogish,"[8] cried Bennie Lee thickly.

"Whut's bogish?" Shug demanded. She and Bennie were step-brother and sister and they had had a lawsuit over the property of his late father and her late mother, so a very little of Bennie's sugar would sweeten Shug's tea and vice versa.

"Ah don't want to lissen to no ole talk 'bout three mens after no one 'oman. It's always more'n three womens after every man."

"Well, de way Ah know de story, there was three mens after de same girl," Shug insisted. "You drunk, Bennie Lee. You done drunk so much of dis ole coon dick till you full of monkies."

"Whut you gointer do?" Bennie demanded. "Whut you gointer do?" No answer was expected to this question. It was just Bennie Lee's favorite retort. "De monkies got me, now whut you gointer do?"

"Ah ain't got you to study about, Bennie Lee. If God ain't payin' you no mo' mind than Ah is, youse in hell right now. Ah ain't talkin' to you nohow. Zora, you wanter hear dis story?"

"Sure, Shug. That's what Ah'm here for."

"Somebody's gointer bleed," Bennie Lee threatened. Nobody paid him any mind.

"God knows Ah don't wanter hear Shug tell nothin'," Bennie Lee complained.

"Ah wish yo' monkies would tell you to go hide in de hammock and forgit to tell you de way home." Shug was getting peeved.

"You better shut up befo' Ah whip yo' head to de red. Ah wish Ah was God. Ah'd turn you into a blamed hawg, and then Ah'd concrete de whole world over so you wouldn't have not one nary place to root."

"Dat's dat two-bits in change you got in yo' pocket now dat's talkin' for you. But befo' de summer's over *you'll* be rootin' lak a hawg. You already lookin' over-plus lak one now. Don't you worry 'bout me."

Bennie Lee tried to ask his well-known question but the coon dick was too strong. He mumbled down into his shirt bosom and went to sleep.

[8]Bogus.

III

"YOUSE in de majority, now Shug," B. Moseley said, seeing Bennie asleep. "Le's hear 'bout dat man wid three women."

Shug said:

Naw, it was three mens went to court a girl, Ah told you. Dis was a real pretty girl wid shiny black hair and coal black eyes. And all dese men wanted to marry her, so they all went and ast her pa if they could have her. He looked 'em all over, but he couldn't decide which one of 'em would make de best husband and de girl, she couldn't make up her mind, so one Sunday night when he walked into de parlor where they was all sittin' and said to 'em, "Well, all y'all want to marry my daughter and youse all good men and Ah can't decide which one will make her de best husband. So y'all be here tomorrow mornin' at daybreak and we'll have a contest and de one dat can do de quickest trick kin have de girl."

Nex' mornin' de first one got up seen it wasn't no water in de bucket to cook breakfas' wid. So he tole de girl's mama to give him de water bucket and he would go to the spring and git her some.

He took de bucket in his hand and then he found out dat de spring was ten miles off. But he said he didn't mind dat. He went on and dipped up de water and hurried on back wid it. When he got to de five-mile post he looked down into de bucket and seen dat de bottom had done dropped out. Then he recollected dat he heard somethin' fall when he dipped up de water so he turned round and run back to de spring and clapped in dat bottom before de water had time to spill.

De ole man thought dat was a pretty quick trick, but de second man says, "Wait a minute. Ah want a grubbin' hoe and a axe and a plow and a harrow." So he got everything he ast for. There was ten acres of wood lot right nex' to de house. He went out dere and chopped down all de trees, grubbed up de roots,

42

ploughed de field, harrowed it, planted it in cow-peas, and had green peas for dinner.

De ole man says "Dat's de quickest trick. Can't nobody beat dat. No use in tryin'. He done won de girl."

De last man said, "You ain't even givin' me a chance to win de girl."

So he took his high-powered rifle and went out into de woods about seben or eight miles until he spied a deer. He took aim and fired. Then he run home, run round behind de house and set his gun down and then run back out in de woods and caught de deer and held 'im till de bullet hit 'im.

So he won de girl.

Robert Williams said:

Ah know another man wid a daughter.

The man sent his daughter off to school for seben years, den she come home all finished up. So he said to her, "Daughter, git yo' things and write me a letter to my brother!" So she did.

He says, "Head it up," and she done so.

"Now tell 'im, 'Dear Brother, our chile is done come home from school and all finished up and we is very proud of her.'"

Then he ast de girl "Is you got dat?"

She tole 'im "yeah."

"Now tell him some mo'. 'Our mule is dead but Ah got another mule and when Ah say (clucking sound of tongue and teeth) he moved from de word.'"

"Is you got dat?" he ast de girl.

"Naw suh," she tole 'im.

He waited a while and he ast her again, "You got dat down yet?"

"Naw suh, Ah ain't got it yet."

"How come you ain't got it?"

"Cause Ah can't spell (clucking sound)."

"You mean to tell me you been off to school seben years and can't spell (clucking sound)? Why Ah could spell dat myself and Ah ain't been to school a day in

mah life. Well jes' say (clucking sound) he'll know what
yo' mean and go on wid de letter."

Henry "Nigger" Byrd said:

I know one about a letter too.
My father owned a fas' horse—I mean a *fast* horse.
We was livin' in Ocala then. Mah mother took sick
and mah father come and said, "Skeet,"—he uster call
me Skeet—"You oughter wire yo' sister in St. Peters-
burg."
"I jus' wired her," I tole him.
"Whut did you put in it?"
I tole 'im.
He says, "Dat ain't right. I'm goin' ketch it." He
went out in de pasture and caught de horse and shod
'im and curried 'im and brushed 'im off good, put de
saddle on 'im and got on 'im, and caught dat telegram
and read it and took it on to mah sister.
Soon as he left de house, mama said, "You chillun
make a fire in de stove and fix somethin' for de ole man
to eat."
Befo' she could git de word out her mouf, him and
mah sister rode up to de do' and said "Whoa!"
By dat time a flea ast me for a shoe-shine so I left.

Armetta said: "Nigger, I didn't know you could lie like
that."
"I ain't lyin', Armetta. We had dat horse. We had a cow too
and she was so sway-backed that she could use de bushy part
of her tail for a umbrella over her head."
"Shet up, Nig!" "Seaboard" Hamilton pretended to be
outraged. "Ah knowed you could sing barytone but Ah
wouldn't a b'lieved de lyin' was in you if Ah didn't hear you
myself. Whut makes you bore wid such a great big augur?"
Little Julius Henry, who should have been home in bed
spoke up. "Mah brother John had a horse 'way back dere in
slavery time."
"Let de dollars hush whilst de nickel speak," Charlie Jones
derided Julius' youth. "Julius, whut make you wanta jump in

a hogshead when a kag[1] will hold yuh? You hear dese hard ole coons lyin' up a nation and you stick in yo' bill."

"If his mouf is cut cross ways and he's two years ole, he kin lie good as anybody else," John French defended. "Blow it, Julius."

Julius spat out into the yard, trying to give the impression that he was skeeting tobacco juice like a man.[2]

De rooster chew t'backer, de hen dip snuff
De biddy can't do it, but he struts his stuff.

Ole John, he was workin' for Massa and Massa had two hawses and he lakted John, so he give John one of his hawses.

When John git to workin' 'em he'd haul off and beat Massa's hawse, but he never would hit his'n. So then some white folks tole ole Massa 'bout John beatin' his hawse and never beatin' his own. So Massa tole John if he ever heard tell of him layin' a whip on his hawse agin he was gointer take and kill John's hawse dead as a nit.

John tole 'im, "Massa, if you kill my hawse, Ah'll beatcher makin' money."

One day John hit ole Massa's hawse agin. Dey went and tole Massa 'bout it. He come down dere where John was haulin' trash, wid a great big ole knife and cut John's hawse's th'oat and he fell dead.

John jumped down off de wagon and skint his hawse, and tied de hide up on a stick and throwed it cross his shoulder, and went on down town.

Ole John was a fortune teller hisself but nobody 'round dere didn't know it. He met a man and de man ast John, "Whut's dat you got over yo' shoulder dere, John?"

"It's a fortune teller, boss."

"Make it talk some, John, and I'll give you a sack of money and a hawse and saddle, and five head of cattle."

John put de hide on de ground and pulled out de

[1] Keg.
[2] This story is of European origin, but has been colored by the negro mouth.

stick and hit 'cross de hawse hide and hold his head down dere to lissen.

"Dere's a man in yo' bed-room behind de bed talkin' to yo' wife."

De man went inside his house to see. When he come back out he said, "Yeah, John, you sho tellin' de truth. Make him talk some mo'."

John went to puttin' de stick back in de hide. "Naw, Massa, he's tired now."

De white man says, "Ah'll give you six head of sheeps and fo' hawses and fo' sacks of money."

John pulled out de stick and hit down on de hide and hold down his head to lissen.

"It's a man in yo' kitchen openin' yo' stove." De man went back into his house and come out agin and tole John, "Yo' fortune-teller sho is right. Here's de things Ah promised you."

John rode on past Ole Massa's house wid all his sacks of money and drivin' his sheeps and cattle, whoopin' and crackin' his whip. "Yee, whoo-pee, yee!" Crack!

Massa said, "John, where did you git all dat?"

John said, "Ah tole you if you kilt mah hawse Ah'd beatcher makin' money."

Massa said to 'im, "Reckon if Ah kilt mah hawse Ah'd make dat much money?"

"Yeah, Massa, Ah reckon so."

So ole Massa went out and kilt his hawse and went to town hollerin', "Hawse hide for sale! Hawse hide for sale!"

One man said, "Hold on dere. Ah'll give you two-bits for it to bottom some chears."

Ole Massa tole 'im, "Youse crazy!" and went on hollerin' "Hawse hide for sale!"

"Ah'll gi' you twenty cents for it to cover some chears," another man said.

"You must be stone crazy! Why, dis hide is worth five thousand dollars."

De people all laughed at 'im so he took his hawse hide and throwed it away and went and bought hisself another hawse.

Ole John, he already rich, he didn't have to work but he jus' love to fool 'round hawses so he went to drivin' hawse and buggy for Massa. And when nobody wasn't wid him, John would let his grandma ride in Massa's buggy. Dey tole ole Massa 'bout it and he said, "John, Ah hear you been had yo' grandma ridin' in mah buggy. De first time Ah ketch her in it, Ah'm gointer kill 'er."

John tole 'im, "If you kill my grandma, Ah'll beatcher makin' money."

Pretty soon some white folks tole Massa dat John was takin' his gran'ma to town in his buggy and was hittin' his hawse and showin' off. So ole Massa come out dere and cut John's gran'ma's th'oat.

So John buried his gran'ma in secret and went and got his same ole hawse hide and keered it up town agin and went 'round talkin' 'bout, "Fortune-teller, fortune-teller!"

One man tole 'im, "Why, John, make it talk some for me. Ah'll give you six head of goats, six sheeps, and a hawse and a saddle to ride 'im wid."

So John made it talk and de man was pleased so he give John more'n he promised 'im, and John went on back past Massa's house wid his stuff so ole Massa could see 'im.

Ole Massa run out and ast, "Oh, John, where did you git all dat?"

John said, "Ah tole you if you kill mah gran'ma Ah'd beatcher makin' money."

Massa said, "You reckon if Ah kill mine, Ah'll make all dat?"

"Yeah, Ah reckon so."

So Massa runned and cut his gran'ma's th'oat and went up town hollerin' "gran'ma for sale! gran'ma for sale!"

Wouldn't nobody break a breath wid him. Dey thought he was crazy. He went on back home and grabbed John and tole 'im, "You made me kill my gran'ma and my good hawse and Ah'm gointer throw you in de river."

John tole 'im, "If you throw me in de river, Ah'll beatcher makin' money."

"Naw you won't neither," Massa tole 'im. "You done made yo' last money and done yo' las' do."

He got ole John in de sack and keered 'im down to de river, but he done forgot his weights, so he went back home to git some.

While he was gone after de weights a toad frog come by dere and John seen 'im. So he hollered and said, "Mr. Hoptoad, if you open dis sack and let me out Ah'll give you a dollar."

Toad frog let 'im out, so he got a soft-shell turtle and put it in de sack wid two big ole bricks. Then ole Massa got his weights and come tied 'em on de sack and throwed it in de river.

Whilst Massa was down to de water foolin' wid dat sack, John had done got out his hawse hide and went on up town agin hollerin', "Fortune-teller! fortune-teller!"

One rich man said "Make it talk for me, John."

John pulled out de stick and hit on de hide, and put his ear down. "Uh man is in yo' smoke-house stealin' meat and another one is in yo' money-safe."

De man went inside to see and when he come back he said, "You sho kin tell de truth."

So John went by Massa's house on a new hawse, wid a sack of money tied on each side of de saddle. Ole Massa seen 'im and ast, "Oh, John, where'd you git all dat?"

"Ah tole you if you throw me in de river Ah'd beatcher makin' money."

Massa ast, "Reckon if Ah let you throw me in de river, Ah'd make all dat?"

"Yeah, Massa, Ah *know* so."

John got ole Massa in de sack and keered 'im down to de river. John didn't forgit *his* weights. He put de weights on ole Massa and jus' befo' he throwed 'im out he said, "Good-bye, Massa, Ah hope you find all you lookin' for."

And dat wuz de las' of ole Massa.

"Dat wuz a long tale for a li'l boy lak you," George Thomas praised Julius.

"Ah knows a heap uh tales," Julius retorted.

Whut is de workinest pill you ever seen? Lemme tell you whut kind of a pill it was and how much it worked.

It wuz a ole man one time and he had de rheumatism so bad he didn't know what to do. Ah tole 'im to go to town and git some of dem conthartic pills.[3]

He went and got de pills lak Ah tole 'im, but on his way back he opened de box and went to lookin' at de pills. He wuz comin' cross some new ground where dey hadn't even started to clear up de land. He drop one of de pills but he didn't bother to pick it up—skeered he might hurt his back stoopin' over.

He got to de house and say, "Ole lady, look down yonder whut a big smoke! Whut is dat, nohow?"

She say, "Ah don't know."

"Well," he say. "Guess Ah better walk down dere and see whut dat big smoke *is* down dere."

He come back. "Guess whut it is, ole lady? One of dem conthartic pills done worked all dem roots out de ground and got 'em burning!"

"Julius, you little but you loud. Dat's a over average lie you tole," Shug laughed. "Lak de wind Ah seen on de East Coast. It blowed a crooked road straight and blowed a well up out de ground and blowed and blowed until it scattered de days of de week so bad till Sunday didn't come till late Tuesday evenin'."

"Shug, Whuss yuh gonna do?" Bennie Lee tried to rise to the surface but failed and slumped back into slumber.

"A good boy, but a po' boy," somebody commented as John French made his mind up.

"Zora, Ah'm gointer tell one, but you be sho and tell de folks Ah tole it. Don't say Seymore said it because he took you on de all-day fishin' trip to Titusville. Don't say Seaboard

[3]Compound cathartic.

Hamilton tole it 'cause he always give you a big hunk of barbecue when you go for a sandwich. Give ole John French
whut's comin' to 'im."

"You gointer tell it or you gointer spend de night tellin' us
you gointer tell it?" I asked.

Ah got to say a piece of litery (literary) fust to git mah
wind on.
Well Ah went up on dat meat-skin
And Ah come down on dat bone
And Ah grabbed dat piece of corn-bread
And Ah made dat biscuit moan.
Once a man had two sons. One was name Jim and de
other one dey call him Jack for short. Dey papa was a
most rich man, so he called de boys to 'im one night
and tole 'em, "Ah don't want y'all settin' 'round waitin'
for me tuh die tuh git whut Ah'm gointer give yuh.
Here's five hundred dollars apiece. Dat's yo' sheer of de
proppity. Go put yo'selves on de ladder. Take and make
men out of yourselves."

Jim took his and bought a big farm and a pair of
mules and settled down.

Jack took his money and went on down de road
skinnin' and winnin'. He won from so many mens till he
had threbbled his money. Den he met a man says,
"Come on, le's skin some." De man says "Money on de
wood" and he laid down a hundred dollars.

Jack looked at de hund'ud dollars and put down five
hund'ud and says, "Man, Ah ain't for no spuddin'.[4] You
playin' wid yo' stuff out de winder.[5] You fat 'round de
heart.[6] Bet some money."

De man covered Jack's money and dey went to
skinnin'. Jack was dealin' and he thought he seen de
other man on de turn so he said, "Five hund'ud mo' my
ten spot is de bes'."

De other man covered 'im and Jack slapped down an-

[4]Playing for small change.
[5]Risking nothing, i.e. hat, coat and shoes out the window so that the
owner can run if he loses.
[6]Scared.

other five hund'ud and said, "Five hund'ud mo' you fall dis time."

De other man never said a word. He put down five hund'ud mo'.

Jack got to singin':
"When yo' card git-uh lucky, oh pardner
You oughter be in a rollin' game."

He flipped de card and bless God it wuz de ten spot! Jack had done fell hisself instead of de other man. He was all put out.

Says, "Well, Ah done los' all mah money so de game is through."

De other man say, "We kin still play on. Ah'll bet you all de money on de table against yo' life."

Jack agreed to play 'cause he figgered he could out-shoot and out-cut any man on de road and if de man tried to kill *him* he'd git kilt hisself. So dey shuffled agin and Jack pulled a card and it fell third in hand.

Den de man got up and he was twelve foot tall and Jack was so skeered he didn't know whut to do. De man looked down on 'im and tole 'im says, "De Devil[7] is mah name and Ah live across de deep blue sea. Ah could kill you right now, but Ah'll give yuh another chance. If you git to my house befo' de sun sets and rise agin Ah won't kill yuh, but if you don't Ah'll be compelled to take yo' life."

Den he vanished.

Jack went on down de road jus' a cryin' till he met uh ole man.

Says, "Whuss de matter, Jack?"

"Ah played skin wid de Devil for mah life and he winned and tole me if Ah ain't to his house by de time de sun sets and rise agin he's gointer take mah life, and he live way across de ocean."

De ole man says, "You sho is in a bad fix, Jack. Dere ain't but one thing dat kin cross de ocean in dat time."

"Whut is dat?"

[7]See glossary.

"It's uh bald eagle. She come down to de edge of de ocean every mornin' and dip herself in de sea and pick off all de dead feathers. When she dip herself de third time and pick herself she rocks herself and spread her wings and mount de sky and go straight across de deep blue sea. And every time she holler, you give her piece uh dat yearlin' or she'll eat you.

"Now if you could be dere wid a yearlin' bull and when she git thru dippin' and pick herself and rock to mount de sky and jump straddle of her back wid dat bull yearlin' you could make it."

Jack wuz dere wid de yearlin' waitin' for dat eagle to come. He wuz watchin' her from behind de bushes and seen her when she come out de water and picked off de dead feather and rocked to go on high.

He jumped on de eagle's back wid his yearlin' and de eagle was out flyin' de sun. After while she turned her head from side to side and her blazin' eyes lit up first de north den de south and she hollered, "Ah-h-h, Ah, ah! One quarter cross de ocean! Don't see nothin' but blue water, uh!"

Jack was so skeered dat instead of him givin' de eagle uh quarter of de meat, he give her de whole bull. After while she say, "Ah-h-h, ah, ah! One half way cross de ocean! Don't see nothin' but blue water!"

Jack didn't have no mo' meat so he tore off one leg and give it to her. She swallowed dat and flew on. She hollered agin, "Ah-h-h. Ah, ha! Mighty nigh cross de ocean! Don't see nothin' but blue water! Uh!"

Jack tore off one arm and give it to her and she et dat and pretty soon she lit on land and Jack jumped off and de eagle flew on off to her nest.

Jack didn't know which way de Devil lived so he ast. "Dat first big white house 'round de bend in de road," dey tole 'im.

Jack walked to de Devil's house and knocked on de do'.

"Who's dat?"

"One of de Devil's friends. One widout uh arm and widout uh leg."

Devil tole his wife, says: "Look behind de do' and hand dat man uh arm and leg." She give Jack de arm and leg and Jack put 'em on.

Devil says, "See you got here in time for breakfas'. But Ah got uh job for yuh befo' you eat. Ah got uh hund'ud acres uh new ground ain't never had uh brush cut on it. Ah want you to go out dere and cut down all de trees and brushes, grub up all de roots and pile 'em and burn 'em befo' dinner time. If you don't, Ah'll hafta take yo' life."

Jus' 'bout dat time de Devil's chillen come out to look at Jack and he seen he had one real pretty daughter, but Jack wuz too worried to think 'bout no girls. So he took de tools and went on out to de wood lot and went to work.

By de time he chopped down one tree he wuz tired and he knowed it would take 'im ten years to clear dat ground right, so Jack set down and went to cryin'. 'Bout dat time de Devil's pretty daughter come wid his breakfas'. "Whuss de matter, Jack?"

"Yo papa done gimme uh job he know Ah can't git through wid, and he's gonna take mah life and Ah don't wanna die."

"Eat yo' breakfas' Jack, and put yo' head in mah lap and go to sleep."

Jack done lak she tole 'im and went to sleep and when he woke up every tree was down, every bush — and de roots grubbed up and burnt. Look lak never had been a blade uh grass dere.

De Devil come out to see how Jack wuz makin' out and seen dat hundred acres cleaned off so nice and said, "Uh, huh, Ah see youse uh wise man, 'most wise as me. Now Ah got another job for yuh. Ah got uh well, uh hundred feet deep and Ah want yuh to dip it dry. Ah mean dry, Ah want it so dry till Ah kin see dust from it and den Ah want you to bring me whut you find at de bottom."

Jack took de bucket and went to de well and went to work but he seen dat de water wuz comin' in faster dan he could draw it out. So he sat down and begin to cry.

De Devil's daughter come praipsin long wid Jack's dinner and seen Jack settin' down cryin'. "Whuss de matter, Jack? Don't cry lak dat lessen you wanta make me cry too."

"Yo' pa done put me to doin' somethin' he know Ah can't never finish and if Ah don't git thru he is gonna take mah life."

"Eat yo' dinner, Jack and put yo' head in mah lap and go to sleep."

Jack done lak she tole 'im and when he woke up de well wuz so dry till red dust wuz boilin' out of it lak smoke. De girl handed 'im a ring and tole 'im "Give papa dis ring. Dat's whut he wanted. It's mama's ring and she lost it in de well de other day."

When de devil come to see whut Jack wuz doin', Jack give 'im de ring and de devil looked and seen all dat dust pourin' out de well. He say, "Ah see youse uh very smart man. Almos' as wise as me. All right, Ah got just one mo' job for you and if you do dat Ah'll spare yo' life and let you marry mah daughter to boot. You take dese two geeses and go up dat cocoanut palm tree and pick 'em, and bring me de geeses when you git 'em picked and bring me every feather dat come off 'em. If you lose one Ah'll have to take yo life."

Jack took de two geeses and clammed up de cocoanut palm tree and tried to pick dem geeses. But he was more'n uh hundred feet off de ground and every time he'd pull uh feather offen one of dem birds, de wind would blow it away. So Jack began to cry agin. By dat time Beatrice Devil come up wid his supper. "Whuss de matter, Jack?"

"Yo' papa is bound tuh kill me. He know Ah can't pick no geeses up no palm tree, and save de feathers."

"Eat yo' supper Jack and lay down in mah lap."

When Jack woke up all both de geeses wuz picked and de girl had all de feathers even; she had done caught dem out de air dat got away from Jack. De Devil said "Well, now you done everything Ah tole you, you kin have mah daughter. Y'all take dat ole house down de road apiece. Dat's where me and her ma got our start."

So Jack and de Devil's daughter got married and went to keepin' house.

Way in de night, Beatrice woke up and shook Jack. "Jack! Jack! Wake up! Papa's comin' here to kill you. Git up and go to de barn. He got two horses dat kin jump a thousand miles at every jump. One is named Hallowed-be-thy-name and de other, Thy-kingdom-come. Go hitch 'em to dat buck board and head 'em dis way and le's go."

Jack run to de barn and harnessed de hawses and headed towards de house where his wife wuz at. When he got to de do' she jumped in and hollered, "Le's go, Jack. Papa's comin' after us!"

When de Devil got to de house to kill Jack and found out Jack wuz gone, he run to de barn to hitch up his fas' hawses. When he seen dat dey wuz gone, he hitched up his jumpin' bull dat could jump five hundred miles at every jump, and down de road, baby!

De Devil wuz drivin' dat bull! Wid every jump he'd holler, "Oh! Hallowed-be-thy-name! Thy-kingdom-come!" And every time de hawses would hear 'im call 'em they'd fall to they knees and de bull would gain on 'em.

De girl say, "Jack, he's 'bout to ketch us! Git out and drag yo' feet backwards nine steps, throw some sand over yo' shoulders and le's go!"

Jack done dat and de hawses got up and off they went, but every time they hear they master's voice they'd stop till de girl told Jack to drag his foot three times nine times and he did it and they gained so fast on de Devil dat de hawses couldn't hear 'im no mo', and dey got away.

De Devil passed uh man and he say, "Is you seen uh man in uh buck board wid uh pretty girl wid coal black hair and red eyes behind two fas' hawses?"

De man said, "No, Ah speck dey done made it to de

mountain and if dey gone to de mountain you can't overtake 'em.'"

Jack and his wife wuz right dere den listenin' to de Devil. When de daughter saw her pa comin' she turned herself and de hawses into goats and they wuz croppin' grass. Jack wuz so tough she couldn't turn him into nothin' so she saw a holler log and she tole 'im to go hide in it, which he did. De Devil looked all around and he seen dat log and his mind jus' tole 'im to go look in it and he went and picked de log up and said, "Ah, ha! Ah gotcher!"

Jack wuz so skeered inside dat log he begin to call on de Lawd and he said, "O Lawd, have mercy."

You know de Devil don't lak tuh hear de name uh de Lawd so he throwed down dat log and said "Damn it! If Ah had of knowed dat God wuz in dat log Ah never would a picked it up."

So he got back in and picked up de reins and hollered to de bull, "Turn, bull, turn! Turn clean roh-hound. Turn bull tu-urn, turn clee-ean round!"

De jumpin' bull turnt so fast till he fell and broke his own neck and throwed de Devil out on his head and kilt 'im. So dat's why dey say Jack beat de Devil.

"Boy, how kin you hold all dat in yo' head?" Jack Jones asked John. "Bet if dat lie was somethin' to do yuh some good yuh couldn't remember it."

Johnnie Mae yawned wide open and Ernest seeing her called out, "Hey, there, Johnnie Mae, throw mah trunk out befo' you shet up dat place!"

This reflection upon the size of her mouth peeved Johnnie Mae no end and she and Ernest left in a red hot family argument. Then everybody else found out that they were sleepy. So in the local term everybody went to the "pad."

Lee Robinson over in the church was leading an ole spiritual, "When I come to Die," to which I listened with one ear, while I heard the parting quips of the story-tellers with the other.

Though it was after ten the street lights were still on. B. Moseley had not put out the lights because the service in the church was not over yet, so I sat on the porch for a while looking towards the heaven-rasping oaks on the back street, towards the glassy sliver of Lake Sabelia. Over in the church I could hear Mrs. Laura Henderson finishing her testimony . . . "to make Heben mah home when Ah come to die. Oh, Ah'll never forget dat day when de mornin' star bust in mah heart! Ah'll never turn back! O evenin' sun, when you git on de other side, tell mah Lawd Ah'm here prayin'."

The next afternoon I sat on the porch again. The young'uns had the grassy lane that ran past the left side of the house playing the same games that I had played in the same

lane years before. With the camphor tree as a base, they played "Going 'Round de Mountain." Little Hubert Alexander was in the ring. The others danced rhythmically 'round him and sang:

> Going around de mountain two by two
> Going around de mountain two by two
> Tell me who love sugar and candy.

Now, show me your motion, two by two
Show me your motion two by two
Tell me who love sugar and candy.

I tried to write a letter but the games were too exciting.

"Little Sally Walker," "Draw a bucket of water," "Sissy in de barn," and at last that most raucous, popular and most African of games, "Chirck, mah Chick, mah Craney crow." Little Harriet Staggers, the smallest girl in the game, was contending for the place of the mama hen. She fought hard, but the larger girls promptly overruled her and she had to take her place in line behind the other little biddies, two-year-old Donnie Brown, being a year younger than Harriet, was the hindmost chick.

During the hilarious uproar of the game, Charlie Jones and Bubber Mimms came up and sat on the porch with me.

"Good Lawd, Zora! How kin you stand all dat racket? Why don't you run dem chaps 'way from here?" Seeing his nieces, Laura and Melinda and his nephew, Judson, he started to chase them off home but I made him see that it was a happy accident that they had chosen the lane as a playground. That I was enjoying it more than the chaps.

That settled, Charlie asked, "Well, Zora, did we lie enough for you las' night?"

"You lied good but not enough," I answered.

"Course, Zora, you ain't at de right place to git de bes' lies. Why don't you go down 'round Bartow and Lakeland and 'round in dere—Polk County? Dat's where they really lies up a mess and dats where dey makes up all de songs and things lak dat. Ain't you never hea'd dat in Polk County de water drink lak cherry wine?"

"Seems like when Ah was a child 'round here Ah heard de folks pickin' de guitar and singin' songs to dat effect."

"Dat's right. If Ah was you, Ah'd drop down dere and see. It's liable to do you a lot uh good."

"If Ah wuz in power[8] Ah'd go 'long wid you, Zora," Bubber added wistfully. "Ah learnt all Ah know 'bout pickin' de box[9] in Polk County. But Ah ain't even got money essence.

[8]Funds.
[9]Playing the guitar.

'Tain't no mo' hawgs 'round here. Ah cain't buy no chickens. Guess Ah have tuh eat gopher.[10]

"Where you gointer git yo' gophers, Bubber?" Charlie asked. "Doc Biddy and his pa done 'bout cleaned out dis part of de State."

"Oh, Ah got a new improvement dat's gointer be a lot of help to me and Doc Biddy and all of us po' folks."

"What is it, Bubber?"

"Ah'm gointer prune a gang of soft-shells (turtles) and grow me some gophers."

The sun slid lower and lower and at last lost its grip on the western slant of the sky and dipped three times into the bloody sea — sending up crimson spray with each plunge. At last it sunk and night roosted on the tree-tops and houses.

Bubber picked the box and Charlie sang me songs of the railroad camps. Among others, he taught me verses of JOHN HENRY, the king of railroad track-laying songs which runs as follows:[11]

> John Henry driving on the right hand side,
> Steam drill driving on the left,
> Says, 'fore I'll let your steam drill beat me down
> I'll hammer my fool self to death,
> Hammer my fool self to death.

> John Henry told his Captain,
> When you go to town
> Please bring me back a nine pound hammer
> And I'll drive your steel on down,
> And I'll drive your steel on down.

> John Henry told his Captain,
> Man ain't nothing but a man,
> And 'fore I'll let that steam drill beat me down
> I'll die with this hammer in my hand,
> Die with this hammer in my hand.

> Captain ast John Henry,
> What is that storm I hear?

[10]Dry land tortoise.
[11]See glossary.

He says Cap'n that ain't no storm,
'Tain't nothing but my hammer in the air,
Nothing but my hammer in the air.

John Henry told his Captain,
Bury me under the sills of the floor,
So when they get to playing good old Georgy skin,
Bet 'em fifty to a dollar more,
Fifty to a dollar more.

John Henry had a little woman,
The dress she wore was red,
Says I'm going down the track,
And she never looked back.
I'm going where John Henry fell dead,
Going where John Henry fell dead.

Who's going to shoe your pretty lil feet?
And who's going to glove your hand?
Who's going to kiss your dimpled cheek?
And who's going to be your man?
Who's going to be your man?

My father's going to shoe my pretty lil feet;
My brother's going to glove my hand;
My sister's going to kiss my dimpled cheek;
John Henry's going to be my man,
John Henry's going to be my man.

Where did you get your pretty lil dress?
The shoes you wear so fine?
I got my shoes from a railroad man,
My dress from a man in the mine,
My dress from a man in the mine.

They talked and told strong stories of Ella Wall, East Coast
Mary, Planchita and lesser jook[12] lights around whom the
glory of Polk County surged. Saw-mill and turpentine bosses
and prison camp "cap'ns" set to music passed over the guitar

[12]A fun house. Where they sing, dance, gamble, love, and compose "blues"
songs incidentally.

strings and Charlie's mouth and I knew I had to visit Polk County right now.

A hasty good-bye to Eatonville's oaks and oleanders and the wheels of the Chevvie split Orlando wide open—headed southwest for corn (likker) and song.

IV

TWELVE MILES below Kissimmee I passed under an arch that marked the Polk County line. I was in the famed Polk County. How often had I heard "Polk County Blues."

"You don't know Polk County lak Ah do.
Anybody been dere, tell you de same thing too."

The asphalt curved deeply and when it straightened out we saw a huge smoke-stack blowing smut against the sky. A big sign said, "Everglades Cypress Lumber Company, Loughman, Florida."

We had meant to keep on to Bartow or Lakeland and we debated the subject between us until we reached the opening, then I won. We went in. The little Chevrolet was all against it. The thirty odd miles that we had come, it argued, was nothing but an appetizer. Lakeland was still thirty miles away and no telling what the road held. But it sauntered on down the bark-covered road and into the quarters just as if it had really wanted to come.

We halted beside two women walking to the commissary and asked where we could get a place to stay, despite the signs all over that this was private property and that no one could enter without the consent of the company.

One of the women was named "Babe" Hill and she sent me to her mother's house to get a room. I learned later that Mrs. Allen ran the boarding-house under patronage of the company. So we put up at Mrs. Allen's.

That night the place was full of men—come to look over the new addition to the quarters. Very little was said directly to me and when I tried to be friendly there was a noticeable disposition to *fend* me off. This worried me because I saw at once that this group of several hundred Negroes from all over the South was a rich field for folk-lore, but here was I figuratively starving to death in the midst of plenty.

Babe had a son who lived at the house with his grandmother and we soon made friends. Later the sullen Babe and

I got on cordial terms. I found out afterwards that during the Christmas holidays of 1926 she had shot her husband to death, had fled to Tampa where she had bobbed her hair and eluded capture for several months but had been traced thru letters to her mother and had been arrested and lodged in Bartow jail. After a few months she had been allowed to come home and the case was forgotten. Negro women *are* punished in these parts for killing men, but only if they exceed the quota. I don't remember what the quota is. Perhaps I did hear but I forgot. One woman had killed five when I left that turpentine still where she lived. The sheriff was thinking of calling on her and scolding her severely.

James Presley used to come every night and play his guitar. Mrs. Allen's temporary brother-in-law could play a good second but he didn't have a box so I used to lend him mine. They would play. The men would crowd in and buy soft drinks and woof at me, the stranger, but I knew I wasn't getting on. The ole feather-bed tactics.

Then one day after Cliffert Ulmer, Babe's son, and I had driven down to Lakeland together he felt close enough to tell me what was the trouble. They all thought I must be a revenue officer or a detective of some kind. They were accustomed to strange women dropping into the quarters, but not in shiny gray Chevrolets. They usually came plodding down the big road or counting railroad ties. The car made me look too prosperous. So they set me aside as different. And since most of them were fugitives from justice or had done plenty time, a detective was just the last thing they felt they needed on that "job."

I took occasion that night to impress the job with the fact that I was also a fugitive from justice, "bootlegging." They were hot behind me in Jacksonville and they wanted me in Miami. So I was hiding out. That sounded reasonable. Bootleggers always have cars. I was taken in.

The following Saturday was pay-day. They paid off twice a month and pay night is big doings. At least one dance at the section of the quarters known as the Pine Mill and two or three in the big Cypress Side. The company works with two kinds of lumber.

You can tell where the dances are to be held by the fires.

Huge bonfires of faulty logs and slabs are lit outside the house in which the dances are held. The refreshments are parched[1] peanuts, fried rabbit, fish, chicken and chitterlings.

The only music is guitar music and the only dance is the ole square dance. James Presley is especially invited to every party to play. His pay is plenty of coon dick, and he *plays*.

Joe Willard is in great demand to call figures. He rebels occasionally because he likes to dance too.

But all of the fun isn't inside the house. A group can always be found outside about the fire, standing around and woofing and occasionally telling stories.

The biggest dance on this particular pay-night was over to the Pine Mill. James Presley and Slim assured me that they would be over there, so Cliffert Ulmer took me there. Being the reigning curiosity of the "job" lots of folks came to see what I'd do. So it was a great dance.

The guitars cried out "Polk County," "Red River" and just instrumental hits with no name, that still are played by all good box pickers. The dancing was hilarious to put it mildly. Babe, Lucy, Big Sweet, East Coast Mary and many other of the well-known women were there. The men swung them lustily, but nobody asked me to dance. I was just crazy to get into the dance, too. I had heard my mother speak of it and praise square dancing to the skies, but it looked as if I was doomed to be a wallflower and that was a new rôle for me. Even Cliffert didn't ask me to dance. It was so jolly, too. At the end of every set Joe Willard would trick the men. Instead of calling the next figure as expected he'd bawl out, "Grab yo' partners and march up to de table and treat." Some of the men did, but some would bolt for the door and stand about the fire and woof until the next set was called.

I went outside to join the woofers, since I seemed to have no standing among the dancers. Not exactly a hush fell about the fire, but a lull came. I stood there awkwardly, knowing that the too-ready laughter and aimless talk was a window-dressing for my benefit. The brother in black puts a laugh in every vacant place in his mind. His laugh has a hundred

[1]Roasted.

meanings. It may mean amusement, anger, grief, bewilderment, chagrin, curiosity, simple pleasure or any other of the known or undefined emotions. Clardia Thornton of Magazine Point, Alabama, was telling me about another woman taking her husband away from her. When the show-down came and he told Clardia in the presence of the other woman that he didn't want her—could never use her again, she tole me "Den, Zora, Ah wuz so outdone, Ah just opened mah mouf and laffed."

The folks around the fire laughed and boisterously shoved each other about, but I knew they were not tickled. But I soon had the answer. A pencil-shaped fellow with a big Adam's apple gave me the key.

"Ma'am, whut might be yo' entrimmins?" he asked with what was supposed to be a killing bow.

"My whut?"

"Yo entrimmins? Yo entitlum?"

The "entitlum" gave me the cue, "Oh, my name is Zora Hurston. And whut may be yours?"

More people came closer quickly.

"Mah name is Pitts and Ah'm sho glad to meet yuh. Ah asted Cliffert tuh knock me down tuh yuh but he wouldn't make me 'quainted. So Ah'm makin' mahseff 'quainted."

"Ah'm glad you did, Mr. Pitts."

"Sho nuff?" archly.

"Yeah. Ah wouldn't be sayin' it if Ah didn't mean it."

He looked me over shrewdly. "Ah see dat las' crap you shot, Miss, and Ah fade yuh."

I laughed heartily. The whole fire laughed at his quick comeback and more people came out to listen.

"Miss, you know uh heap uh dese hard heads wants to woof at you but dey skeered."

"How come, Mr. Pitts? Do I look like a bear or panther?"

"Naw, but dey say youse rich and dey ain't got de nerve to open dey mouf."

I mentally cursed the $12.74 dress from Macy's that I had on among all the $1.98 mail-order dresses. I looked about and noted the number of bungalow aprons and even the rolled down paper bags on the heads of several women. I did look different and resolved to fix all that no later than the next morning.

"Oh, Ah ain't got doodley squat,"[2] I countered. "Mah man brought me dis dress de las' time he went to Jacksonville. We wuz sellin' plenty stuff den and makin' good money. Wisht Ah had dat money now."

Then Pitts began woofing at me and the others stood around to see how I took it.

"Say, Miss, you know nearly all dese niggers is after you. Dat's all dey talk about out in de swamp."

"You don't say. Tell 'em to make me know it."

"Ah ain't tellin' nobody nothin'. Ah ain't puttin' out nothin' to no ole hard head but ole folks eyes and Ah ain't doin' dat till they dead. Ah talks for Number One. Second stanza: Some of 'em talkin' 'bout marryin' you and dey wouldn't know whut to do wid you if they had you. Now, dat's a fack."

"You reckon?"

"Ah know dey wouldn't. Dey'd 'spect you tuh git out de bed and fix dem some breakfus' and a bucket. Dat's 'cause dey don't know no better. Dey's thin-brainded. Now me, Ah wouldn't let you fix me no breakfus'. Ah git up and fix mah own and den, whut make it so cool, Ah'd fix *you* some and set

---

[2]Nothing.

it on de back of de cook-stove so you could git it when you wake up. Dese mens don't even know how to talk to nobody lak you. If you wuz tuh ast dese niggers somethin' dey'd answer you 'yeah' and 'naw.' Now, if you wuz some ole gator-black 'oman dey'd be tellin' you jus' right. But dat ain't de way tuh talk tuh nobody lak *you*. Now you ast *me* somethin' and see how Ah'll answer yuh."

"Mr. Pitts, are you havin' a good time?"

(In a prim falsetto) "Yes, Ma'am. See, dat's de way tuh talk tuh *you*."

I laughed and the crowd laughed and Pitts laughed. Very successful woofing. Pitts treated me and we got on. Soon a boy came to me from Cliffert Ulmer asking me to dance. I found out that that was the social custom. The fellow that wants to broach a young woman doesn't come himself to ask. He sends his friend. Somebody came to me for Joe Willard and soon I was swamped with bids to dance. They were afraid of me before. My laughing acceptance of Pitts' woofing had put everybody at his ease.

James Presley and Slim spied noble at the orchestra. I had the chance to learn more about "John Henry" maybe. So I strolled over to James Presley and asked him if he knew how to play it.

"Ah'll play it if you sing it," he countered. So he played and I started to sing the verses I knew. They put me on the table and everybody urged me to spread my jenk,[3] so I did the best I could. Joe Willard knew two verses and sang them. Eugene Oliver knew one; Big Sweet knew one. And how James Presley can make his box cry out the accompaniment!

By the time that the song was over, before Joe Willard lifted me down from the table I knew that I was in the inner circle. I had first to convince the "job" that I was not an enemy in the person of the law; and, second, I had to prove that I was their kind. "John Henry" got me over my second hurdle.

After that my car was everybody's car. James Presley, Slim and I teamed up and we had to do "John Henry" wherever

[3]Have a good time.

we appeared. We soon had a reputation that way. We went to Mulberry, Pierce and Lakeland.

After that I got confidential and told them all what I wanted. At first they couldn't conceive of anybody wanting to put down "lies." But when I got the idea over we held a lying contest and posted the notices at the Post Office and the commissary. I gave four prizes and some tall lying was done. The men and women enjoyed themselves and the contest broke up in a square dance with Joe Willard calling figures.

The contest was a huge success in every way. I not only collected a great deal of material but it started individuals coming to me privately to tell me stories they had no chance to tell during the contest.

Cliffert Ulmer told me that I'd get a great deal more by going out with the swamp-gang. He said they lied a plenty while they worked. I spoke to the quarters boss and the swamp boss and both agreed that it was all right, so I strowed it all over the quarters that I was going out to the swamp with the boys next day. My own particular crowd, Cliffert, James, Joe Willard, Jim Allen and Eugene Oliver were to look out for me and see to it that I didn't get snake-bit nor 'gator-swallowed. The watchman, who sleeps out in the swamps and gets up steam in the skitter every morning before the men get to the cypress swamp, had been killed by a panther two weeks before, but they assured me that nothing like that could happen to me; not with the help I had.

Having watched some members of that swamp crew handle axes, I didn't doubt for a moment that they could do all that they said. Not only do they chop rhythmically, but they do a beautiful double twirl above their heads with the ascending axe before it begins that accurate and bird-like descent. They can hurl their axes great distances and behead moccasins or sink the blade into an alligator's skull. In fact, they seem to be able to do everything with their instrument that a blade can do. It is a magnificent sight to watch the marvelous co-ordination between the handsome black torsos and the twirling axes.

So next morning we were to be off to the woods.

It wasn't midnight dark and it wasn't day yet. When I awoke the saw-mill camp was a dawn gray. You could see the big saw-mill but you couldn't see the smoke from the chimney. You could see the congregation of shacks and the dim outlines of the scrub oaks among the houses, but you couldn't see the grey quilts of Spanish Moss that hung from the trees.

Dick Willie was the only man abroad. It was his business to be the first one out. He was the shack-rouser. Men are not supposed to over-sleep and Dick Willie gets paid to see to it that they don't. Listen to him singing as he goes down the line.

Wake up, bullies, and git on de rock. 'Tain't quite daylight but it's four o'clock.

Coming up the next line, he's got another song.

Wake up, Jacob, day's a breakin'. Git yo' hoe-cake a bakin' and yo' shirt tail shakin'.

What does he say when he gets to the jook and the long-house?[4] I'm fixing to tell you right now what he says. He raps on the floor of the porch with a stick and says:

"Ah ha! What make de rooster crow every morning at sun-up?

"Dat's to let de pimps and rounders know de workin' man is on his way."

About that time you see a light in every shack. Every kitchen is scorching up fat-back and hoe-cake. Nearly every skillet is full of corn-bread. But some like biscuit-bread better. Break your hoe-cake half in two. Half on the plate, half in the dinner-bucket. Throw in your black-eyed peas and fat meat left from supper and your bucket is fixed. Pour meat grease in your plate with plenty of cane syrup. Mix it and sop it with your bread. A big bowl of coffee, a drink of water from the tin dipper in the pail. Grab your dinner-bucket and hit the grit. Don't keep the straw-boss[5] waiting.

This morning when we got to the meeting place, the fore-man wasn't there. So the men squatted along the railroad track and waited.

[4]See glossary.
[5]The low-paid poor white section boss on a railroad; similar to swamp boss who works the gang that gets the timber to the sawmill.

Joe Willard was sitting with me on the end of a cross-tie when he saw Jim Presley coming in a run with his bucket and jumper-jacket.

"Hey, Jim, where the swamp boss? He ain't got here yet."

"He's ill—sick in the bed Ah hope, but Ah bet he'll git here yet."

"Aw, he ain't sick. Ah bet you a fat man he ain't," Joe said.

"How come?" somebody asked him and Joe answered:

"Man, he's too ugly. If a spell of sickness ever tried to slip up on him, he'd skeer it into a three weeks' spasm."

Blue Baby[6] stuck in his oar and said: "He ain't so ugly. Ye all jus' ain't seen no real ugly man. Ah seen a man so ugly till he could get behind a jimpson weed and hatch monkies."

Everybody laughed and moved closer together. Then Officer Richardson said: "Ah seen a man so ugly till they had to spread a sheet over his head at night so sleep could slip up on him."

They laughed some more, then Clifford Ulmer said:

"Ah'm goin' to talk with my mouth wide open. Those men y'all been talkin' 'bout wasn't ugly at all. Those was pretty men. Ah knowed one so ugly till you could throw him in the Mississippi river and skim ugly for six months."

"Give Cliff de little dog," Jim Allen said. "He done tole the biggest lie."

"He ain't lyin'," Joe Martin tole them. "Ah knowed dat same man. He didn't die—he jus' uglied away."

They laughed a great big old kah kah laugh and got closer together.

"Looka here, folkses," Jim Presley exclaimed. "Wese a half hour behind schedule and no swamp boss and no log train here yet. What yo' all reckon is the matter sho' 'nough?"

"Must be something terrible when white folks get slow about putting us to work."

"Yeah," says Good Black. "You know back in slavery Ole Massa was out in de field sort of lookin' things over, when a shower of rain come up. The field hands was glad it rained so

[6]See glossary.

they could knock off for a while. So one slave named John says:

"More rain, more rest."

"Ole Massa says, 'What's dat you say?'

"John says, 'More rain, more grass.' "

"There goes de big whistle. We ought to be out in the woods almost."

The big whistle at the saw-mill boomed and shrilled and pretty soon the log-train came racking along. No flats for logs behind the little engine. The foreman dropped off the tender as the train stopped.

"No loggin' today, boys. Got to send the train to the Everglades to fetch up the track gang and their tools."

"Lawd, Lawd, we got a day off," Joe Willard said, trying to make it sound like he was all put out about it. "Let's go back, boys. Sorry you won't git to de swamp, Zora."

"Aw, naw," the Foreman said. "Y'all had better g'wan over to the mill and see if they need you over there."

And he walked on off, chewing his tobacco and spitting his juice.

The men began to shoulder jumper-jackets and grab hold of buckets.

Allen asked: "Ain't dat a mean man? No work in the swamp and still he won't let us knock off."

"He's mean all right, but Ah done seen meaner men than him," said Handy Pitts.

"Where?"

"Oh, up in Middle Georgy. They had a straw boss and he was so mean dat when the boiler burst and blowed some of the men up in the air, he docked 'em for de time they was off de job."

Tush Hawg up and said: "Over on de East Coast Ah used to have a road boss and he was so mean and times was so hard till he laid off de hands of his watch."

Wiley said: "He's almost as bad as Joe Brown. Ah used to work in his mine and he was so mean till he wouldn't give God an honest prayer without snatching back 'Amen.' "

Ulmer says: "Joe Wiley, youse as big a liar as you is a man!

Whoo-wee. Boy, you molds 'em. But lemme tell y'all a sho
nuff tale 'bout Ole Massa."

"Go 'head and tell it, Cliff," shouted Eugene Oliver. "Ah
love to hear tales about Ole Massa and John. John sho was
one smart nigger."

So Cliff Ulmer went on.

You know befo' surrender Ole Massa had a nigger
name John and John always prayed every night befo' he
went to bed and his prayer was for God to come git him
and take him to Heaven right away. He didn't even
want to take time to die. He wanted de Lawd to come
git him just like he was—boot, sock and all. He'd git
down on his knees and say: "O Lawd, it's once more
and again yo' humble servant is knee-bent and body-
bowed—my heart beneath my knees and my knees in
some lonesome valley, crying for mercy while mercy kin
be found. O Lawd, Ah'm astin' you in de humblest way
I know how to be *so* pleased as to come in yo' fiery
chariot and take me to yo' Heben and its immortal
glory. Come Lawd, you know Ah have such a hard time.
Old Massa works me *so* hard, and don't gimme no time
to rest. So come, Lawd, wid peace in one hand and
pardon in de other and take me away from this sin-
sorrowing world. Ah'm tired and Ah want to go home."

So one night Ole Massa passed by John's shack and
heard him beggin' de Lawd to come git him in his fiery
chariot and take him away; so he made up his mind to
find out if John meant dat thing. So he goes on up to de
big house and got hisself a bed sheet and come on back.
He throwed de sheet over his head and knocked on de
door.

John quit prayin' and ast: "Who dat?"

Ole Massa say: "It's me, John, de Lawd, done come
wid my fiery chariot to take you away from this sin-sick
world."

Right under de bed John had business. He told his
wife: "Tell Him Ah ain't here, Liza."

At first Liza didn't say nothin' at all, but de Lawd
kept right on callin' John: "Come on, John, and go to

Heben wid me where you won't have to plough no mo' furrows and hoe no mo' corn. Come on, John."

Liza says: "John ain't here, Lawd, you hafta come back another time."

Lawd says: "Well, then Liza, you'll do."

Liza whispers and says: "John, come out from underneath dat bed and g'wan wid de Lawd. You been beggin' him to come git you. Now g'wan wid him."

John back under de bed not saying a mumblin' word. De Lawd out on de door step kept on callin'.

Liza says: "John, Ah thought you was so anxious to get to Heben. Come out and go on wid God."

John says: "Don't you hear him say 'You'll do'? Why don't you go wid him?"

"Ah ain't a goin' nowhere. Youse de one been whoopin' and hollerin' for him to come git you and if you don't come out from under dat bed Ah'm gointer tell God youse here."

Ole Massa makin' out he's God, says: "Come on, Liza, you'll do."

Liza says: "O, Lawd, John is right here underneath de bed."

"Come on John, and go to Heben wid me and its immortal glory."

John crept out from under de bed and went to de door and cracked it and when he seen all dat white standin' on de doorsteps he jumped back. He says: "O, Lawd, Ah can't go to Heben wid you in yo' fiery chariot in dese ole dirty britches; gimme time to put on my Sunday pants."

"All right, John, put on yo' Sunday pants."

John fooled around just as long as he could, changing them pants, but when he went back to de door, de big white glory was still standin' there. So he says agin: "O, Lawd, de Good Book says in Heben no filth is found and I got on dis dirty sweaty shirt. Ah can't go wid you in dis old nasty shirt. Gimme time to put on my Sunday shirt!"

"All right, John, go put on yo' Sunday shirt."

John took and fumbled around a long time changing

his shirt, and den he went back to de door, but Ole Massa was still on de door step. John didn't had nothin' else to change so he opened de door a little piece and says:

"O, Lawd, Ah'm ready to go to Heben wid you in yo' fiery chariot, but de radiance of yo' countenance is *so* bright, Ah can't come out by you. Stand back jus' a li'l way please."

Ole Massa stepped back a li'l bit.

John looked out agin and says: "O, Lawd, you know dat po' humble me is less than de dust beneath yo' shoe soles. And de radiance of yo' countenance is so bright Ah can't come out by you. Please, please, Lawd, in yo' tender mercy, stand back a li'l bit further."

Ole Massa stepped back a li'l bit mo'.

John looked out agin and he says: "O, Lawd, Heben is so high and wese so low; youse so great and Ah'm so weak and yo' strength is too much for us poor sufferin' sinners. So once mo' and agin yo' humber servant is knee-bent and body-bowed askin' you one mo' favor befo' Ah step into yo' fiery chariot to go to Heben wid you and wash in yo' glory—be so pleased in yo' tender mercy as to stand back jus' a li'l bit further."

Ole Massa stepped back a step or two mo' and out dat door John come like a streak of lightning. All across de punkin patch, thru de cotton over de pasture—John wid Ole Massa right behind him. By de time dey hit de cornfield John was way ahead of Ole Massa.

Back in de shack one of de children was cryin' and she ast Liza: "Mama, you reckon God's gointer ketch papa and carry him to Heben wid him?"

"Shet yo' mouf, talkin' foolishness!" Liza clashed at de chile. "You know de Lawd can't outrun yo' pappy—specially when he's barefooted at dat."

Kah, Kah, Kah! Everybody laughing with their mouths wide open. If the foreman had come along right then he would have been good and mad because he could tell their minds were not on work.

Joe Willard says: "Wait a minute, fellows, wese walkin' too

fast. At dis rate we'll be there befo' we have time to talk some
mo' about Ole Massa and John. Tell another one, Cliffert."

"Aw, naw," Eugene Oliver hollered out.

Let *me* talk some chat. Dis is de real truth 'bout Ole
Massa 'cause my grandma told it to my mama and she
told it to me.

During slavery time, you know, Ole Massa had a nigger named John and he was a faithful nigger and Ole
Massa lakted John a lot too.

One day Ole Massa sent for John and tole him, says:
"John, somebody is stealin' my corn out de field. Every
mornin' when I go out I see where they done carried off
some mo' of my roastin' ears. I want you to set in de
corn patch tonight and ketch whoever it is."

So John said all right and he went and hid in de field.

Pretty soon he heard somethin' breakin' corn. So
John sneaked up behind him wid a short stick in his
hand and hollered: "Now, break another ear of Ole
Massa's corn and see what *Ah'll* do to you."

John thought it was a man all dis time, but it was a
bear wid his arms full of roastin' ears. He throwed down
de corn and grabbed John. And him and dat bear!

John, after while got loose and got de bear by the tail
wid de bear tryin' to git to him all de time. So they run
around in a circle all night long. John was so tired. But
he couldn't let go of de bear's tail, do de bear would
grab him in de back.

After a stretch they quit runnin' and walked. John
swingin' on to de bear's tail and de bear's nose 'bout to
touch him in de back.

Daybreak, Ole Massa come out to see 'bout John and
he seen John and de bear walkin' 'round in de ring. So
he run up and says: "Lemme take holt of 'im, John,
whilst you run git help!"

John says: "All right, Massa. Now you run in quick
and grab 'im just so."

Ole Massa run and grabbed holt of de bear's tail and
said: "Now, John you make haste to git somebody to
help us."

John staggered off and set down on de grass and went to fanning hisself wid his hat.

Ole Massa was havin' plenty trouble wid dat bear and he looked over and seen John settin' on de grass and he hollered:

"John, you better g'wan git help or else I'm gwinter turn dis bear aloose!"

John says: "Turn 'im loose, then. Dat's whut Ah tried to do all night long but Ah couldn't."

Jim Allen laughed just as loud as anybody else and then he said: "We better hurry on to work befo' de buckra[7] get in behind us."

"Don't never worry about work," says Jim Presley. "There's more work in de world than there is anything else. God made de world and de white folks made work."

"Yeah, dey made work but they didn't make us do it," Joe Willard put in. "We brought dat on ourselves."

"Oh, yes, de white folks did put us to work too," said Jim Allen.

Know how it happened? After God got thru makin' de world and de varmints and de folks, he made up a great big bundle and let it down in de middle of de road. It laid dere for thousands of years, then Ole Missus said to Ole Massa: "Go pick up dat box, Ah want to see whut's in it." Ole Massa look at de box and it look so heavy dat he says to de nigger, "Go fetch me dat big ole box out dere in de road." De nigger been stumblin' over de box a long time so he tell his wife:

"'Oman, go git dat box." So de nigger 'oman she runned to git de box. She says:

"Ah always lak to open up a big box 'cause there's nearly always something good in great big boxes." So she run and grabbed a-hold of de box and opened it up and it was full of hard work.

Dat's de reason de sister in black works harder than

_____
[7]West African word meaning white people.

anybody else in de world. De white man tells de nigger to work and he takes and tells his wife.

"Aw, now, dat ain't de reason niggers is working so hard," Jim Presley objected.

Dis is de way *dat* was.

God let down two bundles 'bout five miles down de road. So de white man and de nigger raced to see who would git there first. Well, de nigger out-run de white man and grabbed de biggest bundle. He was so skeered de white man would git it away from him he fell on top of de bundle and hollered back: "Oh, Ah got here first and dis biggest bundle is mine." De white man says: "All right, Ah'll take yo' leavings," and picked up de li'l tee-ninchy bundle layin' in de road. When de nigger opened up his bundle he found a pick and shovel and a hoe and a plow and chop-axe and then de white man opened up his bundle and found a writin'-pen and ink. So ever since then de nigger been out in de hot sun, usin' his tools and de white man been sittin' up figger-in', ought's a ought, figger's a figger; all for de white man, none for de nigger.

"Oh lemme spread my mess. Dis is Will Richardson doin' dis lyin'."

You know Ole Massa took a nigger deer huntin' and posted him in his place and told him, says: "Now you wait right here and keep yo' gun reformed and ready. Ah'm goin' 'round de hill and skeer up de deer and head him dis way. When he come past, you shoot."

De nigger says: "Yessuh, Ah sho' will, Massa."

He set there and waited wid de gun all cocked and after a while de deer come tearin' past him. He didn't make a move to shoot de deer so he went on 'bout his business. After while de white man come on 'round de hill and ast de nigger: "Did you kill de deer?"

De nigger says: "Ah ain't seen no deer pass here yet."

Massa says: "Yes, you did. You couldn't help but see him. He come right dis way."

Nigger says: "Well Ah sho' ain't seen none. All Ah seen was a white man come along here wid a pack of chairs on his head and Ah tipped my hat to him and waited for de deer."

"Some colored folks ain't got no sense, and when Ah see 'em like dat," Ah say, "My race but not my taste."

V

Y'ALL ever hear dat lie 'bout big talk?" cut in Joe Wiley.
"Yeah we done heard it, Joe, but Ah kin hear it some 'gin. Tell it, Joe," pleaded Gene Oliver.

During slavery time two ole niggers wuz talkin' an' one said tuh de other one, "Ole Massa made me so mad yistiddy till Ah give 'im uh good cussin' out. Man, Ah called 'im everything wid uh handle on it."

De other one says, "You didn't cuss *Ole Massa*, didja? Good God! Whut did he do tuh you?"

"He didn't do *nothin'*, an' man, Ah laid one cussin' on 'im! Ah'm uh man lak dis, Ah won't stan' no hunchin'. Ah betcha he won't bother *me* no mo'."

"Well, if you cussed 'im an' he didn't do nothin' tuh you, de nex' time he make me mad Ah'm goin' tuh lay uh hearin' on him."

Nex' day de nigger did somethin'. Ole Massa got in behind 'im and he turnt 'round an' give Ole Massa one good cussin' an Ole Massa had 'im took down and whipped nearly tuh death. Nex' time he saw dat other nigger he says tuh 'im, "Thought you tole me, you cussed Ole Massa out and he never opened his mouf."

"Ah did."

"Well, how come he never did nothin' tuh yuh? Ah did it an' he come nigh uh killin' *me*."

"Man, you didn't go cuss 'im tuh his face, didja?"

"Sho Ah did. Ain't dat whut you tole me you done?"

"Naw, Ah didn't say Ah cussed 'im tuh his face. You sho is crazy. Ah thought you had mo' sense than dat. When Ah cussed Ole Massa he wuz settin' on de front porch an' Ah wuz down at de big gate."

De other nigger wuz mad but he didn't let on. Way after while he 'proached de nigger dat got 'im de beatin' an' tole 'im, "Know whut Ah done tuhday?"

"Naw, whut you done? Give Ole Massa 'nother cussin'?"

"Naw, Ah ain't never goin' do dat no mo'. Ah peeped up under Ole Miss's drawers."

"Man, hush yo' mouf! You knows you ain't looked up under ole Miss's clothes!"

"Yes, Ah did too. Ah looked right up her very drawers."

"You better hush dat talk! Somebody goin' hear you and Ole Massa'll have you kilt."

"Well, Ah sho done it an' she never done nothin' neither."

"Well, whut did she say?"

"Not uh mumblin' word, an' Ah stopped and looked jus' as long as Ah wanted tuh an' went on 'bout mah business."

"Well, de nex' time Ah see her settin' out on de porch Ah'm goin' tuh look too."

"Help yo'self."

Dat very day Ole Miss wuz settin' out on de porch in de cool uh de evenin' all dressed up in her starchy white clothes. She had her legs all crossed up and de nigger walked up tuh de edge uh de porch and peeped up under Ole Miss's clothes. She took and hollered an' Ole Massa come out an' had dat nigger almost kilt alive.

When he wuz able tuh be 'bout agin he said tuh de other nigger; "Thought you tole me you peeped up under Ole Miss's drawers?"

"Ah sho did."

"Well, how come she never done nothin' tuh *you*? She got me nearly kilt."

"Man, when Ah looked under Ole Miss's drawers they wuz hangin' out on de clothes line. You didn't go look up in 'em while she had 'em on, didja? You sho is uh fool! Ah thought you had mo' sense than dat, Ah claire Ah did. It's uh wonder he didn't kill yuh dead. Umph, umph, umph. You sho ain't got no sense atall."

"Yeah," said Black Baby, "But dat wasn't John de white folks was foolin' wid. John was too smart for Ole Massa. He never got no beatin'!"

De first colored man what was brought to dis country

was name John. He didn't know nothin' mo' than you
told him and he never forgot nothin' you told him either. So he was sold to a white man.

Things he didn't know he would ask about. They
went to a house and John never seen a house so he
asked what it was. Ole Massa tole him it was his kingdom. So dey goes on into de house and dere was the
fireplace. He asked what was that. Ole Massa told him it
was his flame 'vaperator.

The cat was settin' dere. He asked what it was. Ole
Massa told him it was his round head.

So dey went upstairs. When he got on de stair steps
he asked what dey was. Ole Massa told him it was his
jacob ladder. So when they got up stairs he had a roller
foot bed. John asked what was dat. Ole Massa told him
it was his flowery-bed-of-ease. So dey came down and
went out to de lot. He had a barn. John asked what was
dat. Ole Massa told him, dat was his mound. So he had
a Jack in the stable, too. John asked, "What in de world
is dat?" Ole Massa said: "Dat's July, de God dam."

So de next day Ole Massa was up stairs sleep and John
was smokin'. It flamed de 'vaperator and de cat was
settin' dere and it got set afire. The cat goes to de barn
where Ole Massa had lots of hay and fodder in de barn.
So de cat set it on fire. John watched de Jack kicking up
hay and fodder. He would see de hay and fodder go up
and come down but he thought de Jack was eatin' de
hay and fodder.

So he goes upstairs and called Ole Massa and told
him to get up off'n his flowery-bed-of-ease and come
down on his jacob ladder. He said: "I done flamed the
'vaperator and it caught de round head and set him on
fire. He's gone to de mound and set it on fire, and July
the God dam is eatin' up everything he kin git his mouf
on."

Massa turned over in de bed and ast, "Whut dat you
say, John?"

John tole 'im agin. Massa was still sleepy so he ast
John agin whut he say. John was gittin' tired so he say,
"Aw, you better git up out dat bed and come on down

stairs. Ah done set dat ole cat afire and he run out to de barn and set it afire and dat ole Jackass is eatin' up everything he git his mouf on."

Gene Oliver said: "Y'all hush and lemme tell this one befo' we git to de mill. This ain't no slavery time talk."

Once they tried a colored man in Mobile for stealing a goat. He was so poorly dressed, and dirty—that de judge told him, "Six months on de country road, you stink so."

A white man was standing dere and he said, "Judge, he don't stink, Ah got a nigger who smells worser than a billy goat." De judge told de man to bring him on over so he could smell him. De next day de man took de billy goat and de nigger and went to de court and sent de judge word dat de nigger and de billy goat wuz out dere and which one did he want fust.

The judge told him to bring in de goat. When he carried de goat he smelled so bad dat de judge fainted. Dey got ice water and throwed it in de Judge's face 'til he come to. He told 'em to bring in de nigger and when dey brung in de nigger de goat fainted.

Joe Wiley said: "Ah jus' got to tell this one, do Ah can't rest."

In slavery time dere was a colored man what was named John. He went along wid Ole Massa everywhere he went. He used to make out he could tell fortunes. One day him and his Old Massa was goin' along and John said, "Ole Massa, Ah kin tell fortunes." Ole Massa made out he didn't pay him no attention. But when they got to de next man's plantation Old Massa told de landlord, "I have a nigger dat kin tell fortunes." So de other man said, "Dat nigger can't tell no fortunes. I bet my plantation and all my niggers against yours dat he can't tell no fortunes."

Ole Massa says: "I'll take yo' bet. I bet everything in de world I got on John 'cause he don't lie. If he say he can tell fortunes, he can tell 'em. Bet you my plantation and all my niggers against yours and throw in de wood lot extry."

So they called Notary Public and signed up de bet. Ole Massa straddled his horse and John got on his mule and they went on home.

John was in de misery all that night for he knowed he was gointer be de cause of Ole Massa losin' all he had.

Every mornin' John useter be up and have Old Massa's saddle horse curried and saddled at de door when Ole Massa woke up. But *this* mornin' Old Massa had to git John out of de bed.

John useter always ride side by side with Massa, but on de way over to de plantation where de bet was on, he rode way behind.

So de man on de plantation had went out and caught a coon and had a big old iron wash-pot turned down over it.

There was many person there to hear John tell what was under de wash-pot.

Ole Massa brought John out and tole him, say: "John, if you tell what's under dat wash pot Ah'll make you independent, rich. If you don't, Ah'm goin' to kill you because you'll make me lose my plantation and everything I got."

John walked 'round and 'round dat pot but he couldn't git de least inklin' of what was underneath it. Drops of sweat as big as yo' fist was rollin' off of John. At last he give up and said: "Well, you got de ole coon at last."

When John said that, Ole Massa jumped in de air and cracked his heels twice befo' he hit de ground. De man that was bettin' against Ole Massa fell to his knees wid de cold sweat pourin' off him. Ole Massa said: "John, you done won another plantation fo' me. That's a coon under that pot sho 'nuff."

So he give John a new suit of clothes and a saddle horse. And John quit tellin' fortunes after that.

Going back home Ole Massa said: "Well, John, you done made me vast rich so I goin' to Philly-Me-York and won't be back in three weeks. I leave everything in yo' charge."

So Ole Massa and his wife got on de train and John went to de depot with 'em and seen 'em off on de train and bid 'em goodbye. Then he hurried on back to de plantation. Ole Massa and Ole Miss got off at de first station and made it on back to see whut John was doin'.

John went back and told de niggers, "Massa's gone to Philly-Me-York and left everything in my charge. Ah want one of you niggers to git on a mule and ride three miles north, and another one three miles west and another one three miles south and another one three miles east. Tell everybody to come here—there's gointer be a ball here tonight. The rest of you go into the lot and kill hogs until you can walk on 'em."

So they did. John goes in and dressed up in Ole Massa's swaller-tail clothes, put on his collar and tie; got a box of cigars and put under his arm, and one cigar in his mouth.

When the crowd come John said: "Y'all kin dance and Ah'm goin' to call figgers."

So he got Massa's biggest rockin' chair and put it up in Massa's bed and then he got up in the bed in the chair and begin to call figgers:

"Hands up!" "Four circle right." "Half back." "Two ladies change." He was puffing his cigar all de time.

'Bout this time John seen a white couple come in but they looked so trashy he figgered they was piney woods crackers, so he told 'em to g'wan out in de kitchen and git some barbecue and likker and to stay out there where they belong. So he went to callin' figgers agin. De git Fiddles[1] was raisin' cain over in de corner and John was callin' for de new set:

"Choose yo' partners." "Couples to yo' places like horses to de traces." "Sashay all." "Sixteen hands up." "Swing Miss Sally 'round and 'round and bring her back to me!"

[1] Guitars.

Just as he went to say "Four hands up," he seen Ole Massa comin' out the kitchen wipin' the dirt off his face.

Ole Massa said: "John, just look whut you done done! I'm gointer take you to that persimmon tree and break yo' neck for this—killing up all my hogs and havin' all these niggers in my house."

John ast, "Ole Massa, Ah know you gointer kill me, but can Ah have a word with my friend Jack before you kill me?"

"Yes, John, but have it quick."

So John called Jack and told him; says: "Ole Massa is gointer hang me under that persimmon tree. Now you get three matches and get in the top of the tree. Ah'm gointer pray and when you hear me ast God to let it lightning Ah want you to strike matches."

Jack went on out to the tree. Ole Massa brought John on out with the rope around his neck and put it over a limb.

"Now, John," said Massa, "have you got any last words to say?"

"Yes sir, Ah want to pray."

"Pray and pray damn quick. I'm clean out of patience with you, John."

So John knelt down. "O Lord, here Ah am at de foot of de persimmon tree. If you're gointer destroy Old Massa tonight, with his wife and chillun and everything he got, lemme see it lightnin'."

Jack up the tree, struck a match. Ole Massa caught hold of John and said: "John, don't pray no more."

John said: "Oh yes, turn me loose so Ah can pray. O Lord, here Ah am tonight callin' on Thee and Thee alone. If you are gointer destroy Ole Massa tonight, his wife and chillun and all he got, Ah want to see it lightnin' again."

Jack struck another match and Ole Massa started to run. He give John his freedom and a heap of land and stock. He run so fast that it took a express train running at the rate of ninety miles an hour and six months to bring him back, and that's how come niggers got they freedom today.

Well, we were at the mill at last, as slow as we had walked. Old Hannah[2] was climbing the road of the sky, heating up sand beds and sweating peoples. No wonder nobody wanted to work. Three fried men are not equal to one good cool one. The men stood around the door for a minute or two, then dropped down on the shady side of the building. Work was too discouraging to think about. Phew! Sun and sawdust, sweat and sand. Nobody called a meeting and voted to sit in the shade. It just happened naturally.

Jim Allen said, "Reckon we better go inside and see if they want us?"

"Oh hell, naw!" shouted Lonnie Barnes. "We ain't no mill-hands nohow. Let's stay right where we is till they find us. We got plenty to do—lyin' on Ole Massa and slavery days. Lemme handle a li'l language long here wid de rest. Y'all ever hear 'bout dat nigger dat found a gold watch?"

"Yeah, Ah done heard it," said Cliff, "but go on and tell it, Lonnie, so yo' egg bag kin rest easy."[3]

"Well, once upon a time was a good ole time.

Monkey chew tobacco and spit white lime."

A colored man was walking down de road one day and he found a gold watch and chain. He didn't know what it was, so the first thing he met was a white man, so he showed the white man de watch and ast him what it was. White man said, "Lemme see it in my hand."

De colored man give it to him and de white man said, "Why this is a gold watch, and de next time you find anything kickin' in de road put it in yo' pocket and sell it."

With that he put the watch in his pocket and left de colored man standing there.

So de colored man walked on down de road a piece further and walked up on a little turtle. He tied a string to it and put de turtle in his pocket and let de string hang out.

[2]The Sun.

[3]So you can be at ease. A hen is supposed to suffer when she has a fully developed egg in her.

So he met another colored fellow and the fellow ast him says: "Cap, what time you got?"

He pulled out de turtle and told de man, "It's a quarter past leben and kickin' lak hell for twelve."

Larkins White says: "Y'all been wearin' Ole Massa's southern can⁺ out dis mornin'. Pass him over here to me and lemme handle some grammar wid him."

"You got him, Ah just hope dat straw boss don't come sidlin' 'round here," somebody said.

"Ah got to tell you 'bout Old Massa down in de piney woods."

During slavery uh nigger name Jack run off from his marster and took and hid hisself down in de piney woods.

Ole Massa hunted and hunted but he never could ketch dat nigger.

But Jack had uh good friend on de plantation dat useter slip 'im somethin' t' eat and fetch de banjo down and play 'im somethin' every day so's he could dance some. Jack wuz tryin' to make it on off de mountain where Old Massa couldn't fetch 'im back. So Ole Massa got on to dis other nigger slippin' out to Jack but he couldn't ketch 'im so he tole 'im if he lead 'im to where Jack wuz he'd give 'im a new suit uh clothes. So he said, "All right."

So he tole Old Massa to follow him and do whutever he sing. So Ole Massa said, "All right."

So dat day de nigger took Jack some dinner and de Banjo. So Jack et. Den he tole him, say: "Jack I got uh new song fuh yuh today."

"Play it and lemme dance some."

"It's about Ole Massa."

Jack said, "I don't give uh damn 'bout Ole Massa. Ah don't b'long tuh him no mo'. Play it and lemme dance."

So he started to playin'.

⁺His hips.

"From pine to pine, Mister Pinkney.
From pine to pine, Mister Pinkney."
Jack was justa dancin' fallin' off de log and cuttin' de
pigeon wing—(diddle dip, diddle dip—diddle dip)
"from pine to pine Mr. Pinkney."
White man coming closer all de time.
"Now take yo' time Mister Pinkney.
Now take yo' time Mister Pinkney."
(Diddle dip, diddle dip, diddle dip, diddle dip)
"Now grab 'im now Mister Pinkney
Now grab 'im now Mister Pinkney."
(Diddle dip, diddle dip, diddle dip, diddle dip)
"Now grab 'im now Mister Pinkney."
So they caught Jack and put uh hundred lashes on his
back and put him back to work.

"Now Ah tole dat one for myself, now Ah got to tell one
for my wife."

"Aw, g'wan tell de lie, Larkins, if you want to. You know
you ain't tellin' no lie for yo' wife. No mo' than de rest of us.
You lyin' cause you like it," James Presley put in. "Hurry up
so somebody else kin plough up some literary and lay-by
some alphabets."

Two mens dat didn't know how tuh count good had
been haulin' up cawn and they stopped at de cemetery
wid de last load 'cause it wuz gittin' kinda dark. They
thought they'd git thru instead uh goin' 'way tuh one of
'em's barn. When they wuz goin' in de gate two ear uh
cawn dropped off de waggin, but they didn't stop tuh
bother wid 'em, just then. They wuz in uh big hurry tuh
git home. They wuz justa vidin' it up. "You take dis'n an
Ah'll take dat'un, you take dat'un and Ah'll take dis'un."
An ole nigger heard 'em while he wuz passin' de cemetery an' run home tuh tell ole Massa 'bout it.
"Massa, de Lawd and de devil is down in de cemetery
'vidin' up souls. Ah heard 'em. One say, 'you take that
'un an' Ah'll take dis'un'."
Ole Massa wuz sick in de easy chear, he couldn't git
about by hisself, but he said, "Jack, Ah don't know
whut dis foolishness is, but Ah know you lyin'."

"Naw Ah ain't neither, Ah swear it's so."

"Can't be, Jack, youse crazy."

"Naw, Ah ain't neither; if you don' believe me, come see for yo'self."

"Guess Ah better go see whut you talkin' 'bout; if you fool me, Ah'm gointer have a hundred lashes put on yo' back in de mawnin' suh."

They went on down tuh de cemetery wid Jack pushin' Massa in his rollin' chear, an' it wuz sho dark down dere too. So they couldn't see de two ears uh cawn layin' in de gate.

Sho nuff Ole Massa heard 'em sayin' "Ah'll take dis'un," and de other say, "An' Ah'll take dis'un." Ole Massa got skeered hisself but he wuzn't lettin' on, an' Jack whispered tuh 'im, "Unh hunh, didn't Ah tell you de Lawd an' de devil wuz down here 'vidin' up souls?"

They waited awhile there in de gate listenin' den they heard 'em say, "Now, we'll go git dem two at de gate."

Jack says, "Ah knows de Lawd gwine take you, and Ah ain't gwine let de devil get me—Ah'm gwine home." An' he did an' lef' Ole Massa settin' dere at de cemetery gate in his rollin' chear, but when he got home, Ole Massa had done beat 'im home and wuz settin' by de fire smokin' uh seegar.

Jim Allen began to fidget. "Don't y'all reckon we better g'wan inside? They might need us."

Lonnie Barnes shouted, "Aw naw—you sho is worrysome. You bad as white folks. You know they say a white man git in some kind of trouble, he'll fret and fret until he kill hisself. A nigger git into trouble, he'll fret a while, then g'wan to sleep."

"Yeah, dat's right, too," Eugene Oliver agreed. "Didja ever hear de white man's prayer?"

"Who in Polk County ain't heard dat?" cut in Officer Richardson.

"Well, if you know it so good, lemme hear *you* say it," Eugene snapped back.

"Oh, Ah don't know it well enough to say it. Ah jus' know it well enough to know it."

"Well, all right then, when Ah'm changing my dollars, you keep yo' pennies out."

"Ah don't know it, Eugene, say it for me," begged Peter Noble. "Don't pay Office no mind."

Well, it come a famine and all de crops was dried up and Brother John was ast to pray. He had prayed for rain last year and it had rained, so all de white folks 'sembled at they church and called on Brother John to pray agin, so he got down and prayed:

"Lord, first thing, I want you to understand that this ain't no nigger talking to you. This is a white man and I want you to hear me. Pay some attention to me. I don't worry and bother you all the time like these niggers—asking you for a whole heap of things that they don't know what to do with after they git 'em—so when I do ask a favor, I want it granted. Now, Lord, we want some rain. Our crops is all burning up and we'd like a little rain. But I don't mean for you to come in a hell of a storm like you did last year—kicking up racket like niggers at a barbecue. I want you to come calm and easy. Now, another thing, Lord, I want to speak about. Don't let these niggers be as sassy as they have been in the past. Keep 'em in their places, Lord, Amen."

Larkins White burst out:

And dat put me in de mind of a nigger dat useter do a lot of prayin' up under 'simmon tree, durin' slavery time. He'd go up dere and pray to God and beg Him to kill all de white folks. Ole Massa heard about it and so de next day he got hisself a armload of sizeable rocks and went up de 'simmon tree, before de nigger got dere, and when he begin to pray and beg de Lawd to kill all de white folks, Ole Massa let one of dese rocks fall on Ole Nigger's head. It was a heavy rock and knocked de nigger over. So when he got up he looked up and said: "Lawd, I ast you to kill all de white folks, can't you tell a white man from a nigger?"

Joe Wiley says: "Y'all might as well make up yo' mind to bear wid me, 'cause Ah feel Ah got to tell a lie on Ole Massa for my mamma. Ah done lied on him enough for myself. So Ah'm gointer tell it if I bust my gall tryin'.

Ole John was a slave, you know. And there was Ole Massa and Ole Missy and de two li' children—a girl and a boy.

Well, John was workin' in de field and he seen de children out on de lake in a boat, just a hollerin'. They had done lost they oars and was 'bout to turn over. So then he went and tole Ole Massa and Ole Missy.

Well, Ole Missy, she hollered and said: "It's so sad to lose these 'cause Ah ain't never goin' to have no more children." Ole Massa made her hush and they went down to de water and follered de shore on 'round till they found 'em. John pulled off his shoes and hopped in and swum out and got in de boat wid de children and brought 'em to shore.

Well, Massa and John take 'em to de house. So they was all so glad 'cause de children got saved. So Massa told 'im to make a good crop dat year and fill up de barn, and den when he lay by de crops nex' year, he was going to set him free.

So John raised so much crop dat year he filled de barn and had to put some of it in de house.

So Friday come, and Massa said, "Well, de day done come that I said I'd set you free. I hate to do it, but I don't like to make myself out a lie. I hate to git rid of a good nigger lak you."

So he went in de house and give John one of his old suits of clothes to put on. So John put it on and come in to shake hands and tell 'em goodbye. De children they cry, and Ole Missy she cry. Didn't want to see John go. So John took his bundle and put it on his stick and hung it crost his shoulder.

Well, Ole John started on down de road. Well, Ole Massa said, "John, de children love yuh."

"Yassuh."

"John, I love yuh."

"Yassuh."

"And Missy *like* yuh!"

"Yassuh."

"But 'member, John, youse a nigger."

"Yassuh."

Fur as John could hear 'im down de road he wuz hollerin', "John, Oh John! De children loves you. And I love you. De Missy *like* you."

John would holler back, "Yassuh."

"But 'member youse a nigger, tho!"

Ole Massa kept callin' 'im and his voice was pitiful. But John kept right on steppin' to Canada. He answered Old Massa every time he called 'im, but he consumed on wid his bag.

VI

TOOKIE ALLEN passed by the mill all dressed up in a tight shake-baby.[1] She must have thought she looked good because she was walking that way. All the men stopped talking for a while. Joe Willard hollered at her.

"Hey, Tookie, how do you like your new dress?"

Tookie made out she didn't hear, but anybody could tell that she had. That was why she had put on her new dress, and come past the mill a wringing and twisting—so she could hear the men talking about her in the dress.

"Lawd, look at Tookie switchin' it and lookin' back at it! She's done gone crazy thru de hips." Joe Willard just couldn't take his eyes off of Tookie.

"Aw, man, you done seen Tookie and her walk too much to be makin' all dat miration over it. If you can't show me nothin' better than dat, don't bring de mess up," Cliff Ulmer hooted. "Less tell some more lies on Ole Massa and John."

"John sho was a smart nigger now. He useter git de best of Ole Massa all de time," gloated Sack Daddy.

"Yeah, but some white folks is smarter than you think," put in Eugene Oliver.

For instance now, take a man I know up in West Florida. He hired a colored man to clear off some new ground, but dat skillet blonde[2] was too lazy to work. De white man would show him what to do then he's g'wan back to de house and keep his books. Soon as he turned his back de nigger would flop down and go to sleep. When he hear somebody comin' he'd hit de log a few licks with de flat of de ax and say, "Klunk, klunk, you think Ah'm workin' but Ah ain't."

De white man heard him but he didn't say a word. Sat'day night come and Ole Cuffee went up to de white man to git his pay. De white man stacked up his great

[1] A dress very tight across the hips but with a full short skirt; very popular on the "jobs."
[2] Very black person.

93

big ole silver dollars and shook 'em in his hand and says, "Clink, clink, you think I'm gointer pay you, but I ain't."

By that time somebody saw the straw boss coming so everybody made it on into the mill. The mill boss said, "What are y'all comin' in here for? Ah ain't got enough work for my own men. Git for home."

The swamp gang shuffled on out of the mill. "Umph, umph, umph," said Black Baby. "We coulda *done* been gone if we had a knowed dat."

"Ah told y'all to come an' go inside but you wouldn't take a listen. Y'all think Ah'm an ole Fogey. Young Coon for running but old coon for cunning."

We went on back to the quarters.

When Mrs. Bertha Allen saw us coming from the mill she began to hunt up the hoe and the rake. She looked under the porch and behind the house until she got them both and placed them handy. As soon as Jim Allen hit the steps she said:

"Ah'm mighty proud y'all got a day off. Maybe Ah kin git dis yard all clean today. Jus' look at de trash and dirt! And it's so many weeds in dis yard, Ah'm liable to git snake bit at my own door."

"Tain't no use in you gittin' yo' mouf all primped up for no hoein' and rakin' out of me, Bertha. Call yo' grandson and let him do it. Ah'm too old for dat," said Jim testily.

"Ah'm standin' in my tracks and steppin' back on my abstract[3]—Ah ain't gointer rake up no yard. Ah'm goin' fishin'," Cliffert Ulmer snapped back. "Grandma, you worries mo' 'bout dis place than de man dat owns it. You ain't de Everglades Cypress Lumber Comp'ny sho nuff. Youse just shacking in one of their shanties. Leave de weeds go. Somebody'll come chop 'em some day."

"Naw, Ah ain't gointer leave 'em go! You and Jim would wallow in dirt right up to yo' necks if it wasn't for me."

Jim threw down his jumper and his dinner bucket. "Now, *Ah'm* goin' fishin' too. When Bertha starts her jawin' Ah

[3] I am standing my ground.

can't stay on de place. Her tongue is hung in de middle and works both ways. Come on Cliff, less git de poles!"

"Speck Ah'm gointer have to make a new line for my trout pole," Cliff said. "Dat great big ole fish Ah hooked las' time carried my other line off in his mouth, 'member?"

"Aw, dat wasn't no trout got yo' line; dat's whut you tell us, but dat was a log bit yo' hook dat time." Larkins White twitted.

"Yes dat was a trout, too now. Ah'm a real fisherman. Ah ain't like y'all. Ah kin ketch fish anywhere. All Ah want to know, is there any water. Man, Ah kin ketch fish out a water bucket. Don't b'lieve me, just come on down to de lake. Ah'll bet, Ah'll pull 'em all de fish out de lake befo' y'all git yo' bait dug."

"Dat's a go," shouted Larkins. "Less go! Come on de rest of y'all to see dis thing out. Dis boy 'bout to burst his britches since he been chawin' tobacco reg'lar and workin' in de swamp wid us mens."

Cliff picked up the hoe and went 'round behind the house to dig some bait. Old Jim went inside and got the spool of No. 8 cotton and a piece of beeswax and went to twisting a trout line. He baptized the hook in asafetida and put his hunting knife in his pocket, met Cliffert at the gate and they were off to join the others down by the jook. Big Sweet and Lucy got out their poles and joined us. It was almost like a log-rolling[4] or a barbecue. The quarters were high. The men didn't get off from work every day like this.

We proaged on thru the woods that was full of magnolia, pine, cedar, oak, cypress, hickory and many kinds of trees whose names I do not know. It is hard to know all the trees in Florida. But everywhere they were twined with climbing vines and veiled in moss.

"What's de matter, Ah don't hear no birds?" complained Eugene Oliver. "It don't seem natural."

Everybody looked up at one time like cows in a pasture.

"Oh you know how come we don't hear no birds. It's

[4]When people used to get out logs to build a house they would get the neighbors to help. Plenty of food and drink served. Very gay time.

Friday and de mocking bird ain't here," said Big Sweet after a period of observation.

"What's Friday got to do with the mockin' bird?" Eugene challenged.

"Dat's exactly what Ah want to know," said Joe Wiley.

"Well," said Big Sweet. "Nobody never sees no mockin' bird on Friday. They ain't on earth dat day."

"Well, if they ain't on earth, where is they?"

"They's all gone to hell on Friday with a grain of sand in they mouth to help out they friend." She continued:

> Once there was a man and he was very wicked. He useter rob and steal and he was always in a fight and killin' up people. But he was awful good to birds and mockin' birds was his favorite. This was a long time ago before de man first started to buildin' de Rocky Mountains. Well, 'way after while somebody kilt him, and being he had done lived so bad, when he died he went straight to hell.
>
> De birds all hated it mighty bad when they seen him in hell, so they tried to git him out. But the fire was too hot so they give up—all but de mockin' birds. They come together and decided to tote sand until they squenched de fire in hell. So they set a day and they all agreed on it. Every Friday they totes sand to hell. And that's how come nobody don't never see no mockin' bird[5] on Friday.

Joe Wiley chuckled. "If them mockin' birds ever speck to do dat man any good they better git some box-cars to haul dat sand. Dat one li'l grain they totin' in their bill ain't helpin' none. But anyhow it goes to show you dat animals got sense as well as peoples." Joe went on—

> Now take cat-fish for instances. Ah knows a man dat useter go fishin' every Sunday. His wife begged him not to do it and his pastor strained wid him for years but it didn't do no good. He just would go ketch him a fish every Sabbath. One Sunday he went and just as soon as he got to de water he seen a great big ole cat-fish up

[5]Some say it is a jay bird.

under some water lilies pickin' his teeth with his fins. So de man baited his pole and dropped de hook right down in front of de big fish. Dat cat grabbed de hook and took out for deep water. De man held on and pretty soon dat fish pulled him in. He couldn't git out. Some folks on de way to church seen him and run down to de water but he was in too deep. So he went down de first time and when he come up he hollered — "Tell my wife." By dat time de fish pulled him under again. When he come up he hollered, "Tell my wife —" and went down again. When he come up de third time he said: "Tell my wife to fear God and cat-fish," and went down for de last time and he never come up no mo'.

"Aw, you b'lieve dat old lie?" Joe Willard growled. "Ah don't."

"Well, Ah do. Nobody ain't gointer git me to fishin' on Sunday," said Big Sweet fervently.

"How come nothin' don't happen to all dese white folks dat go fishin' on Sunday? Niggers got all de signs and white folks got all de money," retorted Joe Willard.

"Yeah, but all cat-fish ain't so sensible." Joe Wiley cut in with a sly grin on his face. "One time when Ah was livin' in Plateau, Alabama — dat's right on de Alabama river you know — Ah put out some fish lines one night and went on home. Durin' de night de river fell and dat left de hooks up out de water and when Ah went there next morning a cat-fish had done jumped up after dat bait till he was washed down in sweat."

Jim Presley said, "I know you tellin' de truth, Joe, 'cause Ah saw a coach whip after a race runner one day. And de race runner was running so fast to git away from dat coach whip dat his tail got so hot it set de world on fire, and dat coach whip was running so hard to ketch him till he put de fire out wid his sweat."

Jim Allen said, "Y'all sho must not b'long to no church de way y'all tells lies. Y'all done quit tellin' 'em. Y'all done gone to moldin' 'em. But y'all want to know how come snakes got poison in they mouth and nothin' else ain't got it?"

"Yeah, tell it, Jim," urged Arthur Hopkins.

Old man Allen turned angrily upon Arthur.

"Don't you be callin' me by my first name. Ah'm old enough for yo' grand paw! You respect my gray hairs. Ah don't play wid chillun. Play wid a puppy and he'll lick yo' mouf."

"Ah didn't mean no harm."

"Dat's all right, Arthur. Ah ain't mad. Ah jus' don't play wid chillun. You go play wid Cliff and Sam and Eugene. They's yo' equal. Ah was a man when yo' daddy was born."

"Well, anyhow, Mr. Jim, please tell us how come de snakes got poison."

Well, when God made de snake he put him in de bushes to ornament de ground. But things didn't suit de snake so one day he got on de ladder and went up to see God.

"Good mawnin', God."

"How do you do, Snake?"

"Ah ain't so many, God, you put me down there on my belly in de dust and everything trods upon me and kills off my generations. Ah ain't got no kind of protection at all."

God looked off towards immensity and thought about de subject for awhile, then he said, "Ah didn't mean for nothin' to be stompin' you snakes lak dat. You got to have some kind of a protection. Here, take dis poison and put it in yo' mouf and when they tromps on you, protect yo' self."

So de snake took de poison in his mouf and went on back.

So after awhile all de other varmints went up to God.

"Good evenin', God."

"How you makin' it, varmints?"

"God, please do somethin' 'bout dat snake. He' layin' in de bushes there wid poisin in his mouf and he's strikin' everything dat shakes de bush. He's killin' up our generations. Wese skeered to walk de earth."

So God sent for de snake and tole him:

"Snake, when Ah give you dat poison, Ah didn't

mean for you to be hittin' and killin' everything dat
shake de bush. I give you dat poison and tole you to
protect yo'self when they tromples on you. But you
killin' everything dat moves. Ah didn't mean for you to
do dat."

De snake say, "Lawd, you know Ah'm down here in
de dust. Ah ain't got no claws to fight wid, and Ah ain't
got no feets to git me out de way. All Ah kin see is feets
comin' to tromple me. Ah can't tell who my enemy is
and who is my friend. You gimme dis protection in my
mouf and Ah uses it."

God thought it over for a while then he says:

"Well, snake, I don't want yo' generations all
stomped out and I don't want you killin' everything else
dat moves. Here take dis bell and tie it to yo' tail. When
you hear feets comin' you ring yo' bell and if it's yo'
friend, he'll be keerful. If it's yo' enemy, it's you and
him."

So dat's how de snake got his poison and dat's how
come he got rattles.

Biddy, biddy, bend my story is end.

Turn loose de rooster and hold de hen.

"Don't tell no mo' 'bout no snakes—specially when we
walkin' in all dis tall grass," pleaded Presley. "Ah speck Ah'm
gointer be seein' 'em in my sleep tonight. Lawd, Ah'm
skeered of snakes."

"Who ain't?" cut in Cliff Ulmer. "It sho is gittin' hot. Ah'll
be glad when we git to de lake so Ah kin find myself some
shade."

"Man, youse two miles from dat lake yet, and otherwise it
ain't hot today," said Joe Wiley. "He ain't seen it hot, is he
Will House?"

"Naw, Joe, when me and you was hoboing down in Texas it
was so hot till we saw old stumps and logs crawlin' off in de
shade."

Eugene Oliver said, "Aw dat wasn't hot. Ah seen it so hot
till two cakes of ice left the ice house and went down the
street and fainted."

Arthur Hopkins put in: "Ah knowed two men who went to

Tampa all dressed up in new blue serge suits, and it was so hot dat when de train pulled into Tampa two blue suits got off de train. De men had done melted out of 'em."

Will House said, "Dat wasn't hot. Dat was chilly weather. Me and Joe Wiley went fishin' and it was so hot dat before we got to de water, we met de fish, coming swimming up de road in dust."

"Dat's a fact, too," added Joe Wiley. "Ah remember dat day well. It was so hot dat Ah struck a match to light my pipe and set de lake afire. Burnt half of it, den took de water dat was left and put out de fire."

Joe Willard said "Hush! Don't Ah hear a noise?"

Eugene and Cliffert shouted together, "Yeah—went down to de river—

> Heard a mighty racket
> Nothing but de bull frog
> Pullin' off his jacket!"

"Dat ain't what Ah hea'd," said Joe.

"Well, whut did you hear?"

"Ah see a chigger[6] over in de fence corner wid a splinter in his foot and a seed tick is pickin' it out wid a fence rail and de chigger is hollerin', 'Lawd, have mercy.'"

"Dat brings me to de boll-weevil," said Larkins White. "A boll-weevil flew onto de steerin' wheel of a white man's car and says, 'Mister, lemme drive yo' car.'

"De white man says, 'You can't drive no car.'

"Boll-weevil says: 'Oh yeah, Ah kin. Ah drove in five thousand cars last year and Ah'm going to drive in ten thousand dis year.'

"A man told a tale on de boll-weevil agin. Says he heard a terrible racket and noise down in de field, went down to see whut it was and whut you reckon? It was Ole Man Boll-Weevil whippin' li' Willie Boll-Weevil 'cause he couldn't carry two rows at a time."

Will House said, "Ah know a lie on a black gnat. Me and my buddy Joe Wiley was ramshackin' Georgy over when we

---

[6] A young flea.

come to a loggin' camp. So bein' out of work we ast for a job.
So de man puts us on and give us some oxes to drive. Ah had
a six-yoke team and Joe was drivin' a twelve-yoke team. As we
was comin' thru de woods we heard somethin' hummin' and
we didn't know what it was. So we got hungry and went in a
place to eat and when we come out a gnat had done et up de
six-yoke team and de twelve-yoke team, and was sittin' up on
de wagon pickin' his teeth wid a ox-horn and cryin' for
somethin' to eat."

"Yeah," put in Joe Wiley, "we seen a man tie his cow and
calf out to pasture and a mosquito come along and et up de
cow and was ringin' de bell for de calf."

"Dat wasn't no full-grown mosquito at dat," said Eugene
Oliver. "Ah was travellin' in Texas and laid down and went to
sleep. De skeeters bit me so hard till Ah seen a ole iron wash-
pot, so Ah crawled under it and turned it down over me good
so de skeeters couldn't git to me. But you know dem skeeters
bored right thru dat iron pot. So I up wid a hatchet and
bradded their bills into de pot. So they flew on off 'cross
Galveston bay wid de wash pot on their bills."

"Look," said Black Baby, "on de Indian River we went to
bed and heard de mosquitoes singin' like bull alligators. So
we got under four blankets. Shucks! dat wasn't nothin'.
Dem mosquitoes just screwed off dem short bills, reached
back in they hip-pocket and took out they long bills and
screwed 'em on and come right on through dem blankets
and got us."

"Is dat de biggest mosquito you all ever seen? Shucks!
Dey was li'l baby mosquitoes! One day my ole man took
some men and went out into de woods to cut some fence
posts. And a big rain come up so they went up under a great
big ole tree. It was so big it would take six men to meet
around it. De other men set down on de roots but my ole
man stood up and leaned against de tree. Well, sir, a big old
skeeter come up on de other side of dat tree and bored right
thru it and got blood out of my ole man's back. Dat made
him so mad till he up wid his ax and bradded dat mosquito's
bill into dat tree. By dat time de rain stopped and they all
went home.

"Next day when they come out, dat mosquito had done cleaned up ten acres dying. And two or three weeks after dat my ole man got enough bones from dat skeeter to fence in dat ten acres."

Everybody liked to hear about the mosquito. They laughed all over themselves.

"Yeah," said Sack Daddy, "you sho is tellin' de truth 'bout dat big old mosquito 'cause my ole man bought dat same piece of land and raised a crop of pumpkins on it and lemme tell y'all right now—mosquito dust is de finest fertilizer in de world. Dat land was so rich and we raised pumpkins so big dat we et five miles up in one of 'em and five miles down and ten miles acrost one and we ain't never found out how far it went. But my ole man was buildin' a scaffold inside so we could cut de pumpkin meat without so much trouble, when he dropped his hammer. He tole me, he says, 'Son, Ah done dropped my hammer. Go git it for me.' Well, Ah went down in de pumpkin and begin to hunt dat hammer. Ah was foolin' 'round in there all day, when I met a man and he ast me what Ah was lookin' for. Ah tole him my ole man had done dropped his hammer and sent me to find it for him. De man tole me Ah might as well give it up for a lost cause, he had been lookin' for a double mule-team and a wagon that had got lost in there for three weeks and he hadn't found no trace of 'em yet. So Ah stepped on a pin, de pin bent and dat's de way de story went."

"Dat was rich land but my ole man had some rich land too," put in Will House. "My ole man planted cucumbers and he went along droppin' de seeds and befo' he could git out de way he'd have ripe cucumbers in his pockets. What is the richest land you ever seen?"

"Well," replied Joe Wiley, "my ole man had some land dat was so rich dat our mule died and we buried him down in our bottom-land and de next mornin' he had done sprouted li'l jackasses."

"Aw, dat land wasn't so rich," objected Ulmer. "My ole man had some land and it was so rich dat he drove a stob[7] in de ground at de end of a corn-row for a landmark and next

[7] Stake.

morning there was ten ears of corn on de corn stalk and four ears growin' on de stob."

"Dat lan' y'all talkin' 'bout might do, if you give it plenty commercial-nal[8] but my ole man wouldn't farm no po' land like dat," said Joe Wiley. "Now, one year we was kinda late puttin' in our crops. Everybody else had corn a foot high when papa said, 'Well, chillun, Ah reckon we better plant some corn.' So Ah was droppin' and my brother was hillin' up behind me. We had done planted 'bout a dozen rows when Ah looked back and seen de corn comin' up. Ah didn't want it to grow too fast 'cause it would make all fodder and no roastin' ears so Ah hollered to my brother to sit down on some of it to stunt de growth. So he did, and de next day he dropped me back a note—says: "passed thru Heben yesterday at twelve o'clock sellin' roastin' ears to de angels."

"Yeah," says Larkins White, "dat was some pretty rich ground, but whut is de poorest ground you ever seen?"

Arthur Hopkins spoke right up and said:

"Ah seen some land so poor dat it took nine partridges to holler 'Bob White.' "

"Dat was rich land, boy," declared Larkins. "Ah seen land so poor dat de people come together and 'cided dat it was too poor to raise anything on, so they give it to de church, so de congregation built de church and called a pastor and held de meetin'. But de land was so poor they had to wire up to Jacksonville for ten sacks of commercial-nal before dey could raise a tune on dat land."

The laughter was halted by the sound of a woodpecker against a cypress. Lonnie Barnes up with his gun to kill it, but Lucy stopped him.

"What you want to kill dat ole thing for? He ain't fitten to eat. Save dat shot and powder to kill me a rabbit. Ah sho would love a nice tender cotton-tail. Slim Ellis brought me a great big ole fat ham off a rabbit last night, and Ah lakted dat."

"Ah kin shoot you a rabbit just as good as Slim kin," Lonnie protested. "Ah wasn't gointer kill no ole tough pecker-

[8]Commercial fertilizer.

wood for you to eat, baby. Ah was goin' to shoot dat red-head for his meanness. You know de peckerwood come pretty nigh drownin' de whole world once."

"How was dat?"

Well, you know when de Flood was and dey had two of everything in de ark—well, Ole Nora[9] didn't take on no trees, so de woodpecker set 'round and set 'round for a week or so then he felt like he just had to peck himself some wood. So he begin to peck on de Ark. Ole Nora come to him and tole him, "Don't peck on de Ark. If you peck a hole in it, we'll all drown."

Woodpecker says: "But Ah'm hungry for some wood to peck."

Ole Nora says, "Ah don't keer how hongry you gits don't you peck on dis ark no mo. You want to drown everybody and everything?"

So de woodpecker would sneak 'round behind Ole Nora's back and peck every chance he got. He'd hide hisself way down in de hold where he thought nobody could find him and peck and peck. So one day Ole Nora come caught him at it. He never opened his mouth to dat woodpecker. He just hauled off and give dat pecker-wood a cold head-whipping wid a sledge hammer, and dat's why a peckerwood got a red head today—'cause Ole Nora bloodied it wid dat hammer. Dat's how come Ah feel like shootin' every one of 'em Ah see. Tryin' to drown *me* before Ah was born.

"A whole lot went on on dat ole Ark," Larkins White commented. "Dat's where de possum lost de hair off his tail."

"Now don't you tell me no possum ever had no hair on dat slick tail of his'n," said Black Baby, " 'cause Ah know better."

Yes, he did have hair on his tail one time. Yes, indeed. De possum had a bushy tail wid long silk hair on it. Why, it useter be one of de prettiest sights you ever seen. De possum struttin' 'round wid his great big ole plumey tail. Dat was 'way back in de olden times before de big flood.

[9]Noah.

But de possum was lazy—jus' like he is today. He sleep too much. You see Ole Nora had a son name Ham and he loved to be playin' music all de time. He had a banjo and a fiddle and maybe a guitar too. But de rain come up so sudden he didn't have time to put 'em on de ark. So when rain kept comin' down he fretted a lot 'cause he didn't have nothin' to play. So he found a ole cigar box and made hisself a banjo, but he didn't have no strings for it. So he seen de possum stretched out sleeping wid his tail all spread 'round. So Ham slipped up and shaved de possum's tail and made de strings for his banjo out de hairs. When dat possum woke up from his nap, Ham was playin' his tail hairs down to de bricks and dat's why de possum ain't got no hair on his tail today. Losin' his pretty tail sorta broke de possum's spirit too. He ain't never been de same since. Dat's how come he always actin' shame-faced. He know his tail ain't whut it useter be; and de possum feel mighty bad about it.

"A lot of things ain't whut they useter be," observed Jim Presley. "Now take de 'gator for instance. He been changed 'round powerful since he been made."

"Yeah," cut in Eugene Oliver, "He useter have a nice tongue so he could talk like a nat'chal man, but Brer Dog caused de 'gator to lose his tongue, and dat's how come he hate de dog today."

"Brer 'Gator didn't fall out wid Brer Dog 'bout no tongue," retorted Presley.

Brer Dog done de 'gator a dirty trick 'bout his mouth. You know God made de dog and the 'gator without no mouth. So they seen everybody else had a mouth so they made it up to git theirselves a mouth like de other varmints. So they agreed to cut one 'nothers' mouth, and each one said dat when de other one tole 'em to stop cuttin' they would. So Brer Dog got his mouth first. Brer 'Gator took de razor and cut. Brer Dog tole him, "Stop," which he did. Den Brer Dog took de razor and begin to cut Brer 'Gator a mouth. When his mouth was big as he wanted it, Brer 'Gator

says, "Stop, Brer Dog. Dat'll do, I thank you, please."
But Brer Dog kept right on cuttin' till he ruint Brer
'Gator's face. Brer 'Gator was a very handsome gent'-
man befo' Brer Dog done him that a way, and everytime he look in de lookin' glass he cry like a baby over
de disfiggerment of his face. And dat's how come de
'gator hate de dog.

"My people, my people," lamented Oliver. "They just will
talk whut they don't know."
"Go on Oliver."

De 'gator didn't fall out wid de dog 'bout no mouth
cuttin' scrape. You know all de animals was havin' a ball
down in de pine woods, and so they all chipped in for
refreshments and then they didn't have no music for de
dance. So all de animals what could 'greed to furnish
music. So de dog said he'd be de trumpet in de band,
and de horse and de frog and de mockin' bird and all
said they'd be there and help out all they could. But
they didn't have no bass drum, till somebody said,
"Whut's de matter wid Brer 'Gator, why he don't play
de bass drum for us?" Dey called Brer 'Gator but he
wasn't at de meetin' so de varmints deppitized Brer
Dog to go call on Brer 'Gator and see if he wouldn't
furnish de drum music for de dance. Which he did.

"Good evenin', Brer 'Gator."

"My compliments, Brer Dog, how you makin' out?
Ah'm always glad when folks visit me. Whut you want?"

"Well Brer 'Gator, de varmints is holdin' a big convention tonight in de piney woods and we want you to
furnish us a little bit of yo' drum music."

"It's like this, Brer Dog, tell de other animals dat
Ah'm mighty proud they wants me and de compliments
run all over me, but my wife is po'ly and my chillun is
down sick. But Ah'll lend you my drum if you know
anybody kin play it, and know how to take keer of it
too!"

"Oh, Ah'll do *dat*, Brer 'Gator. You just put it in my
keer. You don't have to worry 'bout dat atall."

So de dog took Brer 'Gator's tongue to de ball dat

night and they beat it for a drum. De varmints lakted de bass drum so well till they didn't play nothin' else hardly. So by daybreak it was wore clean out. Brer Dog didn't want to go tell Brer 'Gator they had done wore his tongue out so he hid from Brer 'Gator. Course de 'gator don't like it 'bout his tongue so he's de sworn enemy of de dog.

Big Sweet says, "Dat's de first time Ah ever heard 'bout de dawg wearin' out de 'gator's tongue, but Ah do know he useter be a pretty varmint. He was pure white all over wid red and yeller stripes around his neck. He was pretty like dat 'till he met up wid Brer Rabbit. Kah, kah, kah! Ah have to laugh everytime Ah think how sharp dat ole rabbit rascal is."

"Yeah," said Sam Hopkins. "At night time, at de right time; Ah've always understood it's de habit of de rabbit to dance in de wood."

"When Ah'm shellin' my corn, you keep out yo' nubbins, Sam," Big Sweet snapped as she spat her snuff.

Ah'm tellin' dis lie on de 'gator. Well, de 'gator was a pretty white varmint wid coal black eyes. He useter swim in de water, but he never did bog up in de mud lak he do now. When he come out de water he useter lay up on de clean grass so he wouldn't dirty hisself all up.

So one day he was layin' up on de grass in a marsh sunnin' hisself and sleepin' when Brer Rabbit come bustin' cross de marsh and run right over Brer 'Gator before he stopped. Brer 'Gator woke up and seen who it was trompin' all over him and trackin' up his pretty white hide. So he seen Brer Rabbit, so he ast him, "Brer Rabbit, what you mean by runnin' all cross me and messin' up my clothes lak dis?"

Brer Rabbit was up behind a clump of bushes peerin' out to see what was after him. So he tole de 'gator, says: "Ah ain't got time to see what Ah'm runnin' over nor under. Ah got trouble behind me."

'Gator ast, "Whut is trouble? Ah ain't never heard tell of dat befo'."

Brer Rabbit says, "You ain't never heard tell of trouble?"

Brer 'Gator tole him, "No."

Rabbit says: "All right, you jus' stay right where you at and Ah'll show you whut trouble is."

He peered 'round to see if de coast was clear and loped off, and Brer 'Gator washed Brer Rabbit's foot tracks off his hide and went on back to sleep agin.

Brer Rabbit went on off and lit him a li'dard knot[10] and come on back. He set dat marsh afire on every side. All around Brer 'Gator de fire was burnin' in flames of fire. De 'gator woke up and pitched out to run, but every which a way he run de fire met him.

He seen Brer Rabbit sittin' up on de high ground jus' killin' hisself laughin'. So he hollered and ast him:

"Brer Rabbit, whut's all dis goin' on?"

"Dat's trouble, Brer 'Gator, dat's trouble youse in."

De 'gator run from side to side, round and round. Way after while he broke thru and hit de water "ker ploogum!" He got all cooled off but he had done got smoked all up befo' he got to de water, and his eyes is all red from de smoke. And dat's how come a 'gator is black today—cause de rabbit took advantage of him lak dat.

---

[10]Lightwood, fat pine. So called because it is frequently used as a torch.

VII

J OE WILEY said, "'Tain't nothin' cute as a rabbit. When they come cuter than him, they got to have 'cute indigestion." He cleared his throat and continued:

Dat's de reason de dog is mad wid de rabbit[1] now— 'cause he fooled de dog.

You know they useter call on de same girl. De rabbit useter g'wan up to de house and cross his legs on de porch and court de girl. Brer Dog, he'd come in de gate wid his banjo under his arm.

"Good evenin', Miss Saphronie."

"My compliments, Brer Dog, come have a chair on de pe-azza."

"No thank you ma'am, Miss Saphronie. B'lieve Ah'll set out here under de Chinaberry tree."

So he'd set out dere and pick de banjo and sing all 'bout:

If Miss Fronie was a gal of mine
She wouldn't do nothin' but starch and iron.

So de girl wouldn't pay no mind to Brer Rabbit at all. She'd be listenin' to Brer Dog sing. Every time he'd stop she'd holler out dere to him, "Wont you favor us wid another piece, Brer Dog? Ah sho do love singin' especially when they got a good voice and picks de banjo at de same time."

Brer Rabbit saw he wasn't makin' no time wid Miss Saphronie so he waylaid Brer Dog down in de piney woods one day and says:

"Brer Dog, you sho is got a mellow voice. You can sing. Wisht Ah could sing like dat, den maybe Miss Fronie would pay me some mind."

"Gawan, Brer Rabbit, you makin' great 'miration at nothin'. Ah can whoop a little, but Ah really do wish Ah could sing enough to suit Miss Fronie."

[1]See glossary.

"Well, dat's de very point Ah'm comin' out on. Ah know a way to make yo' voice sweeter."

"How? Brer Rabbit, how?"

"Ah knows a way."

"Hurry up and tell me, Brer Rabbit. Don't keep me waitin' like dis. Make haste."

"Ah got to see inside yo' throat first. Lemme see dat and Ah can tell you exactly what to do so you can sing more better."

Brer Dog stretched his mouth wide open and the rabbit peered way down inside. Brer Dog had his mouth latched back to de last notch and his eyes shut. So Brer Rabbit pulled out his razor and split Brer Dog's tongue and tore out across de mountain wid de dog right in behind him. Him and him! Brer Rabbit had done ruint Brer Dog's voice, but he ain't had time to stop at Miss Fronie's nor nowhere else 'cause dat dog is so mad he won't give him time.

"Yeah," said Cliff.

De dog is sho hot after him. Run dem doggone rabbits so that they sent word to de dogs dat they want peace. So they had a convention. De rabbit took de floor and said they was tired of runnin', and dodgin' all de time, and they asted de dogs to please leave rabbits alone and run somethin' else. So de dogs put it to a vote and 'greed to leave off runnin' rabbits.

So after de big meetin' Brer Dog invites de rabbit over to his house to have dinner wid him.

He started on thru de woods wid Brer Dog but every now and then he'd stop and scratch his ear and listen. He stop right in his tracks. Dog say:

"Aw, come on Brer Rabbit, you too suscautious. Come on."

Kept dat up till they come to de branch just 'fore they got to Brer Dog's house. Just as Brer Rabbit started to step out on de foot-log, he heard some dogs barkin' way down de creek. He heard de old hound say, "How o-l-d is he?" and the young dogs answer him: "Twenty-one or two, twenty-one or two!" So Brer Rabbit say, "Excuse me, but Ah don't reckon Ah better go home wid you today, Brer Dog."

"Aw, come on, Brer Rabbit, you always gitten scared for nothin'. Come on."

"Ah hear dogs barkin', Brer Dog."

"Naw, you don't, Brer Rabbit."

"Yes, Ah do. Ah know, dat's dogs barkin'."

"S'posin' it is, it don't make no difference. Ain't we done held a convention and passed a law dogs run no mo' rabbits? Don't pay no 'tention to every li'l bit of barkin' you hear."

Rabbit scratch his ear and say,

"Yeah, but all de dogs ain't been to no convention, and anyhow some of dese fool dogs ain't got no better sense than to run all over dat law and break it up. De rabbits didn't go to school much and he didn't learn but three letter, and that's trust no mistake. Run every time de bush shake."

So he raced on home without breakin' another breath wid de dog.

"Dat's right," cut in Larkins White. "De Rabbits run from everything. They held a meetin' and decided. They say, 'Le's all go drown ourselves 'cause ain't nothin' skeered of us.' So it was agreed.

"They all started to de water in a body fast as time could wheel and roll. When they was crossin' de marsh jus' befo' they got to de sea, a frog hollered, 'Quit it, quit it!' So they say, 'Somethin' is 'fraid of us, so we won't drown ourselves.' So they all turnt 'round and went home."

"Dat's as bad as dat goat Ah seen back in South Carolina. We was on de tobacco truck goin' after plants when we passed a goat long side de road. He was jus' chewin' and he looked up and ast, 'Whose truck is dat?' Nobody answered him. When we come on back Ah said, 'Mr. Rush Pinkney's, why?' De goat says, 'Oh nothin'.' and kept right on chewin'."

"Ow, Big Sweet! gimme dat lyin' goat! You know damn

well dat goat ain't broke a breath wid you and nobody else,"
scolded Jim Allen.

"But a goat's got plenty sense, ugly as he is," said Arthur
Hopkins.

Ah know my ole man had a goat and one Sunday
mornin' he got mama to wash his shirt so't would be
clean for him to wear to church. It was a pretty red silk
shirt and my ole man was crazy about it.

So my ole lady washed it and hung it out to dry so
she could iron it befo' church time. Our goat spied pa's
shirt hangin' on de line and et it up tiddy umpty.

My ole man was so mad wid dat goat 'bout his shirt
till he grabbed him and tied him on de railroad track so
de train could run over him and kill him.

But dat old goat was smart. When he seen dat train
bearin' down on him, he coughed up dat red shirt and
waved de train down.

Dad Boykin said: "No ef and ands about it. A goat is a
smart varmint, but my feets sho is tired."

"Dat *was* a long two miles," Jim Allen added. "Ah see de
lake now, and Ah sho am glad."

"Doggone it!" said Lonnie Barnes, "here we is almost at de
lake and Ah ain't got myself no game yet. But maybe Ah'll
have mo' luck on de way back."

"Yeah," Lucy remarked dryly, "dat gun you totin' ain't
doin' you much good! Might just as well left it home."

"He act just like dat nigger did in slavery time wid Ole
Massa's gun," laughed Willie Roberts.

"How as dat?"

Well, you know John was Ole Massa's pet nigger.
He give John de best of everything and John thought
Ole Massa was made outa gold. So one day Massa decided he wanted a piece of deer meat to eat so he
called John and some more of his niggers together and
told 'em:

"Now Ah want y'all to go git me a deer today. Ah'm
goin' to give John my new gun and Ah want de rest of
y'all go 'round and skeer up de deer and head him to-

wards John, and he will shoot him wid de gun." When
de others got there they said, "Did you git him, John?"

He said, "Naw, Ah didn't."

They said, "Well how come you didn't? He come
right dead down de hill towards you."

"Y'all crazy! You think Ah'm gointer sprain Massa's
brand new gun shootin' up hill wid it?"

"Dat's put me in de mind of a gun my ole man had," said
Gene Oliver. "He shot a man wid it one time and de bullet
worked him twice befo' it kilt him and three times after. If
you hold it high, it would sweep de sky; if you hold it level,
it'd kill de devil."

"Oh Gene, stop yo' lyin'! You don't stop lyin' and gone to
flyin'."

"Dat ain't no lie, dat's a fact. One night I fired it myself,"
said Pitts.

"It's a wonder you didn't shoot it off dat time when de
quarters boss was hot behind you."

"Let dat ride! Ah didn't want to kill dat ole cracker. But
one night Ah heard somethin' stumblin' 'round our woodpile, so Ah grabbed de gun, stepped to de back door and fired
it at de woodpile, and went on back to bed. All night long Ah
heard somethin' goin' 'round and 'round de house hummin'
like a nest of hornets. When daybreak come Ah found out
what it was. What you reckon? It was dat bullet. De night was
so dark it was runnin' 'round de house waitin' for daylight so
it could find out which was the way to go!"

"Dat was a mighty gun yo' pa had," agreed Larkins, "but
Ah had a gun dat would lay dat one in the shade. It could
shoot so far till Ah had to put salt down de barrel so de game
Ah kilt wid it would keep till Ah got to it."

"Larkins—" Jim Allen started to protest.

"Mr. Allen, dat ain't no lie. Dat's a fack. Dat gun was so
bad dat all Ah need to do was walk out in de woods wid it to
skeer all de varmints. Ah went huntin' one day and saw three
thousand ducks in a pond. Jus' as Ah levelled dis gun to fire,
de weather turned cold and de water in de lake froze solid
and them ducks flew off wid de lake froze to their feets."

"Larkins, s'posin' you was to die right now, where would

you land?—jus' as straight to hell as a martin to his gourd.
Whew! you sho kin lie. You'd pass slap thru hell proper. Jus' a
bouncin' and a jumpin' and go clear to Ginny Gall, and dat's
four miles south of West Hell; you better stop yo' lyin', man."

"Dat ain't no lie, man. You jus' ain't seen no real guns and
no good shootin'."

"Ah don't want to see none. Less fish. Here we is at de
lake. You can't talk and ketch fish too. You'll skeer all de fish
away."

"Aw, nobody ain't even got a hook baited yet. Leave Larkins lie till we git set!" suggested Joe Wiley. "You gittin' old,
Jim, when you can't stand good lyin'. It's jus' like sound doctrine. Everybody can't stand it."

"Who gittin' old? Not me! Ah laks de lies. All I said is, yo'
talkin' skeers off all de trouts and sheepheads. Ah can't eat no
lies."

"Aw, gran'pa, don't be so astorperious! We all wants to
hear Larkins' tale. I'm goin' ketch you some fish. We ain't off
lak dis often. Tomorrow we'll be back in de swamp 'mong de
cypress knees, de 'gators, and de moccasins, and strainin' wid
de swamp boss," pleaded Cliff. "Go head on, and talk, Larkins, God ain't gonna bother you."

"Well," says Larkins:

A man had a wife and a whole passle of young 'uns,
and they didn't have nothin' to eat.

He told his ole lady, "Well, Ah got a load of ammunition in my gun, so Ah'm gointer go out in de woods
and see what Ah kin bring back for us to eat."

His wife said: "That's right, go see can't you kill us
somethin'—if 'tain't nothin' but a squirrel."

He went on huntin' wid his gun. It was one of dese
muzzle-loads. He knowed he didn't have but one load
of ammunition so he was very careful not to stumble
and let his gun go off by accident.

He had done walked more'n three miles from home
and he ain't saw anything to shoot at. He got worried.
Then all of a sudden he spied some wild turkeys settin'
up in a tree on a limb. He started to shoot at 'em, when
he looked over in de pond and seen a passle of wild

ducks; and down at de edge of de pond he saw a great big deer. He heard some noise behind him and he looked 'round and seen some partiges.

He wanted all of 'em and he didn't know how he could get 'em. So he stood and he thought and he thought. Then he decided what to do.

He took aim, but he didn't shoot at de turkeys. He shot de limb de turkeys was settin' on and de ball split dat limb and let all dem turkeys' feets dropped right down thru de crack and de split limb shet up on 'em and helt 'em right dere. De ball went on over and fell into de pond and kilt all dem ducks. De gun had too heavy a charge in her, so it bust and de barrel flew over and kilt dat deer. De stock kicked de man in de breast and he fell backwards and smothered all dem partiges.

Well, he drug his deer up under de tree and got his ducks out de pond and piled them up wid de turkeys and so forth. He seen he couldn't tote all dat game so he went on home to git his mule and wagon.

Soon as he come in de gate his wife said:

"Where is de game you was gointer bring back? you musta lost yo' gun, you ain't got it."

He told his wife, "Ah wears de longest pants in dis house. You leave me tend to my business and you mind yours. Jus' you put on de pot and be ready. Plenty rations is comin'."

He took his team on back in de woods wid him and loaded up de wagon. He wouldn't git up on de wagon hisself because he figgered his mule had enough to pull without him.

Just as he got his game all loaded on de wagon, it commenced to rain but he walked on beside of the mule pattin' him and tellin' him to "come up," till they got home.

When he got home his wife says: "De pot is boilin'. Where is de game you tole me about?"

He looked back and seen his wagon wasn't behind de mule where it ought to have been. Far as he could see — nothin' but them leather traces, but no wagon.

Then he knowed de rain had done made dem traces

stretch, and de wagon hadn't moved from where he loaded it.

So he told his wife, "De game will be here. Don't you worry."

So he just took de mule out and stabled him and wrapped dem traces 'round de gate post and went on in de house.

De next day it was dry and de sun was hot and it shrunk up dem traces, and about twelve o'clock they brought dat wagon home, "Cluck-cluck, cluck-cluck," right on up to de gate.

In spite of the laughter and talk, Cliff had landed two perch already, so Jim Allen laughed with the rest.

"Now," he said, beaming upon the fish his grandson had hooked, "I'm goin' to tell y'all about de hawk and de buzzard.

You know de hawk and de buzzard was settin' up in a pine tree one day, so de hawk says: "How you get yo' livin', Brer Buzzard?"

"Oh Ah'm makin' out pretty good, Brer Hawk. Ah waits on de salvation of de Lawd."

Hawk says, "Humph, Ah don't wait on de mercy of nobody. Ah takes mine."

"Ah bet, Ah'll live to pick yo' bones, Brer Hawk."

"Aw naw, you won't, Brer Buzzard. Watch me git my livin'."

He seen a sparrer sittin' on a dead limb of a tree and he sailed off and dived down at dat sparrer. De end of de limb was stickin' out and he run his breast right up on de sharp point and hung dere. De sparrer flew on off.

After while he got so weak he knowed he was gointer die. So de buzzard flew past just so—flyin' slow you know, and said, "Un hunh, Brer Hawk, Ah told you Ah was gointer live to pick yo' bones. Ah waits on de salvation of de Lawd."

And dat's de way it is wid some of you young colts."

"Heh, heh, heh! Y'all talkin' 'bout me being old. Ah betcher Ah'll be here when a many of y'all is gone."

Joe Wiley said: "Less table discussion 'bout dyin' and open up de house for new business.

Y'all want to know how come they always use raw-hide on mule, so Ah'm gointer tell you. Whenever they make a whip they gointer have raw-hide on it, if it ain't nothin' but de tip.

A man had a mule you know and he had a ox too. So he used to work 'em together.

Both of 'em used to get real tired befo' knockin' off time but dat ole ox had mo' sense than de mule, so he played off sick.

Every day de mule would go out and work by hisself and de ox stayed in de stable. Every night when de mule come in, he'd ast, "Whut did Massa say 'bout me to-day?"

De mule would say, "Oh nothin'," or maybe he'd say, "Ah heard him say how sorry he was you was sick and couldn't work."

De ox would laugh and go on to sleep.

One day de mule got tired, so he said, "Massa dat ox ain't sick. 'Tain't a thing de matter wid him. He's jus' playin' off sick. Ah'm tired of doin' all dis work by my-self."

So dat night when he got in de stable, de ox ast him, "What did Ole Massa say 'bout me today?"

Mule told him, "Ah didn't hear him say a thing, but Ah saw him talkin' to de butcher man."

So de ox jumped up and said, "Ah'm well. Tell Ole Massa Ah'll be to work tomorrow."

But de next mornin' bright and soon de butcher come led him off.

So he said to de mule, "If you hadn't of told Massa on me, Ah wouldn't be goin' where Ah am. They're gointer kill me, but Ah'll always be war on yo' back."

And that's why they use raw-hide on mule's back—on ac-count of dat mule and dat ox."

"Oh, well, if we gointer go way back there and tell how everything started," said Ulmer, "Ah might just as well tell how come we got gophers."

"Pay 'tention to yo' pole, Cliff," Jim Allen scolded. "You gittin' a bite. You got 'im! A trout too! If dat fool ain't lucky wid fish!"

Old Man Jim strung the trout expertly. "Now, Cliff, you kin do all de talkin' you want, just as long as you ketch me some fish Ah don't keer."

"Well," began Cliff:

God was sittin' down by de sea makin' sea fishes. He made de whale and throwed dat in and it swum off. He made a shark and throwed it in and then he made mullets and shad-fish and cats and trouts and they all swum on off.

De Devil was standin' behind him lookin' over his shoulder.

Way after while, God made a turtle and throwed it in de water and it swum on off. Devil says, "Ah kin make one of those things."

God said, "No, you can't neither."

Devil told him, "Aw, Ah kin so make one of those things. 'Tain't nothin' to make nohow. Who couldn't do dat? Ah jus' can't blow de breath of life into it, but Ah sho kin make a turtle."

God said: "Devil, Ah know you can't make none, but if you think you kin make one go 'head and make it and Ah'll blow de breath of life into it for you."

You see, God was sittin' down by de sea, makin' de fish outa sea-mud. But de Devil went on up de hill so God couldn't watch him workin', and made his outa high land dirt. God waited nearly all day befo' de Devil come back wid his turtle.

As soon as God seen it, He said, "Devil, dat ain't no turtle you done made."

Devil flew hot right off. "Dat ain't no turtle? Who say dat ain't no turtle? Sho it's a turtle."

God shook his head, says, "Dat sho *ain't* no turtle, but Ah'll blow de breath of life into it like Ah promised."

Devil stood Him down dat dat was a turtle.

So God blowed de breath of life into what de devil

had done made, and throwed him into de water. He
swum out. God throwed him in again. He come on out.
Throwed him in de third time and he come out de third
time.

God says: "See, Ah told you dat wasn't no turtle."

"Yes, suh, dat *is* a turtle."

"Devil, don't you know dat all turtles loves de water?
Don't you see whut you done made won't stay in
there?"

Devil said, "Ah don't keer, dat's a turtle, Ah keep a
'tellin' you."

God disputed him down dat it wasn't no turtle. Devil
looked it over and scratched his head. Then he says,
"Well, anyhow it will go for one." And that's why we
have gophers!

"Dat gopher had good sense. He know he was a dry-land
turtle so he didn't try to mix wid de rest. Take for instance de
time they had de gopher up in court.

"De gopher come in and looked all around de place. De
judge was a turtle, de lawyers was turtles, de witnesses was
turtles and they had turtles for jurymen.

"So de gopher ast de judge to excuse his case and let him
come back some other time. De judge ast him how come he
wanted to put off his case and de gopher looked all around de
room and said, 'Blood is thicker than water,' and escused hisself from de place."

"Yeah," said Floyd Thomas, "but even God ain't satisfied
wid some of de things He makes and changes 'em Hisself."

Jim Presley wanted to know what God ever changed, to
Floyd's knowledge.

Well, He made butterflies after de world wuz all finished and thru. You know de Lawd seen so much bare
ground till He got sick and tired lookin' at it. So God
tole 'em to fetch 'im his prunin' shears and trimmed up
de trees and made grass and flowers and throwed 'em all
over de clearin's and dey growed dere from memorial
days.

Way after while de flowers said, "Wese put heah to
keep de world comp'ny but wese lonesome ourselves."

So God said, "A world is somethin' ain't never finished. Soon's you make one thing you got to make somethin' else to go wid it. Gimme dem li'l tee-ninchy shears."

So he went 'round clippin' li'l pieces offa every-thing—de sky, de trees, de flowers, de earth, de var-mints and every one of dem li'l clippin's flew off. When folks seen all them li'l scraps fallin' from God's scissors and flutterin' they called 'em flutter-bys. But you know how it is wid de brother in black. He got a big mouf and a stambling tongue. So he got it all mixed up and said, "butter-fly" and folks been calling 'em dat ever since. Dat's how come we got butterflies of every color and kind and dat's why dey hangs 'round de flowers. Dey wuz made to keep de flowers company.

"Watch out, Cliffert!" yelled Jim Allen. "A 'gator must be on yo' hook! Look at it! It's dived like a duck."

"Aw, 'tain't nothin' but a gar fish on it. Ah kin tell by his bite!" said Cliff.

"You pull him up and see!" Jim commanded.

Cliff hauled away and landed a large gar on the grass.

"See, Ah told you, Gran'pa. Don't you worry. Ah'm gointer ketch you mo' fish than you kin eat. Plenty for Mama and Gran'ma too. Less take dis gar-fish home to de cat."

"Yeah," said Jim Presley. "Y' take de cat a fish, too. They love it better than God loves Gabriel—and dat's His best angel."

"He sho do and dat's how cats got into a mess of trouble—'bout eatin' fish," added Jim Presley.

"How was dat? I done forgot if Ah ever knowed."

"If, if, if," mocked Jim Allen. "Office Richardson, youse always iffin'! If a frog had wings he wouldn't bump his rump so much."

"Gran'pa is right in wid de cats," Cliff teased. "He's so skeered he ain't gointer git all de fish he kin eat, he's just like a watch-dog when de folks is at de table. He'll bite anybody then. Think they cheatin' 'im outa his vittles."

Jim Presley spat in the lake and began:

Once upon a time was a good ole time—monkey chew tobacco and spit white lime.

Well, this was a man dat had a wife and five chillun, and a dog and a cat.

Well, de hongry times caught 'em. Hard times everywhere. Nobody didn't have no mo' then jus' enough to keep 'em alive. First they had a long dry spell dat parched up de crops, then de river rose and drowned out everything. You could count anybody's ribs. De white folks all got faces look lak blue-John[2] and de niggers had de white mouf.[3]

So dis man laid in de bed one night and consulted wid his piller. Dat means he talked it over wid his wife. And he told her, "Tomorrow less git our pole and go to de lake and see kin we ketch a mess of fish. Dat's our last chance. De fish done got so skeerce and educated they's hard to ketch, but we kin try."

They was at de lake bright and soon de next day. De man took de fishin' pole hisself 'cause he was skeered to trust his wife er de chillun wid it. It was they last chance to git some grub.

So de man fished all day long till he caught seven fishes. Not no great big trouts nor mud-cats but li'l perches and brims. So he tole 'em, "Now, Ah got a fish apiece for all of us, but Ah'm gointer keep on till Ah ketch one apiece for our dog and our cat."

So he fished on till sundown and caught a fish for the dog and de cat, and then they went on home and cooked de fish.

After de fish was all cooked and ready de woman said: "We got to have some drinkin' water. Less go down to de spring to git some. You better come help me tote it 'cause Ah feel too weak to bring it by myself."

So de husband got de water bucket off de shelf and went to de spring wid his wife. But 'fore he went, he

[2]Skimmed milk.
[3]A very hungry person is supposed to look ashy-gray around the mouth.

told de chillun, "Now, y'all watch out and keep de cat off de fish. She'll steal it sho if she kin."

De chillun tole him, "Yessuh," but they got to foolin' 'round and playin' and forgot all about de cat, and she jumped up on de table and et all de fish but one. She was so full she jus' couldn't hold another mouthful without bustin' wide open.

When de old folks come back and seen what de cat had done they bust out cryin'. They knowed dat one li'l fish divided up wouldn't save they lives. They knowed they had to starve to death. De man looked at de cat and he knowed dat one mo' fish would kill her so he said, "Ah'm gointer make her greedy gut kill her." So he made de cat eat dat other fish and de man and his wife and chillun and de dog and cat all died.

De cat died first so's he was already in Heben when de rest of de family got there. So when God put de man's soul on de scales to weigh it, de cat come up and was lookin' at de man, and de man was lookin' at de cat.

God seen how they eye-balled one 'nother so He ast de man, "Man, what is it between you and dis cat?"

So de man said, "God, dat cat's got all our nine lives in her belly." And he told God all about de fish.

God looked hard at dat cat for a hundred years, but it seem lak a minute.

Then he said: "Gabriel, Peter, Rayfield, John and Michael, all y'all ketch dat cat, and throw him outa Heben."

So they did and he was fallin' for nine days, and there ain't been no cats in Heben since. But he still got dem nine lives in his belly and you got to kill him nine times befo' he'll stay dead.

> Stepped on a pin, de pin bent
> And dat's de way de story went.

"Dat may be so, Presley," commented Jim Allen, "but if Ah ketch one messin' 'round *my* fish, Ah bet Ah kin knock dat man and woman and dem five chillun, de dog *and* de cat outa any cat Ah ever seen wid one lick."

"Dat's one something, Ah ain't never gointer kill," announced Willard forcefully. "It's dead bad luck."

"Me neither," assented Sack Daddy. "Everybody know it's nine years hard luck. Ah shot a man once up in West Florida, killed him dead for bull-dozin' me in a skin game, and got clean away. Ah got down in de phosphate mines around Mulberry and was doin' fine till Ah shacked up wid a woman dat had a great big ole black cat wid a white star in his bosom. He had a habit of jumpin' up on de bed all durin' de night time. One night Ah woke up and he was on my chest wid his nose right to mine, suckin' my breath.

"Ah got so mad Ah grabbed dat sucker by de tail and bust his brains out against a stanchion. My woman cried and carried on 'bout de cat and she tole me Ah was gointer have bad luck. Man, you know it wasn't two weeks befo' Sheriff Joe Brown laid his hand on my shoulder and tole me, 'Le's go.' Ah made five years for dat at Raiford. Killin' cats is bad luck."

"Talkin' 'bout dogs," put in Gene Oliver, "they got plenty sense. Nobody can't fool dogs much."

"And speakin' 'bout hams;" cut in Big Sweet meaningly, "if Joe Willard don't stay out of dat bunk he was in last night, Ah'm gointer sprinkle some salt down his back and sugar-cure *his* hams."

Joe snatched his pole out of the water with a jerk and glared at Big Sweet, who stood sidewise looking at him most pointedly.

"Aw, woman, quit tryin' to signify."[4]

"Ah kin signify all Ah please, Mr. Nappy-chin, so long as Ah know what Ah'm talkin' about."

"See dat?" Joe appealed to the other men. "We git a day off and figger we kin ketch some fish and enjoy ourselves, but naw, some wimmins got to drag behind us, even to de lake."

"You didn't figger Ah was draggin' behind you when you was bringin' dat Sears and Roebuck catalogue over to my house and beggin' me to choose my ruthers.[5] Lemme tell *you* something, *any* time Ah shack up wid any man Ah gives my-

[4]To show off.
[5]Make a choice.

self de privilege to go wherever he might be, night or day. Ah got de law in my mouth."

"Lawd, ain't she specifyin'!" sniggered Wiley.

"Oh, Big Sweet does dat," agreed Richardson. "Ah knowed she had somethin' up her sleeve when she got Lucy and come along."

"Lawd," Willard said bitterly. " 'My people, my people,' as de monkey said. You fool wid Aunt Hagar's[6] chillun and they'll sho distriminate you and put yo' name in de streets."

Jim Allen commented: "Well, you know what they say—a man can cackerlate his life till he git mixed up wid a woman or git straddle of a cow."

Big Sweet turned viciously upon the old man. "Who you callin' a cow, fool? Ah know you ain't namin' *my* mama's daughter no cow."

"Now all y'all heard what Ah said. Ah ain't called nobody no cow," Jim defended himself. "Dat's just an old time by-word 'bout no man kin tell what's gointer happen when he gits mixed up wid a woman or set straddle of a cow."

"I done heard my gran'paw say dem very words many and many a time," chimed in Larkins. "There's a whole heap of them kinda by-words. Like for instance:

" 'Ole coon for cunnin', young coon for runnin',' and 'Ah can't dance, but Ah know good moves.' They all got a hidden meanin', jus' like de Bible. Everybody can't understand what they mean. Most people is thin-brained. They's born wid they feet under de moon. Some folks is born wid they feet on de sun and they kin seek out de inside meanin' of words."

"Fack is, it's a story 'bout a man sittin' straddle of a cow," Jim Allen went on.

A man and his wife had a boy and they thought so much of him that they sent him off to college. At de end of seven years, he schooled out and come home and de old man and his ma was real proud to have de only boy 'round there dat was book-learnt.

So de next mornin' after he come home, de ma was milkin' de cows and had one young cow dat had never

[6]Negroes are in similie children of Hagar; white folks, of Sarah.

been to de pail befo' and she used to kick every time anybody milked her.

She was actin' extry bad dat mornin' so de woman called her husband and ast him to come help her wid de cow. So he went out and tried to hold her, but she kept on rearin' and pitchin' and kickin' over de milk pail, so he said to his wife: "We don't need to strain wid dis cow. We got a son inside that's been to school for seben years and done learnt everything. He'll know jus' what to do wid a kickin' cow. Ah'll go call him."

So he called de boy and told him.

De boy come on out to de cow-lot and looked everything over. Den he said, "Mama, cow-kickin' is all a matter of scientific principle. You see before a cow can kick she has to hump herself up in the back. So all we need to do is to take the hump out the cow's back."

His paw said, "Son, Ah don't see how you gointer do dat. But 'course you been off to college and you know a heap mo' than me and yo' ma ever will know. Go 'head and take de hump outa de heifer. We'd be mighty much obliged."

De son put on his gold eye glasses and studied de cow from head to foot. Then he said, "All we need to keep this animal from humping is a weight on her back."

"What kinda weight do she need, son?"

"Oh, any kind of a weight, jus' so it's heavy enough, papa," de son told him. "It's all in mathematics."

"Where we gointer git any weight lak dat, son?"

"Why don't you get up there, papa? You're just about the weight we need."

"Son, you been off to school a long time, and maybe you done forgot how hard it is for anybody to sit on a cow, and Ah'm gittin' old, you know."

"But, papa, I can fix that part, too. I'll tie your feet together under her belly so she can't throw you. You just get on up there."

"All right, son, if you say so, Ah'll git straddle of dis cow. You know more'n Ah do, Ah reckon."

So they tied de cow up short to a tree and de ole man

got on by de hardest,[7] and de boy passed a rope under her belly and tied his papa on. De old lady tried to milk de cow but she was buckin' and rearin' so till de ole man felt he couldn't stand it no mo'. So he hollered to de boy, "Cut de rope, son, cut de rope! Ah want to git down."

Instead of de boy cuttin' loose his papa's feet he cut de rope dat had de cow tied to de tree and she lit out 'cross de wood wid de ole man's feet tied under de cow. Wasn't no way for him to git off.

De cow went bustin' on down de back-road wid de ole man till they met a sister he knowed. She was surprised to see de man on de cow, so she ast: "My lawd, Brother So-and-so, where you goin'?"

He tole her, "Only God and dis cow knows."

"Wonder what de swamp boss is studyin' 'bout whilst we out here fishin'?" Oliver wondered.

"Nobody don't know and here's one dat don't keer," Cliff Ulmer volunteered. "Ah done caught me a nice mess of fish and Ah'm gointer bust dat jook wide open tonight."

"Ah was over there last night and maybe de boys didn't get off lyin'! Somebody tole one on de snail.

"You know de snail's wife took sick and sent him for de doctor.

"She was real low ill-sick and rolled from one side of de bed to de other. She was groanin', 'Lawd knows Ah got so much misery Ah hope de Doctor'll soon git here to me.'

"After seben years she heard a scufflin' at de door. She was real happy so she ast, 'Is dat you baby, done come back wid de doctor? Ah'm so glad!'

"He says, 'Don't try to rush me—Ah ain't gone yet.' He had been seben years gettin' to de door."

"Yeah, Ah was over there too," said Larkins White, "and somebody else tole a lie on de snail. A snail was crossin' de road for seben years. Just as he got across a tree fell and barely missed him 'bout a inch or two. If he had a been where he

[7] With great difficulty.

was six months before it would er kilt him. De snail looked back at de tree and tole de people, 'See, it pays to be fast.' "

"Look at de wind risin'!" Willard exclaimed.

"We ain't no hogs, Joe, we can't see no wind."

"You kin see it, if you squirt some sow milk in yo' eyes. Ah seen it one time," Jim Allen announced.

"How did it look, gran'pa? Dat's a sight Ah sho would love to see," cried Cliff.

"Naw, you wouldn't, son. De wind is blood red and when you see it comin' it look lak a bloody ocean rushin' down on you from every side. It ain't got no sides and no top. Youse jus' drownin' in blood and can't help yo'self. When Ah was a li'l chap dey tole me if Ah put hawg milk in mah eyes Ah could see de wind, and——"

"Why they say 'hawg milk'? Can't you try some cow milk?" Cliffert asked.

"De hawg is de onliest thing God ever made whut kin see de wind. Ain't you never seen uh sow take a good look in one direction and go tuh makin' up a good warm nest? She see great winds a comin' a whole day off."

"Well, how didja quit seein' de wind, gran'pa?"

"De sow milk wore outa mah eyes gradual lak, but Ah seen dat wind fo' more'n a week. Dey had to blindfold me tuh keep me from runnin' wild."

Cliff Ulmer said:

De wind is a woman, and de water is a woman too. They useter talk together a whole heap. Mrs. Wind useter go set down by de ocean and talk and patch and crochet.

They was jus' like all lady people. They loved to talk about their chillun, and brag on 'em.

Mrs. Water useter say, "Look at *my* chillun! Ah got de biggest and de littlest in de world. All kinds of chillun. Every color in de world, and every shape!"

De wind lady bragged louder than de water woman: "Oh, but Ah got mo' different chilluns than anybody in de world. They flies, they walks, they swims, they sings, they talks, they cries. They got all de colors from de sun.

Lawd, my chillun sho is a pleasure. 'Tain't nobody got no babies like mine."

Mrs. Water got tired of hearin' 'bout Mrs. Wind's chillun so she got so she hated 'em.

One day a whole passle of her chillun come to Mrs. Wind and says: "Mama, wese thirsty. Kin we go git us a cool drink of water?"

She says, "Yeah chillun. Run on over to Mrs. Water and hurry right back soon."

When them chillun went to squinch they thirst Mrs. Water grabbed 'em all and drowned 'em.

When her chillun didn't come home, de wind woman got worried. So she went on down to de water and ast for her babies.

"Good evenin' Mis' Water, you see my chillun to-day?"

De water woman tole her, "No-oo-oo."

Mrs. Wind knew her chillun had come down to Mrs. Water's house, so she passed over de ocean callin' her chillun, and every time she call de white feathers would come up on top of de water. And dat's how come we got white caps on waves. It's de feathers comin' up when de wind woman calls her lost babies.

When you see a storm on de water, it's de wind and de water fightin' over dem chillun.

"'Bout dat time a flea wanted to get a hair cut, so Ah left."

VIII

Y'ALL been tellin' and lyin' 'bout all dese varmints but you ain't yet spoke about de high chief boss of all de world which is de lion," Sack Daddy commented.

"He's de King of de Beasts, but he ain't no King of de World, now Sack," Dad Boykin spoke up. "He *thought* he was de King till John give him a straightenin'."

"Don't put dat lie out!" Sack Daddy contended. "De lion won't stand no straightenin'."

"Course I 'gree wid you dat everybody can't show de lion no deep point, but John showed it to him. Oh, yeah, John not only straightened him out, he showed dat ole lion where in."

"When did he do all of dis, Dad? Ah ain't never heard tell of it." Dad spoke up:

Oh, dis was way befo' yo' time. Ah don't recolleck myself. De old folks told me about John and de lion. Well, John was ridin' long one day straddle of his horse when de grizzly bear come pranchin' out in de middle of de road and hollered: "Hold on a minute! They tell me you goin' 'round strowin' it dat youse de King of de World."

John stopped his horse: "Whoa! Yeah, Ah'm de King of de World, don't you b'lieve it?" John told him.

"Naw, you ain't no King. Ah'm de King of de World. You can't be no King till you whip me. Git down and fight."

John hit de ground and de fight started. First, John grabbed him a rough-dried brick and started to work de fat offa de bear's head. De bear just fumbled 'round till he got a good holt, then he begin to squeeze and squeeze. John knowed he couldn't stand dat much longer, do he'd be jus' another man wid his breath done give out. So he reached into his pocket and got out his razor and slipped it between dat bear's ribs. De bear turnt loose and reeled on over in de bushes to lay down. He had enough of dat fight.

John got back on his horse and rode on off.

De lion smelt de bear's blood and come runnin' to where de grizzly was layin' and started to lappin' his blood.

De bear was skeered de lion was gointer eat him while he was all cut and bleedin' nearly to death, so he hollered and said: "*Please* don't touch me, Brer Lion. Ah done met de King of de World and he done cut me all up."

De lion got his bristles all up and clashed down at de bear: "Don't you lay there and tell me you done met de King of de World and not be talkin' 'bout me! Ah'll tear you to pieces!"

"Oh, don't tetch me, Brer Lion! Please lemme alone so Ah kin git well."

"Well, don't you call nobody no King of de World but me."

"But Brer Lion, Ah done *met* de King sho' nuff. Wait till you see him and you'll say Ah'm right."

"Naw, Ah won't, neither. Show him to me and Ah'll show you how much King he is."

"All right, Brer Lion, you jus' have a seat right behind dese bushes. He'll be by here befo' long."

Lion squatted down by de bear and waited. Fust person he saw goin' up de road was a old man. Lion jumped up and ast de bear, "Is dat him?"

Bear say, "Naw, dat's Uncle Yistiddy, he's a useter-be!"

After while a li'l boy passed down de road. De lion seen him and jumped up agin. "Is dat him?" he ast de bear.

Bear told him, "Naw, dat's li'l tomorrow, he's a gointer-be, you jus' lay quiet. Ah'll let you know when he gits here."

Sho nuff after while here come John on his horse but he had done got his gun. Lion jumped up agin and ast, "Is dat him?"

Bear say: "Yeah, dat's him! Dat's de King of de World."

Lion reared up and cracked his tail back and forwards

like a bull-whip. He 'lowed, "You wait till Ah git thru wid him and you won't be callin' him no King no mo'."

He took and galloped out in de middle of de road right in front of John's horse and laid his ears back. His tail was crackin' like torpedoes.

"Stop!" de lion hollered at John. "They tell me you goes for de King of de World!"

John looked him dead in de ball of his eye and told him, "Yeah, Ah'm de King. Don't you like it, don't you take it. Here's mah collar, come and shake it!"

De lion and John eye-balled one another for a minute or two, den de lion sprung on John.

Talk about fightin'! Man, you ain't seen no sich fightin' and wrasslin' since de mornin' stars sung together. De lion clawed and bit John and John bit him right back.

Way after while John got to his rifle and he up wid de muzzle right in ole lion's face and pulled de trigger. Long, slim black feller, snatch 'er back and hear 'er beller! Dog damn! Dat was too much for de lion. He turnt go of John and wheeled to run to de woods. John levelled down on him agin and let him have another load, right in his hindquarters.

Dat ole lion give John de book; de bookity book.[1] He hauled de fast mail back into de woods where de bear was laid up.

"Move over," he told de bear. "Ah wanta lay down too."

"How come?" de bear ast him.

"Ah done met de King of de World, and he done ruint me."

"Brer Lion, how you know you done met de King?"

"'Cause he made lightnin' in my face and thunder in my hips. Ah know Ah done met de King, move over."

"Dad, dat lie of your'n done brought up a high wind," said Jim Allen, measuring the weather with his eye. "Look a li'l bit like rain."

"Tain't gonna rain, but de wind's too high for fish to bite.

[1] Sound word meaning running.

Le's go back," suggested Presley. "All them that caught fish
got fish. All them that didn't got another chance."

Everybody began to gather up things. The bait cans were
kicked over so that the worms could find homes. The strings
of fish were tied to pole ends. When Joe Wiley went to
pull up his string of fish, he found a water moccasin stealin'
them and the men made a great ceremony of killin' it. Then
they started away from the water. Cliff had a long string of
fish.

"Look, Gran'pa," he said, "Ah reckon you satisfied, ain't
you?"

"Sho Ah'm satisfied, Ah must *is* got cat blood in me 'cause
Ah never gits tired of fish. Ah knows how to eat 'em too, and
dat's somethin' everybody don't know."

"Oh, anybody can eat fish," said Joe Willard.

"Yeah," Jim conceded grudgingly, "they kin eat it, but they
can't git de real refreshment out de meat like they oughter."

"If you kin git any mo' refreshment off a fish bone than
me, you must be got two necks and a gang of bellies," said
Larkins.

"You see," went on Jim, "y'all ain't got into de technical
apex of de business. When y'all see a great big platter of fried
fish y'all jus' grab hold of a fish and bite him any which way,
and dat's wrong."

"Dat's good enough for me!" declared Willard emphatically. "Anywhere and any place Ah ketch a fish Ah'm ready to
bite him 'ceptin' he's raw."

"Me too."

"See dat?" Jim cried, exasperated. "You young folks is just
like a passle of crows in a corn patch. Everybody talkin' at one
time. Ain't nary one of you tried to learn how to eat a fish
right."

"How you eat 'em, Mr. Allen?" Gene Oliver asked to pacify
him.

"Well, after yo' hands is washed and de blessin' is said, you
look at de fried fish, but you don't grab it. First thing you
chooses a piece of corn-bread for yo' plate whilst youse
lookin' de platter over for a nice fat perch or maybe it's trout.
Nobody wid any manners or home-raisin' don't take de fork
and turn over every fish in de dish in order to pick de best

one. You does dat wid yo' eye whilst youse choosin' yo' pone bread. Now, then, take yo' fork and stick straight at de fish you done choosed, and if somebody ast you to take two, you say 'No ma'am, Ah thank you. This un will do for right now.'

"You see if you got too many fishes on yo' plate at once, folkses, you can't lay 'em out proper. So you take one fish at de time. Then you turn him over and take yo' fork and start at de tail, liff de meat all off de bone clear up to de head, 'thout misplacin' a bone. You eats dat wid some bread. Not a whole heap of bread—just enough to keep you from swallerin' de fish befo' you enjoy de consequences. When you thru on dat side of de fish turn him over and do de same on de other side. Don't eat de heads. Shove 'em to one side till you thru wid all de fish from de platter, den when there ain't no mo' fish wid sides to 'em, you reach back and pull dem heads befo' you and start at de back of de fish neck and eat right on thru to his jaw-bones.

"Now then, if it's summer time, go set on de porch and rest yo'self in de cool. If it's winter time, go git in front of de fireplace and warm yo'self—now Ah done tole you right. A whole heap of people talks about fish-eatin' but Ah done tole you real."

"He's tellin' you right," agreed Dad Boykin. "Ah'm older than he is, 'cause Ah was eighty-one las' November, and Ah was eatin' fish befo' Jim was born, but Ah never did get de gennywine schoolin' till Jim showed me. But Ah teached him somethin' too, didn't Ah, Jim?"

"Yeah, Dad, yo' showed me how to warm myself."

There was a great burst of laughter from the young men, but the two old men scowled upon them.

"You see," Dad said bitingly. "You young poots won't lissen to nothin'! Not a one of you knows how to warm hisself right and youse so hard-headed you don't want to be taught. Any fool kin lam hisself up in a chimbley corner and cook his shins, but when it comes right down to de entrimmins, youse as ig'nant as a hog up under a acorn tree—he eats and grunts and never look up to see where de acorns is comin' from."

"Dad, *please* suh, teach us how to warm ourselves," begged Cliff. "We all wants to know."

"Oh, y'all done wasted too much time, almost back in de quarters now, and de crowd will be scatterin'."

"Dat's all right, Dad," urged Joe Willard soothingly. "We ain't goin' nowhere till we been teached by you."

"Well, then, Ah'll tell y'all somethin'. De real way to git warm is first to git a good rockin' chear and draw it up to de fire. Don't flop yo'self down in it lak a cow in de pasture. Draw it right up in de center of de fireplace 'cause dat's de best. Some folks love to pile into de chimbley corner 'cause they's lazy and feared somebody gointer step on they foots. They don't want to have no trouble shiftin' 'em back and forth. But de center is de best place, so take dat. You even might have to push and shove a li'l bit to git dere, but dat's all right, go 'head.

"When you git yo' chear all set where you wants it, then you walk up to de mantel piece and turn yo' back to de fire— dat's to knock de breezes offen yo' back. You know, all de time youse outside in de weather, li'l breezes and winds is jumpin' on yo' back and crawlin' down yo' neck, to hide. They'll stay right there if you don't do somethin' to git shet of 'em. They don't lak fires, so when you turn yo' back to de fire, de inflamed atmosphere goes up under yo' coat-tails and runs dem winds and breezes out from up dere. Sometimes, lessen you drive 'em off, they goes to bed wid you. Ain't y'all never been so you couldn't git warm don't keer how much kivver you put on?"

"Many's de time I been lak dat."

"Well," went on Dad, "dat because some stray breezes had done rode you to bed. Now dat brings up to de second claw of de subjick. You done got rid of de back breezes, so you git in yo' chear and pull off yo' shoes and set in yo' sock feet. Now, don't set there all spraddle-legged and let de heat just hit you any which way, put yo' feet right close together so dat both yo' big toes is side by side. Then you shove 'em up close to de fire and let 'em git good and hot. Ah know it don't look lak it but dem toes'll warm you all over. You see when Ah was studyin' doctor Ah found out dat you got a leader dat runs from yo' big toe straight to yo' heart, and when you git dem toes hot youse hot all over."

"Yeah, Ah b'lieve youse right, Dad, 'bout dat warmin' business, but Ah wisht somebody'd tell us how to git cool right now."

The party was back in the camp. Everybody began to head for his own shack.

"See you tonight at de jook," Jim Presley called to Willard. "Don't you and Big Sweet put on no roll now. Ah hate to see men and wimmin folks fightin'."

"Me too," said Wiley emphatically. "If a man kin whip his woman and whip her good; all right, but when they don't do nothin' but fight, it makes my stomach turn."

"Well," said Big Sweet crisply. "If Joe Willard try to take dese few fishes he done caught where he shacked up last night, Ah'm gointer take my Tampa switch-blade knife, and Ah'm goin' 'round de hambone lookin' for meat."

"Aw, is *dat* so?" Joe challenged her.

"Ah been baptized, papa, and Ah wouldn't mislead you," Big Sweet told him to his teeth.

"Hey, hey!" Gene Oliver exclaimed. "Big Moose done come down from de mountain. Ah'm gointer be at dat jook tonight to see what Big Sweet and Ella Wall gointer talk about."

"Me too. De time is done come where big britches gointer fit li'l Willie,"[2] Joe Wiley declared significantly.

"Oh, wese all gointer be there," Larkins said. "Say, Big Sweet, don't let de 'gator beat you to de pond,[3] do he'll give you mo' trouble than de day is long."

So everybody got for home.

Back in the quarters the sun was setting. Plenty women over the cook-pot scorching up supper. Lots of them were already thru cooking, with the pots shoved to the back of the stove while they put on fresh things and went out in front of the house to see and be seen.

The fishermen began scraping fish and hot grease began to pop in happy houses. All but the Allens'. Mrs. Allen wouldn't have a thing to do with our fish because Mr. Allen and

[2]Things have come to critical pass.
[3]Don't be out-done; or don't be too slow.

Cliffert had made her mad about the yard. So I fried the fish.
She wouldn't touch a bite, but Mr. Allen, Cliffert and I
pitched into it. Mr. Allen might have eaten by the rules but
Cliffert and I went at it rough-and-tumble with no holds
barred.

But we did sit down on the front porch to rest after the fish
was eaten.

The men were still coming into the quarters from various
parts of the "job." The children played "Shoo-round," and
"Chick-mah-Chick" until Mrs. Williams called her four year
old Frankie and put her to sleep by rocking her and singing
"Mister Frog."

It wasn't black dark, but night was peeping around the corner. The quarters were getting alive. Woofing, threats and
brags up and down the line.

Three figures in the dusk-dark detached themselves from
the railroad track and came walking into the quarters. A tall
black grim-faced man with a rusty black reticule, followed by
two women.

Everybody thought he was a bootlegger and yelled orders
to him to that effect. He paid no attention, but set down his
bag slowly, opened it still slower and took out a dog-eared
Bible and opened it. The crowd quieted down. They knew he
was a travelling preacher, a "stump-knocker" in the language
of the "job".

Some fell silent to listen. Others sucked their teeth and
either went back into their houses or went on to the jook.

When he had a reasonable amount of attention he nodded
to the woman at his left and she raised "Death comes a
Creepin' " and the crowd helped out. At the end the preacher
began:[4]

> You all done been over in Pentecost (got to feeling
> spiritual by singing) and now we going to talk about de
> woman that was taken from man. I take my text from
> Genesis two and twenty-one (Gen. 2:21).
> Behold de Rib!
> Now, my beloved,
> Behold means to look and see.

[4]See glossary.

Look at dis woman God done made,
But first thing, ah hah!
Ah wants you to gaze upon God's previous works.
Almighty and arisen God, hah!
Peace-giving and prayer-hearing God,
High-riding and strong armded God
Walking acrost his globe creation, hah!

Wid de blue elements for a helmet
And a wall of fire round his feet
He wakes de sun every morning from his fiery bed
Wid de breath of his smile
And commands de moon wid his eyes.
And Oh——
Wid de eye of Faith
I can see him
Standing out on de eaves of ether
Breathing clouds from out his nostrils,
Blowing storms from 'tween his lips
I can see!!
Him seize de mighty axe of his proving power
And smite the stubborn-standing space,
And laid it wide open in a mighty gash——

Making a place to hold de world
I can see him——
Molding de world out of thought and power
And whirling it out on its eternal track,
Ah hah, my strong armded God!
He set de blood red eye of de sun in de sky
And told it,
Wait, wait! Wait there till Shiloh come
I can see!
Him mold de mighty mountains
And melting de skies into seas.
Oh, Behold, and look and see! hah
We see in de beginning
He made de bestes every one after its kind,
De birds that fly de trackless air,
De fishes dat swim de mighty deep——
Male and fee-male, hah!
Then he took of de dust cf de earth
And made man in his own image.
And man was alone,
Even de lion had a mate
So God shook his head
And a thousand million diamonds
Flew out from his glittering crown
And studded de evening sky and made de stars.
So God put Adam into a deep sleep
And took out a bone, ah hah!
And it is said that it was a rib.
Behold de rib!
A bone out of a man's side.
He put de man to sleep and made wo-man,
And men and women been sleeping together ever
        since.
Behold de rib!
Brothers, if God
Had taken dat bone out of man's head
He would have meant for woman to rule, hah
If he had taken a bone out of his foot,
He would have meant for us to dominize and rule.
He could have made her out of back-bone

And then she would have been behind us.
But, no, God Amighty, he took de bone out of his
    side
So dat places de woman beside us;
Hah! God knowed his own mind.
Behold de rib!
And now I leave dis thought wid you,
Let us all go marchin' up to de gates of Glory.
Tramp! tramp! tramp!
In step wid de host dat John saw.
Male and female like God made us
Side by side.
Oh, behold de rib!
And less all set down in Glory together
Right round his glorified throne
And praise his name forever.
            Amen.

At the end of the sermon the woman on the preacher's left
raised, "Been a Listenin' All de Night Long", and the
preacher descended from his fiery cloud and lifted the collection in his hat. The singers switched to, "You Can't Hide,
Sinners, You Can't Hide." The sparse contribution taken, the
trio drifted back into the darkness of the railroad, walking
towards Kissimmee.

IX

THE LITTLE DRAMA of religion over, the "job" reverted to the business of amusing itself. Everybody making it to the jook hurriedly or slowly as the spirit moved.

Big Sweet came by and we went over together. I didn't go with Cliffert because it would mean that I'd be considered his property more or less and the other men would keep away from me, and being let alone is no way to collect folk-lore.

The jook was in full play when we walked in. The piano was throbbing like a stringed drum and the couples slow-dragging about the floor were urging the player on to new lows. "Jook, Johnnie, Ah know you kin spank dat ole peanner." "Jook it Johnnie!"[1] "Throw it in de alley!"[2]

The Florida-flip game was roaring away at the left. Four men playing skin game with small piles of loose change.[3]

"High, Jack, game," one side called.

"Low and not ashamed," from the other.

Another deal.

Dealer: (to play at left) "Whut yuh say?"

Player: "Beggin'."

Dealer: "Git up off yo' knees. Go 'head and tell 'em Ah sent you." (I give you one point.)

Dealer: "Pull off, partner."

A frenzied slapping of cards on the table. "Ha! we caught little britches!" (low) "Pull off again!"

"Can't. Ain't seen de deck but one time."

"Aw shucks. Ah got de wrong sign from you. Ah thought you had de king."

"Nope, Ah can't ketch a thing. Ah can't even ketch nobody lookin' at me."

The opponents grin knowingly and one of them sticks the Jack up on his forehead and gloats, "De Jack's a gentleman." It is now the highest card out.

[1] Play the piano in the manner of the jook or "blues."
[2] Get low down.
[3] See glossary.

A furious play to the end of the hand and the dealer cries: "Gone from three. Jus' like Jeff Crowder's eye" (out.)

"Out!" cries the outraged opponents. "Out yo' head! Out wid whut!"

"We played high, low, game!"

"Take dat game right out yo' mouf. We got twenty by tens."

"Le's go to school." (Let's count game.)

One player slyly picks up the deck and tries to mix it with his cards.

"Aw naw, put down dat deck! You can't count it on me."

"Aw, you tryin' to bully de game, but if you ain't prepared to back yo' crap wid hot lead, don't bring de mess up."

Joe Wiley was on the floor in the crap game. He called me to come stand by him and give him luck. Big Sweet left me there and went on over to the skin game.

Somebody had squeezed the alcohol out of several cans of Sterno and added sugar, water and boiled-off spirits of nitre and called it wine. It was dealt out with the utmost secrecy. The quarters boss had a way of standing around in the dark and listening and he didn't allow a drop of likker on the job. Pay-nights used to mean two or three killings but this boss had ended the murders abruptly. And one caught with likker was sent down to Bartow to the jail and bound over to the Big Court. So it had come to the place where "low" wine was about all the quarters could get and the drinker was taking two terrible risks at that—arrest and death.

But there was enough spirits about for things to keep lively. The crap game was frothy. Office had the dice when I walked up. He was shivering the dice and sliding them out expertly.

"Hah! good dice is findin' de money! Six is mah point."

"Whut's yo' come bet?" Blue asked.

"Two bits."

"Two bits you don't six."

Office picked up the dice stealthily, shook them, or rather failed to shake them craftily and slid them out. Blue stopped them. Office threw three times and three times Blue stopped them. Office took out his switch-blade knife and glared at Blue.

"Nigger, don't you stop mah dice befo' dey point."

"You chokin' dem dice. Shake and lemme hear de music."

I wanted to get into the game in a small way but Big Sweet was high balling[4] me to come over to the skin game. I went over to see what she wanted and was given her purse to hold. She wanted to play and she wanted a free hand. It was the liveliest and most intense game in the place. I got all worked up myself watching the falling cards.

A saddle-colored fellow called "Texas Red" was fighting the wine inside him by trying to tenor "Ol' Pal, Why Don't You Answer Me," while he hung over the game watching it. His nasal tones offended Big Sweet, who turned and asked him, "Did somebody hit yuh tuh start yuh? 'Cause if dey did Ah'm goin' ter hit yuh to stop yuh." Texas and Big Sweet did what is locally known as "eye-balling" each other. His eyes fell lower. Her knife was already open, so he strolled on off.

There had been a new deal. Everybody was getting a fresh card.

Dealer: "You want a card, Big Sweet?"

Big Sweet: "Yeah, Ah wanta scoop one in de rough."

Dealer: "Aw right, yo' card is gointer cost you a dollar. Put yo' money on de wood and make de bet go good and then agin, put yo' money in sight and save a fight."

She drew a card from the deck and put it face up beside her, with a dollar bill.

Dealer: "Heah, Hardy, heah's a good card—a queen." He tossed the card to Hardy.

Hardy: "Aw naw, Ah don't play dem gals till way late in de night."

Dealer: "Well take de ace and go to wee-shoppy-tony and dat means East Hell. Ah'm gointer ketch you anyhow."

Hardy: "When you ketch me, you damn sho will ketch a man dat's caught a many one. Ah'm playin' up a nation."

Dealer: "Put down! You all owe de bet a dime. Damn sitters rob St. Peter, rob St. Paul."

Larkins: "Dat nigger is gointer top somebody. He's got a cub.[5] Ah ain't goin' in dat damn steel trap."

<hr />

[4]Waving ahead. A railroad term.

[5]He has arranged the cards so he can deal winning cards to himself and losing cards to others.

Dealer: "Aw naw, Ah ain't! You sap-sucker!" (To Hardy) "You owe de bet a dime if you never pay it."

The dealer starts down the deck, and the singing goes with it. Christopher Jenkins' deep baritone is something to remember.

> "Let de deal go down, boys.[6]
>   Let de deal go down.
>   When yo' card gits lucky, oh padner;
>   You ought to be in a rollin' game."

Each line punctuated by "hah!" and a falling card.
Larkins: "Ah'm dead on de turn."
Dealer: "Ah heard you buddy."
"Ain't had no money, oh padner!"
(To Larkins) "You head-pecked shorty, drive up to de cryin' post and hitch up. You want another card?"
Larkins: "Shuffle and deal and ain't stop fallin' yet." (He means he stays in the game so he takes another hand.)
Dealer: "Put down dat chicken-change quarter you got in yo' hand."
The singing goes on——

> "Ah'm goin' back to de Bama,
>   Won't be worried wid you."

(To Hardy) "De nine" (card dealer holds) "is de best. Is you got air nickel to cry?"

> "Let de deal go down, boys;
>   Let de deal go down."

Big Sweet: "De four" (card she holds) "says a dollar mo'."
Dealer: "Oh hell and brothers! Ah'm strictly a two-bit man."
Big Sweet (arrogantly): "You full of dat ole ism blood. Fat covered yo' heart. Youse skeered to bet. Gamblin' wid yo' stuff out de window."[7]
Dealer: "Dollar mo'."

---

[6] See appendix.
[7] Risking nothing. Ready to run.

Hardy: "Hell broke loose in Georgy!"

Big Sweet: "Ah mean to carry y'all to Palatka and bring yuh back by de way of Winter Park."

Hardy: "Big Sweet, Ah don't b'lieve Ah'll see yo' raise."

Big Sweet: "Oh g'wan and bet. You got mo' sense than me. Look at dem damn kidneys all over yo' head."

"Ain't had no trouble, Lawd padner
   Till Ah stop by here."

Dealer: "Take it and cry, children." (His card falls.) "Dey sent me out by de way of Sandusky. Lemme see kin Ah find me a clean card."

Big Sweet: "Ah caught you guilty lyin'! Make a bet and tell a lie about it."

Hardy: "He done cocked a face card. Look out we don't ketch *you* guilty."

Big Sweet: "He got de cards in his hand."

"Let de deal go down, boys,
   Let de deal go down."

Hardy: "Dat's me. Ah thought dat card was in Bee-luther-hatchee!"[8]

Dealer: "Tell de truth and stay in de church! Ah'm from down in Ginny-Gall where they eat cow-belly, skin and all. Big Sweet, everybody done fell but you. You must be setting on roots."

Big Sweet: "Nope, Ah got my Joe Moore in my hair."[9]

Dealer: "Well, Ah got de cards. I can cheat if I want to and beat you anyway."

Big Sweet: "You mess wid dem cards and see if Ah don't fill you full of looky-deres."

Hardy: "Whut a looky-dere?"

Big Sweet: "A knot on yo' head so big till when you go down de street everybody will point at it and say 'Looky-dere.' "

Dealer: (His card falls.) "Ah'm hot as seven hells."

[8] A mythical place, like "ginny gall."
[9] A piece of gamblers lucky hoodoo.

Big Sweet: "Ah played de last card. Ah don't tell lies all de time. Now, you rich son of a bitch, pay off."

Larkins: "God! She must be sittin' on roots! Luck is a fortune."

Big Sweet raked in the money and passed it to me. She was about to place another bet when we heard a lot of noise outside. Everybody looked at the door at one time.

"Dat *must* be de Mulberry crowd. Nobody else wouldn't keep dat much noise. Ella Wall strowin' it."

"She's plenty propaganda, all right."

Ella Wall flung a loud laugh back over her shoulder as she flourished in. Everybody looked at her, then they looked at Big Sweet. Big Sweet looked at Ella, but she seemed not to mind. The air was as tight as a fiddle string.

Ella wrung her hips to the Florida-flip game. Big Sweet stayed on at the skin game but didn't play. Joe Willard, knowing the imminence of forthright action, suddenly got deep into the crap game.

Lucy came in the door with a bright gloat in her eyes and went straight to Ella. So far as speaking was concerned she didn't see Big Sweet, but she did flirt past the skin game once, overcome with merriment.

"Dat li'l narrer contracted piece uh meatskin gointer make me stomp her right now!" Big Sweet exploded. "De two-faced heifer! Been hangin' 'round me so she kin tote news to Ella. If she don't look out she'll have on her last clean dress befo' de crack of day."

"Ah'm surprised at Lucy," I agreed. "Ah thought you all were de *best* of friends."

"She mad 'cause Ah dared her to jump *you*. She don't lak Slim always playing JOHN HENRY for you. She would have done cut you to death if Ah hadn't of took and told her."

"Ah can see she doesn't like it, but——"

"Neb' mind 'bout ole Lucy. She know Ah backs yo' fallin'. She know if she scratch yo' skin Ah'll kill her so dead till she can't fall. They'll have to push her over. Ella Wall look lak she tryin' to make me kill her too, flourishin' dat ole knife 'round. But she oughter know de man dat made one, made two. She better not vary, do Ah'll be all over her jus' lak gravy over rice."

Lucy and Ella were alternately shoo-shooing[10] to each other and guffawing. Then Ella would say something to the whole table and laugh.

Over at the Florida-flip game somebody began to sing that jook tribute to Ella Wall which has been sung in every jook and on every "job" in South Florida:

Go to Ella Wall
Oh, go to Ella Wall
If you want good boody[11]
Oh, go to Ella Wall

Oh, she's long and tall
Oh, she's long and tall
And she rocks her rider
From uh wall to wall

Oh, go to Ella Wall
Take yo' trunk and all——

"Tell 'em 'bout me!" Ella Wall snapped her fingers and revolved her hips with her hands.

"I'm raggedy, but right; patchey but tight; stringy, but I *will* hang on."

"Look at her puttin' out her brags." Big Sweet nudged me. "Loud-talkin' de place. But countin' from yo' little finger back to the thumb; if she start anything Ah got her some."

I knew that Big Sweet didn't mind fighting; didn't mind killing and didn't too much mind dying. I began to worry a bit. Ella kept on hurling slurs. So I said, "Come on, Big Sweet, we got to go to home."

"Nope, Ah ain't got to do nothin' but die and stay black. Ah stays right here till de jook close if anybody else stay. You look and see how much in dat pocket book."

I looked. "Forty-one dollars and sixty-three cents."

"Just you hold on to it. Ah don't want a thing in mah hands but dis knife."

[10]Whispering.
[11]Sex.

Big Sweet turned to scoop a card in the rough. Just at that moment Ella chose to yell over, "Hey, bigger-than-me!" at Big Sweet. She whirled around angrily and asked me, "Didn't dat storm-buzzard throw a slam at me?"

"Naw, she was hollerin' at somebody else," I lied to keep the peace.

Nothing happening, Ella shouted, "'Tain't nothin' to her. She ain't hit me yet."

Big Sweet heard that and threw in her cards and faced about. "If anything start, Little-Bit, you run out de door like a streak uh lightning and get in yo' car. They gointer try to hurt you too."

I thought of all I had to live for and turned cold at the thought of dying in a violent manner in a sordid saw-mill camp. But for my very life I knew I couldn't leave Big Sweet even if the fight came. She had been too faithful to me. So I assured her that I wasn't going unless she did. My only weapons were my teeth and toe-nails.

Ella crowded her luck. She yelled out, "Lucy, go tell Mr. Lots-of-Papa Joe Willard Ah say come here. Jus' tell 'im his weakness want 'im. He know who dat is."

Lucy started across. Ella stood up akimbo, but everybody knew she was prepared to back her brag with cold steel in some form, or she wouldn't have been there talking like she was.

A click beside me and I knew that the spring blade knife that Big Sweet carried was open.

"Stop right where you is, Lucy," Big Sweet ordered, "lessen you want to see yo' Jesus."

"Gwan Lucy," Ella Wall called out, "'tain't nothin' stoppin' yuh. See nothin', say nothin'."

Big Sweet turned to Ella. "Maybe Ah ain't nothin'. But Ah say Lucy ain't gointer tell Joe Willard nothin'. What you sendin' *her* for? Why don't you go yo'self? Dere he is."

"Well, Ah kin go, now," Ella countered.

Big Sweet took a step forward that would put her right in Ella's path in case she tried to cross the room. "Ah can't hear what you say for yo' damn teeth rattlin'. Come on!"

Then the only thing that could have stopped the killing

happened. The Quarters Boss stepped in the door with a .45 in his hand and another on his hip. Expect he had been eavesdropping as usual.

"What's the matter here, y'all? Big Sweet, what you mean tuh do wid that knife?"

"Ahm jus' 'bout tuh send God two niggers. Come in here bulldozin' me."

The Quarters Boss looked all around and pointed at Ella. "What tha hell *you* doin' in here wid weapons? You don't belong on this job nohow. Git the hell outa here and that quick. This place is for people that works on this job. Git! Somebody'll be in Barton jail in twenty minutes."

"You don't need tuh run her off, Cap'n," Big Sweet said. "Ah can git her tuh go. Jus' you stand back and gimme lief. She done stepped on mah starter and Ahm rearin' tuh go. If God'll send me uh pistol Ah'll send 'im uh man!"

"You ain't gonna kill nobody right under mah nose," the Quarters Boss snorted. "Gimme that knife you got dere, Big Sweet."

"Naw suh! Nobody gits *mah* knife. Ah bought it for dat storm-buzzard over dere and Ah means tuh use it on her, too. As long as uh mule go bareheaded she better not part her lips tuh me. Do Ah'll kill her, law or no law. Don't you touch me, white folks!"

"Aw she ain't so bad!" Ella sneered as she wrung her hips towards the door. "She didn't kill Jesse James."

"Git on 'way from here!" the Boss yelled behind her. "Lessen yuh wanna make time in Barton jail. Git off these premises and that quick! Gimme that knife!" He took the knife and gave Ella a shove. She moved sullenly behind her crowd away from the door, mumbling threats. He followed and stayed outside until the car pulled off. Then he stuck his head back inside and said, "Now you behave yo'self, Big Sweet. Ah don't wanna hafta jail yuh."

Soon as he was gone the mob got around Big Sweet. "You wuz noble!" Joe Willard told her. "You wuz uh whole woman and half uh man. You made dat cracker stand offa *you.*"

"Who wouldn't?" said Presley. "She got loaded muscles. You notice he don't tackle Big Sweet lak he do de rest round here. Dats cause she ain't got uh bit better sense then tuh make 'im kill her."

"Dats right," Big Sweet admitted, "and de nex' time Joe tell his Mulberry woman tuh come here bulldozin' *me*, Ahm gointer beat 'im to death grabbin' at 'im."

Joe Willard affected supreme innocence. "Will you lissen at dis 'oman? Ah ain't sent fuh nobody. Y'all see Ah didn't never go where she wuz, didn't yuh? Come on Big Sweet, less go home. How 'bout uh li'l keerless love? Ahm all ravelled out from de strain."

Joe and Big Sweet went home together and that was that.

When the quarters boss had gone, I saw Box-Car Daddy creeping back in the door. I didn't see him leave the place so I asked him where he had been.

"Had to step off a li'l piece," he told me with an effort at nonchalance.

"He always steps off whenever he see dat Quarters Boss, and he doing right, too," someone said.

"How come?" I asked. "Nobody else don't run."

Everybody laughed but nobody told me a thing. But after a while Box-Car began to sing a new song and I liked the swing of it.

"What's dat you singing, Box-Car?" I asked.

" 'Ah'm Gointer Loose dis Right-hand Shackle from 'Round my Leg.' Dat's a chain-gang song. Thought everybody knowed dat."

"Nope, never heard it. Ain't never been to de gang. How did you learn it?"

"Working on de gang."

"Whut you doin' on de gang, Box-Car? You look like a good boy, but a poor boy."

"Oh, dey put me under arrest one day for vacancy in Bartow. When de judge found out Ah had a job of work. He took and searched me and when he found out Ah had a deck of cards on me, he charged me wid totin' concealed cards, and attempt to gamble, and gimme three months. Then dey made out another charge 'ginst me. 'Cused me of highway shufflin', and attempt to gamble. You know dese white folks sho hates tuh turn a nigger loose, if every dey git dey hands on 'im. And dis very quarters boss was Cap'n on de gang

where Ah wuz. Me and him ain't never gointer set hawses."[12]
So he went on singing:

> All day long, you heard me moan
> Don't you tell my Cap'n which way I gone
> Ah'm gointer lose dis right hand shackle from 'round
>   my leg.

> You work me late, you work me soon
> Some time you work me by de light of de moon
> Ah'm gointer lose dis right hand shackle from 'round
>   my leg.

I learned several other songs. Thanks to James Presley and
Slim; and Gene Oliver and his sister brought me many additional tales.

But the very next pay-night when I went to a dance at the
Pine Mill, Lucy tried to steal me. That is the local term for an
attack by stealth. Big Sweet saved me and urged me to stay
on, assuring me that she could always defend me, but I shivered at the thought of dying with a knife in my back, or having my face mutilated. At any rate, I had made a very fine and
full collection on the Saw-Mill Camp, so I felt no regrets at
shoving off.

The last night at Loughman was very merry. We had a party
at Mrs. Allen's. James Presley and Slim with their boxes; Joe
Willard calling figures in his best mood. Because it was a special occasion and because I was urged, I actually took a sip of
low-wine and found out how very low it was. The dancing
stopped and I was hilariously toted off to bed and the party
moved to my bedroom. We had had a rain flood early in the
afternoon and a medium size rattlesnake had come in out of
the wet. I had thrown away a pile of worn out stockings and
he was asleep upon them there in the corner by the wash-
stand. The boys wanted to kill it, but I begged them not to
hurt my lowly brother. He rattled away for a while, but when
everybody got around the bed on the far end of the room and
got quiet, he moved in the manner of an hour-hand to a
crack where the floor and wall had separated, and popped out
of sight.

[12]Never going to get along. As two horses pull together.

Cliffert told me the last Loughman story around midnight.
"Zora, did yuh ever hear 'bout Jack and de Devil buckin'
'ginst one 'nother to see which one was de strongest?"

"Naw. Ah done heard a lot about de Devil and dat Jack,
but not dat tale *you* know. Tell it."

Jack and de Devil wuz settin' down under a tree one
day arguin' 'bout who was de strongest. De Devil got
tired of talkin' and went and picked up a mule. Jack
went and picked up de same mule. De Devil run to a
great big old oak tree and pulled it up by de roots. Jack
grabbed holt of one jus' as big and pulled it up. De
Devil broke a anchor cable. Jack took it and broke it
agin.

So de Devil says, "Shucks! Dis ain't no sho nuff trial.
Dis is chillun foolishness. Meet me out in dat hund'ed
acre clearin' tomorrow mornin' at nine o'clock and we'll
see who kin throw mah hammer de furtherest. De one
do dat is de strongest."

Jack says, "Dat suits me."

So nex' mawnin' de Devil wuz dere on time wid his
hammer. It wuz bigger'n de white folks church house in
Winter Park. A whole heap uh folks had done come out
tuh see which one would win.

Jack wuz late. He come gallopin' up on hawseback
and reined in de hawse so short till he reared up his
hind legs.

Jack jumped off and says: "Wese all heah, le's go.
Who goin' first?"

De Devil tole 'im, "Me. Everybody stand back and
gimme room."

So he throwed de hammer and it went so high till it
went clean outa sight. Devil tole 'em, "Iss Tuesday now.
Y'all go home and come back Thursday mornin' at nine.
It won't fall till then."

Sho 'nuff de hammer fell on Thursday mornin' at
nine o'clock and knocked out a hole big as Polk
County.

Dey lifted de hammer out de hole and levelled it and
it wuz Jack's time to throw.

Jack took his time and walked 'round de hammer to de handle and took holt of it and throwed his head back and looked up at de sky.

"Look out, Rayfield! Move over, Gabriel! You better stand 'way back, Jesus! Ah'm fixin' to throw." He meant Heaven.

Devil run up to 'im, says, "Hold on dere a minute! Don't you throw mah damn hammer up dere! Ah left a whole lot uh mah tools up dere when dey put me out and Ah ain't got 'em back yet. Don't you *throw* mah hammer up dere!"

X

So I LEFT most of my things at Loughman and ran down in the phosphate country around Mulberry. Around Mulberry, Pierce and Lakeland, I collected a mass of children's tales and games. The company operating the mines at Pierce maintains very excellent living conditions in their quarters. The cottages are on clean, tree-lined streets. There is a good hospital and a nine-months school. They will not employ a boy under seventeen so that the parents are not tempted to put minors to work. There is a cheerful community center with a large green-covered table for crap games under a shady oak.

We held a lying contest out under the trees in the night time, some sitting, some standing, everybody in a jolly mood. Mack C. Ford proved to be a mighty story teller before the Lord.

I found out about creation from him. The tail of the porpoise is on crosswise and he explains the mystery of that.

"Zora, did you ever see a porpoise?"

"Yep. Many times."

"Didja ever notice his tail?"

"Don't b'lieve Ah did. He moves so fast till Ah don't remember much except seeing him turning somersault and shootin' up and down de Indian River like lightnin' thru de trees."

Well, it's on crossways. Every other fish got his tail on straight but de porpoise. His is on crossways and bent down lak dis. (He bent down the fingers of his left hand sharply from the knuckles.)

De reason for dat is, God made de world and de sky and de birds and animals and de fishes. He finished off de stars and de trees.

Den He made a gold track clear 'round de world and greased it, and called de sun to Him and says, "Now Sun, Ah done made everything but Time and Ah want you to make dat. Ah made dat gold track for you to run on and Ah want you to git on it and go 'round de world

153

jus' as fas' as you kin stave it and de time it take you to go and come Ah'm gointer call it 'day' and 'night.'"

De porpoise was standin' 'round and heard God when He spoke to de sun. So he says, "B'lieve Ah'll take dat trip around de world myself."

So de sun lit out and de porpoise took out. Him and him! 'Round de world—lickety split!

So de porpoise beat de sun 'round de world by a hour and three minutes.

When God seen dat He shook His head and says, "Unh, unh! Dis ain't gointer do. Ah never meant for nothin' to be faster than de sun."

So He took out behind dat porpoise and run him for three days and nights befo' He overtook him. But when he *did* ketch dat ole porpoise He grabbed him by de tail and snatched it off and set it back on crossways to slow him up. He can't beat de sun no mo' but he's de next fastest thing in de world.

Everybody laughed one of those blow-out laughs, so Mack Ford said,

Mah lyin' done got good tuh me, so Ahm gointer tell yuh how come de dawg hates de cat.

De dog and de cat used to live next door to one 'nother and both of 'em loved ham. Every time they git a chance they'd buy a slice of ham.

One time both of 'em got holt of a li'l extry change so de dog said to de cat, "Sis Cat, we both got a li'l money, and it would be fine if bofe of us could buy a ham apiece. But neither one of us ain't got enough money to buy a whole ham by ourselves. Why don't we put our money together and buy us a ham together?"

"Aw right, Brer Dawg. T'morrer bein' Sat'day, le's we go to town and git ourselves a ham."

So de next day they went to town and bought de ham. They didn't have no convenience so they had to walk and tote it. De dawg toted it first and he said as he walked up de road wid de ham over his shoulder, "Ours! Ours! Ours! Our ham!"

After while it was de cat's time to tote de meat. She

said, "My ham, my ham, my ham." Dawg heard her but he didn't say nothin'.

When de dawg took it agin he says, "Ours, ours, our ham!" Cat toted it and says, "My ham, my ham."

Dawg says, "Sis Cat, how come you keep on sayin' 'My ham' when you totes our meat. Ah always say, 'Our ham.' "

De Cat didn't turn him no answer, but every time she toted de ham she'd say "My ham" and every time de dawg toted it he'd say "Ours."

When they was almost home, de cat was carryin' de ham and all of a sudden she sprung up a tree and set up there eatin' up de ham. De dawg did all he could to stop her, but he couldn't clim' and so he couldn't do nothin' but bark. But he tole de cat, "You up dat tree eatin' all de ham, and Ah can't git to you. But when you come down ahm gointer make you take dis Indian River for uh dusty road."

"Didja ever pass off much time round de railroad camps, Zora?" asked Mr. Ford.

"Ah been round dere some."

"Ah wuz jus' fixin' tuh tell yuh if you ain't been there you missed some good singin', well ez some good lyin'. Ever hear dat song bout 'Gointer See my Long-haired Babe'?"[1]

"Naw, but ah sho wisht ah had. Can you sing it?"

"Sho can and then ahm gointer do it too, and that one bout 'Oh Lulu, oh Gal.'

"Ah know you want to hear some more stories, don't you? Ah know ah feels lak tellin' some."

"Unh hunh," I agreed.

"Don't you know dat's one word de Devil made up?"

"Nope, Ah had never heard about it. It's a mighty useful word Ah know for lazy folks like me."

"Yes, everybody says 'unh hunh' and Ah'll tell you why." He cleared his throat and continued:

Ole Devil looked around hell one day and seen his place was short of help so he thought he'd run up to

[1]See appendix.

Heben and kidnap some angels to keep things runnin' tell he got reinforcements from Miami.

Well, he slipped up on a great crowd of angels on de outskirts of Heben and stuffed a couple of thousand in his mouth, a few hundred under each arm and wrapped his tail 'round another thousand and darted off towards hell.

When he was flyin' low over de earth lookin' for a place to land, a man looked up and seen de Devil and ast 'im, "Ole Devil, Ah see you got a load of angels. Is you goin' back for mo'?"

Devil opened his mouth and tole 'im, "Yeah," and all de li'l angels flew out his mouf and went on back to Heben. While he was tryin' to ketch 'em he lost all de others. So he went back after another load.

He was flyin' low agin and de same man seen him and says, "Ole Devil, Ah see you got another load uh angels."

Devil nodded his head and said "unh hunh," and dat's why we say it today.

"Dat's a fine story. Tell me some more."

"Ah'm gointer tell you all about Big Sixteen and High Walker and Bloody Bones but first Ah want to ask you a question."

"All right, go ahead and ask me."

"Zora, why do you think dese li'l slim women was put on earth?"

"Couldn't tell you to save my life."

"Well, dese slim ones was put here to beautify de world."

"De big ones musta been put here for de same reason."

"Ah, naw, Zora. Ah don't agree wid you there."

"Well then, what *was* they put here for?"

"To show dese slim girls how far they kin stretch without bustin'."

Everybody out under the trees laughed except Good Bread. She took in a whole lot of breath and added to herself. Then she rolled her eyes and said, "Mack Ford, Ah don't come in yo' conversation atall. You jus' leave me out yo' mouf. And furthermo' Ah don't crack."

"Nobody ain't called yo name, Good Bread, Ah wuz jus' passin' uh joke."

"Oh yes you wuz hintin' at me."

"Aw, nobody ain't studyin' bout yuh. Jus' cause you done set round and growed ruffles round yo' hips nobody can't mention fat 'thout you makin' out they talkin' bout you. Ah wuzn't personatin' yuh, but if de cap fit yuh, wear it."

"G'wan Mack, you know dat a very little uh yo' sugar sweetens mah tea. Don't git *me* started."

"G'wan start something if dats de way yuh feel. You kin be stopped. Now you tryin' to make somebody believe you so bad till you have tuh tote uh pistol tah bed tuh keep from gettin' in uh fight wid yo' self! You got mo' poison in yuh than dat snake dat wuz so poison tell he bit de railroad track and killed de train, hunh?"

"Don't y'all break dis lyin' contest up in no fight," Christopher Jenkins said.

Mah Honey laughed scornfully. "Aw, tain't gointer be no fight. Good Bread jus' feel lak bull woofin' uh little t'night. Her likker told her tuh pick uh fight but let Mack make uh break at her now, and there'll hafta be some good runnin' done befo' dat fight come off. Tain't nothin' tuh her. She know she ugly. She look lak de devil ground up in pieces."

Good Bread jumped up with her pocket knife out. "Who y'all tryin tuh double teen? Trying tuh run de hawg over de wrong one now."

"Aw set down Good Bread, and put dat froe back in yo' pocket. Somebody's liable tuh take dat ole piece uh knife you got and wear it out round yo' own neck."

"Dats what Ah say," Christopher put in. "She always tryin' tuh loud talk somebody. Ah hates women wid men's overalls on anyhow."

"Let her holler all she wants tuh," Ford added off-hand. "Dis is uh holler day. She kin whoop lak de Seaboard and squall lak de A.C.L. Nobody don't keer, long as she don't put her hand on me. Sho as she do dat Ahm gointer light her shuck for her."

Good Bread got to her feet importantly as if she was going

to do something. For a fraction of a second I held my breath in fear. Nobody else paid it the least bit of mind. Good Bread flounced on off.

"Ahm glad she gone," said Mah Honey. "She always pickin' fights and gittin beat. Dat 'oman hates peace and agreement." He looked after her a moment then yelled after her. "Hey, lady, you got all you' bust in de back!" Everybody laughed and Mah Honey went on. "She so mad now she'll stay way and let Mack tell Zora some lies. Gwan, Mack, you got de business."

"Aw, Ah feel lak singin'," Mack Ford said.

"Well nobody don't feel lak hearin' yuh, so g'wan tell dat lie on Big Sixteen. Ah never gits tired uh dat one."

"You ruther hear uh story, Zora?"

"Yeah, g'wan tell it. Dats jus' what Ah'm here for."

"Well alright then:

It was slavery time, Zora, when Big Sixteen was a man. They called 'im Sixteen 'cause dat was de number of de shoe he wore. He was big and strong and Ole Massa looked to him to do everything.

One day Ole Massa said, "Big Sixteen, Ah b'lieve Ah want you to move dem sills Ah had hewed out down in de swamp."

"I yassuh, Massa."

Big Sixteen went down in de swamp and picked up dem 12×12's and brought 'em on up to de house and stack 'em. No one man ain't never toted a 12×12 befo' nor since.

So Ole Massa said one day, "Go fetch in de mules. Ah want to look 'em over."

Big Sixteen went on down to de pasture and caught dem mules by de bridle but they was contrary and balky and he tore de bridles to pieces pullin' on 'em, so he picked one of 'em up under each arm and brought 'em up to Old Massa.

He says, "Big Sixteen, if you kin tote a pair of balky mules, you kin do anything. You kin ketch de Devil."

"Yassuh, Ah kin, if you git me a nine-pound hammer and a pick and shovel!"

Ole Massa got Sixteen de things he ast for and tole 'im to go ahead and bring him de Devil.

Big Sixteen went out in front of de house and went to diggin'. He was diggin' nearly a month befo' he got where he wanted. Then he took his hammer and went and knocked on de Devil's door. Devil answered de door hisself.

"Who dat out dere?"

"It's Big Sixteen."

"What you want?"

"Wanta have a word wid you for a minute."

Soon as de Devil poked his head out de door, Sixteen lammed him over de head wid dat hammer and picked 'im up and carried 'im back to Old Massa.

Ole Massa looked at de dead Devil and hollered, "Take dat ugly thing 'way from here, quick! Ah didn't think you'd ketch de Devil sho 'nuff."

So Sixteen picked up de Devil and throwed 'im back down de hole.

Way after while, Big Sixteen died and went up to Heben. But Peter looked at him and tole 'im to g'wan 'way from dere. He was too powerful. He might git outa order and there wouldn't be nobody to handle 'im. But he had to go somewhere so he went on to hell.

Soon as he got to de gate de Devil's children was playin' in de yard and they seen 'im and run to de house, says, "Mama, mama! Dat man's out dere dat kilt papa!"

So she called 'im in de house and shet de door. When Sixteen got dere she handed 'im a li'l piece of fire and said, "You ain't comin' in here. Here, take dis hot coal and g'wan off and start you a hell uh yo' own."

So when you see a Jack O'Lantern in de woods at night you know it's Big Sixteen wid his piece of fire lookin' for a place to go.

"Give us somethin' to wet our goozles wid, and you kin git some lies, Zora," Jenkins prompted. I stood treats.

"Now g'wan, Mack, and lie some more," I said, and he remarked:

"De mosquitoes mighty bad right now, but down there on de East Coast they used to 'em. Know why we got so many skeeters heah and why we have so many storms?"

"Naw, but Ah'd love to know," I answered eagerly.

Well, one Christmas time, God was goin' to Palatka. De Devil was in de neighborhood too and seen God goin' long de big road, so he jumped behind a stump and hid. Not dat he was skeered uh God, but he wanted to git a Christmas present outa God but he didn't wanta give God nothin'.

So he squatted down behind dis stump till God come along and then he jumped up and said, "Christmas gift!"

God just looked back over his shoulder and said, "Take de East Coast," and kept on walkin'. And dat's why we got storms and skeeters—it's de Devil's property.

I should mention it is a custom in the deep South for the children to go out Christmas morning "catching" people by saying "Christmas gift." The one who says it first gets a present from the other. The adults usually prepare for this by providing plenty of hard candy, nuts, coconuts, fruits and the like. They never try to catch the neighbors' children but let themselves be caught.

"Ah know one mo' story on de devil. Reckon Ah'll tell it now.

"One day de Devil was walkin' along when he met Raw Head."

"Who is Raw Head?" I interrupted to ask. "Ah been hearin' his name called all my life, but never did find out who he was."

"Why, Zora! Ah thought everybody knowed who Raw Head was. Why he was a man dat was more'n a man. He was big and strong like Big Sixteen and he was two-headed. He knowed all de words dat Moses used to make. God give 'im de power to bring de ten plagues and part de Red Sea. He had done seen de Smokey Mountain and de Burnin' Bush. And his head didn't have no hair on it, and it sweated blood all de time. Dat's why he was named Raw Head."[2] Then Mr. Ford told the following story:

As Ah started to say, de Devil met Raw Head and they passed de time of day. Neither one wasn't skeered of de other, so they talked about de work they been doin'.

Raw Head said he had done turnt a man into a ground puppy. Devil said he been havin' a good time breakin' up couples. All over de world de devil had husbands and wives fightin' and partin'.

Tol 'im says, "Devil, youse my cousin and Ah know you got mo' power than me, but Ah know one couple you can't part. They lives cross de big creek in my district, and Ah done everything Ah could but nothin' can't come between 'em."

Devil says, "Dat's because de right one ain't tried yet. Ah kin part any two people. Jus' like Ah kin throw 'em together. You show 'em to me and Ah betcha half of hell Ah'll have 'em fightin' and partin' befo' Sunday."

So de Devil went to where dis couple lived and took up 'round de house.

He done everything he could but they wouldn't fight and they wouldn't part. Devil was real outdone. He had never had such a tussle since they throwed him outer Heben, and it was Friday. He seen he was 'bout to lose half of his kingdom and have to go back on his brag.

He was 'bout to give up and go somewhere else dat night when he met a woman as barefooted as a yard-dog. They spoke and she says, "You don't look so good. You been down sick?"

Devil told her, "Naw, but Ah been tryin' to break up dat lovin' couple up de road a piece there, but Ah can't do it."

De woman says, "Aw shucks, is dat all? Tell you whut: Ah ain't never had a pair of shoes in my life and if you

[2]He was a conjure doctor. They are always referred to as "two-headed doctors," i.e. twice as much sense.

promise to give me a pair of shoes tonight Ah'll part 'em for you."

"If you part 'em you get de shoes, and good ones at dat. But you got to do it first."

"Don't you worry 'bout dat, you jus' meet me at dat sweet-gum tree on de edge of de swamp tomorrer evenin' and bring de shoes."

Next mornin' she got up soon and went past de place to see where de man was workin' at. He was plowin' way off from de house. So she spoke to 'im nice and polite and went on up to de house where de wife was.

De wife asted her in and give her a chair. She took her seat and begin to praise everything on de place. It was de prettiest house she ever seen. It was de bes' lookin' yard in dat part of the state. Dat was de finest dawg she ever laid eyes on. *Nobody* never had no cat as good as dat one was.

De wife thanked her for all her compliments and give her a pound of butter.

De woman told her "Everything you got is pretty, but youse de prettiest of all."

De wife is crazy 'bout her husband and she can't stand to see him left out so she say, "My husband is prettier than Ah ever dared to be."

"Oh, yeah, he's pretty too. Almost as pretty as you. De only thing dat spoil his looks is dat long flesh-mole on his neck. Now if dat was off he'd be de prettiest man in de world."

De wife says, "Ah thinks he's already de prettiest man in de world, but if anything will make 'im *mo'* prettier still, Ah will too gladly do it."

"Well, then, you better cut dat big ole mole offa his neck."

"How kin Ah do dat? He skeered to cut if off. Say he might bleed to death."

"Aw naw, he won't neither. He won't lose more'n a drop of blood if you cut it off right quick wid a sharp razor and then wipe cob-web on de place. It's a pity he won't let you do it 'cause it sho do spoil his looks."

"If Ah knowed jus' how to do it, Ah sho would, 'cause Ah love him so and he is too pretty a man to be spoilt by a mole."

"Why don't you take de razor to bed wid you to-night. Then when he gets to sleep, you chop it off right quick and fix it lak Ah told you. He'll thank you for it next day."

De wife thanked de woman and give her a settin' of eggs and de woman told her good-bye and went on down to de field where de husband was plowin', and sidled up to him. "Good mornin' suh, you sho is a hard-workin' man."

"Yes ma'am, Ah works hard but Ah loves to work so Ah kin do for my wife. She's all Ah got."

"Yeah, and she sho got a man when she got you. 'Tain't many mens dat will hit from sun to sun for a woman."

The man said, "Sho ain't. But ain't no man got no wife as good as mine."

De woman spit on de ground and said, "It's good for a person's mind to be satisfied. But lovin' a person don't make them love you. And youse a pitiful case."

"Why you say dat? Ain't I got de prettiest wife in de world. And what make it so cool, she's de sweetest wife God ever made."

"All Ah got to say is 'Watch out.' "

"Watch out for what? My wife don't need no watchin'. She's pretty, it's true, but Ah don't have to watch her."

"Somebody else done found out she pretty too and she's gointer gid rid of *you*. You better keep a close watch on her and when you go to bed tonight, make out you sleep and see if she don't try to cut yo' throat wid a razor!"

"Git off dis place—lyin' on my wife?"

De woman hid in de bushes outside de fence row and watched. Sho nuff, pretty soon he knocked off and went on towards de house. When he got dere he searched all over de place to see if anybody was there besides his wife. He didn't find nothin' but he watched everybody dat passed de gate, and he didn't say nothin' to his wife.

Dat night he got in bed right after supper and laid there wid his eyes shut. De wife went and got his razor and slipped it to bed wid her. When she thought he was good and sleep she got de cob-web in one hand and de razor in de other and leaned over him to cut his mole off. He had de cover up 'round his neck and soon as she started to ease it back he opened his eyes and grabbed her and took de razor.

"Unh, hunh! Ah was told you was goin' to cut my throat, but Ah didn't b'lieve it. From now on, we ain't no mo' husband and wife."

He dressed and left her cryin' in de bed.

De woman run on down to de sweet-gum tree to git her shoes. De Devil come brought 'em but he took and cut a long sapling and tied de shoe to de end of it and held 'em out to de woman and told her, "You parted 'em all right. Here's de shoes I promised you. But anybody dat kin create mo' disturbance than me is too dangerous. Ah don't want 'em round me. Here, take yo' shoes." And soon as she took 'em he vanished.

Horace Sharp said, "You lemme tell one now, Mack; you been talkin' all night. Tell yuh bout de farmer courtin' a girl.

Well, the startin' of it is, a farmer was courtin' a girl and after he decided to marry her, they married and started home. So when he passed a nice farm he said to the girl: "You see dat nice farm over yonder?" She said, "Yes." He said: "Well, all of these are mine." (Strokes his whiskers.)

Well, they traveled on further and they saw a herd of cattle and he said, "See dat nice herd of cattle?" She said, "Yes." "Well, all of these are mine." He smoothed his whiskers again.

So he traveled on a piece further and come to a big plantation with a big nice house on it, and he said: "All of these are mine."

So he traveled on further. He said, "See dat nice

bunch of sheep?" She said, "Yes." "Well, all of these are mine."

Traveled on further. Come across a nice bunch of hogs and he said: "See dat nice bunch of hogs?" "Yes." "Well, all of these are mine."

So the last go 'round he got home and drove up to a dirty li'l shack and told her to get out and come in.

She says, "You got all those nice houses and want me to come in there? I couldn't afford to come in here. *Why you told me a story.* I'm going back home."

He says, "Why no, I didn't tell you a story. Every-time I showed you those things I said 'all of these were mine' and Ah wuz talkin' bout my whiskers." So the girl jumped out of the wagon and out for home she went.

Goat fell down and skint his chin
Great God A'mighty how de goat did grin.

"You do pretty good, Horace," Mah Honey drawled, "but how come you want to stick in yo' bill when Mack is talkin'? Dat story you told ain't doodly squat."

"Less see *you* tell one better'n dat one, then," Horace slashed back.

"Oh Ah can't tell none worth listenin' tuh and you can't neither. Only difference in us is Ah know Ah can't and you don't. Dat lie you told is po' ez owl harkey. Gwan tell some mo' Mack. Maybe somebody'll come long and help yuh out after while."

"Ah thought Horace's story wuz jus' alright," Lessie Lee Hudson said. "Can't eve'ybody talk de same."

"Course it wuz!" Horace yelled, "it wuz alright wid every-body 'ceptin Mah Honey. He's a nigger wid white folks' head—let *him* tell it. He make out he know every chink in China."

"What you gointer do?" Mah Honey asked. "Ah kin tell yuh fo' yuh part yo' lips. You ain't gointer do nothin' but mildew."

Somebody came along singing, "You Won't Do," and every-body looked round at one time like cows in a pasture.

"Here come A.D. He kin lie good too. Hurry up, A.D. and help Mack out!"

"What Mack doin'?"

"Lyin' up a breeze."

"Awright, lemme git in dis shag-lag. Who lied last?"

"Mack. Youse next."

"Who all know what uh squinch owl[3] is?" Frazier lit out.

"Man, who you reckon it is, *don't* know what dat bad luck thing is?" Christopher Jenkins asked. "Sign uh death every time you hear one hollerin round yo' house. Ah shoots every one Ah kin find."

"You kin stop 'em without shootin' 'em. Jus' tie uh loose knot in uh string and every time he holler you pull de knot uh lil bit tighter. Dat chokes 'im. Keep on you choke 'im tuh death. Go out doors nex' mawnin and look ahround you'll find uh dead owl round dere somewhere," said Mah Honey.

"All you need tuh do is turn somethin' wrong side outuds, pull off yo' coat and turn it or else you kin turn uh pocket," Carrie Jones added. "Me, Ah always pull off uh stockin' and turn it. Dat always drives 'im off."

"Throw some salt on de lamp or stick uh rusty fork in de floor will do de same thing. In fact its de best of all; Ah mean de salt in de lamp. Nothin' evil can't stand salt, let alone burnin' salt."

"Lemme tell y'all how come we got squinch owls and then y'all kin talk all yuh please bout how tuh kill 'em and drive 'em off de house top in de night time," said A.D.

Yuh know Ole Marster had uh ole maid sister that never been married. You know how stringy white folks necks gits when dey gits ole. Well hers had done got that-a-way and more special cause she never been married.

Her name wuz Miss Pheenie and Ole Marster had uh daughter so there wuz young mens round de parlor and de porch. All in de sittin' chairs and in de hammock under de trees. So Miss Pheenie useter stand round and peer at 'em and grin lak uh possum—wishin' she could git courted and married.

[3]Screech owl, sometimes known as a shivering owl.

So one devilish young buck, he seen de feelin' in her so he 'gin tuh make manners wid her and last thing he done, he told her says, "If you go set up on de roof uh de house all night Ah'll marry yuh in de mawnin'."

It wuz uh bitter cold night. De wind searchin' lak de police. So she clambed up dere and set straddle of de highest part cause she couldn't stick nowhere's else. And she couldn't help but shake and shiver. And everytime de clock would strike de hour she'd say, "C-o-o-o-l-d on de housetop, but uh young man in de mawnin'." She kept dat up till de clock struck four, when she tumbled down, froze tuh death. But de very next night after they buried her, she took de shape of uh owl and wuz back dere shivverin' and cryin'. And dats how come us got squinch owls.

"Dat sho waz uh true lie, A.D.," Carrie said. "Ah sho is wished many de time dat Miss Pheenie had uh stayed off de top uh dat house."

"Ah knows one 'bout uh witch woman," A.D. went on. "Ah'll tell dat one too, whilst Ah got mah wind."

"Naw, Ah don't wanta hear bout no witches ridin' nobody," Baby-face Turl objected. "Ah been near rode tuh death in mah time. Can't bear tuh hear tell of it."

"Well then Ah kin tell yuh bout dat talkin' mule.

Ole feller one time had uh mule. His name wuz Bill. Every mornin' de man go tuh ketch 'im he say, "Come 'round, Bill!"

So one mornin' he slept late, so he decided while he wuz drinkin' some coffee he'd send his son tuh ketch Ole Bill.

Told 'im say, "Go down dere, boy, and bring me dat mule up here."

Boy, he sich a fast Aleck, he grabbed de bridle and went on down tuh de lot tuh ketch ole Bill.

He say, "Come round, Bill!"

De mule looked round at 'im. He told de mule, "Tain't no use you rollin' yo' eyes at *me*. Pa want yuh dis mawnin'. Come on round and stick yo' head in dis bridle."

Mule kept on lookin' at 'im and said, "Every mornin' its 'Come round, Bill! Come round, Bill!' Don't hardly git no night rest befo' its 'Come round, Bill!' "

De boy throwed down dat bridle and flew back tuh de house and told his Pa, "Dat mule is talkin'."

"Ah g'wan, boy, tellin' yo' lies! G'wan ketch dat mule."

"Naw suh, Pa, dat mule's done gone tuh talkin'. You hatta ketch dat mule yo' ownself. Ah ain't gwine."

Ole man looked at ole lady and say, "See whut uh lie dat boy is tellin'?"

So he gits out and goes on down after de mule hisself. When he got down dere he hollered, "Come round, Bill!"

Ole mule looked round and says, "Every mornin' its come round, Bill!"

De old man had uh little fice dog useter foller 'im everywhere he go, so he lit out wid de lil fice right behind 'im. So he told de ole lady, "De boy ain't told much of uh lie. Dat mule *is* talkin'. Ah never heered uh mule talk befo'."

Lil fice say, "Me neither."

De ole man got skeered agin. Right through de woods he went wid de fice right behind 'im. He nearly run hisself tuh death. He stopped and commenced blowin' and says, "Ahm so tired Ah don't know whut tuh do."

Lil dog run and set down in front of 'im and went to hasslin'[4] and says, "Me too."

Dat man is runnin' yet.

Everybody agreed that the old man did right by running, only some thought they could have bettered his record both for speed and distance.

"What make you love tuh tell dem skeery lies, A.D.?" Clarence Beale asked.

Lessie Lee snuggled up to Clarence with the eyes of Eve and said, "He skeers me too, Clarence. Less me and you hug

[4]Panting.

up together." Clarence grabbed her and wrapped her up tight.

"Youse jus' all right, A.D. If you know another one skeerier than dat one, Ah'll give yuh five dollars tuh tell it. And then Ah'm gointer git de job uh keepin' de boogers offa Lessie Lee tuhnight. G'wan tell it."

"Yeah man!" Christopher Jenkins chimed in. "All dese frail eels gittin' skittish. Tell some mo' A.D. Skeer Carrie right up on me!"

So A.D. told another one.

This wuz uh man. His name was High Walker. He walked into a boneyard with skull-heads and other bones. So he would call them, "Rise up bloody bones and shake yo'self." And de bones would rise up and come together, and shake theirselves and part and lay back down. Then he would say to hisself, "High Walker," and de bones would say, "Be walkin'."

When he'd git off a little way he'd look back over his shoulder and shake hisself and say, "High Walker and bloody bones," and de bones would shake theirselves. Therefore he knowed he had power.

So uh man sold hisself to de high chief devil. He give 'im his whole soul and body tuh do ez he pleased wid it. He went out in uh drift uh woods[5] and laid down flat on his back beyond all dese skull heads and bloody bones and said, "Go 'way Lawd, and come here Devil and do as you please wid me. Cause Ah want tuh do everything in de world dats wrong and never do nothing right."

And he dried up and died away on doin' wrong. His meat all left his bones and de bones all wuz separated.

And at dat time High Walker walked upon his skull head and kicked and kicked it on ahead of him a many and a many times and said tuh it, "Rise up and shake yo'self. High Walker is here."

Ole skull head wouldn't say nothin'. He looked back

[5] 10,000 "faces" in the turpentine woods, i.e. tree trunks that have been cut on one side to make the sap run from which turpentine is made.

over his shoulder cause he heard some noises behind him and said, "Bloody bones you won't say nothin' yet. Rise tuh de power in de flesh."

Den de skull head said, "My mouf brought me here and if you don't mind, your'n will bring you here."

High Walker went on back to his white folks and told de white man dat a dry skull head wuz talkin' in de drift today. White man say he didn't believe it.

"Well, if you don't believe it, come go wid me and Ah'll prove it. And if it don't speak, you kin chop mah head off right where it at."

So de white man and High Walker went back in de drift tuh find dis ole skull head. So when he walked up tuh it, he begin tuh kick and kick de ole skull head, but it wouldn't say nothin'. High Walker looked at de white man and seen 'im whettin' his knife. Whettin' it hard and de sound of it said rick-de-rick, rick-de-rick, rick-de-rick! So High Walker kicked and kicked dat ole skull head and called it many and many uh time, but it never said nothin'. So de white man cut off High Walker's head.

And de ole dry skull head said, "See dat now! Ah told you dat mouf brought me here and if you didn't mind out it'd bring you here."

So de bloody bones riz up and shook they selves seben times and de white man got skeered and said, "What you mean by dis?"

De bloody bones say, "We got High Walker and we all bloody bones now in de drift together."

The next day was Thursday and I got a letter from Big Sweet saying I must be back at Loughman by Saturday because that was pay night and Thelma and Cliffert were getting married and big doings would be going on.

Friday I arrived in Loughman. Thelma and Cliffert got married on Saturday and everybody that wasn't mad put out to give them a big time.

The biggest crowd was over at the Pine Mill where Jim Presley was playing so I wanted to go there. Big Sweet didn't want to go there much. At least that is what she told everybody, but she told me to go on. She might be over later. She gave me some advice about looking out for myself.

"Don't let nobody bring yuh nothin' tuh eat and drink, and don't let 'em send it neither. They liable tuh put uh spider in yo' dumplin'. Don't let nobody git yuh intuh no fuss, cause you can't do dis kind uh fightin'. You don't know no better'n tuh go face tuh face tuh fight. Lucy and dem ain't gointer fight nobody lak dat. They think it make 'em look big tuh cut yuh. Ah done went tuh her and put mah foot up on her door step and told her dat if she tetch yuh Ah'll gently chain-gang fuh her, but she don't aim tuh lemme ketch her. She mean tuh slip up on yuh sometime and hit yuh uh back hand lick wid her knife and turn her hand over right quick and hit yuh forward wid it and pull it down. Then she aims tuh run cross back yards and jump fences so fast till me and de law neither can't find her."

"Well, Big Sweet, if it's like dat, Ah speck Ah better not go out unless you be wid me," I told her.

"Oh yeah, you go on. You come here tuh see and lissen and Ah means fuh yuh tuh do it. Jus' watch out. Ah could give yuh uh knife tuh tote but dat wouldn't do you no good. You don't know how tuh handle it. Ah got two round here. One real good one Ah got down in Tampa, and one ole froe.[6] But you jus' gwan over dere and mind what Ah tell yuh. Ahm liable tuh be dere tuhreckly mahself. And don't git biggity wid nobody and let yuh head start more than yo' rump kin stand."

I promised sincerely and took Cliffert and Thelma in the car with me to the Pine Mill.

A new man had come from Groveland, where another big sawmill was located, and he was standing behind Jim Presley and Slim, singing new songs, and I was so glad that I had come. It didn't take me long to learn some new ones and I forgot all about Lucy.

Way after midnight Big Sweet came in. The place was hot by then. Everything was done got loud. The music, the dancing, the laughing, and nobody could say a thing even over the

[6]A damaged pocket knife.

card games unless they made it sound something like singing. Heard one woman playing Coon Can sing out:

> Give mah man mah money, tuh play Coon Can
> He lost all mah money but he played his hand.

In a little while I heard her again:

> Befo' Ah'll lose mah rider's change
> Ah'll spread short deuces and tab de game.

Big Sweet nodded me over in a corner and said, "Ah done strowed it over on de other side dat Ahm gone home tuh bed. Jus' wanta see whut might come off."

"Lucy ain't been here atall," I told her. "Believe she skeered you might kill her sho 'nuff."

"She know Ah will lessen she kill me first. Ah hates uh two-facedted heifer lak her. And Ah ain't skeered tuh see Mah Jesus neither cause de Bible say God loves uh plain sinner and he's married tuh de backslider. Ah got jus' as good uh chance at Heben as anybody else. So have yo' correct amount uh fun. Ahm settin' right over dere in dat skin game."

Heard somebody at the Florida Flip game say, "Ahm gone—jus' lak uh turkey through de corn. Deal!"

Heard somebody else in the game say, "Beggin' " and the dealer told him, "Eat acorns."[7]

Heard Blue Baby ask Box-Car, "Who is dat new nigger over dere by de refreshments? God Amighty, ugly got de mug on him wid four wheel brakes."

"He's de new skitter man.[8] He sho' ain't nobody's pretty baby. Bet he have tuh slip up on de dipper tuh git uh drink uh water. B'lieve Ah'll holler at 'im. 'Hey Ugly, who made you? Don't start tuh lyin' on God now.' "

A general laugh followed this. Box-Car, a little proud of his crack grabbed Blue Baby. "Come on less go over dere and marry Cliff and Thelma all over agin. Hey Cliff, you and Thelma git up on de floor and raise yo' right hand. Y'all ain't been hitched right till Box-Car git thew widja." The couple bashfully stood up.

---

[7] I give you one point.
[8] A panther had killed the other one a week earlier.

"Join hands. Alright Cliff, Ahm de preacher—

> Here's yo' woman, here's de ring,
> Here's de banana, here's de skin
> Now you married, go——

A huge burst of laughter drowned out Box Car's voice and when the laugh died out, I could hear Nunkie, "reading the deck" where the flip game used to be. Calling the names of the cards and laying them down rhythmically and dramatically as he read:

> Ace means the first time that Ah met you,
> Deuce means there was nobody there but us two,
> Trey means the third party, Charlie was his name,
> Four spot means the fourth time you tried dat same
>   ole game,
> Five spot is five years you played me for a clown,
> Six spot, six feet of earth when de deal goes down,
> Now, Ahm holdin' de seben spot for each day in de
>   week,
> Eight spot, eight hours you sheba-ed wid yo' sheik,
> Nine spot means nine hours Ah work hard every day,
> Ten spot de tenth of every month Ah brought you
>   home mah pay,
> De Jack is Three Card Charlie who played me for a
>   goat,
> De Queen, dat's you, pretty mama, also tryin' tuh
>   cut mah throat,
> De King, dat hot papa Nunkie, and he's gointer
>   wear de crown,
> So be keerful y'all ain't broke when de deal goes down.

Nunkie looked around belligerently on the last sentence and Joe Willard jumped up and pulled at Big Sweet.

"Play some music, Jim, y'all over dere, and less dance some mo'. Nunkie wants tuh pick uh fight wid Who Flung. Play us uh slow drag. Come on Big Sweet, less me and you have uh schronchuns dance."

"Dance wid Zora, honey, Ah don't choose tuh move from where Ahm at. Ah ain't mad wid nobody, baby, jus' wanta set and look on uh while yet."

Heard the new singing man climbing up on

> Tell me, tell me where de blood red river ru-u-un
> Oh tell me where de blood red river run
> From mah back door, straight to de risin' sun.

Heard Slim's bass strings under the singing throbbing like all Africa and Jim Presley's melody crying like repentance as four or five couples took the floor. Doing the slow drag, doing the schronch. Joe Willard doing a traveling buck and wing towards where I stood against the wall facing the open door.

Just about that time Lucy hopped up in the doorway with an open knife in her hands. She saw me first thing. Maybe she had been outside peeping a long time and there I was leaning against the wall right close to Slim. One door in the place and Lucy standing in it.

"Stop dat music," she yelled without moving. "Don't vip another vop till Ah say so! Ah means tuh turn dis place out right now. Ah got de law in mah mouf."

So she started walking hippily straight at me. She knew I couldn't get out easily because she had me barred and she knew not many people will risk running into a knife blade to stop a fight. So she didn't have to run. I didn't move but I was running in my skin. I could hear the blade already crying in my flesh. I was sick and weak. But a flash from the corner about ten feet off and Lucy had something else to think about besides me. Big Sweet was flying at her with an open blade and now it was Lucy's time to try to make it to the door. Big Sweet kicked her somewhere about the knees and she fell. A doubled back razor flew thru the air very close to Big Sweet's head. Crip, the new skitter man, had hurled it. It whizzed past Big Sweet and stuck in the wall; then Joe Willard went for Crip. Jim Presley punched me violently and said, "Run you chile! Run and ride! Dis is gointer be uh nasty ditch. Lucy been feedin' Crip under rations tuh git him tuh help her. Run clean off dis job! Some uh dese folks goin' tuh judgment and some goin' tuh jail. Come on, less run!"

Slim stuck out the guitar to keep two struggling men from blocking my way. Lucy was screaming. Crip had hold of Big Sweet's clothes in the back and Joe was slugging him loose. Curses, oaths, cries and the whole place was in motion. Blood was on the floor. I fell out of the door over a man lying on the steps, who either fell himself trying to run or got knocked down. I don't know. I was in the car in a second and in high just too quick. Jim and Slim helped me throw my bags into the car and I saw the sun rising as I approached Crescent City.

PART TWO

HOODOO

I

WINTER PASSED and caterpillars began to cross the road again. I had spent a year in gathering and culling over folk-tales. I loved it, but I had to bear in mind that there was a limit to the money to be spent on the project, and as yet, I had done nothing about hoodoo.

So I slept a night, and the next morning I headed my toe-nails toward Louisiana and New Orleans in particular.

New Orleans is now and has ever been the hoodoo capital of America. Great names in rites that vie with those of Hayti in deeds that keep alive the powers of Africa.

Hoodoo, or Voodoo, as pronounced by the whites, is burning with a flame in America, with all the intensity of a suppressed religion. It has its thousands of secret adherents. It adapts itself like Christianity to its locale, reclaiming some of its borrowed characteristics to itself. Such as fire-worship as signified in the Christian church by the altar and the candles. And the belief in the power of water to sanctify as in baptism.

Belief in magic is older than writing. So nobody knows how it started.

The way we tell it, hoodoo started way back there before everything. Six days of magic spells and mighty words and the world with its elements above and below was made. And now, God is leaning back taking a seventh day rest. When the eighth day comes around, He'll start to making new again.

Man wasn't made until around half-past five on the sixth day, so he can't know how anything was done. Kingdoms crushed and crumbled whilst man went gazing up into the sky and down into the hollows of the earth trying to catch God working with His hands so he could find out His secrets and learn how to accomplish and do. But no man yet has seen God's hand, nor yet His finger-nails. All they could know was that God made everything to pass and perish except stones. God made stones for memory. He builds a mountain Himself when He wants things not forgot. Then His voice is heard in rumbling judgment.

Moses was the first man who ever learned God's power-compelling words and it took him forty years to learn ten words. So he made ten plagues and ten commandments. But God gave him His rod for a present, and showed him the back part of His glory. Then too, Moses could walk out of the sight of man. But Moses never would have stood before the Burning Bush, if he had not married Jethro's daughter. Jethro was a great hoodoo man. Jethro could tell Moses could carry power as soon as he saw him. In fact he felt him coming. Therefore, he took Moses and crowned him and taught him. So Moses passed on beyond Jethro with his rod. He lifted it up and tore a nation out of Pharaoh's side, and Pharaoh couldn't help himself. Moses talked with the snake that lives in a hole right under God's foot-rest. Moses had fire in his head and a cloud in his mouth. The snake had told him God's making words. The words of doing and the words of obedience. Many a man thinks he is making something when he's only changing things around. But God let Moses make. And then Moses had so much power he made the eight winged angels split open a mountain to bury him in, and shut up the hole behind them.

And ever since the days of Moses, kings have been toting rods for a sign of power. But it's mostly sham-polish because no king has ever had the power of even one of Moses' ten words. Because Moses made a nation and a book, a thousand million leaves of ordinary men's writing couldn't tell what Moses said.

Then when the moon had dragged a thousand tides behind her, Solomon was a man. So Sheba, from her country where she was, felt him carrying power and therefore she came to talk with Solomon and hear him.

The Queen of Sheba was an Ethiopian just like Jethro, with power unequal to man. She didn't have to deny herself to give gold to Solomon. She had gold-making words. But she was thirsty, and the country where she lived was dry to her mouth. So she listened to her talking ring and went to see Solomon, and the fountain in his garden quenched her thirst.

So she made Solomon wise and gave him her talking ring.

And Solomon built a room with a secret door and everyday he shut himself inside and listened to his ring. So he wrote down the ring-talk in books.

That's what the old ones said in ancient times and we talk it again.

It was way back there—the old folks told it—that Raw-Head-And-Bloody-Bones had reached down and laid hold of the tap-root that points to the center of the world. And they talked about High Walker too. But they talked in people's language and nobody knew them but the old folks.

Nobody knows for sure how many thousands in America are warmed by the fire of hoodoo, because the worship is bound in secrecy. It is not the accepted theology of the Nation and so believers conceal their faith. Brother from sister, husband from wife. Nobody can say where it begins or ends. Mouths don't empty themselves unless the ears are sympathetic and knowing.

That is why these voodoo ritualistic orgies of Broadway and popular fiction are so laughable. The profound silence of the initiated remains what it is. Hoodoo is not drum beating and dancing. There are no moon-worshippers among the Negroes in America.

I was once talking to Mrs. Rachel Silas of Sanford, Florida, so I asked her where I could find a good hoodoo doctor.

"Do you believe in dat ole fogeyism, chile? Ah don't see how nobody could do none of dat work, do you?" She laughed unnecessarily. "Ah been hearin' 'bout dat mess ever since Ah been big enough tuh know mahself, but shucks! Ah don't believe nobody kin do me no harm lessen they git somethin' in mah mouth."

"Don't fool yourself," I answered with assurance. "People can do things to you. I done seen things happen."

"Sho nuff? Well, well, well! Maybe things *kin* be done tuh harm yuh, cause Ah done heard *good* folks—folks dat ought to know—say dat it sho is a fact. Anyhow Ah figger it pays tuh be keerful."

"Oh yeah, Mrs. Rachel, Ah've seen a woman full of scorpions."

"Oh it kin be done, honey, no effs and ands 'bout de thing. There's things that kin be done. Ah seen uh' 'oman wid uh gopher in her belly. You could see 'm movin' 'round in her. And once every day he'd turn hisself clear over and then you could hear her hollerin' for more'n a mile. Dat hard shell would be cuttin' her insides. Way after 'while she took down ill sick from it and died. Ah knowed de man dat done dat trick. Dat wuz done in uh dish of hoppin-john.[1]

Mrs. Viney White, a neighbor, was sitting there so she spoke. "Ah knowed into dat mahself. It wuz done over her breaking de leg of one of his hens dat wuz scratchin' up her garden. When she took down sick Ah went to see her and Ah told her folks right then dat somebody had done throwed at her, but they didn't b'lieve in nothin'. Went and got a Medical doctor, and they can't do them kind of cases no good at all. Fact is it makes it worser." She stopped short and nodded her head apprehensively towards the window. Rachel nodded her head knowingly. "She out dere now, tryin' tuh eavesdrop."

"Who you talkin' 'bout?" I asked.

"De one dat does all de underhand work 'round here. She even throwed at *me* once, but she can't do nothin'. Ah totes mah Big John de Conquerer[2] wid me. And Ah sprinkles mustard seed 'round my door every night before Ah goes tuh bed."

"Yeah, and another thing," Mrs. Rachel said, "Ah keeps her offa me too. She tries tuh come in dis yard so she kin put something down for me too, but air Lawd, Ah got something buried at dat gate dat she can't cross. She done been dere several times, but she can't cross."

"Ah'd git her tuh go if ah wuz you, Rachel," Mrs. Viney said.

"Wisht ah knowed how. Ah'd sho do it."

"You throw salt behind her, everytime she go out of her gate. Do dat nine times and Ah bet she'll move so fast she won't even know where she's going. Somebody salted a

---

[1]Peas and rice cooked together.
[2]A root, extensively used in conjure.

woman over in Georgetown and she done moved so much she done wore out her furniture on de movin' wagon. But looka here, Zora, whut you want wid a two-headed doctor? Is somebody done throwed a old shoe at *you*?"

"Not exactly neither one, Mrs. Viney. Just want to learn how to do things myself."

"Oh, honey, Ah wouldn't mess with it if Ah wuz you. Dat's a thing dat's got to be handled just so, do it'll kill you. Me and Rachel both knows somebody that could teach you if they will. Dis woman ain't lak some of these hoodoo doctors. She don't do nothin' but good. You couldn't pay her to be rottin' people's teeths out, and fillin' folks wid snakes and lizards and spiders and things like dat."

So I went to study with Eulalia, who specialized in Man-and-woman cases. Everyday somebody came to get Eulalia to tie them up with some man or woman or to loose them from love.

Eulalia was average sized with very dark skin and bushy eyebrows. Her house was squatting among the palmettoes and the mossy scrub oaks. Nothing pretty in the house nor outside. No paint and no flowers. So one day a woman came to get tied to a man.

"Who is dis man?" Eulalia wanted to know.

"Jerry Moore," the woman told her. "He want me and Ah know it, but dat 'oman he got she got roots buried and he can't git shet of her—do we would of done been married."

Eulalia sat still and thought awhile. Then she said: "Course Ah'm uh Christian woman and don't believe in partin' no husband and wife but since she done worked roots on him, to hold him where he don't want to be, it tain't no sin for me to loose him. Where they live at?"

"Down Young's Quarters. De third house from dis end."

"Do she ever go off from home and stays a good while durin' de time he ain't there neither?"

"Yas Ma'am! She all de time way from dat house—off fan-footin' whilst he workin' lak a dog! It's a shame!"

"Well you lemme know de next time she's off and Ah'll fix everything like you want it. Put that money back in yo' purse, Ah don't want a thing till de work is done."

Two or three days later her client was back with the news

that the over-plus wife was gone fishing. Eulalia sent her away and put on her shoes.

"Git dat salt-bowl and a lemon," she said to me. "Now write Jerry's name and his wife's nine times on a piece of paper and cut a little hole in the stem end of that lemon and pour some of that gun-powder in de hole and roll that paper tight and shove it inside the lemon. Wrap de lemon and de bowl of salt up and less go."

In Jerry Moore's yard, Eulalia looked all around and looked up at the sun a great deal, then pointed out a spot.

"Dig a little hole right here and bury dat lemon. It's got to be buried with the bloom-end down and it's got to be where de settin' sun will shine on it."

So I buried the lemon and Eulalia walked around to the kitchen door. By the time I had the lemon buried the door was open and we went inside. She looked all about and found some red pepper.

"Lift dat stove-lid for me," she ordered, and I did. She threw some of the pepper into the stove and we went on into the other room which was the bedroom and living-room all in one. Then Eulalia took the bowl and went from corner to corner "salting" the room. She'd toss a sprinkling into a corner and say, "Just fuss and fuss till you part and go away." Under the bed was sprinkled also. It was all over in a minute or two. Then we went out and shut the kitchen door and hurried away. And Saturday night Eulalia got her pay and the next day she set the ceremony to bring about the marriage.

II

Now I was in New Orleans and I asked. They told me Algiers, the part of New Orleans that is across the river to the west. I went there and lived for four months and asked. I found women reading cards and doing mail order business in names and insinuations of well known factors in conjure. Nothing worth putting on paper. But they all claimed some knowledge and link with Marie Leveau. From so much of hearing the name I asked everywhere for this Leveau and everybody told me differently. But from what they said I was eager to know to the end of the talk. It carried me back across the river into the Vieux Carré. All agreed that she had lived and died in the French quarter of New Orleans. So I went there to ask.

I found an oil painting of the queen of conjure on the walls of the Cabildo, and mention of her in the guide books of New Orleans, but I did a lot of stumbling and asking before I heard of Luke Turner, himself a hoodoo doctor, who says that he is her nephew.

When I found out about Turner, I had already studied under five two-headed doctors and had gone thru an initiation ceremony with each. So I asked Turner to take me as a pupil. He was very cold. In fact he showed no eagerness even to talk with me. He feels sure of his powers and seeks no one. He refused to take me as a pupil and in addition to his habitual indifference I could see he had no faith in my sincerity. I could see him searching my face for whatever was behind what I said. The City of New Orleans has a law against fortune tellers, hoodoo doctors and the like, and Turner did not know me. He asked me to excuse him as he was waiting upon someone in the inner room. I let him go but I sat right there and waited. When he returned, he tried to shoo me away by being rude. I stayed on. Finally he named an impossible price for tuition. I stayed and dickered. He all but threw me out, but I stayed and urged him.

I made three more trips before he would talk to me in any way that I could feel encouraged. He talked about Marie

Leveau because I asked. I wanted to know if she was really as great as they told me. So he enlightened my ignorance and taught me. We sat before the soft coal fire in his grate.

"Time went around pointing out what God had already made. Moses had seen the Burning Bush. Solomon by magic knowed all wisdom. And Marie Leveau was a woman in New Orleans.

"She was born February 2, 1827. Anybody don't believe I tell the truth can go look at the book in St. Louis Cathedral. Her mama and her papa, they wasn't married and his name was Christophe Glapion.

"She was very pretty, one of the Creole Quadroons and many people said she would never be a hoodoo doctor like her mama and her grandma before her. She liked to go to the balls very much where all the young men fell in love with her. But Alexander, the great two-headed doctor felt the power in her and so he tell her she must come to study with him. Marie, she rather dance and make love, but one day a rattle-snake come to her in her bedroom and spoke to her. So she went to Alexander and studied. But soon she could teach her teacher and the snake stayed with her always.

"She has her house on St. Anne Street and people come from the ends of America to get help from her. Even Queen Victoria ask her help and send her a cashmere shawl with money also.

"Now, some white people say she hold hoodoo dance on Congo Square every week. But Marie Leveau never hold no hoodoo dance. That was a pleasure dance. They beat the drum with the shin bone of a donkey and everybody dance like they do in Hayti. Hoodoo is private. She give the dance the first Friday night in each month and they have crab gumbo and rice to eat and the people dance. The white people come look on, and think they see all, when they only see a dance.

"The police hear so much about Marie Leveau that they come to her house in St. Anne Street to put her in jail. First one come, she stretch out her left hand and he turn round and round and never stop until some one come lead him away. Then two come together—she put them to running and barking like dogs. Four come and she put them to beating each other with night sticks. The whole station force come. They knock at her door. She know who they are before she ever look. She did work at her altar and they all went to sleep on her steps.

"Out on Lake Pontchartrain at Bayou St. John she hold a great feast every year on the Eve of St. John's, June 24th. It is Midsummer Eve, and the Sun give special benefits then and need great honor. The special drum be played then. It is a cowhide stretched over a half-barrel. Beat with a jaw-bone. Some say a man but I think they do not know. I think the jawbone of an ass or a cow. She hold the feast of St. John's partly because she is a Catholic and partly because of hoodoo.

"The ones around her altar fix everything for the feast. No-body see Marie Leveau for nine days before the feast. But when the great crowd of people at the feast call upon her, she would rise out of the waters of the lake with a great communion candle burning upon her head and another in each one of her hands. She walked upon the waters to the shore. As a little boy I saw her myself. When the feast was over, she went back into the lake, and nobody saw her for nine days again.

"On the feast that I saw her open the waters, she looked hard at me and nodded her head so that her tignon shook. Then I knew I was called to take up her work. She was very old and I was a lad of seventeen. Soon I went to wait upon her Altar, both on St. Anne Street and her house on Bayou St. John's.

"The rattlesnake that had come to her a little one when she was also young was very huge. He piled great upon his altar and took nothing from the food set before him. One night he sang and Marie Leveau called me from my sleep to look at him and see. 'Look well, Turner,' she told me. 'No one shall hear and see such as this for many centuries.'

"She went to her Great Altar and made great ceremony. The snake finished his song and seemed to sleep. She drove me back to my bed and went again to her Altar.

"The next morning, the great snake was not at his altar. His hide was before the Great Altar stuffed with spices and things of power. Never did I know what become of his flesh. It is said that the snake went off to the woods alone after the death of Marie Leveau, but they don't know. This is his skin that I wear about my shoulders whenever I reach for power.

"Three days Marie, she set at the Altar with the great sun candle burning and shining in her face. She set the water upon the Altar and turned to the window, and looked upon the lake. The sky grew dark. The lightning raced to the seventeen quarters of the heavens and the lake heaved like a mighty herd of cattle rolling in a pasture. The house shook with the earth.

"She told me, 'You are afraid. That is right, you should fear. Go to your own house and build an altar. Power will come.' So I hurried to my mother's house and told them.

"Some who loved her hurried out to Bayou St. John and tried to enter the house but she try hard to send them off. They beat upon the door, but she will not open. The terrible strong wind at last tore the house away and set it in the lake. The thunder and lightning grow greater. Then the loving ones find a boat and went out to where her house floats on one side and break a window to bring her out, but she begs, 'NO! Please, no,' she tell them. 'I want to die here in the lake,' but they would not permit her. She did not wish their destruction, so she let herself be drawn away from her altar in the lake. And the wind, the thunder and lightning, and the water all ceased the moment she set foot on dry land.

"That night she also sing a song and is dead, yes. So I have the snake skin and do works with the power she leave me."

"How did Marie Leveau do her work?" I asked feeling that I had gotten a little closer to him.

"She go to her great Altar and seek until she become the same as the spirit, then she come out into the room where she listens to them that come to ask. When they finish she answer them as a god. If a lady have a bad enemy and come to her she go into her altar room and when she come out and take her seat, the lady will say to her:

" 'Oh, Good Mother. I come to you with my heart bowed down and my shoulders drooping, and my spirits broken; for an enemy has sorely tried me; has caused my loved ones to leave me; has taken from me my worldly goods and my gold; has spoken meanly of me and caused my friends to lose faith in me. On my knees I pray to you, Good Mother, that you will cause confusion to reign in the house of my enemy and that you will take their power from them and cause them to be unsuccessful.'

"Marie Leveau is not a woman when she answer the one who ask. No. She is a god, yes. Whatever she say, it will come so. She say:

" 'Oh, my daughter, I have heard your woes and your pains and tribulations, and in the depth of the wisdom of the gods I will help you find peace and happiness.

" 'It is written that you will take of the Vinagredes Four Volle[1] for him, and you will dip into it a sheet of pure parchment paper, and on this sheet you will write the names of your enemies and send it to the house of your enemies, tightly sealed with the wax of the porcupine plant.

" 'Then when the sun shall have risen and gone down three times, you will take of the water of Mars, called War Water, and in front of the house of your enemy you will sprinkle it. This you will do as you pass by. If it be a woman, you will take the egg of a guinea fowl, and put it into the powder of the fruit of cayenne and the dust of Goofer,[2] and you will set it on the fire in your own house and in clear water from the skies you will boil it until it shall be hard. This you will do so that there shall be no fruit from her womb.

" 'And you shall take of the Damnation Powders, two drachmas, and of the water powders, two drachmas and make a package of it and send it to the home of the one who has spoken badly of you and has treated you mean, so that damnation and trouble shall be on the head of your enemy and not on you.

" 'You will do this so that you will undo your enemies and you will take the power to harm you away from your enemies.

" 'Oh daughter, go you in peace and do the works required of you, so that you will have rest and comfort from your enemies and that they will have not the power to harm you and lower you in the sight of your people and belittle you in the sight of your friends. So be it.' "

[1]Four Thieves Vinegar. For paraphernalia of conjure, see appendix.
[2]Dirt taken out of a grave.

By the time that Turner had finished his recitation he wasn't too conscious of me. In fact he gave me the feeling that he was just speaking, but not for my benefit. He was away off somewhere. He made a final dramatic gesture with open hands and hushed for a minute. Then he sank deeper into himself and went on:

"But when she put the last curse on a person, it would be better if that man was dead, yes."

With an impatient gesture he signalled me not to interrupt him.

"She set the altar for the curse with black candles that have been dressed in vinegar. She would write the name of the person to be cursed on the candle with a needle. Then she place fifteen cents in the lap of Death upon the altar to pay the spirit to obey her orders. Then she place her hands flat upon the table and say the curse-prayer.

" 'To The Man God: O great One, I have been sorely tried by my enemies and have been blasphemed and lied against. My good thoughts and my honest actions have been turned to bad actions and dishonest ideas. My home has been disrespected, my children have been cursed and ill-treated. My dear ones have been backbitten and their virtue questioned. O Man God, I beg that this that I ask for my enemies shall come to pass:

" 'That the South wind shall scorch their bodies and make them wither and shall not be tempered to them. That the North wind shall freeze their blood and numb their muscles and that it shall not be tempered to them. That the West wind shall blow away their life's breath and will not leave their hair grow, and that their finger nails shall fall off and their bones shall crumble. That the East wind shall make their minds grow dark, their sight shall fail and their seed dry up so that they shall not multiply.

" 'I ask that their fathers and mothers from their furtherest generation will not intercede for them before the great throne, and the wombs of their women shall not bear fruit except for strangers, and that they shall become extinct. I pray that the children who may come shall be weak of mind and paralyzed of limb and that they themselves shall curse them in their turn for ever turning the breath of life into their bodies.

I pray that disease and death shall be forever with them and that their worldly goods shall not prosper, and that their crops shall not multiply and that their cows, their sheep, and their hogs and all their living beasts shall die of starvation and thirst. I pray that their house shall be unroofed and that the rain, the thunder and lightning shall find the innermost recesses of their home and that the foundation shall crumble and the floods tear it asunder. I pray that the sun shall not shed its rays on them in benevolence, but instead it shall beat down on them and burn them and destroy them. I pray that the moon shall not give them peace, but instead shall deride them and decry them and cause their minds to shrivel. I pray that their friends shall betray them and cause them loss of power, of gold and of silver, and that their enemies shall smite them until they beg for mercy which shall not be given them. I pray that their tongues shall forget how to speak in sweet words, and that it shall be paralyzed and that all about them will be desolation, pestilence and death. O Man God, I ask you for all these things because they have dragged me in the dust and destroyed my good name; broken my heart and caused me to curse the day that I was born. So be it.' "

Turner again made that gesture with his hands that meant the end. Then he sat in a dazed silence. My own spirits had been falling all during the terrible curse and he did not have to tell me to be quiet this time. After a long period of waiting I rose to go. "The Spirit say you come back tomorrow," he breathed as I passed his knees. I nodded that I had heard and went out. The next day he began to prepare me for my initiation ceremony, for rest assured that no one may approach the Altar without the crown, and none may wear the crown of power without preparation. *It must be earned.*

And what is this crown of power? Nothing definite in material. Turner crowned me with a consecrated snake skin. I have been crowned in other places with flowers, with ornamental paper, with cloth, with sycamore bark, with egg-shells. It is the meaning, not the material that counts. The crown without the preparation means no more than a college diploma without the four years' work.

This preparation period is akin to that of all mystics. Clean living, even to clean thoughts. A sort of going to the wilderness in the spirit. The details do not matter. My nine days being up, and possessed of the three snake skins and the new underwear required, I entered Turner's house as an inmate to finish the last three days of my novitiate. Turner had become so sure of my fitness as a hoodoo doctor that he would accept no money from me except what was necessary to defray the actual cost of the ceremony.

So I ate my final meal before six o'clock of the evening before and went to bed for the last time with my right stocking on and my left leg bare.

I entered the old pink stucco house in the Vieux Carré at nine o'clock in the morning with the parcel of needed things. Turner placed the new underwear on the big Altar; prepared the couch with the snake-skin cover upon which I was to lie for three days. With the help of other members of the college of hoodoo doctors called together to initiate me, the snake skins I had brought were made into garments for me to wear. One was coiled into a high headpiece—the crown. One had loops attached to slip on my arms so that it could be worn as a shawl, and the other was made into a girdle for my loins. All places have significance. These garments were placed on the small altar in the corner. The throne of the snake. The Great One[3] was called upon to enter the garments and dwell there.

I was made ready and at three o'clock in the afternoon, naked as I came into the world, I was stretched, face downwards, my navel to the snake skin cover, and began my three day search for the spirit that he might accept me or reject me according to his will. Three days my body must lie silent and fasting while my spirit went wherever spirts must go that seek answers never given to men as men.

I could have no food, but a pitcher of water was placed on a small table at the head of the couch, that my spirit might not waste time in search of water which should be spent in search of the Power-Giver. The spirit must have water, and if none had been provided it would wander in search of it. And evil spirits might attack it as it wandered about dangerous

[3]The Spirit.

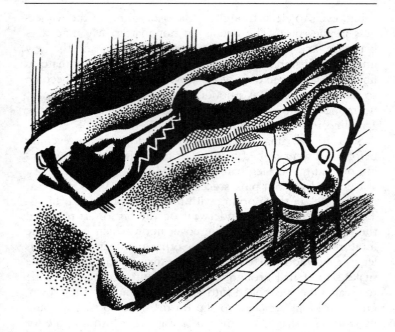

places. If it should be seriously injured, it might never return to me.

For sixty-nine hours I lay there. I had five psychic experiences and awoke at last with no feeling of hunger, only one of exaltation.

I opened my eyes because Turner called me. He stood before the Great Altar dressed ceremoniously. Five others were with him.

"Seeker, come," Turner called.

I made to rise and go to him. Another laid his hand upon me lightly, restraining me from rising.

"How must I come?" he asked in my behalf.

"You must come to the spirit across running water," Turner answered in a sort of chant.

So a tub was placed beside the bed. I was assisted to my feet and led to the tub. Two men poured water into the tub while I stepped into it and out again on the other side.

"She has crossed the dangerous stream in search of the spirit," the one who spoke for me, chanted.

"The spirit does not know her name. What is she called?"

"She has no name but what the spirit gives."

"I see her conquering and accomplishing with the lightning and making her road with thunder. She shall be called the Rain-Bringer."

I was stretched again upon the couch. Turner approached me with two brothers, one on either side of him. One held a small paint brush dipped in yellow, the other bore one dipped in red. With ceremony Turner painted the lightning symbol down my back from my right shoulder to my left hip. This was to be my sign forever. The Great One was to speak to me in storms.

I was now dressed in the new underwear and a white veil was placed over my head, covering my face, and I was seated in a chair.

After I was dressed, a pair of eyes was painted on my cheeks as a sign that I could see in more ways than one. The sun was painted on my forehead. Many came into the room and performed ceremonial acts, but none spoke to me. Nor could I speak to them while the veil covered my face. Turner cut the little finger of my right hand and caught the gushing blood in a wine cup. He added wine and mixed it with the blood. Then he and all the other five leaders let blood from themselves also and mixed it with wine in another glass. I was led to drink from the cup containing their mingled bloods, and each of them in turn beginning with Turner drank mine. At high noon I was seated at the splendid altar. It was dressed in the center with a huge communion candle with my name upon it set in sand, five large iced cakes in different colors, a plate of honeyed St. Joseph's bread, a plate of serpent-shaped breads, spinach and egg cakes fried in olive oil, breaded Chinese okra fried in olive oil, roast veal and wine, two huge yellow bouquets, two red bouquets and two white bouquets and thirty-six yellow tapers and a bottle of holy water.

Turner seated me and stood behind me with his ceremonial hat upon his head, and the crown of power in his hand. "Spirit! I ask you to take her. Do you hear me, Spirit? Will

you take her? Spirit, I want you to take her, she is worthy!"
He held the crown poised above my head for a full minute. A
profound silence held the room. Then he lifted the veil from
my face and let it fall behind my head and crowned me with
power. He lit my candle for me. But from then on I might be
a candle-lighter myself. All the candles were reverently lit. We
all sat down and ate the feast. First a glass of blessed oil was
handed me by Turner. "Drink this without tasting it." I
gulped it down and he took the glass from my hand, took a
sip of the little that remained. Then he handed it to the
brother at his right who did the same, until it went around
the table.

"Eat first the spinach cakes," Turner exhorted, and we did.
Then the meal began. It was full of joy and laughter, even
though we knew that the final ceremony waited only for the
good hour of twelve midnight.

About ten o'clock we all piled into an old Studebaker sedan—all but Turner who led us on a truck. Out Road No. 61
we rattled until a certain spot was reached. The truck was
unloaded beside the road and sent back to town. It was a
little after eleven. The swamp was dismal and damp, but after
some stumbly walking we came to a little glade deep in the
wood, near the lake. A candle was burning at each of the four
corners of the clearing, representing the four corners of the
world and the four winds. I could hear the occasional slap-
slap of the water. With a whispered chant some twigs were
gathered and tied into a broom. Some pine straw was collected. The sheets of typing paper I had been urged to bring
were brought out and nine sheets were blessed and my petition written nine times on each sheet by the light from a
shaded lantern. The crate containing the black sheep was
opened and the sheep led forward into the center of the
circle. He stood there dazedly while the chant of strange syllables rose. I asked Turner the words, but he replied that in
good time I would know what to say. It was not to be taught.
If nothing came, to be silent. The head and withers of the
sheep were stroked as the chanting went on. Turner became
more and more voluble. At last he seized the straw and
stuffed some into the sheep's nostrils. The animal struggled.
A knife flashed and the sheep dropped to its knees, then fell

prone with its mouth open in a weak cry. My petition was thrust into its throat that he might cry it to the Great One. The broom was seized and dipped in the blood from the slit throat and the ground swept vigorously—back and forth, back and forth—the length of the dying sheep. It was swept from the four winds toward the center. The sweeping went on as long as the blood gushed. Earth, the mother of the Great One and us all, has been appeased. With a sharp stick Turner traced the outline of the sheep and the digging commenced. The sheep was never touched. The ground was dug from under him so that his body dropped down into the hole. He was covered with nine sheets of paper bearing the petition and the earth heaped upon him. A white candle was set upon the grave and we straggled back to the road and the Studebaker.

I studied under Turner five months and learned all of the Leveau routines; but in this book all of the works of any doctor cannot be given. However, we performed several of Turner's own routines.

Once a woman, an excited, angry woman wanted something done to keep her husband true. So she came and paid Turner gladly for his services.

Turner took a piece of string that had been "treated" at the altar and gave it to the woman.

"Measure the man where I tell you. But he must never know. Measure him in his sleep then fetch back the string to me."

The next day the woman came at ten o'clock instead of nine as Turner had told her, so he made her wait until twelve o'clock, that being a good hour. Twelve is one of the benign hours of the day while ten is a malignant hour. Then Turner took the string and tied nine knots in it and tied it to a larger piece of string which he tied about her waist. She was completely undressed for the ceremony and Turner cut some hair from under her left armpit and some from the right side of the groin and put it together. Then he cut some from the right arm-pit and a tuft from the left groin and it was all placed on the altar, and burned in a votive light with the wish for her husband to love her and forget all others. She went away quite happy. She was so satisfied with the work that she returned with a friend a few days later.

Turner, with this toothless mouth, his Berber-looking face, said to the new caller:

"I can see you got trouble." He shivered. "It is all in the room. I feel the pain of it; Anger, Malice. Tell me who is this man you so fight with?"

"My husband's brother. He hate me and make all the trouble he can," the woman said in a tone so even and dull that it was hard to believe she meant what she said. "He must leave this town or die. Yes, it is much better if he is dead." Then she burst out, "Yeah, he should be dead long time ago. Long before he spy upon me, before he tell lies, lies, lies. I should be very happy for his funeral."

"Oh I can feel the great hate around you," Turner said. "It follow you everywhere, but I kill nobody, I send him away if you want so he never come back. I put guards along the road in the spirit world, and these he cannot pass, no. When he go, never will he come back to New Orleans. You see him no more. He will be forgotten and all his works."

"Then I am satisfied, yes," the woman said. "When will you send him off?"

"I ask the spirit, you will know."

She paid him and he sent her off and Turner went to his snake altar and sat in silence for a long time. When he arose, he sent me out to buy nine black chickens, and some Four Thieves Vinegar.[+] He himself went out and got nine small sticks upon which he had me write the troublesome brother-in-law's name—one time on each stick. At ten that night we went out into the small interior court so prevalent in New Orleans and drove nine stakes into the ground. The left leg of a chicken was tied to each stake. Then a fire was built with the nine sticks on which the name had been written. The ground was sprinkled all over with the Four Thieves Vinegar and Turner began his dance. From the fire to the circle of flutter-ing chickens and back again to the fire. The feathers were picked from the heads of the chickens in the frenzy of the dance and scattered to the four winds. He called the victim's

---

[+]A conjure mixture. See appendix.

name each time as he whirled three times with the chicken's head-feathers in his hand, then he flung them far.

The terrified chickens flopped and fluttered frantically in the dim firelight. I had been told to keep up the chant of the victim's name in rhythm and to beat the ground with a stick. This I did with fervor and Turner danced on. One by one the chickens were seized and killed by having their heads pulled off. But Turner was in such a condition with his whirling and dancing that he seemed in a hypnotic state. When the last fowl was dead, Turner drank a great draught of wine and sank before the altar. When he arose, we gathered some ashes from the fire and sprinkled the bodies of the dead chickens and I was told to get out the car. We drove out one of the main highways for a mile and threw one of the chickens away. Then another mile and another chicken until the nine dead chickens had been disposed of. The spirits of the dead chickens had been instructed never to let the trouble-maker pass inward to New Orleans again after he had passed them going out.

One day Turner told me that he had taught me all that he could and he was quite satisfied with me. He wanted me to stay and work with him as a partner. He said that soon I would be in possession of the entire business, for the spirit had spoken to him and told him that I was the last doctor that he would make; that one year and seventy-nine days from then he would die. He wanted me to stay with him to the end. It has been a great sorrow to me that I could not say yes.

III

ANATOL PIERRE, of New Orleans, was a middle-aged octoroon. He is a Catholic and lays some feeble claim to
kinship with Marie Leveau.

He had the most elaborate temple of any of the practitioners. His altar room was off by itself and absolutely sac-
rosanct.

He made little difficulty about taking me after I showed
him that I had worked with others.

Pierre was very emotional and sometimes he would be
sharp with his clients, indifferent as to whether they hired him
or not. But he quickly adjusted himself to my being around
him and at the end of the first week began to prepare me for
the crown.

The ceremony was as follows:

On Saturday I was told to have the materials for my initiation bath ready for the following Tuesday at eleven o'clock. I
must have a bottle of lavender toilet water, Jap honeysuckle
perfume, and orange blossom water. I must get a full bunch
of parsley and brew a pint of strong parsley water. I must have
at hand sugar, salt and Vacher Balm. Two long pink candles
must be provided, one to be burned at the initiation, one to
be lit on the altar for me in Pierre's secret room.

He came to my house in Belville Court at a quarter to
eleven to see if all was right. The tub was half-filled with
warm water and Pierre put in all of the ingredients, along
with a handful of salt and three tablespoons of sugar.

The candles had been dressed on Saturday and one was
already burning on the secret altar for me. The other long
pink candle was rolled around the tub three times, "In no-
mina patria, et filia, et spiritu sanctus, Amen." Then it was
marked for a four day burning and lit. The spirit was called
three times. "Kind spirit, whose name is Moccasin, answer
me." This I was told to repeat three times, snapping my
fingers.

Then I, already prepared, stepped into the tub and was
bathed by the teacher. Particular attention was paid to my

head and back and chest since there the "controls" lie. While in the tub, my left little finger was cut a little and his finger was cut and the blood bond made. "Now you are of my flesh and of the spirit, and neither one of us will ever deny you."

He dried me and I put on new underwear bought for the occasion and dressed with oil of geranium, and was told to stretch upon the couch and read the third chapter of Job night and morning for nine days. I was given a little Bible that had been "visited" by the spirit and told the names of the spirits to call for any kind of work I might want to perform. I am to call on Great Moccasin for all kinds of power and also to have him stir up the particular spirit I may need for a specific task. I must call on Kangaroo to stop worrying; call on Jenipee spirit for marriages; call on Death spirit for killing, and the seventeen "quarters"[1] of spirit to aid me if one spirit seems insufficient.

I was told to burn the marked candle every day for two hours—from eleven till one, in the northeast corner of the room. While it is burning I must go into the silence and talk to the spirit through the candle.

On the fifth day Pierre called again and I resumed my studies, but now as an advanced pupil. In the four months that followed these are some of the things I learned from him:

A man called Muttsy Ivins came running to Pierre soon after my initiation was over. Pierre looked him over with some instinctive antipathy. So he wouldn't help him out by asking questions. He just let Mr. Muttsy tell him the best way he could. So he began by saying, "A lot of hurting things have been done to me, Pierre, and now it's done got to de place Ah'm skeered for mah life."

"That's a lie, yes," Pierre snapped.

"Naw it 'tain't!" Muttsy insisted. "Ah done found things 'round mah door step and in mah yard and Ah know who's doin' it too."

"Yes, you find things in your yard because you continue to sleep with the wife of another man and you are afraid because he has said that he will kill you if you don't leave her alone.

[1]See appendix.

You are crazy to think that you can lie to me. Tell me the truth and then tell me what you want me to do."

"Ah want him out de way—kilt, cause he swear he's gointer kill me. And since one of us got to die, Ah'd ruther it to be him than me."

"I knew you wanted a death the minute you got in here. I don't like to work for death."

"Please, Pierre, Ah'm skeered to walk de streets after dark, and me and de woman done gone too far to turn back. And he got de consumption nohow. But Ah don't wanter die before he do. Ah'm a well man."

"That's enough about that. How much money have you got?"

"Two hundred dollars."

"Two fifty is my terms, and I ain't a bit anxious for the job at that."

Pierre turned to me and began to give me a list of things to get for my own use and seemed to forget the man behind him.

"Maybe Ah kin git dat other fifty dollars and maybe not. These ain't no easy times. Money is tight."

"Well, goodbye, we're busy folks here. You don't have to do this thing anyway. You can leave town."

"And leave mah good trucking business? Dat'll never happen. Ah kin git yo' money. When yo' goin' ter do de work?"

"You pay the money and go home. It is not for you to know how and when the work is done. Go home with faith."

The next morning soon, Pierre sent me out to get a beef brain, a beef tongue, a beef heart and a live black chicken. When I returned he had prepared a jar of bad vinegar. He wrote Muttsy's enemy's name nine times on a slip of paper. He split open the heart, placed the paper in it, pinned up the opening with eighteen steel needles, and dropped it into the jar of vinegar, point downward.

The main altar was draped in black and the crudely carved figure of Death was placed upon it to shield us from the power of death.

Black candles were lit on the altar. A black crown was made and placed on the head of Death. The name of the man to die was written on paper nine times and placed on the altar one degree below Death, and the jar containing the heart was set on this paper. The candles burned for twelve hours.

Then Pierre made a coffin six inches long. I was sent out to buy a small doll. It was dressed in black to represent the man and placed in the coffin with his name under the doll. The coffin was left open upon the altar. Then we went far out to a lonely spot and dug a grave which was much longer and wider than the coffin. A black cat was placed in the grave and the whole covered with a cloth that we fastened down so that the cat could not get out. The black chicken was then taken from its confinement and fed a half glass of whiskey in which a paper had been soaked that bore the name of the man who was to die. The chicken was put in with the cat, and left there for a full month.

The night after the entombment of the cat and the chicken, we began to burn the black candles. Nine candles were set to burn in a barrel and every night at twelve o'clock we would go to the barrel and call upon the spirit of Death to follow the man. The candles were dressed by biting off the bottoms, as Pierre called for vengeance. Then the bottom was lighted instead of the top.

At the end of the month, the coffin containing the doll was carried out to the grave of the cat and chicken and buried upon their remains. A white bouquet was placed at the head and foot of the grave.

The beef brain was placed on a plate with nine hot peppers around it to cause insanity and brain hemorrhages, and placed on the altar. The tongue was slit, the name of the victim inserted, the slit was closed with a pack of pins and buried in the tomb.

"The black candles must burn for ninety days," Pierre told me. "He cannot live. No one can stand that."

Every night for ninety days Pierre slept in his holy place in a black draped coffin. And the man died.

Another conjure doctor solicited trade among Pierre's clients and his boasts of power, and his belittling comments of Pierre's power vexed him. So he said to me one day: "That fellow boasts too much, yes. Maybe if I send him a swelling he won't be out on the banquette bragging so much."

So Pierre took me with him to steal a new brick. We took the brick home and dressed nine black candles by writing the offensive doctor's name on each. His name was written nine times on a piece of paper and placed face down on the brick. It was tied there securely with twine. We put the black candles to burn, one each day for nine days, and then Pierre dug a well to the water table and slipped the brick slowly to the bottom. "Just like the brick soaks up the water, so that man will swell."

IV

I HEARD of Father Watson the "Frizzly Rooster" from afar, from people for whom he had "worked" and their friends, and from people who attended his meetings held twice a week in Myrtle Wreath Hall in New Orleans. His name is "Father" Watson, which in itself attests his Catholic leanings, though he is formally a Protestant.

On a given night I had a front seat in his hall. There were the usual camp-followers sitting upon the platform and bustling around performing chores. Two or three songs and a prayer were the preliminaries.

At last Father Watson appeared in a satin garment of royal purple, belted by a gold cord. He had the figure for wearing that sort of thing and he probably knew it. Between prayers and songs he talked, setting forth his powers. He could curse anybody he wished—and make the curse stick. He could remove curses, no matter who had laid them on whom. Hence his title The Frizzly Rooster. Many persons keep a frizzled chicken in the yard to locate and scratch up any hoodoo that may be buried for them. These chickens have, no doubt, earned this reputation by their ugly appearance—with all of their feathers set in backwards. He could "read" anybody at sight. He could "read" anyone who remained out of his sight if they but stuck two fingers inside the door. He could "read" anyone, no matter how far away, if he were given their height and color. He begged to be challenged.

He predicted the hour and the minute, nineteen years hence, when he should die—without even having been ill a moment in his whole life. God had told him.

He sold some small packets of love powders before whose powers all opposition must break down. He announced some new keys that were guaranteed to unlock every door and remove every obstacle in the way of success that the world knew. These keys had been sent to him by God through a small Jew boy. The old keys had been sent through a Jew man. They were powerful as long as they did not touch the floor—but if you ever dropped them, they lost their power.

These new keys at five dollars each were not affected by being dropped, and were otherwise much more powerful.

I lingered after the meeting and made an appointment with him for the next day at his home.

Before my first interview with the Frizzly Rooster was fairly begun, I could understand his great following. He had the physique of Paul Robeson with the sex appeal and hypnotic what-ever-you-might-call-it of Rasputin. I could see that women would rise to flee from him but in mid-flight would whirl and end shivering at his feet. It was that way in fact.

His wife Mary knew how slight her hold was and continually planned to leave him.

"Only thing that's holding me here is this." She pointed to a large piece of brain-coral that was forever in a holy spot on the altar. "That's where his power is. If I could get me a piece, I could go start up a business all by myself. If I could only find a piece."

"It's very plentiful down in South Florida," I told her. "But if that piece is so precious, and you're his wife, I'd take it and let *him* get another piece."

"Oh my God! Naw! That would be my end. He's too powerful. I'm leaving him," she whispered this stealthily. "You get me a piece of that—you know."

The Frizzly Rooster entered and Mary was a different person at once. But every time that she was alone with me it was "That on the altar, you know. When you back in Florida, get me a piece. I'm leaving this man to his women." Then a quick hush and forced laughter at her husband's approach.

So I became the pupil of Reverend Father Joe Watson, "The Frizzly Rooster" and his wife, Mary, who assisted him in all things. She was "round the altar"; that is while he talked with the clients, and usually decided on whatever "work" was to be done, she "set" the things on the altar and in the jars. There was one jar in the kitchen filled with honey and sugar. All the "sweet" works were set in this jar. That is, the names and the thing desired were written on paper and thrust into this jar to stay. Already four or five hundred slips of paper had accumulated in the jar. There was another jar called the "break up" jar. It held vinegar with some unsweetened coffee added. Papers were left in this one also.

When finally it was agreed that I should come to study with them, I was put to running errands such as "dusting" houses, throwing pecans, rolling apples, as the case might be; but I was not told why the thing was being done. After two weeks of this I was taken off this phase and initiated. This was the first step towards the door of the mysteries.

My initiation consisted of the Pea Vine Candle Drill. I was told to remain five days without sexual intercourse. I must remain indoors all day the day before the initiation and fast. I might wet my throat when necessary, but I was not to swallow water.

When I arrived at the house the next morning a little before nine, as per instructions, six other persons were there, so that there were nine of us—all in white except Father Watson who was in his purple robe. There was no talking. We went at once to the altar room. The altar was blazing. There were three candles around the vessel of holy water, three around the sacred sand pail, and one large cream candle burning in it. A picture of St. George and a large piece of brain coral were in the center. Father Watson dressed eight long blue candles and one black one, while the rest of us sat in the chairs around the wall. Then he lit the eight blue candles one by one from the altar and set them in the pattern of a moving serpent. Then I was called to the altar and both Father Watson and his wife laid hands on me. The black candle was placed in my hand; I was told to light it from all the other candles. I lit it at number one and pinched out the flame, and re-lit it at number two and so on till it had been lit by the eighth candle. Then I held the candle in my left hand, and by my right was conducted back to the altar by Father Watson. I was led through the maze of candles beginning at number eight. We circled numbers seven, five and three. When we reached the altar he lifted me upon the step. As I stood there, he called aloud, "Spirit! She's standing here without no home and no friends. She wants you to take her in." Then we began at number one and threaded back to number eight, circling three, five and seven. Then back to the altar again. Again he lifted me and placed me upon the step of the altar. Again the

spirit was addressed as before. Then he lifted me down by
placing his hands in my arm-pits. This time I did not walk at
all. I was carried through the maze and I was to knock down
each candle as I passed it with my foot. If I missed one, I was
not to try again, but to knock it down on my way back to the
altar. Arrived there the third time, I was lifted up and told to
pinch out my black candle. "Now," Father told me, "you are
made Boss of Candles. You have the power to light candles
and put out candles, and to work with the spirits anywhere on
earth."

Then all of the candles on the floor were collected and one
of them handed to each of the persons present. Father took
the black candle himself and we formed a ring. Everybody was
given two matches each. The candles were held in our left
hands, matches in the right; at a signal everybody stooped at
the same moment, the matches scratched in perfect time and
our candles lighted in concert. Then Father Watson walked
rhythmically around the person at his right. Exchanged
candles with her and went back to his place. Then that person
did the same to the next so that the black candle went all
around the circle and back to Father. I was then seated on a
stool before the altar, sprinkled lightly with holy sand and
water and confirmed as a Boss of Candles.

Then conversation broke out. We went into the next room
and had a breakfast that was mostly fruit and smothered
chicken. Afterwards the nine candles used in the ceremony

were wrapped up and given to me to keep. They were to be used for lighting other candles only, not to be just burned in the ordinary sense.

In a few days I was allowed to hold consultations on my own. I felt insecure and said so to Father Watson.

"Of course you do now," he answered me, "but you have to learn and grow. I'm right here behind you. Talk to your people first, then come see me."

Within the hour a woman came to me. A man had shot and seriously wounded her husband and was in jail.

"But, honey," she all but wept, "they say ain't a thing going to be done with him. They say he got good white folks back of him and he's going to be let loose soon as the case is tried. I want him punished. Picking a fuss with my husband just to get chance to shoot him. We needs help. Somebody that can hit a straight lick with a crooked stick."

So I went in to the Frizzly Rooster to find out what I must do and he told me, "That a low fence." He meant a difficulty that was easily overcome.

"Go back and get five dollars from her and tell her to go home and rest easy. That man will be punished. When we get through with him, white folks or no white folks, he'll find a tough jury sitting on his case." The woman paid me and left in perfect confidence of Father Watson.

So he and I went into the workroom.

"Now," he said, "when you want a person punished who is already indicted, write his name on a slip of paper and put it in a sugar bowl or some other deep something like that. Now get your paper and pencil and write the name; alright now, you got it in the bowl. Now put in some red pepper, some black pepper—don't be skeered to put it in, it needs a lot. Put in one eightpenny nail, fifteen cents worth of ammonia and two door keys. You drop one key down in the bowl and you leave the other one against the side of the bowl. Now you got your bowl set. Go to your bowl every day at twelve o'clock and turn the key that is standing against the side of the bowl. That is to keep the man locked in jail. And every time you turn the key, add a little vinegar. Now I know this will do the job. All it needs is for you to do it in faith. I'm trusting this job to you entirely. Less see what you going to do. That can wait another minute. Come sit with me in the outside room and hear this woman out here that's waiting."

So we went outside and found a weakish woman in her early thirties that looked like somebody had dropped a sack of something soft on a chair.

The Frizzly Rooster put on his manner, looking like a brown, purple and gold throne-angel in a house.

"Good morning, sister er, er——"

"Murchison," she helped out.

"Tell us how you want to be helped, Sister Murchison."

She looked at me as if I was in the way and he read her eyes.

"She's alright, dear one. She's one of us. I brought her in with me to assist and help."

I thought still I was in her way but she told her business just the same.

"Too many women in my house. My husband's mother is there and she hates me and always puttin' my husband up to fight me. Look like I can't get her out of my house no ways I try. So I done come to you."

"We can fix that up in no time, dear one. Now go take a flat onion. If it was a man, I'd say a sharp pointed onion. Core the onion out, and write her name five times on paper and stuff it into the hole in the onion and close it back with the cut-out piece of onion. Now you watch when she leaves the house and then you roll the onion behind her before anybody else crosses the door-sill. And you make a wish at the same time for her to leave your house. She won't be there two weeks more." The woman paid and left.

That night we held a ceremony in the altar room on the case. We took a red candle and burnt it just enough to consume the tip. Then it was cut into three parts and the short lengths of candle were put into a glass of holy water. Then we took the glass and went at midnight to the door of the woman's house and the Frizzly Rooster held the glass in his hands and said, "In the name of the Father, in the name of the Son, in the name of the Holy Ghost." He shook the glass three times violently up and down, and the last time he threw the glass to the ground and broke it, and said, "Dismiss this woman from this place." We scarcely paused as this was said and done and we kept going and went home by another way because that was part of the ceremony.

Somebody came against a very popular preacher. "He's getting too rich and big. I want something done to keep him down. They tell me he's 'bout to get to be a bishop. I sho' would hate for that to happen. I got forty dollars in my pocket right now for the work."

So that night the altar blazed with the blue light. We wrote the preacher's name on a slip of paper with black ink. We took a small doll and ripped open its back and put in the paper with the name along with some bitter aloes and cayenne pepper and sewed the rip up again with the black thread. The hands of the doll were tied behind it and a black veil tied over the face and knotted behind it so that the man it represented would be blind and always do the things to keep himself from progressing. The doll was then placed in a kneeling position in a dark corner where it would not be disturbed. He would be frustrated as long as the doll was not disturbed.

When several of my jobs had turned out satisfactorily to Father Watson, he said to me, "You will do well, but you need the Black Cat Bone. Sometimes you have to be able to walk invisible. Some things must be done in deep secret, so you have to walk out of the sight of man."

First I had to get ready even to try this most terrible of experiences—getting the Black Cat Bone.

First we had to wait on the weather. When a big rain started, a new receptacle was set out in the yard. It could not be put out until the rain actually started for fear the sun might shine in it. The water must be brought inside before the weather faired off for the same reason. If lightning shone on it, it was ruined.

We finally got the water for the bath and I had to fast and "seek," shut in a room that had been purged by smoke. Twenty-four hours without food except a special wine that was fed to me every four hours. It did not make me drunk in the accepted sense of the word. I merely seemed to lose my body, my mind seemed very clear.

When dark came, we went out to catch a black cat. I must catch him with my own hands. Finding and catching black cats is hard work, unless one has been released for you to find. Then we repaired to a prepared place in the woods and a circle drawn and "protected" with nine horseshoes. Then the fire and the pot were made ready. A roomy iron pot with a lid. When the water boiled I was to toss in the terrified, trembling cat.

When he screamed, I was told to curse him. He screamed three times, the last time weak and resigned. The lid was clamped down, the fire kept vigorously alive. At midnight the lid was lifted. Here was the moment! The bones of the cat must be passed through my mouth until one tasted bitter.

Suddenly, the Rooster and Mary rushed in close to the pot and he cried, "Look out! This is liable to kill you. Hold your nerve!" They both looked fearfully around the circle. They communicated some unearthly terror to me. Maybe I went off in a trance. Great beast-like creatures thundered up to the circle from all sides. Indescribable noises, sights, feelings. Death was at hand! Seemed unavoidable! I don't know. Many times I have thought and felt, but I always have to say the same thing. I don't know. I don't know.

Before day I was home, with a small white bone for me to carry.

V

D R. DUKE is a member of a disappearing school of folk
    magic. He spends days and nights out in the woods and
swamps and is therefore known as a "swamper." A swamper is
a root-and-conjure doctor who goes to the swamps and gath-
ers his or her own herbs and roots. Most of the doctors buy
their materials from regular supply houses.

He took me to the woods with him many times in order
that I might learn the herbs by sight and scent. Not only
is it important to be able to identify the plant, but the
swamper must know when and how to gather it. For instance, the most widely used root known as John de Conqueror must be gathered before September 21st. Wonder of
the World Root must be spoken to with ceremony before it is
disturbed, or forces will be released that will harm whoever
handles it. Snakes guard other herbs and roots and must not
be killed.

He is a man past fifty but very active. He believes his power
is unlimited and that nothing can stand against his medicine.

His specialty is law cases. People come to him from a great
distance, and I know that he received a fee of one hundred
and eighty five dollars from James Beasley, who was in the
Parish prison accused of assault with attempt to murder.

For that particular case we went first to the cemetery. With
his right hand he took dirt from the graves of nine children. I
was not permitted to do any of this because I was only a
beginner with him and had not the power to approach spirits
directly. They might kill me for my audacity.

The dirt was put in a new white bowl and carried back to
the altar room and placed among the burning candles, facing
the east. Then I was sent for sugar and sulphur. Three teaspoons each of sugar and sulphur were added to the graveyard
dirt. Then he prayed over it, while I knelt opposite him. The
spirits were asked to come with power more than equal to a
man. Afterwards, I was sent out to buy a cheap suit of men's
underclothes. This we turned wrong side out and dressed
with the prepared graveyard dust. I had been told to buy a

new pair of tan socks also, and these were dressed in the same way.

As soon as Dr. Duke had been retained, I had been sent to the prison with a "dressed" Bible and Beasley was instructed to read the Thirty-fifth Psalm every day until his case should be called.

On the day he came up for trial, Dr. Duke took the new underclothes to the jail and put them on his client just before he started to march to the court room. The left sock was put on wrongside out.

Dr. Duke, like all of the conjure masters, has more than one way of doing every job. People are different and what will win with one person has no effect upon another. We had occasion to use all of the other ways of winning law suits in the course of practice.

In one hard case the prisoner had his shoes "dressed with the court." That was to keep the court under his control.

We wrote the judge's name three times, the prisoner's name three times, the district attorney's name three times, and folded the paper small, and the prisoner was told to wear it in his shoe.

Then we got some oil of rose geranium, lavender oil, verbena oil. Put three drops of oil of geranium in one-half ounce Jockey Club. Shook it and gave it to the client. He must use seven to nine drops on his person in court, but we had to dress his clothes, also. We went before court set to dress the court room and jury box and judge's stand, and have our client take perfume and rub it on his hand and rub from his face down his whole front.

To silence opposing witnesses, we took a beef tongue, nine pins, nine needles, and split the beef tongue. We wrote the names of those against our man and cut the names out and crossed them up in slit of tongue with red pepper and beef gall, and pinned the slit up with crossed needles and pins. We hung the tongue up in a chimney, tip up, and smoked the tongue for thirty-six hours. Then we took it down and put it in ice and lit on it from three to four black candles stuck in ice. Our client read the Twenty-second Psalm and Thirty-fifth also, because it was for murder. Then we asked the spirits for power more than equal to man.

So many people came to Dr. Duke to be uncrossed that he took great pains to teach me that routine. He never let me perform it, but allowed me to watch him do it many times.

Take seven lumps of incense. Take three matches to light the incense. Wave the incense before the candles on the altar. Make client bow over the incense three times. Then circle him with a glass of water three times, and repeat this three times. Fan him with the incense smoke three times—each time he bows his head. Then sprinkle him seven times with water, then lead him to and from the door and turn him around three times over incense that has been placed at the door. Then seat the client and sprinkle every corner of the room with water, three times, and also three times down the middle of the room, then go to another room and do the same. Smoke his underclothes and dress them. Don't turn the client's hand loose as he steps over the incense. Smoke him once at the door and three times at each corner. The room must be thoroughly smoked—even under the furniture—before the client leaves the room. After the evil has been driven out of him, it must also be driven from the room so it cannot return to him.

So much has been said and written about hoodoo doctors driving people away from a place that we cannot omit mentioning it. This was also one of Dr. Duke's specialties.

A woman was tired of a no-good husband; she told us about it.

"He won't work and make support for me, and he won't git on out the way and leave somebody else do it. He spend up all my money playing coon-can and kotch and then expect me to buy him a suit of clothes, and then he all the time fighting me about my wages."

"You sure you don't want him no more?" Dr. Duke asked her. "You know women get mad and say things they takes back over night."

"Lawd knows I means this. I don't want to meet him riding nor walking."

So Dr. Duke told her what to do. She must take the right foot track of her hateful husband and parch it in an old tin frying pan. When she picks it up she must have a dark bottle

with her to put the track in. Then she must get a dirt dauber
nest, some cayenne pepper and parch that together and add it
to the track. Put all of this into a dirty sock and tie it up. She
must turn the bundle from her always as she ties it. She must
carry it to the river at twelve noon. When she gets within
forty feet of the river, she must run fast to the edge of the
water, whirl suddenly and hurl the sock over her left shoulder
into the water and never look back, and say, "Go, and go
quick in the name of the Lord."

So she went off and I never saw her again.

Dr. Samuel Jenkins lives across the river in Marrero, Louisiana. He does some work, but his great specialty is reading
the cards. I have seen him glance at people without being
asked or without using his cards and making the most startling statements that all turned out to be true.

A young matron went out with me to Dr. Jenkins's one day
just for the sake of the ride. He glanced at her and told her
that she was deceiving her husband with a very worthless fellow. That she must stop at once or she would be found out.
Her husband was most devoted, but once he mistrusted her
he would accept no explanations. This was late in October,
and her downfall came in December.

Dr. Charles S. Johnson, the well-known negro sociologist
came to New Orleans on business while I was there and since
I had to see Dr. Jenkins, he went with me. Without being
asked, Dr. Jenkins told him that he would receive a sudden
notice to go on a long trip. The next day, Dr. Johnson received a wire sending him to West Africa.

Once Dr. Jenkins put a light on a wish of mine that a certain influential white woman would help me, and assured me
that she would never lose interest in me as long as she lived.
The next morning at ten o'clock I received a wire from her
stating that she would stand by me as long as she lived. He
did this sort of thing day after day, and the faith in him is
huge. Let me state here that most of his clients are white and
upper-class people at that.

In appearance he is a handsome robust dark-skinned man
around forty.

*   *   *

There are many superstitions concerning the dead.

All over the South and in the Bahamas the spirits of the dead have great power which is used chiefly to harm. It will be noted how frequently graveyard dust is required in the practice of hoodoo, goofer dust as it is often called.

It is to be noted that in nearly all of the killing ceremonies the cemetery is used.

The Ewe-speaking peoples[1] of the west coast of Africa all make offerings of food and drink—particularly libations of palm wine and banana beer upon the graves of the ancestor. It is to be noted in America that the spirit is always given a pint of good whiskey. He is frequently also paid for his labor in cash.

It is well known that church members are buried with their feet to the east so that they will arise on that last day facing the rising sun. Sinners are buried facing the opposite direction. The theory is that sunlight will do them harm rather than good, as they will no doubt wish to hide their faces from an angry God.

Ghosts cannot cross water—so that if a hoodoo doctor wishes to sic a dead spirit upon a man who lives across water, he must first hold the mirror ceremony to fetch the victim from across the water.

People who die from the sick bed may walk any night, but Friday night is the night of the people who died in the dark— who were executed. These people have never been in the light. They died with the black cap over the face. Thus, they are blind. On Friday nights they visit the folks who died from sick beds and they lead the blind ones wherever they wish to visit.

Ghosts feel hot and smell faintish. According to testimony all except those who died in the dark may visit their former homes every night at twelve o'clock. But they must be back in the cemetery at two o'clock sharp or they will be shut out by the watchman and must wander about for the rest of the night. That is why the living are frightened by seeing ghosts at times. Some spirit has lingered too long with the living person it still loves and has been shut out from home.

Pop Drummond of Fernandina, Fla., says they are not

[1] A West African nation from which many slaves came to America.

asleep at all. They "Sings and has church and has a happy time, but some are spiteful and show themselves to scare folks." Their voices are high and thin. Some ghosts grow very fat if they get plenty to eat. They are very fond of honey. Some who have been to the holy place wear seven-starred crowns and are very "suscautious" and sensible.

Dirt from sinners' graves is supposed to be very powerful, but some hoodoo doctors will use only that from the graves of infants. They say that the sinner's grave is powerful to kill, but his spirit is likely to get unruly and kill others for the pleasure of killing. It is too dangerous to commission.

The spirit newly released from the body is likely to be destructive. This is why a cloth is thrown over the face of a clock in the death chamber and the looking glass is covered over. The clock will never run again, nor will the mirror ever cast any more reflections if they are not covered so that the spirit cannot see them.

When it rains at a funeral it is said that God wishes to wash their tracks off the face of the earth, they were so displeasing to him.

If a murder victim is buried in a sitting position, the murderer will be speedily brought to justice. The victim sitting before the throne is able to demand that justice be done. If he is lying prone he cannot do this.

A fresh egg in the hand of a murder victim will prevent the murderer's going far from the scene. The egg represents life, and so the dead victim is holding the life of the murderer in his hand.

Sometimes the dead are offended by acts of the living and slap the face of the living. When this happens, the head is slapped one-sided and the victim can never straighten his neck. Speak gently to ghosts, and do not abuse the children of the dead.

It is not good to answer the first time that your name is called. It may be a spirit and if you answer it, you will die shortly. They never call more than once at a time, so by waiting you will miss probable death.[2]

[2]See Appendix for superstitions concerning sudden death.

VI

Before telling of my experiences with Kitty Brown I want to relate the following conjure stories which illustrate the attitude of negroes of the Deep South toward this subject.

Old Lady Celestine went next door one day and asked her neighbor to lend her a quarter.

"I want it all in nickels, please, yes."

"Ah don't have five nickels, Tante Celestine, but Ah'll send a boy to get them for you," the obliging neighbor told her. So she did and Celestine took the money with a cold smile and went home.

Soon after another neighbor came in and the talk came around to Celestine.

"Celestine is not mad any more about the word we had last week. She was just in to pay me a visit."

"Humph!" snorted the neighbor, "maybe she come in to dust yo' door step. You shouldn't let people in that hate you. They come to do you harm."

"Oh no, she was very nice. She borrowed a quarter from me."

"Did she ask for small change?"

"Yes."

"Then she is still mad and means to harm you. They always try to get small change from the ones they wish to harm. Celestine always trying to hurt somebody."

"You think so? You make me very skeered."

"Go send your son to see what she is doing. Ah'll bet she has a candle on yo' money now."

The boy was sent and came running back in terror. "Oh Mamma, come look at what Tante Celestine is doin'."

The two women crept to the crack in old Celestine's door. There in midsummer was the chimney ablaze with black candles. A cup in front of each candle, holding the money. The old woman was stretched out on her belly with her head in the fire-place twirling a huge sieve with a pair of shears stuck in the mesh, whirling and twirling the sieve and muttering the name of the woman who had loaned her the five nickels.

"She is cutting my heart with the shears!" the woman gasped; "the murderer should die." She burst into the house without ceremony and all the Treme[1] heard about the fight that followed.

Mrs. Grant lived down below Canal Street and was a faithful disciple of Dr. Strong, a popular hoodoo doctor who lived on Urquhart Street near St. Claude.

One hot summer night Mr. Grant couldn't sleep, so he sat on the upper balcony in his underwear chewing tobacco. Mrs. Grant was in bed.

A tall black woman lived two blocks down the street. She and Mrs. Grant had had some words a few days past and the black woman had been to a hoodoo doctor and bought a powder to throw at Mrs. Grant's door. She had waited till the hour of two in the morning to do it. Just as she was "dusting" the door, Mr. Grant on the balcony spit and some of the tobacco juice struck the woman.

She had no business at the Grant house at all, let alone at two o'clock in the morning throwing War Powder against the door. But even so, she stepped back and gave Mr. Grant a piece of her mind that was highly seasoned. It was a splendid bit of Creole invective art. He was very apologetic, but Mrs. Grant came to the door to see what was the trouble.

Her enemy had retreated, but as soon as she opened the door she saw the white powder against the door and on the steps. Moreover, there was an egg shell on each step.

Mrs. Grant shrieked in terror and slammed the door shut. She grabbed the chamber pot and ran out of the back door. Next door were three boys. She climbed into their back yard and woke up the family. She must have some urine from the boys. This she carried through the neighbor's front gate to her own door and dashed it over the door and steps. One of the boys was paid to take the egg shells away. She could not enter her front door until the conjure was removed. The neighborhood was aroused—she must have a can of lye. She must have some river water in which to dissolve the lye. All this was dashed against the door and steps.

Early next morning she was at the door of Dr. Strong. He

[1]The old French quarter of New Orleans.

congratulated her on the steps she had already taken, but told her that to be sure she had counteracted all the bad work, she must draw the enemy's "wine". That is, she must injure her enemy enough to draw blood.

So Mrs. Grant hurried home and half-filled three quart bottles with water. She put these in a basket, and the basket on her arm, and set out for the restaurant where the night-sprinkler-of-powders was a cook.

She asked to speak to her, and as soon as she appeared — bam! bam! bam! went the bottles over her head and the "wine" flowed. But she fought back and in the fracas she bit Mrs. Grant's thumb severely, drawing *her* "wine."

This complicated affairs again. Something must be done to neutralize this loss of blood. She hurried home and called one of the boys next door and said: "Son, here's five dollars. Go get me a black chicken — not a white feather on him — and keep the change for your trouble."

The chicken was brought. She seized her husband's razor and split the live bird down the breast and thrust her fist inside. As the hot blood and entrails enveloped her hand, she went into a sort of frenzy, shouting: "I got her, I got her, I got her now!"

A wealthy planter in Middle Georgia was very arrogant in his demeanor towards his Negro servants. He boasted of being "unreconstructed" and that he didn't allow no niggers to sass him.

A Negro family lived on his place and worked for him. The father, it seems, was the yard man, the mother, the cook. The boys worked in the field and a daughter worked in the house and waited on the table.

There was a huge rib-roast of beef one night for dinner. The white man spoke very sharply for some reason to the girl and she sassed right back. He jumped to his feet and seized the half-eaten roast by the naked ribs and struck her with the vertebrate end. The blow landed squarely on her temple and she dropped dead.

The cook was attracted to the dining-room door by the tumult. The white man resumed his seat and was replenishing his plate. He coolly told the mother of the dead girl to "Call Dave and you all take that sow up off the floor."

Dave came and the parents bore away the body of their daughter, the mother weeping.

Now Dave was known to dabble in hoodoo. The negroes around both depended upon him and feared him.

He came back to clear away the blood of the murdered girl. He came with a pail and scrubbing brush. But first he sopped his handkerchief in the blood and put it into his pocket. Then he washed up the floor.

That night the Negro family moved away. They knew better than to expect any justice. They knew better than to make too much fuss about what had happened.

But less than two weeks later, the planter looked out of his window one night and thought he saw Dave running across the lawn away from the house. He put up the window and called to demand what he was doing on his place, but the figure disappeared in the trees. He shut the window and went to his wife's room to tell her about it and found her in laughing hysteria. She laughed for three days despite all that the doctors did to quiet her. On the fourth day she became maniacal and attacked her husband. Shortly it was realized that she was hopelessly insane and she had to be put in an institution. She made no attempt to hurt anyone except her husband. She was gentleness itself with her two children.

The plantation became intolerable to the planter, so he decided to move to more cheerful surroundings with his children. He had some friends in South Carolina, so he withdrew his large account at the bank and transferred it to South Carolina and set up a good home with the help of a housekeeper.

Two years passed and he became more cheerful. Then one night he heard steps outside his window and looked out. He saw a man—a Negro. He was sure it was Old Dave. The man ran away as before. He called and ran from the house in pursuit. He was determined to kill him if he caught him, for he began to fear ambush from the family of the girl he had murdered. He ran back to get his son, his gun and the dogs to trail the Negro.

As he burst into the front door he was knocked down by a blow on the head, but was not unconscious. His twenty year old son was raving and screaming above him with a poker in his hand. He struck blow after blow, his father dodging and covering himself as best he could. The housekeeper rushed up and caught the poker from behind and saved the man on the floor. The boy was led away weeping by the woman, but renewed his attack upon his father later in the night. This kept up for more than a month before the devoted parent would consent to his confinement in an institution for the criminally insane.

This was a crushing blow to the proud and wealthy ex-planter. He once more gathered up his goods and moved away. But a year later the visitation returned. He saw Dave. He was sure of it. This time he locked himself in his room and asked the housekeeper through the door about his daughter. She reported the girl missing. He decided at once that his black enemies had carried off his daughter Abbie. He made ready to pursue. He unlocked his door and stepped into the hall to put on his overcoat. When he opened the closet his daughter pointed a gun in his face and pulled the trigger. The gun snapped. It happened to be unloaded. She had hidden in the closet to shoot him whenever he emerged from his room. Her disordered brain had overlooked the cartridges.

So he moved to Baltimore—out in a fashionable neighborhood. The nurse who came to look after his deranged daughter had become his mistress. He skulked about, fearful of every Negro man he saw. At no time must any Negro man come upon his premises. He kept guns loaded and handy, but hidden from his giggling, simpering daughter, Abbie, who now and then attacked him with her fists. His love for his children was tremendous. He even contrived to have his son released in his charge. But two weeks later, as he drove the family out, the young man sitting in the rear seat attacked him from behind and would have killed him but for the paramour and a traffic officer.

"When I was a boy[2] about ten years old there was a man named Levi Conway whom I knew well. He operated a ferry and had money and was highly respected by all. He was very

[2]Told by Pierre Landeau of New Orleans.

careful about what he wore. He was tall and brown and wore a pompadour. He usually wore a broad-brimmed Stetson.

"He began to change. People thought he was going crazy. He owned lots of residential property but he quickly lost everything in some way that nobody seemed to understand. He grew careless in his dress and became positively untidy. He even got to the point where he'd buy ten cents worth of whiskey and drink it right out of the bottle.

"He began to pick up junk—old boilers, stones, wheels, pieces of harness, etc., and drag it around for miles every day. Then he'd bring it home and pile it in his backyard. This kept up for ten years or more.

"Finally he got sick in bed and couldn't get up.

"Tante Lida kept house for him. She was worried over his sickness, so she decided to get a woman from the Treme to find out what was wrong. The woman came. She was about fifty with a sore on her nose.

"She looked at Levi in the bed. Then she came out to Tante Lida. 'Sure, something has been done. I don't believe I can do anything to save him now, but I can tell you who did the work. You fix a place for me to stay here tonight and in the morning I will tell you.'

"Early next morning she sent for a heart of sheep or beef. She had them get her a package of needles and a new kettle. She lit a wood fire in the yard and filled the kettle one-third full of water and stood over the pot with the heart. She stuck the needles in one by one, muttering and murmuring as she stuck them in. When the water was boiling hard she dropped the heart in. It was about eleven o'clock in the morning.

" 'Now we shall know who has done this thing to Levi. In a few minutes the one who did it will come and ask for two things. Don't let him have either.'

"In a few minutes in came Pere Voltaire, a man whom all of us knew. He asked how Levi was. They told him pretty bad! He asked would they let him have two eggs and they said they had none. Then he asked would they lend him the wheelbarrow, and they said it wasn't there. The old woman winked and said, 'That is he.'

"He went on off. Then she told them to look into the pot, and they did. The heart was gone.

"A week later Levi died.

"This is the funny part. Some time after that my older brother, my cousin and I rowed over to the west bank of the river. Just knocking about as boys will, we found an old leaky boat turned upside down on the bank just out of reach of the water. I wondered who owned the piece of trash. My brother told me it belonged to Pere Voltaire. I said: 'Why doesn't he get a decent boat? This is too rotten to float.'

"I turned it over and found a great deal of junk under it— bundles tied up in rags, old bottles and cans and the like. So I started to throwing the stuff into the water and my cousin helped me. We pushed the boat in, too. My brother tried to stop us.

"I forget now how it was that Pere Voltaire knew we did that. But two days later I began to shake as if I had an ague. Nothing the doctors could do stopped me. Two days later my cousin began to shake and two days after that my brother started to shake. It was three or four months before we could be stopped. But my brother stopped first. Then my cousin, then at last I stopped."

VII

KITTY BROWN is a well-known hoodoo doctor of New Orleans, and a Catholic. She liked to make marriages and put lovers together. She is squat, black and benign. Often when we had leisure, she told funny stories. Her herb garden was pretty full and we often supplied other doctors with plants. Very few raise things since the supply houses carry about everything that is needed. But sometimes a thing is wanted fresh from the ground. That's where Kitty's garden came in.

When the matter of my initiation came up she said, "In order for you to reach the spirit somebody has got to suffer. I'll suffer for you because I'm strong. It might be the death of you."

It was in October 1928, when I was a pupil of hers, that I shared in a hoodoo dance. This was not a pleasure dance, but ceremonial. In another generation African dances were held in Congo Square, now Beauregard Square. Those were held for social purposes and were of the same type as the fire dances and jumping dances of the present in the Bahamas. But the hoodoo dance is done for a specific purpose. It is always a case of death-to-the-enemy that calls forth a dance. They are very rare even in New Orleans now, even within the most inner circle, and no layman ever participates, nor has ever been allowed to witness such a ceremony.

This is how the dance came to be held. I sat with my teacher in her front room as the various cases were disposed of. It was my business to assist wherever possible, such as running errands for materials or verifying addresses; locating materials in the various drawers and cabinets, undressing and handling patients, writing out formulas as they were dictated, and finally making "hands".[1] At last, of course, I could do all of the work while she looked on and made corrections where necessary.

This particular day, a little before noon, came Rachael Roe. She was dry with anger, hate, outraged confidence and desire

[1] Manufacturing certain luck charms.

for revenge. John Doe had made violent love to her; had lain in her bed and bosom for the last three years; had received of Rachael everything material and emotional a woman can give. They had both worked and saved and had contributed to a joint savings account. Now, only the day before yesterday, he had married another. He had lured a young and pretty girl to his bed with Rachael's earnings; yes. Had set up housekeeping with Rachael's sweat and blood. She had gone to him and he had laughed at his former sweetheart, yes. The police could do nothing, no. The bank was sorry, but they could do nothing, no. So Rachael had come to Kitty.

Did she still love her John Doe? Perhaps; she didn't know. If he would return to her she should strive to forget, but she was certain he'd not return. How could he? But if he were dead she could smile again, yes — could go back to her work and save some more money, yes. Perhaps she might even meet a man who could restore her confidence in menfolk.

Kitty appraised her quickly. "A dance could be held for him that would carry him away right now, but they cost something."

"How much?"

"A whole lot. How much kin you bring me?"

"I got thirty-seven dollars."

"Dat ain't enough. Got to pay de dancers and set de table."

One hundred dollars was agreed upon. It was paid by seven o'clock that same night. We were kept very busy, for the dance was set from ten to one the next day, those being bad hours. I ran to certain addresses to assemble a sort of college of bishops to be present and participate. The table was set with cake, wine, roast duck and barbecued goat.

By nine-thirty the next morning the other five participants were there and had dressed for the dance. A dispute arose about me. Some felt I had not gone far enough to dance. I could wait upon the altar, but not take the floor. Finally I was allowed to dance, as a delegate for my master who had a troublesome case of neuritis. The food was being finished off in the kitchen.

Promptly on the stroke of ten Death mounted his black draped throne and assumed his regal crown, Death being represented by a rudely carved wooden statue, bust length. A box was draped in black sateen and Kitty placed him upon it and set his red crown on. She hobbled back to her seat. I had the petition and the name of the man written on seven slips of paper—one for each participant. I was told to stick them in Death's grinning mouth. I did so, so that the end of each slip protruded. At the command I up-ended nine black tapers that had been dressed by a bath in whiskey and bad vinegar, and bit off the butt end to light, calling upon Death to take notice. As I had been instructed, I said: "Spirit of Death, take notice I am fixing your candles for you. I want you to hear me." I said this three times and the assembly gave three snaps with the thumb and middle finger.

The candles were set upside down and lighted on the altar, three to the left of Death, three to the right, and three before him.

I resumed my seat, and everyone was silent until Kitty was possessed. The exaltation caught like fire. Then B. arose drunkenly and danced a few steps. The clapping began lightly. He circled the room, then prostrated himself before the altar, and, getting to his hands and knees, with his teeth pulled one of the slips from the jaws of Death. He turned a violent somersault and began the dance, not intricate, but violent and muscle-twitching.

We were to dance three hours, and the time was divided equally, so that the more participants the less time each was called upon to dance. There were six of us, since Kitty could not actively participate, so that we each had forty minutes to dance. Plenty of liquor was provided so that when one appeared exhausted the bottle was pressed to his lips and he danced on. But the fury of the rhythm more than the stimulant kept the dancers going. The heel-patting was a perfect drum rhythm, and the hand clapping had various stimulating breaks. At any rate no one fell from exhaustion, though I know that even I, the youngest, could not have danced continuously on an ordinary dance floor unsupported by a partner for that length of time.

Nearly all ended on the moment in a twitchy collapse, and the next most inspired prostrated himself and began his dance with the characteristic somersault. Death was being continuously besought to follow the footsteps of John Doe. There was no regular formula. They all "talked to him" in their own way, the others calling out to the dancer to "talk to him." Some of the postures were obscene in the extreme. Some were grotesque, limping steps of old men and women. Some were mere agile leapings. But the faces! That is where the dedication lay.

When the fourth dancer had finished and lay upon the floor retching in every muscle, Kitty was taken. The call had come for her. I could not get upon the floor quickly enough for the others and was hurled before the altar. It got me there and I danced, I don't know how, but at any rate, when we sat about the table later, all agreed that Mother Kitty had done well to take me.

I have neglected to say that one or two of the dancers remained upon the floor "in the spirit" after their dance and had to be lifted up and revived at the end.

Death had some of all the food placed before him. An uncorked pint of good whiskey was right under his nose. He was paid fifteen cents and remained on his throne until one o'clock that night. Then all of the food before him was taken up with the tablecloth on which it rested and was thrown into the Mississippi River.

The person danced upon is not supposed to live more than nine days after the dance. I was very eager to see what would happen in this case. But five days after the dance John Doe deserted his bride for the comforting arms of Rachael and she hurried to Mother Kitty to have the spell removed. She said he complained of breast pains and she was fearfully afraid for him. So I was sent to get the beef heart out of the cemetery (which had been put there as part of the routine), and John and Rachael made use of the new furniture bought for his bride. I think he feared that Rachael might have him fixed, so he probably fled to her as soon as the zest for a new wife had abated.

Kitty began by teaching me various ways of bringing back a man or woman who had left his or her mate. She had plenty to work on, too. In love cases the client is often told what to do at home. Minnie Foster was the best customer Kitty had. She wanted something for every little failing in her lover.

Kitty said to her one day, "You must be skeered of yourself with that man of yours."

"No, Ma'am, I ain't. But I love him and I just want to make sure. Just you give me something to make his love more stronger."

"Alright, Minnie, I'll do it, but you ain't got no reason to be so unsettled with me behind you. Do like I say and you'll be alright.

"Use six red candles. Stick sixty pins in each candle—thirty on each side. Write the name of your sweetheart three times on a small square of paper and stick it underneath the candle. Burn one of these prepared candles each night for six nights. Make six slips of paper and write the name of the loved one once on each slip. Then put a pin in the paper on all four sides of the name. Each morning take up the sixty pins left from the burning of the candles, and save them. Then smoke the slip of paper with the four pins in it in incense smoke and bury it with the pins under your door step. The piece of paper with the name written on it three times, upon which each candle stands while burning, must be kept each day until the last candle is burned. Then bury it in the same hole with the rest. When you are sticking the pins in the candles, keep repeating: 'Tumba Walla, Bumba Walla, bring Gabe Staggers back to me.'"

Minnie paid her five dollars, thanked her loudly and hurried off to tighten the love-shackles on her Gabriel. But the following week she was back again.

"Ain't you got dat man to you wishes, yet, Minnie?" Kitty asked, half in fun and half in impatience.

"He love me, I b'lieve, but he gone off to Mobile with a construction gang and I got skeered he might not come back. Something might delay him on his trip."

"Oh, alright Minnie, go do like I say and he'll sure be back. Write the name of the absent party six times on paper. Put the paper in a water glass with two tablespoons full of quicksilver on it. Write his or her name three times each on six candles and burn one on a window sill in the daytime for six days."

Minnie paid and went home, but a week later she was back, washed down in tears. So Kitty gave her a stronger help.

"This is bound to bring him. Can't help it, Minnie. Now go home and stop fretting and do this:

"Write his name three times. Dig a hole in the ground. Get a left-foot soiled-sock from him secretly. His hatband may be used also. Put the paper with the name in the hole first. Then the sock or hatband. Then light a red candle on top of it all and burn it. Put a spray of Sweet Basil in a glass of water beside the candle. Light the candle at noon and burn until one. Light it again at six P. M. and burn till seven. (Always pinch out a candle—never blow it.) After the candle is lit, turn a barrel over the hole. When you get it in place, knock on it three times to call the spirit and say: 'Tumba Walla, Bumba Walla, bring Gabriel Staggers home to me.' "

We saw nothing of Minnie for six weeks, then she came in another storm of tears.

"Miss Kitty, Gabriel done got to de place I can't tell him his eye is black. What can I do to rule de man I love?"

"Do like I say, honey, and you can rule. Get his sock. Take one silver dime, some hair from his head or his hatband. Lay the sock out on a table, bottom up. Write his name three times and put it on the sock. Place the dime on the name and the hair or hatband on the dime. Put a piece of 'he' Lodestone[2] on top of the hair and sprinkle it with steel dust. As you do this, say, 'Feed the he, feed the she.' That is what you call feeding the Lodestone. Then fold the sock heel on the toe and roll it all up together, tight. Pin the bundle by crossing two needles. Then wet it with whiskey and set it up over a door. And don't 'low him to go off no more, do you going to lose all control.

"Now listen, honey, this is the way to change a man's mind about going away: Take the left shoe, set it up straight, then roll it one-half over first to the right, then to the left. Roll it to a coming-in door and point it straight in the door, and he can't leave. Hatband or sock can be made into a ball and rolled the same way: but it must be put under the sill or over the door."

*   *   *

[2]Magnetic iron ore.

Once Sis Cat got hongry and caught herself a rat and set herself down to eat 'im. Rat tried and tried to git loose but Sis Cat was too fast and strong. So jus' as de cat started to eat 'im he says, "Hol' on dere, Sis Cat! Ain't you got no manners atall? You going set up to de table and eat 'thout washing yo' face and hands?"

Sis Cat was mighty hongry but she hate for de rat to think she ain't got no manners, so she went to de water and washed her face and hands and when she got back de rat was gone.

So de cat caught herself a rat again and set down to eat. So de Rat said, "Where's yo' manners at, Sis Cat? You going to eat 'thout washing yo' face and hands?"

"Oh, Ah got plenty manners," de cat told 'im. "But Ah eats mah dinner and washes mah face and uses mah manners afterwards." So she et right on 'im and washed her face and hands. And cat's been washin' after eatin' ever since.

I'm sitting here like Sis Cat, washing my face and usin' my manners.

GLOSSARY

JACK OR JOHN (not John Henry) is the great human culture hero in Negro folk-lore. He is like Daniel in Jewish folk-lore, the wish-fulfillment hero of the race. The one who, nevertheless, or in spite of laughter, usually defeats Ole Massa, God and the Devil. Even when Massa seems to have him in a hopeless dilemma he wins out by a trick. Brer Rabbit, Jack (or John) and the Devil are continuations of the same thing.

WOOFING is a sort of aimless talking. A man half seriously flirts with a girl, half seriously threatens to fight or brags of his prowess in love, battle or in financial matters. The term comes from the purposeless barking of dogs at night.

TESTIMONY. There is a meeting called a "love-feast" in the Methodist Church and an "experience meeting" with the Baptists. It is held once a month, either on a week-night or a Sunday morning preceding the Communion service. It is a Protestant confessional. No one is supposed to take communion unless he is on good terms with all of the other church members and is free from sin otherwise. The love-feast gives opportunity for public expression of good-will to the world. There are three set forms with variations. (1) The person who expects to testify raises a hymn. After a verse or two he or she speaks expressing (a) love for everybody, (b) joy at being present, (c) tells of the determination to stay in the field to the end. (2) Singing of a "hot" spiritual, giving the right hand of fellowship to the entire church, a shouting, tearful finish. (3) (a) Expresses joy at being present, (b) recites incident of conversion, telling in detail the visions seen and voices heard, (c) expresses determination to hold out to the end.

It is singular that God never finds fault, never censures the Negro. He sees faults but expects nothing different. He is

229

lacking in bitterness as is the Negro story-teller himself in circumstances that ordinarily would call for pity.

The devil is not the terror that he is in European folk-lore. He is a powerful trickster who often competes successfully with God. There is a strong suspicion that the devil is an extension of the story-makers while God is the supposedly impregnable white masters, who are nevertheless defeated by the Negroes.

JOHN HENRY. This is a song of the railroad camps and is suited to the spiking rhythm, though it is, like all the other work songs, sung in the jooks and other social places. It is not a very old song, being younger by far than Casey Jones and like that song being the celebration of an incidence of bravery. John Henry is not as widely distributed as "Mule on de Mount," "Uncle Bud" or several of the older songs, though it has a better air than most of the work songs. *John Henry has no place in Negro folk-lore except in this one circumstance.* The story told in the ballad is of John Henry, who is a great steel-driver, growing jealous when the company installs a steam drill. He boasts that he can beat the steam drill hammering home spikes, and asks his boss for a 9-pound hammer saying that if he has a good hammer he can beat the steam drill driving. The hammer is provided and he attempts to beat the drill. He does so for nearly an hour, then his heart fails him and he drops dead from exhaustion. It is told in direct dialogue for the greater part. The last three verses show internal evidence of being interpolated from English ballads. Judge the comparative newness of the song by the fact that he is competing with something as recent as a steam drill. For music for "John Henry" see Appendix.

LONG HOUSE. Another name for jook. Sometimes means a mere bawdy house. A long low building cut into rooms that all open on a common porch. A woman lives in each of the rooms.

BLUE BABY. Nicknames such as this one given from appearances or acts, i.e. "Blue Baby" was so black he looked blue. "Tush Hawg," a rough man; full of fight like a wild boar.

One notes that among the animals the rabbit is the trickster hero. Lacking in size, strength and natural weapons such as teeth and claws, he continues to overcome by cunning. There are other minor characters that are heroic, but Brer Rabbit is first. In Florida, Brer Gopher, the dry-land tortoise, is also a hero and perhaps nearly equal to the rabbit.

The colored preacher, in his cooler passages, strives for grammatical correctness, but goes natural when he warms up. The "hah" is a breathing device, done rhythmically to punctuate the lines. The congregation wants to hear the preacher breathing or "straining."

GEORGIA SKIN GAME. Any number of "Pikers" can play at a time, but there are two "principals" who do the dealing. Both of them are not dealing at the same time, however. But when the first one who deals "falls" the other principal takes the deal. If he in turn falls it goes back to the first dealer. The principals draw the first two cards. The pikers draw from the third card on. Unless a player or players want to "scoop one in the rough," he can choose his own card which can be any card in the deck except the card on top of the deck and that one goes to the dealer. The dealer charges anything he pleases for the privilege of "scooping," the money being put in sight. It is the player's bet. After the ones who wish to have scooped, then the dealer begins to "turn" the cards. That is, flipping them off the deck face upwards and the pikers choose a card each from among those turned off to bet on. Sometimes several pikers are on the same card. When all have selected their cards and have their bets down, they begin to chant "Turn 'em" to the dealer. He turns them until a player falls. That is, a card like the one he is holding falls. For instance one holds the 10 of hearts. When another 10 falls he loses. Then the players cry "hold 'em" until the player selects another clean card, one that has not fallen. The fresh side bets are down and the chant "turn 'em" and the singing "Let de deal go Down" until the deck is run out.

I

NEGRO SONGS WITH MUSIC

JOHN HENRY

1 John Henry driving on the right hand side,
Steam drill driving on the left,
Says, 'fore I'll let your steam drill beat me down
I'll hammer my fool self to death,
Hammer my fool self to death.

2 John Henry told his Captain,
When you go to town
Please bring me back a nine pound hammer
And I'll drive your steel on down.
And I'll drive your steel on down.

3 John Henry told his Captain,
Man ain't nothing but a man,
And 'fore I'll let that steam drill beat me down
I'll die with this hammer in my hand,
Die with this hammer in my hand.

4 Captain ast John Henry,
What is that storm I hear?
He says Cap'n that ain't no storm,
'Tain't nothing but my hammer in the air,
Nothing but my hammer in the air.

5 John Henry told his Captain,
Bury me under the sills of the floor,
So when they get to playing good old Georgy skin,
Bet 'em fifty to a dollar more,
Fifty to a dollar more.

6 John Henry had a little woman,
   The dress she wore was red,
   Says I'm going down the track,
   And she never looked back.
   I'm going where John Henry fell dead,
   Going where John Henry fell dead.

7 Who's going to shoe your pretty li'l' feet?
   And who's going to glove your hand?
   Who's going to kiss your dimpled cheek?
   And who's going to be your man?
   Who's going to be your man?

8 My father's going to shoe my pretty li'l' feet;
   My brother's going to glove my hand;
   My sister's going to kiss my dimpled cheek;
   John Henry's going to be my man,
   John Henry's going to be my man.

9 Where did you get your pretty li'l' dress?
   The shoes you wear so fine?
   I got my shoes from a railroad man,
   My dress from a man in the mine,
   My dress from a man in the mine.

JOHN HENRY

(Work Song Series)

From the Zora Neale Hurston Collection of Negro Folk-lore   Arranged by C. Spencer Tocus

1. John Hen-ry driv-ing on the right hand side,

Steam drill driv-ing on the left, Says, 'fore I'll let your steam drill

beat me down I'll ham-mer my fool self to

death,   Ham-mer my fool self   to   death.

REFRAIN

Hm ....   Hm .... hah!   *(spoken)*

Hm..........................   Hm.. 2. John' Hm.... Hah
                                      3. The
                                      4. John

D.S. | *Last time (spoken)*

D.S.

EAST COAST BLUES

1 Don't you hear that East Coast when she blows,
   Oh, don't you hear that East Coast when she blows,
   Ah, don't you hear that East Coast when she blows.

2 I'm going down that long lonesome road,
   Oh, I'm going down that long lonesome road,
   Ah, I'm going down that long lonesome road.

3 I'm going where the chilly winds don't blow,
   Oh, I'm going where the chilly winds don't blow,
   Ah, I'm going where the chilly winds don't blow.

4 You treat me mean you sho going see it again,
   Oh, you treat me mean you sho going see it again,
   Ah, you treat me mean you sho going see it again.

5 I love you honey but your woman got me barred,
   Oh, I love you honey but your woman got me barred,
   Ah, I love you honey but your woman got me barred.

6 Love ain't nothing but the easy going heart disease,
   Oh, love ain't nothing but the easy going heart disease,
   Ah, love ain't nothing but the easy going heart disease.

EAST COAST BLUES

(Social Song Series)

From the Zora Neale Hurston Collection Negro Folk-lore

Po' gal long ways from home............

Po' gal long ways from home.......... oh ....

I'm po' gal a long ways from home ....

PLEASE DON'T DRIVE ME

(Convict Song)

From the Zora Neale Hurston Collection of Negro Folk-lore   Arranged by PORTER GRAINGER

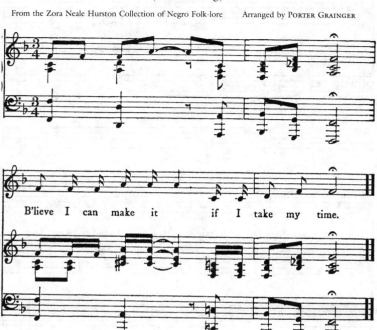

B'lieve I can make it   if I take my time.

1 Please don't drive me because I'm blind,
  B'lieve I kin make it if I take my time.

2 Lift up de hammer and let it fall down,
  It's a hard rocky bottom and it must be found.

3 De cap'n say hurry, de boss say run,
  I got a damn good notion not to do nary one.

COLD RAINY DAY

Cold rain-y day. Some old cold rain-y day I'll be back some old cold rain-y day. Old Smok-ey Joe Lawd, he died on the road Say-ing I'll be back some day.

Cold rain-y day. Some old cold rain-y day I'll be back some old cold

rain-y day. All I want is my rail - road fare, Take me back

where I was born. Oh, the rocks may be my pil-low, Lawd, the sand may

be my bed. I'll be back some old cold rain-y day.   Cold rain-y day,

Some old cold rain-y day, I'll be back some old cold rain-y day.

1 Cold rainy day, some old cold, rainy day,
   I'll be back some old cold, rainy day.

2 All I want is my railroad fare,
   Take me back where I was born.

3 Ole Smoky Joe, Lawd, he died on the road
   Saying I'll be back some day.

4 Oh, the rocks may be my pillow
   Lawd, the sand may be my bed,
   I'll be back some old cold, rainy day.

GOING TO SEE MY LONG-HAIRED BABE

SOLOIST:
Oh Lulu! Oh Gal!
Want to see you, so bad.

CHORUS:
Going to see my long-haired babe;
Going to see my long-haired babe,
Oh Lawd I'm going 'cross the water
See my long-haired babe.

SOLOIST:
What you reckon Mr. Treadwell
Said to Mr. Goff,
Lawd I b'lieve I'll go South,
Pay them poor boys off.

CHORUS:

SOLOIST:
Lawd I ast that woman
Lemme be her kid,
And she looked at me
And began to smile.

CHORUS:

SOLOIST:
Oh Lulu! Oh Gal!

ALL:
Want to see you, so bad.

GOING TO SEE MY LONG-HAIRED BABE

(Spiking Rhythm)

wa - ter see my long - haired babe. Lawd, I ast dat wom-an

lem - me be— her kid And she looked at me—and be - gan to smile.

After last verse

Oh, - Lu - lu, Oh gal, Want to see you so bad.

CAN'T YOU LINE IT?

NOTE: This song is common to the railroad camps. It is suited to the "lining" rhythm. That is, it fits the straining of the men at the lining bars as the rail is placed in position to be spiked down.

1 When I get in Illinois
  I'm going to spread the news about the Florida boys.
  Chorus: (All men straining at rail in concert.)
  Shove it over! Hey, hey, can't you line it?
  (Shaking rail.) Ah, shack-a-lack-a-lack-a-lack-a-lack-a-
      lack.
  (Grunt as they move rail.) Can't you move it? Hey, hey,
      can't you try.

2 Tell what the hobo told the bum,
  If you get any corn-bread save me some.
CHORUS:

3 A nickle's worth of bacon, and a dime's worth of lard,
  I would buy more but the time's too hard.
CHORUS:

4 Wonder what's the matter with the walking boss,
  It's done five-thirty and he won't knock off.
CHORUS:

5 I ast my Cap'n what's the time of day,
  He got mad and throwed his watch away.
CHORUS:

6 Cap'n got a pistol and he try to play bad,
  But I'm going to take it if he make me mad.
CHORUS:

7 Cap'n got a burner* I'd like to have,
  A 32:20 with a shiny barrel.
CHORUS:

*Gun.

8 De Cap'n can't read, de Cap'n can't write,
   How do he know that the time is right?
CHORUS:

9 Me and my buddy and two three more,
   Going to ramshack Georgy everywhere we go.
CHORUS:

10 Here come a woman walking 'cross the field,
   Her mouth exhausting like an automobile.

CAN'T YOU LINE IT?

(Work Song Series)

From the Zora Neale Hurston Collection of Negro Folk-lore   Arranged by PORTIA D. DUHART

THERE STANDS A BLUE BIRD (Children)

Another version: Going around de mountain, two by two (actions suit words).

1 There stands a blue-bird, tra la, la, la.
There stands a blue-bird, tra la, la, la.
Gimme sugar, coffee and tea.

2 Now trip around the ocean, tra, la, la, la.
Now trip around the ocean, tra, la, la, la.
Gimme sugar, coffee and tea (one in ring dances around
    ring).

3 Show me your motion, tra, la, la, la (does solo dance).
Show me your motion, tra, la, la, la.
Gimme sugar, coffee and tea.

4 Show me a better one, tra, la, la, la (second solo step).
Show me a better one, tra, la, la, la.

5 Choose your partner, tra, la, la, la.
Choose your partner, tra, la, la, la.
Gimme sugar, coffee and tea.

(One in ring chooses partner and the new chosen partner takes his place in the ring and the other comes out.)

THERE STANDS A BLUE BIRD

(Children's Game)

From the Zora Neale Hurston Collection of Negro Folk-lore   Arranged by C. Spencer Tocus

There stands a blue-bird, tra la la la —, There stands a blue-bird

tra la la la,   Gim - me su - gar   cof - fee and   tea.   Now

skip a-round the o - cean,   tra la la la —,   Skip a-round the o - cean.

tra la la la —,   Gim - me su - gar,   cof - fee and   tea.

MULE ON DE MOUNT

NOTE: The most widely distributed and best known of all Negro work songs. Since folk songs grow by incremental repetition the diversified subject matter that it accumulates as it ages is one of the evidences of its distribution and usage. This has everything in folk life in it. Several stories to say nothing of just lyric matter. It is something like the Odyssey, or the Iliad.

1 Cap'n got a mule, mule on the Mount called Jerry
  Cap'n got a mule, mule on the Mount called Jerry
  I can ride, Lawd, Lawd, I can ride.
  (He won't come down, Lawd; Lawd, he won't come
      down, in another version.)

2 I don't want no cold corn bread and molasses,
  I don't want no cold corn bread and molasses,
  Gimme beans, Lawd, Lawd, gimme beans.

3 I don't want no coal-black woman for my regular,
  I don't want no coal-black woman for my regular,
  She's too low-down, Lawd, Lawd, she's too low-down.

4 I got a woman, she's got money 'cumulated,
  I got a woman, she's got money 'cumulated,
  In de bank, Lawd, Lawd, in de bank.

5 I got a woman she's pretty but she's too bulldozing,
  I got a woman she's pretty but she's too bulldozing,
  She won't live long, Lawd, Lawd, she won't live long.

6 Every pay day, pay day I gits a letter,
  Every pay day, pay day I gits a letter,
  Son come home, Lawd, Lawd, son come home.

7 If I can just make June, July and August,
  If I can just make June, July and August,
  I'm going home, Lawd, Lawd, I'm going home.

8 Don't you hear them, coo-coo birds keep a'hollering,
  Don't you hear them, coo-coo birds keep a'hollering,
  It's sign of rain, Lawd, Lawd, it's sign of rain.

9 I got a rain-bow wrapped and tied around my shoulder,
   I got a rain-bow wrapped and tied around my shoulder,
   It ain't goin' rain, Lawd, Lawd, it ain't goin' rain.

MULE ON DE MOUNT

(Work Song Series)

From the Zora Neale Hurston Collection of Negro Folk-lore   Arranged by C. SPENCER TOCUS

VOICE
Very slow

Cap'-'n got a mule, mule on the Mount call-ed Jer - ry,

PIANO

Cap'-'n got a mule, mule on the Mount called Jer - ry I can

ride, Lawd,...... Lawd, I can ride.................

8va.

LET THE DEAL GO DOWN
(Gaming song suited to the action of Georgia Skin Game.)

SOLOIST:
    1 When your card gits lucky, oh partner,
      You ought to be in a rolling game.

CHORUS:
      Let the deal go down, boys,
      Let the deal go down.

SOLOIST:
    2 I ain't had no money, Lawd, partner,
      I ain't had no change.

CHORUS:

SOLOIST:
    3 I ain't had no trouble, Lawd, partner,
      Till I stop by here.

CHORUS:

SOLOIST:
    4 I'm going back to de 'Bama, Lawd, partner,
      Won't be worried with you.

LET THE DEAL GO DOWN

Slowly

When your card gits luck - y, oh, part - ner,
You ought to be in a roll - ing game.

CHORUS

Let the deal go down, boys, Let the deal go down.

II

FORMULAE OF HOODOO DOCTORS [1]

Concerning Sudden Death

1. Put an egg in a murdered man's hand and the murderer can't get away. He will wander right around the scene.

2. If a murder victim falls on his face, the murderer can't escape punishment. He will usually be executed.

3. If the blood of the victim is put in a jug and buried at the north corner of his house, the murderer will be caught and convicted.

4. Bury the victim with his hat on and the murderer will never get away.

5. If you kill and step backwards over the body, they will never catch you.

6. If you are murdered or commit suicide, you are dead before your time comes. God is not ready for you, and so your soul must prowl about until your time comes.

7. If you suspect that a person has been killed by hoodoo, put a cassava stick in the hand and he will punish the murderer. If he is killed by violence, put the stick in one hand and a knife and fork in the other. The spirit of the murdered one will first drive the slayer insane, and then kill him with great violence.

8. If people die wishing to see someone, they will stay limp and warm for days. They are waiting.

9. If a person dies who has not had his fling in this world, he will turn on his face in the grave.

10. If a person dies without speaking his mind about matters, he will purge (foam at the mouth after death). Hence the expression: "I ain't goin' to purge when I die (I shall speak my mind)."

To Rent a House

Tie up some rice and sycamore bark in a small piece of goods. Tie six fig leaves and a piece of John de Conquer root in another piece. Cheesecloth is good. Boil both bundles in a quart of water at the same time. Strain it out. Now sprinkle the rice and sycamore bark mixed together in front of the house. Put the fig leaves and John de Conquer root in a corner of the house and scrub the house with the water they were boiled in. Mix it with a pail of scrub water.

[1] The formulae, paraphernalia and prescriptions of conjure are reprinted through the courtesy of the Journal of American Folk-Lore.

For Bad Work—(Death)

Take a coconut that has three eyes. Take the name of the person you want to get rid of and write it on the paper like a coffin. (Put the name all over the coffin.) Put this down in the nut. (Pour out water.) Put beef gall and vinegar in the nut and the person's name all around the coconut. Stand nut up in sand and set one black candle on top of it. Number the days from one to fifteen days. Every day mark that coconut at twelve o'clock A.M. or P.M., and by the fifteenth day they will be gone. Never let the candle go out. You must light the new candle and set it on top of the old stub which has burnt down to a wafer.

Court Scrapes

a. Take the names of all the *good* witnesses (for your client), the judge and your client's lawyer. Put the names in a dish and pour sweet oil on them and burn a white candle each morning beside it for one hour, from nine to ten. The day of the trial when you put it upon the altar, don't take it down until the trial is over.

b. Take the names of the opponent of your client, his witnesses and his lawyer. Take all of their names on one piece of paper. Put it between two whole bricks. Put the top brick crossways. On the day of the trial set a bucket or dishpan on top of the bricks with ice in it. That's to freeze them out so they can't talk.

c. Take the names of your client's lawyer, witnesses and lawyer on paper. Buy a beef tongue and split it from the base towards the tip, thus separating top from bottom. Put the paper with names in the split tongue along with eighteen pods of hot pepper and pin it through and through with pins and needles. Put it in a tin pail with plenty of vinegar and keep it on ice until the day of court. That day, pour kerosene in the bucket and burn it, and they will destroy themselves in court.

d. Put the names of the judge and all those *for* your client on paper. Take the names of the twelve apostles after Judas hung himself and write each apostle's name on a sage leaf. Take six candles and burn them standing in holy water. Have your client wear six of the sage leaves in each shoe and the jury will be made for him.

e. Write all the enemies' names on paper. Put them in a can. Then take soot and ashes from the chimney of your client and mix it with salt. Stick pins crosswise in the candles and burn them at a good hour. Put some ice in a bucket and set the can in it. Let your client recite the One Hundred Twentieth Psalm before Court and in Court.

f. To let John the conqueror win your case; take one-half pint whiskey, nine pieces of John the Conqueror Root one inch long. Let it soak thirty-eight hours till all the strength is out. (Gather all roots before September 21.) Shake up good and drain off roots in another bottle. Get one ounce of white rose or Jockey Club perfume and pour into the mixture. Dress your client with this before going to Court.

To Kill and Harm

Get bad vinegar, beef gall, filet gumbo with red pepper, and put names written across each other in bottles. Shake the bottle for nine mornings and talk and tell it what you want it to do. To kill the victim, turn it upside down and bury it breast deep, and he will die.

Running Feet

To give anyone the running feet: Take sand out of one of his tracks and mix the sand with red pepper; throw some into a running stream of water and this will cause the person to run from place to place, until finally he runs himself to death.

To Make a Man Come Home

Take nine deep red or pink candles. Write his name three times on each candle. Wash the candles with Van-Van. Put the name three times on paper and place under the candles, and call the name of the party three times as the candle is placed at the hours of seven, nine or eleven.

To Make People Love You

Take nine lumps of starch, nine of sugar, nine teaspoons of steel dust. Wet it all with Jockey Club cologne. Take nine pieces of ribbon, blue, red or yellow. Take a dessertspoonful and put it on a piece of ribbon and tie it in a bag. As each fold is gathered together call his name. As you wrap it with yellow thread call his name till you finish. Make nine bags and place them under a rug, behind an armoire, under a step or over a door. They will love you and give you everything they can get. Distance makes no difference. Your mind is talking to his mind and nothing beats that.

To Break Up a Love Affair

Take nine needles, break each needle in three pieces. Write each person's name three times on paper. Write one name backwards and one forwards and lay the broken needles on the paper. Take five black candles, four red and three green.

Tie a string across the door from it, suspend a large candle upside down. It will hang low on the door; burn one each day for one hour. If you burn your first in the daytime, keep on in the day; if at night, continue at night. A tin plate with paper and needles in it must be placed to catch wax in.

When the ninth day is finished, go out into the street and get some white or black dog dung. A dog only drops his dung in the street when he is running and barking, and whoever you curse will run and bark likewise. Put it in a bag with the paper and carry it to running water, and one of the parties will leave town.

III

PARAPHERNALIA OF CONJURE

It would be impossible for anyone to find out all the things that are being used in conjure in America. Anything may be conjure and nothing may be conjure, according to the doctor, the time and the use of the article.

What is set down here are the things most commonly used.

1. Fast Luck: Aqueous solution of oil of Citronella. It is put in scrub water to scrub the house. It brings luck in business by pulling customers into a store.
2. Red Fast Luck: Oil of Cinnamon and Oil of Vanilla, with wintergreen. Used as above to bring luck.
3. Essence of Van Van: Ten percent. Oil of Lemon Grass in alcohol. (Different doctors specify either grain, mentholated, or wood alcohol), used for luck and power of all kinds. It is the most popular conjure drug in Louisiana.
4. Fast Scrubbing Essence: A mixture of thirteen oils. It is burned with incense for fish-fry luck, i. e., business success. It includes:
   Essence Cinnamon
   Essence Wintergreen
   Essence Geranium
   Essence Bergamot
   Essence Orange Flowers, used also in initiation baths
   Essence Lavender; used also in initiation baths
   Essence Anice
   Essence St. Michael
   Essence Rosemary.
5. Water Notre Dame: Oil of White Rose and water. Sprinkle it about the home to make peace.
6. War Water: Oil of Tar in water (filtered). Break a glass of it on the steps wherever you wish to create strife. (It is sometimes made of creolin in water.)
7. Four Thieves Vinegar. It is used for breaking up homes, for making a person run crazy, for driving off. It is sometimes put with a name in a bottle and the bottle thrown into moving water. It is used also to "dress" cocoanuts to kill and drive crazy.

8. Egyptian Paradise Seed (Amonium Melegreta). This is used in seeking success. Take a picture of St. Peter and put it at the front door and a picture of St. Michael at the back door. Put the Paradise seeds in little bags and put one behind each saint. It is known as "feeding the saint."

9. Guinea Paradise seed. Use as above.

10. Guinea pepper. This may also be used for feeding saints; also for breaking up homes or protecting one from conjure.

11. White Mustard seed. For protection against harm.

12. Black Mustard seed. For causing disturbance and strife.

13. Has-no-harra: Jasmine lotion. Brings luck to gamblers.

14. Carnation, a perfume. As above.

15. Three Jacks and a King. A perfume. As above.

16. Narcisse. As above but mild.

17. Nutmegs, bored and stuffed with quicksilver and sealed with wax, and rolled in Argentorium are very lucky for gamblers.

18. Lucky Dog is best of all for gamblers' use.

19. Essence of Bend-over. Used to rule and have your way.

20. Cleo-May, a perfume. To compel men to love you.

21. Jockey Club, a perfume. To make love and get work.

22. Jasmine Perfume. For luck in general.

23. White Rose. To make peace.

24. French Lilac. Best for vampires.

25. Taper Oil: perfumed olive oil. To burn candles in.

26. St. Joseph's Mixture:
    Buds from the Garden of Gilead
    Berries of the Fish
    Wishing Beans
    Juniper Berries
    Japanese scented Lucky Beans
    Large Star Anice

27. Steel dust is sprinkled over black load stone in certain ceremonies. It is called "feeding the he, feeding the she."

28. Steel dust is attracted by a horse-shoe magnet to draw people to you. Used to get love, trade, etc.

29. Gold and silver magnetic sand. Powdered silver gilt used with a magnet to draw people to you.

30. *Saltpetre* is dissolved in water and sprinkled about to ward off conjure.

31. Scrub waters other than the Fast Lucks (See above, 1 and 2) are colored and perfumed and used as follows: red, for luck and protection; yellow, for money; blue, (always colored with copperas), for protection and friends.

32. Roots and Herbs are used freely under widespread names:

    Big John the Conqueror.

    Little John the Conqueror. It is also put in Notre Dame Water or Waterloo in order to win.

    World-wonder Root. It is used in treasure-hunts. Bury a piece in the four corners of the field; also hide it in the four corners of your house to keep things in your favor.

    Ruler's Root. Used as above.

    Rattlesnake Root.

    Dragon's Blood (red root fibres). Crushed. Used for many purposes.

    Valerian Root. Put a piece in your pillow to quiet nerves.

    Adam and Eve Roots (paid). Sew together in bag and carry on person for protection.

    Five-fingered grass. Used to uncross. Make tea, strain it and bathe in it nine times.

    Waste Away Tea. Same as above.

33. Pictures of Saints, etc., are used also.

    St. Michael, the Archangel. To Conquer.

    St. Expedite. For quick work.

    St. Mary. For cure in sickness.

    St. Joseph with infant Jesus. To get job.

    St. Peter without the key. For success.

    St. Peter with the key. For great and speedy success.

    St. Anthony de Padua. For luck.

    St. Mary Magdalene. For luck in love (for women).

    Sacred Heart of Jesus. For organic diseases.

34. Crosses. For luck.

35. Scapular. For protection.

36. Medals. For success.

37. Candles are used with set meanings for the different colors. They are often very large, one candle costing as much as six dollars.

    White. For peace and to uncross and for weddings.

    Red. For victory.

    Pink. For love (some say for drawing success).

    Green. To drive off (some say for success).

    Blue. For success and protection (for causing death also).

    Yellow. For money.

    Brown. For drawing money and people.

    Lavender. To cause harm (to induce triumph also).

    Black. Always for evil or death.

    Valive candles. For making Novenas.

38. The Bible. All hold that the Bible is the great conjure book in the world. Moses is honored as the greatest conjurer. "The names he knowed to call God by was what give him the power to conquer Pharaoh and divide the Red Sea."

IV
PRESCRIPTIONS OF ROOT DOCTORS

Folk medicine is practiced by a great number of persons. On the "jobs," that is, in the sawmill camps, the turpentine stills, mining camps and among the lowly generally, doctors are not generally called to prescribe for illnesses, certainly, nor for the social diseases. Nearly all of the conjure doctors practice "roots," but some of the root doctors are not hoodoo doctors. One of these latter at Boga-loosa, Louisiana, and one at Bartow, Florida, enjoy a huge patron-age. They make medicine only, and white and colored swarm about them claiming cures.

The following are some prescriptions gathered here and there in Florida, Alabama and Louisiana:

GONORRHEA

a. Fifty cents of iodide potash in two quarts of water. Boil down to one quart. Add two teaspoons of Epsom salts. Take a big swallow three times a day.

b. Fifty cents iodide potash to one quart sarsaparilla. Take three teaspoons three times a day in water.

c. A good handful of May pop roots; one pint ribbon cane syrup; one-half plug of Brown's Mule tobacco cut up. Add fifty cents iodide potash. Take this three times a day as a tonic.

d. Parch egg shells and drink the tea.

e. For Running Range (Claps): Take blackberry root, sheep weed, boil together. Put a little blueing in (a pinch) and a pinch of laundry soap. Put all this in a quart of water. Take one-half glass three times a day and drink one-half glass of water behind it.

f. One quart water, one handful of blackberry root, one pinch of alum, one pinch of yellow soap. Boil together. Put in last nine drops of turpentine. Drink it for water until it goes through the bladder.

SYPHILIS

a. Ashes of one good cigar, fifteen cents worth of blue ointment. Mix and put on the sores.

b. Get the heart of a rotten log and powder it fine. Tie it up in a muslin cloth. Wash the sores with good castile soap and powder them with the wood dust.

c. When there are blue-balls (buboes), smear the swellings with mashed up granddaddies (daddy-long-legs) and it will bring them to a head.

d. Take a gum ball, cigar, soda and rice. Burn the gum ball and cigar and parch the rice. Powder it and sift and mix with vaseline. It is ready for use.

e. Boil red oak bark, palmetto root, fig root, two pinches of alum, nine drops of turpentine, two quarts of water together to one quart. Take one-half cup at a time. (Use no other water.)

FOR BLADDER TROUBLE

One pint of boiling water, two tablespoons of flaxseed, two tablespoons of cream of tartar. Drink one-half glass in the morning and one-half at night.

FISTULA

Sweet gum bark and mullen cooked down with lard. Make a salve.

RHEUMATISM

Take mullen leaves (five or six) and steep in one quart of water. Drink three to four wine glasses a day.

SWELLING

Oil of white rose (fifteen cents), oil of lavender (fifteen cents), Jockey Club (fifteen cents), Japanese honeysuckle (fifteen cents). Rub.

FOR BLINDNESS

a. Slate dust and pulverized sugar. Blow it in the eyes. (It must be finely pulverized to remove film.)

b. Get somebody to catch a catfish. Get the gall and put it in a bottle. Drop one drop in each eye. Cut the skin off. It gives the sight a free look.

LOCK-JAW

a. Draw out the nail. Beat the wound and squeeze out all the blood possible. Then take a piece of fat bacon, some tobacco and a penny and tie it on the wound.

b. Draw out the nail and drive it in a green tree on the sunrise side, and the place will heal.

FLOODING[1]

One grated nutmeg, pinch of alum in a quart of water (cooked). Take one-half glass three times daily.

SICK AT STOMACH

Make a tea of parched rice and bay leaves (six). Give a cup at a time. Drink no other water.

LIVE THINGS IN STOMACH (FITS)

Take a silver quarter with a woman's head on it. Stand her on her head and file it in one-half cup of sweet milk. Add nine parts of garlic. Boil and give to drink after straining.

MEDICINE TO PURGE

Jack of War tea, one tablespoon to a cup of water with a pinch of soda after it is ready to drink.

LOSS OF MIND

Sheep weed leaves, bay leaf, sarsaparilla root. Take the bark and cut it all up fine. Make a tea. Take one tablespoon and put in two cups of water and strain and sweeten. You drink some and give some to patient.

Put a fig leaf and poison oak in shoe. (Get fig leaves off a tree that hasn't borne fruit. Stem them so that nobody will know.)

TO MAKE A TONIC

One quart of wine, three pinches of raw rice, three dusts of cinnamon (about one heaping teaspoon), five small pieces of the hull of pomegranate about the size of a fingernail, five tablespoons of sugar. Let it come to a boil, set one-half hour and strain. Dose: one tablespoon.

(When the pomegranate is in season, gather all the hulls you can for use at other times in the year.)

POISONS

There are few instances of actual poisoning. When a conjure doctor tells one of his patients, "Youse poisoned nearly to death," he does not necessarily mean that poison has been swallowed. He might mean that, but the instances are rare. He names that something has

[1]Menstruation.

been put down for the patient. He may be: (1) "buried in the grave-yard"; (2) "throwed in de river"; (3) "nailed up in a tree"; (4) put into a snake, rabbit, frog or chicken; (5) just buried in his own yard; (6) or hung up and punished. Juice of the nightshade, extract of polk root, and juice of the milkweed have been used as vegetable poisons, and poisonous spiders and powdered worms and insects are used as animal poisons. I have heard of one case of the poison sac of the rattlesnake being placed in the water pail of an enemy. But this sort of poisoning is rare.

It is firmly held in such cases that doctor's medicine can do the patient no good. What he needs is a "two-headed" doctor, that is, the conjure man. In some cases the hoodoo man does effect a cure where the physician fails because he has faith working with him. Often the patient is organically sound. He is afraid that he has been "fixed," and there is nothing that a medical doctor can do to remove that fear. Besides, some poisons of a low order, like decomposed reptiles and the like, are not listed in the American pharmacopoeia. The doctor would never suspect their presence and would not be prepared to treat the patient if he did.

TELL MY HORSE

Ascending the Sacred Waterfalls at Saut d'Eau

TO
CARL VAN VECHTEN
GOD'S IMAGE OF A FRIEND

Contents

APPENDIX

Illustrations

Chapter I

The Rooster's Nest

JAMAICA, British West Indies, has something else besides its mountains of majesty and its quick, green valleys. Jamaica has its moments when the land, as in St. Mary's, thrusts out its sensuous bosom to the sea. Jamaica has its "bush." That is, the island has more usable plants for medicinal and edible purposes than any other spot on earth. Jamaica has its Norman W. Manley, that brilliant young barrister who looks like the younger Pitt in yellow skin, and who can do as much with a jury as Darrow or Leibowitz ever did. The island has its craze among the peasants known as Pocomania, which looks as if it might be translated into "a little crazy." But Brother Levi says it means "something out of nothing." It is important to a great number of people in Jamaica, so perhaps we ought to peep in on it a while.

The two greatest leaders of the cult in Jamaica are Mother Saul, who is the most regal woman since Sheba went to see Solomon, and Brother Levi, who is a scrontous-looking man himself.

Brother Levi said that this cult all started in a joke but worked on into something important. It was "dry" Pocomania when it began. Then it got "spirit" in it and "wet." What with the music and the barbaric rituals, I became interested and took up around the place. I witnessed a wonderful ceremony with candles. I asked Brother Levi why this ceremony and he said, "We hold candle march after Joseph. Joseph came from cave where Christ was born in the manger with a candle. He was walking before Mary and her baby. You know Christ was not born in the manger. Mary and Joseph were too afraid for that. He was born in a cave and He never came out until He was six months old. The three wise men see the star but they can't find Him because He is hid in cave. When they can't find Him after six months, they make a magic ceremony and the angel come tell Joseph the men wanted to see Him.

That day was called 'Christ must day' because it means 'Christ must find today,' so we have Christmas day, but the majority of people are ignorant. They think Him born that day."

I went to the various "tables" set in Pocomania, which boils down to a mixture of African obeah and christianity enlivened by very beautiful singing. I went to a "Sun Dial"—that is a ceremony around the clock (24 hours long). The place was decorated from the gate in, with braided palm fronds and quacca bush. Inside the temple, the wall behind the altar was papered with newspapers.

There, the ceremony was in the open air. A long table covered with white. Under this table, on the ground, lighted candles to attract the spirits. There was a mysterious bottle which guaranteed "the spirit come." The Shepherd entered followed by the Sword Boy, carrying a wooden sword. After him came the Symbol Boy with a cross, chanting. Then came the Unter Boy with a supple jack, a switch very much like a rattan cane in his hand. During the ceremony he flogged those who were "not in spirit" that is, those who sat still. They are said to "cramp" the others who are in spirit. The Governess followed the Unter Boy. She has charge of all the women, but otherwise she functions something like the Mambo of Haiti. She aids the Shepherd and generally fires the meeting by leading the songs and whipping up the crowd. There followed then the Shepherd Boy who is the "armor-bearer" to the Shepherd.

Their ceremony is exciting at times with singing, marching, baptisms at sacred pools in the yard. Miraculous "cures" (Mother Saul actually sat down upon a screaming Chinese boy to cure him of insanity); and the dancing about the tables with that tremendous exhalation of the breath to set the rhythm. That is the most characteristic thing of the whole ceremony. That dancing about the lighted candle pattern on the ground and that way of making a rhythmic instrument of the breathing apparatus—such is Pocomania, but what I have discussed certainly is not all of it.

These "Balm yards" are deep in the lives of the Jamaican peasants. A Balm Yard is a place where they give baths, and the people who operate these yards are to their followers both doctor and priest. Sometimes he or she diagnoses a case as a natural ailment, and a bath or series of baths in infusions of secret plants is prescribed. More often the diagnosis is that the patient has been "hurt" by a duppy, and the bath is given to drive the spirit off. The Balm Yard with a reputation is never lacking for business. These anonymous rulers of the common people have decreed certain rules and regulations for events in life that are rigidly adhered to. For instance the customs about birth and death. The childbed and the person of the newborn baby must be protected from the dead by marks made with bluing. When it is moved from this room, the open Bible must precede it to keep off the duppies, and so on.

Tables are usually set because something for which a ceremony has been performed is accomplished. The grateful recipient of favor from the gods then sets a table of thanksgiving. No one except the heads of the Balm Yard and the supplicants are told what it is for. Most of the country products are served with plenty of raw rum. The first and most important thing is a small piece of bread in a small glass of water as a symbol of plenty.

And then Jamaica has its social viewpoints and stratifications which influence so seriously its economic direction.

Jamaica is the land where the rooster lays an egg. Jamaica is two per cent white and the other ninety-eight per cent all degrees of mixture between white and black, and that is where the rooster's nest comes in. Being an English colony, it is very British. Colonies always do imitate the mother country more or less. For instance some Americans are still aping the English as best they can even though they have had one hundred and fifty years in which to recover.

So in Jamaica it is the aim of everybody to talk English, act English and *look* English. And that last specification is where the greatest difficulties arise. It is not so difficult to put a coat of European culture over African culture, but it is next to impossible to lay a European face over an African face in the same generation. So everybody who has any hope at all is looking out for the next generation and so on. The color line in Jamaica between the white Englishman and the blacks is not as sharply drawn as between the mulattoes and the blacks.

To avoid the consequences of posterity the mulattoes give the blacks a first class letting alone. There is a frantic stampede white-ward to escape from Jamaica's black mass. Under ordinary circumstances the trend would be towards the majority group, of course. But one must remember that Jamaica has slavery in her past and it takes many generations for the slave derivatives to get over their awe for the master-kind. Then there is the colonial attitude. Add to that the negro's natural aptitude for imitation and you have Jamaica.

In some cases the parents of these mulattoes have been properly married, but most often that is not the case. The mixed-blood bears the name with the bar sinister. However, the mulatto has prestige, no matter how he happened to come by his light skin. And the system of honoring or esteeming his approach to the Caucasian state is so elaborate that first, second, third and fourth degrees of illegitimacy are honored in order of their nearness to the source of whiteness. Sometimes it is so far fetched, that one is reminded of that line from "Of Thee I Sing," where the French Ambassador boasts, "She is the illegitimate daughter of the illegitimate son of the illegitimate nephew of the great Napoleon." In Jamaica just substitute the word Englishman for Napoleon and you have the situation.

Perhaps the Jamaican mixed bloods are logical and right, perhaps the only answer to the question of what is to become of the negro in the Western world is that he must be absorbed by the whites. Frederick Douglass thought so. If he was right, then the strategy of the American Negro is all wrong, that is, the attempt to achieve a position equal to the white population in every way but each race to maintain its separate identity. Perhaps we should strike our camps and make use of the cover of night and execute a masterly retreat under white skins. If that is what must be, then any way at all of getting more whiteness among us is a step in the right direction. I do not pretend to know what is wise and best. The situation presents a curious spectacle to the eyes of an American Negro. It is as if one stepped back to the days of slavery or the generation immediately after surrender when negroes had little else to boast of except a left-hand kinship with the master, and the privileges that usually went with it of being house servants instead of field hands. Then, as in Jamaica at present, no shame was attached to a child born "in a carriage with no top." But the pendulum has swung away over to the other side of our American clock. Even in His Majesty's colony it may work out to everybody's satisfaction in a few hundred years, if the majority of the population, which is black, can be persuaded to cease reproduction. That is the weak place in the scheme. The blacks keep on being black and reminding folk where mulattoes come from, thus conjuring up tragi-comic dramas that bedevil security of the Jamaican mixed bloods.

Everywhere else a person is white or black by birth, but it is so arranged in Jamaica that a person may be black by birth but white by proclamation. That is, he gets himself declared legally white. When I used the word black I mean in the American sense where anyone who has any colored blood at all, no matter how white the appearance, speaks of himself as black. I was told that the late John Hope, late President of Atlanta University, precipitated a panic in Kingston on his visit there in 1935, a few months before his death. He was quite white in appearance and when he landed and visited the Rockefeller Institute in Kingston and was so honored by them, the "census white" Jamaicans assumed that he was of pure white blood. A great banquet was given him at the Myrtle Bank Hotel, which is the last word in swank in Jamaica. All went well until John Hope was called upon to respond to a toast. He began his reply with, "We negroes—." Several people all but collapsed. John Hope was whiter than any of the mulattoes there who had had themselves ruled white. So that if a man as white as that called himself a negro, what about them? Consternation struck the banquet like a blight. Of course, there were real white English and American people there too, and I would have loved to have read their minds at that moment. I certainly would.

The joke about being white on the census records and colored otherwise has its curious angles. The English seem to feel that "If it makes a few of you happy and better colonials to be officially white, very well. You are white on the census rolls." The Englishman keeps on being very polite and cordial to the legal whites in public, but ignores them utterly in private and social life. And the darker negroes do not forget how they came to be white. So I wonder what really is gained by it. George Bernard Shaw on his recent tour observed this class of Jamaicans and called them "those pink people" of Jamaica.

That brings us to the matter of the rooster's nest again. When a Jamaican is born of a black woman and some English or Scotsman, the black mother is literally and figuratively kept out of sight as far as possible, but no one is allowed to forget that white father, however questionable the circumstances of birth. You hear about "My father this and my father that, and my father who was English, you know," until you get the impression that he or she *had* no mother. Black skin is so utterly condemned that the black mother is not going to be mentioned nor exhibited. You get the impression that these virile Englishmen do not require women to reproduce. They just come out to Jamaica, scratch out a nest and lay eggs that hatch out into "pink" Jamaicans.

But a new day is in sight for Jamaica. The black people of Jamaica are beginning to respect themselves. They are beginning to love their own things like their songs, their Anansi stories and proverbs and dances. Jamaican proverbs are particularly rich in philosophy, irony and humor. The following are a few in common use:

1. Rockatone at ribber bottom no know sun hot. (The person in easy circumstances cannot appreciate the sufferings of the poor.)

2. Seven year no 'nough to wash speckle off guinea hen back. (Human nature never changes.)

3. Sharp spur mek maugre horse cut caper. (The pinch of circumstances forces people to do what they thought impossible.)

4. Sickness ride horse come, take foot go away. (It is easier to get sick than it is to get well.)

5. Table napkin want to turn table cloth. (Referring to social climbing.)

6. Bull horn nebber too heavy for him head. (We always see ourselves in a favorable light.)

7. Cock roach nebber in de right befo' fowl. (The oppressor always justifies his oppression of the weak.)

8. If you want fo' lick old woman pot, you scratch him

back. (The masculine pronoun is always used for female. Use flattery and you will succeed.)

9. Do fe do make guinea nigger come a' Jamaica. (Fighting among themselves in Africa caused the negroes to be sold into slavery in America.)

10. Dog run for him character; hog run for him life. (It means nothing to you, but everything to me.)

11. Finger nebber say, "look here," him say "look dere." (People always point out the shortcomings of others but never their own.)

12. Cutacoo on man back no yerry what kim massa yerry. (The basket on a man's back does not hear what he hears.)

Up until three years ago these proverbs and everything else Jamaican have been lumped with black skins and utterly condemned.

There is Mrs. Norman W. Manley, a real Englishwoman who is capturing Jamaican form in her sculpture. Her work has strength of conception and a delicate skill in execution. Because she used native models, she has been cried down by the "census whites" who know nothing about art but know that they do not like anything dark, however great the art may be. Mrs. Manley's work belongs in New York and London and Paris. It is wasted on Kingston for the most part, but the *West Indian Review*, which is the voice of thinking Jamaica, has found her. That is a very hopeful sign. And there is the yeast of the Bailey Sisters and the Meikle Brothers and their leagues, and influences like the Quill and Ink Club which is actively inviting Jamaica's soul to come out from its hiding place. The Rooster's Nest is bound to be less glamorous in the future.

Chapter II

Curry Goat

THE VERY best place to be in all the world is St. Mary's parish, Jamaica. And the best spot in St. Mary's is Port Maria, though all of St. Mary's is fine. Old Maker put himself to a lot of trouble to make that part of the island of Jamaica, for everything there is perfect. The sea is the one true celestial blue, and the shore, the promontories, the rocks and the grass are the models for the rest of the world to take pattern after. If Jamaica is the first island of the West Indies in culture, then St. Mary's is the first parish of Jamaica. The people there are alert, keen, well-read and hospitable.

They did something for me there that has never been done for another woman. They gave me a curry goat feed. That is something utterly masculine in every detail. Even a man takes the part of a woman in the "shay shay" singing and dancing that goes on after the feed.

It was held on a Wednesday night at the house of C. I. Magnus. His bachelor quarters sat upon a hill that overlooked his large banana plantation. I heard that Dr. Leslie, Claude Bell, Rupert Meikle and his two big, handsome brothers and Larry Coke and some others bought up all those goats that were curried for the feed. I have no way of knowing who all chipped in to buy things, but the affair was lavish.

We set out from Port Maria in Claude Bell's car, containing Claude, Dr. Leslie and I. Then Larry Coke overtook us and we ambled along until we ran into something exciting. Just around a bend in the road we came to an arch woven of palm fronds before a gate. There were other arches of the same leading back to a booth constructed in the same manner. It was not quite finished. Men were seated in the yard braiding more palm fronds. A great many people were in the yard, under the palm booth and in the house. Three women with elaborate cakes upon their heads were dancing under the arch at the gate. The cakes were of many layers and one of the cakes was decorated with a veil. The cake-bearers danced and turned under the arch, and turned and danced and sang with the others something about "Let the stranger in." This kept up until an elderly woman touched one of the dancers. Then the one who was touched whirled around gently, went inside the yard and on into the house. Another was touched and turned and she went in and then the third.

"What is going on here?" I asked Claude Bell, and he told me that this was a country wedding. That is, it was the preparation for one. Claude Bell is the Superintendent of Public Works in St. Mary's, so that everybody knows him. He went over and said that we wished to come in and the groom-to-be made us welcome. I asked how was it that they all knew at once who the groom was and they said that he would always be found out front being very proud and expansive and doing all the greeting and accepting all the compliments.

We went inside the house and saw the cakes arranged to keep their vigil for the night. A lighted candle was placed beside the main cake, and it was kept burning all that night. It did add something to the weight of the occasion to drape that bride's cake in a white lace veil and surround it with lights for a night. It made one spectator at least feel solemn about marriage. After being introduced to the shy little bride and shaking hands with the proud groom we went off after promising to come back to the wedding next day.

So on to the Magnus plantation and the curry goat feed. It was after sundown when we arrived. Already some of the others were there before us. Around a fire under a clump of mango trees, two or three Hindoos were preparing the food. Magnus was setting out several dozen quarts of the famous T. T. L. rum, considered the best in Jamaica. They told me that a feed without T. T. L. was just nothing at all. It must be served or it is no proper curry goat feed. The moon rose full and tropical white and under it I could see the musicians huddled under another clump of trees waiting until they should be told to perform.

Finally there were about thirty guests in all including some very pretty half-Chinese girls. The cooks announced and we went inside to eat. Before that everybody had found congenial companions and had wandered around the grounds warming themselves by the moonlight.

It appeared that there must be a presiding officer at a curry goat. Some wanted the very popular Larry Coke, but it seemed that more wanted the more popular Dr. Leslie, so it went that way. He sat at the head of the table and directed the fun. There was a story-telling contest, bits of song, reminiscences that were side splitting and humorous pokes and jibes at each other. All of this came along with the cock soup. This feast is so masculine that chicken soup would not be allowed. It must be soup from roosters. After the cock soup comes ram goat and rice. No nanny goat in this meal either. It is ram goat or nothing. The third spread was banana dumpling with dip-and-flash. That is, you dip your boiled banana in the suruwa sauce, flash off the surplus and take a bite. By that time the place was on fire with life. Every course was being washed down with T. T. L. Wits were marvelously sharpened; that very pretty Lucille Woung was eating out of the same spoon with J. T. Robertson; Reginald Beckford kept on trying to introduce somebody and the others always howled him down because he always got wound up and couldn't find his way out. Finally Dr. Leslie asked him why he never finished and he said "Being a banana man, I have to go around the corner before I get my target." The award for the best storyteller went to Rupert Meikle, but his brother H. O. S. Meikle ran him a close second.

The band began playing outside there in the moonlight and we ran away from the table to see it. You have to see those native Jamaica bands to hear them. They are doing almost as much dancing with the playing as they are playing. As I said before no woman appears with the players, though there is a woman's part in the dancing. That part is taken by a man especially trained for that. The whole thing is strong meat, but compelling. There is some barbaric dancing to magnificent rhythms. They played that famous Jamaican air, "Ten Pound Ten," "Donkey Want Water," "Salaam," and "Sally Brown." All strong and raw, but magnificent music and dancing. It is to be remembered that curry goat is a strong feed, so they could not have femalish music around there.

We got home in time to sleep a little before going on to the wedding the next afternoon.

The wedding was at the church and the guests all finally got there by sending one car back and forth several times.

The bride came in the last load. There were many, many delays, but finally the couple were married and everybody went back to the house for the reception.

At the house it came to me what a lot of trouble these country people were taking to create the atmosphere of romance and mystery. Here was a couple who were in late middle life, who had lived together so long that they had grown children and were just getting married. Seemingly it all should have been rather drab and matter of fact. Surely there could be no mystery and glamor left for them to find in each other. But the couple and all the district were making believe that there was. It was like sewing ruffles on fence rails. The will to make life beautiful was strong. It happens this way frequently in Jamaica. That is, many couples live together as husband and wife for a generation and then marry. They explain that they always intended to marry, but never had the money. They do not mean by that that they did not have the price of the marriage license. They mean that they did not have the money for the big wedding and all that it means. So they go on raising their children on the understanding that if and when they can afford it they will have the wedding. Sometimes, as in this case, the couple is along in years and with grown children before the money can be spared. In the meanwhile, they live and work together like any two people who have been married by the preacher.

Back at the house everything was very gay with cake and wine and banter. There was a master of ceremonies. The bride's face was covered with her veil. In fact it had never been uncovered. She was made to stand like that and the master of ceremonies received bids on who was to lift her veil first. The highest bidder got the first peep. The first man to peep had bid six shillings. I thought that that was very high for a poor man until I found that on such occasions it was agreed that the word shilling is substituted for pence. It would sound too poor to say pence. He paid his sixpence amid great applause and lifted the bride's veil and peeped and put it back in place. Then the bidding began again and kept up until the master of ceremonies put a stop to it. The bidding had gone on for some time and everyone pretended a curiosity about the youth and glamor they imagined to be hidden under the veil.

After the unveiling of the bride we left. The groom made us promise that we would be present at the "turn thanks." That is a ceremony held at the church on the Sunday after the eighth day after the wedding. Again everybody goes to the church to see the bride again in her finery. The pastor and the Justice of the Peace are there and give the happy couple a lecture on how to live together. But the bride does not wear her veil this time, she is resplendent in her "turn-thanks" hat. The couple are turning thanks for the blessing of getting married.

But we did not go to the turn-thanks. Something happened in Claude Bell's summer house that rushed me off in another direction.

The next morning after the wedding I was lounging in the summer house and looking at the sea when a young man of St. Mary's dropped in. I do not remember how we got around to it, but the subject of love came up somehow. He let it be known that he thought that women who went in for careers were just so much wasted material. American women, he contended, were destroyed by their brains. But they were only a step or two worse off than the rest of the women of the western world. He felt it was a great tragedy to look at American women whom he thought the most beautiful and vivacious women on earth, and then to think what little use they were as women. I had been reclining on my shoulderblades in a deck chair, but this statement brought me up straight. I assured him that he was talking about what he didn't know.

"Oh, yes, I do," he countered, "I was not born yesterday and my light has not been kept under a bushel, whatever that is."

"You are blaspheming, of course, but go ahead and let me see what you are driving at."

"Oh, these wisdom-wise western women, afraid of their function in life, are so tiresomely useless! We men do not need your puny brains to settle the affairs of the world. The truth is, it is yet to be proved that you have any. But some of you are clever enough to run mental pawnshops, that is you loan out a certain amount of entertainment and hospitality on

some masculine tricks and phrases and later pass them off as
your own. Being a woman is the only thing that you can do
with any real genius and you refuse to do that."

I tried to name some women of genius but I was cut short.
The man was vehement.

"You self-blinded women are like the hen who lived by a
sea-wall. She could hear the roar of the breakers but she never
flew to the top of the wall to see what it was that made the
sound. She said to herself and to all who would listen to her,
'The world is something that makes a big noise.' Having arrived at that conclusion, she thought that she had found a
great truth and was satisfied for the rest of her life. She died
without ever hopping upon the sea-wall to look and see if
there was anything to the world besides noise. She had lived
beside the biggest thing in the world and never saw it."

"So you really feel that all women are dumb, I see."

"No, not all women. Just those who think that they are the
most intelligent, as a rule. And the occidental men are stupid
for letting you ruin yourselves and the men along with you."

Of course I did not agree with him and so I gave him my
most aggravating grunt. I succeeded in snorting a bit of scorn
into it. I went on to remark that western men, especially
American men, probably knew as much about love as the next
one.

Then *he* snorted scornfully. He went on to say that the men
of the west and American men particularly knew nothing
about the function of love in the scheme of life. I cut in to
mention Bernarr McFadden. He snorted again and went on.
Even if a few did have some inkling, they did not know how
to go about it. He was very vehement about it. He said we
insulted God's intentions so grossly that it was a wonder that
western women had not given up the idea of mating and marriage altogether. But many men, and consequently women, in
Jamaica were better informed. I wanted to know how it was
that these Jamaicans had been blessed beyond all others on
this side of the big waters, and he replied that there were
oriental influences in Jamaica that had been at work for generations, so that Jamaica was prepared to teach continental
America something about love. Saying this, he left the summer house and strode towards his car which was parked in the

drive. But he could not say all that to me and then walk off like that. I caught him on the running board of his car and carried him back. When I showed a disposition to listen instead of scoffing, we had a very long talk. That is, he talked and I listened most respectfully.

Before he drove away he had told me about the specialists who prepare young girls for love. This practise is not universal in Jamaica, but it is common enough to speak of here. I asked to be shown, and he promised to use his influence in certain quarters that I might study the matter at close range. It was arranged for me to spend two weeks with one of the practitioners and learn what I could in that time. There are several of these advisors scattered about that section of Jamaica, but people not inside the circle know nothing about what is going on.

These specialists are always women. They are old women who have lived with a great deal of subtlety themselves. Having passed through the active period and become widows, or otherwise removed from active service, they are re-inducted in an advisory capacity.

The young girl who is to be married shortly or about to become the mistress of an influential man is turned over to the old woman for preparation. The wish is to bring complete innocence and complete competence together in the same girl. She is being educated for her life work under experts.

For a few days the old woman does not touch her. She is taking her pupil through the lecture stages of instruction. Among other things she is told that the consummation of love cannot properly take place in bed. Soft beds are not for love. They are comforts for the old and lack-a-daisical. Also she is told that her very position must be an invitation. When her lord and master enters the chamber she must be on the floor with only her shoulders and the soles of her feet touching the floor. It is *so* that he must find her. Not lying sluggishly in bed like an old cow, and hiding under the covers like a thief who has snatched a bit of beef from the market stall. The exact posture is demonstrated over and over again. The girl must keep on trying until she can assume it easily. In addition she is instructed at length on muscular control inside her body and out, and this also was rehearsed again and again, until it was certain that the young candidate had grasped all that was meant.

The last day has arrived. This is the day of the wedding. The old woman gives her first a "balm bath," that is a hot herb bath. Only these old women know the secret of which herbs to use to steep a virgin for marriage. It is intended, this bath is, to remove everything mental, spiritual and physical that might work against a happy mating. No soap is used at this point. It is a medicinal sweating tub to open the pores and stimulate the candidate generally. Immediately that the virgin leaves the bath she is covered and sweated for a long time. Then she is bathed again in soapy water.

Now the subtleties begin. Jamaica has a grass called khus khus. The sweet scent from its roots is the very odor of seduction. Days before the old woman has prepared an extract from these roots in oil and it is at hand in a bowl. She begins and massages the girl from head to foot with this fragrant unction. The toes, the fingers, the thighs, and there is a special motional treatment for every part of the body. It seemed to me that the breasts alone were ignored. But when the body massage is over, she returns to the breasts. These are bathed several times in warm water in which something special had been steeped. After that they are massaged every so lightly with the very tips of the fingers dipped in khus khus. This fingertip motion is circular and moves ever towards the nipple. Arriving there, it begins over and over again. Finally the breasts are cupped and the nipples flicked with a warm feather back and forth, back and forth until there was a reaction to stimulation. The breasts stiffened and pouted, while the rest of the body relaxed.

But the old woman is not through. She carries this same light-fingered manipulation down the body and the girl swoons. She is revived by a mere sip of rum in which a single leaf of ganga has been steeped. Ganga is that "wisdom weed" which has been brought from the banks of the sacred Ganges to Jamaica. The girl revives and the massage continues. She swoons again and is revived. But she is not aware of the work-a-day world. She is in a twilight state of awareness, cushioned on a cloud of love thoughts.

Now the old woman talks to her again. It is a brief summation of all that has been said and done for the past week.

"You feel that you are sick now but that is because the reason for which you were made has not been fulfilled. You cannot be happy nor complete until that has happened. But the success of everything is with you. You have the happiest duty of any creature on earth and you must perform it well. The whole duty of a woman is love and comfort. You were never intended for anything else. You are made for love and comfort. Think of yourself in that way and no other. If you do as I teach you, heaven is with you and the man who is taking you to his house to love and comfort him. He is taking you there for that reason and for no other. That is all that men ever want women for, love and softness and peace, and you must not fail him."

The old instructor ran over physical points briefly again. She stressed the point that there must be no fear. If the girl experienced any pain, then she had failed to learn what she had been taught with so much comfort and repetition. *There was nothing to fear.* Love killed no one. Rather it made them beautiful and happy. She said this over and over again.

Still stressing relaxed muscles, the old woman took a broad white band of cloth and wound it tightly about the loins of the girl well below the navel. She circled the body with the band perhaps four times and then secured it with safety pins. It was wound very tightly and seemed useless at first. All the time that this was being done the girl was crying to be taken to her future husband. The old woman seemingly ignored her and massaged her here and there briefly.

They began to put her wedding clothes upon the girl. The old woman was almost whispering to her that she was the most important part of all creation, and that she must accept her role gladly. She must not make war on her destiny and creation. The impatient girl was finally robed for her wedding and she was led out of the room to face the public and her man. But here went no frightened, shaking figure under a veil. No nerve-racked female behaving as if she approached her doom. This young, young thing went forth with the assurance of infinity. And she had such eagerness in her as she went!

Chapter III
Hunting the Wild Hog

IF YOU GO to Jamaica you are going to want to visit the Maroons at Accompong. They are under the present rule of Colonel Rowe, who is an intelligent, cheerful man. But I warn you in advance not to ride his wall-eyed, pot-bellied mule. He sent her to meet me at the end of the railroad line so that I would not have to climb that last high peak on foot. That was very kind of Colonel Rowe, and I appreciate his hospitality, but that mule of his just did not fall in with the scheme somehow. The only thing that kept her from throwing me, was the fact that I fell off first. And the only thing that kept her from kicking me, biting me and trampling me under foot after I fell off was the speed with which I got out of the way after the fall. I think she meant to chase me straight up that mountain afterwards, but one of Colonel Rowe's boys grabbed her bridle and held her while I withdrew. She was so provoked when she saw me escaping, that she reared and pitched till the saddle and everything else fell off except the halter. Maybe it was that snappy orange-colored four-in-hand tie that I was wearing that put her against me. I hate to think it was my face. Whatever it was, she started to rolling her pop-eyes at me as soon as I approached her. One thing I will say for her, she was not deceitful. She never pretended to like me. I got upon her back without the least bit of co-operation from her. She was against it from the start and let me know. I was the one who felt we might be sisters under the skin. She corrected all of that about a half mile down the trail and so I had to climb that mountain into Accompong on my own two legs.

The thing that struck me forcefully was the feeling of great age about the place. Standing on that old parade ground, which is now a cricket field, I could feel the dead generations crowding me. Here was the oldest settlement of freedmen in the Western world, no doubt. Men who had thrown off the bands of slavery by their own courage and ingenuity. The courage and daring of the Maroons strike like a purple beam across the history of Jamaica. And yet as I stood there looking into the sea beyond Black river from the mountains of St. Catherine, and looking at the thatched huts close at hand, I could not help remembering that a whole civilization and the mightiest nation on earth had grown up on the mainland since the first runaway slave had taken refuge in these mountains. They were here before the Pilgrims landed on the bleak shores of Massachusetts. Now, Massachusetts had stretched from the Atlantic to the Pacific and Accompong had remained itself.

I settled down at the house of Colonel Rowe to stay a while. I knew that he wondered about me—why I had come there and what I wanted. I never told him. He told me how Dr. Herskovits had been there and passed a night with him; how some one else had spent three weeks to study their dances and how much money they had spent in doing this. I kept on day by day saying nothing as to why I had come. He offered to stage a dance for me also. I thanked him, but declined. I did not tell him that I was too old a hand at collecting to fall for staged-dance affairs. If I do not see a dance or a ceremony in its natural setting and sequence, I do not bother. Self-experience has taught me that those staged affairs are never the same as the real thing. I had been told by some of the Maroons that their big dance, and only real one, came on January 6th. That was when they went out to the wooded peaks the day before and came back with individual masques and costumes upon them. They are summoned from their night long retreat by the Abeng, or Conk-shell. Then there is a day of Afro-Karamante' dancing and singing, and feasting on jerked pork.

What I was actually doing was making general observations. I wanted to see what the Maroons were like, really. Since they are a self-governing body, I wanted to see how they felt about education, transportation, public health and democracy. I wanted to see their culture and art expressions and knew that if I asked for anything especially, I would get something out of context. I had heard a great deal about their primitive medicines and wanted to know about that. I was interested in vegetable poisons and their antidote. So I just sat around and waited.

There are other Maroon settlements besides Accompong, but England made treaty with Accompong only. There are now about a thousand people there and Colonel Rowe governs the town according to Maroon law and custom. The whole thing is very primitive, but he told me he wished to bring things up to date. There is a great deal of lethargy, however, and utter unconsciousness of what is going on in the world outside.

For instance, there was not a stove in all Accompong. The cooking, ironing and whatever else is done, is done over an open fire with the women squatting on their haunches inhaling the smoke. I told Rowe that he ought to buy a stove himself to show the others what to do. He said he could not afford one. Stoves are not customary in Jamaica outside of good homes in the cities anyway. They are imported luxuries. I recognized that and took another tack. We would build one! I designed an affair to be made of rock and cement and Colonel Rowe and some men he gathered undertook to make it. We sent out to the city and bought some sheet tin for the stove pipe and the pot-holes. I measured the bottoms of the pots and designed a hole to fit each of the three. The center hole was for the great iron pot, and then there were two other holes of different sizes. Colonel Rowe had some lime there, and he sent his son and grandchildren out to collect more rocks. His son-in-law-to-be mixed the clay and lime and in a day the furnace-like stove was built. The kitchen house lacking a floor anyway, the stove was built clear across one side of the room so that there was room on top of it for pots and pans not in use. The pot-holes were lined with tin so that the pots would not break the mortar. Then we left it a day to dry. We were really joyful when we fired it the next day and found out that it worked. Many of the Maroons came down to look at the miracle. There were pots boiling on the fire; no smoke in the room, but a great column of black smoke shooting out of the stove pipe which stuck out of the side of the house.

In the building of the stove I came to know little Tom, the Colonel's grandson. He is a most lovable and pathetic little figure. He is built very sturdy and is over strong for his age. He lives at the house of his grandfather because he has no mother and his father will not work for himself, let alone for his son. He is not only lazy and shiftless, he is disloyal to Colonel Rowe who has wasted a great deal of money on him. Little Tom is there among more favored grandchildren and his life is wretched. The others may strike him, kick him, I even saw one of them burn him without being punished for it. He is fed last and least and is punished severely for showing any resentment towards the treatment he gets from his cousins. They are the children of the Colonel's favorite child, his youngest daughter, and she is there to watch and see that her three darlings are not in any way annoyed by Tom. He was so warmed by the little comfort he got out of me that I wished very much to adopt him. He is just full of love and goodwill and nowhere to use it. It was most pointedly scorned when he offered it. When I asked why all this cruelty to such a small child, they answered with that excuse of all cruel people, "He is a very bad child. He has criminal tendencies. If we do not treat him harshly he will grow up to be nothing but a brute." So they abuse him and beat him and scorn him for his future good.

It was not long before I noticed people who were not Maroons climbing the mountain road past the Colonel's gate. I found that they were coming to Accompong for treatment. Colonel Rowe began to tell me about it and soon after that I met the chief medicine man. Colonel Rowe told me he was a liar and over ambitious politically, but that he really knew his business as a primitive doctor. Later I found that to be true. He was a wonderful doctor, but he wanted to be the chief. At one time he had seized the treaty that was signed long ago between England and the Maroons and attempted to make himself the chief. This had failed and he was still not too sincere in his dealings with Colonel Rowe, but their outward relations were friendly enough. So he took to coming around to talk with me.

First we talked about things that are generally talked about in Jamaica. Brother Anansi, the Spider, that great culture hero of West Africa who is personated in Haiti by Ti Malice and in the United States by Brer Rabbit. About duppies and how and where they existed, and how to detect them. I learned that they lived mostly in silk-cotton trees and in almond trees.

One should never plant either of those trees too close to the house because the duppies will live in them and "throw heat" on the people as they come and go about the house. One can tell when a duppy is near by the feeling of heat and the swelling of the head. A duppy can swell one's head to a huge thing just by being near. But if one drinks tea from that branch of the snake weed family known as Spirit Weed, duppies can't touch you. You can walk into a room where all kinds of evil and duppies are and be perfectly safe.

The Whooping Boy came up. Some say that the Whooping Boy is the great ghost of a "penner" (a Cow-herd). He can be seen and heard only in August. Then he can be heard at a great distance whooping, cracking his whip and "penning" his ghost cows. He frightens real cows when he "pauses" (cracks) his whip.

The Three-leg-Horse manifests himself just before Christmas, a woman said that "him drag hearse when him was alive." (He was used to pull a hearse when he was alive) and that he did not appear until one in the morning. From then until four o'clock he ranged the highways and might attack a wayfarer if he chanced to meet one. If he chases you, you can only escape by running under a fence. If you climb over it, he will jump the fence after you.

But the men all looked at each other and laughed. They denied that the Three-leg-Horse ever hurt any one. Girls they said, were afraid of it, but it was not dangerous. He appeared around Christmas time to enjoy himself. When the country people masque with the horse head and cow head for the parades, the three-legged-Horse wrapped himself up in a sheet and went along with them in disguise. But if one looked close he could be distinguished from the people in masques, because he was two legs in front and one behind. His gait is a jump and a leap that sounds "Te-coom-tum! Te-coom-tum!" In some parts of Jamaica he is called "The Three-legged Aurelia," and they, the people, dance in the road with the expectation that the spirit horse will come before seven o'clock at night, and pass the night revelling in masquerade. Two main singers and dancers lead the rest in this outdoor ceremony and it is all quite happy.

All in all from what I heard, I have the strong belief that the

Three-legged-Horse is a sex symbol and that the celebration
of it is a fragment of some West African puberty ceremony for
boys. All the women feared it. They had all been told to fear
it. But none of the men were afraid at all. Perhaps under those
masques and robes of the male revellers is some culture secret
worth knowing. But it was quite certain that my sex barred
me from getting anything more than the other women knew.
(I found the "Société Trois-jambe" in Haiti also but could
learn nothing definite of its inner meaning.)

But the Rolling-Calf is the most celebrated of all the appa-
ritions in Jamaica. His two great eyes are balls of fire, he
moves like lightning and "he has no abiding city." He wan-
ders all over Jamaica. The Rolling-Calf is a plague put upon
the earth to trouble people, and he will always be here. He
keeps chiefly to the country parts and comes whirling down
hills to the terror of the wayfarer. But the biggest harm that
he does is to spoil the shape of the female dog. He harms the
dog; she squeals and the owner goes into the yard and sees
nothing but a flame of fire vanishing in the distance. The
dog's shape is ruined, and she will never have puppies again.
Rolling-Calf can be seen most any moonlight night roving
the lanes of the countryside.

After a night or two of talk, the medicine man began to
talk about his profession and soon I was a spectator while he
practised his arts. I learned of the terrors and benefits of Cow-
itch and of that potent plant known as Madame Fate. "It is a
cruel weed," he told me, and I found he had understated its
powers. I saw him working with the Cassada bean, the Sleep-
and-Wake, Horse Bath and Marjo Bitters. Boil five leaves of
Horse Bath and drink it with a pinch of salt and your kidneys
are cleaned out magnificently. Boil six leaves and drink it and
you will die. Marjo Bitter is a vine that grows on rocks. Take a
length from your elbow to your wrist and make a tea and it is
a most excellent medicine. Boil a length to the palm of your
hand and you are violently poisoned. He used the bark of a
tree called Jessamy, well boiled for a purgative. Twelve minutes after drinking the wine glass of medicine the purge begins and keeps up for five days without weakening the patient
or griping.

I went with him to visit the "God wood" tree (Birch

Gum). It is called "God Wood" because it is the first tree that ever was made. It is the original tree of good and evil. He had a covenant with that tree on the sunny side. We went there more than once. One day we went there to prevent the enemies of the medicine man from harming him. He took a strong nail and a hammer with him and drove the nail into the tree up to the head with three strokes; dropped the hammer and walked away rapidly without looking back. Later on, he sent me back to fetch the hammer to him.

He proved to me that all you need to do to poison a person and leave them horribly swollen was to touch a chip of this tree to their skin while they were sweating. It was uncanny.

We went to see a girl sick in bed. The medicine man was not in high favor with the mother; but Accompong is self-sufficient. They keep to their primitive medicine particularly. He went in and looked down on the sick girl and said that it was a desperate case, but he could cure her. But first the mother must chop down the papaya tree that was growing just outside of the bed-room window. The mother objected. That was the only tree that she had and that she needed the fruit for food. The medicine man said that she *must* cut it down. It was too close to the house to begin with. It sapped the strength of the inmates. And it was a tall tree, taller than the house and she ought to know that if a paw paw or papaya tree were allowed to grow taller than the house, that somebody would die. The mother hooted that off. That tree had nothing to do with the sickness of her daughter. If he did not know what to do for her, let him say so and go on about his business and she would call in someone else. If he knew what to do, get busy and stop wasting time on the paw paw tree.

Day by day the young woman grew weaker in spite of all that was done for her. Finally she called her mother to the bed and said, "Mama, cut the tree for me, please."

"I will do anything to make you well again, daughter, but cutting that tree is so unnecessary. It is nothing but a belief of ignorant people. Why must I cut down the tree that gives us so much food?"

Several times a day, now the girl begged her mother to cut

the tree. She said if she were strong enough she would find the machete and chop it down herself. She cried all the time and followed her mother with her eyes pleading.

"Mama, I am weaker today than I was yesterday. Mama, please chop down the tree. Since I was a baby I have heard that the paw paw was an unlucky tree."

"And ever since you were a baby you have been eating the fruit," the mother retorted. "I spend every ha' penny I can find to make you well, and now you want me to do a foolish thing like killing my tree. No!"

"Mama if it is cut I will live. If you don't cut it I will die."

The girl grew weaker and finally died. The grief stricken mother rushed outside with the machete and chopped down the tree. It was lying in the yard full of withered leaves and fruit when the girl was buried. But even then the woman was not completely convinced. She thinks often that it might have been coincidence. I passed her house on my way to visit the daughter of Esau Rowe, who is the brother of the Colonel. The mourning mother was looking down at the great mass of withered fruit when I spoke to her. She did not exactly ask me for a little money, but she opened the way for me to offer it. I gave her three shillings with the utmost joy because I knew she needed it.

"Thank you," she said half choked with tears. "My girl is dead. I-I don't know—" she looked down at the tree, "I don't know if it was I who could have saved her. I wish I could know. Have you noticed how hungry a person can be the next day after a funeral? But I don't suppose you could know about such things at all."

One night Colonel Rowe, Medicine Man and I sat on what is going to be a porch when the Colonel finds enough money to finish it, looking down on the world and talking. The tree frogs on the mountainside opposite were keeping up a fearful din. Colonel Rowe said it was a sign of rain. I said I hoped not, for then all Accompong would become a sea of sticky mud. I expressed the wish that the frogs shut up. Colonel Rowe said that Medicine Man could make them hush but that would have no effect upon the weather.

"He can stop those frogs over on that other peak?" I asked.

"Yes, he can stop them at will. I have seen him do it, many times."

"Can you, really?" I turned to Medicine Man.

"That is very easy to do."

"Do it for me, then. I'd like to see that done."

He stood up and turned his face toward the mountain peak opposite and made a quick motion with one hand and seemed to inhale deeply from his waist up. He held this pose stiffly for a moment, then relaxed. The millions of frogs in the trees on that uninhabited peak opposite us ceased chirping as suddenly as a lightning flash. Medicine Man sat back down and would have gone on telling me the terrible things that the milk from the stalk of the paw paw tree does to male virility, but I stopped him. I had to listen to this sudden silence for a while.

"Oh they will not sing again until I permit them," Medicine Man assured me. "They will not sing again until I pass the house of Esau on my way home. When I get there I will whistle so that you will know that I am there. Then they will commence again."

We talked on awhile about the poisonous effect of Dumb Cane and of bissy (Kola nut) as an antidote, and how to kill with horse hair and bamboo dust. I was glad, however, when Medicine Man rose to go.

"Oh you need not worry," Colonel Rowe told me, "he can do what he says."

He walked out of Colonel's tumbledown gate and began to climb the mountain in that easy way that Maroons have from a life time of mountain climbing, and grew dim in the darkness. After a few minutes we heard the whistle way up the path and like an orchestra under the conductor's baton, the frog symphony broke out. And it was certainly going on when I finally dropped off to sleep.

I kept on worrying the Colonel about jerked pig. I wanted to eat some of it. The jerked pig of the Maroons is famous beyond the seas. He explained to me that the Maroons did not jerk domestic pork. It was the flesh of the wild hog that they dressed that way. Why not kill a wild hog then, and jerk it, I wanted to know.

"Mama! That is much harder than you think. Wild hog is

very sensible creature. He does not let you kill him so easily. Besides, he lives in the Cock-Pit country and that is hard travelling even for us here who are accustomed to rocks and mountains."

"And there are not so many now as there use to be. We have killed many and then the mongoose also kill some," Medicine Man added.

"A mongoose kill a wild hog? I cannot believe it!" I exclaimed.

"Oh that mongoose, he a terrible insect," Medicine Man said. "He is very destroyfull, Mama! If the pig is on her feet she will tear that mongoose to pieces, Mama! But when she is giving birth the mongoose run there and seize the little pig as it is born and eat it. So we do not have so many wild pig now."

But I kept on talking and begging and coaxing until a hunting party was organized. A hunting party usually consists of four hunters, the dogs and the baggage boy, but this one was augmented because few of the men had much work to do at the moment, and then I was going, and women do not go on hog hunts in Accompong. If I had had more sense I would not have gone either, but you live and learn. The party was made up of Colonel Rowe, his brother Esau, Tom Colly, his two sons-in-law, his prospective son-in-law, his son who acted as baggage boy and your humble servant.

The day before, old machetes were filed down to spear heads and made razor sharp. Then they were attached to long handles and thus became spears. All of this *had* to be done the day before, especially the sharpening of all blades. If you sharpen your cutting weapons on the day of the hunt, your dogs will be killed by the hog.

We were up before dawn the day of the hunt, and with all equipment, food for several days, cooking utensils, weapons, and the like, we found our way by stealth to the graveyard. Medicine Man was to meet us there and he was true to his word. There the ancestors of all the hunters were invoked to strengthen their arms. The graves are never marked in Accompong for certain reasons, and thus if a person does not himself know the graves of his relatives there is no way of finding out. One of the men had been away in Cuba for several years and could not find his father's grave. That was considered not so good, but not too bad either. No attempt was made to guess at it for fear of waking up the wrong duppy who might do him harm. So the ceremony over, it was necessary for us to be out and gone before anyone in Accompong should speak to us. That would be the worst of luck. In fact, we were all prepared to turn back in case it happened to us. Some of us would be expected to be killed before we returned.

The baggage-boy was carrying our food which was not very heavy for the Maroons are splendid human engines. Not a fat person in all Maroon town. That comes, I suppose, from climbing mountains and a simple diet. They are lean, tough and durable. They can march, fight or work for hours on a small amount of food. The food on the hunt was corn pone, Cassada-by-me (Cassava bread), green plantain, salt, pimento and other spices to cure the hog when and if we caught him, *and* coffee. The baggage boy carried the iron skillet and the coffee pot also. The hunters carried their own guns and blades. I stumbled along with my camera and note book and a few little womanish things like comb and tooth brush and a towel.

We struck out back of the cemetery and by full sun-up we were in the Cock-Pit country. There is no need for me to try to describe the Cock-Pits. They are great gaping funnel-shaped holes in the earth that cover miles and miles of territory in this part of Jamaica. They are monstrous things that have never been explored. The rock formations are hardly believable. Mr. Astly Clerk is all for exploiting them as a tourist lure. But very few tourists have the stamina necessary to visit even one of them let alone descend into these curious, deep openings. They are monstrous.

By the time we reached the first of the Cock-Pits I was tired but I did not let on to the men. I thought that they would soon be tired too and I could get a rest without complaining. But they marched on and on. The dogs ran here and there but no hog sign. As the country became more rocky and full of holes and jags and points and loose looking boulders, I thought more and more how nice it would be to be back in Accompong.

Around noon, we halted briefly, ate and marched on. I suggested to Colonel Rowe that perhaps all the hogs had been killed already and we might be wasting our time. I let him know that I would not hold the party responsible if they killed no hogs. We had tried and now we could return with colors flying. He just looked at me and laughed. "Why," he said, "this is too soon to expect to find hog sign. Sometimes we are out four days before we even pick up the sign. If we pick up the hog sign tomorrow before night, we will have a luck."

And four more hours till sun-down!

We picked up no hog sign that day, but the men found a nest of wild bees in a tree growing out of the wall down inside a Cock-Pit. Everybody was delighted over the find. I asked them how would they get it. They tried several times to climb down to it but the wall was too sheer and the tree leaned too far out to climb into it. So Colly let himself be swung head foremost over the precipice by his heels and he was pulled up with the dripping honey combs. I had to look away. It was too much for my nerves, but no one else seemed to think anything of the feat.

While they were eating the honey, I sprawled out on a big hot rock to rest and the Colonel noticed it and ordered the men to build a hut for the night. It was near sun-down anyway.

The men took their machetes and chopped down enough branches to make a small shack and inside of an hour it was ready for use.

We found no hog sign the second day and I lost my Kodak somewhere. Maybe I threw it away. My riding boots were chafing my heels and I was sore all over. But those Maroons were fresh as daisies and swinging along singing their Karamante' songs. The favorite one means "We we are coming, oh." It says in Karamanti, "Blue Yerry, ai! Blue Yerry Gallo, Blue Yerry!"

It was near dark on the third day the dogs picked up the hog sign. No sight of him, you understand. They struck a scent and began to dash about like ferrets hungry for blood. But it was too late for even a Maroon to do anything about it.

The men built the hut dead on the trail and we settled down for the night. Esau explained that they built the hut on the trail for a purpose. He said that the wild hog is an enchanted beast. He has his habits and does not change them. He has several hiding places along one trail and works from one to the other. When he reaches the limit of his range, he is bound to double back on his trail, seeking one of his other hide-aways. He can go a long time without food but he must have water. And so if the dogs keep after him he has no time to hunt water. When there is little rain and the waterholes are dried up, he will climb the rocks and drink the water from Wild Pines (a species of orchid). But it takes time for him to find these plants. He cannot do it with dogs at his heels. The hunters must not sleep too soundly during the night as the hog will repass and they will not know it. He is very shrewd. When he gets near the camp and smells the smoke he will climb higher and pass the camp higher up the mountain and be lost before morning.

We did not sleep much that night. And I suppose it was mostly my fault that we didn't. I was inside the hut by myself for one thing and I was a little scared because the men had told me scary things about hogs. They had said that when a wild boar, harassed by the dogs and hunter turns back down the trail, you must be prepared to give him the trail or kill him. His hide was tough and unless the bullet struck squarely and in a vital spot, it might be deflected. Then the men had to go in with their knives and spears and kill or be killed. I was afraid that the men would go to sleep and the boar be upon us before we knew it. So I kept awake and kept the others awake by talking and asking questions. We could hear the dogs at a distance, barking and charging and parrying. So the night passed.

The next day the chase was really hot. About noon the party divided. Colonel Rowe with three men went ahead to catch up with the dogs and see if the hog had made a stand. Esau, Colly and Tom stayed with me. That is, they stayed back to tackle the brute in case he doubled back on his track. We heard a great deal of noise far ahead, but no sound of shots nor anything conclusive. By three o'clock, however, the sounds were coming nearer, and the men looked after their guns. Then we heard a terrific and prolonged battle and the barking of the dogs ceased.

"Sounds like he has killed the dogs," said Esau.

"Killed five dogs?" I asked.

"If he is a big one, that would not be hard for him to do," Esau said. "When he gets desperate he will kill anything that stands in his way. But he will not kill the dogs if he can get at the hunter. He knows that the hunter is his real enemy. Sometimes he will charge the dogs, and swerve so fast that the hunter is caught off guard, and attack. A man is in real danger there."

It was not long after that, that we heard deep panting. It was a long way off but it seemed upon us. There was a huge boulder over to the right and I moved nearer to it so that I might hide behind it if necessary after seeing the wild boar approach and pass. The panting came nearer. Now we could hear him trotting and dislodging small stones. The men got ready to meet the charge. The boar with his huge, curving tusks dripping with dogs' blood came charging down upon us. I had never pictured anything so huge, so fierce nor so fast. Everybody cleared the way. He had come too fast for Esau to get good aim on a vital spot.

Just around a huge rock he whirled about. He made two complete circles faster than thought and backed into a small opening in the rock. He had made his stand and resolved to fight. Only his snout was visible from where we were. The men crept closer and Esau chanced a shot. The bullet nicked his nose and the shocking power of it knocked the hog to his knees. We rushed forward, the men expecting to finish him off with the knives. At that moment he leaped up and charged the crowd. I raced back to the big rock and scrambled up. What was going on behind my back I did not know until I got on top of the rock and looked back. Tom had scurried to safety also. Colly had not quite made it. The hog had cut the muscle in the calf of his leg and he was down. But Esau rushed in and almost pressed the muzzle of his rifle against the head of the boar and fired. The hog made a half turn and fell. Esau shot him again to make sure and he scarcely twitched after that.

While we were doing the best we could for Colly, the others came. They had heard the shooting. As soon as Colly was made as comfortable as possible, the men supported him and all made a circle around the fallen boar. They shook each other's hand most solemnly across the body of the hog and kissed each other for dangers past. All this was done with the utmost gravity. Finally Colonel Rowe said, "Well, we got him. We have a luck."

Then all of the men began to cut dry wood for a big fire. When the fire began to be lively, they cut green bush of a certain kind. They put the pig into the fire on his side and covered him with green bush to sweat him so that they could scrape off the hair. When one side was thoroughly cleaned, they scraped the other side and then washed the whole to a snowy white and gutted the hog. Everything was now done in high good humor. No effort was made to save the chitterlings and hasslets which were referred to as "the fifth quarter," because there was no way to handle it on the march. All of the bones were removed, seasoned and dried over the fire so that they could be taken home. The meat was then seasoned with salt, pepper and spices and put over the fire to cook. It was such a big hog that it took nearly all night to finish cooking. It required two men to turn it over when necessary. While it was being cooked and giving off delicious odors, the men talked and told stories and sang songs. One told the story of Paul Bogle, the Jamaican hero of the war of 1797 who made such a noble fight against the British. Unable to stop the fighting until they could capture the leader, they finally appealed to their new allies, the Maroons, who some say betrayed Bogle into the hands of the English. Paul Bogle never knew how it was that he was surprised by the English in a cave and taken. He was hanged with his whole family and the war stopped.

Towards morning we ate our fill of jerked pork. It is more delicious than our barbecue. It is hard to imagine anything better than pork the way the Maroons jerk it. When we had eaten all that we could hold, the rest was packed up with the bones and we started the long trek back to Accompong. My blistered feet told me time and time again that we would never get there, but we finally did. What was left of the wild pig was given to the families and friends of the hunters. They never sell it because they say they hunt for fun. We came marching in singing the Karamante' songs.

Blue yerry, ai
Blue yerry
Blue yerry, gallo
Blue yerry!

Chapter IV
Night Song After Death

THE MOST universal ceremony in Jamaica is an African survival called "The Nine Night." Minor details vary according to parish and district, but in the main it is identical all over the island. In reality it is old African ancestor worship in fragmentary form. The West African tradition of appeasing the spirit of the dead lest they do the living a mischief.

Among the upper classes it has degenerated into something that approximates the American wake, with this one difference: when the people who attend wakes leave the house of mourning they always call out a cheerful goodbye to the family. In Jamaica any form of goodbye is taboo. Even the family and housemates, after everyone else is gone, go to their separate rooms without taking leave of each other. Then one by one the windows and doors are slowly closed in silence. The lights in the various rooms go out in the same way so that the house is gradually darkened. The dead is dismissed.

But the barefoot people, the dwellers in wattled huts, the donkey riders, are at great pains to observe every part of the ancient ceremony as it has been handed down to them. Let me speak of one that I saw in St. Thomas.

This man had died in the hospital some distance from home. He was as poor in death as he had been in life. He had walked barefooted all his days so now there would be no hearse, no car, no cart—not even a donkey to move this wretched clay. Well then, a rude stretcher was made out of a sheet and two bamboo poles and men set out on foot to bring the body home. There are always more men than donkeys.

According to custom, several people from the district went along with the body-bearers to sing along the road with the body. The rest of the district were to meet them halfway. It is a rigid rule that the whole district must participate in case of death. All kinds of bad feelings are suspended for the time being so that they sing together with the dead.

The news of his death had come to his woman near sun-

down so that many things had to be done at night that are
usually done in daylight. That is, make coffee, mix butter-
dough, provide rum and bread for the "set up." Some folks
had to stay behind to look after this.

The bearers and these folks had been gone a long time
when we others set out to meet them half way. Two or three
naked lights or flambeaux were among us but nobody felt the
need of them. A little cement bridge had been agreed upon as
the halfway mark, so we halted there to wait. Perhaps it
seemed longer than it really was because people saved up the
entertainment inside them for the time when the body would
arrive. So we were a sort of sightless, soundless, shapeless,
stillness there in the dark, wishing for life.

At last a way-off whisper began to put on flesh. In the space
of a dozen breaths the keening harmony was lapping at our
ears. Somebody among us struck matches and our naked
lights flared. The shapeless crowd-mass became individuals. A
hum seemed to rise from the ground around us and became
singing in answer to the coming singers and in welcome to
the dead.

The corpse might have been an African monarch on safari,
the way he came borne in his hammock. The two crowds
became one. Fresh shoulders eagerly took up the burden and
all voices agreed on one song. Then there was a jumbled motion that finally straightened out into some sort of a marching
order with singing. Harmony rained down on sea and shore.
The mountains of St. Thomas heaved up in the moonlessness;
the smoking flambeaux splashed the walking herd; bare feet
trod the road in soundless rhythm and the dead man rode like
a Pharaoh—his rags and his wretchedness gilded in glory.

The less fortunate of the district who for one reason or
another could not help with the singing on the road were
waiting for us at the house. The widow stood in the inner
door and cried in a ceremonial way. Her head was draped in a
bath towel in such a way that at a short distance it looked like
a shaggy white wig.

Everything that could be done was already done because
the Nanas, or old nurses of the district had charge. There
was a strong flavor of matriarchal rule about the place. Unconscious or not, an acknowledgment of the priestess ran

through it all. There was one who seemed especially to have authority over the rest. She conferred with the wife in a whisper for a moment and then ordered several women to make a shirt for the dead man out of cloth that she produced from nowhere it seemed. She turned from that to other things. But even in the midst of the much-do she had time to observe that only one woman was working on the shirt. To be sure the lone worker was most skillful with her needle, but the Nana stopped her and glared all about her at the other women.

"One woman no make shirt for dead." She accused the others with a look. "What for do?" (What can I do about it?) asked the efficient seamstress. "Them don't help me."

Everybody knew it was bad luck for only one woman to sew a garment for the dead. It exposed her to spite-work from the ghost of the departed. They were being a little lazy, that was all. But they did go to work with a will when the Nana got in behind them. "I tell you to make shirt, and you *make* shirt!" she scolded. "My word must stand for dominate." (My word must rule.)

The other nanas were washing the body. The Nana-Superior stopped them while the body was being dried with a towel. They did nothing right unless she watched them every minute, she complained. Where were the lime and the nutmeg, she demanded to know? Could a person be called ready for burial when his nose, mouth, under his arms and between his legs had not been rubbed with slices of lime and a nutmeg? Of course not! The women explained to her that lime and nutmeg had not been provided by the wife of the deceased. What could they do about it? Nana ran somebody out to pick some off of anybody's tree. The messenger was not to come back without it. The body must be prepared in the ceremonial way, and no other, Must do!

The burial was to take place in the yard as is usual among the common people of Jamaica, but the grave could not be opened until morning. So Nana sent men out to gather lumber for the coffin. Boards were bought until there was no more money. Then the rest were gifts from backyards, or just scraped up from here and there until the coffin was ready for the body.

When it came time to place the body in the coffin there was a great deal of talk back and forth. Some few said that he had been a fairly good man and that they were sure that once buried, he would not return. All the trouble of keeping the ghost, or duppy in the grave was unnecessary. But the majority were for taking no chances. Every precaution for keeping duppies in graves must be taken. So as soon as the body was placed in the coffin, the pillow with the parched peas, corn and coffee beans sewed inside it was placed under his head. Then they took stronger methods. They took four short nails and drove one in each cuff of the shirt as close to the hand as possible to hold the hands firmly in place. The heel of each sock was nailed down in the same way. Now the duppy was "nailed hand and foot."

The brother of the corpse was summoned and he spoke to the dead and said, "We nail you down hand and foot. You must stay there till judgment. If we want you we come wake you." Some salt mixed with "compellance" powder was sprinkled in the coffin and it was finally closed.

Followed activities of the set-up. The leader tracked out sankeys. (Methodist hymns.) Then he looked about him and asked, "Who is the treble?" That is, who is raising the hymns? A willing volunteer obliged and the rest of us sang. There were periods of short prayers, a little story-telling, a period of eating and the like until the last cock-crow. (5 A. M.)

Several bottles of rum were handed over to the grave-diggers early that morning and after sprinkling the ground with rum they all drank some and began digging with a will. After that, every bottle that was opened, the first drink out of it was poured into the grave for the dead. Soon the grave was opened, the parched corn and peas thrown in and the coffin lowered with proper rituals and patted to rest in the earth. The train of salt and ground coffee was laid from the grave to the house door to prevent the return of the duppy and people went on home.

A sort of wake is held every night after this until the ninth night after death, but it is understood that practically no one except the family and old friends will bother to come again until the "nine night." But all being new to me, I decided to miss nothing. So each night I came bringing some white rum for folks to talk by, I made bold to ask the reason for the nine night. With everybody helping out with detail they told me.

It all stems from the firm belief in survival after death. Or rather that there *is no death*. Activities are merely changed from one condition to the other. One old man smoking jack-ass rope tobacco said to me in explanation: "One day you see a man walking the road, the next day you come to his yard and find him dead. Him don't walk, him don't talk again. He is still and silent and does none of the things that he used to do. But you look upon him and you see that he has all the parts that the living have. Why is it that he cannot do what the living do? It is because the thing that gave power to these parts is no longer there. That is the duppy, and that is the most powerful part of any man. Everybody has evil in them, and when a man is alive, the heart and the brain controls him and he will not abandon himself to many evil things. But when the duppy leaves the body, it no longer has anything to restrain it and it will do more terrible things than any man ever dreamed of. It is not good for a duppy to stay among living folk. The duppy is much too powerful and is apt to hurt people all the time. So we make nine night to force the duppy to stay in his grave."

"Where is the duppy until nine night?" I asked. "Doesn't it stay in its grave at all until then?"

"Oh, yes. The duppy goes into the grave with the body and it stays in there the first day and the next. But the third day at midnight it rises from the grave."

The eyes of a youngish matron flew wide open. "Eh, eh!" she exclaimed, "True, sah?" (Is that true?)

"Sure, I see it myself," said the narrator.

"Eh, eh," the matron said sliding forward in her seat, "Tell, make see" (Explain it to us).

"It was when I was a pickney (small child) my uncle died and was buried in the yard. I had heard tell that the duppy rises on the third night at cock-crow, so I got up out of my bed and went into the yard on the third night after his death and climbed a big mango tree where I could see the grave. I heard the cock-crow and felt the midnight breeze. Then I saw some thick mist come from the grave and make a huge white ball that lifted itself free from the earth for a moment, then sat down on top of the grave. I was just a pickney, so I got frightened and I climbed down from the mango tree and ran into the house. The duppy, him go dream to mama (appeared to her in a dream) and tell her and she told me not to do that again. One must never spy on a duppy, because it vexes him. The duppy told mama that if I had not been a part of the family he would have hurt me."

This narrative excited everybody. They all began to tell what they knew about duppies.

"A pickney duppy is stronger than the duppy of a man," one said.

"Oh, no. A coolie duppy is stronger than all other duppies."

"No, man, a Chinee duppy is strongest of all."

"Well," the man who started it all summed up, "all duppies got power to hurt you. He can breathe on you and make you sick. If he touches you, you will have fits."

"But," somebody defended the duppies, "Duppies will never come inside your yard to hurt you unless somebody send him. It is a rude (wicked) person who set duppies on folks."

"Oh, many people are cruel, man. Some goes to the cemetery with rum and threepence and a calabash stick. They throw the rum and the money on the grave for the duppy and then they beat the grave with the calabash stick. Then they throw themselves down upon the grave and they roll on the grave and they beat it and call the duppy and tell him, 'You see what advantage so-and-so takes of me! You see how I punish (how I suffer). I want you to follow so-and-so. I want you to lick him! I want you to lick him so!' (The grave is beaten violently with the stick) And the duppy comes out of the grave and does what he is paid to do. Otherwise he would stay in his grave."

"But some duppy is rude, man. Some duppy will come even if nobody don't send call him. If he is not tied down he will come. Some duppy take a big strong chain to hold him down. I see a grave chained like that up in Manchester. They have to send to England to get a chain strong enough to tie him.

"Duppy is strong, but no matter how strong he is, he can't

come in the house if you put tobbacco seed over the door. He can't come in until he count all the seed, and duppy can't count more than nine. If you put more than ten, duppy will never come inside. The duppy counts with a jerk and when he gets to nine he wails, 'Lord, I miss!' And then he have to start all over again. He will keep that up until last cock-crow and then duppy *must* go back to his grave."

Somebody contends that duppies *can* count and do anything else if they have salt. Salt, they said, makes sense. That is why nobody gives salt to duppies because with salt, they are too strong for mortals. Somebody else shouts that that is not the reason at all. Duppies, he says do not like salt. Salt gives "temper" to mortal food and duppies are not mortal any longer so they do not need salt. When he leaves off being mortal, the duppy does not need anything to temper his vittles. Another says that salt is *not* given because salt is heavy. It holds duppies to the ground. He cannot fly and depart if he has salt. Once Africans could all fly because they never ate salt. Many of them were brought to Jamaica to be slaves, but they never were slaves. They flew back to Africa. Those who ate salt had to stay in Jamaica and be slaves, because they were too heavy to fly. A woman was positive that duppies do not like salt. She said that salt vexed duppies. If a duppy sees salt around a place he will keep away. He will run right back to his grave.

The Nana said that was true and moreover, a duppy was in bad danger if he did not get back to his grave. He positively must be there by last cock-crow. And that is how a duppy can be punished for leaving the grave to hurt people. She said that if you meet a duppy in the road and you are wearing a felt hat, take off the hat and fold it four times and sit on it and the duppy cannot come close enough to you to hurt you, and neither can he run back to his grave. He is tied until you let him go. So you can hold him from his grave until after cock-crow and make him a homeless duppy forever.

"I never heard of sitting on a hat to hold a duppy," an old man said, "so I would not trust a hat. A river stone is what will tie a duppy." There was a great groan of agreement to this. "You take two river stones. You must have one stone from the bed of the river to sit on, and one little flat river stone to place on top of your head and the duppy cannot come up to you and he cannot go back to his grave."

"True, true, that is very true," the room agreed. So the man went on.

"One worthless woman died and soon after her duppy came to harm the family in the next yard to where she use to live. The family had a daughter, and she being a very young girl, they sent her always for water. One night they sent her for water after dark. Soon she run back in the house and fell in a fit. She had many fits and foamed at the mouth."

"If they foam at the mouth, that is a sign of duppy."

"Eh, eh, that sure is duppy."

"So the father gave her salt to eat and made a cross on her forehead with chalk. Then he rubbed under her arms with garlic and she got better and was able to talk. She said that she saw the old woman who had died and the duppy came up to her and laughed in her face and threw heat on her and touched her. Then she had fits and knew nothing until she was revived. The father grew very mad when he heard this. He went outside and got two river stones to trap the duppy. He sat very still with the river-stones on his head and under him. The duppy came and saw him and tried to run back to the grave, but she could not go. Then the duppy tried to rush upon him and hurt him, but she could not do that either. So the duppy advanced, and the duppy backed up. This went on for quite a while. Then she began to plead, 'Do, Bucky Massa, let me go! Let me go back to the grave. I won't do it again! Do, Bucky Massa, please let me go!' But the man said, 'No, you worthless duppy, I'll keep you until day.' He meant to do so, but he fell asleep after awhile and the top rock fell off of his head. The duppy saw it and quick as lightning, it ran back to the grave and never came out again. Nobody ever saw that duppy again."

"But some duppies wish to stay in their graves," Nana said, "and it is a most cruel thing to wake them after they are gone. Let them rest. They don't need to come back for nothing after they are gone. God gives the duppy nine days after death to do and take with him what he wants. After that let him rest."

Then I wanted to ask a question. "You tell me that the

duppy rises on the third night after death and that he does
not depart until the ninth night. But where is he all this
time?" I asked.

"Oh, the duppy goes back and forth from the grave to his
house where he use to live. He is in the yard and he visits all
the places where he use to go. On the ninth night he goes
back to the apartment (room) where he lived last and where
he breathed his last breath and takes with him the shadow of
of everything he wants. We know that he is there, so we prepare everything for him in that dead room that he wants so
that he will go away happy and not come back and harm us.
We know that he likes singing and to see his family and
friends for the last time. The whole district comes to make
him happy so that he will rest well and not come back again."

The talk went on and on all about duppies caught in
bottles; duppies caught in pimento sticks to make a terrible
weapon; duppies sitting on beds of the sick and "throwing
heat" on them; duppies paid to throw the sick out of bed;
duppies raining showers of stones in the houses; duppies forcing men to turn around and walk with them from town to
town. So the nights ran together and made nine.

On that ninth night Joe Forsythe and I came to the familiar
yard. People stood about in small collections talking. A great
table at the far left was loaded with foodstuffs. Fried fish, rice,
rum, bread, coffee, wet sugar for the coffee, fowl, and what
not. A sizable tarpaulin had been stretched on tall poles from
one house wall. Chairs and boxes were spaced around the
edge of the covered area and boards were laid between these
to make plenty of seats. A small deal table was in the center
and a four-spouted naked light hung directly over the table.
There was a chair for the leader when the time should arrive
for him to "track out" the hymn for the rest to sing. The
beginning of everything was there, but nothing had shaped
up yet. I went inside to pay my respects to the widow.

Most of the patriarchs had already arrived and were in the
dead room. The feast for the duppy was spread. There was
white rum and white rice without salt and white fowl also
saltless. The wooden bath bowl was full of water and placed
in the center of the floor. A glass of drinking water was on the
white draped table with the food which was not in plates at

all, but spread on banana leaves. The bed was snowy white in its cleanliness.

The intimates sat and talked casually. Now and then one of the old women looked out of the door and bawled at some girl whom she considered too free with the boys. But mostly they had the air of just waiting around for something. I could hear a great hub-bub of talking from the outside and looked out to find that the yard was full of people.

Suddenly one Nana removed her clay pipe from her lips and stared pointedly at the door for a moment, then nudged her neighbor to look. She looked in the same direction and in turn nudged her neighbor. Calling-attention gestures swept the room in the silence. Everything was conveyed by gesture. The first Nana led the "seeing." Her eyes went from door to bed, from bed to bath bowl, from bath bowl to table, and all eyes followed hers. Little nodes of gratification as the duppy was observed to eat or drink, or bathe, or take the shadow of his bed and meal. Finally he was seen to take a seat to enjoy the evening. Then the leader arose and spoke to him.

"We know you come," he said with gracious courtesy. "We glad you come. Myself two times."

All others nod and murmur in agreement. The duppy is assured of a welcome in every way. "We do the best we can."

The leader went outside and took his place under the four-pronged naked light and began tracking out the songs. The "treble" raised the song. He had a dramatic falsetto with un-canny qualifications. It could not be called a good voice, but it did things to those who could sing. It seemed to search out the hidden roads to harmony so the others could find them. The night song had begun. It kept up hour after hour. The monotony varied only by the new inventions in melody and harmony on the same song.

Way late the leader cried "Sola!" That was an invitation for those who had special or favorite songs to track the verses out for the others to sing the chorus. Ten or more people were instantly tracking out. The leader gave precedence to a girl. She was a penny brown girl with high lights in her eyes. She acted out the verses of a song and raised the singing to a frenzied pitch.

Inside the room the old ones kept the duppy entertained with Anansi stories. Now and then they sang a little. A short squirt of song and then another story would come. Its syllables would behave like tambour tones under the obligato of the singing outside. It fitted together beautifully because Anansi stories are partly sung anyway. So rhythmic and musical is the Jamaican dialect that the tale drifts naturally from words to chant and from chant to song unconsciously. There was Brer Anansi and Brer Grassquit; Brer Anansi and the Chatting Pot; Brer Frog's dissatisfaction with his flat behind and Anansi's effort to teach him how to make stiffening for it. And how all the labor was lost on account of Brer Frog's boasting and ingratitude. "So Frog don't learn how to make him behind stick out like other animals. Him still have round behind with no shape because him don't know how to make the stiffening." A great burst of laughter. This is the best liked tale and it is told more than once.

Eleven o'clock arrives and "tea" is served. When this is over it is still a half hour till midnight. Plaintive tunes, mournful songs are sung now. A new and most doleful arrangement of "Lead Kindly Light" fairly drips tears. Then "Good Night" sung over and over. Finally the leader signals a halt. He then solemnly invites all the family and close friends together in the dead room to help discharge the dead.

I was signalled to come too so I went. Inside the tiny room it was very crowded and solemn. The brother of the dead man was selected to preside. He tracked out "There is rest for the Weary" and after that he prayed:

"Lord we come to send off the spirit of our dear one to thee. We know him is with thee for him is thy child and not Satan child. So him is not with Satan in Hell but with thee in Heaven. Accept him there, Lord. Don't drive him out of thy Kingdom. And whether him is gone to thee or to Satan, help we to discharge him from this house forever. The living has no right with the dead. Amen." He tracked out a sankey and then addressed the duppy directly.

"We know you come and we make you welcome. We give you white fowl; we give you rice and leave your bed for you. We leave you water and we do *everything* for you. Done!!! Go

on to your rest now and no do we no harm. We no want to
see you again. You must left and you not to come again. *No
come back!* Mind now, you come again we plant you!"

Now this closest male relative of the dead man seizes the
sheet from the bed and casts it to the floor. The mattress
follows. Eager hands help gather up the slats and take the bed
down completely. The slats are thrown to the floor with a
great clatter. The brother takes one of the slats and beats the
pile of bedding on the floor before it is taken outdoors. The
women seize the banana leaves with the food heaped on them
and throw them out of the window. The water follows. A
Nana looks at the door and nudges. They all "see" the duppy
depart. The duppy that was once a man can have no more
friendly relationship with mortals.

Instantly outside the tempo changes. They grow jubilant. A
"village lawyer" holds up his hand in restraint. "It no finish
yet! It no finish yet!"

"Yes, man, it finish. Him gone. Bed is outside."

"Then what about the chalk marks? Make I see." (Show
them to me.)

In their eagerness to begin play, some have overlooked or
forgotten this last necessity. The know-it-all takes a piece of
white chalk and with an air of importance makes a cross mark
on all the windows and doors. The recent activities inside
have driven the duppy out. The cross marks are meant to
keep him out. It is finished.

A play spirit seized the yard. Men hunted up rocks with
which to play "Dollyman." A game where fingers get crushed
and fights commence. Temporary love affairs were developing
right and left. In spite of the older women who tried to keep
an eye on the girls, there were numerous love-lit excursions
into the outer darkness. Two men with cow-cords under their
arms swaggered about very conscious of the weapon they carried. But a "bad stick" under the arm of a stocky, grim looking fellow was regarded with awe.

This was one of the far-famed "Ebolite" sticks. They are
made from pimento wood, which become "prementa" on the
lips of the peasant. A stick of pimento about a yard long is
cut. It is roasted in a fire with great skill so that the bark sheds
completely without injuring the wood beneath. A little more

roasting and the stick becomes a beautiful, dark, glistening thing. The stick is buried in a grave, a coolie grave is the preference, and allowed to remain there for two or three weeks. In this time, the duppy of the person buried there has come to live in the stick. After it is dug up it is polished and the two ends and sometimes the middle of the stick is wound with brass wire. The stick is ready for its baptism after the wire and it is given a name. This name is always feminine. It is named for some mule or horse or obeah woman. Soon everyone in the district knows this stick just as well as if it were justice of the peace. People whisper its name as if it were a person. "Me see Alice in the yard," and no man however full of rum would jostle the owner of Alice in the yard. But rum was talking thru several men there. "Red men licking a black man," is the way the one woman spoke of it.

I was standing in the swirl of all this when Joe touched my arm. "Let's go," he said.

"No, I don't want to go. Look, one man has got his fingers mashed over there at dollyman game. I think it's going to be a fight. I want to see it."

"Plenty fight, man. But I take you to see Koo-min-ah. That's the best kind of nine night. It don't happen often. It's a nine night but it don't happen until the person been dead a year and a half. The Africans do this with the Maroons. I take great trouble to fix it so you can come see. Come on. They make two 'house' tonight."

When we reached the yard where the Koo-min-ah was being held we found that we were early for the Koo-min-ah but late for a magnificent Congo. Both the drumming and the muscular subtleties were extraordinary.

Zachariah, "The Power," came forward and received me and later explained that they built the house for the duppy after he was gone eighteen months because it was not certain that the spirit had definitely settled down in his new home before then. If the house which in reality is a cement tomb were built earlier than that, it might be closed while the duppy happened to be out, and then he would become a wandering spirit.

Back of us was an elaborate palm booth. Off to one side the Maroons were jerking a pig. Close by the Africans were preparing a goat with all fragrant herbs. Four or five persons in full ceremonials appeared out of a house there in the back. The Power hurriedly left us and went into the house. The intriguing monotony of the Congo died down and people began to collect around the great booth. There is a bustle inside there but the flambeau hanging from a palm stem is not yet lighted.

The Power appears for a moment at the door and the light flares. Four men who look like African nabobs I find are the drummers, and the four less panoplied men with them are the "rackling" men. That is the men who play the triple rhythm on the back of the drum with little sticks. There are two "shuckers," the men who play the cha cha.

There under the booth are two "houses" for the dead. Between them is a wooden bath bowl which contains a large calabash full of water. That is all. I wonder about the bowl and the calabash but the time is past for asking questions, because the drummers are pounding the drumheads with hammers and turning pegs in tuning their instruments.

There is the thunder of drums subtley rubbed with bare heels, and the ferocious attack of the rackling men. The thing has begun. They are "making house for duppy." The hands of the drummers weave their magic and the drums speak of old times and old things.

A few warming-up steps by some dancers. Then a woman breaks through the dancers with a leap like a lioness emerging from cover. Just like that. She sings with gestures as she challenges the drummers, a lioness defying the tribesmen.

"Ah minnie wah oh, Ah minnie wah oh!"

And the men at the instruments reply:

"Saykay ah brah ay."

She makes some liquid movements of her upper body and cries again:

"Yekko tekko, yekko tekko, Yahm pahn sah ay!"

The men:

"Ah yah yee-ai, Ah yah yee-ai, ah say oh!"

She danced thru one furious movement and cried again:

"Yekko tekko, ah pah ahah ai!"

This whole thing was repeated many times with more singers and dancers entering into it each time. Now the scores of dancers circled the tombs. It was asymmetric dancing that yet had balance and beauty. It was certainly most compelling. There was a big movement and a little movement. The big movement was like a sunset in its scope and color. The little movement had the almost imperceptible ripple of a serpent's back. It was a cameo in dancing.

One male dancer suddenly ceases and demands rum. All the others join him. Zachariah hesitates and fools around a bit, but they insist and he produces a bottle. The oldest man among the Africans is summoned. It is the law that he must have the first drink that is poured. It is handed to him with deference. Zachariah takes the next drink himself, then the woman singer-dancer who I learn is called "The Governess." Then the drummers, then the rackling men and the shuckers, then the dancers. Lastly, these who just stand and sing. They don't really belong, so if nothing is left for them no harm is done.

The dancing begins in earnest now. The Governess is like an intoxicating spirit that whips up the crowd. Those rackling men become fiends from hell. The shuckers do a magnificent muscle dance which they tell me is African. The drums and the movements of the dancers draw so close together that the drums become people and the people become drums. The pulse of the drum is their shoulders and belly. Truly the drum is inside their bodies. More rum, more fire.

"Hand a' bowl, Knife a' throat
 Rope a' tie me, Hand a' bowl

"Hand a' bowl, Day a' light
 Wango doe, doe, Knife a' throat

"Hand a' bowl, Knife a' throat
 Want ingwalla, Fum dees ah"

Now Zachariah proved the magnificent dancer that he was. He dominated the group with his skill. The whole performance rose to a pitch. They all followed him in spirit and ferocity if not in skill. It was the goat song that was being sung. The Governess was speaking for the sacrificial one, and Zachariah was dancing the priest. Women began to "cramp."

They flung themselves about and fell quivering. It is law that they be not allowed to lie on the ground and they were instantly seized up by men and the tempo increased. Clothes were torn away unconsciously. Two or three hot, wet bodies collided with me. I saw women picked up by their buttocks, their bodies bent backwards so limply that their heads and heels trailed the ground. Their faces were bathed in rum to revive them. If it took too long, they were carried outside of the lighted circle somewhere to be revived. The drummers, the shuckers, the rackling men had played their faces into ferocious masks. Ecstatic body movements went with every throb.

Zachariah leaped over both graves, over the seated drummers, whirled his body in mid-air, fell on his back, arched his back until only his head and toes touched the ground, held the pose in trembling ecstasy for a long moment, then hurled his lower body up and seized a cramping woman with his thighs and brought her down. Somebody rushed in and broke his scissors hold and the dance went on.

Too late I saw the goat dragged up between the tombs and the knife in Zachariah's hand. In a flash he was catching the blood from its throat in a glass. There was a great pressing forward for a drop of his wonder-working blood, but the crowd was driven back. Still in motion, Zachariah took a deep drink from the glass, then allowed each drummer a little sip. "The Power" then danced with the glass and finally with a leap and a cry, hurled it as far from him as he could. Some of the crowd motioned to follow the glass and take it up, but "The Power" shook his head in warning and chanted without ceasing to dance, "Who want to take it up, take it up, but it is trouble to do so." That halted the rush instantly. Not a soul ventured to go.

After a magnificent flourish that coincided with sounds of the drums, "The Power" went into a cramp himself and sank to the ground. Nobody touched him. Then I saw the rising calabash. There before my eyes the calabash full of water rose from the bath bowl and slowly mounted to the top of the palm booth and as slowly sank again. The drums went on and on. They sang on and on.

Hand a' bowl. . . . Cocks crowing raucously. . . . Day a'
light. . . . Night took on a deathly look. . . . Want ingwalla. . . . The spirit went out of the drums. . . . Fum dee
ah. . . . The sun came up walking sideways.

Chapter V

Women in the Caribbean

IT IS a curious thing to be a woman in the Caribbean after you have been a woman in these United States. It has been said that the United States is a large collection of little nations, each having its own ways, and that is right. But the thing that binds them all together is the way they look at women, and that is right, too. The majority of men in all the states are pretty much agreed that just for being born a girl-baby you ought to have laws and privileges and pay and perquisites. And so far as being allowed to voice opinions is concerned, why, they consider that you are born with the law in your mouth, and that is not a bad arrangement either. The majority of the solid citizens strain their ears trying to find out what it is that their womenfolk want so they can strain around and try to get it for them, and that is a *very* good idea and the right way to look at things.

But now Miss America, World's champion woman, you take your promenading self down into the cobalt blue waters of the Caribbean and see what happens. You meet a lot of darkish men who make vociferous love to you, but otherwise pay you no mind. If you try to talk sense, they look at you right pitifully as if to say, "What a pity! That mouth that was made to supply some man (and why not me) with kisses, is spoiling itself asking stupidities about banana production and wages!" It is not that they try to put you in your place, no. They consider that you never had any. If they think about it at all, they think that they are removing you from MAN'S place and then granting you the privilege of receiving his caresses and otherwise ministering to his comfort when he has time to give you for such matters. Otherwise they flout your God-given right to be the most important item in the universe and assume your prerogatives themselves. The usurpers! Naturally women do not receive the same educational advantages as the men.

This sex superiority is further complicated by class and color ratings. Of course all women are inferior to all men by

God and law down there. But if a woman is wealthy, of good family and mulatto, she can overcome some of her drawbacks. But if she is of no particular family, poor and black, she is in a bad way indeed in that man's world. She had better pray to the Lord to turn her into a donkey and be done with the thing. It is assumed that God made poor black females for beasts of burden, and nobody is going to interfere with providence. Most assuredly no upper class man is going to demean himself by assisting one of them with a heavy load. If he were caught in such an act he probably would become an outcast among his kind. It is just considered down there that God made two kinds of donkeys, one kind that can talk. The black women of Jamaica load banana boats now, and the black women used to coal ships when they burned coal.

The old African custom of polygamy is rampant down there. The finer touches of keeping mistresses come from Europe, however. The privileges those men have of several families at the same time! And their wives don't like it a bit better than we do, but the whole national set-up favors him and crushes her. If one woman is protected in breaking into her husband's arrangements and regulating his pleasures, what is to hinder the others? The thing might become general and that would be a sad state of affairs! No, selfish, jealous wives must be discouraged.

Women get no bonus just for being female down there. She can do the same labors as a man or a mule and nobody thinks anything about it. In Jamaica it is a common sight to see skinny-looking but muscular black women sitting on top of a pile of rocks with a hammer making little ones out of big ones. They look so wretched with their bare black feet all gnarled and distorted from walking barefooted over rocks. The nails on their big toes thickened like a hoof from a life time of knocking against stones. All covered over with the gray dust of the road, those feet look almost saurian and repellent. Of course their clothing is meager, cheap and ugly. But they sit by the roadside on their enormous pile of rocks and crack down all day long. Often they build a slight shelter of palm leaves to protect them from the sun. The government buys the crushed rock to use in road-building and maintenance. It is said that a woman who sticks to her business with the help of a child or two can average about one dollar and a half per week. It is very hard, but women in Jamaica must eat like everywhere else. And everywhere in the Caribbean women carry a donkey's load on their heads and walk up and down mountains with it.

But the upper class women in the Caribbean have an assurance that no woman in the United States possesses. The men of her class are going to marry inside their class. They will have their love affairs and their families wherever they will or may. But seldom does one contract a marriage outside of his class. Here in the United States a man is liable to marry wherever he falls in love. The two things are tied together in his mind. But in the Caribbean it is different. Love and marriage need not be related at all. What is shocking to an American mind is that the man has no obligation to a girl outside of his class. She has no rights which he is bound to respect. What is worse, the community would be shocked if he did respect them. Fatherhood gives no upper class man the license to trample down conventions and crash lines, nor shades-of-color lines by marrying outside his class.

Here is an example of this from Jamaica. A pretty girl, but definitely brown, boarded a train to come down to Kingston to work for the United Fruit Company as a typist. A young man, a mulatto, was already on the train travelling in the same class as the girl. He was immediately attracted to the girl's lush appeal and laid siege. This went on for months after she was established in Kingston and her mother had come to join her. The girl was thrilled at his attentions even though he never took her out to meet his friends. She began to dream the impossible, that this mulatto of good family had honorable intentions towards her mama's daughter. Now then, her girl friend in whom she confided her great hope and greater love, began to tell her that rumors were about that he was engaged to a girl of his own set. The lovelorn little country bird charged him but he denied it in the most positive manner. She believed him and kept up the female game of advance and retreat to lure him into the golden circle of matrimony.

Then one Sunday night he did not call to take her for a country ride as usual. He did not come until Tuesday night.

He did not come into the house then. He stayed in the car and called her to come and go for a ride. As soon as she was in the car she said, "George, my friend says that you are going to be married. She says that the girl's mother came to borrow cake pans from my friend's mother early Monday morning, saying that you were going to marry her daughter tomorrow. Is it true?" "No, it is not true, darling, I love no one but you. Do you think I would be taking you for a drive tonight if I expected to marry someone else tomorrow?" He drove faster up into the wooded heights and away from Kingston.

Up in a safe little spot he induced her to leave the car after a struggle and possessed her. Afterwards, standing above her he said humbly, "I lied to you dear. I *am* getting married tomorrow as they told you. But I just had to have you. I could have no peace of mind for thinking of you. I had to do it tonight because tomorrow I will be married and I can not continue calling on you. Come on, get into the car. I've got to get on back to town and attend to several things for tomorrow."

And he drove like the wind to her door and never even alighted to help her, but rushed her out of the car. In the struggle before getting out of the car before her seduction she had lost one of her pumps. Evidently not wishing to leave any clues for his bride to find, he discovered the shoe a short distance from the house of the ravished girl and threw it in the road where it was found later by her friend and returned to her.

His wedding, next day, was considered one of the great social events of the year. But that is not the end. A year or two later this same man heard that the girl he had ravished was about to marry. He told the other man of his own experience with her and asked in a scornful tone, "You don't want second-hand goods, do you?" The other man did not. She is still around Kingston drinking too much and generally being careless of herself. But what becomes of her is unimportant. The honor of two men has been saved, and men's honor is important in the Caribbean.

In Haiti the law says that a woman may accuse no man of being the father of her child unless she is married to him. Thus unattached men who have been out for a few nights of pleasure need fear no embarrassment from girls who come to complain of consequences. Furthermore several intelligent Haitian women have told me that a man may marry a girl but if he wishes to do so, he can return her to her parents by saying simply, "I was not the first." Then he can vindicate his honor by getting a divorce and marry the woman he prefers. So far as the discarded bride is concerned, she has no redress. She cannot refute his statement. What could she offer as proof? The marriage would have to be consummated before the husband could have grounds for his complaint. And after that the bride is in a difficult position to make out a case for her virginity before marriage. It is barely possible that some girls, not really wanted as wives, but unattainable otherwise have been traduced out of their good names and their husband's homes at the same time after satiation. Who knows?

Take the case of Mr. A. He was a widower in his late forties. A spinster in her early thirties worked in a store very near his place of business. They fell in love and he proposed marriage. They married quietly and went to Leogane to spend their honeymoon. Leogane is a small town about twelve miles south of Port-au-Prince. During the night he accused her of having lost her virgin status and not only drove her from the bed, but he also drove her from the house. She, in this great distress of mind started out to walk back to Port-au-Prince because she had no other way of getting there, turned out penniless and barehanded the way she was. But her virtuous husband considered that she was getting off too light. He went outside himself and gathered up a band of rowdies and paid them to follow her all the way to Port-au-Prince beating drums, and dish pans and five-gallon cans, while they made announcements about the state of affairs to everyone they met. This outraged man whose honor had nearly been tampered with secured a divorce and married a sister of a well known physician in Port-au-Prince. The allegedly unvirtuous wife hid around a year or two and died. Perhaps she suffered some but then he was a man and therefore sacred and his honor must be protected even if it takes forty women to do it.

Chapter VI

Rebirth of a Nation

FOR four hundred years the blacks of Haiti had yearned for peace. For three hundred years the island was spoken of as a paradise of riches and pleasures, but that was in reference to the whites to whom the spirit of the land gave welcome. Haiti has meant spilt blood and tears for blacks. So the Haitians got no answer to their prayers. Even when they had fought and driven out the white oppressors, oppression did not cease. They sought peace under kingdoms and other ruling names. They sought it in the high, cold, beautiful mountains of the island and in the sudden small alluvial plains, but it eluded them and vanished from their hands.

A prophet could have foretold it was to come to them from another land and another people utterly unlike the Haitian people in any respect. The prophet might have said, "Your freedom from strife and your peace shall come when these symbols shall appear. There shall come a voice in the night. A new and bloody river shall pour from a man-made rock in your chief city. Then shall be a cry from the heart of Haiti—a great cry, a crescendo cry. There shall be survivors, and they shall have a look and a message. There shall be a Day and the Day shall mother a Howl, and the Howl shall be remembered in Haiti forever and nations beyond the borders shall hear it and stir. Then shall appear a Plume against the sky. It shall be a black plume against the sky which shall give fright to many at its coming, but it shall bring peace to Haiti. You who have hopes, watch for these signs. Many false prophets shall arrive who will promise you peace and faith, but they are lacking in the device of peace. Wait for the plume in the sky."

THE VOICE IN THE NIGHT

A whisper ran along the edge of the dawn. A young girl heard rifle shots spattering the darkness of a night that was holding its breath. The girl stirred in fright and went to waken her father and her family where they were, but there was no need. All Haiti was awake and listening for shots. The father ordered the family to dress in haste and questioned the girl nervously. "Your ears are younger than mine. Did it seem to you that those shots came from the direction of the palace? For if they came from the palace or *near* the palace, the people in the prison—go see if the door is secure."

The girl went to the door but instead of seeing to the fastening, she eased the door open and crept outside. A band of Cacos passed swinging machetes. There were signs on many gates announcing that foreigners occupied those houses.

"But this is a street of foreigners," said one of the Cacos to his fellows. "Let us go into a street of Haitians so that we may kill some people." The girl drew her Haitian face back into the shadows and the little band of knife-men went on the business of hunting work.

The girl crept out onto the sidewalk again straining to translate the whisper of the night. Outside the ominous pulsation of the city was more definite. The voice of the night rose higher to say what it would. This night *must* say something, the political situation was too tense to pass another day undefined, and every house in Haiti had an ear strained with fear or with hope. Behind her, Fannie heard her father find the unlatched door by his gasp of terror. Across the street she saw someone all but crawling along the sidewalk as close to the wall as possible. She found that it was the son of a neighbor around her own age. She hailed him in a whisper, and he beckoned her to cross the street to where he was. He seemed to be afraid for her.

"What are you doing outside, Fannie?"

"I heard shots, Etienne. Why are you outside tonight? It is very dangerous. I saw Cacos walking."

The boy crept close to her in the dark to give tongue to the speechless something that was reeking in the air.

"Sh-sh-Fannie; The people in the prison are dead!"

"How do you know that, Etienne?"

"A whisper came to our door. A Voice—nobody saw who spoke. But it is certain. The people in the prison are dead."

THE BLOODY RIVER

The people and the women of Port-au-Prince came to the prison that dawn morning. Winged tongues had whispered at every door, "The people in the prison are dead! Our people in the prison are dead!" A very few worried the bone of whether Jean Vilbrun Guillaume Sam was still president in the palace or a fugitive in the French Legation. But nobody listened to them talk. The collected mass said, "The people in the prison are dead." Or some said it like a question, "Are our people dead in the prison?"

Some blamed the political foes who had harried President Sam to the point where he had seized nearly two hundred men, all members of good families, and imprisoned them more as hostages for the good behavior of the leaders than as politicians suspected of plotting the overthrow of the Sam administration. Some denounced the machinations of Sam and his adherents. President Sam, they said, was a cheat and a fraud. He was a man of no honor. He had not the politesse. He had no regard for established rules of occupying the palace. He did not respect the conventions. He was a greedy and detestable criminal. He had been in the palace for five months, or nearly so. That was sufficient time for him to "assure his future," if he had been alert and intelligent about the national funds. Why then must the monster resist the efforts of other desiring men to improve their fortunes? When Sam had captured the principal cities, had not Theodore sailed away like a gentleman? Now that General Bobo had marched from the north and invested the capitol, why did Sam ignore the conventions governing the situation? Clearly the man was a greedy, stupid pig lacking in good manners. A man like that deserved no loyalty and allegiance from cultured folk. He must expect revolution. The men in the prison were heroes for having resisted him. This was the opinion of the majority. A few still felt that Sam having gained the presidency should not be deposed by violence, and that his resistance was justified. Moreover, the nation wanted peace. The people were weary of the "generals" and their endless revolutions and counter-revolution. Their greed and ambition were destroying the nation. They breathed a great prayer for Peace! But where in Haiti?

They had heard shots and the President had issued orders
to kill the political prisoners in the prison at the first shots of
the opposing forces. And now it was generally agreed that the
shots had come from the Champ de Mars and that the
President's Caco army on which he had depended, had answered weakly before it deserted the President's cause. So
now the families of the prisoners were there and they must go
into the jail. Screams and groans had been reported with
muffled shots. The families must know if the unhappy sounds
pertained to their own. Someone said that fifteen bloody men
with bloody blades had just left the jail. But Charles Oscar
Etienne, Chief military officer of the government, could not
be found to be questioned. Chocotte and Paul Herard were
inside, rumor said, but no one could enter to question them.
But dawn discovered a drain from the inside of the prison
flowing with gouts and clots of blood. The doors crashed
open before the fury of families and friends of families and
they surged to the cells of their relatives to be reassured of
their safety.

THE CRESCENDO CRY

There in the cells in huddled stillness were shot bodies and
cut bodies. Skulls crushed in by machetes' blows and bowels
ripped away by blades. Men with machetes had been ordered
to follow the rifle men. The finished youth of the three sons
of Polynice in their helplessness called out to pity and retribu-
tion. The hunks of human flesh screamed of outrage. The
blood screamed. The women screamed. The great cry went
up from the bloody cells and hung over Haiti like smoke over
a ruin. And the sun rushed up from his slot in the horizon to
listen.

THE SURVIVORS

They lifted the heaps of the dead and found a man. He
screamed and muttered and screamed. He was mad. Another
one could talk, "I heard them when they said 'fifteen men,
forward march!'" Then he whispered, "I heard Chocotte, the
adjutant say, 'fire close to the ground. A bullet in the head for
each man. Every one of the political prisoners must die. The
arrondissement's orders are that not one be left standing.

They don't know the kind of man that General Vilbrun is.' But I am still alive, am I not? The slaughter of July 27 is past and I am still alive." They led out Stephen Alexis; they led out a mad man and they led out another. These three had survived the massacre. "But where is the body of Charles Oscar Etienne?" Polynice cried. "He cannot be alive or this butchery could not have happened. He is the Chief military officer of Haiti with the care and protection of these unarmed and helpless people."

"He is the friend of Guillaume Sam," someone answered him.

"But honor lays a greater obligation than friendship; and if friendship made such a monster of a man, then it is a thing vile indeed. No, Oscar Etienne is dead. Only over his dead body could such a thing have happened. Show me the body of Etienne. Look near the bodies of my three young sons. It must be there. He could not have betrayed them out of their young lives in so wretched a manner. Look well and find the body of this honorable man who died in defense of his own honor and the helplessness of his prisoners. We must bury him with honor like our great ones. Like L'Ouverture he died defending Haiti from brutality and butchery."

So Polynice went about among the dismembered parts of bodies to which no one could give a name, searching for one small piece of the protector of the helpless that he might do it honor and thus wash his own grief, which was a terrible thing. After a while someone told him, "But Oscar Etienne is not dead. He was seen to leave the prison before five o'clock. It was he who ordered the massacre. He has taken refuge in the Dominican legation. He will not come out for any reason at all."

"Then I must go and bring him out. It will be a great kindness to him after this terrible end of my sons. He will not wish to live and remember his defeat in the carrying out of his duty. I must hurry to relieve him of his memories."

Polynice rushed to the Dominican legation and dragged out the cringing Etienne who went limp with terror when he saw the awful face of the father of the Polynices. He mumbled "mistakes" and "misunderstanding" and placed the blame upon President Vilbrun Sam. But it is doubtful if Polynice heard a word. He dragged him to the sidewalk and gave him three calming bullets, one for each of his murdered sons and stepped over the dead body where it lay and strode off. The crowd followed him to the home of Etienne where they stripped it first and then levelled it to its foundation. In their rage they left nothing standing that one might say "Here is the remains of the house of Etienne who betrayed and slaughtered defenseless men under his protection for the crime of difference of politics." His heart retched terribly as he went through the city that was weeping and washing the dead as he made his way to the French legation to see if he might not speak with General Sam. The weepers and Polynice were the survivors with the mad man and Stephen Alexis and that other one who did not die.

THE DAY AND THE HOWL

All that day of the massacre the families washed bodies and wept and hung over human fragments asking of the bloody lumps, "Is it you, my love, that I touch and hold?" And in that desperate affection every lump was carried away from the prison to somebody's heart and a loving burial. They knew that Vilbrun Guillaume Sam hid in the French legation after fighting his way out of the palace with something of the courage of Christophe and the ferocity of Dessalines. But this day was the day of the dead. It was not the day of thinking of Vilbrun Sam. This was the day of feeling. The next day the one hundred and sixty-seven martyrs would be buried. With their bodies out of sight, perhaps they could think again. So another night of whispers and sleeplessness and the funeral processions streamed to the churches from all directions. People fell into the processions as they passed grim and solemn. Men called out encouragement from houses along the way. Women wept at windows. Body after body climbed toward the great church of the Sacred Heart. Funeral met funeral at the door. Peasant women with their weeping handkerchiefs tied tight about their loins wailed all about the doors along the routes. The people who had not been able to get into the church stopped the processions of bodies as they were carried from the church and wept over them.

One black peasant woman fell upon her knees with her arms outstretched like a crucifix and cried, "They say that the white man is coming to rule Haiti again. The black man is so cruel to his own, *let the white man come!*"

With the bodies in the earth, with the expectation of American intervention, with the prong of such cries in their hearts, the people moved toward the French legation. They were not to be balked. For this day and this act amenities national and inter-national were suspended. The outraged voice of Haiti had changed from a sob to a howl. They dragged General Jean Vilbrun Guillaume Sam, until the dawn of the day of the massacre, president of the Republic, from his hiding place. They chopped his hand that tried in its last desperation to save him from the massed frenzy outside the legation gates. They dragged him through the door into the court and there a woman whose dainty hands had never even held a broom, struck him a vicious blow with a machete at the root of his neck, and he was hurled over the gate to the people who chopped off his parts and dragged his torso in the streets.

THE PLUME AGAINST THE SKY

They were like that when the black plume of the American battleship smoke lifted itself against the sky. They were like that when Admiral Caperton from afar off gazed at Port-au-Prince through his marine glasses. They were so engaged when the U. S. S. Washington arrived in the harbor with Caperton in command. When he landed, he found the head of Guillaume Sam hoisted on a pole on the Champ de Mars and his torso being dragged about and worried by the mob. This dead and mutilated corpse seemingly useless to all on earth except those who might have loved it while it was living. But it should be entombed in marble for it was the deliverer of Haiti. L'Ouverture had beaten back the outside enemies of Haiti, but the bloody stump of Sam's body was to quell Haiti's internal foes, who had become more dangerous to Haiti than anyone else. The smoke from the funnels of the U. S. S. Washington was a black plume with a white hope. This was the last hour of the last day of the last year that ambitious

and greedy demagogues could substitute bought caco blades
for voting power. It was the end of the revolution and the
beginning of peace.

Chapter VII

The Next Hundred Years

PEEPS at personalities in the Black Republic.

Haiti has always been two places. First it was the Haiti of the masters and slaves. Now it is Haiti of the wealthy and educated mulattoes and the Haiti of the blacks. Haiti of the Champ de Mars and Haiti of the Bolosse. Turgeau against the Salines. Under this present administration, the two Haities are nearer one than at any time in the history of the country. The mulattoes began their contention for equality with the whites at least a generation before freedom for the blacks was even thought of. In 1789 it was estimated that the mulattoes owned at least ten per cent of the productive land and held among them over 50,000 black slaves. Therefore when they sent representatives to France to fight for their rights and privileges, they would have been injuring themselves to have asked the same thing for the blacks. So they fought only for themselves.

In 1791 under Boukmann, Biasson and Jean-François, the blacks began their savage lunge for freedom and in 1804 they were free. Their bid for freedom had to have lunge and it had to be savage, for every man's hand was against them. Certainly their kinfolks, the mulattoes, could see no good for themselves in freedom for the blacks. Thus the very stream of Haitian liberty had two sources. It was only the white Frenchman's scorn of the mulattoes and his cruelty that forced Petion and his followers into the camp of the blacks.

Since the struggle began, L'Ouverture died in a damp, cold prison in France, Dessalines was assassinated by the people whom he helped to free, Christophe was driven to suicide, three more presidents have been assassinated, there have been fourteen revolutions, three out-and-out kingdoms established and abolished, a military occupation by a foreign white power which lasted for nineteen years. The occupation is ended and Haiti is left with a stable currency, the beginnings of a system of transportation, a modern capitol, the nucleus of a modern army.

So Haiti, the black republic, and where does she go from

here? That all depends. It depends mostly upon the action of a group of intelligent young Haitians grouped around Dividnaud, the brilliant young Minister of the Interior. These young men who hold the hope of a new Haiti because they are vigorous thinkers who have abandoned the traditional political tricks.

In the past, as now, Haiti's curse has been her politicians. There are still too many men of influence in the country who believe that a national election is a mandate from the people to build themselves a big new house in Petionville and Kenscoff and a trip to Paris.

It is not that Haiti has had no able men in the presidential chair in the past. Several able and high minded men have been elected to office at various times. But their good intentions have been stultified by self-seekers and treasury-raiders who surrounded them. So far there has been little recognition of compromise, which is the greatest invention of civilization and its corollary, recognition of the rule of the majority which is civilization's most useful tool of government. Of course, it is more difficult to discover the will of the majority in a nation where less than ten per cent of the population can read and write. Still there is a remarkable lack of agreement among those few who do read and write.

Of course Haiti is not now and never has been a democracy according to the American concept. It is an elected monarchy. The President of Haiti is really a king with a palace, with a reign limited to a term of years. The term republic is used very loosely in this case. There is no concept of the rule of the majority in Haiti. The majority being unable to read and to write, have not the least idea of what is being done in their name. Haitian class consciousness and the universal acceptance of the divine right of the crust of the upper crust is a direct denial of the concept of democracy. Neither is the Haitian chambers of Senate and deputies the same sort of thing as our Senate and House. No man may seek either of those offices in Haiti unless he has the approval of the Palace.

In addition to the self seekers who continually resorted to violence to improve their condition—they always called themselves patriots—Haiti has suffered from another internal enemy. Another brand of patriot. Out of office, he continually did everything possible to chock the wheels of government. In office himself, he spent his time waving the flag and orating on Haiti's past glory. The bones of L'Ouverture, Christophe and Dessalines were rattled for the poor peasants' breakfast, dinner and supper, never mentioning the fact that the constructive efforts of these three great men were blocked by just such "patriots" as the present day patriots. No one mentioned that all three died miserably because of their genuine love of country. Less worthy men have lived to rob, oppress, and sail off to Jamaica on their way to Paris and the boulevards. These talking patriots, who have tried to move the wheels of Haiti on wind from their lungs are blood brothers to the empty wind bags who have done so much to nullify opportunity among the American Negroes. The Negroes of the United States have passed through a tongue-and-lung era that is three generations long. These "Race Men's" claim to greatness being the ability to mount any platform at short notice and rattle the bones of Crispus Attucks; tell what great folks the thirteenth and fourteenth amendments to the constitution had made out of us; and *never* fail to quote, "We have made the greatest progress in sixty years of any people on the face of the globe." That always brought the house down. Even the white politicians found out what a sure-fire hit that line was and used it always when addressing a Negro audience. It made us feel so good that the office seeker did not need to give out any jobs. In fact I am told that some white man way back there around the period of the Reconstruction invented the line. It has only been changed by bringing it up to date with the number of years mentioned. Perhaps the original demagogue reared back with one hand in his bosom and the other one fumbling in his coat tails for a handkerchief and said, "You have made the greatest progress in ten years, etc." But America has produced a generation of Negroes who are impatient of the orators. They want to hear about more jobs and houses and meat on the table. They are resentful of opportunities lost while their parents sat satisfied and happy listening to crummy orators. Our heroes are no longer talkers but doers. This leaves some of our "race" men and women of yesterday puzzled and hurt. "Race leaders" are simply obsolete. The man and woman of today in America is the one who makes us believe he can make our side-meat taste like ham.

These same sentiments are mounting in Haiti. But they have not spread as rapidly as in the United States because so few of the Haitian population can read and write. But it is there and growing. There is a group of brilliant young men who have come together to form a scientific society under the leadership of Dr. Camille Lherisson who is a great grandson of a Lowell of Massachusetts. He is a graduate of Magill University in Canada and Harvard, and head of the Department of Biology in the Medical School at Port-au-Prince, and on the staff of the hospital. Dr. Dorsainville, Dr. Louis Mars, and several other men of high calibre meet in the paved court of Dr. Lherisson's home once every week to listen to foreign scientists who happen to be visiting Haiti at the time, or to provoke discussion among themselves. These men with Dividnaud, who is the most politically conscious of them all, are the realists of Haiti. Dr. Rulx Leon, Director General of the Public Health Department, is definitely of these thinking men who hold the future of Haiti in their hands. One has only to look through the Service d'Hygiene and visit the hospitals to realize what a great man is Dr. Leon. The finest medical men in Haiti are on his staff. He does not even permit his own feelings toward the men to influence him. Every one in Port-au-Prince knows that he is the personal enemy of the most brilliant man of his staff and yet he retains him. "The man is a genius. Haiti needs his talents," Dr. Leon explained. "It is not for me to thrust my personal disagreements before the welfare of the country. I am trying to keep this department up to the standard set by the American doctors of the Occupation. Unfortunately there is so little money with which to work." And the man in question is just as big as Dr. Leon. He gives everything in him to his work. Everything in the National Medical Service there is evidence of great talent and high character.

It is touching to go through the hospital and visit the maternity ward. Young Dr. Sam has charge there. He is the son of the President Guillaume Sam, whose horrible death brought on the Occupation in 1915. Nowhere is there a more earnest physician than Dr. Sam. How he loves those babies

Rex Hardy, Jr.

Dr. Ruix Leon and Family

that are delivered under his care! This is real devotion. His face is so fine and intelligent, and he is so careful with the very poorest of the peasant mothers who come to his out-patient clinic! Nothing is finer in all Haiti than Dr. Sam at work. The same thing, but not so obvious, is felt about Dr. Seide. The Service d'Hygiene is full of character and talent and that is another way of saying that Dr. Leon is a big man. Any little-souled man would be too petty to hire such men. The man evidently has no fear of being dwarfed by his subordinates.

Among these men, and Elie Lescot, Haitian minister at Washington is of them, one sees the real tragedy of Haiti. Here are clear headed, honest men of ability who see what is to be done for the salvation of Haiti, but there are "so many ways that wind and wind" and there is so much red tape, so many bad political habits that must be forgotten before they can be at all effective. People are beginning to say that the most promising man in Haiti to untangle this snarl-upon-snarl in government is the dynamic young Dividnaud. He is not only intelligent, he has force in his makeup and a world of courage. He conducts the affairs of his department with a brisk celerity. He is no dreamer, no rattler-of-bones, no demagogue. The Minister of the Interior is a man of action if ever one lived. And he is continually spoken of as the most audacious man in all Haiti. It has been proven conclusively that he cannot be bluffed and bullied. The President knows that and the people know that the President knows it. There is a spirit in him and others that is opposed to the old-style Haitian who has his eyes closed to fact and keeps chanting to himself that Haiti has a glorious past and that everything is just lovely. They know that everything is *not* lovely; that what happened in 1804 was all to Haiti's glory, but this is another century and another age. The patriots of 1804 did what was necessary then. It is now another time that calls for patriotism. They feel that they must do those things which will prove that they deserve their freedom. It is said over and over that they are weary of the type of politician who does everything to benefit himself and nothing to benefit his country but who is the first to rush to press to "defend" Haiti from criticism. These "defenses" are the only returns that Haiti receives for the money the "defender" is allowed to squander

and the opportunities for national advancement that he ignores or prostitutes to his own advantage. The honest and
earnest of Haiti do not want Haiti apologized for. They want
to make these apologies unnecessary. So they are now laying
the groundwork for greater unity and progress in the future.

They realize that internal matters are not so glory-getting
as foreign wars, but they are even more necessary. They see
that all is *not* well, that public education, transportation and
economics need more attention, much more than do the
bones of Dessalines. The peasants of Haiti are so hungry, and
relief would not be difficult with some planning. They are
refusing to see the glorified Haiti of the demagogue's tongue.
These few intellectuals must struggle against the blind political pirates and the inert mass of illiterates.

That brings us to the most striking phenomenon in Haiti
to a visiting American. That habit of lying! It is safe to say
that this art, pastime, expedient or whatever one wishes to call
it, is more than any other factor responsible for Haiti's tragic
history. Certain people in the early days of the Republic took
to deceiving first themselves and then others to keep from
looking at the dismal picture before them. For it was dismal,
make no mistake about that, if it is looked at from the viewpoint of the educated mulatto and the thinking blacks. This
freedom from slavery only looked like a big watermelon cutting and fish-fry to the irresponsible blacks, those people who
have no memory of yesterday and no suspicion of tomorrow.
L'Ouverture, Christophe, Petion and Dessalines saw it as the
grave problem it was. No country has ever had more difficult
tasks. In the first place Haiti had never been a country. It had
always been a colony so that there had never been any real
government there. So that the victors were not taking over an
established government. They were trying to make a government of the wreck of a colony. And not out of the people
who had at least been in the habit of thinking of government
as something real and tangible. They were trying to make a
nation out of very diffident material. These few intelligent
blacks and mulattoes set out to make a nation out of slaves to
whom the very word government sounded like something
vague and distant. Government was something, they felt, for
masters and employers to worry over while one rested from

the ardors of slavery. It has not yet come to be the concern of the great mass of Haitians.

It must have been a terrible hour for each of the three actual liberators of Haiti, when having driven the last of the Frenchmen from their shores, they came at last face to face with the people for whom they had fought so ferociously and so long. Christophe, Dessalines and Petion were realists. Every plan they laid out attests this. They tried to deal with things as they were. But Dessalines was murdered; Christophe killed himself mercifully to prevent the people for whom he had fought so valiantly from doing it in a more brutal manner. Petion saw his co-leaders fall and abandoned his great plans for restoration of the coffee and sugar estates and other developments that had once brought such great wealth to the colony of Saint Domingue.

Perhaps it was in this way that Haitians began to deceive themselves about actualities and to throw a gloss over facts. Certainly at the present time the art of saying what one would like to be believed instead of the glaring fact is highly developed in Haiti. And when an unpleasant truth must be acknowledged a childish and fantastic explanation is ready at hand. More often it is an explanation that nobody but an idiot could accept but it is told to intelligent people with an air of gravity. This lying habit goes from the thatched hut to the mansion, the only differences being in the things that are lied about. The upper class lie about the things for the most part that touch their pride. The peasant lies about things that affect his well-being like work, and food, and small change. The Haitian peasant is a warm and gentle person, really. But he often fancies himself to be Ti Malice, the sharp trickster of Haitian folk-lore.

The Haitian people are gentle and lovable except for their enormous and unconscious cruelty. It is the peasants who tie the feet of chickens and turkeys together and sling the bundle over their shoulders with the heads of the fowls hanging down and walk for miles down mountains to the market. The sun grows hot and the creatures all but perish of thirst and they do faint from their unnatural and unhappy position. I have bought chickens from women who came into my yard and found them unconscious. Sometimes the skin would be rubbed from their thighs from being tied too tight. They bore holes in the rumps of the donkeys by prodding them with sharp sticks to make them hurry when they have been driving donkeys for centuries and should know by now that the little animals are not inclined to speed. I have seen great pieces of hide scraped off the rumps and thighs of these patient little beasts, yet they were still being driven. There are thousands of donkeys in Haiti whose ears have been beaten off in an effort to hurry them. I have seen horses raw from their withers to their rumps, scalded by saddles and still being worked.

I say Haitian people are unconsciously cruel instead of merely the peasants. I know that the upper classes do not sell chickens nor drive donkeys, but they do rule the country and make the laws. If they were conscious of the cruelty of the thing, they would forbid it. I spoke of this one day to Jules Faine when I visited him and found him chasing some boys away who were trying to kill birds with stones. I said that he was the first Haitian whom I had noticed who seemed to care about such things.

"Why should these peasants be tender with animals?" he asked gently. "No one has been tender with them."

"Why do you Americans always speak of our cruelty to animals?" the editor of the Le Matin asked me. "You are cruel also. You boil live lobsters."

"Yes," I said, "but the people who sell them would not be permitted to drag them by the legs from Massachusetts to Virginia, nor to half-skin them on the way."

"It is all the same," he shied away from actuality and went on.

Then again under the very sound of the drums, the upper class Haitian will tell you that there is no such thing as voodoo in Haiti, and that all that has been written about it is nothing but the malicious lies of foreigners. He knows that is not so and should know that you know that it is not true. Down in his heart he does not hate voodoo worship. Even if he is not an adept himself he sees it about him every day and takes it for a matter of course, but he lies to save his own and the national pride. He has read the fantastic things that have been written about Haitian voodoo by people who know nothing at all about it. Consequently, there are the stereo-typed tales of virgin worship, human sacrifice and other elements borrowed from European origins. All this paints the Haitian as a savage and he does not like to be spoken of like that. So he takes refuge in flight. He denies the knowledge and the existence of the whole thing. But a peasant who has been kindly treated will answer frankly if he is not intimidated by the presence of a Gros Negre or a policeman. That is, if the policeman is strange to him or is known to be self-conscious about voodoo. But that same peasant who answered you so freely and so frankly about voodoo, if you paid him in advance for the simplest service would not return with your change. The employer class in Haiti continually warn their foreign friends not to pay for any service in advance nor to send anyone off with change. The peasant does not consider this as stealing. He prides himself on having put over a smart business deal. What he might lose by it in future business never occurs to him. And while this applies particularly to the servant class, it is just as well not to pay any money in advance to *anyone* in Haiti unless you know them very well indeed.

This self deception on the upper levels takes another turn. It sounds a good deal like wishful thinking out loud. They would like to say that Haiti is a happy and well-ordered country and so they just say it, obvious facts to the contrary. There is the marked tendency to refuse responsibility for anything that is unfavorable. Some outside influence, they say, usually the United States or Santo Domingo, is responsible for all the ills of Haiti. For example in June and July I learned that thousands of Haitian laborers were being expelled from Cuba and returned to Haiti. Knowing that work was scarce and hunger plentiful already I asked what was going to be done about providing jobs for these additional hands. Among answers I got was "What can we do? We are a poor country that has been made poorer by an Occupation forced upon us by the United States. So now we have no money to provide work for our laborers." "But," I countered, "you and many others have told me that the Occupation brought a great deal of money here which you were sorry to lose." "Oh, perhaps they did make jobs for a few hundred people, but what is that when they robbed the country so completely? You *see* that we have nothing left, and besides they are still holding our customs and so we cannot sell our coffee to any advantage. France will always buy our coffee if only they would make decent terms with France. Then there would be work for all our people." "But I have just heard that France has attempted to collect more for her debt than your country actually owed her and the American fiscal agents would not permit it. Is that not true?" "We know nothing, Mlle. All we know is that the Marines saw that our country was rich and so they came and robbed us until we grew tired of it and drove them away."

"You evidently were very slow to wrath because they stayed here nineteen years, I believe," I said.

"Yes, and we would have let them stay here longer but the Americans have no politeness so we drove them out. They knew that they had no right to come here in the beginning."

"But, didn't you have some sort of disturbance here, and were you not in embarrassing debt to some European nations? It seems that I heard something of the sort."

"We never owed any debts. We had plenty of gold in our bank which the Americans took away and never returned to us. They claimed that we owed debts so that they could have an excuse to rob us. When they had impoverished the country they left, and now our streets are full of beggars and the whole country is very poor. But what can a weak country like Haiti do when a powerful nation like your own forces its military upon us, kills our citizens and steals our money?"

"No doubt you are correct in what you say. However, an official of your own government told me that Haiti borrowed $40,000,000 to pay off these same foreign debts which you tell never existed at all."

"Mlle., I swear on the head of my mother that we had no debts. The Americans did force us to borrow the money so that they could steal it from us. That is the truth. Poor Haiti has suffered much."

All this was spoken with the utmost gravity. There was a dash of self pity in it. He was patently sorry for himself and all of the citizens who had suffered so much for love of country. If I did not know that every word of it was a lie, I would have been bound to believe him, his lies were that bold and brazen. His statements presupposed that I could not read and even if I could that there were no historical documents in existence that dealt with Haiti. I soon learned to accept these insults to my intelligence without protest because they happened so often.

With all the grave problems in Haiti to be dealt with, President Stenio Vincent, himself, finds time to indulge in the national pastime of blowing up a hurricane with his tongue. He has fabricated a conqueror's role for himself and struts as the second deliverer of Haiti, thus ranking himself with L'Ouverture, Dessalines and Christophe. He goes about it by having himself photographed with the frowning mien of a conqueror and looking for all the world like a ferocious rabbit. Without cracking a smile he announces himself as the Second Deliverer of Haiti. He bases his claim on the fact that President Roosevelt, in keeping with his good-neighbor policy, withdrew the Marines from Haiti during Vincent's administration. He knows that the N.A.A.C.P., The Nation and certain other organizations had a great deal more to do with the withdrawal of the Marines than Vincent did and much more than they are given credit for. In fact they are never mentioned when Vincent orates about Second Independence and honors himself as the Second Liberator. The story of how he drove out the Marines all by himself is a great one, the way he tells it. He even holds a celebration about it every year on August 21st. For the 1937 celebration he is supposed to have spent 80,000 gourds (about $16,000) to illumine the city of Port-au-Prince in celebration of an event that never took place.

But in spite of the great cost, something seemed lacking. Not a great number of people turned out and those who did come did not effervesce. It went off with more spirit in 1936 when the people were not so hungry as they had become a year later. The Haitian people naturally love fetes, and under normal circumstances they are happy to join in celebrating anything at all. No one in Haiti actually believes that President Vincent drove out the Marines, because even the humblest peasant knows that there was no fighting on the occasion of their departure and from past experience they know if there had been any fighting the Marines would have been on top as usual. But if the President wished to celebrate something, why not? After all the imagination is a beautiful thing.

Now in 1937 hunger and want were stalking the land. There were people who did not have a garment of any kind to cover their nakedness so that they could not come out of doors at all. As far back as November 1936 there were scared whispers about prisoners starving to death in the prison in Port-au-Prince. The jobless peasant still felt hungry after his meal of sour oranges. They had nothing really against a celebration for any reason whatsoever, but some "pois rouge et dee wee" (red beans and rice) would have suited their mood better than the electric lights, especially in celebration of a fiction. A great many expressed resentment toward the whole thing. Why celebrate the leaving of the Marine corps when nobody wanted the Marines to go anyway? Their era of prosperity had left with the Marines. If President Vincent had arranged for them to go, then he was no friend to the people. The man they wanted to honor was the one who could bring them back. A great many of them had their doubts as to whether the $16,000 stated actually was spent. "They don't spend all of this money as they tell us. The Gros Negre only find more excuse to take money for themselves." The Champ de Mars was full of suspicion and doubt that night.

It is a well known fact, and freely acknowledged in Haiti, that before the withdrawal of the American Marines, Colonel Little and the officers of the Occupation prepared a Haitian fighting force of three thousand men under Colonel Calixe. With so many trained men, and with the equipment left by the Americans plus that bought by the Haitian government, it would seem that some effective resistance could be made to an invasion from Santo Domingo if necessary. Therefore it is astonishing to read the recent statements of President Vincent that Haiti is defenseless before the onslaughts of Santo Domingo. That statement is far from true and very puzzling until one considers the reports of starvation among the Haitian peasants and the rumors of uprisings. One revolt was reported definitely under way at Cayes in the south when the massacre took place on the border. That whole department was said to be seething with revolt at the results of hunger. Does Presi-

Rex Hardy, Jr.

The American Minister and President Stenio Vincent (right)

dent Vincent think it better to allow the Dominicans to kill a few thousand Haitian peasants than to arm the peasants and risk being killed himself? Does he fear that if the stores of ammunition in the basement of the palace were issued to the army that his own days in the palace would be numbered? From actual conditions in Haiti these questions are not too far fetched. President Vincent practically acknowledged it himself in his statement to Quentin Reynolds in which he said that the Garde d'Haiti was only large enough to police Haiti. Are his own people more to be feared than Trujillo? Does he reason that after all those few thousands of peasants are dead and gone and he is still President in the palace? But if the arms and the ammunition in the basement of the palace ever got out of his control in his attempt to avenge their massacre, he might find himself "sailing for Jamaica" like many other Haitian ex-presidents have done?

Another significant figure in Haitian life is Colonel Calixe, chief of the Garde d'Haiti, which means that he is the number one man in the military forces of Haiti. He is a tall, slender black man around forty with the most beautiful hands and feet that I have ever beheld on a man. He is truly loved and honored by the three thousand men under him. His officers are well-trained professional men—doctors, engineers, lawyers and the like. There is no doubt that the military love their chief. But it is apparent that others fear his influence. Perhaps they think he might be moved to seize executive power, for he is bound by a curious oath. Not only must he refrain from moving against the Palace, he is further under threat of punishment of death if anything should happen to the President in any way at all. More than that, the ammunition is kept in the basement of the Palace under the special eye of Col. Armand, mulatto choice of the President for military chief. But the Garde d'Haiti was trained and established under the American military officers of the Occupation, and it is said that Colonel Little selected Calixe as the most able of all the Haitian officers available and had insisted on him as chief. Someone told me that the American officers had preferred Calixe, but also that President Vincent had felt that the appointment was wise because Colonel Calixe was a hero among the blacks and also because he is from the North. He is a native of Fort Liberty, a small town near Cape Haitian, and the North has always played an important part in the history of Haiti. This was then an attempt to soften the differences between the blacks and the mulattoes and recognize the importance of the North. Otherwise the administration would have preferred the mulatto Colonel André or La Fontant if Armand was not appointed. To his great credit it must be said that in the face of great opposition, the President has taken many steps to destroy this antagonism between the mulattoes and the blacks which has been the cause of so much bloodshed in Haiti's past and has been one of the major obstacles to national unity. But the end is not yet in sight. Anyway, there is Colonel Calixe with his long tapering fingers and his beautiful slender feet, very honest and conscientious and doing a beautiful job of keeping order in Haiti. If he is conscious of the jitters he inspires in other office holders and men of ambitions, he does not show it. He has told me that he is a man of arms and wishes no other job than the one he has. In fact we have a standing joke between us that when I become President of Haiti, he is going to be my chief of the army and I am going to allow him to establish state farms in all of the departments of Haiti, a thing which he has long wanted to do in order to eliminate the beggars from the streets of Port-au-Prince, and provide food for the hospitals, jails and other state institutions, since there is not enough tax money to do these things well. He is pathetically eager to clear the streets of Haiti of beggars and petty thieves and to make his department shine generally. If he has ambitions outside of his office, he dissembles well. And what a beautifully polished Sam Brown belt on his perfect figure and what lovely, gold-looking buckles on his belt!

There is somebody else in Haiti that the people cannot forget. He is not there in person, but his shadow walks around like a man. That is the shadow of Trujillo, President of neighboring Santo Domingo. Trujillo is not in Haiti; he is not even a Haitian but he has connections that reach all around. He has relatives there and numerous friends and admirers. All day long, Haitians are pointing to the Man of Santo Domingo. Some of them with fear, the rest with admiration. Some Haitians even speak of him with hope. They reason that if he can bring peace and advancement to Santo Domingo, he can contrive something of the kind in Haiti. They remember his resplendent visit to Haiti in 1936 and afterwards his gift of food and provisions to the Haitian peasants. Trujillo is *really* among those present in Haiti. Moreover, the Haitian who cannot find work in his own country, immediately thinks of migrating to Santo Domingo. Before the recent border trouble, there were thousands of Haitians in Santo Domingo because of better working and living conditions. With this condition in mind, Trujillo is supposed to have made a speech in which he threatened in a veiled manner to clean up the Haitian end of the island. His contention being, perhaps, that his own country always had to share the burden of Haiti's poor economic arrangement. So that Santo Domingo's own strides toward advancement were being shortened by having to absorb great numbers of the unemployed of her practically static neighbor. So the poor people of Haiti see more in Trujillo than just the President of a neighboring country.

Among the whispered angles of the notorious case of Joseph Jolibois, Fils, is the one that Jolibois, Fils, was the friend of Trujillo, and that when the president of Santo Domingo learned of his mysterious death in jail, he burst into a rage and expelled the Haitian Minister from his country. He is said to have accused someone very high in Haitian National life of murdering his friend Jolibois, Fils, to get him out of the way because he was becoming too popular with the people and too open in his opposition to the Administration. That was in 1936. Since then people whisper: "They say that Jolibois was poisoned in that prison. Jolibois was accused of shooting Elie Elius to death but there was no proof. They say that both men were troublesome and were liquidated for that reason. They say that Trujillo is in a great rage over the death of his friend and means to avenge him. Soon now, perhaps, he will come with his great army to punish the Haitian government for the death of Jolibois. Who knows?"

These new and vigorous young Haitian intellectuals feel that Santo Domingo's great advancement should spur Haiti out of her fog of self-deception, internal strife and general backwardness. They are advocating universal free grammar schools as in the United States and a common language. As things stand, the upper class Haitians speak French and the peasants speak Creole. M. Sejourné rightfully contends that the barrier of language is a serious thing in a nation. It makes for division and distrust through lack of understanding. He thinks that either French must speedily be taught to all, or that Haiti must adopt Creole as its official language and commission some of its scholars like Jules Faine to reduce the patois to writing. Then there is the matter of religion. Nominally Haiti is a Catholic country, but in reality it is deeply pagan. Some of the young men are ceasing to apologize for this. They feel that the foreign Catholic priests do the country much more harm than voodoo does. They are eager for the day when they shall expel the French and Belgian priests whom they say foster and propagate "War between the skins." They mean by that, that they encourage differences among the mulattoes and the blacks, besides impoverishing the country by the great sums that they collect and send to Rome and France. Also they say that the priests in order to crush a powerful rival, place all the evils of politics and what not upon the shoulders of voodoo.

The politicians, to cover up their mistakes, have also seized upon this device. As someone in America said of whiskey, voodoo has more enemies in public and more friends in private than anything else in Haiti. None of the sons of voodoo who sit in high places have yet had the courage to defend it publicly, though they know quite well and acknowledge privately that voodoo is a harmless pagan cult that sacrifices domestic animals at its worst. The very same animals that are killed and eaten every day in most of the civilized countries of the world. So since voodoo is openly acknowledged by the humble only, it is safe to blame all the ill of Haiti on voodoo. I predict that this state of affairs will not last forever. A feeling of nationalism is growing in Haiti among the young. They admire France less and less, and their own native patterns more. They are contending that voodoo is not what is wrong with Haiti. The thing fettering the country is its politics and those foreign priests.

Well, anyway, there is Haiti as it is, and there is this class of new and thinking young Haitians who are on the side lines for the most part at the moment, becoming more and more world-and-progress conscious all the time. And always there is the dynamic and forceful Trujillo, the Ever-Ready, gazing across the frontier with a steely eye. Whither Haiti?

Chapter VIII

The Black Joan of Arc

HAITI, the black daughter of France, also has its Joan of Arc. Celestina Simon stands over against The Maid of Orleans. Both of these young women sprung alike from the soil. Both led armies and came to unbelievable power by no other right than communion with mysterious voices and spirits. Both of these women stood behind weak ruling chairs, and both departed their glory for ignominy. The Duke of Burgundy burned Joan at the stake. The conquering hordes of Michel Cincinnatus Leconte drove Celestina Simon from the Haitian palace and doomed her to a dark and dishonored old age. But if Celestina and her father were driven out of power and public life, they have not lost their places in the minds of the people. More legends surround the name of Simon than any other character in the history of Haiti.

History says that General Francois Antoine Simon became President of Haiti in 1908, but practically the whole country agrees that he never should have been. There are countless tales of this crude soldier peasant's stumbling and blunders in the palace where he had no right to be. His not knowing what to do in matters of state; what to say to foreign diplomats; and how to behave amid the luxuries of the palace, all are told and told again. But these possibilities have never been considered by the men who made him president in a desperate effort to cut short the reforms instituted by the noble Nord Alexis. It was near the end of the presidential term of Nord Alexis and he was full of years. He did not wish to run for office again, but he was favoring a man who was pledged to continue his policies of honesty in government and the development of Haiti. This seemed a waste of money and opportunity to certain politicians. They had enough of the stringent honesty of President Alexis and wanted no more of the like. So they engineered General Simon into the palace. They knew he was too ignorant and boorish to make much of a president. But they did not shove him into the palace to do any governing. He was put there as a device. His "advisors" knew perfectly well what to do about matters of state. At least they knew what they *wanted* to do about such things. And the great benefits to be derived from having the perfect tool in office as a facade were too great to be lost on account of the tool's bad social form. What the "advisors" had not reckoned with was Celestina Simon and Simalo, the goat.

It was not that no one had ever heard of Celestina's powers as a Mambo. That was no secret. Everybody around Aux Cayes and the Department of the South generally knew that General Francois Antoine Simon was a great follower of the loa, and that his daughter Celestina was his trusted priestess. No one was surprised at this, for while Simon was the military governor of the Department of the South, it was well known that he had come up the military ladder from the most humble beginnings. Also, practically everyone had heard of his pet goat Simalo. It was claimed by the soldiers of Simon's army that they were invincible because of the presence of the priestess Celestina and her consort, Simalo, in the front ranks of the force. Their combined powers utterly routed the government forces at Ansa-a-veau, so they said.

General Simon, it is recalled, had taken the field because he had been removed from office by Nord Alexis. He had been removed because he let it be known that he had presidential ambitions and President Alexis had his own ideas as to who should follow him in office. So he determined to squelch Simon be demoting him. But as Nord Alexis well knew, Simon was being prompted by others with more intelligence but less courage. And Simon won the battle of Ansa-a-veau and won his way into the national palace only because the government was betrayed and because others had uses for a man like Simon. But Simon brought along with his usefulness, himself, his daughter Celestina, and Simalo, the goat. There are tales and tales of the services to the loa on that march from Aux Cayes to Port-au-Prince, especially the services that Celestina made to Ogoun Feraille, the god of war, to make the men of her army impervious to bullet and blade. The army came marching into the capital carrying their coco macaque sticks to which had been tied a red handkerchief. This was a sign that Ogoun was protecting them. The stories of Celestina's part in the battles, of her marching in advance of the men and firing them by her own ferocious attack upon the enemy had all preceded the army to the capital. The populace therefore made a great clamor as she entered the city at the head of the men of arms and called her the black Joan of Arc.

When her father became president, her prestige increased, and the flattery about her became almost hysterical when it was discovered that President Simon did and granted whatever Celestina approved. She was not only loved as a daughter, she was revered and respected as a great houngan. Nevertheless there was a great deal of laughter behind sophisticated hands in Port-au-Prince at the antics of the attachments of the president to his daughter and his goat.

But the laughter died very quickly. In the first place Simon was not as manageable as anticipated. He took flattery seriously and it bloated him. It was impossible to ignore the fact that the saying of Celestina and the behavior of Simalo were of greater importance to him than any other national affairs, for indeed, the woman and the goat had come to be affairs of the nation.

The disgust and the fear of the upper class Haitians grew with their astonishment. For instance when it was common knowledge that voodoo services and the ceremonies were being held in the national palace, many of them decided to keep as far away as possible and to have nothing at all to do with such persons, but President Simon thought differently. He gave great dinners and other state functions and the aristocrats dared not refuse his invitations. They knew the temper of the man too well for that. So they came at his thinly veiled command, ate, drank, and danced. Before his face they laughed loudly at all of his jokes and made the appearance of happiness. The moment his back was turned they looked at each other fearfully. They also looked with dread suspicion at the food and the wine. "Are we drinking wine or dirty *blood* and wine?" they asked each other in quick whispers. Dare they leave the potage untasted? Is this roast really beef or is it——? But just then the face of the president was turned toward them and they chewed and swallowed with fear and made out somehow to smile and flatter. Often it was said that a Voodoo ceremony was going on in the basement chambers while the state function was glittering its farcical way in the salon.

The Mountain House, the summer palace of President Simon was the scene of the greatest ceremonies, however. It was rumored that there took place the celebrations of the dread Sect Rouge and that years later the blood stains on the walls and floor of one room were so ghastly that they were difficult to cover with paint. There Simon, and all those in the high places who believed with him, gathered for these services under the priestess Celestina and Simalo.

The most dramatic story of all tells about the breaking of Simalo's heart. Rumor had it that years before there had been a "marriage" between Celestina and Simalo. A houngan had mysteriously tied them together for many causes and the power of each depended upon the other. All had gone happily until they were elevated to the palace. Then the flattery of many men gave Simon hope that his black daughter might capture a man of position and wealth. His and her ears heard only the flattery. They heard none of the fear and loathing that was increasing about them. Simon and Celestina saw nothing to prevent an advantageous marriage, so they began to plan for it. So far as they could see, the only barrier was the previous betrothal to Simalo. So they set about getting a divorce.

A powerful houngan whom Simon had brought from the South with him was said to have officiated at this ceremony. At the same time an elaborate function was going on in the salon of the palace. It was to be a celebration of the freeing of Celestina from her vows to the goat so that she might marry a man. Celestina herself was kept in her own bedroom until the ceremony was over. It was said to be a terrible wrench to her and she supported the sorrow with difficulty. It was only the prospect of a brilliant marriage, now that she was the daughter of the president, that sustained her in grief.

President Simon himself went from salon to basement several times watching the progress in his impatience to report the "liberation" of Celestina, feeling of course that several men of wealth and education were ready to prostrate themselves before his daughter. And each time that he left the room, the uneasy crowd above stairs exchanged hurried looks and whispers about the ceremony going on beneath them. It was one of those secrets that everyone had gotten hold of.

Finally, as he started below again, an attendant met him in the corridor and whispered that the ceremony was over and "Celestina est libre." The President sought his daughter and led her into the great salon, announcing, "Celestina is free. She may marry anyone she chooses now."

The news was received in great embarrassment. There was a polite show of joy, but no man rushed forward to take the widow of Simalo. One young deputy who escorted her on several occasions was fired on from ambush and killed; it was never made clear just why. At any rate, she has never married a man.

As for Simalo, it is said that his grief over the divorce was so great that he did not linger long after that. Some say, of course, that he was killed by the houngan that same day. A few days later there were as many whispers about the manner of his death as there would have been about the archbishop. It was certain that he was dead and both Simon and Celestina were sodden with grief. It is said that they could not bear the thought of Simalo being dumped in a hole and buried like any other dead animal. He must be buried like a man who had obligations to a god and hopes of eternity. So a priest and the Catholic church were tricked into giving him a Christian burial. The body of Simalo in a closed coffin was borne to the Cathedral in great pomp and glory. It was represented to the priest that a close relative of the president had passed away. There were great bouquets of flowers, smoking censora, the chanted mass for the dead and great weeping. A most impressive funeral, all in all. It was only when the services were completely over that the priest became suspicious and discovered that all this holy service had been performed over a goat. He was furious and the scandal spread over all Haiti. Some contend that the ill luck that attended Simon after was because of his treatment of Simalo. Perhaps this elaborate funeral was an act of atonement. Perhaps Simon was hiding his heartbreak in the rites. It might have been the first flinching from the price of ambition. After all these years educated folk of Port-au-

Prince are still laughing at the clown who occupied their palace for two years. But there is pathos too in the story.

It is the story of a peasant who gained the palace but lost his goat. He sacrificed his best friend to ambition which turned upon him and mocked his happiness to death. In the fog of flattery, he lost sight of the fact that goats and peasants are seldom the helms of empire.

Of this triumvirate, Celestina, Simon and Simalo who had come up from the south to the capital of Haiti, perhaps Simalo, by his early death, came off best. There was President Simon in the palace, there by the grace of corrupt politicians who planned to use him to their own advantage, believing that he was there by the magic powers of his daughter and his goat.

Here he was making every social, diplomatic and political blunder conceivable, and thinking that he was cutting a great figure. And all the while, his make-believe paradise was dissolving before harsh reality. His simple faith like the priests of Baal was in his daughter and in his gods and they failed him.

It must have been disheartening to the peasant-General-Governor-President Simon when, confident of victory on account of the powers of Ogoun, he took the field against Leconte, to find that the most numerous and best directed bullets always win battles in spite of the gods. But it is said that he never lost faith in the powers of Celestina and the loa. He firmly believed, but for her he never would have become governor of the South.

There are many to agree with him in this. It is said that Celestina was possessed of the greatest courage and urged her father to fight at every challenge. It was because of this prompt and strong action that he pulled himself up by his boot straps. Of course, they say his way of explanation that Celestina had this great courage was because she had such power from the loa. They never failed her until she broke her vows. But, anyway, it is a matter of history that she not only had great personal bravery, she was able to inspire others with the same, her father and his soldiers being the first to feel her personality.

The people laugh and laugh at the capers of President

Simon in the palace. They do not laugh at Celestina. She is today an elderly woman living in poverty in the South and she is still to the thinking Haitian a sinister figure. The glory of the days when she had a special military attaché of her own (General André Chevalier) and wielded power absolute from the palace are gone. She is a surly figure of the past. Some say that she pronounced a terrible curse against the man whose victorious army drove Simon from power. So that when the palace was blown up and Leconte killed, they said it was the power of Celestina still at work.

There are numerous accounts of Simon's grief at the loss of his goat. He used to weary his listeners with his memories of the feats of Simalo in military campaigns. It was plain that he considered the goat more than beast, more than man, more than just a friend. There was something of worship there.

It is said that one Sunday after the death of Simalo, Simon had the cabinet members and several other persons of importance assembled at the palace. He delivered one of the orations that he delighted to make and having embarrassed himself by making a faux pas, dismissed them. But a few intimates were allowed to remain and wander about informally. The President was moving towards his private apartments when he ran into the Minister of War, General Septimus Marius. He stopped suddenly as if he had seen a ghost and then broke into tears and said, "My dear Marius, as soon as I see your long beard, I think of my dear Simalo." And he wept so hard that the other guests felt that they had better weep with him.

There seems to be no doubt that Celestina and Simon enjoyed their places of power in the palace. Also that the young Amazon stirred something heroic in the hearts of Haiti for a time. She brought a whiff of the battle field with her as she came and made virile man think again of Christophe and Dessalines.

But soon the tales of the "services" in the palace, the sacrifices at Mountain House, the cruelty of Celestina and the affairs of the goat filled Haiti's cup of disgust to the brim. Insurrections began. Simon and Celestina confident in their loa marched out to conquer as before. Simon beat down one uprising only to be met by others. He was living over the life of Macbeth and his lady, both betrayed by their mysteries. After many harried months, he bowed before that which he could no longer oppose with conviction. So Simon like many other presidents of Haiti sailed for Jamaica.

In his exile the peasant who had become a soldier, then a general, then a governor, then a president must have thought about his march from himself into the capital, into other men's hopes and schemes. In a foreign land there he had no army, no importance, no daughter, no goat. He had nothing but time for weapons and friends and the chances are he had never learned how to use time in bulk. Probably he used what he could of it in remembering, and no doubt he remembered the days when he was governor of Aux Cayes when he, his priestess daughter and his goat were happy rulers, before ambition tricked them into the palace.

"Oh well," they conclude, "what can you expect? One cannot expect to prosper who breaks his vows to the loa. If President Simon had not killed Simalo——"

Ah Bo Bo!

Chapter IX

Death of Leconte

THIS is the story of the death of President Leconte the way the people tell it. The history books all say Cincinnatus Leconte died in the explosion that destroyed the palace, but the people do not tell it that way. Not one person, high or low, ever told me that Leconte was killed by the explosion. It is generally accepted that the destruction of the palace was to cover up the fact that the President was already dead by violence.

There are many reasons given for the alleged assassination, and each one of these motives has its own cast of characters in the tragedy. But the main actors always remain the same. These men were ambitious and stood to gain political power and what goes with it in Haiti by the death of President Leconte.

For example, some tell a story of the little son of Leconte who was said to be a love child. He loved the boy with a great love, but that seemed not to be reason enough to cause him to marry the mother of his child. She belonged to a high caste family and there was said to be a great deal of hard feeling between the family of the young woman and the President. Those who contend that this friction was behind the assassination point out that the child was not in the palace when the explosion took place. He was at the home of his mother's people.

All the other reasons given for his alleged assassination were political. The only differences in the accounts were, whose political aspirations were being choked off by Leconte's actions.

It is not to be inferred from this that Leconte was a tyrant. On the contrary he is credited with beginning numerous reforms and generally taking progressive steps. He was merely in the way of other men's ambition by virtue of the office he held.

The first person who told me about it said that he was not even killed in the executive Mansion. He said that a message came to the president to visit his little son who was with his mother at the time. He disguised himself and entered the bus driven by the aged coachman of the palace called Edmond, whose loyalty to Leconte was doubtful. Rumor says that they left the palace by the gate called Port Salnave, and that Leconte left the conveyance at the house of the father of his child's mother, whose father was one of his Ministers, and never came out again. That is, he never came out alive. The family whose honor had been outraged by the refusal of Leconte to marry the daughter of the house had secretly joined forces with the president's political enemies. Some of them were in the house when Leconte arrived. The arrangement for the body to be carried out on the Plain-Cul-de-Sac to be buried had already been made. It is said that he was killed after a short altercation. The body was wrapped up, placed in the bus and driven out to the estate of one of the conspirators to be buried. The old coachman was rewarded and the palace blown up. The very next person that I told this version to, agreed that Leconte did get into the bus and he did leave the palace by the gate Salnave. But they maintained that he was lured out by the coachman whom he trusted. This Edmond came to the President with a tale of his cabinet gathered at a certain place on the Plain-Cul-de-Sac and plotting the downfall of the president at that very moment. President Leconte must come and see this infamy with his own eyes. The President slightly disguised entered the bus and was driven off. Out on the Plain, the bus was surrounded and he was killed and buried out there on the estate of a powerful man who himself had presidential ambitions.

But I kept on talking to people and asking questions about Leconte and they kept on telling me things. So I came to hear from many people a story that was the same in all the essential points. Minor details differed of course. But the happenings that follow were repeated to me by numerous persons.

Sansarique, Leconte's Minister of the Interior was most faithful to his chief and loved him like a brother. He got wind of a conspiracy against the life of Leconte and warned him time and again to be careful. But the President was not inclined to take these warnings too seriously. He knew that he was very popular with the people and went to work building

Casernes and planning other improvements. But the conspirators grew bold by seeming immunity. They began to move
with more assurance. Rumors of plots and conspiracies increased. Definite plans seemed to have been made and the
Minister of the Interior began to be really alarmed and rushed
to the President and mentioned names. He accused Tancred
Auguste, Volcius Nerette, Chef de Sureté, and La Roche,
Minister of Agriculture of plotting to overthrow the regime
of Leconte and to make Auguste president in his stead. He
urged the President to lose no time in arresting Auguste and
Nerette. But such was the confidence of Leconte in his well-
being that he refused to believe this advice. He put it down to
over anxiety on the part of a friend. This was the state of
affairs for some time before the night of the explosion.

One man told me what he saw on the night of August 7,
1912. It was the habit of many men of the upper class to
gather at Thibeaut's Café on the Champ-de-Mars to eat, sip
drinks, and play dice, practically every night. This night of
August 7th, the crowd who loved a game of chance for moderate stakes gathered as usual. Because, he explained "when
the tambour sounds, the hounsi come." Meaning those who
love a thing will follow it.

But this particular evening, there was to be no dice. Thibeaut served the many social and political lights their coffee
and some one called for the dice. Thibeaut's face went very
stern. "Gentlemen, no dice tonight. You will please leave early
as I wish to close the Café and get to bed at a good hour.
Good evening, gentlemen."

The men were naturally surprised at this unusual announcement. They left the Café reluctantly in little groups and
went elsewhere. My informant says that from the Champ-
de-Mars, he and three associates looked towards the palace
and saw the President standing alone on the balcony of the
Palace. "Look at Conte Conte" somebody said, using the
familiar name of affection that the people had made for him.
The President was just standing there outlined by the Palace
lights as if in deep thought. Across from the Palace and
watching it closely was Tancred Auguste mounted on his grey
horse.

The young men balked of their dice game and social

evening soon left the Champ-de-Mars and the pensive President behind and went on their way seeking other amusements.

This is what they say was going on inside the Palace. Some time during the night the Chief de Sureté came to the Palace accompanied by several men. He sent word to Leconte that he must see him on a matter of vital importance and thus persuaded the President to receive him at such an unusual hour. He said it was a matter which necessitated the greatest secrecy and Leconte hearing this took the party to the telegraph room where Nerette knew he always went when he wished to receive secret reports. This room was not only built sound proof, but it was detached from the Palace building proper for greater secrecy.

Inside the locked room Nerette began a recital of having discovered a plot against the President's regime. He began a rambling narrative that not only lacked any evidence of a plot, but the jumble of words was lacking in sense. Leconte asked the Chef to tell him what he meant by these disconnected statements and began to pace up and down, no doubt trying to figure out for himself why he had been disturbed to listen to such a senseless tale. He knew there was something behind it. There were several minutes of silence while Leconte paced up and down, puzzled and annoyed. Nerette and his men huddled at one end of the room, the president pacing up and down. One time when Leconte had reached the end farthest away from Nerette, that plotter whispered to the men "Qu'est que vous attendez?" (What are you waiting for?) The frightened men still huddled where they were and Nerette grew angry, "Eh, bien, Messieurs, Ca n ap'tan?" The armed butchers were lashed into action so that when the President's back was again turned to them they drew their knives and did what they had come there to do. They did in desperation that which they were afraid not to do. They butchered Leconte.

When the hacking and slashing was over, the body was removed through the Salnave door and carried to the house of one of the assassins. The work was done. Leconte was dead and his body actually removed from the palace without the faithful guard suspecting that he was not safely in bed. The conspirators most concerned were sent for and came hurriedly to the house to verify the information. The body was carefully

examined. There was no mistake. The late President of Haiti
was there at the feet of the men who toasted the success of
the coup in rum. Then plans for the coming "elections" were
rehearsed again. That settled, the final details that would dispose of the body and cover the evidence of the assassination
were gone over for the last time. The body was left in the care
and in the house of the same man where it now was. He was
loyal to the conspirators and they had his assurance that the
body would be disposed of as planned. The higher ups might
go on and look to the matter of "elections." He knew they
would remember him when making the new appointments.
They could rest assured the body would never be seen again.
Most certainly it would not be seen by anyone who favored
Leconte in his life time. So some of the conspirators hurried
away to attend to matters of state while others remained there
in the house with the body of Leconte, waiting. It was kept
there until a man was found to take it away on a donkey. At
first the body was wrapped and thrown across the donkey's
back. But it was too bloody—too apt to attract attention in
that way. So the peasant cut it up with his machete and
loaded it in a sac paille (straw bag with two huge pockets. A
sort of pannier for carrying loads on a donkey) and he was
then ordered to dispose of it on an estate on the Plain-Cul-
de-Sac. This peasant was paid, sworn to secrecy and dismissed. But soon he was bragging about his part in the crime.
He would display his machete and explain proudly "This is
the knife that cut up the body of Leconte." During the administration that followed Leconte, it is said that he was
ordered killed by a strychnine injection. But the President
himself died of poisoning before it happened.

The conspirator to whose house the body of Leconte was
taken before it was finally disposed of, from a nothing and a
nobody, was given a government position immediately after
the next administration came to power. Even his grandmother was given a pension. Indeed, the man is said to hold a
government position at this moment. He seems to have fared
better than anyone else who figured in the murder plot. For
the candidate alleged to be at the bottom of the whole matter
was himself assassinated by poisoning less than a year after
taking office. Volcius Nerette was one of the 167 who were

butchered in the prison by Sam and Etienne in 1915. The eight men with knives who did the actual killing of Leconte were arrested on a trumped-up charge and taken out side of the harbor in a boat and killed and their bodies thrown overboard. The man who cut up the body and hauled it away became an idiot. He still goes about the city laughing his laugh and showing the Machete and gloating. But nobody listens.

When the word came back to the conspirators waiting in the house that the body had been disposed of, the brains of the plot hurried forth to find the man to carry out the final detail to cover up the murder of Leconte. He called on a young electrician named Faine (no relation to the well-known writer, Jules Faine) and dragged him from his bed. Faine was told nothing about what had gone on before. He was ordered to blow up the palace at once or die. It is to be remembered that great stores of ammunition were hoarded in the palace. He was forced to rig up a device to set off this immense hoard of explosives. It is said that only fear of certain death persuaded the young man to do the work.

Thus early in the morning of August 8, 1912, the city of Port-au-Prince was rocked by an explosion that completely wrecked the palace. Other buildings near by were also injured. People were thrown out of their beds in Belair and even in Petionville, approximately six miles away. Nearly three hundred soldiers, the palace guard, were belched out of the eruption, headless, legless, armless, eyes burnt out by the powder and just bodies and parts of bodies, mangled and mingled.

The people of Port-au-Prince awakened like that out of their sleep all rushed out doors because everybody thought it was an earthquake. When they got outside they saw it was the palace and came running, putting their cries of surprise and terror with the hurt and harmed who were crawling off from the wreckage. Sansarique rushed into the ruins seeking his friend Leconte, who was not there and would not have been able to answer him if he had been. Nobody could stop the Minister of the Interior. He tore off the hands that held him. He rushed about through the smoking ruins calling Leconte, hoping he could save him. He kept crying out that he had warned him against his enemies. Finding no way to help Le-

conte, finding nothing in the likeness of his friend, he wept
for him bitterly. He was like old David at the gates when they
brought home Absalom. They say that the friendship between
Sansarique and Leconte was a beautiful thing. Here was another Damon and Pythias, another David and Jonathan. He
alone of all those near to Leconte was not concerned with his
political future. He had rushed into the ruins to do those
things which become a man and a friend. No matter who tells
the story and how, they dwell on the nobility of Sansarique.
And indeed, it is a thing to make songs about.

When the daylight came they picked up something that nobody could say with any certainty was President Leconte and
held a funeral. But then the way things were nobody could
say the formless matter was not the late president either. So
they held a state funeral and buried it.

All that being settled, right away, Tancred Auguste, with
the help of his friends, was elected President of Haiti. Perhaps
he could feel that divinity had pointed him to power. One day
there had been Leconte occupying the Palace, popular with
the people, and going on about building things like Solomon.
Seemingly this man was to occupy the National palace for
many years to come. The people willed it to be that way.
They had elected him and turned their thoughts towards
peace.

But evidently God did not agree with the Haitian people,
for behold God repudiated their candidate by belching him
out of the Palace. The poor taste of the people was corrected,
and Tancred Auguste became their ruler. The sight of the explosion must have affected him deeply if rumor is true that he
took to talking to himself. Also, they say he disliked to pass
the ruins and avoided doing so until one day he attended a
wedding and the carriages were passing the ruins before he
realized it. The sight of the tragic spot must have touched his
compassion too deeply, for he began to mutter aloud and
almost left the carriage. At any rate, the palace food proved
too rich for him, for less than a year after he had taken office
he died of a digestive disturbance that his enemies called poison. So God must have changed His mind about him also.
And while he was being buried, even before his body left the
Cathedral for the cemetery, the mourners heard shots being

fired from different parts of the City of Port-au-Prince. The successor to Tancred Auguste was being "elected."

This is what they say in Port-au-Prince about the death of President Leconte, who built the great Casernes.

Ah Bo Bo!

Chapter X
Voodoo and Voodoo Gods

D R. HOLLY says that in the beginning God and His woman went into the bedroom together to commence creation. That was the beginning of everything and Voodoo is just as old as that. It is the old, old mysticism of the world in African terms. Voodoo is a religion of creation and life. It is the worship of the sun, the water and other natural forces, but the symbolism is no better understood than that of other religions and consequently is taken too literally.

Thus the uplifted forefinger in greeting in Voodoo is really phallic and that means the male attributes of the Creator. The handclasp that ends in the fingers of one hand encircling the thumb of the other signifies the vulva encircling the penis, denoting the female aspect of deity. "What is the truth?" Dr. Holly asked me, and knowing that I could not answer him he answered himself through a Voodoo ceremony in which the Mambo, that is the priestess, richly dressed is asked this question ritualistically. She replies by throwing back her veil and revealing her sex organs. The ceremony means that this is the infinite, the ultimate truth. There is no mystery beyond the mysterious source of life. The ceremony continues on another phase after this. It is a dance analogous to the nuptial flight of the queen bee. The Mambo discards six veils in this dance and falls at last naked, and spiritually intoxicated to the ground. It is considered the highest honor for all males participating to kiss her organ of creation, for Damballa, the god of gods has permitted them to come face to face with truth.

Some of the other men of education in Haiti who have given time to the study of Voodoo esoterics do not see such deep meanings in voodoo practices. They see only a pagan religion with an African pantheon. And right here, let it be said that the Haitian gods, mysteres, or loa are not the catholic calendar of saints done over in black as has been stated by casual observers. This has been said over and over in print because the adepts have been seen buying the lithographs of saints, but this is done because they wish some visual representation of the invisible ones, and as yet no Haitian artist has given them an interpretation or concept of the loa. But even the most illiterate peasant knows that the picture of the saint is only an approximation of the loa. In proof of this, most of the houngans require those who place themselves under their tutelage in order to become hounci to bring a composition book for notes, and in this they must copy the houngan's concept of the loa. I have seen several of these books with the drawings, and none of them even pretend to look like the catholic saints. Neither are their attributes the same.

Who are the loa, then? I would not pretend to call the name of every mystere in Haiti. *No one* knows the name of every loa because every major section of Haiti has its own local variation. It has gods and goddesses of places and forces that are unknown fifty miles away. The heads of "families" of gods are known all over the country, but there are endless variations of the demigods even in the same localities. It is easy to see the unlettered meeting some unknown natural phenomenon and not knowing how to explain it, and a new local demigod is named. It is always added to the "family," to which it seems, by the circumstances, to belong. Hence, the long list of Ogouns, Erzulies, Cimbies, Legbas, and the like. All over Haiti, however, it is agreed that there are two *classes* of deities, the Rada or Arada and the Petro. The Rada gods are the "good" gods and are said to have originated in Dahomey. The Petro gods are the ones who do evil work and are said to have been brought over from the Congo, some say Guinea and the Congo have provided the two sets of gods but place names of Dahomey are included in the names of the Rada deities. Perhaps there is a mingling of several African localities and spirits under the one head in Haiti. Damballah or Dambala Ouedo Freda Tocan Dahomey, to give him his full name, heads the Rada gods. Baron Samedi (Lord of Saturday) Baron Cimeterre (Lord of the Cemetery) and Baron Crois (Lord of the cross), one spirit with three names is the head of the Petro loa. Let us first meet the Rada designations.

DAMBALA, OF DAMBALLAH OUEDO
(PRONOUNCED WAY-DOE)

Damballah Ouedo is the supreme Mystere and his signature is the serpent. Though the picture that is bought of him is that of St. Patrick, he in no way resembles that Irish saint. The picture of St. Patrick is used because it has the snakes in it which no other saint has. All over Haiti it is well established that Damballah is identified as Moses, whose symbol was the serpent. This worship of Moses recalls the hard-to-explain fact that wherever the Negro is found, there are traditional tales of Moses and his supernatural powers that are not in the Bible, nor can they be found in any written life of Moses. The rod of Moses is said to have been a subtle serpent and hence came his great powers. All over the Southern United States, the British West Indies and Haiti there are reverent tales of Moses and his magic. It is hardly possible that all of them sprang up spontaneously in these widely separated areas on the blacks coming in contact with Christianity after coming to the Americas. It is more probable that there is a tradition of Moses as the great father of magic scattered over Africa and Asia. Perhaps some of his feats recorded in the Pentateuch are the folk beliefs of such a character grouped about a man for it is well established that if a memory is great enough, other memories will cluster about it, and those in turn will bring their suites of memories to gather about this focal point, because perhaps, they are all scattered parts of the one thing like Plato's concept of the perfect thing. At any rate, concerning Moses' rod and the serpent, they say that many witch doctors in Africa can so hypnotize a snake that it can be made rigid and seemingly lifeless and carried as a cane and brought to life again at the will of the witch doctor. They contend that that was why the rod of Aaron, which was none other than the rod of Moses, was such a cane thrust into the hand of Aaron at the right moment. Such were the "rods" of the magicians of the Pharaoh. But Moses knew that his "rod" fed on the variety that the king's men of magic used, so he knew what would happen the moment that the magicians turned their "rods" into snakes.

This serpent signature of Damballah, also spelt Damballa

Rex Hardy, Jr.
The Voodoo Altar, Piled with Sacred Objects and Food

and Dambala, is responsible for the belief by the casual observer that the snake is worshipped in Haiti. This is not accurate. There is no actual worship of the snake as such in Haiti. It is treated with reverence because it is considered the servant of Damballah. Everywhere I found an altar to Damballah, I found either an iron representation of the snake beside the pool, or an actual green snake which lived in a special place upon the altar. And in each instance I asked about the divinity of the snake and they told me that the snake was not a god but the "bonne" (maid servant) of Damballah and was therefore protected and honored.

Damballah is the highest and most powerful of all the gods, but never is he referred to as the father of the gods as was Jupiter, Odin and great Zeus and while he is not spoken of as the father of the gods, whenever any of the other gods meet him they bow themselves and sing, "Ohe,' Ohe'! Ce Papa nous qui pe' passe'!" ("It is our papa who passes.") He is the father of all that is powerful and good. The others are under him in power, that is all. He never does "bad" work. If you make a ceremony to any of the other gods and ask favors, they must come to Damballah to get the permission and the power to do it. Papa Damballah is the *great source.*

Around Damballah is grouped the worship of the beautiful in nature. One must offer him flowers, the best perfumes, a pair of white chickens; his "mange" sec (dry food) consisting of corn meal and an egg which must be placed on the altar on a white plate. He is offered cakes, french melons, watermelons, pineapples, rice, bananas, grapes, oranges, apples and the like. There must be a porcelain pot with a cover on the altar, desserts and sweet liquors, and olive oil. There must be a representation of Damballah within the oratory, a small crucifix, a bouquet, a bottle of liquor, a glass of oil to keep his lamps burning on his day. He brings good luck to those who make offerings to him regularly and faithfully. "It is possible for you to have a grand situation and it is even possible to become a minister or the president if you serve Papa Damballah faithfully. But yes!" His day is Wednesday in the afternoon of every week and his sacrifice is a pair of white chickens, hen and cock. The average houngan says that he is given the white cock and hen because he guards domestic happiness. Dr.

Holly says it is another acknowledgment of the bi-sexual concept of the Creator, and that Damballah with the subtle wisdom and powers represented by the snake is to the Africans
something of a creator, if not actively, certainly The Source.
His color is white. His woman is Aida Ouedo. His signature is
the ascending snakes on a rod or a crucifix. He is the fourth in
the order of the service being preceded by (1) Papa Legba,
opener of gates (opportunities), (2) Loco Attison, Mystere of
work and knowledge, (3) Mah-lah-sah, the guardian of the
doorsill. None of these are so important as Damballah. But
the order has been established to have things ready when he
arrives through possession of some of the persons taking part
in the ceremony. There is a definite behavior for the possession of each of the gods. The houngan (Voodoo priest) or the
mambo or priestess can say at once what god possesses a person present. Perhaps the wrong impression is conveyed by the
expression that the other gods precede Damballah in the services. Actually, they are his suite and surround him and go
before or after him in order to more quickly serve his commands. In the Voodoo temple or peristyle, the place of Damballah, there must also be the places of Legba, Ogoun, Loco,
the cross of Guedé who is the messenger of the gods, of Erzulie, Mademoiselle Brigitte and brave Guedé. Damballah re-
sides within the snake on the altar in the midst of all these
objects. The construction must face the rising sun and there
must be a door which looks toward the west.

Songs to Damballah

NO. 1

Me roi *e'* Damballah Ouedo, ou ce gran moun, ho, ho,
    ho, me roi *e'*.
Damballah Ouedo ou ce' gran moun la k'lle ou.
(My king is Damballah Ouedo. You are a great man, ho, ho,
    ho, my king is.)

NO. 2

Ah Damballah, bon jour, bon jour, bon jour, Damballah
    Ouedo!

Apres Manday, Damballah ou mah ou yeah, oh, oh, oh oui
    may lah, Damballah,
Ouido, moin, ah may Vinant lauh yo.

There is in Voodoo worship a reverent remoteness where
Damballah is concerned. There are not the numerous personal anecdotes about him as about some of the lesser and
more familiar gods. I asked why they did not ask more things
of him, and I was told that when they make "services" to the
other gods they are making them to Damballah indirectly for
none of the others can do anything unless he gives them the
power. There is the feeling of awe. One approaches the lesser
gods and they in turn approach the great one. The others
must listen and take sides in the neighborhood disputes, jeal-
ousies and feuds. One comes to Damballah for advancement
and he is approached through beauty. Give Damballah his
sweet wine and feed his wisdom with white pigeons.

ERZULIE FREIDA

Nobody in Haiti ever really told me who Erzulie Freida
was, but they told me what she was like and what she did.
From all of that it is plain that she is the pagan goddess of
love. In Greece and Rome the goddesses of love had husbands and bore children, Erzulie has no children and her husband is all the men of Haiti. That is, anyone of them that she
chooses for herself. But so far, no one in Haiti has formulated
her. As the perfect female she must be loved and obeyed. She
whose love is so strong and binding that it cannot tolerate a
rival. She is the female counterpart of Damballah. But high
and low they serve her, dream of her, have visions of her as of
the Holy Grail. Every Thursday and every Saturday millions
of candles are lighted in her honor. Thousands of beds, pure
in their snowy whiteness and perfumed are spread for her.
Desserts, sweet drinks, perfumes and flowers are offered to
her and hundreds of thousands of men of all ages and classes
enter those pagan bowers to devote themselves to this spirit.
On that day, no mortal woman may lay possessive hands upon
these men claimed by Erzulie. They will not permit themselves to be caressed or fondled even in the slightest manner,

even if they are married. No woman may enter the chamber
set aside for her worship except to clean it and prepare it for
the "service." For Erzulie Freida is a most jealous female
spirit. Hundreds of wives have been forced to step aside entirely by her demands.

She has been identified as the Blessed Virgin, but this is far
from true. Here again the use of the pictures of the Catholic
saints have confused observers who do not listen long
enough. Erzulie is not the passive queen of heaven and
mother of anybody. She is the ideal of the love bed. She is so
perfect that all other women are a distortion as compared to
her. The Virgin Mary and all of the female saints of the
Church have been elevated, and celebrated for their absti-
nence. Erzulie is worshipped for her perfection in giving herself to mortal man. To be chosen by a goddess is an exaltation
for men to live for. The most popular Voodoo song in all
Haiti, outside of the invocation to Legba, is the love song to
Erzulie.

Erzulie is said to be a beautiful young woman of lush appearance. She is a mulatto and so when she is impersonated
by the blacks, they powder their faces with talcum. She is
represented as having firm, full breasts and other perfect female attributes. She is a rich young woman and wears a gold
ring on her finger with a stone in it. She also wears a gold
chain about her neck, attires herself in beautiful, expensive
raiment and sheds intoxicating odors from her person. To
men she is gorgeous, gracious and beneficent. She promotes
the advancement of her devotees and looks after their welfare
generally. She comes to them in radiant ecstasy every Thursday and Saturday night and claims them.

Toward womankind, Erzulie is implacable. It is said that no
girl will gain a husband if an altar to Erzulie is in the house.
Her jealousy delights in frustrating all the plans and hopes of
the young woman in love. Women do not "give her food"
unless they tend toward the hermaphrodite or are elderly
women who are widows or have already abandoned the hope
of mating. To women and their desires, she is all but maliciously cruel, for not only does she choose and set aside for
herself, young and handsome men and thus bar them from
marriage, she frequently chooses married men and thrusts

Door of Room to Erzulie

herself between the woman and her happiness. From the time that the man concludes that he has been called by her, there is a room in her house that the wife may not enter except to prepare it for her spiritual rival. There is a bed that she must make spotless, but may never rest upon. It is said that the most terrible consequences would follow such an act of sacrilege and no woman could escape the vengeance of the enraged Erzulie should she be bold enough to do it. But it is almost certain that no male devotee of the goddess would allow it to occur.

How does a man know that he has been called? It usually begins in troubled dreams. At first his dreams are vague. He is visited by a strange being which he cannot identify. He cannot make out at first what is wanted of him. He touches rich fabrics momentarily but they flit away from his grasp. Strange perfumes wisp across his face, but he cannot know where they came from nor find a name out of his memory for them. The dream visitations become more frequent and definite and sometimes Erzulie identifies herself definitely. But more often, the matter is more elusive. He falls ill, other unhappy things befall him. Finally his friends urge him to visit a houngan for a consultation. Quickly then, the visitor is identified as the goddess of love and the young man is told that he has been having bad luck because the goddess is angry at his neglect. She behaves like any other female when she is spurned. A baptism is advised and a "service" is instituted for the offended loa and she is placated and the young man's ill fortune ceases.

But things are not always so simply arranged. Sometimes the man chosen is in love with a mortal woman and it is a terrible renunciation he is called upon to make. There are tales of men who have fought against it valiantly as long as they could. They fought until ill luck and ill health finally broke their wills before they bowed to the inexorable goddess. Death would have ensued had they not finally given in, and terrible misfortune for his earthly inamorata also. However, numerous men in Haiti do not wait to be called. They attach themselves to the cult voluntarily. It is more or less a vow of chastity certainly binding for specified times, and if the man is not married then he can never do so. If he is married

his life with his wife will become so difficult that separation
and divorce follows. So there are two ways of becoming an
adept of Erzulie Freida—as a "reclame'" meaning, one called
by her, and the other way of voluntary attachment through
inclination. Besides this merely amorous goddess, there is another Erzulie, or perhaps another aspect of the same deity.
She is the terrible Erzulie, ge-rouge (Erzulie, the red-eyed)
but she does not belong to the Rada. She belongs to the
dreaded Petro phalanx. She is described as an older woman
and terrible to look upon. Her name has been mentioned in
connection with the demon worship of the Bocors and the
Sect Rouge.

The "baptism" or initiation into the cult of Erzulie is perhaps the most simple of all the voodoo rites. All gods and
goddesses must be fed, of course, and so the first thing that
the supplicant must do is to "give food" to Erzulie. There must
be prepared a special bread and Madeira wine, rice-flour, eggs,
a liqueur, a pair of white pigeons, a pair of chickens. There
must be a white pot with a cover to it. This food is needed at
the ceremony during which the applicant's head is "washed."

This washing of the head is necessary in most of their ceremonies. In this case the candidate must have made a natte
(mat made of banana leaf-stems) or a couch made of fragrant
branches of trees. He must dress himself in a long white night
shirt. The houngan places him upon the leafy couch and recites three Ave Maria's, three Credos and the Confiteor three
times. Then he sprinkles the couch with flour and a little
syrup. The houngan then takes some leafy branches and dips
them in the water in the white pot which has been provided
for washing the head of the candidate. While the priest is
sprinkling the head with this, the hounci and the Canzos are
singing:

> "Erzulie Tocan Freida Dahomey, Ce ou qui faut
>   ce' ou qui bon
>   Erzulie Freida Tocan Maitresse m'ap monte'
>   Ce' ou min qui Maitresse."

The hounci and the adepts continue to sing all during the
consecration of the candidate unassisted by the drums. The

drums play *after* a ceremony to Erzulie, *never during* the service. While the attendants are chanting, the houngan very carefully parts the hair of the candidate who is stretched upon the couch. After the parted hair is perfumed, an egg is broken on the head, some Madeira wine, cooked rice placed thereon, and then the head is wrapped in a white handkerchief large enough to hold everything that has been heaped upon the head. The singing keeps up all the while. A chicken is then killed on the candidate's head and some of the blood is allowed to mingle with the other symbols already there. The candidate is now commanded to rise. This is the last act of the initiation. Sometimes a spirit enters the head of the new-made adept immediately. He is "mounted" by the spirit of Erzulie who sometimes talks at great length, giving advice and making recommendations. While this is going on a quantity of plain white rice is cooked—a portion sufficient for one person only, and he eats some of it. What he does not eat is buried before the door of his house.

The candidate now produces the ring of silver, because silver is a metal that has wisdom in it, and hands it to the houngan who takes it and blesses it and places it upon the young man's finger as in a marriage ceremony. Now, for the first time since the beginning of the ceremony, the priest makes the libation. The five wines are elevated and offered to the spirits at the four cardinal points and finally poured in three places on the earth for the dead, for in this as in everything else in Haiti, the thirst of the dead must be relieved. The financial condition of the applicant gauges the amount and the variety of the wines served on this occasion. It is the wish of all concerned to make it a resplendent occasion and there is no limit to the amount of money spent if it can be obtained by the applicant. Enormous sums have been spent on these initiations into the cult of Erzulie Freida. It is such a moment in the life of a man! More care and talent have gone into the songs for this occasion than any other music in Haiti. Haiti's greatest musician, Ludoric Lamotte, has worked upon these folk songs. From the evidence, the services to Erzulie are the most idealistic occasions in Haiti. It is a beautiful thing. Visualize a large group of upper class Haitians all in white, their singing voices muted by exaltation doing service to man's

eternal quest, a pure life, the perfect woman, and all in a setting as beautiful and idyllic as money and imagination available can make it. "Erzulie, Nin Nin, Oh'!" is Haiti's favorite
folk song.

1

"Erzulie ninnin, oh! hey! Erzulie ninnin oh, hey!
    Moin senti ma pe' monte', ce moin minn yagaza.

2

"General Jean—Baptiste, oh ti parrain
    Ou t'entre' lan caille la, oui parrain
    Toutes mesdames yo a genoux, chapelette you
    Lan main yo, yo pe' roule' mise' yo
    Ti mouns yo a' genoux, chapelette you
    Erzulie ninninm oh, Hey gran Erzulie Freida
    Dague, Tocan, Miroize, nan nan ninnin oh, hey
    Moin senti ma pe' monte' ce' moin minn yagaza."

3

(Spoken in "Langage" recitative)
"Oh Aziblo, qui dit qui dit ce' bo yo
    Ba houn bloco ita ona yo, Damballah Ouedo
    Tocan, Syhrinise o Agoue', Ouedo, Pap Ogoun oh,
    Dambala, O Legba Hypolite, Oh
    Ah Brozacaine, Azaca, Neque, nago, nago pique cocur yo
    Oh Loco, co loco, bel loco Ouedo, Loco guinea
    Ta Manibo, Doçu, Doça, D agoue' moinminn
    Negue, candilica calicassague, ata, couine des
    Oh mogue', Clemezie, Clemeille, papa mare' yo.

4

"Erzulie, Ninninm oh, hey grann' Erzulie
    Freida dague, Tocan Miroize, maman, ninninm oh, hey!
    Moin senti ma pe' monte', ce moin mimm yagaza, Hey!"

More upper class Haitians "make food" for Erzulie Freida
than for any other loa in Haiti. Forever after the consecration,

Rex Hardy, Jr.

Drums and Drummers

they wear a gold chain about their necks under their shirts and a ring on the finger with the initials E. F. cut inside of it. I have examined several of these rings. I know one man who has combined the two things. He has a ring made of a bit of gold chain. And there is a whole library of tales of how this man and that was "reclamé" by the goddess Erzulie, or how that one came to attach himself to the Cult. I have stood in one of the bedrooms, decorated and furnished for a visit from the invisible perfection. I looked at the little government employee standing there amid the cut flowers, the cakes, the perfumes and the lace covered bed and with the spur of imagination, saw his common clay glow with some borrowed light and his earthiness transfigured as he mated with a goddess that night—with Erzulie, the lady upon the rock whose toes are pretty and flowery.

PAPA LEGBA ATTIBON

Legba Attibon is the god of the gate. He rules the gate of the hounfort, the entrance to the cemetery and he is also Baron Carrefour, Lord of the crossroads. The way to all things is in his hands. Therefore he is the first god in all Haiti in point of service. Every service to whatever loa for whatever purpose must be preceded by a service to Legba. The peasants say he is an old man that moves about with a sac paille (large pouch woven of straw) and therefore the houngan must take everything to be used in his service in the Sac paille called Macout. They say he has a brother, however, who eats his food from a kwee, which is a bowl made from half a calabash.

The picture of John the Baptist is used to represent Papa Legba. The rooster offered to him must be Zinga, what we would call a speckled black and white rooster. All of his food must be roasted. He eats roasted corn, peanuts, bananas, sweet potatoes, chicken, a tobacco pipe for smoking, some tobacco, some soft drinks. All these things must be put in the Macoute and tied to the limb of a tree that has been baptized in the name of Papa Legba.

Of all the Haitian gods, Legba is probably best known to the foreigners for no one can exist in Haiti very long without

hearing the drums and the chanting to Papa Legba asking him
to open the gate.

> "Papa Legba, ouvirier barriere pour moi agoe
> Papa Legba, ouvirier barriere pour moi
> Attibon Legba, ouvirier barriere pour moi passer
> Passer Vrai, loa moi passer m' a remerci loa moin."

There are several variations of this prayer-chant. In fact at
every different place that I heard the ceremony I heard another version, but always it is that prayer song to the god of
the gates to permit them and the loa to pass. The other loa
cannot enter to serve them unless Legba permits them to do
so. Hence the fervent invocation to him. Another often sung
invocation is:

> "Legba cli-yan, cli-yan Zandor, Zandor, Attibon Legba,
> Zander immole'
> Legba cli-yan, cli-yan Zand-Zandor Attibon Legba
> Zander immole'."

Legba's altar is a tree near the hounfort, preferably with the
branches touching the hounfort. His offering is made in the
branches and his repository is at the foot of the tree. Legba is
a spirit of the fields, the woods and the general outdoors.
There is one important distinction between offering a chicken
to Legba and offering it to the other loa. With the others his
head is bent back and his throat is cut, but for Legba his neck
must be wrung.

Papa Legba has no special day. All of the days are his, since
he must go before all of the ceremonies. Loco Atisou follows
Legba in the service, and is in fact "saluted" in the Legba
ceremony. This is absolutely necessary. If it is not done Loco
will be offended and the gods called in the invocation will not
come.

Loco Atisou gives knowledge and wisdom to the houngan
and indicates to them what should be done. In case clients
come to them Loco shows the houngan what leaves and me-
dicaments to use for treating the ailments. Either in the hounfort or anywhere else, the houngan can take his Asson and

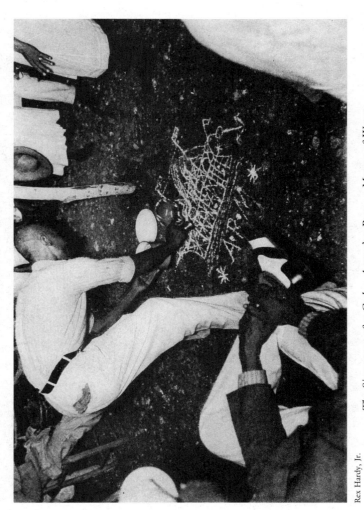

Rex Hardy, Jr.

The Signature of a God — Agoue'ta-Royo — Master of Waters

call Papa Loco and he will indicate the malady of the patient if the sickness is natural. If it is unnatural, he will advise the houngan.

Loco is the god of medicine and wisdom, but at the same time a great drinker of rum. Sacrifice to him a gray cock. His day is Wednesday. The image of St. Joseph is used for Loco Atisou.

SONG OF LOCO ATISOU

Va, Loco, Loco Valadi', Va, Loco, Loco Valadi
Va, Loco, Loco Valadi', Va, Loco, Loco Valadi
Man, Jean Valou Loco, Loco Valadi.

Most of the other gods of national importance will be briefly explained as they occur in ceremonies. This work does not pretend to give a full account of either voodoo or voodoo gods. It would require several volumes to attempt to cover completely the gods and Voodoo practices of one vicinity alone. Voodoo in Haiti has gathered about itself more detail of gods and rites than the Catholic church has in Rome.

A study of the Marassas and the Dossou or Dossa, the twin gods represented by the little joined plates are worthy of a volume in themselves. The same could be said of the Ogouns, the Cimbys, and the ramifications of Agoue'ta-Royo, the Master of Waters, the Erzulies, the Damballas and the Locos. I am merely attempting to give an effect of the whole in the round. It is unfortunate for the social sciences that an intelligent man like Dr. Dorsainville has not seen fit to do something with Haitian mysticism comparable to Frazier's "The Golden Bough." The history of the Asson would be a most interesting thing in itself. The layman as well as the scientist would like to know how this gourd sheathed in beads and snake vertebrae, and sometimes containing a human bone, came to be the fixed and honored object that it is. It has its commandments as the voice of the gods and certainly it is hallowed. How did it get that way? Who began it? Where exactly?

Chapter XI
Isle de La Gonave

EVERYBODY knows that La Gonave is a whale that lingered so long in Haitian waters that he became an island. He bears a sleeping woman on his back. Any late afternoon anyone in Port-au-Prince who looks out to sea can see her lying there on her back with her hands folded across her middle sleeping peacefully. It is said that the Haitians prayed to Damballa for peace and prosperity. Damballa was away on a journey accompanied by his suite including two wives, Aida and Cilla. When the invocations reached Damballa where he was travelling in the sky, he sent his woman Cilla with a message to his beloved Haitians. He commanded Agoue'ta-Royo to provide a boat for his wife and to transport her safely to Port-au-Prince so that she could give the people the formula for peace. Papa Agoue' sent a great whale to bear Cilla and instructed him to transport the woman of Damballa with safety and speed and comfort. The whale performed everything that the Master of Waters commanded him. He rode Madame Cilla so quickly and so gently that she fell asleep, and did not know that she arrived at her destination. The whale dared not wake her to tell her that she was in Haiti. So every day he swims far out to sea and visits with his friends. But at sundown he creeps back into the harbor so that Madame Cilla may land if she should awake. She has the formula of peace in her sleeping hand. When she wakes up, she will give it to the people.

From the house of George de Lespinasse high in Pacot I watched the island of La Gonave float out of the harbor with the sun each day and return at sundown. And I wanted to go out there where it was. William Seabrook in his "Magic Island" had fired my imagination with his account of The White King of La Gonave. I wanted to see the Kingdom of Faustin Wirkus. Then two weeks before Christmas of 1936 a friend of mine, Frank Crumbie, Jr. of Nyack, New York, suggested that we go over together and do some investigation.

He knew people and Creole and I knew methods. So we made preparations to go.

Frank Crumbie, or Junior, as he was known among his intimates, knew where to find a boat. He engaged a small sailing boat known as a shallop to take us across the eighteen miles of bay water to La Gonave. The captain told us to be ready to sail between eight and nine at night because the wind would be right then. Then is the only time a sailing vessel can put out from Port-au-Prince for La Gonave. Mr. and Mrs. Scott drove us down to the waterfront with our army cots and other paraphernalia and saw us off. The captain and his crew of one other man poled the boat out into deep water and we began our all night voyage to the island of the sleeping woman.

The wind did not catch the sails at once. The men rowed and rowed. I looked at the big stars blazing so near overhead sunk in a sky that was itself luminous. Junior was already getting sea sick and trying to get comfortable. The men began a song and I asked Junior what it was they were singing so earnestly. He said, "A song to Papa Agoue', the Master of the Waters. They are asking him for a wind." The wind rose and soon we swept past the Bissotone Navy Yard and on our way. The stars soon lost themselves in clouds and down came a heavy shower of rain. I put on my rain coat and big straw hat. Junior took refuge in his sleeping bag, but we got dampish just the same. The men took no notice of the downpour. The lights of Port-au-Prince had faded when the sky cleared. Then we saw the luminous sea! It glowed like one vast jewel. It glittered like bushels and bushels of gems poured into the casket that God keeps right behind His throne for beauty. The moving fish put on their gilding. It was a privilege to move upon this liquid radiance. Junior was sick by this time but the men who were used to Haitian night seas did not pay attention. I had the feeling of being adrift in a boat alone.

All night the captain and the crew talked, smoked cigarettes we gave them and sailed and talked so that daylight found us off the coast of La Gonave. We saw two or three little thatched houses. The captain told the crew to announce our arrival. He took a conk shell and stood up on the prow and blew several mingled rhythms and tones, "Tell them two ti

blancs (unimportant whites or mulattoes) are coming." The
crew blew again and sat down as the sun was rising. At 11:00
o'clock we landed at Ansa-a-galets.

La Gonave's well advertised mosquitoes met us at the landing. That same landing that Faustin Wirkus had built during
his reign. But away from the mangrove swamps the town rose
high and dry and the mosquitoes ceased to be important.

The days went by and we made acquaintances. The chief of
police there and his subordinates were very kind and entertaining. I saw Haitian folk games played and began to hear
the folk tales around Ti Malice and Bouke'. For the first time
I heard about the sacred stones of Voodoo. I found on this
remote island a peace I have never known anywhere else on
earth. La Gonave is the mother of peace. Its outlines which
from Port-au-Prince look like a sleeping woman are prophetic.
And the moonlight tasted like wine.

One of the Lieutenants of the Garde d'Haiti was collecting
sacred stones for Faustin Wirkus. He was telling Junior about
it in my presence so I asked questions. The Haitian peasants
come upon the stone implements of the dead and gone ab-
origines and think that they are stones inhabited by the loa.
In Africa they have a god of thunder called Shango or
Shangor. He hurls his bolts and makes stones that are full of
power. They think that these stones in Haiti were made by
their god Shango and that the various gods of voodoo reside
in them. The moment that they see a stone of a certain shape
and color they say that it belongs to a certain god because
they have come to be associated that way. This one is Damballa. That one is Agoue'. Another is Ogoun. And so on.
When one finds one of these stones it is considered very
lucky. It is said, "You have found a loa." When the finder
acquires enough money to pay for the ceremony, the stone is
baptized in the rites of the god to whom it is dedicated and
placed upon the little shrine in the home upon a white plate
and treated with the greatest respect. At stated times it is
bathed in oil and little things are offered to it. Some of these
stones have been in certain families for generations. No
amount of money could buy them. The way to tell whether a
stone has a loa or not is to cup it in the hand and breathe

upon it. If it sweats then it has a spirit in it. If not, then it is useless.

We heard about one famous stone that had so much power that it urinated. It was identified as Papa Guedé who had ordered it to be clothed, so it wore a dress. It attracted so many people and caused so much disturbance indoors that the owner had it chained outside the door. One of the American officers of the Occupation named Whitney saw it and finally got it for himself. It was a curious idol and he wanted it for his desk. The Haitian guard attached to Whitney's station told him that it would urinate and not to put it on his desk but he did so in spite of warning and on several occasions he found his desk wet and then he removed it to the outdoors again. They said he took it away to the United States with him when he left.

At Ansa-a-galets I met the black marine. A sergeant of the Garde d'Haiti lived in the house beside mine and I kept hearing "Jesus Christ!" and "God Damn!" mixed up with whatever he was saying in Creole. When we became friendly enough to converse, I told him that I had heard him and said that it was remarkable to hear the ejaculations from him.

"Oh," he said, "I served with the Marines when they were here."

"I see," I replied facetiously, "then you are a black Marine."

"But yes," he replied proudly, "I am a black Marine. I speak like one always. Perhaps you would like me to kill something for you. I kill that dog for you." It was a half-starved dog that had taken to hanging around me.

"No, no, don't kill it. Poor thing!" He put his pistol back into its holster. "Jesus Christ! God Damn! I kill something," he swaggered. I learned afterwards that he had told all his friends and associates that he must be just like an American Marine because the femme American had recognized the likeness at once. Perhaps by this time he has promoted himself to Colonel Little.

I met Madame Lamissier Mille from Archahaie, that rich alluvial plain going north from Port-au-Prince which is called the granary of Haiti. There are so many wealthy and pro-

ductive plantations of bananas, coconuts and garden produce
that the whole place is swathed in rich green foliage. From
this Lamissier I heard the name Vixama which is hard to hear
even in Haiti. You hear much about the mythical man in the
mountain near St. Marc, but few know and breathe the name
Vixama. What was more important than the secret name of a
legendary figure, was the invitation to visit a real Bocor who
has his hounfort at Archahaie whom she said was a "parent"
of hers which means in Creole that they were related. This
was the opening I had wished for, so I eagerly accepted. We
passed Christmas day in Ansa-a-galets, and I had stewed goat
with the Chief of Police. The next night our party of five
marched single file down the stony path to the sea in the
white light of a gross old moon and embarked for Port-au-
Prince. When the sun arose the next morning it was pleasant
to stretch myself along the gunwale and look far down into
the water and see the animal life down there. I saw a huge
shark point his nose up and lazily follow it to the surface; I
saw a great ray swimming about and numerous parrot fish. It
rained on us twice, but that night around nine o'clock, we
landed in Port-au-Prince, and the next day Lamissier went off
to Archahaie to find out when her cousin, the Bocor, would
receive me. I was very eager for him to admit me, because
Archahaie is the greatest place known in Haiti for Voodoo.

Chapter XII

Archahaie and What It Means

EARLY in January I went to Archahaie to the Hounfort of Dieu Donnez St. Leger. He has a large following and owns large plantations himself. He lives in a compound like an African chief with the various family connections in smaller houses within the enclosure. About one hundred people are under him as head of the family or clan. He is very intelligent, reads and writes well and sees to it that all of the children in his compound go to school. The arch above the door to the hounfort and peristyle were both painted in stripes alternating green, white, blue and orange. The walls were green and red.

He was extremely kind in allowing me to attend all of their ceremonies and in making explanations. He had his Mambo, Madame Isabel Etienne take great pains with me to conduct me through the rites step by step and to teach me the songs of the services. I was in a fortunate position, for his place has such a large following that there were ceremonies nearly every day. Sometimes two or three in the same day. Red cocks were tied before the door of the mysteries awaiting the hour of sacrifice. I was learning many things and being astonished at the elaborate rituals that voodoo has developed in Haiti. After the ceremonies the drums played for Congo dances and men and women helped to teach me the steps. First, of course, was the Jean Valou, the Congo and then the Mascaron. Other steps were introduced as the occasion demanded until I could follow whatever they did in the dance and singing.

One night something very interesting and very terrifying came to pass. A houngan had died and Dieu Donnez was to officiate at the Wete' loa non tete yum mort (taking the spirit from the head of the dead). This ceremony is also called the Manger des morts (The food or feast of the dead) or the Courir Zinc (To run the Zinc fish hook of the dead). This ceremony is not always in honor of a houngan. It is also celebrated for a dead hounci or canzo.

That day a pair of white pigeons were obtained, some olive oil, flour, more than thirty pieces of fat pine wood, a pair of chickens, some coarse corn meal, and a saddle blanket, and a large white plate. Two chairs were placed under the peristyle and the dead body of the houngan was placed on them and covered with the saddle blanket.

The chickens and the pigeons were killed and cooked without seasoning. They were very careful that no salt whatever should touch anything. This reminded me of my experiences in Jamaica and how it was felt that salt was offensive to the dead. The coarse corn meal was put in a pan and parched or roasted as one would roast peanuts or coffee. Every minute or two the assistant would pick up the pan and shake it to make it roast evenly. When it was finished, it was placed in the white plate. Then slivers of pine wood were lighted and placed for illumination instead of candles.

Dieu Donnez himself made a sparkling fire under the peristyle and when it burned hot and fierce, he took the white plate with the corn meal in one hand and the white pot with the chickens in the other and approached the fire chanting:

"Har'au Va Erique Dan, Sobo Dis Vou qui nan
  Ce' bon Die qui maitre, Afrique Guinin, tous les morts
  Hai' 'an Va erique dan."

The body of the dead man sat up with its staring eyes, bowed its head and fell back again and then a stone fell at the feet of Dieu Donnez, and it was so unexpected that I could not discover how it was done. There it was, and its presence excited the hounci, the canzo and the visitors tremendously. But its presence meant that the loa or mystere which had lived in the dead man and controlled him was separated from him. He could go peacefully to rest and the loa would be employed by someone else. If the spirit were not taken away from the head of the dead, then it would have to go and dwell at the bottom of the water until this ceremony is performed. Some say that the spirit of the houngan must pass one year at the bottom of the water anyway. When the ceremony is finished, after the man has been buried, the two chairs are dressed with the saddle cover, but are otherwise unoccupied except in a spiritual way, if you want to look at it like that.

Rex Hardy, Jr.

The Jean Valou about the Sacred Center Pole

Mambo Etienne, Archahaie

Houngan in Full Ceremonials with Drapeaux (Flags)

Dieu Donnez then addressed the dead spirit in the African jargon called "langage." That is a private matter with each houngan and it varies with each time he employs it because different loa dictate different things to him. So that is always new. But the opening prayer which is taken from the Catholic church remains fixed. No one knows what was said to the dead man to get him to relinquish the mystere but he had sat up, bowed his head with its unchanging eyes and laid back down and the stone had fallen at the feet of Dieu Donnez St. Leger. Now he produced a fish hook made of zinc and passed it through the flames three times. This is the "Zinc" of the dead that is his no longer. The power it held will pass on to his successor, which in this case was his son.

Then all of the assistants began to march around the two dressed-up chairs, each with a flaming pine torch in his or her hands and it was a most impressive sight. Mambo Etienne rattled her asson and began the singing. The whole crowd sang lustily and well. The two Petro drums began their rhythmic march from Guinea across the seas and the three Rada drums answered them in exultation.

The chickens cooked in olive oil without salt were placed on a white plate and Dieu Donnez offered them to the dead with tremendous earnestness and dignity. After that the plates were paraded around the two chairs and buried with the food on them.

It was then the thing of terror happened. There were some odd noises from a human throat somewhere in the crowd behind me. Instantly the triumphant feeling left the place and was succeeded by one of fear. A man was possessed, it seemed, and began crashing things and people as he cavorted toward the center of things. There was a whisper that an evil spirit had materialized and from appearances, this might well have been true, for the face of the man had lost itself in a horrible mask. It was unbelievable in its frightfulness. But that was not all. A feeling had entered the place. It was a feeling of unspeakable evil. A menace that could not be recognized by ordinary human fears, and the remarkable thing was that everybody seemed to feel it simultaneously and recoiled from the bearer of it like a wheat field before a wind.

Instantly Dieu Donnez faced this one with his ascon and

other signs of office to drive it away from there, but it did not submit at once. He uttered many prayers and the terror of the crowd grew as the struggle dragged out. The fear was so humid you could smell it and feel it on your tongue. But the amazing thing was that the people did not take refuge in flight. They pressed nearer Dieu Donnez and at last he prevailed. The man fell. His body relaxed and his features untangled themselves and became a face again. They wiped his face and head with a red handkerchief and put him on a natte where he went to sleep soundly and woke up after a long while with a weary look in his eyes.

They poured libations for the dead and the ceremony ended.

It was explained to me later that the Courir Zinc is not a difficult ceremony to perform, but that it is dangerous for any except a full fledged and experienced houngan to try it for fear that evil spirits may appear and do great harm before the good loa can be summoned to drive them off. The happening confirmed the belief of the people that Dieu Donnez St. Leger is a great and a powerful houngan. It is said that he is also a powerful Bocor when he serves in that capacity.

Life had plenty of flip for me at Archahaie. I could put my army cot under the peristyle during the day and lie there in the cool and rest and watch the people come to Dieu Donnez for various things. Several sick persons were there at all times. The sick men sat around under the trees or laid on their nattes in long shirts without any trousers. Sometimes I visited among them and practised up on Creole. But usually I was wherever Madame Etienne was. Not because she was next to Dieu Donnez himself in importance but because she is a kindly person, very entertaining and an amazing dancer for all of her bulk. She has charge of running the establishment and no one dares disobey her. All of the food for the hundred or more people in the compound is prepared at a common point. The work is divided up by Madame Etienne and supervised by her. She works as hard as anybody.

Leaving the professional aspect of the place aside it is one of those patriarchal communities so numerous in Haiti. It is the African compound where the male head of the family rules over all of the ramifications of the family and looks after

Rex Hardy, Jr.

Enter the Sabre and the Drapeaux
(The sword and the ceremonial flags)

them. It is a clan. Dieu Donnez has a little house all to himself where he can retire and rest after tiresome and strenuous work. He would send for me to come there so that he could instruct me. There is nothing primitive about the man away from his profession. He is gentle but intelligent and businesslike. All of his lectures had to be written. He took ashes and drew the signatures of the loa on the ground and I had to copy them until he was satisfied. Sometimes abruptly he would leave the hounfort and go on a tour of inspection of his extensive banana and coconut plantations. I have a suspicion that he is a person who likes solitude and that it was a way he had of escaping from the nig-nagging of crowds. He inherited his office of priest from his father, who many say was a greater houngan than Dieu Donnez is. Anyway, Dieu Donnez is a hereditary houngan and that is considered the real and the true way in Haiti. One day I said that I must go to Port-au-Prince to see about my mail and he let me go saying that nothing important was in prospect for the time being anyway. So I rode one of those bone-racking, liver-shaking camions back to the capital and Lucille who was always so anxious about my safety whenever I was out of her sight.

But I was not in Port-au-Prince many days before the Master sent for me by a young man who is part of the clan and is also of the palace guard. Dieu Donnez said for me to be there within three days to bring a bottle of toilet water, a fountain pen for him and a bottle of ink. I went with portable stove, army cot and the things that Dieu Donnez wanted. And I am very glad that I went. He was going to set up a hounfort and make a houngan and these things would call for many ceremonies. I was very glad about it all. My Creole was getting pretty good by now.

The next day after my arrival at Archahaie, we set out for the place where the new hounfort was to be established. Dieu Donnez said that I could wait until next morning and come by camion but I said I'd rather walk with the rest. We set out gaily near sundown with great quantities of everything including the spirit of laughter. We sang as the dusk closed in on us plodding down the dusty road. We joked and frolicked. Madame De Grasse Celestin was riding her donkey amid two great sac paille full of good things for the trip. After a while I rode some too and Mambo Etienne's son walked alongside and joked and sang and kept the little animal moving. So we went on like this for hours into the night. It was a dark night but nobody cared. We were like a happy army stealing a march.

We came to a point of huge mango trees where a man was standing beside the road. It was the place to leave the highway and go down a twining path across running water that chuckled among the greenery. Now and then houses hid behind the trees. We walked two miles perhaps and the straggling army halted again. We had reached our destination, the compound of Année La Cour, who is a cousin of Dieu Donnez and for whom the Master was going to set up the hounfort. We had halted because there were formalities that required it.

A canzo came out with a torch light and brought corn meal and water and a houngan made the signature of a loa upon the ground, and threw the water three times upon the ground for the dead. Mambo Etienne did the same. They went through a ritual proper to the occasion, but brief. The other canzo came after and threw water ceremonially. Then the hounci. After that we all went inside.

We found great piles of palm fronds piled under the peristyle and a quantity of gay colored paper. The women were waiting to be told what to do and Mambo Etienne put us all to work stripping the palm fronds into strips so fine that when it was done, it looked like a great, cream and green ostrich plume. Mambo Etienne and Annee' La Cour cut the fringe away from the central stalks and draped the "plumes" over the back of a chair. These were going to be cut into smaller pieces and used to decorate the peristyle and the various repositories of the gods. More work was going on out under the great elm tree that was to be dedicated to Loco and late in the night I went out there and spread up my bed to sleep. The next morning Dieu Donnez himself arrived with the rest of the clan in tow, and there was a great ceremony at the entrance for him. We were given some delicious hot tea called channelle before breakfast and it was a most refreshing and surprising thing. Channelle tea is a lovely habit for anybody to have. I was put to work cutting up the colored paper to be strung across the peristyle to decorate it and spent the entire morning at it. By that time a crowd was beginning to collect. When the peristyle was all decorated, I went out to the cooking place where the women were cooking great quantities of food. I noticed that Madame Etienne found the rocks herself to support the large cooking pots, and that she marked each rock with a cross mark in charcoal. She answered me that this was done to keep them from breaking when they were heated.

Soon Dieu Donnez sent for me to come to him under the peristyle. He was breaking up the Asson. That must be done to remake it for a new Canzo or a houngan. He wanted me to see how it was done. I was allowed to help him restring the beads and snake-bones that surround the gourd that becomes the most sacred object in Haiti outside of the stones which contain loa. Each important god has a bead of a different color dedicated to him or her and these are represented in the arrangement of the beads on the Asson and in the grand necklace that is worn by all the grades from a hounci to a houngan. The Collier hounci is neither as long nor as elaborate as the Collier Canzo or houngan. The necklace of the houngan is a splendid affair that is looped about his shoulders in a specific manner. It must be very long for that.

That afternoon the ceremonies began. The drums and the hounfort were dedicated. But of course, the very first ceremony was to Papa Legba. I ought to explain that while the people always say and sing "legba," the scholars tell me that the African word is Lecbah or Letbah. Perhaps the people are in error. All I know is they sing "Papa Legba, ouvrier barriere por moi passer." Anyway out in the courtyard of the hounfort of Annee' La Cour, the great preparation was going on. The drapeaux done in blue and white with the symbols in blue and red on it was flying from a pole high on the hounfort with its roasted ear of corn for the god who loves it. I saw the red rooster tied out in front of the house of ceremony. I saw the great tree well decorated with lacyfied palm fronds. Pieces of this stripped palm fronds were everywhere. In the hounfort were niches for the different gods. The pole with an iron serpent beside it for Damballa, "Li qui retti en ciel," (He who lives in the sky) and whose symbol on earth is the serpent. In the second room were the things dedicated to the congos with their resplendent colors. The congo and the Rada should not occupy the same room but they should be under the same roof.

Soon now, we were summoned to the hounfort to begin, and Mambo Etienne tied my red and yellow handkerchief on my head in the proper loose knot at the back of my head. We removed our shoes and went into the hounfort where Dieu Donnez, Annee La Cour were already. The altar was set. Dieu Donnez was seated in a very low chair facing the altar. When we were all in that the place could hold, he covered his head with his ceremonial handkerchief and began the monotonous Litany:

Dieu Donnez: Ela Grand-Pere Eternel,
  Us: Ela Grand-Pere, Eternel, sin dior e'
    Ela Grand-Pere Eternel, Sin dior docor Ague'
    Ela Grand-Pere Eternel Sime nan-min bon O sain'en.
Dieu Donnez: Ela Saint Michel.
Us: Ela Saint Michel, sin dior e', and so on as before.

This continued until Saint Gabriel, Raphael, Nicolas, Joseph, John the Baptist, Saint Peter, Paul, Andre', Jacques, Jean, Phillipe', Come et Damien, Luc, Marc, Louis, Augustine, Vincent, Thomas, Laurent, Sainte Marie, Mere De Dieu, Saint Vierge Marie (A distinction between Virgin Mary and the mother of God), Sainte Catherine, Saintes Lucie, Cecile, Agnes and Agatha. These were all on the christian side and the same response was sung for each name. Now the houngan began to chant the names of the Voodoo gods, and we responded as before including the pagan deities in our chants.

"Ela Lecba Atibon, Sin Dior e', Ela Lecba Atibon, Sin dior docor Ague', Ela Lecba Atibon si' m nan min bon Dieu O Sain 'en."

We were led on to chant to Loco Atisson, Ela Aizan Velequiete, Ela Sobo, Ela Badere, Ela Agassou, Ela Ague' Ta-Royo, Ela Bosou, Ela Agaron, Ela Azacca, Ela Erzulie Freda, Ela Ogoun Bodagris, Ela Ogoun Feraille, Ela Ogoun Shango, Ela Ogoun Taus Sam, Ela Ogoun Achade', Ela Ogoun Palama, Ela Ossage, Ela Baron Carrefour, Ela Baron La Croix, Ela Baron Cimeterre, Ela Guede' Nibo, Ela Papa Cimby, Ela Nanchon Congo, Ela Nanchon Sine'gal, Ela Nanchon Ibo,

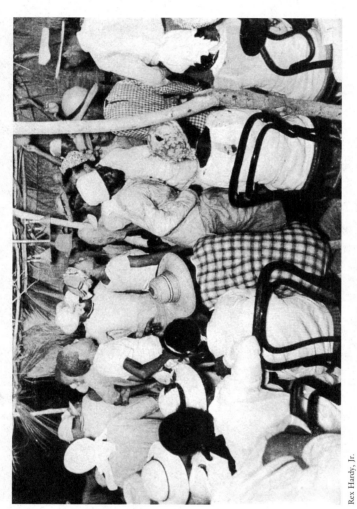

Rex Hardy, Jr.

Jean Valou Dance—Voodoo Ceremony

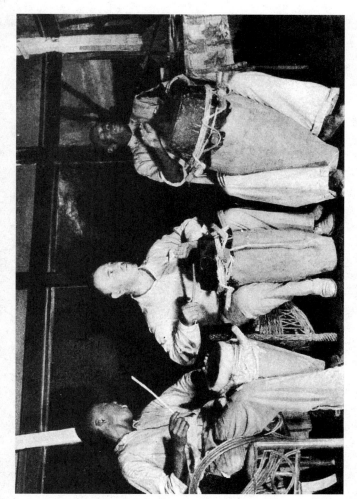

The Drums Woke Up

Ela Nanchon Caplarou, Ela Nanchon Annine, Ela Papa Brise', Ela Contes Loas Petros, Ela Contes Boccos, Ela Contes Houngenicons, Ela Contes Laplaces, Ela Contes Port-Drapeaux, Ela Contes Ounci Canzos, Ela Ounci Dessounins, Ela Contes Ounci Bossales, Ela Contes Hounfort, Ela Contes Oganiers.

Now inside a room of the hounfort, decorated for the occasion, we found a large table on which was placed food and drinks of all the gods to be honored along with the food of Legba, for Legba is never honored alone. He opens the gate so that the other gods come to their worshippers. All over the table there were plates, couis (pronounced Kwee) bottles and flacons. Under the table were the terrines, that is the baked clay containers like crude plates, cruches (little baked clay water-jugs), the chickens dedicated to the different gods, the perfumes and aromatics and leaves which would be used in the ceremonies. All of these were grouped about a watch light whose fuel is olive oil.

Here there was an interruption. Three women entered all dressed in black. They looked like a mother and her two daughters. The service was promptly stopped and the Mambo sent them away almost harshly. The older woman tried to argue, but they were hustled on out. I asked in a whisper why this was done and they said, "They have on black for mourning and so they cannot come in here. This is for the living. Baron Samedi must not be present."

I asked, "But suppose he manifests himself in some of the adepts? There must be some here consecrated to him."

"In that case, we would make a ceremony to drive him away. This is not the day of the dead. This is for the living. All the work would go wrong if he were here."

Dieu Donnez sprinkled the water in the direction of the four quarters of the world. The Canzos and the houncis followed his example. They all faced the door which looks toward the north and chanted, "Afrique-Guinin Atibon Legba, ouvrir barriere pour nous." Dieu Donnez then took the coui of corn meal and drew a design on the ground in the center of which he poured a little of each of the drinks dedicated to Legba. He took a piece of the baked banana, herring, a few grains of corn, a bit of watermelon, a bit of cake and placed them all in a single little heap within the design. Until then Dieu Donnez had done all these things seated in a very low chair. Now he arose and took two "poule Zinga" (speckled chickens), one in each hand. These he elevated to the east, the west, the north and the south in turn, saying: "Au nom du Grand Maitre, Tocan Frieda Dahomey, Marassas, Dossou, Dossa, toute l'Esprits, Atibon, Ogoun, Locos, Negue, fait, Negue Defait." The assistants knelt down. The houngan passed the two chickens over the heads of the kneeling Canzos and houncis. Then he turned to a niche dedicated to Legba and saluted it. Returning then to that north-facing door, he took the two chickens in one hand and a firebrand in the other, and set fire to the three heaps of gunpowder placed around the design or signature of Legba while the adepts were chanting:

"Ce Letbah, qui ap vini, ce papa Legba laissez barriere l'ouvri."

The moment had come to consecrate the chickens to Legba. Dieu Donnez knelt and kissed the earth. He kissed three times the signature of Legba. The whole crowd followed his example. The drums woke up. First the tenor boulatier, then the sirgonh and last the thundering hountah, which controls the mood and the movement of the dancers. Some of the hounci began the Jean Valou. Dieu Donnez broke the wings of one of the chickens, then its legs, holding the throat of the fowl in such a way that it did not cry out as the sickening sound of cracking bones broke through the singing. Then he wrung its neck. In every other ceremony the throat is cut. The supposedly dead bird was placed upon the signature, but after what seemed like a full minute, even with its broken thighs, it leaped in its death agony and crashed into me. My heart flinched and my flesh drew up like tripe. With averted eyes I heard the next song begin with the rattle of the Asson:

"Ouanga te' papa Legba, Legba Touton, Legba Atibon—" they began with a lust and ended, "Toute hounci fait Croix."

The order of the ceremonies to the gods continued according to the rhythm of the offerings. The next god honored was Aisan who walks with the Marassas, Yumeaux ad Trumeaux and the child who follows the twins which is called the

Rex Hardy, Jr.

In Full Ritual the Houngan Kisses the Sword

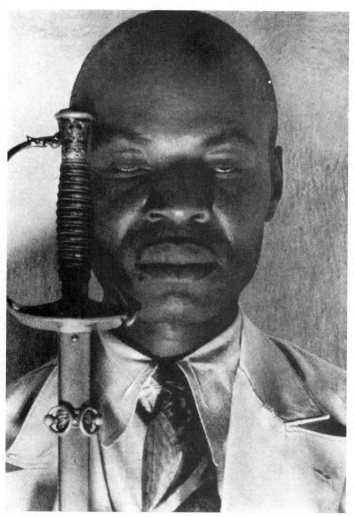

Rex Hardy, Jr.

The Loa "Mounts" the Houngan

Dossou. They are the gods of the little joined plates that one finds displayed all over Haiti. The full name is Marassas Cinigal (black twins) Dahomey.

Mambo Etienne shook her Asson and sang:

> "Aisan, hey! Ou ape' laisse' coule'
> Aisan, hey! Oua te' Corone' Gis."

We were now in full ceremony. Dieu Donnez bowed himself twice toward the altar. He took a white pigeon and lifted it to the four quarters of the earth before he killed it. Then all of the good angels and twins were supposed to enter the hounfort. This ceremony to the twins is observed by all who have or have had twins in the family. It is believed that twins have some special power to harm if they are not appeased. It seems that everyone in Haiti has been involved with twins in one way or another, so that the ceremony is universal. The food was all on white plates and divided into two parts. One part for the Marassas and the other for the adepts.

Mambo Mabo Aizan who walks with the Marassas, the twins, is the wife of Papa Loco whose full name is Loco Atison Goue' Azambloguide', Loa Atinoque', and he is always accompanied by a Nanchon-Aan-Hizo-Yan-go. In the ceremonies of the days of Grand Fete, when all of the mysteries are honored and saluted, the ceremony to Loco comes immediately after the Marassas. So Dieu Donnez took a grayish cock in his two hands and lifted it toward the altar at the same time that he bowed himself. Then he turned toward the east, toward the south and toward the west. He poured the libation of rum and clairin on the ground and chanted:

> "Loco Anbe'! Ce Loco Azambloguidi
> Loca Anbe'! Loco Atinogue' Apoyoci
> Loco, Loco Atinis do guidi, Loco
> Azamblonguidi Atinogue', Loco he'!"

The houngan saluted the white pot on the altar that was dedicated to Loco. The Mambo and several servitors became possessed and the crowd became excited because they were glad that the god was manifesting himself so freely. In this

exalted condition these "horses" of Loco dressed an altar to
him. They placed a table and placed on it the sacred stone
dedicated to Loco, his white pot, chapilets, images of St. Joseph and his drinks. A visiting houngan became possessed and
the cry went up that "Papa Loco 'Amarre les points' "—that
is, he was "tying the points." That means that the loa was
personally taking a hand in the execution of the things asked
of him by his followers. For instance, a man came to Dieu
Donnez to make good in a business venture. He had come to
the houngan to find out what he must do to insure success.
He wanted the houngan to invoke the "Master of his head,"
to give him the information and assistance needed. The houngan summoned his loa and he came and it was Papa Loco. He
demanded certain articles and indicated to Dieu Donnez
which ceremony to observe and how to conduct it. The loa
then left the houngan and he informed the man who had
asked the favor what the loa had demanded. The man gave
the houngan the money to buy the things and to celebrate
the ceremony. The supplicant, of course, would not be
present at this. But when Dieu Donnez went to perform the
rites, Loco took possession of the body of the houngan and
performed the ceremony himself. Then he was "tying the
points." The reason it was known that Loco was there himself, was because he said with the lips of the houngan, "Vivant
yo pas rainmin loa, yo rahi voodoo ce' ouanga yo rainmin."

But Loco can be terrible sometimes. He refuses to answer
when he pleases. He refused to answer the very next applicant. The man was very eager for an answer but the houngan
told him to wait until another time. But for two women who
had asked health favors of Loco Papa Loco indicated a ceremony out under the tree that was his repository. So we took
our chairs and went out under the tree. We marched three
times around the tree carrying the chairs and singing. The
little baskets with the offerings were hanging from the limbs.
The houngans intoned the ceremony and we answered. Two
live chickens were passed all about the heads and the shoulders of the two kneeling women. Dieu Donnez made a cross
on top of the heads of both women with the corn meal. Both
women were made to stand and were faced both ways as they
danced around the tree. When they had danced so far, the

Altar to Ogoun Feraille, God of War.
Old Iron and Other Metals Are Offered to Him

priest faced them the other way. Finally the chicken of each woman was surrendered to the priest and killed with a knife—their heads bent far back to expose their throats. More singing with four women marching around the tree picking the chickens as they went. The loose feathers in the lamp light made a pattern of a loose tumbling circle in the air like playful little clouds or like suntracks in the sky. Some of the cooked chicken was returned and the two women executed a wild dance about the tree and the signature of Loco on the ground. Then some of the food was put in the hollow of the tree for the god.

There was a new note on the Rada drums. We went into the hounfort to the altar of Ogoun. There are many Ogouns. Ogoun Badagris, Ogoun Ferraille, Ogoun Shango or Chango, Ogoun Balingio. But this ceremony was to Ogoun Badagris. Before his altar there were eggs and corn meal, the signs of fertility. There were sweets, and parched corn and peanuts. Of course, the water dedicated to the dead and the liqueurs, cognac, red wine, rum clairin and a red cock. The same one that I had seen tied all day by one leg before the bath house of ceremony. I felt I knew that rooster because another had attacked him while he was tethered there and while he showed plenty of courage, being tied by the leg hindered his movements, and I had driven off his assailant. I looked into his round brown eye in the hounfort and looked away. A sword was stuck into the earth at the central pole and a round black hat something like a Turkish fez was hung on the handle of it. Joswee, the sabreur (sword-bearer) who belonged to the compound of Dieu Donnez engaged Pierre Charles the sabreur of Annee La Cour in mock combat. It was a very lively encounter and brought wild cheering. As Pierre Charles was forced to give away before Joswee, a figure leaped into the door. It was all in blazing red from head to foot. The skirts of the robes were very full and trimmed in white lace. This figure rushed forward, put on the fez, seized the sword and challenged Joswee fiercely. The crowd went mad as the clever dance went on. Neither really conquered the other. It was not done to prove strength and courage. It was done as a symbol of

Ogoun's power to help warriors and for the magnificent and spirited grotesque.

The Man in red dress was Ogoun. At a point, both lowered their blades and Ogoun planted a ceremonial kiss on the brow of Joswee. The drums commenced to walk with the songs and Dieu Donnez took the red rooster from Joswee. He surprised the fowl by setting off a little heap of gunpowder near him and the rooster leaped high. The crowd called that "foula poule." The servitors following Mambo Etienne knelt and kissed the earth. One female hounci, when she knelt before Madame Etienne received a good kick in the behind for not behaving properly. The second prayer was chanted and the tongue of the red rooster is torn out before it is killed with a sharp knife. Some of its blood is smeared on the wall with a cluster of feathers from the throat. The body of the rooster was placed before the altar. The drums changed their tempo and Dieu Donnez left the hounfort and crossed the peristyle followed by everybody because he was going to salute all the repositories in the place. Several servitors became possessed during this part of the ceremony. There was a great deal of spirited dancing under the peristyle after the repositories had been honored. The figure of Ogoun dominated the movement. Dieu Donnez was beating the hountah, the greatest Rada drum, women wishing children prostrated themselves before Ogoun and when he danced with them in a way to symbolize sex and procreation there was joy and even ecstasy in their faces. He did not always approach them from the front. He sometimes approached them from the rear as they danced face to face with someone else and made his motions of promise.

We then honored Damballa, the great and the pure. He was given the sweet soft drinks and white chickens. He it is who looks after peace and love in the home so that a pair of white chickens, a hen and a rooster are offered him. They must be bought a month in advance and dedicated to his intention. When they have been sacrificed, they are laid side by side before the altar.

The last deity to be honored was Brave Guedé, who is a sort of messenger of all the gods. Then we danced for the rest of the night. We knew that the next day a Petro ceremony, "A

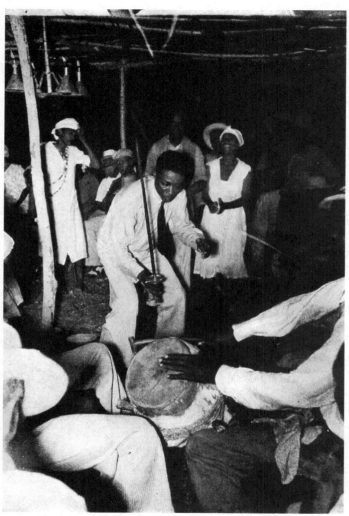

Rex Hardy, Jr.

The Sabreur Before the Gods

The Mambo Offers to Damballa

"Horse" Mounted by Papa Guedé

day of promise" was in store for us but we danced the sun out of bed just the same. After daylight, the nattes or sleeping mats were full of people that looked like dead bodies getting some sleep before the ceremonies of the day should begin. Lamissier woke me up to hand me a cup of chanelle tea and to tell me that Dieu Donnez wanted me.

I had about two hours of instruction in the nature of the gods and something about their origins. I had some practise in drawing with corn meal the ververs or signatures of various loa. Then he let me see him work on the Paquettes de Congo. They are those figures which must be present at a baptism and the new drapeaux (flags) and the new sabre were to be baptized on Sunday.

Before we go into the description of the outdoor altar to Petro, let me give you some idea of the differences between a Rada god and a Petro divinity.

As has been said before, Damballa and his suite are high and pure. They do only good things for people, but they are slow and lacking in power. The Petro gods on the other hand are terrible and wicked, but they are more powerful and quick. They can be made to do good things, however, as well as evil. They give big doses of medicine and effect quick cures. So these Petro gods are resorted to by a vast number of people who wish to gain something but fear them at the same time. The Rada spirits demand nothing more than chickens and pigeons, and there are no consequences or hereafter to what they do for you, while the Petros demand hogs, goats, sheep, cows, dogs and in some instances they have been known to take dead bodies from the tombs. The Petros work for you only if you make a promise of service to them. You can promise a service to be fulfilled as far away as thirty years, but at the end of that time, the promise *must* be kept or the spirits begin to take revenge. It seems that they actually do collect on the debt owed to them, for first the domestic animals of the family begin to die and when all these are gone, the children fall ill and die if the service is still not done and finally the head of the house. If you make a promise to the Petros *it is going to be kept.*

The Petros and the Congos, who sometimes unite are the cults who make use of charms, ouangas (pronounced wanga).

The Petro Quita Sec have the power to take human life. There is a long list of these spirits who have the same names as the Rada gods except that the second name distinguishes them from the rada. "Ge-rouge" after a name places that god in the Petros or the Congos. For instance we find Damballa Ge-rouge which means "red-eyed," Erzulle, ge-rouge, Ogoun ge-rouge, Damballa-la-flambeau. The list included the Congos Savanne, that is Congos of the open field or woods, such as Congo Mazambi, Congo Zandor, Marinette-pied-seche (dry foot), Erzulie Mapiangue, Bacca loup-gerow, Petit Jean Petro. They are recognized as evil, but one must feed them to have better luck than others. Louis Romain says, "All these mysteres make big cures and do heavy work. When you have a big sickness case about which Rada mysteres are too helpless to bring recovery Petro will undertake the treatment and *cure* the party. They give you luck to find a job or to start any kind of trading. They lend you big support or give you something to protect you in order that nothing will happen to you and that no one will cause you to be sick, and the demons or the devil will be unable to do you anything at night."

Therefore, since these evil mysteres are so useful, it is necessary for the houngan to have them under his control. Many, many families have their day of promise to the Petros for health, wealth or advancement in life.

The Petros make great use of fire. When a Petro ceremony is going on, there is always a big fire close by the hounfort with a bar of iron stuck into the middle of the flames.

Every Christmas, the Petros fix baths for all of those for whom they have worked during the year. They also give them "guards." Some times they dose their followers with machettas. Sometimes they cut a piece out of your body and put something in the hole and close it up. Two minutes afterwards, you feel nothing and know nothing about the wound. Neither can anyone see it again.

No Petro ceremony is held in the hounfort where the niche or repository of Damballa is. Even the door to the hounfort must be kept closed while the Petro service is going on. Neither can the two services be held in the same day.

The Petro *ceremony of promise* or of service to Petro is held in the open air.

Two large draperies or curtains are joined together at one end by a large hoop or circle of some kind and suspended from a limb of a tree. Beside this is a partition built to that end formed by the two sides of the niche. The loose ends opposite fall about a table which is covered by the curtains. A picture representing Maitresse Erzulie, St. Joseph and Loco is hung at the bottom of the niche which is decorated by a knot of red ribbon. A white plate is on the table with a knife, fork and spoon. As many different kinds of perfume as the suppli-cant can afford are on the table also with bouquets of flowers. At a little distance from the draped niche is the tonnelle, a palm thatched shed open on all sides which contains the two Petro drums. It must be ten metres from the niche. That dis-tance is fixed.

The animals consecrated to Petro Quita Mondong are the pig, the goat, male and female; and the dog.

During the afternoon we saw the niche, the tonnelle being built and three holes being dug not far from the niche. Every-thing was ready by night time. The houngan went into the court to see that everything was ready and it was. The fire, the niche, the tonnelle, the animals, the family who wished to make the promise to Petro and the Canzos and houncis. See-ing all this, he had the animals led up to the holes and began the services.

First came the Litany to Saint Joseph, then the Pater-Noster. These being intoned and finished, he demanded to know as a matter of form if the animals had been bought for the ceremony. A Canzo answered that they had been bought and they were now present. He then asked if they had been bathed. He was told that they had been bathed. He next asked if they had been perfumed. He was told that all of the animals present had been perfumed also. Since these things had been attended to, he said that they must be dressed. Then a sort of cape, or tunic was thrown over the back of each animal and tied with a ribbon about the neck and an-other under its tail. The heads of the animals were wrapped in a white cloth.

The officiating houngan gave the word after the voodoo prayers had been said, and the procession with the animals began. It circled the niche, the tonnelle, the three holes and a house of ceremony. The three holes were illuminated by a dozen white candles. Here before the holes Dieu Donnez drew his sabre from its scabbard and cut off the testicles of the pig, which he first elevated for the edification of the crowd, then placed on a white plate prepared to receive this sacred burden. The houngan turned again to the groaning animal and stuck him in the throat and caught the blood, or part of it in the white soup plate. Then he drank some blood from the wound himself. Then the family who was making the promise was brought forward and placed money, gold money, in the plate with the blood. It could not be less than five dollars somebody told me.

The family drank some of the blood from the plate and crossing themselves dipped their fingers in the blood and drew a cross on their foreheads and on napes of their necks in the hot blood of the pig. They put a cruche with wine in it in one of the end holes and a cruche with liquor in the other. The middle hole received the blood and the testicles of the hog. At that moment an adept knelt, kissed the earth three times and stated the demands of the family upon the gods.

The pig is always sacrificed the first day of the ceremony. The next day was the day of Quita and in a ceremony essentially the same, the male and female goat were sacrificed. The male goat was brought under the tonnelle in its little flowered cape, but he was most unwilling. We chanted, we sang, and effort was made to lead the goat gaily about the center pole but he balked and had to be pushed every step of the way in the procession. The red-clad Ogoun bestrode him and the crowd yelled and pushed and pulled but the goat was emphatic in his desire to have nothing to do with the affair. The crowd sang and shouted exultantly but I could hear the pathetic, frightened bleat of the goat beneath it all, as he was buffeted and dragged to make a grand spectacle of his death.

The next day was spent in the chants and dances to Petro Quita and on which day a bull was sacrificed. Dressed in the

Offering to Congo Savanne

ruffled cape tied upon its back it was led about and the world ran behind it chanting:

> "Wah, wah, wah, wah, wah O bay
> Wah, wah, wah, wah, wah O bay
> Wah, wah, wah, wah, wah O bay
> Pas Tombé."

During the procession with the bull I heard the most beautiful song that I heard in all Haiti. The air was exquisite and I promised myself to keep it in mind. The sound of the words stayed with me long enough to write them down, but to my great regret the tune that I intended to bring home in my mouth to Harry T. Burleigh escaped me like the angels out of the Devil's mouth. The words they chanted as they followed the bull which was unwilling, like the goat, to go were:

> Bah day, bah day, oh man jah ee!
> Bah day, bah day, oh man jah ee!
> Bah day, bah day, oh man jah ee!
> Oh bah day, oh way, oh man jah ee.

The thing that the adepts seemed to enjoy most was the drink of Petro. That is a mixture of pig blood, fresh from the wound, white wine, red wine, a pinch of flour, cannelle and nutmeg. All of this is put in a bowl and whipped well. It was most agreeable to the participants, and eagerly quaffed. In fact it seemed extremely good and even a small sip was jealously sought.

The next morning, I received a message from my good friend Louis Romain to come to Port-au-Prince to witness a Canzo ceremony, so I got the first camion and did not see the end of the Petro at Archahaie. However I did see a Petro Mondong ceremony in which they sacrificed a dog.

That ceremony was the same except that the dog was not killed so soon in this instance. Only part of one of his ears was cut off by the priest. Then an assistant pulled the teeth of the dog and finally he was buried alive. The god had indicated that he desired his food thus.

I was under the wing of Louis Romain and his wife, who is

herself a Mambo and they were extremely kind and consider-
ate of me. Louis has the gift of making you understand in one
sentence more than most people can with a page. I found
every word he ever told me to be true. Never once did he
attempt to mislead me. He saw to it that I went places and
saw things. He was preparing me to "go Canzo" myself. That
is the second degree of initiation in the department of the
West. It is the second step towards the priesthood.

The usual routine is this:

The spirit enters the head of a person. He is possessed of
this spirit and sometimes he or she is troubled by it because
the possession comes at times and places that are, perhaps,
embarrassing. On advice, he goes to a houngan and the spirit
is identified and the "horse" is advised to make food for the
loa who is the master of his head. As soon as the person is
financially able, he or she goes through the ceremony of baptism known as "getting the head washed." Three days before
the reception of the degree, the candidate presents himself to
the houngan, who receives him and makes certain libations to
the spirit who has claimed the candidate. The libation varies
according to the god. It is a sweet liquor if it is Damballa,
rum for Ogoun, Loco or Legba. The candidate is dressed in a
long white shirt with sleeves to the wrists. The head of the
applicant is wrapped in a large white handkerchief and he is
put to bed on a natte where he must remain for seventy-two
hours. The last day, which is the day of consecration, his head
is washed, and he is given something to eat and drink. He
usually rises possessed of his loa who continues the service in
place of the houngan. Then he is a hounci bossal, the first
step of the way to the priesthood. This does not mean that all
houncis become houngans. Far from it. Only a small proportion ever take the second step which is the Canzo.

The Canzo is a hounci who "brule son zinc" (burns his
zinc fish hook). The second degree renders the hounci invul-
nerable to fire. Like the candidate for the first degree, the
hounci who wishes to be Canzo presents himself at the hounfort of the houngan seven days before the service is to be
finished. He carries with him a long white night gown. He is
put to bed in the first room of the hounfort on a bed of
Mimbon leaves. But an odd number of candidates cannot

Rex Hardy, Jr.

The Priest Opens the Ceremony with a Chant

take the degree at the same time. It must be an even number, or one must wait, because the hounci are put to bed in pairs. The two men who sleep together thus are called brothers-in-law. If it is a pair of women, they are sisters-in-law. They are given nothing to eat except fresh fruits, milk and the like. The Mambo or the priest lies down occasionally to instruct the candidates, and they are cautioned to relax and to permit the spirit to dominate them.

When the seventh day, which is the day of consecration arrives, a great fire is built and a large kettle of water put on it and allowed to boil. A small stone or a piece of money is thrown in the pot by the houngan. The houngan, after saluting the gods of the candidates, sounds the Asson and pronounces the sacred words: "Ce grand Maitre qui passe avant nous, tous les saints, les morts, Marassas, Afrique Guinin, Ce yo qui fait, qui defait" (This Grand Master, that is Lord of Lords, who passes before us, all the saints, the dead, the twins, African gods, that which they do, they are able to undo.) The adepts, the houncis, the Canzos already consecrated salute with the drums the newly elected.

The houngan pours the libations, some into the flames. He places a small amount of gunpowder near the small kettle; he approaches it with a fire brand in his hand, and sets it off. He sets off a small amount of gunpowder in the hand of each candidate. Then he himself, to the great astonishment of the crowd puts both hands into the boiling pot and takes out the stone or the money there without burning himself.

Then the brule zinc begins. The four little clay pots are put on three iron pegs for each pot. The pine wood is set and a blazing fire under each pot is kept up. Two small chickens are torn to death and some of the feathers dipped in their blood are stuck to each pot. The drums are beating and the Canzo who has been assigned to each candidate conducts him or her in line. A huge sheet or cloth is spread over the Canzos and candidates. They dance around the blazing pots from one to the other. The boiling chickens have been removed from the water and cornmeal added. One servitor takes the boiling corn meal from a pot, rolls it into balls with his hands and passes them quickly to a candidate who passes it along. They are instructed to anoint their hands from the white plate of olive oil so that they will not burn themselves from the hot corn meal mush. They proceed from pot to pot. The left foot and the left hand of each candidate is thrust into the fire, but they are not burned. It is to prove to them that they are impervious to fire that the food and the hand are exposed to flame. All this time the drums are beating furiously and the crowd of servitors and hounci are dancing round in the circle behind the Canzos with their candidates. When the fiery ordeal is over, the corn meal balls, the knife, fork and white plate, with a piece of white calico, the iron bars called "piedszin" all tied up together with the calico and some leaves, and they are buried in a large hole. Pieces of the pine wood (bois pins) and some of all the food, a glass, one of the ounzin, some money, rum and clairin and all are buried. The houngan orders the houncis to cover the hole. They toss in the dirt and stamp it down with the left foot. The next day, the houngan invests the new Canzo who are all dressed in new white things, with grand colliers (necklaces) and the Assons. Now they may hold consultations and serve the houngans most directly. It is a very joyful time for everybody. The peristyle of the hounfort fairly glitters with the crowds all dressed in new white for the final details.

The next step is to become a priest, but that is for the few. The way most acceptable to become a priest is by inheritance. But many are "claimed" by the gods. There are still others who just take up the trade.

The most famous houngans in Haiti are:

Do-See-Mah (sound spelling) of Cotes De Fer, a horse back ride up in the hills from the Sea. Port-de-Paix is the nearest large town. Do-See-Mah is the houngan of the upper classes. He is said to be so independent that he will not see anyone about his profession on Sunday no matter how urgent the case.

Ti Cousin (Little Cousin) of Leogane. Said to be the richest houngan in all Haiti. He has applied business methods to his profession and certainly has prospered. He is overlord of great stretches of land and many people. Some say that he is more often a Bocor than a houngan.

Dieu Donnez St. Leger, of Archahaie. He is not a rich man,

Mme. Romain, a Mambo

but he is not a poor one either. Every young person under his care must attend school.

Di Di, a little beyond Archahaie on the north.

Archahaie is the most famous and the most dreaded spot in all Haiti for Voodoo work. It is supposed to be the great center of the Zombie trade. But Kenscoff and many other localities have their names in the mouths of the people.

Ah Bo Bo!

Chapter XIII

Zombies

WHAT IS the whole truth and nothing else but the truth about Zombies? I do not know, but I know that I saw the broken remnant, relic, or refuse of Felicia Felix-Mentor in a hospital yard.

Here in the shadow of the Empire State Building, death and the graveyard are final. It is such a positive end that we use it as a measure of nothingness and eternity. We have the quick and the dead. But in Haiti there is the quick, the dead, and then there are Zombies.

This is the way Zombies are spoken of: They are the bodies without souls. The living dead. Once they were dead, and after that they were called back to life again.

No one can stay in Haiti long without hearing Zombies mentioned in one way or another, and the fear of this thing and all that it means seeps over the country like a ground current of cold air. This fear is real and deep. It is more like a group of fears. For there is the outspoken fear among the peasants of the work of Zombies. Sit in the market place and pass a day with the market women and notice how often some vendeuse cries out that a Zombie with its invisible hand has filched her money, or her goods. Or the accusation is made that a Zombie has been set upon her or some one of her family to work a piece of evil. Big Zombies who come in the night to do malice are talked about. Also the little girl Zombies who are sent out by their owners in the dark dawn to sell little packets of roasted coffee. Before sun up their cries of "Cafe grille" can be heard from dark places in the streets and one can only see them if one calls out for the seller to come with her goods. Then the little dead one makes herself visible and mounts the steps.

The upper class Haitians fear too, but they do not talk about it so openly as do the poor. But to them also it is a horrible possibility. Think of the fiendishness of the thing. It is not good for a person who has lived all his life surrounded by a degree of fastidious culture, loved to his last breath by family and friends, to contemplate the probability of his resurrected body being dragged from the vault—the best that love and means could provide, and set to toiling ceaselessly in the banana fields, working like a beast, unclothed like a beast, and like a brute crouching in some foul den in the few hours allowed for rest and food. From an educated, intelligent being to an unthinking, unknowing beast. Then there is the helplessness of the situation. Family and friends cannot rescue the victim because they do not know. They think the loved one is sleeping peacefully in his grave. They may motor past the plantation where the Zombie who was once dear to them is held captive often and again and its soulless eyes may have fallen upon them without thought or recognition. It is not to be wondered at that now and then when the rumor spreads that a Zombie has been found and recognized, that angry crowds gather and threaten violence to the persons alleged to be responsible for the crime.

Yet in spite of this obvious fear and the preparations that I found being made to safeguard the bodies of the dead against this possibility, I was told by numerous upper class Haitians that the whole thing was a myth. They pointed out that the common people were superstitious, and that the talk of Zombies had no more basis in fact than the European belief in the Werewolf.

But I had the good fortune to learn of several celebrated cases in the past and then in addition, I had the rare opportunity to see and touch an authentic case. I listened to the broken noises in its throat, and then, I did what no one else had ever done, I photographed it. If I had not experienced all of this in the strong sunlight of a hospital yard, I might have come away from Haiti interested but doubtful. But I saw this case of Felicia Felix-Mentor which was vouched for by the highest authority. So I know that there are Zombies in Haiti. People have been called back from the dead.

Now, why have these dead folk not been allowed to remain in their graves? There are several answers to this question, according to the case.

A was awakened because somebody required his body as a beast of burden. In his natural state he could never have been hired to work with his hands, so he was made into a Zombie

because they wanted his services as a laborer. B was summoned to labor also but he is reduced to the level of a beast
as an act of revenge. C was the culmination of "ba' Moun"
ceremony and pledge. That is, he was given as a sacrifice to
pay off a debt to a spirit for benefits received.

I asked how the victims were chosen and many told me
that any corpse not too old to work would do. The Bocor
watched the cemetery and went back and took suitable bodies. Others said no, that the Bocor and his associates knew
exactly who was going to be resurrected even before they
died. They knew this because they themselves brought about
the "death."

Maybe a plantation owner has come to the Bocor to "buy"
some laborers, or perhaps an enemy wants the utmost in revenge. He makes an agreement with the Bocor to do the
work. After the proper ceremony, the Bocor in his most powerful and dreaded aspect mounts a horse with his face toward
the horse's tail and rides after dark to the house of the victim.
There he places his lips to the crack of the door and sucks out
the soul of the victim and rides off in all speed. Soon the
victim falls ill, usually beginning with a headache, and in a few
hours is dead. The Bocor, not being a member of the family is
naturally not invited to the funeral. But he is there in the
cemetery. He has spied on everything from a distance. He is
in the cemetery but does not approach the party. He never
even faces it directly, but takes in everything out of the corner
of his eye. At midnight he will return for his victim.

Everybody agrees that the Bocor is there at the tomb at
midnight with the soul of the dead one. But some contend
that he has it in a bottle all labelled. Others say no, that he
has it in his bare hand. That is the only disagreement. The
tomb is opened by the associates and Bocor enters the tomb,
calls the name of the victim. He *must* answer because the
Bocor has the soul there in his hand. The dead man answers
by lifting his head and the moment he does this, the Bocor
passes the soul under his nose for a brief second and chains
his wrists. Then he beats the victim on the head to awaken
him further. Then he leads him forth and the tomb is closed
again as if it never had been disturbed.

The victim is surrounded by the associates and the march

to the hounfort (voodoo temple and its surroundings) begins. He is hustled along in the middle of the crowd. Thus he is screened from prying eyes to a great degree and also in his half-waking state he is unable to orientate himself. But the victim is not carried directly to the hounfort. First he is carried past the house where he lived. *This* is always done. *Must* be. If the victim were not taken past his former house, later on he would recognize it and return. But once he is taken past, it is gone from his consciousness forever. It is as if it never existed for him. He is then taken to the hounfort and given a drop of a liquid, the formula for which is most secret. After that the victim is a Zombie. He will work ferociously and tirelessly without consciousness of his surroundings and conditions and without memory of his former state. He can never speak again, unless he is given salt. "We have examples of a man who gave salt to a demon by mistake and he come man again and can write the name of the man who gave him to the loa," Jean Nichols told me and added that of course the family of the victim went straight to a Bocor and "gave" the man who had "given" their son.

Now this "Ba Moun" (give man) ceremony is a thing much talked about in Haiti. It is the old European belief in selling one's self to the devil but with Haitian variations. In Europe the man gives himself at the end of a certain period. Over in Haiti he gives others and only gives himself when no more acceptable victims can be found. But he cannot give strangers. It must be a real sacrifice. He must give members of his own family or most intimate friends. Each year the sacrifice must be renewed and there is no avoiding the payments. There are tales of men giving every member of the family, even his wife after nieces, nephews, sons and daughters were gone. Then at last he must go himself. There are lurid tales of the last days of men who have gained wealth and power thru "Give man."

The wife of one man found him sitting apart from the family weeping. When she demanded to know the trouble, he told her that he had been called to go, but she was not to worry because he had put everything in order. He was crying because he had loved her very much and it was hard to leave her. She pointed out that he was not sick and of course it was ridiculous for him to talk of death. Then with his head in her lap he told her about the "services" he had made to obtain the advantages he had had in order to surround her with increasing comforts. Finally she was the only person left that he could offer but that he would gladly die himself rather than offer her as a sacrifice. He told her of watching the day of the vow come and go while his heart grew heavier with every passing hour. The second night of the contract lapsed and he heard the beasts stirring in their little box. The third night which was the one just past, a huge and a terrible beast had emerged in the room. If he could go to the Bocor that same day with a victim, he still could go another year at least. But he had no one to offer except his wife and he had no desire to live without her. He took an affectionate farewell of her, shut himself in his own room and continued to weep. Two days later he was dead.

Another man received the summons late one night. Bosu Tricorne, the terrible three-horned god had appeared in his room and made him know that he must go. Bosu Tricorne bore a summons from Baron Cimiterre, the lord of the cemetery. He sprang from his bed in terror and woke up his family by his fear noises. He had to be restrained from hurling himself out of the window. And all the time he was shouting of the things he had done to gain success. Naming the people he had given. The family in great embarrassment dragged him away from the window and tried to confine him in a room where his shouts could not be heard by the neighbors. That failing, they sent him off to a private room in a hospital where he spent two days confessing before he died. There are many, many tales like that in the mouths of the people.

There is the story of one man of great courage who, coming to the end of his sacrifices, feeling that he had received what he bargained for, went two days ahead and gave himself up to the spirit to die. But the spirit so admired his courage that he gave him back all of the years he had bargained to take.

Why do men allegedly make such bargains with the spirits who have such terrible power to reward and punish?

When a man is ambitious and sees no way to get there, he becomes desperate. When he has nothing and wants prosperity he goes to a houngan and says, "I have nothing and I am disposed to do anything to have money."

The houngan replies, "He who does not search, does not find."

"I have come to you because I wish to search," the man replies.

"Well, then," the houngan says, "we are going to make a ceremony, and the loa are going to talk with you."

The houngan and the man go into the hounfort. He goes to a small altar and makes the symbol with ashes and gunpowder (indicating that it is a Petro invocation), pours the libation and begins to sing with the Asson and then asks the seeker, "What loa you want me to call for you?"

The man makes his choice. Then the houngan begins in earnest to summon the loa wanted. No one knows what he says because he is talking "langage" that is language, a way of denoting the African patter used by all houngans for special occasions. The syllables are his very own, that is something that cannot be taught. It must come to the priest from the loa. He calls many gods. Then the big jars under the table that contain spirits of houngans long dead begin to groan. These spirits in jars have been at the bottom of the water for a long time. The loa was not taken from their heads at death and so they did not go away from the earth but went to the bottom of the water to stay until they got tired and demanded to be taken out. All houngans have one or more of these spirit jars in the hounfort. Some have many. The groaning of the jars gets louder as the houngan keeps calling. Finally one jar speaks distinctly, "Pourquoi, ou derange' moi?" (Why do you disturb me?) The houngan signals the man to answer the loa. So he states his case.

"Papa, loa, ou mem, qui connais toute baggaye ou mem qui chef te de l'eau, moi derange' ou pour mande' ou servir moi." (Papa, loa, yourself, who knows all things, you yourself who is master of waters, I disturb you to ask you to serve me.)

The Voice: Ma connais ca ou besoin. Mais, ou dispose pour servir moi aussi? (I know what you want, but are you disposed to serve me also?)

The Man: Yes, command me what you want.

Voice: I am going to give you all that you want, but you must make all things that I want. Write your name in your own blood and put the paper in the jar.

The houngan still chanting pricks the man's finger so sharply that he cries out. The blood flows and the supplicant dips a pen in it and writes his name and puts the paper in the jar. The houngan opens a bottle of rum and pours some in the jar. There is the gurgling sound of drinking.

The Voice: And now I am good (I do good) for you. Now I tell you what you must do. You must give me someone that you love. Today you are going into your house and stay until tomorrow. On the eighth day you are returning here with something of the man that you are going to give me. Come also with some money in gold. The voice ceases. The houngan finishes presently after repeating everything that the Voice from the jar has said and dismisses the man. He goes away and returns on the day appointed and the houngan calls up the loa again.

The Voice: Are you prepared for me?

The Man: Yes.

The Voice: Have you done all that I told you?

The Man: Yes.

The Voice (to houngan): Go out. (To man) Give me the gold money.

(The man gives it.)

The Voice: Now, you belong to me and I can do with you as I wish. If I want you in the cemetery I can put you there.

The Man: Yes, I know you have all power with me. I put myself in your care because I want prosperity.

The Voice: That I will give you. Look under the table. You will find a little box. In this box there are little beasts. Take this little box and put it in your pocket. Every eighth day you must put in it five hosts (Communion wafers). *Never forget to give the hosts.* Now, go to your house and put the little box in a big box. Treat it as if it were your son. It is now your son. Every midnight open the box and let the beasts out. At four o'clock he will return and cry to come in and you will open for him and close the box again. And every time you give the beasts the communion, immediately after, you will receive large sums of money. Each year on this date you will come to me with another man that you wish to give me. Also you must bring the box with the beasts. If you do not come, the third night after the date, the beasts in the box will become great huge animals and execute my will upon you for your failure to keep your vow. If you are very sick on that day that the offering falls due say to your best friend that he must bring the offering box for you. Also you must send the name of the person you intend to give me as pay for working for you and he must sign a new contract with me for you.

All is finished between the Voice and the man. The houngan re-enters and sends the man away with assurance that he will commence the work at once. Alone he makes ceremony to call the soul of the person who is to be sacrificed. No one would be permitted to see that. When the work in the hounfort is finished, then speeds the rider on the horse. The rider who faces backwards on the horse, who will soon place his lips to the crack of the victim's door and draw his soul away. Then will follow the funeral and after that the midnight awakening. And the march to the hounfort for the drop of liquid that will make him a Zombie, one of the living dead.

Some maintain that a real and true priest of Voodoo, the houngan, has nothing to do with such practices. That it is the bocor and priests of the devil—worshipping cults who do these things. But it is not always easy to tell just who is a houngan and who is a bocor. Often the two offices occupy the same man at different times. There is no doubt that some houngans hold secret ceremonies which their usual following know nothing of. It would be necessary to investigate every houngan and bocor in Haiti rigidly over a period of years to determine who was purely houngan and who was purely Bocor. There is certainly some overlapping in certain cases. A well known houngan of Leogane, who has become a very wealthy man by his profession is spoken of as a bocor more often than as a houngan. There are others in the same category that I could name. Soon after I arrived in Haiti a young woman who was on friendly terms with me said, "You know, you should not go around alone picking acquaintances with these houngans. You are liable to get involved in something

that is not good. You must have someone to guide you." I
laughed it off at the time, but months later I began to see
what she was hinting at.

What is involved in the "give man" and making of Zombies
is a question that cannot be answered anywhere with legal
proof. Many names are called. Most frequently mentioned in
this respect is the Man of Trou Forban. That legendary character who lives in the hole in the mountain near St. Marc. He
who has enchanted caves full of coffee and sugar plantations.
The entrance to this cave or this series of caves is said to be
closed by a huge rock that is lifted by a glance from the master. The Marines are said to have blown up this great rock
with dynamite at one time, but the next morning it was there
whole and in place again. When the master of Trou Forban
walks, the whole earth trembles. There are tales of the master
and his wife, who is reputed to be a greater Bocor than he.
She does not live with him at Trou Forban. She is said to have
a great hounfort of her own on the mountain called Tapion
near Petit Gouave. She is such a great houngan that she is
honored by Agoue' te Royo, Maitre l'eau, and walks the waters with the same ease that others walk the earth. But she
rides in boats whenever it suits her fancy. One time she took a
sailboat to go up the coast near St. Marc to visit her husband,
Vixama. She appeared to be an ordinary peasant woman and
the captain paid her no especial attention until they arrived on
the coast below Trou Forban. Then she revealed herself and
expressed her great satisfaction with the voyage. She felt that
the captain had been extremely kind and courteous, so she
went to call her husband to come down to the sea to meet
him. Realizing now who she was, the captain was afraid and
made ready to sail away before she could return from the long
trip up the mountain. But she had mounted to the trou very
quickly and returned with Vixama to find the captain and his
crew poling the boat away from the shore in the wildest terror. The wind was against them and they could not sail away.
Mme. Vixama smiled at their fright and hurled two grains of
corn which she held in her hand, on to the deck of the boat
and they immediately turned into golden coin. The captain
was more afraid and hastily brushed them into the sea. They
sailed south all during the night, much relieved that they had

broken all connections with Vixama and his wife. But at first light the next morning he found four gold coins of the same denomination as the two that he had refused the day before. Then he knew that the woman of Vixama had passed the night on board and had given them a good voyage as well—the four gold coins were worth twenty dollars each.

There are endless tales of the feats of the occupant of this hole high up on this inaccessible mountain. But in fact it has yet to be proved that anyone has ever laid eyes on him. He is like the goddess in the volcano of Hawaii, and Vulcan in Mt. Vesuvius. It is true that men, taking advantage of the legend and the credulous nature of the people, have set up business in the mountain to their profit. The name of this Man of Trou Forban is known by few and rarely spoken by those who know it. This whispered name is Vixama, which in itself means invisible spirit. He who sits with a hive of honey-bees in his long flowing beard. It is he who is reputed to be the greatest buyer of souls. His contact man is reputed to be Mardi Progres. But we hear too much about the practice around Archahaie and other places to credit Trou Forban as the headquarters. Some much more accessible places than the mountain top is the answer. And some much more substantial being than the invisible Vixama.

If embalming were customary, it would remove the possibility of Zombies from the minds of the people. But since it is not done, many families take precaution against the body being disturbed.

Some set up a watch in the cemetery for thirty-six hours after the burial. There could be no revival after that. Some families have the bodies cut open, insuring real death. Many peasants put a knife in the right hand of the corpse and flex the arm in such a way that it will deal a blow with the knife to whoever disturbs it for the first day or so. But the most popular defense is to poison the body. Many of the doctors have especially long hypodermic needles for injecting a dose of poison into the heart, and sometimes into other parts of the body as well.

A case reported from Port du Paix proves the necessity of this. In Haiti if a person dies whose parents are still alive, the mother does not follow the body to the grave unless it is an only child. Neither does she wear mourning in the regular sense. She wears that coarse material known as "gris-blanc." The next day after the burial, however, she goes to the grave to say her private farewell.

In the following case everything had seemed irregular. The girl's sudden illness and quick death. Then, too, her body stayed warm. So the family was persuaded that her death was unnatural and that some further use was to be made of her body after burial. They were urged to have it secretly poisoned before it was interred. This was done and the funeral went off in routine manner.

The next day like Mary going to the tomb of Jesus, the mother made her way to the cemetery to breathe those last syllables that mothers do over their dead, and like Mary she found the stones rolled away. The tomb was open and the body lifted out of the coffin. It had not been moved because it was so obviously poisoned. But the ghouls had not troubled themselves to rearrange things as they were.

Testimony regarding Zombies with names and dates come from all parts of Haiti. I shall cite a few without using actual names to avoid embarrassing the families of the victims.

In the year 1898 at Cap Haitian a woman had one son who was well educated but rather petted and spoiled. There was some trouble about a girl. He refused to accept responsibility and when his mother was approached by a member of the girl's family she refused to give any sort of satisfaction. Two weeks later the boy died rather suddenly and was buried. Several Sundays later the mother went to church and after she went wandering around the town—just walking aimlessly in her grief, she found herself walking along Bord Mer. She saw some laborers loading ox carts with bags of coffee and was astonished to see her son among these silent workers who were being driven to work with ever increasing speed by the foreman. She saw her son see her without any sign of recognition. She rushed up to him screaming out his name. He regarded her without recognition and without sound. By this time the foreman tore her loose from the boy and drove her away. She went to get help, but it was a long time and when she returned she could not find him. The foreman denied that there had ever been anyone of that description around. She never saw him again, though she haunted the water front and coffee warehouses until she died.

A white protestant Missionary Minister told me that he had a young man convert to his flock who was a highly intelligent fellow and a clever musician. He went to a dance and fell dead on the floor. The missionary conducted the funeral and saw the young man placed in the tomb and the tomb closed. A few weeks later another white minister of another protestant denomination came to him and said, "I had occasion to visit the jail and who do you suppose I saw there? It was C. R."

"But it is not possible. C. R. is dead. I saw him buried with my own eyes."

"Well, you just go down to the prison and see for yourself. He is there for nobody knows I saw him. After I had talked with a prisoner I went there to see, I passed along the line of cells and saw him crouching like some wild beast in one of the cells. I hurried here to tell you about it."

The former pastor of C. R. hurried to the prison and made some excuse to visit in the cell block. And there was his late convert, just as he had been told. This happened in Port-au-Prince.

Then there was the case of P., also a young man. He died and was buried. The day of the funeral passed and the mother being so stricken some friends remained overnight in the house with her and her daughter. It seems that the sister of the dead boy was more wakeful than the rest. Late in the night she heard the subdued chanting, the sound of blows in the street approaching the house and looked out of the window. At the moment she did so, she heard the voice of her brother crying out: "Mama! mama! Sauvez moi!" (Save me!) She screamed and aroused the house and others of the inside looked out and saw the procession and heard the cry. But such is the terror inspired by these ghouls, that no one, not even the mother or sister dared go out to attempt a rescue. The procession moved on out of sight. And in the morning the young girl was found to be insane.

But the most famous Zombie case of all Haiti is the case of Marie M. It was back in October 1909 that this beautiful young daughter of a prominent family died and was buried. Everything appeared normal and people generally forgot about the beautiful girl who had died in the very bloom of her youth. Five years passed.

Then one day a group of girls from the same school which Marie had attended went for a walk with one of the Sisters who conducted the school. As they passed a house one of the girls screamed and said that she had seen Marie M. The Sister tried to convince her she was mistaken. But others had seen her too. The news swept over Port-au-Prince like wild fire. The house was surrounded, but the owner refused to let any-one enter without the proper legal steps. The father of the supposedly dead girl was urged to take out a warrant and have the house searched. This he refused to do at once. Finally he was forced to do so by the pressure of public opinion. By that time the owner had left secretly. There was no one nor noth-ing in the house. The sullen action of the father caused many to accuse him of complicity in the case. Some accused her uncle and others her god father. And some accused all three. The public clamored for her grave to be opened for inspec-tion. Finally this was done. A skeleton was in the coffin but it was too long for the box. Also the clothes that the girl had been buried in were not upon the corpse. They were neatly folded beside the skeleton that had strangely outgrown its coffin.

It is said that the reason she was in the house where she was seen was that the houngan who had held her had died. His wife wanted to be rid of the Zombies that he had collected. She went to a priest about it and he told her these people must be liberated. Restitution must be made as far as possible. So the widow of the houngan had turned over Marie M. among others to this officer of the church and it was while they were wondering what steps to take in the matter that she was seen by her school mates. Later dressed in habit of a nun she was smuggled off to France where she was seen later in a Convent by her brother. It was the most notorious case in all Haiti and people still talk about it whenever Zombies are mentioned.

In the course of a conversation on November 8, 1936, Dr. Rulx Leon, Director-General of the Service d'Hygiene told me that a Zombie had been found on the road and was now at the hospital at Gonaives. I had his permission to make an investigation of the matter. He gave me letters to the officers of the hospital. On the following Sunday I went up to Gonaives and spent the day. The Chief of staff of the hospital was very kind and helped me in every way that he could. We found the Zombie in the hospital yard. They had just set her dinner before her but she was not eating. She hovered against the fence in a sort of defensive position. The moment that she sensed our approach, she broke off a limb of a shrub and began to use it to dust and clean the ground and the fence and the table which bore her food. She huddled the cloth about her head more closely and showed every sign of fear and expectation of abuse and violence. The two doctors with me made kindly noises and tried to reassure her. She seemed to hear nothing. Just kept on trying to hide herself. The doctor uncovered her head for a moment but she promptly clapped her arms and hands over it to shut out the things she dreaded.

I said to the doctor that I had permission of Dr. Leon to take some pictures and he helped me to go about it. I took her first in the position that she assumed herself whenever left alone. That is cringing against the wall with the cloth hiding her face and head. Then in other positions. Finally the doctor forcibly uncovered her and held her so that I could take her face. And the sight was dreadful. That blank face with the dead eyes. The eyelids were white all around the eyes as if they had been burned with acid. It was pronounced enough to come out in the picture. There was nothing that you could say to her or get from her except by looking at her, and the sight of this wreckage was too much to endure for long. We went to a more cheerful part of the hospital and sat down to talk. We discussed at great length the theories of how Zombies come to be. It was concluded that it is not a case of awakening the dead, but a matter of the semblance of death induced by some drug known to a few. Some secret probably brought from Africa and handed down from generation to generation. These men know the effect of the drug and the antidote. It is evident that it destroys that part of the brain which governs speech and will power. The victims can move and act but cannot formulate thought. The two doctors expressed their desire to gain this secret, but they realize the impossibility of doing so. These secret societies are secret. They will die before they will tell. They cited instances. I said I was willing to try. Dr. Legros said that perhaps I would find myself involved in something so terrible, something from which I could not extricate myself alive and that I would curse the day that I had entered upon my search. Then we came back to the case in hand, and Dr. Legros and Dr. Belfong told me her story.

Her name is Felicia Felix-Mentor. She was a native of Ennery and she and her husband kept a little grocery. She had one child, a boy. In 1907 she took suddenly ill and died and was buried. There were the records to show. The years passed. The husband married again and advanced himself in life. The little boy became a man. People had forgotten all about the wife and mother who had died so long ago.

Then one day in October 1936 someone saw a naked woman on the road and reported it to the Garde d'Haiti. Then this same woman turned up on a farm and said, "This is the farm of my father. I used to live here." The tenants tried to drive her away. Finally the boss was sent for and he came and recognized her as his sister who had died and been buried twenty-nine years before. She was in such wretched condition that the authorities were called in and she was sent to the hospital. Her husband was sent for to confirm the identification, but he refused. He was embarrassed by the matter as he was now a minor official and wanted nothing to do with the affair at all. But President Vincent and Dr. Leon were in the neighborhood at the time and he was forced to come. He did so and reluctantly made the identification of this woman as his former wife.

How did this woman, supposedly dead for twenty-nine years come to be wandering naked on a road? Nobody will tell who knows. The secret is with some bocor dead or alive. Sometimes a missionary converts one of these bocors and he gives up all his paraphernalia to the church and frees his captives if he has any. They are not freed publicly, you understand, as that would bring down the vengeance of the community upon his head. These creatures, unable to tell anything—for almost always they have lost the power of speech forever, are found wandering about. Sometimes the

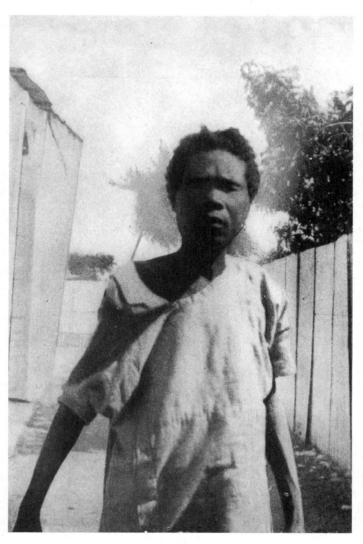

Felicia Felix-Mentor, the Zombie

bocor dies and his widow refuses their responsibility for various reasons. Then again they are set free. Neither of these happenings is common.

But Zombies are wanted for more uses besides field work. They are reputedly used as sneak thieves. The market women cry out continually that little Zombies are stealing their change and goods. Their invisible hands are believed to provide well for their owners. But I have heard of still another service performed by Zombies. It is in the story that follows:

A certain matron of Port-au-Prince had five daughters and her niece also living with her. Suddenly she began to marry them off one after the other in rapid succession. They were attractive girls but there were numerous girls who were more attractive whose parents could not find desirable husbands for. People began to marvel at the miracle. When madame was asked directly how she did it, she always answered by saying, "filles ce'marchandies peressables" (Girls are perishable goods, it is necessary to get them off hand quickly). That told nobody anything, but they kept on wondering just the same.

Then one morning a woman well acquainted with the madame of the marrying daughters got up to go to the lazy people's mass. This is celebrated at 4:00 A. M. and is called the lazy people's mass because it is not necessary to dress properly to attend it. It is held mostly for the servants anyway. So people who want to go to mass and want no bother, get up and go and come back home and go to sleep again.

This woman's clock had stopped so she guessed at the hour and got up at 2:00 A. M. instead of 3:00 A. M. and hurried to St. Anne's to the mass. She hurried up the high steps expecting to find the service about to begin. Instead she found an empty church except for the vestibule. In the vestibule she found two little girls dressed for first communion and with lighted candles in their hands kneeling on the floor. The whole thing was too out of place and distorted and for a while the woman just stared. Then she found her tongue and asked, "What are you two little girls doing here at such an hour and why are you dressed for first communion?"

She got no answer as she asked again, "Who are you anyway? You must go home. You cannot remain here like this."

Then one of the little figures in white turned its dead eyes on her and said, "We are here at the orders of Madame M. P., and we shall not be able to depart until all of her daughters are married."

At this the woman screamed and fled.

It is told that before the year was out all of the girls in the family had married. But already four of them had been divorced. For it is said that nothing gotten through "give man" is permanent.

Ah Bo Bo!

Chapter XIV

Sect Rouge

I<small>F YOU</small> stay in Haiti long enough and really mingle with the people, the time will come when you hear secret societies mentioned. Nobody, of course sits down and gives lectures on these dread gatherings. It is not in any open way that you come to know. You hear a little thing here and see a little thing there that seem to have no connection at first. It takes a long time and a mass of incidents before it all links up and gains significance. To bring it down to a personal thing, I came at it backwards. I did not move from cause to effect. I saw the effect and it aroused my curiosity to go seek the cause.

For instance, I kept meeting up with an unreasoning fear. Repeated incidents thrust upon my notice a fear out of all proportion to the danger. That is to what seemed to be the danger. Some of the things I heard and saw seemed crazy until I realized that it was all too simple to be nothing more than it showed from the outside. The first of these incidents came after I had been in Haiti less than a month.

I had taken my little house in the suburbs of Port-au-Prince with the excellent maid that Mme. Jules Faine had found for me. One night I heard drums throbbing at a distance. They came from the mountain that rose as a sort of backdrop behind the village. Immediately the sounds caught my attention, not just because they were drum tones. I had heard plenty drum music since I had been there. You cannot avoid hearing the drums in Haiti. Besides M. Clement Magliore, publisher of Le Matin and other friends had taken me to Saturday night bomboches and I had heard the rada drums. But the drum that I was hearing this night did not have the deep singing quality of the rada. This was a keen, high-pitched sound that was highly repetitious. I resolved to go and see this new kind of dance, or whatever it was.

I began to dress and woke up Lucille, the maid. I told her what I planned to do and told her to get dressed. She got up and dressed readily enough, but she refused to go. She refused to go outside the door. Lucille went even further than that. She went and stood guard and would not let me go outside of the door either. And all the explanation she would give was, "It is very bad to go there, Mlle. Do not search for the drums. Anyway the drum is not near. It is far away. But such things are very bad."

Since I could not do anything to make her go with me, I had to stay home. This incident struck me as strange, the more I thought about it. It was not usual for Lucille not to want to do anything I wanted done because she loved to please. Already I was beginning to love her and to depend upon her. Later on I put her on the roster of my few earthly friends and gave her all my faith. Lucille with her great heart, her willingness to help, her sympathy under varying conditions and her great honesty. The treasury of the United States could be left in her hands with absolute safety. In addition she is extremely kind. Thinking the incident of the drum over for several days I asked Lucille what she meant. Why was it bad for me to go to the music-makers? She knew that I had been to other native gatherings. Why not this one also? She gave some sort of a general answer. I have asked her many times since, but to this day, she has never said anything more definite than "Some things are very dangerous to see Mlle. There are many good things for you to learn. I am well content if you do not run to every drum that you hear." That was the first instance.

The second incident came shortly afterwards and was more pointed. After two months I grew tired of my landlord swindling me and moved to Pacot. There Joseph bestowed himself upon me as a yard-boy. Two days after I agreed to keep him, he moved his wife and infant child into his room that was in a sort of basement. All went well for a week or two. One night I was propped up in bed writing as usual, when I smelled an odor of something burning. It smelled awful. Like rubber and several other things equally disagreeable smouldering. I stood it as long as I could in bed, and then I got up and called Lucille, who slept in the room next to mine. We went about looking for the source. When we got to the salon which was directly over Joseph's room the smell was overwhelming, so I concluded he was responsible for it.

I called down to Joseph and demanded to know what on earth was going on. He told me he was burning something to drive off bad things. What bad things, I wanted to know. I was good and angry about the thing. He said not to be angry, please. But cochon gris (gray pigs) qui mange' moun, (who eat people) were after his baby and he "was make a little ceremony to drive them away." I told him to come into the house and tell me about it, but he refused. He was not going to open his room door until daylight. The house was so arranged that he must come into the yard, round the corner of the house and mount a high flight of steps before he could enter the house. This he refused to do. He begged me not to be angry, but he could not come out until daylight.

When I came down to breakfast the next morning and looked down at the yard and saw Joseph's wife sitting there in the sunlight calmly nursing her child, Joseph's explanations of the night before seemed so ridiculous that I grew very peevish and I made myself a promise to give him a highly seasoned piece of my mind. But he did not wait for me to summon him. As soon as he saw me at the table he came of his own accord. He told me that he had seen figures in white robes and hoods, no, some of them had red gowns and hoods, lurking in the paraseuse (hedge) the night before. He thought the cochons gris knew that he had a very young baby and they wanted to take it and eat it.

"Now Joseph," I objected, "you are trying to excuse yourself for disturbing me by telling a fantastic lie. In the first place I have never seen a grey pig and do not believe they exist. In the second place, hogs do not go about in robes of any sort and neither do they go about eating babies. Pas capab'."

"But yes, Mlle, there are very bad thing that go about at night. I have great fear from what I see last night. I want you to take my baby in the house with you. Then nobody can steal him."

"No, Joseph, your baby is too young. He would cry all of the time and disturb me. I must have quiet to write a book."

"But he is very little, Mlle. He cannot cry much. Take him to sleep at night, please, Mlle. If you don't want baby in the house, then please give me seven gourds and I put my wife and baby on the boat and send them to Petit Goave. My family will take care of them. Then I come back and I work for you very good because then I will not worry about my baby die. First they make him die, then they take him from the grave."

The discussion was broken off there because an upper class Haitian came at that moment for a morning visit. The Haitian peasant is very humble before his betters, so Joseph shut up quickly and went on back to cleaning up the yard. The gentleman and I went on the front gallery that commands such a magnificent view of Port-au-Prince and the sea, and sat down. I laughed and told him the fantastic explanation that Joseph had made. He laughed briefly, then he said he was thirsty. He would neither permit me to go for a glass of water for him, nor call Lucille to bring it. He would just go out to the kitchen and let Lucille give it to him there. After he went to the rear, I thought I'd join him and offer him a drink of rum. When I reached the end of the salon I saw that he was not asking Lucille for water at all. He was on the back gallery speaking to Joseph in the yard. He was speaking in Creole and calling Joseph every kind of a stupid miscreant. He ended his tirade by saying that since Joseph had been so foolish as to tell a foreigner, who might go off and say bad things about Haiti, such things, he was going to see that the Garde d'Haiti gave him a good beating with a coco-macaque. Knowing that I would embarrass my friend by letting him know that I had heard, I went back to the porch as quietly as I could and waited until he returned before I mentioned the rum.

When he came back to where I sat he accepted the rum and then explained to me with all the charm that an upper class Haitian is so full of, that the peasants of Haiti were a poetical group. They loved the metaphor and the simile. They had various figures of speech that could easily be misunderstood by those who did not know their ways. For example: It was the habit of the peasant to say "mange' moun" (eat a man) when he really meant to kill. Had I never heard the Haitian threat "map mange' ou sans cel" (I'll eat you without salt)? It is of course the same exaggerated threat that is commonly used in the United States by white and black. "I'll eat you up! I'll eat you alive; I'll chew you up!"

I acknowledged that I had heard the expression in the market several times. I added that we Negroes of America also employed the figures of speech continuously. Very well then, he replied, I would understand, and not take the mode of speech of the peasants literally. He never referred directly to Joseph and neither did I. He sipped his rum, and I drank coconut water and we studied the magnificent panorama before us and spent a pleasant morning. But the thing left me quivering with curiosity and I wanted to call Joseph and ask questions. I did not do this because I knew that the time had passed for him to answer me truthfully. He was visibly cowed by that gros Negre. I would have given most anything to know what it was Joseph had started to explain.

A little later I told a very intelligent young Haitian woman that I was going to the mountains shortly to study voodoo practices. We had come to be very close to each other. We had gotten to the place where neither of us lied to each other about our respective countries. I freely admitted gangsters, corrupt political machines, race prejudice and lynchings. She as frankly deplored bad politics, overemphasized class distinctions, lack of public schools and transportation. We neither of us apologized for voodoo. We both acknowledged it among us, but both of us saw it as a religion no more venal, no more impractical than any other.

So when I told her that I was going to Archahaie to live in the compound of a Bocor in order to learn all I could about voodoo, I did not expect her to take the attitude of the majority of the Haitian elite who have become sensitive about any reference to voodoo in Haiti. In a way they are justified in this because the people who have written about it, with one exception, that of Dr. Melville Herskovits, have not known the first thing about it. After I had spoken she sat very still for a while, and then she asked me if I knew the man well that I was going to study with. I said no, not very well, but I had reports from many directions that he was powerful. She was very slow about talking, but she said that I was not to go about trusting myself to people that I knew nothing about. Furthermore it was not possible for me to know who to trust without advice. All was not gold that glittered. There were different kinds of priests. Some of them worked with two hands. Some things were good to know and some things were not. I must make no contacts nor must I go anywhere to stay unless I let my friends advise me. She was as solemn and specific about the warning as she was vague about what I was to fear. But she showed herself a friend in that she introduced me to an excellent Mambo (Priestess) whom I found sincere in all her dealings with me.

A physician of very high calibre said the same thing to me at Gonaives the day that I visited the Zombie there at the hospital and photographed her, or it. Over the coffee cups we discussed the possibility of a drug being used to produce this semblance of death. That is his theory of the matter. He said that he would give much to know the secret of it. It was his belief that many scientific truths were hidden in some of these primitive practices that have been brought from Africa. But the knowledge of the plants and formulae are secret. They are usually kept in certain families, and nothing will induce the guardians of these ancient mysteries to divulge them. He had met up with some startling things in primitive chemistry by reason of his position at the hospital, but never had he been able to break down the resistance of the holders of those secrets. One man was placed in prison and threatened with a long term unless he told. The prisoner produced a fever temperature much higher than any mortal man is supposed to be able to stand to force the prison authorities to release him. But this they refused to do. Then he sent another prisoner to get a little pouch of powdered leaves which he had hidden in his clothes. He refused to let either the doctors or the gendarmes get it for him. When he had it, he mixed a pinch of it with water, allowed it to stand for a few minutes and drank the mixture. In three hours his temperature was perfectly normal. Soon they released him without being able to gain one word of information out of him. He merely stated that what they asked was a family secret brought over from Guinea. He could not reveal it. That was final. He left the prison and the hospital as he had come.

Hearing this, I determined to get at the secret of Zombies. The doctor said that I would not only render a great service to Haiti, but to medicine in general if I could discover this secret. But it might cost me a great deal to learn. I said I was

devoted to the project and willing to try no matter how difficult. He hesitated long and then said, "Perhaps it will cost
you more than you are willing to pay, perhaps things will be
required of you that you cannot stand. Suppose you were
forced to— Could you endure to see a human being killed?
Perhaps nothing like that will ever happen, but no one on the
outside could know what might be required. Perhaps one's
humanity and decency might prevent one from penetrating
very far. Many Haitian intellectuals have curiosity but they
know if they go to dabble in such matters, they may disappear
permanently. But leaving possible danger aside, they have
scruples."

Things like this kept on happening. Like Arius and Lucille
having one of those quarrels over jurisdiction that all Haitian
servants seem to be having eternally, and during which Arius
saying that she had better be careful how she insulted him.
She must know whom she was dealing with before she went
too far. On hearing this, Lucille was as terrified as if he had
pointed a gun at her heart. She came to me and wanted to
leave. I persuaded her against it and chided Arius a little. But
the next day when an old man entered the yard with his black
head covered with a red handkerchief, Lucille fled the place
and went down to the nearest police station for protection.
Then at La Gonave I heard references to things done by some
society in a village across the Morne from Ansa-a'-galets
which the Garde d'Haiti was going to suppress. Then on one
of those little sailboats that matches itself against wind and
tide for eighteen miles between Ansa-a'-galets and Port-au-
Prince, I heard some more puzzling talk. Things mentioned,
not by name, but by insinuation, and only briefly at that.
Then that quick hush of uneasiness. But in all this time, not
one single individual had ever mentioned directly the existence of secret societies let alone put a name to one. What had
been conveyed was a feeling of fear of something that nobody
wanted to discuss.

Then one afternoon in the Tourist Bar, a man who is a
Haitian and also not a Haitian said something that suddenly
connected all of these happenings and gave them a meaning
beside. So I began to see a great deal of him. From time to
time he told me many things and without knowing it, put me

on the trail of what to look for. One N'gan (houngan) with whom I was particularly friendly answered my questions quite frankly and took me to a house in the Belair district where the cobblestones of the floor were polished like marble from the passage of so many feet and so many generations that they inspired awe in themselves. There first I saw and examined a paper, yellow with age that bore the "mot de passage" (pass word) and discovered that Cochon Gris was a name of a society.

On the way back home I remarked that I had seen no altar and hounfort as I was accustomed to in Voodoo worship. There were a few things about, but I knew what to expect and the regular set-up was not there. There were a dozen bottles on a table, some cruches, or clay water jugs. The place of honor was given to an immense black stone that was attached to a heavy chain, which was itself held by an iron bar whose two ends were buried in the masonry of the wall. A well used cuvette was before the stone that had the same look of age and memory as an ancient gibbet. When we first entered, the Bocor had touched the stone proudly and said, "This is for Petro. It has the power to do all things—the good and the evil." Certainly neither of us disputed the statement. But when we were clear of the place, I said I knew that the Bocor had lied to us. The houngan was proud of me, then, as a pupil because I had noticed the difference. He said that it really was not a place of Voodoo. That the Cochon Gris was a secret society and a thing forbidden by law and detested by all except the members. That they used the name of Voodoo to cloak their gatherings and evade arrest and extinction.

Later on I introduced the subject in a conversation with a well known physician of Port-au-Prince and he discussed the matter most intelligently.

"Our history has been unfortunate. First we were brought here to Haiti and enslaved. We suffered great cruelties under the French and even when they had been driven out, they left here certain traits of government that have been unfortunate for us. Thus having a nation continually disturbed by revolution and other features not helpful to advancement we have not been able to develop economically and culturally as many of us have wished. These things being true, we have not been able to control certain bad elements because of a lack of a sufficient police force."

"But," I broke in, "with all the wealth of the United States and all the policing, we still have gangsters and the Ku Klux Klan. Older European nations still have their problems of crime."

"Thank you for your understanding. We have a society that is detestable to all the people of Haiti. It is known as the Cochon Gris, Sect Rouge and the Vinbrindingue and all of these names mean one and the same thing. It is outside of, and has nothing to do with Voodoo worship. They are banded together to eat human flesh. Perhaps they are descended from the Mondongues and other cannibals who were brought to this Island in the Colonial days. These terrible people were kept under control during the French period by the very strictures of slavery. But in the disturbances of the Haitian period, they began their secret meetings and were well organized before they came to public notice. It is generally believed that the society spread widely during the administration of President Fabre Geffrard (1858–1867). Perhaps it began much earlier, we are not sure. But their evil practices had made them thoroughly hated and feared before the end of this administration. It is not difficult to understand why Haiti has not even yet thoroughly rid herself of these detestable creatures. It is because of their great secrecy of movement on the one hand and the fear that they inspire on the other. It is like your American gangsters. They intimidate the common people so that even when they could give the police actual proof of their depredations, they are afraid to appear in court against them.

"The cemeteries are the places where they display the most horrible aspects of their inclinations. Some one dies after a short illness, or a sudden indisposition. The night of the burial, the Vinbrindingues go to the cemetery, the chain around the tomb is broken and the grave profaned. The coffin is pulled out and opened and the body spirited away. And now, if you are friendly to Haiti as you say you are, you must speak the truth to the world. Many white writers who have passed a short time here have heard these things mentioned,

and knowing nothing of the Voodoo religion except the
Congo dances, they conclude that the two things are the
same. That gives a wrong impression to the world and makes
Haiti a subject for slander."

Dr. Melville Herskovits heard this society mentioned at
Mirablais as the "Bissage," and "Cochon sans poils." (Life in
a Haitian Valley, page 243) He quotes Dr. Elsie Clewes Par-
sons as saying that the peasants around Jacmel told her
"people *do* eat people at Aux Cayes. I *know* it." Her informant went on to tell of human finger nails being found on
what had been sold as pigs feet (pages 246, 247).

"But how can I say these things until I am very sure?" I
asked him. I had participated in many ceremonies, and had
never seen anything that even bordered on human sacrifice,
but I knew that I did not know every voodoo ceremony in
Haiti. How could I say unless I eliminated the possibility of
an occasional sacrifice. Later I found what he said to be true.

Then I found out about another secret society. It is composed of educated, upper class Haitians who are sworn to destroy the Red Sect in Haiti. They are now taking the first step
of the program. That is to drive the adepts of the organization out from under the cloak of Voodooism so that they may
be recognized and crushed by the government. Naturally,
there are laws against murder in Haiti, however committed.
In addition the penal code contains provisions against magic
practices which can be invoked when evil traits are discovered.
Official Haiti knows of the Sect Rouge and frowns upon it,
but one must have legal proof to gain a conviction. A high
official of the Garde d'Haiti told me that he has every known
member in the neighborhood of Port-au-Prince under surveil-
lance. "But one cannot arrest a man for what he believes," he
said, "one must have proof that the suspect has put his belief
to action. And when we have that, ah, you shall see something." My attention was called to the trial and conviction of
the sorceress in the affair of Jeanne Nelie, "That affair which
gave place to a trial which echoed around the world." The
effect of this conviction was to cause the adepts of Sect Rouge
to take refuge under the greatest secrecy which has since been
axiomatic. Now they give themselves names of the Petros, the
Erzulies and the Locos, and perhaps many other Voodoo loas.

I witnessed one such fraudulent ceremony myself one night on the Plain Cul-de-Sac. In company with a man who knew all about voodoo in that part of Haiti, I was returning from a Congo dance when we approached a small cluster of houses where a ceremony was in progress. I asked to stop and see it and we did. I got a very disagreeable surprise, because they sacrificed a dog. This must be some new cult of voodoo, I concluded, so I asked. They told me it was a service to Mondongue, who always made his appearance in the form of a great dog, and when one beheld such a manifestation, it was certainly a time for fear. My friend and I soon left. When we were far away, he said to me, "They do not make a voodoo service at all. Mondongue is not a loa of voodoo. They do not always content themselves with dog, I am afraid." He showed the strongest feeling of revulsion to the whole matter and I was glad because then I did not need to hide my own distaste. I had not read St. Mery at that time and had never heard the name Mondongue pronounced in all Haiti:

"Never has there been a character more hideous than that of these last (The Mondongues) whose depravities have reached the execrable of excesses, that of to eat their fellows. There were brought to Saint Dominique (Haiti) some of these butchers of human flesh (for at the houses of these butchers the flesh of humans has been sold as veal) and here (in Haiti) they caused as in Africa, the horror of the other Negroes.—One is convinced that these people have kept up their odious inclinations. Notably in 1786 a Negress was confined in a hospital on a plantation in the vicinity of Jeremy. The proprietor having remarked that the greater part of the Negro babies perished in the first eight days after their birth, spied upon the midwife whom he surprised eating one of these infants who had recently been buried. She confessed that she caused them to die for this purpose."*

The most celebrated meeting place in the Department of the West used to be the bridge across the lake at Miragoane. An awful sight to the late traveller! The bridge covered with candles, the brilliantly costumed figures, themselves bearing multiple candles and the little coffin that is their object of

*Tome Premier, page 39, L. E. Moreau de St. Mery.

worship, in the center of the floor of the bridge, the sharp piercing voice of the little drum and the wildly dancing horde.

This is how a meeting was held.

The two marked stones were struck together, the whispered word was sent secretly, but swiftly by word of mouth to all of the adepts. A full meeting was to be held in a town some miles south of Port-au-Prince. This distance is a bit tiresome even by automobile, considering the condition of the roads. But one of the remarkable things concerning the members of the Red Sect is their great mobility. They cover great distances with incredible speed.

The meeting is in a sort of court surrounded by several small cailles (thatched houses). There is a huge silk cotton tree in the open space, and behind the houses, fields and fields of cane.

The night was very dark but starry. Only a homemade lamp made simply and crudely from a condensed milk can fought against the blackness. Members came in like shadows from all directions. One came down a narrow path from the main road. Two more came into the opening from cane fields, parting the rustling leaves so skillfully that there was no sound. They kept coming like this and every member carried his sac paille which held his trappings. There was subdued talk but no whispers. The time had not come for expression, that was all. They kept coming until perhaps a hundred persons were gathered there. Looking around the court, they were just ordinary looking people. Might be anybody at all getting ready for a prayer meeting or a country dance.

All of the officers came at last and the word went around for every one to robe themselves. This was quickly done and the drab crowd became a shining assembly in red and white with bared heads. Some began to leap and dance, imitating the motions of various animals. The singing and dancing became general and the head coverings were put on. The adepts were now all transformed into demons with tails and horns, cows, hogs, dogs and goats. Some even became cocks, and all of a most terrifying aspect. Standing silently in that dimlit courtyard they were enough to strike terror into the breast of the most courageous. But now they began to dance and sing. The little, high pitched drum resounded and the Emperor, a most fearful sight, took the center of the group and began to sing and the President, the Minister, the Queen, the cuisineres, the officers, the servants, bourresouse, and all the grades joined in and the sound and the movement was like hell boiling over. Over and anew they sang to the drums.

Carrefour tingindingue, mi haut, mi bas-e'
Carrefour tingindingue, mi haut, mi bas-e'
Oun prali' tingindingue, mi haut, mi bas, tingindingue
Oun prali' tingindingue, mi haut, mi bas, tingindingue
Oun prali' tingindingue, mi haut, mi bas, tingindingue

Now the whole body prepared to depart. Every member lighted a candle and chanting to the drums, they struck a rhythmic half dance, half trot and marched forth to a certain cross-road not more than a mile away. The Sect Rouge was going to the cross-roads to do honor to the loa who rules there. What they wished for tonight would be in his realm. They were going there to give food and drink and money to Maitre Carrefour (Lord of the Cross Roads) and after that they were going to ask favors of him.

As the fearsome procession pranced on down the highway, it halted before several doors and danced furiously. The doors opened and other figures leaped out, red-robed like the rest. They had candles blazing on top of their heads, on the backs of their hands and planted on their feet. They joined the dancing and marched off with the band. These turned out to be honorary members, who partake in the dancing only until a further degree is conferred upon them. The honorary members are those who are in sympathy with the society, but for one reason or another are not yet fully initiated. The group moves on with the little coffin being carried in the very middle of the procession. It is brilliant with candles. This was the soul about which everything moved.

At the cross-roads, Maitre Carrefour was given food and drink and money. But only the copper one cent pieces of Haitian money known as "cob." The coffin was set down in the very center of the cross roads and the ceremony performed. After Maitre Carrefour had been well fed and his thirst slaked, he was asked for powers. He was asked to grant powers to find victims on the road and he was asked for powers to overtake and overpower these victims. Finally the Master of the Cross-roads gave a sign of assent by entering the head of one of the female adepts. She became possessed. The entire body of the society became jubilant of success and concluded the service and marched off to a cemetery not too far away.

They were going there to do honor to Baron Maitre Cimiterre and to ask him for powers similar to those already granted by Maitre Carrefour, that is, success in their maneuvers, fortune to find victims, and power to catch and to eat them.

They were singing again, but the song had changed. Now they were singing and whirling as they went.

"Sortie Nan Cimiterre, toute corps moin senti malingue'
Sortie Nan Cimiterre, toute corps moin senti malingue'
Sortie Nan Cimiterre, toute corps moin senti malingue,'
Sortie Nan Cimiterre, toute corps moin senti malingue' "

And so singing and dancing they arrived at the gate of the cemetery. The main body halted at the gate while the queen entered and went to a grave that had evidently been selected in advance and began to dance about it. This she did five times, but stopped at the head of the tomb to sing each time that she arrived there. After the fifth turn she took a bottle of clairin and with it outlined a large cross upon the stone and placed a candle at the head and a kwee (bowl made by cutting a calabash in half lengthwise) with blood seasoned with condiments in it at the foot of the cross. The cross is the emblem of Baron Cimiterre, who is also called Baron Samedi, and Baron Croix. She danced some more and sang a song that began with

"Cote' toute moun" (where are all men, or everybody).

Then everybody entered the cemetery in single file, each person with his or her hand on the hip of the person before and with a lighted candle in the other. The youngest adept is selected and stretched upon the tomb and all the lighted candles are placed around him. The kwee, a bowl made of half a calabash, is set upon his navel. Everybody around the tomb place the palms of their hands together and sing, moving around the tomb until each person returns again to stand before their own candle. The invocation was made and when

Altar to Baron Cimeterre

it was felt Baron Samedi had granted the request, the queen announces "The powers are joined with the degrees!" All others bowed and covered their eyes so that nobody knew the exact moment that she left the cemetery. Nor which way she went. Then the youngest adept arose and went and none saw him go either. Then all the rest ran out in every direction as fast as they could because all feared that Baron Cimiterre would select him or her as a victim. But soon the whole convoy was joined together again not far from the cemetery. The last two men came out of the gate walking backwards brandishing well sharpened machetes, defending the rear from an attack by the Lord of the Dead.

Now it was decided that the convoy should proceed to a certain bridge over a stream that crossed the highway near a sedgy lake. This it seems, had long been a favorite rendezvous. At the bridge, more candles were brought forth and every part of the structure was brilliantly illuminated, even to the rails at the sides. The little coffin was set down in the center of the floor of the bridge. It was an awful sight. This bridge lighted up by hundreds of flickering candles, peopled by a horde of fantastic creatures with the coffin, the symbol of their strange appetites and endeavors in the midst.

A strong guard for defense was stationed along the road on either side of the bridge to prevent attacks from enemies. There had been trouble on other occasions. The Brave Guedé, servants of Baron Samedi, who are particularly numerous in that neighborhood, and who consider this bridge their particular place of worship, had fallen upon the Sect Rouge in the midst of their celebration in times past and inflicted serious injuries. So these guards, armed with machetes were thrown out along the road to deal with these people without mercy in case they attempted to dislodge the Red Sect this night.

Now the members of the society went running and dancing along the routes hunting for victims. They had been granted all powers and every thing else was arranged. The higher officers remained on the bridge relatively inactive. They would intercept any luckless person who tried to pass that point. Woe be to the wayfarer who had no "mot de passage" who approached that bridge that night.

The bourresouse, the advance guard, ran fast and hunted farther afield than all the rest. The success of the whole matter rests upon the courage, discretion, and efficiency of this advance guard. They are beautifully trained stealthy scouts. They faded off into the darkness swiftly like so many leopards with their cords in their hands. These cords are made from the dried and well cured intestines of human beings who have been the victims of other raids. They are light and have the tensile strength of cello strings. The gut of one victim drags to his death his successor. Except in special cases no particular person is hunted. The advance guard, cord in hand ready for instant use stalks the quarry. And the amount of territory that these guards can cover in a short time is unbelievable. When a victim is located, he is surrounded and the cord is whipped about his throat to silence him first. Then he is bound and led before the main convoy.

The main convoy waited there on the bridge relatively inactive until the word came that some one was approaching from the west on horse back. At any moment the rider might have been dragged from his horse without giving him an opportunity for resistance, but knowing that he must cross that bridge the guards and the other servants allowed him to proceed. Just before he reached the brilliantly lighted bridge, he dismounted and hesitated a long time, evidently considering turning back. But finally he, a well dressed young man, approached with the utmost diffidence and was challenged. Dripping with terror, he first made the sign of the cross, before he thought to answer, "Si lili te' houmba, min dia, mi haut." It was a glorious thing that that handsome, well dressed young man knew that fantastic sentence. The emperor was favorably impressed by him also. He was almost paternal in his manner as he bade the boy proceed.

Soon after, one detail of the bourresouse returned with game from the chase and led their victim before the Emperor, the Queen, the President, the minister and all of the other officers. Finally all of the guards returned, but that took hours. When all were in, the whole convoy moved back to the original meeting place. Then the ceremony began to change the three victims into beef. That is, one was "turned" into a "cow" and two into "pigs." And under these terms they were killed, and divided. Everyone received their share of the game except the honorary members. They serve without being allowed a taste.

By that time dawn is nigh. The animals and demons are "transformed" again into human beings who may walk anywhere without attracting the least attention. After the happenings of the night one might expect the sun to rise on Judgment Day. But no, it was just a common day outside in the court.

The identities of the Sect Rouge, Cochon Gris, Vinbrindingue are really secret, hence the difficulty for the Garde d'Haiti to cope with it. Like the American gangster and racketeer, their deeds are well-known. But the difficulty is to prove it in court. And like the American racketeer, the Sect Rouge takes care that its members do not talk. It is a thing most secret and it stays that way. The very lives of the members depend upon it. There is swift punishment for the adept who talks. When suspicion of being garrulous falls upon a member, he or she is thoroughly investigated, but with the utmost secrecy without the suspect knowing that he is suspect. But he is followed and watched until he is either accounted innocent or found guilty. If he is found guilty, the executioners are sent to wait upon him. By hook or crook, he is gotten into a boat and carried out beyond aid and interference from the shore. After being told the why of the thing, if indeed that is necessary, his hands are seized by one man and held behind him, while another grips his head under his arm. A violent blow with a rock behind the ear stuns him and at the same time serves to abraise the skin. A deadly and quick-acting poison is then rubbed into the wound. There is no antidote for this poison and the victim knows it. However well he might know how to swim, when he is thrown overboard, he knows it would be useless. He would never be alive long enough to reach the shore. When his body strikes the water, the incident is closed.

Ah Bo Bo!

Chapter XV
Parlay Cheval Ou (Tell My Horse)

Gods always behave like the people who make them. One can see the hand of the Haitian peasant in that boisterous god, Guedé, because he does and says the things that the peasants would like to do and say. You can see him in the market women, in the domestic servant who now and then appears before her employer "mounted" by this god who takes occasion to say many stinging things to the boss. You can see him in the field hand, and certainly in the group of women about a public well or spring, chattering, gossipping and dragging out the shortcomings of their employers and the people like him. Nothing in Haiti is quite so obvious as that this loa is the deification of the common people of Haiti. The mulattoes give this spirit no food and pay it no attention at all. He belongs to the blacks and the uneducated blacks at that. He is a hilarious divinity and full of the stuff of burlesque. This manifestation comes as near a social criticism of the classes by the masses as anything in all Haiti. Guedé has another distinction. It is the one loa which is entirely Haitian. There is neither European nor African background for it. It sprang up or was called up by some local need and now is firmly established among the blacks.

This god of the common people has no hounfort. A cross at the head of a tomb inside the yard of the hounfort is his niche. If there is none there it is enough for the houngan to plant a cross dedicated to him.

The apparel of this god is in keeping with his people. He likes to dress himself in an old black overcoat, a torn old black hat with a high crown and worn-out black pants. He loves to smoke a cigar. He cavorts about, making coarse gestures, executing steps like the prancing of a horse, drinking and talking.

His drink is very special. This god likes clairin well seasoned with hot peppers, to which powdered nutmeg is added at times. The grated nutmeg should always be in this strong, raw rum infusion, but when it is not to be had, Guedé will content himself with the pepper in alcohol. He also drinks

494

pure clairin, that raw white rum of Haiti. He eats roasted peanuts, and parched corn which is placed at the foot of the cross on a plate. No white cloth is used in this offering as in others.

There is no real service or ritual for Guedé. One places a circle of twenty white candles about the cross dedicated to him. Some adepts offer him an old redingote or an old pair of pants, but roasted peanuts and parched corn are customary. The people who created Guedé needed a god of derision. They needed a spirit which could burlesque the society that crushed him, so Guedé eats roasted peanuts and parched corn like his devotees. He delights in an old coat and pants and a torn old hat. So dressed and fed, he bites with sarcasm and slashes with ridicule the class that despises him.

But for all his simple requirements, Guedé is a powerful loa. He has charge of everyone within the regions of the dead, and he presides over all that is done there. He is a grave-digger and opens the tombs and when he wishes to do so he takes out the souls and uses them in his service.

Guedé is never visible. He manifests himself by "mounting" a subject as a rider mounts a horse, then he speaks and acts through his mount. The person mounted does nothing of his own accord. He is the horse of the loa until the spirit departs. Under the whip and guidance of the spirit-rider, the "horse" does and says many things that he or she would never have uttered un-ridden.

"Parlay Cheval Ou" (Tell my Horse), the loa begins to dictate through the lips of his mount and goes on and on. Sometimes Guedé dictates the most caustic and belittling statements concerning some pompous person who is present. A prominent official is made ridiculous before a crowd of peasants. It is useless to try to answer Guedé because the spirit merely becomes angry and may reprove the important person by speaking of some compromising event in the past in the coarsest language or predicting something of the sort in the near future to the great interest of the listening peasants who accept every word from the lips of the horse of Guedé as gospel truth. On several occasions, it was observed that Guedé seemed to enjoy humbling his betters. On one occasion Guedé reviled a well-dressed couple in a car that passed. Their names were called and the comments were truly devastating to say the least.

With such behavior one is forced to believe that some of the valuable commentators are "mounted" by the spirit and that others are feigning possession in order to express their resentment general and particular. That phrase "Parlay cheval ou" is in daily, hourly use in Haiti and no doubt it is used as a blind for self expression. There are often many drunken people in the cemeteries who claim to be "mounted." The way to differentiate between the persons really "mounted" and the frauds is to require them to swallow some of the drink of Guedé and to wash their whole face in it. The fakir will always draw back because he fears to get that raw rum and hot pepper in his eyes, while the subject really mounted will do it. They do it without being told and it never seems to injure them. So one is forced to the conclusion that a great deal of the Guedé "mounts" have something to say and lack the courage to say it except under the cover of Brave Guedé.

Down in the neighborhood of Port-au-Prince behind St. Joseph's I witnessed one of these simulated possessions. A man was crying "Tell my horse" again and again and defaming many persons. A girl approached. He called her Erzulie and shouted "Erzulie, don't you remember I have connections with you for a cake?" The girl was chagrined no end and looked pathetic. One of the men took a hand and cried, "Shoo!" as if he were shooing chickens. Immediately the fakir started to run. He stopped after a step or two and looked about him and asked "Who did that to me?" Everybody laughed. I asked why he seemed afraid. They explained that the majority of such characters are chicken thieves and they live in fear of the police. They knew the nasty accusation against the girl was inspired by malice at being refused, so they knew the way to stop it and did. The "mount" moved on away looking like a wet chicken.

A tragic case of a Guedé mount happened near Pont Beudet. A woman known to be a Lesbian was "mounted" one afternoon. The spirit announced through her mouth "Tell my horse I have told this woman repeatedly to stop making love to women. It is a vile thing and I object to it.

Tell my horse that this woman promised me twice that she would never do such a thing again, but each time she has broken her word to me as soon as she could find a woman suitable for her purpose. But she has made love to women for the last time. She has lied to Guedé for the last time. Tell my horse to tell that woman I am going to kill her today. She will not lie again." The woman pranced and galloped like a horse to a great mango tree, climbed it far up among the top limbs and dived off and broke her neck.

But the peasants believe that the things that "mounts" claim to see in the past and future are absolutely accurate. There are thousands of claims of great revelations. They are identical for the most part, however, with the claims that the believers in fortune-tellers make in the United States.

The spirit Guedé (pronounced geeday) originated at Miragoane and its originators' especial meeting place was the bridge across the lake at Miragoane where the Departments of the South and the West meet. These people who originated this cult were Bossals who were once huddled on the waterfront in Port-au-Prince in the neighborhood of the place where all of the slaves were disembarked from the ships. There came to be a great huddle of these people living on a very low social and economic level in the stretch flanking the bay. For some cause, these folk had gained the despisement of the city, and the contempt in which they were held caused a great body of them to migrate to the vicinity of Miragoane, and there the cult arose. It is too close to the cult of Baron Cimeterre not to be related. It is obvious that it is another twist given to the functions of that loa. The spirit of Guedé is Baron Cimeterre with social consciousness, plus a touch of burlesque and slapstick.

It is interesting to note that this cult does not exist in the North nor in the Artibonite. He belongs to the South and the West, and the people in the West and South who do not make food for Guedé are careful not to anger him or to offend in anyway. It is dangerous to make his spirit angry. When a "mount" of this spirit is making devastating revelations the common comment is "Guedé pas drah." (Guedé is not a sheet), that is Guedé covers up nothing. It seems to be his mission to expose and reveal. At any rate, Guedé is a whimsical

deity, and his revelations are often most startlingly accurate and
very cruel. Papa Guedé is almost identical with Baron Cimeterre, Baron Samedi and Baron Croix, who is one god with
three epithets, and all of them mean the Lord of the dead.
Perhaps that is natural for the god of the poor to be akin
to the god of the dead for there is something about poverty
that smells of death.

One man stood out against all the rest and insisted that
Baron Cimeterre and Baron Samedi were separate deities.
Maybe so, but I do not blame the others who think that they
are the same. The general belief is that both, if one could
consider them separately, live in the cemetery. This physician
who says that he is an authority, maintains that Baron Cimeterre has his abode in an elm tree, lives always in the forest,
and may be worshipped anywhere in the woods. Baron Samedi lives in the cemetery or anywhere else he chooses. Baron
Cimeterre speaks with authority like a great lord while Baron
Samedi always announces his presence with "Ca ou vley?"
(What do you want of me?) Both of them, like Guedé can
open tombs and command the dead to do their bidding.
Baron Cimeterre is absolute ruler of the cemetery and Baron
Samedi is also. This authority says that both of these gods are
doctors and point out roots and herbs to be used, and that
they give specific directions as to how they must be used.
Sometimes he prescribes leaves and states that they must be
powdered; at other times he might use those same leaves as a
tea; at other times he might use the same leaves as a poultice.
But Louis Romain who is a great houngan says that this
god is not a doctor. Papa Loco is the god of medicine and
knowledge.

Some say that you must talk to Baron Samedi or Cimeterre
with a cow foot. That is necessary because you must place
your hand in his while you make your request of him. When
he leaves, he will take away with him whatever he is holding.
So you get the foreleg of a cow with a foot attached and offer
that as your hand. He holds to the foot and when he leaves
you, merely let go of the other end and all is well. You do not
lose your hand and arm as you would have done, had you not
taken care.

Baron Samedi delights in dressing his "horses" in shabby

and fantastic clothes like Papa Guedé. Women dressed like men and men like women. Often the men, in addition to wearing female clothes, thrust a calabash up under their skirts to simulate pregnancy. Women put on men's coats and prance about with a stick between their legs to imitate the male sex organs. Baron Samedi is a very facetious god like Guedé. He is simple in his tastes also. Since he craves neither hounfort nor altar, when the houngan wishes to summon him to ask a service, he goes into the court and to the tree which is the repository of Baron Samedi and sprinkles the ground with clairin or rum and lights either three or thirteen white candles.

The people love Samedi because he knows the herbs and roots to make them well and because he is a loquacious god and gives them plenty of detail along with the medicine. Sometimes he sends the dead on a mission. Sometimes he will not permit a soul to leave the cemetery because he will not permit them to be used to do a mischief to a person he has chosen, nor to one who has placed himself under his protection. Baron Samedi has no especial offering. When the houngan wishes to summon him outside of the hounfort as in the woods or the plains, a shot fired in the air will summon him and he will appear and ask, "Ca ou vley?" In certain parts of Haiti, however, they offer Baron Samedi a black goat or a black chicken. It is placed on a plate and placed beneath the tree for him. Beside the plate they place an ear of corn, a bottle of clairin and three bottles of Kola.

Baron Cimeterre is also very popular all over Haiti. He is also a doctor of medicine and prescribes a great number of healing baths for the sick people under his care. He is very powerful but also temperamental and full of whimsy.

The houngan who wishes to summon him, goes to the elm tree consecrated to him and raps three times with the baguette of a Rada drum and recites the prayer common in all voodoo ceremonies. He then demands of Damballah the authority or permission to enter into communication with Baron Cimeterre. He says to Baron Cimeterre "Ce ou minn, Baron moi vley. Chretiens besoin concones ou." (It is you that I call for or want. Living people need you.) Then he sings a song to Baron Cimeterre. Baron becomes incarnate in

the houngan or in a canzo. Sometimes he employs the dead.
It is Baron Cimeterre that one invokes to draw a dead man
from his tomb. Without this formality, one could not leave
the cemetery with the souls one had invoked.

One offers Baron Cimeterre a black goat or a black chicken,
which is prepared and placed at the roots of the tree. At the
moment of invocation one pours rum or clairin on the roots
of the tree.

November first and second are great days of obligation to
these spirits. The houngan and the Mambo go to the cemetery on the night of the first to begin the invocation for All
Saints Day which follows. The graveyard is blazing with
lighted candles for this important celebration. It must have
been a joyful thing to the Africans newly arrived in Saint
Dominique to find their worship of the dead confirmed in the
European All Saints Day, but the services to Baron Samedi or
Cimeterre is more than just an expansion of Halloween. The
Christian Church has merely given the cult an annual feast
day. The rest of it has come out of Africa with adaptations on
Haitian soil. This cult of the dead has so many ramifications
that it touches in some way the majority of the voodoo cults
and services.

CEREMONY OF THE TETE L'EAU

In Haiti spirits inhabit the heads of streams, known as
sources, the cascades, and the grottoes. Sometimes the spot
has a master, or a mistress and sometimes it has both. The loa
most commonly found in possession of these nooks and grottoes are Papa Badere, Cimby Apaca, Papa Sobo, Papa Pierre,
and the white woman, Mademoiselle Charlotte.

Spirits occupy all of the sources, cascades and grottoes, but
certain places in Haiti are ruled by spirits who are known
to reside there by everyone in the country. For instance,
the grotto at Leogane is inhabited by Madam Anacaona.
Papa Sobo rules the grotto at Turgean and Cimby-Apaca-
endeux-eaux.

The ceremony Tete l'eau (Head of the water) is a thing to
induce the belief in gods and spirits. It is held on a night
when the moon is shining full and white—and in Haiti the
moonlight is a white that the temperate zones never could

believe possible. The ceremony is held from nine to ten
o'clock at night; that is, the ceremony does not begin until
that hour. About that time the adepts and the invited guests
begin to arrive at the source. There is a large white table cloth
and sometimes two. Dishes and silver sufficient to serve all of
the company is provided.

The houngan opens the ceremony by invoking the Master
of the source. As always he salutes first the superior spirits. He
invokes The Master of All Things, then Jesus, Mary, Joseph
and John the Baptist. He recites the Ave Maria, the credo, the
Pater Noster. The adepts respond with the prayers. Then the
houngan sprinkles the source, the cascade or the grotto, as
the case might be, with flour, breaks three to thirteen eggs in
the source or cascade. He turns himself towards the four cardinal points successively, and taking in his hands the sealed
bottles of fine wines, he offers them with an air of majesty to
the spirit. Opening then the bottles, he pours some from each
on the ground all around the source. The different wines are
poured separately and in turn. At this moment of making the
libation the houngan approaches the source, strikes three
blows upon the Rada drums and the resonance rolls over the
moonlit water and the towering rocks sheathed in verdure.
He strikes three other notes from the Petro drums which sing
so humanly and the rhythmic sound departs in pursuit of the
other music fleeing over the hills. A gun is fired and all of the
assistants bow themselves toward the source and remain with
the head bowed while the houngan intones the liturgic song:

> "Maitre, Maitre, L'Afrique Guinin ce' protection
> Nous Ap Mande', ce d'lo qui poti mortel, protection
> Maitre d'lo pour-toute petites li"

(Master, African Master of Guinea, we ask your protection.
The water which is able to hear mortals, we ask protection for
all of us children.)

At this exhortation the crowd responds. Then the houngan
commands the houncis and the canzos present to prepare a
plate for the spirit who protects the place. They immediately
spread the table cloth beside the source and lay the plates for
all, but they are careful to reserve a particular plate for the
god or goddess. This plate that the houngan carries himself to

the source before anyone touches anything to eat, is thrown
into the water with all that it contains. It must contain a piece
of everything served at the feast for the main course and a
piece of each of the cakes for the dessert. Only after this is
done may the adepts and the guests approach the table to eat.
And there is plenty to eat and to drink! There is roast turkey,
chicken, beef, goat and white rice. Great plates of different
kinds of bread and several kinds of cakes. To drink there is
champagne, red wine, white wine, beer, clairin, tafia and various liqueurs. Nearly always, the spirit becomes embodied in
the houngan and thus takes part in all of the eating and drinking. There is music and happiness. The feast usually continues
until three or four o'clock in the morning.

This ceremony is a lovely and impressive affair when conducted by a member of the upper class. Like the ceremony to
Erzulie, it loses in beauty and purpose when it is celebrated
by people too poor to make the proper provisions. Many
wealthy people who do not wish to make a public announcement that they make food for Voodoo gods, merely announce
to their friends that "A repast is offered on the banks of such
and such a river *very* near the source," or often the servants of
the family organize the service if not too many outsiders are
asked. In this case the food is merely served on a plate at the
source and the drinks poured. This ceremony is so beautiful
in setting and spirit that it is necessary to participate in it to
fully appreciate it.

The most famous cascade in all Haiti is at Saut D'eau, a
triple waterfall just above Ville Bonheur. Every year, people
make a pilgrimage from all over the country to this beautiful
waterfall which translates into "leap of the water." Up until
about three years ago there were two divisions of the falls, but
since the flood in Haiti of 1933 there are now three beautiful
torrents tumbling down from their great heights that men
might see and worship.

My sister-in-law, Emma Williams, wife of Dr. Leonard Williams of Brooklyn was visiting me in Haiti when the day in
July came for everybody to go up to Haiti's holy place of
miracles. Hermann Pape had offered to drive us in his car,
and we so gladly accepted. It was a lively party in Hermann's
sedan with plenty of food and things to drink. We bumped

along the rocky road and passed people walking briskly with youth. Old people padded along and stepped aside to let us pass. Women and men rode bourriques and horses. They went anyway they could, but they went. It is the great annual "going up" in Haiti. When it came time to ford a river with the car, we paused. The men went in for a swim and the women spread the table beside the stream and we ate, ascended spiritually a little on the beauty of the scenery and drove on to Ville Bonheur.

We got to Ville Bonheur after dark and found a great number of little booths selling candy, Kola and the things that people usually buy when they go off gala. There was music of different kinds. Hermann got into one of the many dice games that were going on. It was very strange to me because they played it with three dice in a cup instead of two in the hand the way I had been taught. We were all tired but the great crowds, the flambeaux and candle-lighted places kept us moving from one excitement to another. It was like a fair only less hard and brittle. There is a softness and gentleness of manner about the Haitian peasant that makes itself felt whenever and wherever you get near him. The ground was practically paved with mango seeds and everybody was looking for a place to sleep. The insides of the few houses of the town had already been taken, for many people had come the day before. The women who were selling candles were doing a great business. Many of them were pushing about through the crowd selling the new prayers to the miraculous virgin and the two others. These printed prayers to the three women of miracles were printed partly in Spanish and partly in French to accommodate both the Haitians and the Dominicans. We bought both prayers and candles.

Finally Hermann found us a place to sleep. It was under the porch of a little caille. The car was moved over there and we got out our folding cots. Hermann slept on the natte beside us. The other young man who had come along to help Hermann with the driving as well as to enjoy the trip finally wandered off and we simmered off to sleep at last.

We woke and found several peasants standing around us in utter silence and gazing down on us in our riding breeches and boots. As soon as we stirred, they were happy to help us find water to wash our faces and get ourselves fixed up. We were going up to the spot where the miraculous virgin lit in a palm tree. At daylight throngs were pouring into the enclosure where the church stood and slowly trickling out again.

We had that small cup of coffee that all Haitians take in the morning. But first we must get all six of the persons in our party together. We found the two ladies easily but that other young man remained invisible until Hermann met Ti Jean and he told him that our missing companion had found a lady friend to sleep with and was late abed. Hermann led us all to the house and was all for us peeping in but we declined and waited until he came out of his own accord.

We had coffee and waded through the sellers of candles and amulets. These amulets were little heart-shaped affairs made of printed cotton with a string to wear about the neck. Some were selling colored cords to hang as an offering upon the sacred tree at the falls. We bought things and went into the enclosure where an unfinished church was standing. This is where the sacred palm tree once stood. On either side of the path were blackened stones, and each one of these stones was surrounded by an ecstastic crowd anointing themselves with the candle grease that sobbed down over the stones from the votive candles. They anointed their faces and their arms and their bare breasts. Some had ailing feet and legs and they anointed them. Several women were rubbing their buttocks and thighs without any self-consciousness at all. And thousands upon thousands poured into the place and up to the church and back again. The mass was celebrated at an early hour and when we entered the enclosure the people were pouring out of the church. There was Ti Cousin, the great houngan of Leogane striding past all in snowy white linen; Dieu Donnez St. Leger, the great one of famed Archahaie going toward the church. The scene was like a great place of flame in that no part of it was still at any time and it had so many different movements making up the whole. And it had its changing colors like fire too and one could feel the inner heat from the people.

This great shrine of Haiti got its first breath of life in 1884, they say. In that year a beautiful, luminous virgin lit in the fronds of a palm tree there and waved her gorgeous wings

Saut d'Eau. Disrobing to Ascend the Falls

and blessed the people. She paused there a long time and the whole countryside saw her. Seeing the adoration of the people, the Catholic Priest of the parish came out to drive off the apparition. Finally she sang a beautiful song and left of her own volition. She had not been disturbed at all by the priest. People came to the palm tree and were miraculously cured and others were helped in various ways. The people began to worship the tree. The news spread all over Haiti and more and more people came. The Catholic Church was neglected. So the priest became so incensed that he ordered the palm tree to be chopped down, but he could find no one who would chop it. Finally he became so incensed at the adoration of the people for the tree that he seized a machete and ran to the tree to cut it down himself. But the first blow of the blade against the tree caused the machete to bounce back and strike the priest on the head and wound him so seriously that he was taken to the hospital in Port-au-Prince where he soon died of his wound. Later on the tree was destroyed by the church and a church was built on the spot to take the place of the palm tree, but it is reported that several churches have burned on that site. One was destroyed by lightning. That is the story of the Virgin of Ville Bonheur.

The cascade at Saut d'Eau attracts as many people as the palm tree. From Ville Bonheur they mount on horseback to the falls. There the people drape their offerings of colored cotton cords on the sacred tree, undress and climb the misted rocks so that the sacred water may wet their bodies. Immediately many of them become possessed. The spirit Ague' T'Royo enters their heads and they stagger about as if they are drunk. Some of them talk in the unknown tongues. Louis Romain, the houngan of the Bolosse who was preparing me for initiation at the time begged me not to enter the water. He said, and others agreed with him that Ague' T' Royo, the Maitre L'Eau (Master of waters) might enter my head and since I was not baptized he might just stay in my head for years and worry me.

The belief is widespread in Haiti that Ague' T'Royo carries off people whom he chooses to a land beneath the waters. One woman told me that she had lived there for seven years. There are thousands who say that they have been there. They say they have no memory of how they got there nor how they left. There is a great belief in a land beneath the waters. Some say it is not beneath the waters, but one must pass through the waters to get there. One man told me that there is a place in Haiti where a great cave has been hollowed out by a water-fall and that if one knows the way they may pass under the fall and enter this great cave. He says that there is an opening from the cave like a chimney that permits one to emerge again and that this is where people have been taken who speak of having been under the water for years. He promised several times to show me this place, but he never got around to it. Some day when I have a great deal of leisure, I shall visit Haiti for the express purpose of visiting the kingdom of Ague' T' Royo and see things for myself.

There was a fly in the ointment that day. The local priest who is a Haitian had used his influence to station a gendarme at the falls. Therefore there were few cases of possession. There was a lavish denunciation of the priest though. High and low were there and all felt that a police at the waterfall at Saut d'Eau was a desecration, but expressions of fervor were not to be suppressed entirely and the hundreds of people entering the eternal mists from the spray and ascending the sacred stones and assuming all possible postures of adoration made a picture that might have been painted by Doré. It was very beautiful and fitting. Whether they had the words to fit their feelings or not, it was a moving sight to see these people turning from sordid things once each year to go into an ecstasy of worship of the beautiful in waterforms. Perhaps the priest has some good reason for attempting to break-up this annual celebration at the waterfalls. I only heard that the Church does not approve and so it must be stopped if possible.

I fail to see where it would have been more uplifting for them to have been inside a church listening to a man urging them to "contemplate the sufferings of our Lord," which is just another way of punishing one's self for nothing. It is very much better for them to climb the rocks in their bare clean feet and meet Him face to face in their search for the eternal in beauty.

Saut d'Eau. After the Touch of the Sacred Stream

MANGER YIAMM (FEAST OF THE YAMS)

Another simple and lovely ceremony that I had the pleasure of witnessing is the Feast of the Yams. It is celebrated in all parts of Haiti and is compulsory with all the cults of Voodoo. The Rada cult, the Congo, the Petro, the Ibo and Congo Petro, all must do honor to the Yam once each year. It is not an expensive feast, fortunately, so that everybody can look forward to it with pleasure. It falls on the day before the day of the great animal sacrifices.

We had to buy the yams for the feast on the last day in October. We must also buy a piece of salt fish to go along with the yams. Plenty of olive oil and white candles too. The olive oil to cook the yams and the fish with. The candles for illumination and because they are required in the rites.

The Feast of the Yams is a ceremony that must be done annually. If one is an adept of any Voodoo cult at all, then he must observe Manger Yiamm. I was glad that it had to be done while I was there.

The ceremony was celebrated this way. We gathered under the peristyle. The houngan invoked the mysteries beginning with that long formula in which a long list of the Christian saints are called first, and then a long list of the more important loa of Voodoo. The adepts responding behind each name. Each was saluted and the favorite drink of each loa was poured on the ground around the center post for the dead. Then the hounci gathered around and the houngan approached the repositories of all of the loa in the hounfort whom he saluted with equal reverence. The houncis now gathered up all the yams that had been brought by the crowd and prepared to cook them. The service went on with prayers and the whole assembly chanting the Pater Noster, the Credo and the Confiteor. Then they began to sing the airs dedicated to the various loa. They sang songs to Papa Legba, Papa Loco, Papa Cimby, to some Congos, to Maitre Grand Bois, Papa Badere, Manchon Ibo, but the most beautiful ones it seemed to me were dedicated to Grand Erzulie.

All this time the yams and fish were being prepared. Some adepts were sent out to cut a great quantity of banana leaves. These were arranged into a sort of bed and the whole thing surrounded by candles. Then everybody assembled upon this couch of leaves to wait for the yams to be served. The candles were lighted and it was very agreeable to lie on the fresh cool leaves surrounded by light.

When the word came that the yams were ready, the houngan sprinkled flour all around the couch. Then he went into the hounfort and the food was carried in to him and he offered some of it to the loa. Then everyone was served and we passed the rest of the night singing and amusing ourselves. Several people were possessed during the singing and dancing. Three or four loa presented themselves at the same time through different people. A great many prophetic statements were made and some of those present were profoundly moved by the revelations. One spirit identified as Grande Libido entered one of his servants and forced him to chase away a guest whom he had especially invited. The loa said that the guest was a stranger to true Voodoo worship, but he was given to demon-worship. This revelation was most embarrassing to the guest who tried to deny it. But his friend, possessed of his loa began to announce dates, places and incidents of his practices and he ran out of the place in the greatest haste and confusion. Soon after the loa left the friend who had driven him out and as soon as he came to himself, he asked for his friend and was much distressed at what had taken place. He left us singing and dancing and went off to seek him.

Chapter XVI

Graveyard Dirt and Other Poisons

THEY take dirt from a graveyard to maim and kill. And the principle behind this practice is more subtle than the surface shows. It is hardly probable that more than one per cent of the people who dig into an old grave to get a handful of dirt to destroy an enemy, or the enemy of a client, know what they do. To most of them it is a superstition connected in their minds with the idea of ghosts and the belief in their power to harm. But soil from deep in an old grave has prestige wherever the negro exists in the Western world. In the United States it is called goofer dust and there is a great deal of laughter among educated people over it. The idea of some old witch doctor going to a cemetery at dead of night to dig arm-length deep in a grave for dirt with which to harm and kill does seem ridiculous. Now, wait just a moment before you laugh too hard at this old hoodoo man or woman of magic. Listen to some men of science on the same subject.

Sir Spencer Wells, ("The Disposal of the Dead") "Shane found germs of scarlatina in the soil surrounding a grave after thirty years."

Dr. Domingo Foriero of Rio de Janeiro, "If each corpse is the bearer of millions of organisms specific of ill, imagine what a cemetery must be in which new foci are forming around each body! More than twenty years after the death of a body, Shane found the germs of yellow fever, scarlatina, typhoid and other infectious diseases."

Pasteur: "What outlooks are opened to the mind in regards to the possible influence of soil with the etiology of disease and the probable danger of the earth of cemeteries!"

So it appears that instead of being a harmless superstition of the ignorant, the African men of magic found out the deadly qualities of graveyard dirt. In some way they discovered that the earth surrounding a corpse that had sufficient time to thoroughly decay was impregnated with deadly power. It happened ages before the idea gained ground in the civilized areas. It might in some accidental way, come out of the ancestor worship of West Africa. That is a mere shot in the dark, but what it illuminates is the great interest in subtle ways of providing death, and this brings up the whole matter of poisons and poisonings, not only in Haiti, but wherever the negro exists in the Western world.

Naturally, this cult of poisoning that has come in fragmentary form from Africa has built up an alertness and caution that is extreme in certain quarters. Naturally the accusations far out-number the actual cases. But who knows what the actual cases are? Even in countries with the most efficient crime detection agencies and with medical science, many, many cases of poisoning escape detection as has been proven by police records. There have been many instances where poisoners were detected only because they killed too many in the same way. In the United States great masses of young negro children are taught to eat and drink nowhere except at home. There is the gravest suspicion of unsolicited foods. In Jamaica, British West Indies, people carry bissy (Kola Nut) as an antidote. In Haiti there is extreme wariness and precaution. One educated man told me that he never orders the same drink at the same saloon on consecutive visits so that it is impossible to anticipate his order and prepare a bottle for him.

What is most interesting is that the use of poisons follows the African pattern rather than the European. It is rare that the poison is bought at a drug store. In most cases it is a vegetable poison which makes them harder to detect than the mineral poisons so often used by the Europeans. And when the European poison is used it is seldom employed in the same fashion. Who has made all of these experiments and not only found out the poisonous plants in the New World, but found the most efficient use of them? It is a clear case of an African survival distorted by circumstances.

For example let us look at death by hair. Kossula (Cudjoe Lewis) who was brought over from Africa in 1859 to be a slave, and who died in Mobile, Alabama in 1934 told me that his King in Africa was a good man and did not like wicked things. So he allowed no man to keep the head of a leopard. I asked him what was wicked about possessing the head of a leopard? He said that men made bad medicine and killed people with it. Just how, he could not say, because, he explained, he was only a boy when he was brought away and he had not learned. But it was very bad for a man to keep the head of a leopard. If one killed a leopard and did not bring the head to the King, then everybody knew that he was a wicked man who meant to do evil, and so he was executed at once before he had a chance to do it. I met Chief Justice Johnson of Liberia and asked him for a leopard skin. He said that he would send me one, but that it was certain that he could not get me one with the head, because the native chiefs always kept the heads of all leopards killed in their territory. Duke, an African dancer in New York, told me that the head was important because of the whiskers. Duke is a Fanti from Gold Coast and he said that there also, it was a capital crime to keep the head of a leopard. And when the head was brought to the king, before the hunter was allowed to leave, the leopard's whiskers were counted and not one must be missing on pain of death. The assumption that if the hunter has kept one, then he intends to kill someone with it and so he is a murderer already by intent so they execute him at once. The whiskers, he stated most positively were deadly poison, not a quick violent death, but very sure. How and why, he could not, or would not tell me.

Now, there are no leopards in Jamaica or Haiti. But in both places, when I asked about poisons, I was told about *chopped hair from the tail of a horse*. Chop it up short and mix it in something like mush and give it to the one you wish to kill and their stomach and intestines will become full of sores and death is certain. The short bits of hair will penetrate the tissues like so many needles and each bit will first irritate, then puncture the intestine. A clear adaptation of the African leopard whisker method of killing. There is a variation of this in Jamaica also. They curry a horse and clean off the curry comb in the food of the victim. He not only gets the hair, he gets all the germs from the skin and hair of the horse. A violent and fatal vomiting is said to follow this.

Kossula, who was a Takkoi, a country in Nigeria, "three sleeps" from the Abomey, capital city of Dahomey, Chief Justice Johnson of Liberia and Duke from the Gold Coast all reporting the same practise in their separate areas. And these areas are all inside the territory from which the greater part of the slaves were drawn for service in the Americas. Leopard whiskers not being available, those adept in the practise of killing by hair looked for a substitute and found the coarse, stiff hair of the horse's tail.

Duke also told me of the poison to be found in the rudimentary legs of a rock python and the gall-bladder of a crocodile. In Jamaica I heard of the poisonous qualities of the gallbladder of the alligator. Dried and powered lizards in Africa and powered lizards in Jamaica, Haiti and Florida. And the numerous vegetable poisons that had been worked out as to application, dosage and deadliness in Africa had to find substitutes in the Western world. And the fact that so many have been found, the tremendous quantity of experimentation that has been done, which again proves the inclination of the seekers.

There is no way of knowing how many other plants are used as poisons, but the following were checked and re-checked in different areas of the West Indies!

1. Night Shade (Jamaica). Antidote—Bissy (Kola Nut).
2. Red Head (Jamaica). Antidote—Bissy (Kola Nut).
3. Bitter Cassava (Jamaica). Antidote—Mix clay and water and drink.
4. Dumb cane (Jamaica). Antidote—None known. (The juice from this plant attacks the throat first and so constricts the vocal cords that the victim cannot speak. A flood of saliva pours from the mouth and drenches the lower part of the face. Terrible skin eruptions occur wherever this poisoned saliva has touched.)
5. Rose Apple (root is black and very poisonous). Antidote—None known.
6. Dogwood root (Haiti, Jamaica, Bahamas). Antidote—None known.
7. Black sage (Haiti, Jamaica, Bahamas). Antidote—None known.
8. Dust of Bamboo (Haiti, Jamaica, Bahamas). Antidote—None known.

ANIMAL DERIVATIVES

1. Horse hair
2. Dried gallowass (a poisonous lizard).
3. Dried Mabolier (Haitian lizard).
4. Spiders, worms and insects.
5. The gleanings from a curry comb after currying a horse.

MINERAL DERIVATIVES

1. Ground bottle glass.
2. Calomel. (Applied externally. The drug is mixed with water and the under garments of the victim is soaked in the solution for an hour or two and dried without rinsing. It is absorbed through the skin when the wearer perspires and produces a dangerous swelling.)
3. Arsenic. (Dr. Rulx Leon in defending Haiti from the charge of primitive poisonings estimated that most of the poisoning done in Haiti is done by Arsenic. He says that during the last days of slavery that a quantity of Arsenic was stolen by the slaves from some plantation owners and was later parcelled out. That was around 1793 and it is hardly probable that the original supply has lasted until the present. Anyway there is bountiful evidence of other poisons being used. In 1934, however, there was an attempt to assassinate President Stenio Vincent by Arsenic. It was established that thirty grains of Arsenic was bought in Santo Domingo for the purpose by the conspirators. It was bought outside Haiti to cover the trail, but it was traced to the purchaser nevertheless. It had been ordered in the name of a legislator who knew nothing of the matter. Names very big in the political life of Haiti were mentioned in connection with this attempt upon the life of the President. But the affair occurred just before the visit of President Roosevelt and so the matter was hushed up quickly. Eighteen grains of the thirty purchased are still unaccounted for. A grocery store on the Champ de Mars failed because it was rumored that a member of the family which owned the business had actual possession, or access to the missing eighteen grains of Arsenic. No one but the family traded at *that* store. It goes without saying that few would be concerned very much about this particular eighteen grains if great quan-

tities of the same thing were known to be loose in Haiti already. There is a poison which the Cacos used to treat the blades of their machetes before a battle.)

The subject of poisons and poisonings in the whole area of the Caribbean is too important to omit altogether, though a thorough study of the matter would require years of investigation. It has such an immense background and an infinite sinister future. There are the various reasons for poisoning and the accompanying temptation. There is the age-old inclination; there is the security of secrecy and the ease of gaining the weapon that exists in all countries. In addition to death by poisoning, in Haiti there is the necessity of poisoning the bodies of the dead against the ravages of the Zombie-makers and the Societie ge Rouge (Red-eyed society, another name for the Sect Rouge).

Ah Bo Bo!

Chapter XVII
Doctor Reser

A THING is mighty big when time and distance cannot shrink it. That is how vivid my memory is of the colorful Dr. Reser of Pont Beudet. I am breaking a promise by writing this, and maybe the cocks are crowing because of it, but all the cocks in creation can crow three times if they must. I am going to say something about Dr. Reser. A piece about Haiti without Dr. Reser would be lacking in flavor.

I heard many things about Dr. Reser before I met him. A great deal is said about the white man who is a houngan (Voodoo priest). All of the foreigners living in Port-au-Prince know him and like him. A great many Haitians admit that he is deep in the inner secrets of Voodoo, and startling legends have grown up about him. Some say that he belongs to the Societie de Couleve (Snake Society) which is supposed to be headed by Dr. Arthur Holly. Its object is said to be the extermination of the Sect Rouge and the devil worshippers in Haiti. One young man assured me that they all wore a snake tattooed on their fore arms. He had seen the snake on Dr. Reser's arm. It had life. He had seen Dr. Reser feed it eggs. After I met Reser I asked to see this symbol. It turned out to be a dragon which he had had tattooed on his arm when he was in the navy. But to many Haitians it is a sacred snake that eats eggs and performs miracles of magic.

Therefore it was not long before I went out to Pont Beudet and found this much-talked-of man. But then everybody finds Dr. Reser as soon as they land in Port-au-Prince. He is one of the show pieces of Haiti like the Citadel. This white American is better known than any other living character in Haiti.

As officer in charge of the state insane asylum at Pont Beudet, Dr. Reser has a comfortable house with a large well screened veranda. He has three sets of bed springs suspended by chains with comfortable mattresses on this screened porch. And these contraptions make good swings in the day time and good beds at night. He is a gracious host and serves good native food at his table and tall, cool fruit drinks on his porch.

He is a facile conversationalist on an amazing number of subjects. Philosophy, esoterics, erotica, travel, physics, psychology, chemistry, geology, religions, folk lore and many subjects I have heard him discuss in a single afternoon.

So I took to spending time on his porch when I was not busy otherwise. We would play cards and talk and swap tales and listen to the harmless lunatics who wandered about the grounds and occasionally came up to the screened porch to beg a cigarette or say something that seemed important to their crippled minds. It was very nice to lie sprawled on my back on one of those swing-beds and pass the day. His house boy, Telemarque, was sure to appear with lemonade or orange juice about once every hour. The insane patients would be depended upon to yell something startling ever so often and then Dr. Reser talks well. He has been in Haiti eleven years by the calendar but in soul he came from Africa with the rest of the people.

Seeing how the Haitian people, high and low, far and near, love and trust him, I tackled him one day on the business of being a white king of Haiti.

"Doctor Reser," I called over from one swing-bed to the other.

"I am not a doctor, you know. I am a pharmacist's mate, first class, retired U. S. N. They began to call me doctor while I was in the Public Health service at Port-de-Paix and they have just kept it up."

"I stand corrected, but getting back to what I started to say, Doctor, the people all seem to love you so much. Now in all the adventure tales I have ever read, the natives finding a white man among them, always assume that he is a god, and at *least* make him a king. Here you have been in Haiti for eleven years according to your own story. You are on the most friendly terms with the Haitians of any white man in Haiti and still no kingly crown. How is that?"

"Well, I tell you, Zora, if you show yourself sincere, the Haitians will make a good friend of a white man, but hardly a king. They just don't run to royalty."

"Not even a *white* man?"

"Not even a white man, and the Haitians who made themselves kings did not fare so well, either, if you will recall."

I sat bolt upright at that. He had his mouth open and he was making broad statements.

"But on the island of La Gonave they made a king out of a sergeant of Marines."

"Oh, no they didn't."

"But King Faustin Wirkus——"

"All I have to say about Wirkus and that white king business is that he had a good collaborator. Let's have another round of orange juice."

"You mean to say he was no king at all?"

"I mean just that."

"May I quote you as saying that?"

"Certainly. Now, how about that orange juice?"

"With pleasure, Doctor. Can I change the subject and talk about you instead?"

"I suppose so."

"Why is it then that the Haitians and the Haitian peasants particularly love *you* so much?"

"They are infinitely kind and gentle and all that I have ever done to earn their love is to return their unfailing courtesy."

One tall lanky patient of the asylum hung around the porch and kept reciting the tales of Fontaine. It was a steady monotonous flow of syllables with his eyes fixed on us. It was a curious thing to see his mouth so active and the upper part of his face so still. It was plain that the upper part of his face did not know what the lower part was doing. One Syrian, formerly a merchant in Port-au-Prince, kept standing with his face against the porch wishing Dr. Reser well.

"Doctor Reser! Doctor Reser!" he kept calling. "I like for you to eat a very good eating. The very best eating in the United States."

"Thank you very much," Dr. Reser answered each time.

"Dr. Reser, I was driving very fast to Port-au-Prince—about sixty meters an hour and I make three times around a pork (pig). I tell the man, 'You pay five dollars duty to American government every time you leave pork in the street.'"

"Yes, yes," Dr. Reser answered with feigned interest. "Perhaps you want to go and look after the chickens for me."

The man hurried off very happy in the thought of performing a service for Dr. Reser and the conversation took up again on the porch.

I was speaking of returning to Port-au-Prince but Dr. Reser would not hear of it. They were expecting Joseph White, the American Vice-Consul and his little new wife; M. C. Love, of the West India Oil Company, Frank Crumbie, Jr. of Nyack New York; Mr. and Mrs. Scott and John Lassiter, American fiscal agents to the Haitian government; all were coming out that night with some newly arrived officials of the Pan American Airways.

Dr. Reser was giving a Voodoo dance for them and he was asking me to stay. I was on very friendly terms with all of them and so I was grateful to Dr. Reser for asking me. Cicerone, the greatest drummer in all Haiti performed upon the *Hountah*, the great thundering rada drum that night. Everyone who cannot go to Africa should go to Pont Beudet, Haiti, to hear Cicerone play. He is not much to look at. He is past middle life, and is small and black and sort of shaggy. The magic of him is in those hands. The sun-stuff that places him among the geniuses of the timpani is found in those fingers that have actually been modified by their association with the taut heads of drums. Ah, yes, one must hear Cicerone of Pont-Beudet!

It was all very glinty and strong what went on that night. The white visitors, whether they would have had it different or not, were a sort of audience around the walls. Strong action in the center. Many of Dr. Reser's Haitian friends came in. Some were upper class, educated men who received the introduction with poise and charm. Some were the peasants who were going to participate in the dance. They were all so glad to see Dr. Reser and made extravagant expressions of pleasure. One dark brown man with aquiline feature told him, "It is *such* a pleasure to see you again. I would have been hump-backed if I had not met you!" All of this was spoken in Creole, of course.

The evening got under way. Cicerone and the other drummers paid many of the guests the compliment of playing a special salute for each, after which the guest paid the drummers the compliment of a round of drinks or the cash for the purpose. The evening rose in spirit—the drumming, the singing, the dancers and the dancing. I was taught the Jean Valou. Midnight dashed past us on the run. Finally the others left and I was put to bed in Dr. Reser's bedroom while he and the others who lived there slept in the swing-beds on the porch.

The crowing of roosters, the small waking noises of the world, and the little dawn wind, all acknowledging the receipt of the new day got me up. It took shape out of a ropy white mist, but there it was, the very last day that God had made, and it went about the business of changing people the way days always do. I got up to go home at once.

But I did not go as I had planned. A young woman came to bring a message to Dr. Reser. It was from Aux Cayes in the south. It had been passed along by word of mouth of market women until it came to the young woman in Port-au-Prince, and it was an invitation to attend a ceremony in the South. What kind of ceremony was it going to be? It was to be a ceremony where the food was to be cooked without fire. Real food? Yes, a great pot of real food — enough to feed all of the people attending the ceremony would be cooked without fire. Was such a thing *possible*? The young woman asked for a cup and saucer, a piece of laundry blue, a cup of cold water and a fresh egg. No, she did not wish to acquire the egg herself for fear that we might believe that she had one prepared. Dr. Reser went out and got one himself and gave it to her. She placed it in the cup at once. Poured some of the cold water on it and covered the cup with the saucer and made a cross mark on the saucer with the bluing. Then she bowed her head and mumbled a prayer for a few minutes. None of us could catch the exact words of what she said in that prayer. When it was over, she lifted the saucer and offered the egg to Dr. Reser with a diffident smile and told him to break it. He refused on the grounds that he had on his best gray suit and did not wish to have it spattered with egg. She assured him time and time again that the egg would not spatter over his clothes. At last he broke the egg very carefully and found it done. That was startling enough. But the realest surprise came when the egg was found to be harder in the center than anywhere else. The young woman now begged him to eat the egg. He was so reluctant to do so that it was necessary for her to coax him a great deal, but she prevailed at last and he ate the egg. Then she assured him that he would never die of poisoning. He would always be warned in time to avoid eating poisoned food or touching poisoned surfaces. Would he now accept the invitation to the ceremony? He would with great unction and avidity. I asked to come along and so it was arranged. A few days later we jolted over the rocky road south to Aux Cayes. It was night when our party arrived. A guard stood beside the main highway to guide us to the hounfort. After the proper little ceremonies of greeting an important guest and the one of entering was over we were assigned sleeping space and went to bed. On our nattes under a great mimbo tree.

Their ceremony was held in the court of a great hounfort and the members of the society all came bearing foodstuffs. There were great heaps of peas, carrots, cabbage, string beans, onions, corn meal, rice and egg-plant.

The next morning the women were up preparing the little cups of coffee that everyone drinks in Haiti before breakfast. Then there was breakfast. After that the women went about dressing the food for the ceremony while the men amused themselves with a game of dice that is played with three "bones" instead of the two that we used in the United States.

Many, many things came to pass in a ceremonial way and then the "cooking" of the food without fire began. All that I could see, and afterwards when I talked it over with Dr. Reser, he confirmed my impression, was that the people formed a circle about the big iron pot that contained the mingled food. The Mambo began to sing, with the Asson of course, and then the drums began to sound. At the first note of the boulatier, the smallest of the Rada drums, the men took off their hats and the women the colored handkerchiefs that every woman wears to a ceremony and began to dance, circling the pot. As they went they chanted and waved their hats and handkerchiefs at the pot as if fanning an invisible flame. This went on and on. When the houngan and the Mambo concluded the ritual, the food was dipped up with a wooden spoon and served to all. Everybody ate with their fingers for it is an unbreakable law of this ceremony that no metal except the pot must touch this food, so knives, forks and spoons are forbidden.

How was the food cooked? I do not know. Dr. Reser and I

tried bribery and everything else in our power to learn the secret, but it belongs to that small group and nothing we could devise would do any good. Dr. Reser knew the girl who had boiled the egg in cold water very well indeed. I would say that they are very intimate friends. He concentrated upon her finally, but all she would say was that it was a family secret brought from Africa which could not be divulged. He kept at her and she yielded enough to say that she could not tell him until he had been baptised in a certain ceremony. He went to the trouble and expense to have the baptism. After that was over, she returned to her original position that it was an inherited secret which she could not divulge under pain of death. So that is as far as we got on the food-without-fire ceremony. This is an annual affair and some day I shall try again.

I visited Dr. Reser many more times and polished my shoulder in his bed-swings and listened and ate. But one thing I never did. I never went to him for the information that I had come to Haiti to seek. One reason for this was that everyone who goes to Haiti to find out something makes a bee line for Dr. Reser and tries to pump out of him all that they can in a few weeks and then they sail off and write as if they had seen something. Be it said right here that Dr. Reser tells no more than he wants to, so what they get is bound to be limited first by Dr. Reser's own information, which is bound to be limited by the nature of Haiti's vastly complicated and variegated lore, and second by what he chooses to give out to the lazy mind-pickers who descend upon him. Since he has plans of his own for the future, he gives out nothing of any great importance. Thus they waste their time in Haiti on him. But the most important reason why I never tried to get my information second-handed out of Dr. Reser was because I consider myself amply equipped to go out in the field and get it myself. So my association with him was fifty per cent social and fifty per cent a study of the man himself. I wanted to know all I could about this educated, widely travelled man, this ex-navy man who could so completely find his soul and his peace in the African rituals of Haiti. I have seen him in the grip of the African loa (spirits) known as possession: that is, the spirits have entered his head and driven his own consciousness out. I have seen him reeling as if he were drunk under the spirit possession like any Haitian peasant and I was trying to reconcile the well-read man of science with the credulous man of emotions. A man who could break off a discussion of Aristotle to show me, with child-like eagerness a stone that he had found which contained a loa. So I spent as much time as I could spare from other things on his porch sprawled upon one of his bed-swings. Besides he is a very fine and generous person; and then again, so many things happened around his place.

He is very kind and tender with the unfortunate people in the asylum. Though many have applied for his job, he is still considered by the Chief of the Service d'Hygiene the best man for the place. Of course, the criminally insane and the violent ones are strictly confined, but the harmless have a measure of liberty. And some days they hang around Dr. Reser's porch and say things and say things. He never drives them away nor speaks to one of them harshly.

One afternoon on the porch I fell to wondering what part of the United States Dr. Reser came from. I had tried to place him by his accent but I was not sure. So I asked, "Where are you from, Dr. Reser."

"I am from Lapland, Zora."

"Why, Dr. Reser, I thought you said you were an American."

"I am, but I am from Lapland just the same."

I fell to wondering if Lapland had become an American colony while my back was turned. He saw my bewilderment and chuckled.

"Yes, I am from Lapland—where Missouri laps over on Arkansas."

Naturally I laughed at that and he went on in the brogue of the hill-billy reciting about folk-heroes: "Yes, I'm the guy that chewed the wad the goat eat that butted the bull off the bridge!"

Just then the Syrian hurried up to the porch and called:

"Dr. Reser! Dr. *Reser!* The soldiers of Monte Carlo killed the Dead Sea, then they built the Casino!"

"Thanks for the information," Dr. Reser replied.

The patient who spent all of his waking hours quoting

Fontaine's fables came to the porch too. I had laughed heartily at Dr. Reser's quotations from the folk lore of the Ozarks, and perhaps our merriment attracted them. Another patient came up and began to babble the Haitian folk tales around Brother Bouki and Ti Malice.

Dr. Reser went on: "Raised on six shooters till I got big enough to eat growed shotguns. I warm up the Gulf of Mexico and bathe therein. I mount the wild ass and hop from crag to crag. I swim the Mississippi River from end to end with five hundred pound shot in my teeth! Airy dad gummed man that don't believe it, I'll hold him by the neck and leave him wiggle his fool self to death."

"Dr. Reser! Dr. *Reser!*" The Syrian attracts attention to himself. "They have horse racing in Palestine. The horses have contracts in Jewish, and Arabic and English and the Jewish horse *must* be second. It's political."

The man who recited Fontaine pointed his stagnant eyes on the porch and babbled on as if he raced with the man who was talking about Ti Malice and Bouki, but he had a weaker voice. So we heard very distinctly:

"Of course, Bouki was very angry with Ti Malice for what he had done and Ti Malice was afraid, so he ran away very fast until he came to a fence. The fence had a hole in it, but the hole was not very big, but Malice tried to go through——"

"Dr. Reser! Dr. *Reser!* Never speak to person with tired physinomic! I drive car five years without license and the United States Government was very content."

"Are they annoying you?" Dr. Reser asked me. "They never worry *me* at all."

"Oh no," I answered. "It is very interesting. Let them go on."

"All right, then. It will soon be time for them to go to bed anyway."

The Syrian was very close to the screen now. "When you write to the president, every amigo here remember you." He was advising us. "Dr. Reser, what is love?"

"I really don't know," Reser replied. "What is it?"

"Love is the heart. And what is the heart? It is the communication of the body."

The sun was setting and I lifted my eyes as the father of

worlds dropped towards the horizon. In the near distance a
royal palm flaunted itself above the other foliage with its stiff
rod of a new leaf making assignation with life.

"Dr. Reser, I know love what it is," the Syrian went on. "I
go in Cuba once and they have a house there. The bell ring
'ting!!' and you go in and they shake you like this and in the
morning you come out and you know about life."

The Syrian turned suddenly and walked over to the shrub-
bery and began to gather hibiscus blooms. Dr. Reser sent the
man who always quoted Fontaine to stop him from denuding
the plants. Then we could hear the other one still telling his
story of Malice and Bouki. "—Malice was stuck in the hole in
the fence and he could not go forward neither could he back
out. His behind was too big to pass through. So Bouki found
him there but he did not know it. He saw this great behind
stuck in the fence but he was impatient to overtake Malice so
he slapped it and said:

" 'Behind, have you seen Malice?'

"The behind said, 'Push me and I'll tell you.'

"So Brother Bouki gave a great shove and pushed Ti Malice through the hole and he ran away. It was only after he was
gone that Bouki knew it was Malice, so——"

He received the signal that supper was being served so he
abruptly left us. In a short while we saw a file of men being
conducted through the grounds to their sleeping quarters.
Several women stood about within their enclosure, which was
fenced in by heavy chicken wire. As the line of men came
abreast of the space where the women were standing, one of
the women walked up to the fence, suddenly lifted her skirts
up around her waist and presented herself. Instantly one of
the men broke from the line and ran to her. It was all un-
planned, simple and instinctive. Presently the guard who was
marching in front heard the commotion and looked around.
He rushed back and dragged the man away with the help
of two others. The woman stumbled back to a stool and
drooped down in a sort of apathy. The man was forced to his
cell and could be heard cursing and howling all night long.

As for us, we waited outside until the black curtain ran all
the way around the hoop of the horizon. Then Telemarque
announced and we went inside and ate the delicious bits of

lean cured pork that Telemarque knows how to cook. We ate jean-jean and rice which is Haiti's most delicious native dish. Jean-jean is a little wild mushroom that grows there and Mme. Jules Faine prepares jean-jean and rice better than anyone else in Haiti.

Dr. Reser was discussing tides and the movement of ocean current for a while. Then somehow we got off on determining the sex of children before birth. He stated positively that it could be done by means of a gold ring suspended on a chain. From there he went precipitately into the occult and the occult in Haiti. He offered as justification for his firm belief in the power of the Voodoo gods several instances of miraculous cures, warnings, foretelling of events and prophecies. Some of them were striking. He told of visions of Prepti. He promised to introduce me to Prepti but we never did arrange it. Prepti was secretary to Charlemagne Peralt, one of the leaders of the Caco rebellion. Prepti was an educated and cultivated man and had no desire to perform any such service for Charlemagne Peralt, but he was kidnapped by Peralt and tortured and forced to serve him for three years as his secretary. He was forced to accompany Peralt during all of the fighting in the rebellion. Running away from an engagement with the Marines, Prepti fell over a cliff into a crevice from which he could not extricate himself. The sides were too sheer and steep. He struggled until he realized that escape was impossible. Then he cried out but there was no one to hear him. He grew hungry and thirsty and after the second day resigned himself to die. But during the night as he lay against the rocks in his extremity, came a vision of Ogoun with his red robes and long white beard. He assured Prepti that he would not die there, and that he would be found and rescued. Then came a vision of Erzulie, the goddess of love, who comforted him and also promised him that he would be rescued. Prepti stayed there several days. He was dried up and starved when they found him, but so much alive he completely recovered from his exposure and starvation. He had another vision also in which God sent two angels with needles and thread to make dolls and the movement of these figures showed him what would happen. And it all happened that way.

Dr. Reser began to tell of his experiences while in the psychological state known as possession. Incident piled on incident. A new personality burned up the one that had eaten supper with us. His blue-gray eyes glowed, but at the same time they drew far back into his head as if they went inside to gaze on things kept in a secret place. After awhile he began to speak. He told of marvelous revelations of the Brave Guedé cult. And as he spoke, he moved farther and farther from known land and into the territory of myths and mists. Before our very eyes, he walked out of his nordic body and changed. Whatever the stuff of which the soul of Haiti is made, he was that. You could see the snake god of Dahomey hovering about him. Africa was in his tones. He throbbed and glowed. He used English words but he talked to me from another continent. He was dancing before his gods and the fire of Shango played about him. Then I knew how Moses felt when he beheld the burning bush. Moses had seen fires and he had seen bushes, but he had never seen a bush with a fiery ego and I had never seen a man who dwelt in flame, who was coldly afire in the pores. Perhaps some day I shall visit his roomy porch again and drink his orangeade and listen to him discourse on Aristotle, but even in the midst of it, I shall remember his hour of fire.

Ah Bo Bo!!

Chapter XVIII

God and the Pintards

WITH ALL of their ineptitude for certain concepts that the Anglo-Saxon holds sacred, the Haitian people have a tremendous talent for getting themselves loved. They are drenched in kindliness and beaming out with charm. They are like the pintards of God that Dr. Reser told me about. That is a Haitian folk tale that somebody told to him. A pintard is a guinea-fowl.

God planted a rice field one year. It was a rice field that was equal to His station and circumstances. It began to ripen and God began to look forward to the day of reaping.

One day a message came to God saying, "God, the pintards are eating up all of your rice. If you don't do something about it, there won't be any rice to reap."

So God called the Angel Michael and told him, "Here, Michael, you take this gun and go down to my rice fields and kill those pintards. They are eating up all of my rice and I did not plant rice for them. Go and shoot enough of them to scare off the rest. I meant to have a great crop this year."

The Angel Michael took the gun and went on down to God's rice fields to shoot the pintards as he had been told. When he was about there the pintards saw him coming with God's gun and they all flew up into a huge mimbon tree and began to sing and clap their wings together in rhythm. Michael came up to the tree and pointed the shot-gun at the great mass of pintards crowded into the tree singing and making rhythm. But the song and the rhythm were so compelling that he forgot to pull the trigger. With the gun still pointing he began to keep time with the wing clapping. Then he went to dancing and finally he laid the gun down and danced until he was exhausted. Then he took up the gun and went away and told God saying, "God, I could not shoot those pintards. They were too happy and made too beautiful a dance-song for me to kill them." With a shamed face, because he had not done what God sent him to do, Michael put the gun down and went away.

God called Gabriel and said, "Gabriel, I don't aim to have all of my rice eaten up by those pintards. You take this gun and go down there and shoot them, and otherwise drive them away from my rice fields. I sent Michael and he never did a thing. Now you go and hurry up. I want some rice this year."

So Gabriel took the gun and went on down to God's rice field to shoot the pintards, but they saw him coming too and flew up into the mimbon tree and began to clap wings and sing, and Gabriel began to dance and forgot all about God's rice field for a whole day. When he saw the sun going down he remembered why he had been sent and he was so ashamed of himself that he couldn't bear to face God. So he met Peter and handed him the gun and said, "Please take God His gun for me. I am ashamed to go back."

Peter took the gun and told God what Gabriel had said. So God sent Peter and told him, "You go and *kill* those pintards! I do not plant rice for pintards and don't intend to have my crop all ruined by them, either. Go and clear them out." Peter took the gun and went down in a hurry to do God's will. But he got all charmed by the song and the dance and when he went back with the gun he was too ashamed to talk.

So God took the gun and went down to His rice fields Himself. The pintards saw Him coming and left the rice and flew up into the tree again. They saw it was God Himself, so they sang a new song and put on a double rhythm and then they doubled it again. God aimed the gun but before He knew it He was dancing and because of the song, He didn't care whether He saved any rice or not. So He said, "I can't kill these pintards—they are too happy and joyful to be killed. But I do want my rice fields so I know what I will do. There is the world that I have made and so far it is sad and nobody is happy there and nothing goes right. I'll send these pintards down there to take music and laughter so the world can forget its troubles."

And that is what He did. He called Shango, the god of thunder and lightning and he made a shaft of lightning and the pintards slid down it and landed in Guinea. So that is why music and dancing came from Guinea—God sent it there first.

Songs of Worship to Voodoo Gods

MAITRESSE ERSULIE

Ersulie nain nain oh! Ersulie nain nain oh! Ersulie ya gaga gaaza,
La roseé fait brodè tou temps soleil par lévé
La roseé fait brode tou temps soleil par lévé
Ersulie nain nain oh! Ersulie nain nain oh! Ersulie ya gaza.

No. 1

Er - su - lie nain nain oh! Er - su - lie nain nain oh!..

.... Er - su - lie ya... ga-ga... ga - a - za, La ro-seé fait bro-

dè tou temps so - leil par lé - vé La ro seé fait bro-

de tou temps so - leil par lé - vé Er - su - lie nain nain oh!....

Er - su lie nain nain oh!.... Er su - lie ya ga - za..........

FÉRAILLE

Féraille oh! nan main, qui moun ma quité baquiya
laquan moin rété m'songé Ogoun Féraille
ma consolé ma prend courail oh!
relé nan qui temps rou si malade oh
cor wa nouyé nan qui temps nan qui temps oh!
Cor wa nouyé ma console' ma prend courail oh!
so bé guim as sura.

RADA

Coté ma prend Coté ma prend Médi oh!
Anago Coté ma prend Coté ma prend Medi oh!
Anago . . .

RADA

Bonjour papa Legba bonjour ti moun moin yo
Bonjour papa Legba bonjour ti moun moin yo
ma pé mandé ou con man non yé
ma pé mandé ou con man non yé
bonjour papa Legba bonjour ti moun moin yo Bon.

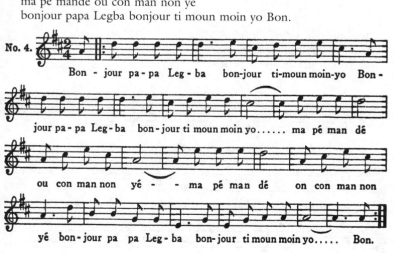

JANVALO (JEAN VALDO)

Adia ban moin zui potó tou félé
Adia ban moin zui potó tou félé
Adia ban moin zui zui ya ma qué félé
Adia ban moin zui zui ya ma qué félé
Adia ban moin zui potó tout félé.

A - dia ban moin zui po - tó..... tou fé - lé

A - dia ban moin zui po - té.... tou fé - lé   A - dia ban moin

zui zui ya ma qué fé - lé   A - dia ban moin zui zui

ya ma qué fé - lé   A - dia ban moin zui po - té..... tout fé - lé.

JANVALO

Adi bon ça ma dit si ma dènié oh!
gadé misè ya cé pou do moins
adi bon ça ma dit si ma dénié oh!
gade misè ya cé pou do moins.

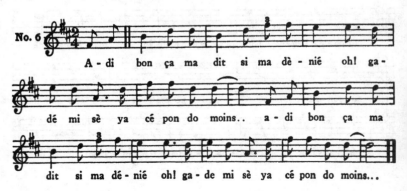

A - di bon ça ma dit si ma dè - nié oh! ga -

dé mi sè ya cé pon do moins..   a - di bon ça ma

dit si ma dé - nié oh! ga - de mi sè ya cé pon do moins...

SAINT JACQUES

St. Jacques pas là St. Jacques pas là St. Jacques pas là
cé moin qui là St. Jacques pas là oh! chien ya modé moin.

PETRO

Nous vley wè Don Pétro Nous vley wé oh!
Nous vley wè si ya quité caille la tombé
Nous vley wè Don Petro Nous vley wè oh!
Nous vley wè oh! Si ya quité caille là tombé elan oh!

PETRO

Salut moin oh! Salut moin oh! Salut moins
Nous sévi lan rent nan caille là oh! Salut moins.
oh a diĕ salut moins oh Salut moins oh Salut moins
nous sèvi lan rent nan caille la oh! Salut moins Salut.

IBO

Ibo Lélé Ibo Lélé Iyanman
ça ou gain yen conça Ibo Lélé
cé con ça moin dansé Ibo Iyanman oh! Anan Iyanman
Con ça m'dansé Ibo Iyanman oh! Anan Iyanman.

No. 10

I - bo Lé - lé........ I - bo Lé - lé I-yan-man

ça ou gain yen çon - ça I bo Lé - lé........ cé con

ça moin dan-té I - bo I-yan-man oh! An - an I-yan-man

Con çam dan- té I bo I-yan-man oh! An an I-yan man...

IBO

Ibo moin youn oh! Ibo moin youn oh!
Ibo moin youn oh! m'pa gan guin man man guidé moin
Grand Ibo moin youn oh! m'pa gan guin man man guidé moin.

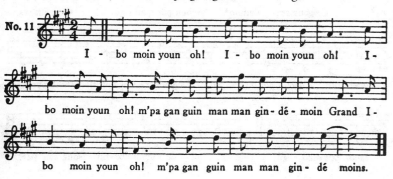

No. 11

I - bo moin youn oh! I - bo moin youn oh! I-

bo moin youn oh! m'pa gan guin man man gin - dé - moin Grand I-

bo moin youn oh! m'pa gan guin man man gin - dé moins.

DAMBALLA

Fiolé por Dambalá Dambala Wèdo
Fiolé oh! Dambala Wèdo Fiolé por Dambala
Dambala Wédo Fiolé por Dambala.

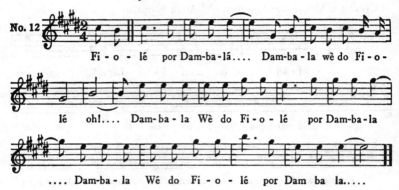

Fi - o - lé   por Dam-ba-lá....   Dam-ba - la wè do Fi - o -

lé   oh!.... Dam-ba - la Wè do Fi - o - lé   por Dam-ba-la

.... Dam-ba - la   Wé do Fi - o - lé   por Dam ba la.....

OGOUN

Ogoun travail oh! Ogoun por mangé
Ogoun travail oh! Ogoun por mangé
Ogoun travail tout nan nuit por Ogoun por mangé
yiĕre soi Ogoun dormi sans souper.

O - goun tra   vail oh!   O-goun por man - gé......   O - goun tra -

vail oh!   O-goun por man - gé   O - goun tra vail tout nan nuit por O -

goun por man - gé   yiĕ - re soi O - goun dor mi sans sou per.

SALONGO

Zin zin zin zin zin zin Ba yan min oh! Saya Pimba
zin zin zin zin zin zin Ba yan min oh! Saya Pimba

No. 14

Zin zin zin zin zin zin Ba yan min oh! Sa-ya Pim ba

zin zin zin zin zin zin Ba yan min oh! Sa-ya Pim-ba.....

SALONGO

Tousa Tousa rèlè Tou Salonggo
Tou sa Tou sa rèlè Tou Salonggo
Tousa Tou sa rèlè Tou Salonggo.

No. 15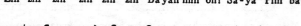

Tou - sa Tou-sa rè lè Tou Sa-long-go Tou sa Tou

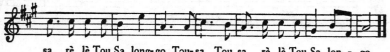

sa rè lè Tou Sa long-go Tou-sa Tou sa rè lè Tou Sa lon - go.

LOCO

Loco Mabia Ebon Azacan Loco Mabia Ello oh!
Loco Mabia Ello Azagan Loco Mabia Ello oh!
Jean valou Moin Jean valou
Moin Loco Loco Mabia Ello . . .

No. 1

Lo-co Ma - bia E - bon.... A - za - can... Lo-co Ma-

bia El - lo oh!.... Lo-co Ma - bia El - lo..... A - za gan..

.... Lo - co Ma- bia El - lo oh!... Jean va-lou Moin.... Jean va-lou

Moin Lo - co.... Lo-co Ma- bia El-lo..... Lo-co Ma- Lo.

MAMBO ISAN

Mambo Isan ma pralé Oh! Ma pralé quéléfré
m'pralé chaché fammil moin yo Mambo Isan ma pralé
Oh! Ma pralé quéléfré m'pralé chaché fammil moin yo
Mambo Isan oh! cé rou qui maré moin Mambo Isan oh!
cé rou qui maré moin cé rou qua laqué'm oh!

No. 2

Mam-bo I - san ma pra - lé.... Oh!... Ma pra-lé qué-lé-fré

.... m'pra-lé cha-ché fammil - moin yo... Mam bo I-san ma pra - lé..

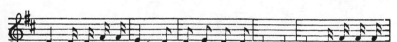

..... Oh!.... Ma pra lé qué-lé-fré... m'pra lé cha-ché fammil moin

yo... Mambo I - sanoh! cé ron... qui ma-ré   moin...Mam-bo I san

oh! cé - ron qui ma ré moin cé ron   qua la - qué'm oh!.....

DAMBALA

Filé na filé fem Dambala Wèdo
Filé na filé Dambala Wèdo cé coulèv oh! . . .

AGOË (AGOUÉ TE ROYO)

Aroquè si ou gain yen chanson nivo pou ou chanté
wa chanté l'nan hounfort ou
Piga ou montre creole chanson nivo
va gaté moyen ou Agoë ta royo
neg bas sin bleu neg dlo salé neg coqui doré
Si ou gain yen chanson nivo pou ou chanté
Wa chanté l'nan hounfor ou Piga ou montré creole chanson
    nivo.

A - ro - què si ou gain yen chan-son ni - vo..... pon ou chan-

té..... wa chan té...'l'nan hounfort ou - d ro - nan hounfort ou Pi -

gaon mon tre cri - ole than son ni vo Pi - Vo on cri - ole

va ga té mo yenou.... A- goë ta ro ´yo neg bas sin bleu neg dlo sa-lé neg

co-qui do- ré...... Si ou gain yen chan-son ni vo...... pon ou chan -

té.... Wa chan tél-nan houn for ou Pi ga ou mon tré cre-ole cha n son ni vo.

SOBO

Gué Manyan manyan gadé hounfort
wa gadé hounfor wa Sobo gué manyan be!
O gué Manyan Manyan gadé hounfor wa Sobo
Gadé hounfor wa Sobo Gué Manyan bé!

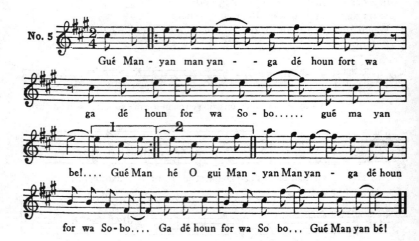

OGOUN

Alou man dia hé! Ogoun oh! ohsans yo oh! aho!
Alou man O sange ba coule qui mande drapo o
Sange ba coulé qui mandé drapo lila Ogoun bare I baba.

Miscellaneous Songs

SECT ROUGE

Carrefour, tingindingue, mi haut, mi bas-é
Carrefour, tingindingue, mi haut, mi bas-é
Oun pralé, tingindingue, mi haut, mi bas, tingindingue
Oun pralé, tingindingue, mi haut, mi bas, tingindingue
Oun pralé, tingindingue, mi haut, mi bas, tingindingue

SECT ROUGE

Sortie nan cimiterre, toute corps moin sentie malingue
Sortie nan cimiterre, toute corps moin sentie malingue
Sortie nan cimiterre, toute corps moin sentie malingue
Sortie nan cimiterre, toute corps moin sentie malingue

CHANT BEGINNING ALL RADA CEREMONIES

Héla grand pere étérnel sin joé
Héla grand pere étérnel sin jozé do co agué
Héla grand pere éternel sin'nam min bon Diĕ o Saint yen.

TUNE TO CALL THE "LOA"

LA MYSTÉRIEUSE, MÉRINGUE

A. L. Duroseau

ETONNEMENT, MÉRINGUE CARACTÉRISTIQUE

A. Herandez

—BONNE HUMEUR—
MÉRINGUE HAITÏENNE
à Miss Zora Neale Hurston

Arthur L. Duroseau

OLGA, MÉRINGUE PAR

Arthur Lyncíe Duroseau

Arthur Lyncíe Duroseau

CHANSON DE CALICOT

LA DOUCEUR

Méringue Haïtienne par Arthur L. Duroseau

—JANVALHO—

DUST TRACKS ON A ROAD

Contents

I

My Birthplace

LIKE the dead-seeming, cold rocks, I have memories within that came out of the material that went to make me. Time and place have had their say.

So you will have to know something about the time and place where I came from, in order that you may interpret the incidents and directions of my life.

I was born in a Negro town. I do not mean by that the black back-side of an average town. Eatonville, Florida, is, and was at the time of my birth, a pure Negro town—charter, mayor, council, town marshal and all. It was not the first Negro community in America, but it was the first to be incorporated, the first attempt at organized self-government on the part of Negroes in America.

Eatonville is what you might call hitting a straight lick with a crooked stick. The town was not in the original plan. It is a by-product of something else.

It all started with three white men on a ship off the coast of Brazil. They had been officers in the Union Army. When the bitter war had ended in victory for their side, they had set out for South America. Perhaps the post-war distress made their native homes depressing. Perhaps it was just that they were young, and it was hard for them to return to the monotony of everyday being after the excitement of military life, and they, as numerous other young men, set out to find new frontiers.

But they never landed in Brazil. Talking together on the ship, these three decided to return to the United States and try their fortunes in the unsettled country of South Florida. No doubt the same thing which had moved them to go to Brazil caused them to choose South Florida.

This had been dark and bloody country since the mid-seventeen hundreds. Spanish, French, English, Indian, and American blood had been bountifully shed.

The last great struggle was between the resentful Indians and the white planters of Georgia, Alabama, and South Carolina. The strong and powerful Cherokees, aided by the conglomerate Seminoles, raided the plantations and carried off Negro slaves into the Spanish-held Florida. Ostensibly they were carried off to be slaves to the Indians, but in reality the Negro men were used to swell the ranks of the Indian fighters against the white plantation owners. During lulls in the long struggle, treaties were signed, but invariably broken. The sore point of returning escaped Negroes could not be settled satisfactorily to either side. Who was an Indian and who was a Negro? The whites contended all who had negro blood. The Indians contended all who spoke their language belonged to the tribe. Since it was an easy matter to teach a slave to speak enough of the language to pass in a short time, the question could never be settled. So the wars went on.

The names of Oglethorpe, Clinch and Andrew Jackson are well known on the white side of the struggle. For the Indians, Miccanopy, Billy Bow-legs and Osceola. The noble Osceola was only a sub-chief, but he came to be recognized by both sides as the ablest of them all. Had he not been captured by treachery, the struggle would have lasted much longer than it did. With an offer of friendship, and a new rifle (some say a beautiful sword) he was lured to the fort seven miles outside of St. Augustine, and captured. He was confined in sombre Fort Marion that still stands in that city, escaped, was recaptured, and died miserably in the prison of a fort in Beaufort, South Carolina. Without his leadership, the Indian cause collapsed. The Cherokees and most of the Seminoles, with their Negro adherents, were moved west. The beaten Indians were moved to what is now Oklahoma. It was far from the then settlements of the Whites. And then too, there seemed to be nothing there that White people wanted, so it was a good place for Indians. The wilds of Florida heard no more clash of battle among men.

The sensuous world whirled on in the arms of ether for a generation or so. Time made and marred some men. So into this original hush came the three frontier-seekers who had been so intrigued by its prospects that they had turned back after actually arriving at the coast of Brazil without landing. These young men were no poor, refuge-seeking, wayfarers. They were educated men of family and wealth.

The shores of Lake Maitland were beautiful, so they chose the northern end and settled. There one of the old forts— built against the Indians, had stood. It had been commanded by Colonel Maitland, so the lake and the community took their names in memory of him. It was Mosquito County then and the name was just. It is Orange County now for equally good reason. The men persuaded other friends in the north to join them, and the town of Maitland began to be in a great rush.

Negroes were found to do the clearing. There was the continuous roar of the crashing of ancient giants of the lush woods, of axes, saws and hammers. And there on the shores of Lake Maitland rose stately houses, surrounded by beautiful grounds. Other settlers flocked in from upper New York state, Minnesota and Michigan, and Maitland became a center of wealth and fashion. In less than ten years, the Plant System, later absorbed into the Atlantic Coast Line Railroad, had been persuaded to extend a line south through Maitland, and the private coaches of millionaires and other dignitaries from North and South became a common sight on the siding. Even a president of the United States visited his friends at Maitland.

These wealthy homes, glittering carriages behind blooded horses and occupied by well-dressed folk, presented a curious spectacle in the swampy forests so dense that they are dark at high noon. The terrain swarmed with the deadly diamond-back rattlesnake, most potent reptile on the North American continent. Huge, centuries-old bull alligators bellowed their challenge from the uninhabited shores of lakes. It was necessary to carry a lantern when one walked out at night, to avoid stumbling over these immense reptiles in the streets of Maitland.

Roads were made by the simple expedient of driving buggies and wagons back and forth over the foot trail, which ran for seven miles between Maitland and Orlando. The terrain was as flat as a table and totally devoid of rocks. All the road-makers had to do was to curve around the numerous big pine trees and oaks. It seems it was too much trouble to cut them down. Therefore, the road looked as if it had been laid out by a playful snake. Now and then somebody would chop down a troublesome tree. Way late, the number of tree stumps along the route began to be annoying. Buggy wheels bumped and jolted over them and took away the pleasure of driving. So a man was hired to improve the road. His instructions were to round off the tops of all stumps so that the wheels, if and when they struck stumps, would slide off gently instead of jolting the teeth out of riders as before. This was done, and the spanking rigs of the bloods whisked along with more assurance.

Now, the Negro population of Maitland settled simultaneously with the White. They had been needed, and found profitable employment. The best of relations existed between employer and employee. While the White estates flourished on the three-mile length of Lake Maitland, the Negroes set up their hastily built shacks around St. John's Hole, a lake as round as a dollar, and less than a half mile wide. It is now a beauty spot in the heart of Maitland, hard by United States Highway Number 17. They call it Lake Lily.

The Negro women could be seen every day but Sunday, squatting around St. John's Hole on their haunches, primitive style, washing clothes and fishing, while their men went forth and made their support in cutting new ground, building, and planting orange groves. Things were moving so swiftly that there was plenty to do, with good pay. Other Negroes in Georgia and West Florida heard of the boom in South Florida from Crescent City to Cocoa and they came. No more back-bending over rows of cotton; no more fear of the fury of the Reconstruction. Good pay, sympathetic White folks and cheap land, soft to the touch of a plow. Relatives and friends were sent for.

Two years after the three adventurers entered the primeval forests of Mosquito County, Maitland had grown big enough, and simmered down enough, to consider a formal city government.

Now, these founders were, to a man, people who had risked their lives and fortunes that Negroes might be free. Those who had fought in the ranks had thrown their weight behind the cause of Emancipation. So when it was decided to hold an election, the Eatons, Lawrences, Vanderpools, Hurds, Halls, the Hills, Yateses and Galloways, and all the rest including Bishop Whipple, head of the Minnesota diocese, never for a moment considered excluding the Negroes from participation. The Whites nominated a candidate and the Negroes, under the aggressive lead of Joe Clarke, a muscular, dynamic Georgia Negro, put up Tony Taylor as their standard-bearer.

I do not know whether it was the numerical superiority of the Negroes, or whether some of the Whites, out of deep feeling, threw their votes to the Negro side. At any rate, Tony Taylor became the first Mayor of Maitland with Joe Clarke winning out as town Marshal. This was a wholly unexpected turn, but nobody voiced any open objections. The Negro Mayor and Marshal and the White City Council took office peacefully and served their year without incident.

But during that year, a yeast was working. Joe Clarke had asked himself, why not a Negro town? Few of the Negroes were interested. It was too vaulting for their comprehension. A pure Negro town! If nothing but their own kind was in it, who was going to run it? With no White folks to command them, how would they know what to do? Joe Clarke had plenty of confidence in himself to do the job, but few others could conceive of it.

But one day by chance or purpose, Joe Clarke was telling of his ambitions to Captain Eaton, who thought it a workable plan. He talked it over with Captain Lawrence and others. By the end of the year, all arrangements had been made. Lawrence and Eaton bought a tract of land a mile west of Maitland for a town site. The backing of the Whites helped Joe Clarke to convince the other Negroes, and things were settled.

Captain Lawrence at his own expense erected a well-built church on the new site, and Captain Eaton built a hall for general assembly and presented it to the new settlement. A little later, the wife of Bishop Whipple had the first church rolled across the street and built a larger church on the same spot, and the first building was to become a library, stocked with books donated by the White community.

So on August 18, 1886, the Negro town, called Eatonville, after Captain Eaton, received its charter of incorporation from the state capital at Tallahassee, and made history by becoming the first of its kind in America, and perhaps in the world. So, in a raw, bustling frontier, the experiment of self-government for Negroes was tried. White Maitland and Negro Eatonville, have lived side by side for fifty-five years without a single instance of enmity. The spirit of the founders has reached beyond the grave.

The whole lake country of Florida sprouted with life—mostly Northerners, and prosperity was everywhere. It was in the late eighties that the stars fell, and many of the original settlers date their coming "just before, or just after the stars fell."

II

My Folks

Iᴺᵀᴏ this burly, boiling, hard-hitting, rugged-individualistic setting, walked one day a tall, heavy-muscled mulatto who resolved to put down roots.

John Hurston, in his late twenties, had left Macon County, Alabama, because the ordeal of share-cropping on a southern Alabama cotton plantation was crushing to his ambition. There was no rise to the thing.

He had been born near Notasulga, Alabama, in an outlying district of landless Negroes, and Whites not too much better off. It was "over the creek," which was just like saying on the wrong side of the railroad tracks. John Hurston had learned to read and write somehow between cotton-choppings and cotton-picking, and it might have satisfied him in a way. But somehow he took to going to Macedonia Baptist Church on the right side of the creek. He went one time, and met up with dark-brown Lucy Ann Potts, of the land-owning Richard Potts, which might have given him the going habit.

He was nearly twenty years old then, and she was fourteen. My mother used to claim with a smile that she saw him looking and looking at her up there in the choir and wondered what he was looking at her for. She wasn't studying about *him*. However, when the service was over and he kept standing around, never far from her, she asked somebody, "Who is dat bee-stung yaller nigger?"

"Oh, dat's one of dem niggers from over de creek, one of dem Hurstons—call him John I believe."

That was supposed to settle that. Over-the-creek niggers lived from one white man's plantation to the other. Regular hand-to-mouth folks. Didn't own pots to pee in, nor beds to push 'em under. Didn't have no more pride than to let themselves be hired by poor white trash. No more to 'em than the stuffings out of a zero. The inference was that Lucy Ann Potts had asked about nothing and had been told.

Mama thought no more about him, she said. Of course,

567

she couldn't help noticing that his grey-green eyes and light
skin stood out sharply from the black-skinned, black-eyed
crowd he was in. Then, too, he had a build on him that made
you look. A stud-looking buck like that would have brought a
big price in slavery time. Then, if he had not kept on hanging
around where she couldn't help from seeing him, she would
never have remembered that she had seen him two or three
times before around the cotton-gin in Notasulga, and once in
a store. She had wondered then who he was, handling bales
of cotton like suitcases.

After that Sunday, he got right worrisome. Slipping her
notes between the leaves of hymn books and things like that.
It got so bad that a few months later she made up her mind
to marry him just to get rid of him. So she did, in spite of the
most violent opposition of her family. She put on the little
silk dress which she had made with her own hands, out of
goods bought from egg-money she had saved. Her ninety
pounds of fortitude set out on her wedding night alone, since
none of the family except her brother Jim could bear the
sight of her great come-down in the world. She who was considered the prettiest and the smartest black girl was throwing
herself away and disgracing the Pottses by marrying an over-
the-creek nigger, and a bastard at that. Folks said he was a
certain white man's son. But here she was, setting out to walk
two miles at night by herself, to keep her pledge to him at the
church. Her father, more tolerant than her mother, decided
that his daughter was not going alone, nor was she going to
walk to her wedding. So he hitched up the buggy and went
with her. Nobody much was there. Her brother Jim slipped
in just before she stood on the floor.

So she said her words and took her stand for life, and went
off to a cabin on a plantation with him. She never forgot how
the late moon shone that night as his two hundred pounds of
bone and muscle shoved open the door and lifted her in his
arms over the door-sill.

That cabin on a white man's plantation had to be all for the
present. She had been pointedly made to know that the Potts
plantation was nothing to her any more. Her father soon softened and was satisfied to an extent, but her mother, never.
To her dying day her daughter's husband was never John

Hurston to her. He was always "dat yaller bastard." Four years after my mother's marriage, and during her third pregnancy, she got to thinking of the five acres of cling-stone peaches on her father's place, and the yearning was so strong that she walked three miles to get a few. She was holding the corners of her apron with one hand and picking peaches with the other when her mother spied her, and ordered her off the place.

It was after his marriage that my father began to want things. Plantation life began to irk and bind him. His over-the-creek existence was finished. What else was there for a man like him? He left his wife and three children behind and went out to seek and see.

Months later he pitched into the hurly-burly of South Florida. So he heard about folks building a town all out of colored people. It seemed like a good place to go. Later on, he was to be elected Mayor of Eatonville for three terms, and to write the local laws. The village of Eatonville is still governed by the laws formulated by my father. The town clerk still consults a copy of the original printing which seems to be the only one in existence now. I have tried every way I know how to get this copy for my library, but so far it has not been possible. I had it once, but the town clerk came and took it back.

When my mother joined papa a year after he had settled in Eatonville, she brought some quilts, her feather bed and bedstead. That was all they had in the house that night. Two burlap bags were stuffed with Spanish moss for the two older children to sleep on. The youngest child was taken into the bed with them.

So these two began their new life. Both of them swore that things were going to better, and it came to pass as they said. They bought land, built a roomy house, planted their acres and reaped. Children kept coming—more mouths to feed and more feet for shoes. But neither of them seemed to have minded that. In fact, my father not only boasted among other men about "his house full of young'uns" but he boasted that he had never allowed his wife to go out and hit a lick of work for anybody a day in her life. Of weaknesses, he had his share, and I know that my mother was very unhappy at times, but neither of them ever made any move to call the thing off. In fact, on two occasions, I heard my father threaten to kill my mother if she ever started towards the gate to leave him. He was outraged and angry one day when she said lightly that if he did not want to do for her and his children, there was another man over the fence waiting for his job. That expression is a folk saying and Papa had heard it used hundreds of times by other women, but he was outraged at hearing it from Mama. She definitely understood, before he got through carrying on, that the saying was not for her lips.

On another occasion Papa got the idea of escorting the wife of one of his best friends, and having the friend escort Mama. But Mama seemed to enjoy it more than Papa thought she ought to—though she had opposed the idea when it was suggested—and it ended up with Papa leaving his friend's wife at the reception and following Mama and his friend home, and marching her into the house with the muzzle of his Winchester rifle in her back. The friend's wife, left alone at the hall, gave both her husband and Papa a good cussing out the next day. Mama dared not laugh, even at that, for fear of stirring Papa up more. It was a month or so before the two families thawed out again. Even after that, the subject could never be mentioned before Papa or the friend's wife, though both of them had been red-hot for the experiment.

My mother rode herd on one woman with a horse whip about Papa, and "spoke out" another one. This, instead of making Papa angry, seemed to please him ever so much. The woman who got "spoken out" threatened to whip my mother. Mama was very small and the other woman was husky. But when Papa heard of the threats against Mama, he notified the outside woman that if she could not whip him too, she had better not bring the mess up. The woman left the county without ever breaking another breath with Papa. Nobody around there knew what became of her.

So, looking back, I take it that Papa and Mama, in spite of his meanderings, were really in love. Maybe he was just born before his time. There was nothing then to hinder impulses. They didn't have these zippers on pants in those days, guaranteed to stay locked no matter what the strain. From what I can learn, those button-up flies were mighty tricky and betraying. Maybe if I ask around, somebody will tell me what modern invention has done for a lot of morals.

We lived on a big piece of ground with two big chinaberry trees shading the front gate . . . Cape jasmine bushes with hundreds of blooms on either side of the walks. I loved the fleshy, white, fragrant blooms as a child but did not make too much of them. They were too common in my neighborhood. When I got to New York and found out that the people called them gardenias, and that the flowers cost a dollar each, I was impressed. The home folks laughed when I went back down there and told them. Some of the folks did not want to believe me. A dollar for a Cape jasmine bloom! Folks up north there must be crazy.

There were plenty of orange, grapefruit, tangerine, guavas and other fruits in our yard. We had a five acre garden with things to eat growing in it, and so we were never hungry. We had chicken on the table often; home-cured meat, and all the eggs we wanted. It was a common thing for us smaller children to fill the iron tea-kettle full of eggs and boil them, and lay around in the yard and eat them until we were full. Any leftover boiled eggs could always be used for missiles. There was plenty of fish in the lakes around the town, and so we had all that we wanted. But beef stew was something rare. We were all very happy whenever Papa went to Orlando and brought back something delicious like stew-beef. Chicken and fish were too common with us. In the same way, we treasured an apple. We had oranges, tangerines and grapefruit to use as hand-grenades on the neighbors' children. But apples were something rare. They came from way up north.

Our house had eight rooms, and we called it a two-story house; but later on I learned it was really one story and a jump. The big boys all slept up there, and it was a good place to hide and shirk from sweeping off the front porch or raking up the back yard.

Downstairs in the dining room there was an old "safe," a punched design in its tin doors. Glasses of guava jelly, quart jars of pear, peach and other kinds of preserves. The leftover cooked foods were on the lower shelves.

There were eight children in the family, and our house was

noisy from the time school turned out until bedtime. After
supper we gathered in Mama's room, and everybody had to
get their lessons for the next day. Mama carried us all past
long division in arithmetic, and parsing sentences in grammar,
by diagrams on the black-board. That was as far as she had
gone. Then the younger ones were turned over to my oldest
brother, Bob, and Mama sat and saw to it that we paid attention. You had to keep on going over things until you did
know. How I hated the multiplication tables—especially the
sevens!

We had a big barn, and a stretch of ground well covered
with Bermuda grass. So on moonlight nights, two-thirds of
the village children from seven to eighteen would be playing
"hide and whoop," "chick-mah-chick," "hide and seek," and
other boisterous games in our yard. Once or twice a year we
might get permission to go and play at some other house. But
that was most unusual. Mama contended that we had plenty
of space to play in; plenty of things to play with; and, furthermore, plenty of us to keep each other's company. If she had
her way, she meant to raise her children to stay at home. She
said that there was no need for us to live like no-count negroes and poor white trash—too poor to sit in the house—
had to come outdoors for any pleasure, or hang around
somebody else's house. Any of her children who had any tendencies like that must have got it from the Hurston side. It
certainly did not come from the Pottses. Things like that gave
me my first glimmering of the universal female gospel that all
good traits and leanings come from the mother's side.

Mama exhorted her children at every opportunity to "jump
at de sun." We might not land on the sun, but at least we
would get off the ground. Papa did not feel so hopeful. Let
well enough alone. It did not do for Negroes to have too
much spirit. He was always threatening to break mine or kill
me in the attempt. My mother was always standing between
us. She conceded that I was impudent and given to talking
back, but she didn't want to "squinch my spirit" too much
for fear that I would turn out to be a mealy-mouthed rag doll
by the time I got grown. Papa always flew hot when Mama
said that. I do not know whether he feared for my future,
with the tendency I had to stand and give battle, or that he

felt a personal reference in Mama's observation. He predicted
dire things for me. The white folks were not going to stand
for it. I was going to be hung before I got grown. Somebody
was going to blow me down for my sassy tongue. Mama was
going to suck sorrow for not beating my temper out of me
before it was too late. Posses with ropes and guns were going
to drag me out sooner or later on account of that stiff neck I
toted. I was going to tote a hungry belly by reason of my
forward ways. My older sister was meek and mild. She would
always get along. Why couldn't I be like her? Mama would
keep right on with whatever she was doing and remark, "Zora
is my young'un, and Sarah is yours. I'll be bound mine will
come out more than conquer. You leave her alone. I'll tend
to her when I figger she needs it." She meant by that that
Sarah had a disposition like Papa's, while mine was like hers.

Behind Mama's rocking chair was a good place to be in
times like that. Papa was not going to hit Mama. He was two
hundred pounds of bone and muscle and Mama weighed
somewhere in the nineties. When people teased him about
Mama being the boss, he would say he could break her of her
headstrong ways if he wanted to, but she was so little that he
couldn't find any place to hit her. My Uncle Jim, Mama's
brother, used to always take exception to that. He maintained
that if a woman had anything big enough to sit on, she had
something big enough to hit on. That was his firm conviction, and he meant to hold on to it as long as the bottom end
of his backbone pointed towards the ground—don't care
who the woman was or what she looked like, or where she
came from. Men like Papa who held to any other notion were
just beating around the bush, dodging the issue, and otherwise looking like a fool at a funeral.

Papa used to shake his head at this and say, "What's de use
of me taking my fist to a poor weakly thing like a woman?
Anyhow, you got to submit yourself to 'em, so there ain't no
use in beating on 'em and then have to go back and beg 'em
pardon."

But perhaps the real reason that Papa did not take Uncle
Jim's advice too seriously, was because he saw how it worked
out in Uncle Jim's own house. He could tackle Aunt Caroline, all right, but he had his hands full to really beat her. A

knockdown didn't convince her that the fight was over at all. She would get up and come right on in, and she was nobody's weakling. It was generally conceded that he might get the edge on her in physical combat if he took a hammer or a trace-chain to her, but in other ways she always won. She would watch his various philandering episodes just so long, and then she would go into action. One time she saw all, and said nothing. But one Saturday afternoon, she watched him rush in with a new shoe box which he thought that she did not see him take out to the barn and hide until he was ready to go out. Just as the sun went down, he went out, got his box, cut across the orange grove and went on down to the store.

He stopped long enough there to buy a quart of peanuts, two stalks of sugar cane, and then tripped on off to the little house in the woods where lived a certain transient light of love. Aunt Caroline kept right on ironing until he had gotten as far as the store. Then she slipped on her shoes, went out in the yard and got the axe, slung it across her shoulder and went walking very slowly behind him.

The men on the store porch had given Uncle Jim a laughing sendoff. They all knew where he was going and why. The shoes had been bought right there at the store. Now here came "dat Cal'line" with her axe on her shoulder. No chance to warn Uncle Jim at all. Nobody expected murder, but they knew that plenty of trouble was on the way. So they just sat and waited. Cal'line had done so many side-splitting things to Jim's lights of love—all without a single comment from her—that they were on pins to see what happened next.

About an hour later, when it was almost black dark, they saw a furtive figure in white dodging from tree to tree until it hopped over Clarke's strawberry patch fence and headed towards Uncle Jim's house until it disappeared.

"Looked mightily like a man in long drawers and nothing else," Walter Thomas observed. Everybody agreed that it did, but who and what could it be?

By the time the town lamp which stood in front of the store was lighted, Aunt Caroline emerged from the blackness that hid the woods and passed the store. The axe was still over her shoulder, but now it was draped with Uncle Jim's pants, shirt and coat. A new pair of women's oxfords were dangling from the handle by their strings. Two stalks of sugar cane were over her other shoulder. All she said was, "Good evening, gentlemen," and kept right on walking towards home.

The porch rocked with laughter. They had the answer to everything. Later on when they asked Uncle Jim how Cal'line managed to get into the lady's house, he smiled sourly and said, "Dat axe was her key." When they kept on teasing him, he said, "Oh, dat old stubborn woman I married, you can't teach her nothing. I can't teach her no city ways at all."

On another occasion, she caused another lady who couldn't give the community anything but love, baby, to fall off of the high, steep church steps on her head. Aunt Cal'line might have done that just to satisfy her curiosity, since it was said that the lady felt that anything more than a petticoat under her dresses would be an incumbrance. Maybe Aunt Caroline just wanted to verify the rumor. The way the lady tumbled, it left no doubt in the matter. She was really a free soul. Evidently Aunt Caroline was put out about it, because she had to expectorate at that very moment, and it just happened to land where the lady was bare. Aunt Caroline evidently tried to correct her error in spitting on her rival, for she took her foot and tried to grind it in. She never said a word as usual, so the lady must have misunderstood Aunt Caroline's curiosity. She left town in a hurry—a speedy hurry—and never was seen in those parts again.

So Papa did not take Uncle Jim's philosophy about handling the lady people too seriously. Every time Mama cornered him about some of his doings, he used to threaten to wring a chair over her head. She never even took enough notice of the threat to answer. She just went right on asking questions about his doings and then answering them herself until Papa slammed out of the house looking like he had been whipped all over with peach hickories. But I had better not let out a giggle at such times, or it would be just too bad.

Our house was a place where people came. Visiting preachers, Sunday school and B.Y.P.U. workers, and just friends. There was fried chicken for visitors, and other such hospitality as the house afforded.

Papa's bedroom was the guest room. Store-bought towels would be taken out of the old round-topped trunk in Mama's room and draped on the wash-stand. The pitcher and bowl were scrubbed out before fresh water from the pump was put in there for the use of the guest. Sweet soap was company soap. We knew that. Otherwise, Octagon laundry soap was used to keep us clean. Bleached-out meal sacks served the family for bath towels ordinarily, so that the store-bought towels could be nice and clean for visitors.

Company got the preference in toilet paper, too. Old newspapers were put out in the privy house for family use. But when company came, something better was offered them. Fair to middling guests got sheets out of the old Sears, Roebuck catalogue. But Mama would sort over her old dress patterns when really fine company came, and the privy house was well scrubbed, lime thrown in, and the soft tissue paper pattern stuck on a nail inside the place for the comfort and pleasure of our guests. It was not that regular toilet paper was unheard of in our house. It was just unthought of. It was right there in the catalogue for us to see. But as long as we had Mr. Sears, Roebuck's catalogue, we had no need for his toilet paper.

III

I Get Born

THIS is all hear-say. Maybe, some of the details of my birth as told me might be a little inaccurate, but it is pretty well established that I really did get born.

The saying goes like this. My mother's time had come and my father was not there. Being a carpenter, successful enough to have other helpers on some jobs, he was away often on building business, as well as preaching. It seems that my father was away from home for months this time. I have never been told why. But I did hear that he threatened to cut his throat when he got the news. It seems that one daughter was all that he figured he could stand. My sister, Sarah, was his favorite child, but that one girl was enough. Plenty more sons, but no more girl babies to wear out shoes and bring in nothing. I don't think he ever got over the trick he felt that I played on him by getting born a girl, and while he was off from home at that. A little of my sugar used to sweeten his coffee right now. That is a Negro way of saying his patience was short with me. Let me change a few words with him—and I am of the word-changing kind—and he was ready to change ends. Still and all, I looked more like him than any child in the house. Of course, by the time I got born, it was too late to make any suggestions, so the old man had to put up with me. He was nice about it in a way. He didn't tie me in a sack and drop me in the lake, as he probably felt like doing.

People were digging sweet potatoes, and then it was hog-killing time. Not at our house, but it was going on in general over the country, like, being January and a bit cool. Most people were either butchering for themselves, or off helping other folks do their butchering, which was almost just as good. It is a gay time. A big pot of hasslits cooking with plenty of seasoning, lean slabs of fresh-killed pork frying for the helpers to refresh themselves after the work is done. Over and above being neighborly and giving aid, there is the food, the drinks and the fun of getting together.

So there was no grown folks close around when Mama's water broke. She sent one of the smaller children to fetch Aunt Judy, the mid-wife, but she was gone to Woodbridge, a mile and a half away, to eat at a hog-killing. The child was told to go over there and tell Aunt Judy to come. But nature, being indifferent to human arrangements, was impatient. My mother had to make it alone. She was too weak after I rushed out to do anything for herself, so she just was lying there, sick in the body, and worried in mind, wondering what would become of her, as well as me. She was so weak, she couldn't even reach down to where I was. She had one consolation. She knew I wasn't dead, because I was crying strong.

Help came from where she never would have thought to look for it. A white man of many acres and things, who knew the family well, had butchered the day before. Knowing that Papa was not at home, and that consequently there would be no fresh meat in our house, he decided to drive the five miles and bring a half of a shoat, sweet potatoes, and other garden stuff along. He was there a few minutes after I was born. Seeing the front door standing open, he came on in, and hollered, "Hello, there! Call your dogs!" That is the regular way to call in the country because nearly everybody who has anything to watch, has biting dogs.

Nobody answered, but he claimed later that he heard me spreading my lungs all over Orange County, so he shoved the door open and bolted on into the house.

He followed the noise and then he saw how things were, and being the kind of a man he was, he took out his Barlow Knife and cut the navel cord, then he did the best he could about other things. When the mid-wife, locally known as a granny, arrived about an hour later, there was a fire in the stove and plenty of hot water on. I had been sponged off in some sort of a way, and Mama was holding me in her arms.

As soon as the old woman got there, the white man unloaded what he had brought, and drove off cussing about some blankety-blank people never being where you could put your hands on them when they were needed.

He got no thanks from Aunt Judy. She grumbled for years about it. She complained that the cord had not been cut just right, and the belly-band had not been put on tight enough. She was mighty scared I was going to have a weak back, and that I would have trouble holding my water until I reached puberty. I did.

The next day or so a Mrs. Neale, a friend of Mama's, came in and reminded her that she had promised to let her name the baby in case it was a girl. She had picked up a name somewhere which she thought was very pretty. Perhaps, she had read it somewhere, or somebody back in those woods was smoking Turkish cigarettes. So I became Zora Neale Hurston.

There is nothing to make you like other human beings so much as doing things for them. Therefore, the man who grannied me was back next day to see how I was coming along. Maybe it was pride in his own handiwork, and his resourcefulness in a pinch, that made him want to see it through. He remarked that I was a God damned fine baby, fat and plenty of lung-power. As time went on, he came infrequently, but somehow kept a pinch of interest in my welfare. It seemed that I was spying noble, growing like a gourd vine, and yelling bass like a gator. He was the kind of a man that had no use for puny things, so I was all to the good with him. He thought my mother was justified in keeping me.

But nine months rolled around, and I just would not get on with the walking business. I was strong, crawling well, but showed no inclination to use my feet. I might remark in passing, that I still don't like to walk. Then I was over a year old, but still I would not walk. They made allowances for my weight, but yet, that was no real reason for my not trying.

They tell me that an old sow-hog taught me how to walk. That is, she didn't instruct me in detail, but she convinced me that I really ought to try.

It was like this. My mother was going to have collard greens for dinner, so she took the dishpan and went down to the spring to wash the greens. She left me sitting on the floor, and gave me a hunk of corn bread to keep me quiet. Everything was going along all right, until the sow with her litter of pigs in convoy came abreast of the door. She must have smelled the corn bread I was messing with and scattering crumbs about the floor. So, she came right on in, and began to nuzzle around.

My mother heard my screams and came running. Her heart must have stood still when she saw the sow in there, because hogs have been known to eat human flesh.

But I was not taking this thing sitting down. I had been placed by a chair, and when my mother got inside the door, I had pulled myself up by that chair and was getting around it right smart.

As for the sow, poor misunderstood lady, she had no interest in me except my bread. I lost that in scrambling to my feet and she was eating it. She had much less intention of eating Mama's baby, than Mama had of eating hers.

With no more suggestions from the sow or anybody else, it seems that I just took to walking and kept the thing a'going. The strangest thing about it was that once I found the use of my feet, they took to wandering. I always wanted to go. I would wander off in the woods all alone, following some inside urge to go places. This alarmed my mother a great deal. She used to say that she believed a woman who was an enemy of hers had sprinkled "travel dust" around the doorstep the day I was born. That was the only explanation she could find. I don't know why it never occurred to her to connect my tendency with my father, who didn't have a thing on his mind but this town and the next one. That should have given her a sort of hint. Some children are just bound to take after their fathers in spite of women's prayers.

IV

The Inside Search

G ROWN PEOPLE know that they do not always know the why of things, and even if they think they know, they do not know where and how they got the proof. Hence the irritation they show when children keep on demanding to know if a thing is so and how the grown folks got the proof of it. It is so troublesome because it is disturbing to the pigeon-hole way of life. It is upsetting because until the elders are pushed for an answer, they have never looked to see if it was so, nor how they came by what passes for proof to their acceptances of certain things as true. So, if telling their questioning young to run off and play does not suffice for an answer, a good slapping of the child's bottom is held to be proof positive for anything from spelling Constantinople to why the sea is salt. It was told to the old folks and that had been enough for them, or to put it in Negro idiom, nobody didn't tell 'em, but they heard. So there must be something wrong with a child that questions the gods of the pigeon-holes.

I was always asking and making myself a crow in a pigeon's nest. It was hard on my family and surroundings, and they in turn were hard on me. I did not know then, as I know now, that people are prone to build a statue of the kind of person that it pleases them to be. And few people want to be forced to ask themselves, "What if there is no me like my statue?" The thing to do is to grab the broom of anger and drive off the beast of fear.

I was full of curiosity like many other children, and like them I was as unconscious of the sanctity of statuary as a flock of pigeons around a palace. I got few answers from other people, but I kept right on asking, because I couldn't do anything else with my feelings.

Naturally, I felt like other children in that Death, destruction and other agonies were never meant to touch me. Things like that happened to other people, and no wonder. They were not like me and mine. Naturally, the world and the firmaments careened to one side a little so as not to inconvenience me. In fact, the universe went further than that—it was happy to break a few rules just to show me preferences.

For instance, for a long time I gloated over the happy secret that when I played outdoors in the moonlight, the moon followed me, whichever way I ran. The moon was so happy when I came out to play, that it ran shining and shouting after me like a pretty puppy dog. The other children didn't count.

But, I was rudely shaken out of this when I confided my happy secret to Carrie Roberts, my chum. It was cruel. She not only scorned my claim, she said that the moon was paying me no mind at all. The moon, my own happy private-playing moon, was out in its play yard to race and play with her.

We disputed the matter with hot jealousy, and nothing would do but we must run a race to prove which one the moon was loving. First, we both ran a race side by side, but that proved nothing because we both contended that the moon was going that way on account of us. I just knew that the moon was there to be with me, but Carrie kept on saying that it was herself that the moon preferred. So then it came to me that we ought to run in opposite directions so that Carrie could come to her senses and realize the moon was mine. So we both stood with our backs to our gate, counted three and tore out in opposite directions.

"Look! Look, Carrie!" I cried exultantly. "You see the moon is following me!"

"Aw, youse a tale-teller! You know it's chasing me."

So Carrie and I, parted company, mad as we could be with each other. When the other children found out what the quarrel was about, they laughed it off. They told me the moon always followed them. The unfaithfulness of the moon hurt me deeply. My moon followed Carrie Roberts. My moon followed Matilda Clarke and Julia Mosely, and Oscar and Teedy Miller. But after a while, I ceased to ache over the moon's many loves. I found comfort in the fact that though I was not the moon's exclusive friend, I was still among those who showed the moon which way to go. That was my earliest conscious hint that the world didn't tilt under my foot-falls, nor careen over one-sided just to make me glad.

But no matter whether my probings made me happier or sadder, I kept on probing to know. For instance, I had a stifled longing. I used to climb to the top of one of the huge Chinaberry trees which guarded our front gate, and look out over the world. The most interesting thing that I saw was the horizon. Every way I turned, it was there, and the same distance away. Our house then, was in the center of the world. It grew upon me that I ought to walk out to the horizon and see what the end of the world was like. The daring of the thing held me back for a while, but the thing became so urgent that I showed it to my friend, Carrie Roberts, and asked her to go with me. She agreed. We sat up in the trees and disputed about what the end of the world would be like when we got there—whether it was sort of tucked under like the hem of a dress, or just was a sharp drop off into nothingness. So we planned to slip off from our folks bright and soon next morning and go see.

I could hardly sleep that night from the excitement of the thing. I had been yearning for so many months to find out about the end of things. I had no doubts about the beginnings. They were somewhere in the five acres that was home to me. Most likely in Mama's room. Now, I was going to see the end, and then I would be satisfied.

As soon as breakfast was over, I sneaked off to the meeting place in the scrub palmettoes, a short way from our house and waited. Carrie didn't come right away. I was on my way to her house by a round-about way when I met her. She was coming to tell me that she couldn't go. It looked so far that maybe we wouldn't get back by sundown, and then we would both get a whipping. When we got big enough to wear long dresses, we could go and stay as long as we wanted to. Nobody couldn't whip us then. No matter how hard I begged, she wouldn't go. The thing was too bold and brazen to her thinking. We had a fight, then. I had to hit Carrie to keep my heart from stifling me. Then I was sorry I had struck my friend, and went on home and hid under the house with my heartbreak. But, I did not give up the idea of my journey. I

was merely lonesome for someone brave enough to undertake
it with me. I wanted it to be Carrie. She was a lot of fun, and
always did what I told her. Well, most of the time, she did.
This time it was too much for even her loyalty to surmount.
She even tried to talk me out of my trip. I couldn't give up. It
meant too much to me. I decided to put it off until I had
something to ride on, then I could go by myself.

So for weeks I saw myself sitting astride of a fine horse. My
shoes had sky-blue bottoms to them, and I was riding off to
look at the belly-band of the world.

It was summer time, and the mocking birds sang all night
long in the orange trees. Alligators trumpeted from their
stronghold in Lake Belle. So fall passed and then it was
Christmas time.

Papa did something different a few days before Christmas.
He sort of shoved back from the table after dinner and asked
us all what we wanted Santa Claus to bring us. My big brothers wanted a baseball outfit. Ben and Joel wanted air rifles. My
sister wanted patent leather pumps and a belt. Then it was my
turn. Suddenly a beautiful vision came before me. Two things
could work together. My Christmas present could take me to
the end of the world.

"I want a fine black riding horse with white leather saddle
and bridles," I told Papa happily.

"You, what?" Papa gasped. "What was dat you said?"

"I said, I want a black saddle horse with . . ."

"A saddle horse!" Papa exploded. "It's a sin and a shame!
Lemme tell you something right now, my young lady; you
ain't white.* Riding horse!! Always trying to wear de big hat!
I don't know how you got in this family nohow. You ain't like
none of de rest of my young'uns."

"If I can't have no riding horse, I don't want nothing at
all," I said stubbornly with my mouth, but inside I was suck-
ing sorrow. My longed-for journey looked impossible.

"I'll riding-horse you, Madam!" Papa shouted and jumped
to his feet. But being down at the end of the table big
enough for all ten members of the family together, I was near

*That is a Negro saying that means "Don't be too ambitious. You are a
Negro and they are not meant to have but so much."

the kitchen door, and I beat Papa to it by a safe margin. He chased me as far as the side gate and turned back. So I did not get my horse to ride off to the edge of the world. I got a doll for Christmas.

Since Papa would not buy me a saddle horse, I made me one up. No one around me knew how often I rode my prancing horse, nor the things I saw in far places. Jake, my puppy, always went along and we made great admiration together over the things we saw and ate. We both agreed that it was nice to be always eating things.

I discovered that I was extra strong by playing with other girls near my age. I had no way of judging the force of my playful blows, and so I was always hurting somebody. Then they would say I meant to hurt, and go home and leave me. Everything was all right, however, when I played with boys. It was a shameful thing to admit being hurt among them. Furthermore, they could dish it out themselves, and I was acceptable to them because I was the one girl who could take a good pummeling without running home to tell. The fly in the ointment there, was that in my family, it was not lady-like for girls to play with boys. No matter how young you were, no good could come of the thing. I used to wonder what was wrong with playing with boys. Nobody told me. I just mustn't, that was all. What was wrong with my doll-babies? Why couldn't I sit still and make my dolls some clothes?

I never did. Dolls caught the devil around me. They got into fights and leaked sawdust before New Year's. They jumped off the barn and tried to drown themselves in the lake. Perhaps, the dolls bought for me looked too different from the ones I made up myself. The dolls I made up in my mind, did everything. Those store-bought things had to be toted and helped around. Without knowing it, I wanted action.

So I was driven inward. I lived an exciting life unseen. But I had one person who pleased me always. That was the robust, grey-haired, white man who had helped me get into the world. When I was quite small, he would come by and tease me and then praise me for not crying. When I got old enough to do things, he used to come along some afternoons and ask to take me with him fishing. He said he hated to bait his own hook and dig worms. It always turned out when we got to some lake back in the woods that he had a full can of bait. He baited his own hooks. In between fishing business, he would talk to me in a way I liked—as if I were as grown as he. He would tell funny stories and swear at every other word. He was always making me tell him things about my doings, and then he would tell me what to do about things. He called me Snidlits, explaining that Zora was a hell of a name to give a child.

"Snidlits, don't be a nigger," he would say to me over and over.* "Niggers lie and lie! Any time you catch folks lying, they are skeered of something. Lying is dodging. People with guts don't lie. They tell the truth and then if they have to, they fight it out. You lay yourself open by lying. The other fellow knows right off that you are skeered of him and he's more'n apt to tackle you. If he don't do nothing, he starts to looking down on you from then on. Truth is a letter from courage. I want you to grow guts as you go along. So don't you let me hear of you lying. You'll get 'long all right if you do like I tell you. Nothing can't lick you if you never get skeered."

My face was all scratched up from fighting one time, so he asked me if I had been letting some kid lick me. I told him how Mary Ann and I had started to fighting and I was doing fine until her older sister Janie and her brother Ed, who was about my size, had all doubleteened me.

"Now, Snidlits, this calls for talking. Don't you try to fight three kids at one time unlessen you just can't get around it. Do the best you can, if you have to. But learn right now, not to let your head start more than your behind can stand. Measure out the amount of fighting you can do, and then do it. When you take on too much and get licked, folks will pity you first and scorn you after awhile, and that's bad. Use your head!"

"Do de best I can," I assured him, proud for him to think I could.

*The word Nigger used in this sense does not mean race. It means a weak, contemptible person of any race.

"That's de ticket, Snidlits. The way I want to hear you talk. And while I'm on the subject, don't you never let nobody spit on you nor kick you. Anybody who takes a thing like that ain't worth de powder and shot it takes to kill 'em, hear?"

"Yessir."

"Can't nothing wash that off, but blood. If anybody ever do one of those things to you, kill dead and go to jail. Hear me?"

I promised him I would try and he took out a peanut bar and gave it to me.

"Now, Snidlits, another thing. Don't you never threaten nobody you don't aim to fight. Some folks will back off of you if you put out plenty threats, but you going to meet some that don't care how big you talk, they'll try you. Then, if you can't back your crap with nothing but talk, you'll catch hell. Some folks puts dependence in bluffing, but I ain't never seen one that didn't get his bluff called sooner or later. Give 'em what you promise 'em and they'll look up to you even if they hate your guts. Don't worry over that part. Somebody is going to hate you anyhow, don't care what you do. My idea is to give 'em a good cause if it's got to be. And don't change too many words if you aim to fight. Lam hell out of 'em with the first lick and keep on lamming. I've seen many a fight finished with the first lick. Most folks can't stand to be hurt. But you must realize that getting hurt is part of fighting. Keep right on. The one that hurts the other one the worst wins the fight. Don't try to win no fights by calling 'em low-down names. You can call 'em all the names you want to, after the fight. That's the best time to do it, anyhow."

I knew without being told that he was not talking about my race when he advised me not to be a nigger. He was talking about class rather than race. He frequently gave money to Negro schools.

These talks went on until I was about ten. Then the hard-riding, hard-drinking, hard-cussing, but very successful man, was thrown from his horse and died. Nobody ever expected him to die in bed, so that part was all right. Everybody said that he had been a useful citizen, just powerful hot under the collar.

He was an accumulating man, a good provider, paid his

debts and told the truth. Those were all the virtues the community expected. Any more than that would not have been
appreciated. He could ride like a centaur, swim long distances, shoot straight with either pistol or guns, and allowed
no man to give him the lie to his face. He was supposed to be
so tough, it was said that once he was struck by lightning and
was not even knocked off his feet, but that lightning went off
through the woods limping. Nobody found any fault with a
man like that in a country where personal strength and courage were the highest virtues. People were supposed to take
care of themselves without whining.

For example, two men came before the justice of the peace
over in Maitland. The defendant had hit the plaintiff three
times with his fist and kicked him four times. The justice of
the peace fined him seven dollars—a dollar a lick. The defendant hauled out his pocketbook and paid his fine with a smile.
The justice of the peace then fined the plaintiff ten dollars.

"What for?" he wanted to know. "Why, Mr. Justice, that
man knocked me down and kicked me, and I never raised my
hand."

"That is just what I'm fining you for, you yellow-bellied
coudar!* Nobody with any guts would have come into court
to settle a fist fight."

The community felt that the justice had told him what was
right. In a neighborhood where bears and alligators raided
hog-pens, wild cats fought with dogs in people's yards, rattlesnakes as long as a man and as thick as a man's forearm were
found around back doors, a fist fight was a small skimption.
As in all frontiers, there was the feeling for direct action. Decency was plumb outraged at a man taking a beating and then
swearing out a warrant about it. Most of the settlers considered a courthouse a place to "law" over property lines and
things like that. That is, you went to law over it if neither
party got too abusive and personal. If it came to that, most
likely the heirs of one or the other could take it to court after
the funeral was over.

So the old man died in high favor with everybody. He had
done his cussing and fighting and drinking as became a man,

*A coudar is a fresh-water terrapin.

taken care of his family and accumulated property. Nobody thought anything about his going to the county seat frequently, getting drunk, getting his riding-mule drunk along with him, and coming down the pike yelling and singing while his mule brayed in drunken hilarity. There went a man!

I used to take a seat on top of the gate post and watch the world go by. One way to Orlando ran past my house, so the carriages and cars would pass before me. The movement made me glad to see it. Often the white travelers would hail me, but more often I hailed them, and asked, "Don't you want me to go a piece of the way with you?"

They always did. I know now that I must have caused a great deal of amusement among them, but my self-assurance must have carried the point, for I was always invited to come along. I'd ride up the road for perhaps a half mile, then walk back. I did not do this with the permission of my parents, nor with their foreknowledge. When they found out about it later, I usually got a whipping. My grandmother worried about my forward ways a great deal. She had known slavery and to her, my brazenness was unthinkable.

"Git down offa dat gate post! You li'l sow, you! Git down! Setting up dere looking dem white folks right in de face! They's gowine to lynch you, yet. And don't stand in dat doorway gazing out at 'em neither. Youse too brazen to live long."

Nevertheless, I kept right on gazing at them, and "going a piece of the way" whenever I could make it. The village seemed dull to me most of the time. If the village was singing a chorus, I must have missed the tune.

Perhaps a year before the old man died, I came to know two other white people for myself. They were women.

It came about this way. The whites who came down from the North were often brought by their friends to visit the village school. A Negro school was something strange to them, and while they were always sympathetic and kind, curiosity must have been present, also. They came and went, came and went. Always, the room was hurriedly put in order, and we were threatened with a prompt and bloody death if we cut one caper while the visitors were present. We always sang a spiritual, led by Mr. Calhoun himself. Mrs. Calhoun always stood in the back, with a palmetto switch in her hand as a squelcher. We were all little angels for the duration, because we'd better be. She would cut her eyes and give us a glare that meant trouble, then turn her face towards the visitors and beam as much as to say it was a great privilege and pleasure to teach lovely children like us. They couldn't see that palmetto hickory in her hand behind all those benches, but we knew where our angelic behavior was coming from.

Usually, the visitors gave warning a day ahead and we would be cautioned to put on shoes, comb our heads, and see to ears and fingernails. There was a close inspection of every one of us before we marched in that morning. Knotty heads, dirty ears and fingernails got hauled out of line, strapped and sent home to lick the calf over again.

This particular afternoon, the two young ladies just popped in. Mr. Calhoun was flustered, but he put on the best show that he could. He dismissed the class that he was teaching up at the front of the room, then called the fifth grade in reading. That was my class.

So we took our readers and went up front. We stood up in the usual line, and opened to the lesson. It was the story of Pluto and Persephone. It was new and hard to the class in general, and Mr. Calhoun was very uncomfortable as the readers stumbled along, spelling out words with their lips, and in mumbling undertones before they exposed them experimentally to the teacher's ears.

Then it came to me. I was fifth or sixth down the line. The story was not new to me, because I had read my reader through from lid to lid, the first week that Papa had bought it for me.

That is how it was that my eyes were not in the book, working out the paragraph which I knew would be mine by counting the children ahead of me. I was observing our visitors, who held a book between them, following the lesson. They had shiny hair, mostly brownish. One had a looping gold chain around her neck. The other one was dressed all over in black and white with a pretty finger ring on her left hand. But the thing that held my eyes were their fingers. They were long and thin, and very white, except up near the tips. There they were baby pink. I had never seen such hands. It was a fascinating discovery for me. I wondered how they felt. I would have given those hands more attention, but the child before me was almost through. My turn next, so I got on my mark, bringing my eyes back to the book and made sure of my place. Some of the stories, I had reread several times, and this Greco-Roman myth was one of my favorites. I was exalted by it, and that is the way I read my paragraph.

"Yes, Jupiter had seen her (Persephone). He had seen the maiden picking flowers in the field. He had seen the chariot of the dark monarch pause by the maiden's side. He had seen him when he seized Persephone. He had seen the black horses leap down Mount Aetna's fiery throat. Persephone was now in Pluto's dark realm and he had made her his wife."

The two women looked at each other and then back to me. Mr. Calhoun broke out with a proud smile beneath his bristly moustache, and instead of the next child taking up where I had ended, he nodded to me to go on. So I read the story to the end where flying Mercury, the messenger of the Gods, brought Persephone back to the sunlit earth and restored her to the arms of Dame Ceres, her mother, that the world might have springtime and summer flowers, autumn and harvest. But because she had bitten the pomegranate while in Pluto's kingdom, she must return to him for three months of each year, and be his queen. Then the world had winter, until she returned to earth.

The class was dismissed and the visitors smiled us away and went into a low-voiced conversation with Mr. Calhoun for a few minutes. They glanced my way once or twice and I began to worry. Not only was I barefooted, but my feet and legs were dusty. My hair was more uncombed than usual, and my nails were not shiny clean. Oh, I'm going to catch it now. Those ladies saw me, too. Mr. Calhoun is promising to 'tend to me. So I thought.

Then Mr. Calhoun called me. I went up thinking how awful it was to get a whipping before company. Furthermore, I heard a snicker run over the room. Hennie Clark and Stell Brazzle did it out loud, so I would be sure to hear them. The smart-aleck was going to get it. I slipped one hand behind me and switched my dress tail at them, indicating scorn.

"Come here, Zora Neale," Mr. Calhoun cooed as I reached the desk. He put his hand on my shoulder and gave me little pats. The ladies smiled and held out those flower-looking fingers towards me. I seized the opportunity for a good look.

"Shake hands with the ladies, Zora Neale," Mr. Calhoun prompted and they took my hand one after the other and smiled. They asked me if I loved school, and I lied that I did. There was *some* truth in it, because I liked geography and reading, and I liked to play at recess time. Whoever it was invented writing and arithmetic got no thanks from me. Neither did I like the arrangement where the teacher could sit up there with a palmetto stem and lick me whenever he saw fit. I hated things I couldn't do anything about. But I knew better than to bring that up right there, so I said yes, I *loved* school.

"I can tell you do," Brown Taffeta gleamed. She patted my head, and was lucky enough not to get sandspurs in her hand. Children who roll and tumble in the grass in Florida, are apt to get sandspurs in their hair. They shook hands with me again and I went back to my seat.

When school let out at three o'clock, Mr. Calhoun told me to wait. When everybody had gone, he told me I was to go to the Park House, that was the hotel in Maitland, the next afternoon to call upon Mrs. Johnstone and Miss Hurd. I must tell Mama to see that I was clean and brushed from head to feet, and I must wear shoes and stockings. The ladies liked me, he said, and I must be on my best behavior.

The next day I was let out of school an hour early, and went home to be stood up in a tub of suds and be scrubbed and have my ears dug into. My sandy hair sported a red ribbon to match my red and white checked gingham dress, starched until it could stand alone. Mama saw to it that my shoes were on the right feet, since I was careless about left and right. Last thing, I was given a handkerchief to carry, warned again about my behavior, and sent off with my big brother, John, to go as far as the hotel gate with me.

First thing, the ladies gave me strange things, like stuffed dates and preserved ginger, and encouraged me to eat all that I wanted. Then they showed me their Japanese dolls and just talked. I was then handed a copy of *Scribner's Magazine*, and asked to read a place that was pointed out to me. After a paragraph or two, I was told with smiles, that that would do.

I was led out on the grounds and they took my picture under a palm tree. They handed me what was to me then, a heavy cylinder done up in fancy paper, tied with a ribbon, and they told me goodbye, asking me not to open it until I got home.

My brother was waiting for me down by the lake, and we hurried home, eager to see what was in the thing. It was too heavy to be candy or anything like that. John insisted on toting it for me.

My mother made John give it back to me and let me open it. Perhaps, I shall never experience such joy again. The nearest thing to that moment was the telegram accepting my first book. One hundred goldy-new pennies rolled out of the cylinder. Their gleam lit up the world. It was not avarice that moved me. It was the beauty of the thing. I stood on the mountain. Mama let me play with my pennies for a while, then put them away for me to keep.

That was only the beginning. The next day I received an Episcopal hymn-book bound in white leather with a golden cross stamped into the front cover, a copy of *The Swiss Family Robinson*, and a book of fairy tales.

I set about to commit the song words to memory. There was no music written there, just the words. But there was to my consciousness music in between them just the same. "When I survey the Wondrous Cross" seemed the most beautiful to me, so I committed that to memory first of all. Some of them seemed dull and without life, and I pretended they were not there. If white people liked trashy singing like that, there must be something funny about them that I had not noticed before. I stuck to the pretty ones where the words marched to a throb I could feel.

A month or so after the two young ladies returned to Minnesota, they sent me a huge box packed with clothes and books. The red coat with a wide circular collar and the red tam pleased me more than any of the other things. My chums pretended not to like anything that I had, but even then I knew that they were jealous. Old Smarty had gotten by them again. The clothes were not new, but they were very good. I shone like the morning sun.

But the books gave me more pleasure than the clothes. I had never been too keen on dressing up. It called for hard scrubbings with Octagon soap suds getting in my eyes, and none too gentle fingers scrubbing my neck and gouging in my ears.

In that box was Gulliver's Travels, Grimm's Fairy Tales, Dick Whittington, Greek and Roman Myths, and best of all, Norse Tales. Why did the Norse tales strike so deeply into my soul? I do not know, but they did. I seemed to remember seeing Thor swing his mighty short-handled hammer as he sped across the sky in rumbling thunder, lightning flashing from the tread of his steeds and the wheels of his chariot. The great and good Odin, who went down to the well of knowledge to drink, and was told that the price of a drink from that fountain, was an eye. Odin drank deeply, then plucked out one eye without a murmur and handed it to the grizzly keeper, and walked away. That held majesty for me.

Of the Greeks, Hercules moved me most. I followed him eagerly on his tasks. The story of the choice of Hercules as a boy when he met Pleasure and Duty, and put his hand in that of Duty and followed her steep way to the blue hills of fame and glory, which she pointed out at the end, moved me profoundly. I resolved to be like him. The tricks and turns of the other Gods and Goddesses left me cold. There were other thin books about this and that sweet and gentle little girl who gave up her heart to Christ and good works. Almost always they died from it, preaching as they passed. I was utterly indifferent to their deaths. In the first place I could not conceive of death, and in the next place they never had any funerals that amounted to a hill of beans, so I didn't care how soon they rolled up their big, soulful, blue eyes and kicked the bucket. They had no meat on their bones.

But I also met Hans Andersen and Robert Louis Stevenson. They seemed to know what I wanted to hear and said it in a way that tingled me. Just a little below these friends was Rudyard Kipling in his Jungle Books. I loved his talking snakes as much as I did the hero.

I came to start reading the Bible through my mother. She

gave me a licking one afternoon for repeating something I had overheard a neighbor telling her. She locked me in her room after the whipping, and the Bible was the only thing in there for me to read. I happened to open to the place where David was doing some mighty smiting, and I got interested. David went here and he went there, and no matter where he went, he smote 'em hip and thigh. Then he sung songs to his harp a while, and went out and smote some more. Not one time did David stop and preach about sins and things. All David wanted to know from God was who to kill and when. He took care of the other details himself. Never a quiet moment. I liked him a lot. So I read a great deal more in the Bible, hunting for some more active people like David. Except for the beautiful language of Luke and Paul, the New Testament still plays a poor second to the Old Testament for me. The Jews had a God who laid about Him when they needed Him. I could see no use waiting till Judgment Day to see a man who was just crying for a good killing, to be told to go and roast. My idea was to give him a good killing first, and then if he got roasted later on, so much the better.

In searching for more Davids, I came upon Leviticus. There were exciting things in there to a child eager to know the facts of life. I told Carrie Roberts about it, and we spent long afternoons reading what Moses told the Hebrews not to do in Leviticus. In that way I found out a number of things the old folks would not have told me. Not knowing what we were actually reading, we got a lot of praise from our elders for our devotion to the Bible.

Having finished that and scanned the Doctor Book, which my mother thought she had hidden securely from my eyes, I read all the things which children write on privy-house walls. Therefore, I lost my taste for pornographic literature. I think that the people who love it, got cheated in the matter of privy-houses when they were children.

In a way this early reading gave me great anguish through all my childhood and adolescence. My soul was with the gods and my body in the village. People just would not act like gods. Stew beef, fried fat-back and morning grits were no ambrosia from Valhalla. Raking back yards and carrying out chamber pots, were not the tasks of Hercules. I wanted to be

away from drabness and to stretch my limbs in some mighty
struggle. I was only happy in the woods, and when the ecstatic Florida springtime came strolling from the sea, trance-
glorifying the world with its aura. Then I hid out in the tall
wild oats that waved like a glinty veil. I nibbled sweet oat
stalks and listened to the wind soughing and sighing through
the crowns of the lofty pines. I made particular friendship
with one huge tree and always played about its roots. I named
it "the loving pine," and my chums came to know it by that
name.

In contrast to everybody about me, I was not afraid of
snakes. They fascinated me in a way which I still cannot explain. I got no pleasure from their death.

I do not know when the visions began. Certainly I was not
more than seven years old, but I remember the first coming
very distinctly. My brother, Joel, and I had made a hen take
an egg back and been caught as we turned the hen loose. We
knew we were in for it and decided to scatter until things
cooled off a bit. He hid out in the barn, but I combined
discretion with pleasure, and ran clear off the place. Mr.
Linsay's house was vacant at the time. He was a neighbor
who was off working somewhere. I had not thought of stopping there when I set out, but I saw a big raisin lying on the
porch and stopped to eat it. There was some cool shade on
the porch, so I sat down, and soon I was asleep in a strange
way. Like clearcut stereopticon slides, I saw twelve scenes
flash before me, each one held until I had seen it well in every
detail, and then be replaced by another. There was no conti-
nuity as in an average dream. Just disconnected scene after
scene with blank spaces in between. I knew that they were all
true, a preview of things to come, and my soul writhed in
agony and shrunk away. But I knew that there was no shrink-
ing. These things had to be. I did not wake up when the last
one flickered and vanished, I merely sat up and saw the Methodist Church, the line of moss-draped oaks, and our strawberry patch stretching off to the left.

So when I left the porch, I left a great deal behind me. I
was weighed down with a power I did not want. I had knowledge before its time. I knew my fate. I knew that I would be
an orphan and homeless. I knew that while I was still helpless,

that the comforting circle of my family would be broken, and that I would have to wander cold and friendless until I had served my time. I would stand beside a dark pool of water and see a huge fish move slowly away at a time when I would be somehow in the depth of despair. I would hurry to catch a train, with doubts and fears driving me and seek solace in a place and fail to find it when I arrived, then cross many tracks to board the train again. I knew that a house, a shot-gun built house that needed a new coat of white paint, held torture for me, but I must go. I saw deep love betrayed, but I must feel and know it. There was no turning back. And last of all, I would come to a big house. Two women waited there for me. I could not see their faces, but I knew one to be young and one to be old. One of them was arranging some queer-shaped flowers such as I had never seen. When I had come to these women, then I would be at the end of my pilgrimage, but not the end of my life. Then I would know peace and love and what goes with those things, and not before.

These visions would return at irregular intervals. Sometimes two or three nights running. Sometimes weeks and months apart. I had no warning. I went to bed and they came. The details were always the same, except in the last picture. Once or twice I saw the old faceless woman standing outdoors beside a tall plant with that same off-shape white flower. She turned suddenly from it to welcome me. I knew what was going on in the house without going in, it was all so familiar to me.

I never told anyone around me about these strange things. It was too different. They would laugh me off as a story-teller. Besides, I had a feeling of difference from my fellow men, and I did not want it to be found out. Oh, how I cried out to be just as everybody else! But the voice said no. I must go where I was sent. The weight of the commandment laid heavy and made me moody at times. When I was an ordinary child, with no knowledge of things but the life about me, I was reasonably happy. I would hope that the call would never come again. But even as I hoped I knew that the cup meant for my lips would not pass. I must drink the bitter drink. I studied people all around me, searching for someone to fend it off. But I was told inside myself that there was no one. It gave me a feeling of terrible aloneness. I stood in a world of vanished communion with my kind, which is worse than if it had never been. Nothing is so desolate as a place where life has been and gone. I stood on a soundless island in a tideless sea.

Time was to prove the truth of my visions, for one by one they came to pass. As soon as one was fulfilled, it ceased to come. As this happened, I counted them off one by one and took consolation in the fact that one more station was past, thus bringing me nearer the end of my trials, and nearer to the big house, with the kind women and the strange white flowers.

Years later, after the last one had come and gone, I read a sentence or a paragraph now and then in the columns of O. O. McIntyre which perhaps held no meaning for the millions who read him, but I could see through those slight revelations that he had had similar experiences. Kipling knew the feeling for himself, for he wrote of it very definitely in his *Plain Tales from the Hills.* So I took comfort in knowing that they were fellow pilgrims on my strange road.

I consider that my real childhood ended with the coming of the pronouncements. True, I played, fought and studied with other children, but always I stood apart within. Often I was in some lonesome wilderness, suffering strange things and agonies while other children in the same yard played without a care. I asked myself why me? Why? Why? A cosmic loneliness was my shadow. Nothing and nobody around me really touched me. It is one of the blessings of this world that few people see visions and dream dreams.

V

Figure and Fancy

NOTHING that God ever made is the same thing to more than one person. That is natural. There is no single face in nature, because every eye that looks upon it, sees it from its own angle. So every man's spice-box seasons his own food.

Naturally, I picked up the reflections of life around me with my own instruments, and absorbed what I gathered according to my inside juices.

There were the two churches, Methodist and Baptist, and the school. Most people would say that such institutions are always the great influences in any town. They would say that because it sounds like the thing that ought to be said. But I know that Joe Clarke's store was the heart and spring of the town.

Men sat around the store on boxes and benches and passed this world and the next one through their mouths. The right and the wrong, the who, when and why was passed on, and nobody doubted the conclusions. Women stood around there on Saturday nights and had it proven to the community that their husbands were good providers, put all of his money in his wife's hands and generally glorified her. Or right there before everybody it was revealed that he was keeping some other woman by the things the other woman was allowed to buy on his account. No doubt a few men found that their wives had a brand new pair of shoes oftener than he could afford it, and wondered what she did with her time while he was off at work. Sometimes he didn't have to wonder. There were no discreet nuances of life on Joe Clarke's porch. There was open kindnesses, anger, hate, love, envy and its kinfolks, but all emotions were naked, and nakedly arrived at. It was a case of "make it and take it." You got what your strengths would bring you. This was not just true of Eatonville. This was the spirit of that whole new part of the state at the time, as it always is where men settle new lands.

For me, the store porch was the most interesting place that

I could think of. I was not allowed to sit around there, naturally. But, I could and did drag my feet going in and out whenever I was sent there for something to allow whatever was being said to hang in my ear. I would hear an occasional scrap of gossip in what to me was adult double talk, but which I understood at times.

There would be, for instance, sly references to the physical condition of women, irregular love affairs, brags on male potency by the parties of the first part, and the like. It did not take me long to know what was meant when a girl was spoken of as "ruint" or "bigged." For instance somebody would remark, "Ada Dell is ruint, you know." "Yep, somebody was telling me. A pitcher can go to the well a long time, but its bound to get broke sooner or later." Or some woman or girl would come switching past the store porch and some man would call to her, "Hey Sugar! What's on de rail for de lizard?" Then again I would hear some man say that "I got to have my ground-rations. If one woman can't take care of it, I gits me another one." One man told a woman to hold her ear close, because he had a bug to put in her ear. He was sitting on a box. She stooped over to hear whatever it was he had to whisper to her. Then she straightened up sharply and pulled away from him. "Why, you!" she exclaimed. "The idea of such a thing! Talking like dat to me, when you know I'm a good church-worker, and you a deacon!" He didn't seem to be ashamed at all. "Dat's just de point I'm coming out on, sister. Two clean sheets can't dirty one 'nother, you know." There was general laughter, as the deacon moved his foot so that I could get in the store door. I happened to hear a man talking to another in a chiding manner and say, "To save my soul, I can't see what you fooled with her for. She'd have a shake if somebody was to hold his head for her! I'd just as soon pick up a old tin can out of the trash pile." The other one stroked his chin and said, "On de average, I'd say de same thing. But last night, I had de feeling dat anything hot and hollow would do. Just like Uncle Bud."

One afternoon my oldest brother was on the store porch with the men. He was proudly stroking two or three hairs on his top lip. A married man in his late twenties was giving him some advice about growing a big, thick mustache. I went on inside. When I was coming out, I heard something about getting his finger wet from a woman and wiping it on his lip. Best mustache-grower God ever made. They all grew theirs that way. It was a good thing my brother let them know so he could be told the inside secret. I emerged from the door and the porch fell silent. Later on, I asked my brother what they were talking about, and he slapped me all over the place. He and my second brother, John, were in secret session upstairs in their room. I went on down and crept back to listen and heard John asking how old the woman had to be? It seemed that Bob was not sure. He had forgotten to ask. But it was evident that some great discovery had been made, and they were both most eager to grow big, manly moustaches. It was still mysterious to me. I was out of college and doing research in Anthropology before I heard all about it. Then I heard that a man's moustache was given him by a woman anyway. It seems that Adam came to feel that his face needed more decoration than it had. Eve, obligingly, took a spot of hair from where she had no particular use for it—it didn't show anyway, and slapped it across Adam's mouth, and it grew there. So what Bob was being told, was regular knowledge he was supposed to get when he approached manhood. Just as I learned at puberty that a girl is supposed to catch water-beetles and let one bite her on each breast if she wants a full bosom. There was another way, of course. You could let a boy—anywhere from sixteen to sixty—do what the boys call, "steal a feel" on you, but of course that would not be nice. Almost as bad as having a baby, and not being married.

But what I really loved to hear was the menfolks holding a "lying" session. That is, straining against each other in telling folk tales. God, Devil, Brer Rabbit, Brer Fox, Sis Cat, Brer Bear, Lion, Tiger, Buzzard, and all the wood folk walked and talked like natural men. The wives, of the story-tellers I mean, might yell from backyards for them to come and tote some water, or chop wood for the cook-stove and never get a move out of the men. The usual rejoinder was, "Oh, she's got enough to go on. No matter how much wood you chop, a woman will burn it all up to get a meal. If she got a couple of pieces, she will make it do. If you chop up a whole boxful, she will burn every stick of it. Pay her no mind." So the story telling would go right on. And I often hung around and listened while Mama waited on me for the sugar or coffee to finish off dinner, until she lifted her voice over the tree tops in a way to let me know that her patience was gone: "You Zora-a-a! If you don't come here, you better!" That had a promise of peach hickories in it, and I would have to leave. But I would have found out from such story-tellers as Elijah Moseley, better known as "Lige," how and why Sis Snail quit her husband, for instance. You may or may not excuse my lagging feet, if you know the circumstances of the case:

One morning soon, Lige met Sis Snail on the far side of the road. He had passed there several times in the last few years and seen Sis Snail headed towards the road. For the last three years he had stepped over her several times as she crossed the road, always forging straight ahead. But this morning he found her clean across, and she seemed mighty pleased with herself, so he stopped and asked her where she was headed for.

"Going off to travel over the world," she told him. "I done left my husband for good."

"How come, Sis Snail? He didn't ill-treat you in no ways, did he?"

"Can't exactly say he did, Brother Lige, but you take and take just so much and then you can't take no more. Your craw gits full up to de neck. De man gits around too slow to suit me, and look like I just can't break him of it. So I done left him for good. I'm out and gone. I gits around right fast, my ownself, and I just can't put up with nobody dat gits around as slow as he do."

"Oh, don't leave de man too sudden, Sis Snail. Maybe he might come to move round fast like you do. Why don't you sort of reason wid de poor soul and let him know how you feel."

"I done tried dat until my patience is all wore out. And this last thing he done run my cup over. You know I took sick in de bed—had de misery in my side so bad till I couldn't rest in de bed. He heard me groaning and asked me what was de matter. I told him how sick I was. Told him, 'Lawd, I'm so sick!' So he said 'If youse sick like dat, I'll go git de doctor for you.' I says, 'I sho would be mighty much obliged if you

would.' So he took and told me, 'I don't want you laying
there and suffering like dat. I'll go git de doctor right away.
Just lemme go git my hat.'

"So I laid there in de bed and waited for him to go git de
doctor. Lawd! I was so sick! I rolled from pillar to post. After
seven I heard a noise at de door, and I said, 'Lawd, I'm so
glad! I know dats my husband done come back wid de
doctor.' So I hollered out and asked, 'Honey, is dat you done
come back wid de doctor?' And he come growling at me and
giving me a short answer wid, 'Don't try to rush me. I ain't
gone yet.' It had done took him seven years to git his hat and
git to de door. So I just up and left him."

Then one late afternoon, a woman called Gold, who had
come to town from somewhere else, told the why and how of
races that pleased me more than what I learned about race
derivations later on in Ethnology. This was her explanation:

God did not make folks all at once. He made folks sort of
in His spare time. For instance one day He had a little time
on his hands, so He got the clay, seasoned it the way He
wanted it, then He laid it by and went on to doing something
more important. Another day He had some spare moments,
so He rolled it all out, and cut out the human shapes, and
stood them all up against His long gold fence to dry while He
did some important creating. The human shapes all got dry,
and when He found time, He blowed the breath of life in
them. After that, from time to time, He would call everybody
up, and give them spare parts. For instance, one day He called
everybody and gave out feet and eyes. Another time He give
out toe-nails that Old Maker figured they could use. Anyhow,
they had all that they got up to now. So then one day He
said, "Tomorrow morning, at seven o'clock *sharp*, I aim to
give out color. Everybody be here on time. I got plenty of
creating to do tomorrow, and I want to give out this color
and get it over wid. *Everybody* be 'round de throne at seven
o'clock tomorrow morning!"

So next morning at seven o'clock, God was sitting on His
throne with His big crown on His head and seven suns circling around His head. Great multitudes was standing around
the throne waiting to get their color. God sat up there and
looked, east, and He looked west, and He looked north and

He looked Australia, and blazing worlds were falling off His teeth. So He looked over to His left and moved His hands over a crowd and said, "Youse yellow people!" They all bowed low and said, "Thank you, God," and they went on off. He looked at another crowd, moved His hands over them and said, "Youse red folks!" They made their manners and said, "Thank you, Old Maker," and they went on off. He looked towards the center and moved His hand over another crowd and said, "Youse white folks!" They bowed low and said, "Much obliged, Jesus," and they went on off. Then God looked way over to the right and said, "Look here, Gabriel, I miss a lot of multitudes from around the throne this morning." Gabriel looked too, and said, "Yessir, there's a heap of multitudes missing from round de throne this morning." So God sat there an hour and a half and waited. Then He called Gabriel and said, "Looka here, Gabriel, I'm sick and tired of this waiting. I got plenty of creating to do this morning. You go find them folks and tell 'em they better hurry on up here and they expect to get any color. Fool with me, and I won't give out no more."

So Gabriel run on off and started to hunting around. Way after while, he found the missing multitudes lying around on the grass by the Sea of Life, fast asleep. So Gabriel woke them up and told them "You better get up from there and come on up to the throne and get your color. Old Maker is might wore out from waiting. Fool with Him and He won't give out no more color."

So as the multitudes heard that, they all jumped up and went running towards the throne hollering, "Give us our color! We want our color! We got just as much right to color as anybody else." So when the first ones got to the throne, they tried to stop and be polite. But the ones coming on behind got to pushing and shoving so till the first ones got shoved all up against the throne so till the throne was careening all over to one side. So God said "Here! Here! Git back! Git back!" But they was keeping up such a racket that they misunderstood Him, and thought He said "Git black!" So they just got black, and kept the thing agoing.

In one way or another, I heard dozens more of these tales. My father and his preacher associates told the best stories on the church. Papa, being moderator of the South Florida Baptist Association, had numerous preacher visitors just before the Association met, to get the politics of the thing all cut and dried before the meetings came off. After it was decided who would put such and such a motion before the house, who would second it, and whom my father would recognize first and things like that, a big story-telling session would get under way on our front porch, and very funny stories at the expense of preachers and congregations would get told.

No doubt, these tales of God, the Devil, animals and natural elements seemed ordinary enough to most people in the village. But many of them stirred up fancies in me. It did not surprise me at all to hear that the animals talked. I had suspected it all along. Or let us say, that I wanted to suspect it. Life took on a bigger perimeter by expanding on these things. I picked up glints and gleams out of what I heard and stored it away to turn it to my own uses. The wind would sough through the tops of the tall, long-leaf pines and said things to me. I put in the words that the sounds put into me. Like "woo woo, you wooo!" The tree was talking to me, even when I did not catch the words. It was talking and telling me things. I have mentioned the tree, near our house that got so friendly I named it "the loving pine." Finally all of my playmates called it that too. I used to take a seat at the foot of that tree and play for hours without any other toys. We talked about everything in my world. Sometimes we just took it out in singing songs. That tree had a mighty fine bass voice when it really took a notion to let it out.

There was another tree that used to creep up close to the house around sundown and threaten me. It used to put on a skull-head with a crown on it every day at sundown and make motions at me when I had to go out on the back porch to wash my feet after supper before going to bed. It never bothered around during the day. It was just another pine tree about a hundred feet tall then, standing head and shoulders above a grove. But let the dusk begin to fall, and it would put that crown on its skull and creep in close. Nobody else ever seemed to notice what it was up to but me. I used to wish it would go off somewhere and get lost. But every evening I would have to look to see, and every time, it would be right there, sort of shaking and shivering and bowing its head at me. I used to wonder if sometime it was not going to come in the house.

When I began to make up stories I cannot say. Just from one fancy to another, adding more and more detail until they seemed real. People seldom see themselves changing. It is like going out in the morning, or in the springtime to pick flowers. You pick and you wander till suddenly you find that the light is gone and the flowers are withered in your hand. Then, you say that you must turn back home. But you have wandered into a place and the gates are closed. There is no more sharp sunlight. Gray meadows are all about you where blooms only the asphodel. You look back through the immutable gates to where the sun still shines on the flowered fields with nostalgic longing, but God pointed men's toes in one direction. One is surprised by the passage of time and the distance travelled, but one may not go back.

So I was making little stories to myself, and have no memory of how I began. But I do remember some of the earliest ones.

I came in from play one day and told my mother how a bird had talked to me with a tail so long that while he sat up in the top of the pine tree his tail was dragging the ground. It was a soft beautiful bird tail, all blue and pink and red and green. In fact I climbed up the bird's tail and sat up the tree and had a long talk with the bird. He knew my name, but I didn't know how he knew it. In fact, the bird had come a long way just to sit and talk with me.

Another time, I dashed into the kitchen and told Mama how the lake had talked with me, and invited me to walk all over it. I told the lake I was afraid of getting drowned, but the lake assured me it wouldn't think of doing *me* like that. No, indeed! Come right on and have a walk. Well, I stepped out on the lake and walked all over it. It didn't even wet my feet. I could see all the fish and things swimming around under me, and they all said hello, but none of them bothered me. Wasn't that nice?

My mother said that it was. My grandmother glared at me like open-faced hell and snorted.

"Luthee!" (She lisped.) "You hear dat young'un stand up

here and lie like dat? And you ain't doing nothing to break her of it? Grab her! Wring her coat tails over her head and wear out a handful of peach hickories on her back-side! Stomp her guts out! Ruin her!"

"Oh, she's just playing," Mama said indulgently.

"Playing! Why dat lil' heifer is lying just as fast as a horse can trot. Stop her! Wear her back-side out. I bet if I lay my hands on her she'll stop it. I vominates (abominate) a lying tongue."

Mama never tried to break me. She'd listen sometimes, and sometimes she wouldn't. But she never seemed displeased. But her mother used to foam at the mouth. I was just as sure to be hung before I got grown as gun was iron! The least thing Mama could do to straighten me out was to smack my jaws for me. She outraged my grandmother scandalously by not doing it. Mama was going to be responsible for my downfall when she stood up in judgment. It was a sin before the living justice, that's what it was. God knows, grandmother would break me or kill me, if she had her way. Killing me looked like the best one, anyway. All I was good for was to lay up and wet the bed half of the time and tell lies, besides being the spitting image of dat good-for-nothing yaller bastard. I was the punishment God put on Mama for marrying Papa. I ought to be thrown in the hogslops, that's what. She could beat me as long as I last.

I knew that I did not have to pay too much attention to the old lady and so I didn't. Furthermore, how was she going to tell what I was doing inside? I could keep my inventions to myself, which was what I did most of the time.

One day, we were going to have roasting-ears for dinner and I was around while Mama was shucking the corn. I picked up an inside chuck and carried it off to look at. It was such a delicate, blushy green. I crawled under the side of the house to love it all by myself.

In a few minutes, it had become Miss Corn-Shuck, and of course needed some hair. So I went back and picked up some corn silk and tied it to the pointed end. We had a lovely time together for a day or two, and then Miss Corn-Shuck got lonesome for some company.

I do not think that her lonesomeness would have come

down on her as it did, if I had not found a cake of sweet soap in Mama's dresser drawer. It was a cake of Pear's scented soap. It was clear like amber glass. I could see straight through it. It delighted my senses just as much as the tender green corn-shuck. So Miss Corn-Shuck fell in love with Mr. Sweet Smell then and there. But she said she could not have a thing to do with him unless he went and put on some clothes. I found a piece of red and white string that had come around some groceries and made him a suit of clothes. Being bigger in the middle than he was on either end, his pants kept falling off—sometimes over his head and sometimes the other way. So I cut little notches in his sides around the middle and tied his suit on. To other people it might have looked like a cake of soap with a bit of twine tied around it, but Miss Corn-Shuck and I knew he had on the finest clothes in the world. Every day it would be different, because Mr. Sweet Smell was very particular about what he wore. Besides he wanted Miss Corn-Shuck to admire him.

There was a great mystery about where Mr. Sweet Smell came from. I suppose if Mama had been asked, she would have said that it was the company soap, since the family used nothing but plain, yellow Octagon laundry soap for bathing. But I had not known it was there until I happened to find it. It might have been there for years. Whenever Miss Corn-Shuck asked him where his home was, he always said it was a secret which he would tell her about when they were married. It was not very important anyway. We knew he was some very high-class man from way off—the farther off the better.

But sad to say, Miss Corn-Shuck and Mr. Sweet Smell never got married. They always meant to, but before very long, Miss Corn-Cob began to make trouble. We found her around the kitchen door one day, and she followed us back under the house and right away started her meanness. She was jealous of Miss Corn-Shuck because she was so pretty and green, with long silky hair, and so Miss Corn-Cob would make up all kinds of mean stories about her. One day there was going to be a big party and that was the first time that the Spool People came to visit. They used to hop off of Mama's sewing machine one by one until they were a great congregation—at least fifteen or so. They didn't do anything much besides second the motion on what somebody else did and said, so they must have been the common people.

Reverend Door-Knob was there, too. He used to live on the inside of the kitchen door, but one day he rolled off and came under the house to be with us. Unconsciously he behaved a lot like Mayor Joe Clarke. He was roundish and reddish brown, and used to laugh louder than anything when something funny happened. The Spool People always laughed whenever he laughed. They used to cry too, whenever Mr. Sweet Smell or Miss Corn-Shuck cried. They were always doing whatever they saw other people do. That was the way the Spool People were.

When Mr. Sweet Smell left his fine house in the dresser drawer that day, he came through the kitchen and brought a half can of condensed milk for the refreshments. Everybody liked condensed milk for refreshment. Well, Miss Corn-Cob sneaked around and ate up all the refreshments and then she told everybody that Miss Corn-Shuck ate it. That hurt Mr. Sweet Smell's feelings so bad till he went home and so he didn't marry Miss Corn-Shuck that day. Reverend Door-Knob was so mad with Miss Corn-Cob that he threw her clear over the house and she landed in the horse trough, which everybody said, served her just right.

But not getting married that day sort of threw Mr. Sweet Smell in a kind of fever. He was sick in the bed for several days. Miss Corn-Shuck went to see him every day, and that was very nice. He rubbed off some of his smell on her because she was so nice to come to see him.

Some people might have thought that Miss Corn-Shuck's green dress had faded and her silky hair all dried up. But that was because they didn't know any better. She just put on a brownish cloak over it, so it wouldn't get dirty. She would let me see it any time I wanted to. That was because she liked me better than anyone else except Mr. Sweet Smell. She lay under the mattress of my bed every night. Mr. Sweet Smell always went home to the dresser drawer. The Spool People slept on the sill under the house because Reverend Door-Knob used to sleep there. They couldn't do a thing unless they saw somebody else doing it. They wore a string around their waist, trying to dress up like Mr. Sweet Smell.

Miss Corn-Cob played a very mean trick once. Miss Corn-Shuck and Mr. Sweet Smell were going to get married down by the lake. The lake had kindly moved into the wash-basin for the occasion. A piece of cold cornbread had turned into a magnificent cake. Plenty of egg-nogg had come out of a cake of shaving soap. The bride and groom were standing side by side and ready. Then what did Miss Corn-Cob do? She shoved Reverend Door-Knob into the lake, because she knew he couldn't swim. Here everybody was waiting and nobody would have known where the preacher was if one of the Spool People had not seen him kicking down at the bottom of the lake and rescued him.

While he was getting dry and putting on a fresh suit of clothes, Miss Corn-Cob sent our old dominecker rooster to steal the wedding cake. So the wedding had to be put off until Christmas because then there would be plenty of cake for everybody. The Spool People said they were glad of it, because there ought to be enough cake to go around if you wanted a really nice wedding. The lake told everybody good-bye, jumped out in the yard and went on home. It could not stay off too long, because it would be missed and people would not know what to think.

Miss Corn-Cob went and hid down a gopher hole for a whole week. Every night she used to cry so loud, that we could hear her at the house. You see she was scared of the dark. Her mama gave her a good whipping when she got back home and everybody stood around and said "Goody! Goody! Goody! Goody! Goody!" Because that makes everybody feel bad. That is, no child likes to hear another one gloating "Goody!" when he is in trouble.

They all stayed around the house for years, holding funerals and almost weddings and taking trips with me to where the sky met the ground. I do not know exactly when they left me. They kept me company for so long. Then one day they were gone. Where? I do not know. But there is an age when children are fit company for spirits. Before they have absorbed too much of earthy things to be able to fly with the unseen things that soar. There came a time when I could look back on the fields where we had picked flowers together but they, my friends, were nowhere to be seen. The sunlight where I had lost them was still of Midas gold, but that which touched me where I stood had somehow turned to gilt. Nor could I return to the shining meadow where they had vanished. I could not ask of others if they had seen which way my company went. My friends had been too shy to show themselves to others. Now and then when the sky is the right shade of blue, the air soft, and the clouds are sculptured into heroic shapes, I glimpse them for a moment, and believe again that the halcyon days have been.

When inanimate things ceased to commune with me like natural men, other dreams came to live with me. Animals took on lives and characteristics which nobody knew anything about except myself. Little things that people did or said grew into fantastic stories.

There was a man who turned into an alligator for my amusement. All he did was live in a one-room house by himself down near Lake Belle. I did the rest myself. He came into the village one evening near dusk and stopped at the store. Somebody teased him about living out there by himself, and said that if he did not hurry up and get married, he was liable to go wild.

I saw him tending his little garden all day, and otherwise just being a natural man. But I made an image of him for after dark that was different. In my imagination, his work-a-day hands and feet became the reptilian claws of an alligator. A tough, knotty hide crept over him, and his mouth became a huge snout with prong-toothed, powerful jaws. In the dark of the night, when the alligators began their nightly mysteries behind the cloaking curtain of cypress trees that all but hid Lake Belle, I could see him crawling from his door, turning his ugly head from left to right to see who was looking, then gliding down into the dark waters to become a 'gator among 'gators. He would mingle his bellow with other bull 'gator bellows and be strong and terrible. He was the king of 'gators and the others minded him. When I heard the thunder of bull 'gator voices from the lake on dark nights, I used to whisper to myself, "That's Mr. Pendir! Just listen at him!"

I kept adding detail. For instance, late one afternoon, my mother had taken me for a walk down around Lake Belle. On our way home, the sun had set. It was good and dark when we came to the turning-off place that would take us straight home. At that spot, the trees stood apart, and the surface of the lake was plain. I saw the early moon laying a shiny track across the water. After that, I could picture the full moon laying a flaming red sword of light across the water. It was a road of yellow-red light made for Mr. Pendir to tread. I could see him crossing the lake down this flaming road wrapped in his awful majesty, with thousands on thousands of his subject-'gators moving silently along beside him and behind him in an awesome and mighty convoy.

I added another chapter to the Pendir story when a curious accident happened in the village. One old woman, Mrs. Bronson, went fishing in Blue Sink late one afternoon and did not return. The family, who had opposed the idea of a woman of Mrs. Bronson's age going off to Blue Sink to fish so late in the day, finally became worried and went out to hunt for her. They went around the edge of the lake with lanterns and torches and called and called, but they could not see her, and neither did she answer. Finally, they found her, though people were beginning to be doubtful about it. Blue Sink drops down abruptly from its shores, and is supposed to be bottomless. She was in the lake, at the very edge, still alive, but unable to crawl out. She did not even cry out when she heard herself being called and could discern the moving lanterns. When she was safely home in bed, she said that she had sat there till sundown because she knew the fish would begin to bite. She did catch a few. But just as black dark came on, a terrible fear came on her somehow, and something like a great wind struck her and hurled her into the water. She had fallen on the narrow inside rim of the lake, otherwise she would have sunk into the hidden deeps. She said that she screamed a few times for help, but something rushed across Blue Sink like a body-fied wind and commanded her to hush-up. If she so much as made another sound, she would never get out of that lake alive. That was why she had not answered when she was called, but she was praying inside to be found.

The doctor came and said that she had suffered a stroke. One whole side of her body was paralyzed, so when she tumbled over into the lake, she could not get out. Her terror and fear had done the rest. She must have had two or three

horrible hours lying there in the edge of the water, hard put
to it to keep her face above water, and expecting the attack of
an alligator, water moccasin, gar fish, and numerous other
creatures which existed only in her terrified mind. It is a wonder that she did not die of fright.

Right away, I could see the mighty tail of Mr. Pendir slapping Old Lady Bronson into the lake. Then he had stalked
away across the lake like the Devil walking up and down in
the earth. But when she had screamed, I pictured him re-
crossing to her, treading the red-gold of his moon-carpet,
with his mighty minions swimming along beside him, his feet
walking the surface like a pavement. The soles of his feet
never even being damp, he drew up his hosts around her and
commanded her to hush.

The old woman was said to dabble in hoodoo, and some
said that Pendir did too. I had heard often enough that it was
the pride of one hoodoo doctor to "throw it back on the one
that done it." What could be more natural then than for my
'gator-man to get peeved because the old lady had tried to
throw something he did back on him? Naturally, he slapped
her in to the lake. No matter what the doctor said, I knew the
real truth of the matter.

I told my playmates about it and they believed it right
away. I got bold and told them how I had seen Mr. Pendir
turning into a 'gator at night and going down into the lake
and walking the water. My chums even believed part of it in a
way. That is they liked the idea and joined in the game. They
became timid in the presence of the harmless little man and
on the sly, would be looking for 'gator signs on him. We
pretended a great fear of him. We might meet him in 'gator
form some night and get carried off into the lake, and die on
that terrible road of light.

I told them how he couldn't die anyway. That is, he
couldn't die anymore. He was not a living man. He had died
a long time ago, and his soul had gone to the 'gators. He had
told me that he had no fear of death because he had come
back from where other folks were going.

The truth of the matter was, that poor Mr. Pendir was the
one man in the village who could not swim a lick. He died a
very ordinary death. He worked too long in the hot sun one

day, and some said on an empty stomach, and took down sick. Two days later he just died and was buried and stayed where he was put. His life had not agreed with my phantasy at any point. He had no female relatives around to mourn loud and make his funeral entertaining, even, and his name soon ceased to be called. The grown folks of the village never dreamed what an exciting man he had been to me. Even after he was dead and buried, I would go down to the edge of Lake Belle to see if I could run across some of his 'gator hides that he had sloughed off at daybreak when he became a man again. My phantasies were still fighting against the facts.

VI

Wandering

I KNEW that Mama was sick. She kept getting thinner and thinner and her chest cold never got any better. Finally, she took to bed.

She had come home from Alabama that way. She had gone back to her old home to be with her sister during her sister's last illness. Aunt Dinky had lasted on for two months after Mama got there, and so Mama had stayed on till the last.

It seems that there had been other things there that worried her. Down underneath, it appeared that Grandma had never quite forgiven her for the move she had made twenty-one years before in marrying Papa. So that when Mama suggested that the old Potts place be sold so that she could bring her share back with her to Florida, her mother urged on by Uncle Bud, Mama's oldest brother, refused. Not until Grandma's head was cold, was an acre of the place to be sold. She had long since quit living on it, and it was pretty well run down, but she wouldn't, that was all. Mama could just go on back to that yaller rascal she had married like she came. I do not think that the money part worried Mama as much as the injustice and spitefulness of the thing.

Then Cousin Jimmie's death seemed to come back on Mama during her visit. How he came to his death is an unsolved mystery. He went to a party and started home. The next morning his headless body was found beside the railroad track. There was no blood, so the train couldn't have killed him. This had happened before I was born. He was said to have been a very handsome young man, and very popular with the girls. He was my mother's favorite nephew and she took it hard. She had probably numbed over her misery, but going back there seemed to freshen up her grief. Some said that he had been waylaid by three other young fellows and killed in a jealous rage. But nothing could be proved. It was whispered that he had been shot in the head by a white man unintentionally, and then beheaded to hide the wound. He

615

had been shot from ambush, because his assailant mistook him for a certain white man. It was night. The attacker expected the white man to pass that way, but not Jimmie. When he found out his mistake, he had forced a certain Negro to help him move the body to the railroad track without the head, so that it would look as if he had been run over by the train. Anyway, that is what the Negro wrote back after he had moved to Texas years later. There was never any move to prove the charge, for obvious reasons. Mama took the whole thing very hard.

It was not long after Mama came home that she began to be less active. Then she took to bed. I knew she was ailing, but she was always frail, so I did not take it too much to heart. I was nine years old, and even though she had talked to me very earnestly one night, I could not conceive of Mama actually dying. She had talked of it many times.

That day, September eighteenth, she had called me and given me certain instructions. I was not to let them take the pillow from under her head until she was dead. The clock was not to be covered, nor the looking-glass. She trusted me to see to it that these things were not done. I promised her as solemnly as nine years could do, that I would see to it.

What years of agony that promise gave me! In the first place, I had no idea that it would be soon. But that same day near sun-down, I was called upon to set my will against my father, the village dames and village custom. I know now that I could not have succeeded.

I had left Mama and was playing outside for a little while when I noted a number of women going inside Mama's room and staying. It looked strange. So I went on in. Papa was standing at the foot of the bed looking down on my mother, who was breathing hard. As I crowded in, they lifted up the bed and turned it around so that Mama's eyes would face the east. I thought that she looked to me as the head of the bed was reversed. Her mouth was slightly open, but her breathing took up so much of her strength that she could not talk. But she looked at me, or so I felt, to speak for her. She depended on me for a voice.

The Master-Maker in His making had made Old Death. Made him with big, soft feet and square toes. Made him with a face that reflects the face of all things, but neither changes itself, nor is mirrored anywhere. Made the body of Death out of infinite hunger. Made a weapon for his hand to satisfy his needs. This was the morning of the day of the beginning of things.

But Death had no home and he knew it at once.

"And where shall I dwell in my dwelling?" Old Death asked, for he was already old when he was made.

"You shall build you a place close to the living, yet far out of the sight of eyes. Wherever there is a building, there you have your platform that comprehends the four roads of the winds. For your hunger, I give you the first and last taste of all things."

We had been born, so Death had had his first taste of us. We had built things, so he had his platform in our yard.

And now, Death stirred from his platform in his secret place in our yard, and came inside the house.

Somebody reached for the clock, while Mrs. Mattie Clarke put her hand to the pillow to take it away.

"Don't!" I cried out. "Don't take the pillow from under Mama's head! She said she didn't want it moved!"

I made to stop Mrs. Mattie, but Papa pulled me away. Others were trying to silence me. I could see the huge drop of sweat collected in the hollow at Mama's elbow and it hurt me so. They were covering the clock and the mirror.

"Don't cover up that clock! Leave that looking-glass like it is! Lemme put Mama's pillow back where it was!"

But Papa held me tight and the others frowned me down. Mama was still rasping out the last morsel of her life. I think she was trying to say something, and I think she was trying to speak to me. What was she trying to tell me? What wouldn't I give to know! Perhaps she was telling me that it was better for the pillow to be moved so that she could die easy, as they said. Perhaps she was accusing me of weakness and failure in carrying out her last wish. I do not know. I shall never know.

Just then, Death finished his prowling through the house on his padded feet and entered the room. He bowed to Mama in his way, and she made her manners and left us to act out our ceremonies over unimportant things.

I was to agonize over that moment for years to come. In

the midst of play, in wakeful moments after midnight, on the way home from parties, and even in the classroom during lectures. My thoughts would escape occasionally from their confines and stare me down.

Now, I know that I could not have had my way against the world. The world we lived in required those acts. Anything else would have been sacrilege, and no nine-year-old voice was going to thwart them. My father was with the mores. He had restrained me physically from outraging the ceremonies established for the dying. If there is any consciousness after death, I hope that Mama knows that I did my best. She must know how I have suffered for my failure.

But life picked me up from the foot of Mama's bed, grief, self-despisement and all, and set my feet in strange ways. That moment was the end of a phase in my life. I was old before my time with grief of loss, of failure, of remorse of failure. No matter what the others did, my mother had put her trust in me. She had felt that I could and would carry out her wishes, and I had not. And then in that sunset time, I failed her. It seemed as she died that the sun went down on purpose to flee away from me.

That hour began my wanderings. Not so much in geography, but in time. Then not so much in time as in spirit.

Mama died at sundown and changed a world. That is, the world which had been built out of her body and her heart. Even the physical aspects fell apart with a suddenness that was startling.

My oldest brother was up in Jacksonville in school, and he arrived home after Mama had passed. By then, she had been washed and dressed and laid out on the ironing board in the parlor.

Practically all of the village was in the front yard and on the porch, talking in low tones and waiting. They were not especially waiting for my brother Bob. They were doing that kind of waiting that people do around death. It is a kind of sipping up the drama of the thing. However, if they were asked, they would say it was the sadness of the occasion which drew them. In reality it is a kind of feast of the Passover.

Bob's grief was awful when he realized that he was too late. He could not conceive at first that nothing could be done to straighten things out. There was no ear for his excuse nor explanation—no way to ease what was in him. Finally it must have come to him that what he had inside, he must take with him wherever he went. Mama was there on the cooling board with the sheet draped over her blowing gently in the wind. Nothing there seemed to hear him at all.

There was my sister Sarah in the kitchen crying and trying to quiet Everett, who was just past two years old. She was crying and trying to make him hush at the same time. He was crying because he sensed the grief around him. And then, Sarah, who was fifteen had been his nurse and he would respond to her mood, whatever it was. We were all grubby bales of misery, huddled about lamps.

I have often wished I had been old enough at the time to look into Papa's heart that night. If I could know what that moment meant to him, I could have set my compass towards him and been sure. I know that I did love him in a way, and that I admired many things about him. He had a poetry about him that I loved. That had made him a successful preacher. He could hit ninety-seven out of a hundred with a gun. He could swim Lake Maitland from Maitland to Winter Park, and no man in the village could put my father's shoulders to the ground. We were so certain of Papa's invincibility in combat that when a village woman scolded Everett for some misdemeanor, and told him that God would punish him, Everett, just two years old, reared back and told her, "He better not bother me. Papa will shoot Him down." He found out better later on, but that goes to show you how big our Papa looked to us. We had seen him bring down bears and panthers with his gun, and chin the bar more times than any man in competing distance. He had to our knowledge licked two men who Mama told him had to be licked. All that part was just fine with me. But I was Mama's child. I knew that she had not always been happy, and I wanted to know just how sad he was that night.

I have repeatedly called up that picture and questioned it. Papa cried some too, as he moved in his awkward way about the place. From the kitchen to the front porch and back again. He kept saying, "Poor thing! She suffered so much." I do not know what he meant by that. It could have been love and pity for her suffering ending at last. It could have been remorse mixed with relief. The hard-driving force was no longer opposed to his easy-going pace. He could put his potentialities to sleep and be happy in the laugh of the day. He could do next year or never, what Mama would have insisted must be done today. Rome, the eternal city, meant two different things to my parents. To Mama, it meant, you must build it today so it could last through eternity. To Papa, it meant that you could plan to lay some bricks today and you have the rest of eternity to finish it. With all that time, why hurry? God had made more time than anything else, anyway. Why act so stingy about it?

Then too, I used to notice how Mama used to snatch Papa. That is, he would start to put up an argument that would have been terrific on the store porch, but Mama would pitch in with a single word or a sentence and mess it all up. You could tell he was mad as fire with no words to blow it out with. He would sit over in the corner and cut his eyes at her real hard. He was used to being a hero on the store porch and in church affairs, and I can see how he must have felt to be always outdone around home. I know now that that is a griping thing to a man—not to be able to whip his woman mentally. Some women know how to give their man that conquesting feeling. My mother took her over-the-creek man and bare-knuckled him from brogans to broadcloth, and I am certain that he was proud of the change, in public. But in the house, he might have always felt over-the-creek, and because that was not the statue he had made for himself to look at, he resented it. But then, you cannot blame my mother too much if she did not see him as his entranced congregations did. The one who makes the idols never worships them, however tenderly he might have molded the clay. You cannot have knowledge and worship at the same time. Mystery is the essence of divinity. Gods must keep their distances from men.

Anyway, the next day, Sam Moseley's span of fine horses, hitched to our wagon, carried my mother to Macedonia Baptist Church for the last time. The finality of the thing came to me fully when the earth began to thud on the coffin.

That night, all of Mama's children were assembled together for the last time on earth. The next day, Bob and Sarah went back to Jacksonville to school. Papa was away from home a great deal, so two weeks later, I was on my way to Jacksonville, too. I was under age, but the school had agreed to take me in under the circumstances. My sister was to look after me, in a way.

The midnight train had to be waved down at Maitland for me. That would put me into Jacksonville in the daytime.

As my brother Dick drove the mile with me that night, we approached the curve in the road that skirts Lake Catherine, and suddenly I saw the first picture of my visions. I had seen myself upon that curve at night leaving the village home, bowed down with grief that was more than common. As it all flashed back to me, I started violently for a minute, then I moved closer beside Dick as if he could shield me from those others that were to come. He asked me what was the matter, and I said I thought I heard something moving down by the lake. He laughed at that, and we rode on, the lantern showing the roadway, and me keeping as close to Dick as I could. A little, humped-up, shabby-backed trunk was behind us in the buckboard. I was on my way from the village, never to return to it as a real part of the town.

Jacksonville made me know that I was a little colored girl. Things were all about the town to point this out to me. Street cars and stores and then talk I heard around the school. I was no longer among the white people whose homes I could barge into with a sure sense of welcome. These white people had funny ways. I could tell that even from a distance. I didn't get a piece of candy or a bag of crackers just for going into a store in Jacksonville as I did when I went into Galloway's or Hill's at Maitland, or Joe Clarke's in Eatonville.

Around the school I was an awful bother. The girls complained that they couldn't get a chance to talk without me turning up somewhere to be in the way. I broke up many good "He said" conferences just by showing up. It was not my intention to do so. What I wanted was for it to go full steam ahead and let me listen. But that didn't seem to please. I was not in the "he said" class, and they wished I would kindly please stay out of the way. My underskirt was hanging, for instance. Why didn't I go some place and fix it? My head looked like a hoo-raw's nest. Why didn't I go comb it? If I took time enough to match my stockings, I wouldn't have time to be trying to listen in on grown folk's business. These venerable old ladies were anywhere from fifteen to eighteen.

In the classroom I got along splendidly. The only difficulty was that I was rated as sassy. I just had to talk back at established authority and that established authority hated back talk worse than barbed-wire pie. My brother was asked to speak to me in addition to a licking or two. But on the whole, things went along all right. My immediate teachers were enthusiastic about me. It was the guardians of study-hour and prayer meetings who felt that their burden was extra hard to bear.

School in Jacksonville was one of those twilight things. It was not dark, but it lacked the bold sunlight that I craved. I worshipped two of my teachers and loved gingersnaps with cheese, and sour pickles. But I was deprived of the loving pine, the lakes, the wild violets in the woods and the animals I used to know. No more holding down first base on the team with my brothers and their friends. Just a jagged hole where my home used to be.

At times, the girls of the school were lined up two and two and taken for a walk. On one of these occasions, I had an experience that set my heart to fluttering. I saw a woman sitting on a porch who looked at a distance like Mama. Maybe it *was* Mama! Maybe she was not dead at all. They had made some mistake. Mama had gone off to Jacksonville and they thought that she was dead. The woman was sitting in a rocking chair just like Mama always did. It must be Mama! But before I came abreast of the porch in my rigid place in line, the woman got up and went inside. I wanted to stop and go in. But I didn't even breathe my hope to anyone. I made up my mind to run away someday and find the house and let Mama know where I was. But before I did, the hope that the woman really was my mother passed. I accepted my bereavement.

VII

Jacksonville and After

M Y SISTER moped a great deal. She was Papa's favorite child, and I am certain that she loved him more than anything on earth, my baby brother Everett being next in her love. So two months after I came to school, Sarah said that she was sick and wanted to go home. Papa arranged for her to leave school.

That had very tragic results for Sarah. In a week or two after she left me in Jacksonville, she wrote back that Papa had married again. That hurt us all, somehow. But it was worse for Sarah, for my step-mother must have resented Papa's tender indulgence for his older daughter. It was not long before the news came back that she had insisted that Papa put Sarah out of the house. That was terrible enough, but it was not satisfactory to Papa's new wife. Papa must go over and beat Sarah with a buggy whip for commenting on the marriage happening so soon after Mama's death. Sarah must be driven out of town. So Sarah just married and went down on the Manatee River to live. She took Everett with her. She probably left more behind her than she took away.

What Papa and Sarah felt during these times, I have never heard from either of them. I know that it must have ploughed very deep with both of them.

God, how I longed to lay my hands upon my stepmother's short, pudgy hulk! No gun, no blade, no club would do. Just flesh against flesh and leave the end of the struggle to the hidden Old Women who sit and spin.

Papa had honored his first-born daughter from the day of her birth. If she was not fore-told, she was certainly fore-wished. Three sons had come, and he was glad of their robust health, but after the first one, he wanted a little girl child around the house. For several years then, it had been a wish deferred. So that when she did arrive, small, under-sized, but a girl, his joy was boundless. He changed and washed her diapers. She was not allowed to cry as an infant, and when she

624 DUST TRACKS ON A ROAD

grew old enough to let on, her wishes did not go unregarded. What was it Papa's girl-baby wanted to eat? She wanted two dolls instead of one? Bless her little heart! A cheeky little rascal! Papa would bring it when he came. The two oldest boys had to get out of their beds late one night and stay outdoors for an hour or more because little three-year-old Sarah woke up and looked out of the window and decided that she wanted to see the stars outdoors. It was no use for the boys to point out that she could see stars aplenty through the window. Papa thundered, "Get up and take dat young'un out doors! Let her look at de stars just as long as she wants to. And don't let me hear a mutter out of you. If I hear one *grumble*, I'll drop your britches below your hocks and bust de hide on you!"

Sarah was diminutive. Even when she was small, you could tell that she never would grow much. She would be short like Papa's mother, and her own mother. She had something of both of them in her face. Papa delighted in putting the finest and the softest shoes on her dainty feet; the fluffiest white organdy dresses with the stiffest ribbon sashes. "Dat's a switching little gal!" he used to gloat.

She had music lessons on the piano. It did not matter that she was not interested in music, it was part of his pride. The parlor organ was bought in Jacksonville and shipped down as a surprise for Sarah on her tenth birthday. She had a gold ring for her finger, and gold earrings. When I begged for music lessons, I was told to dry up before he bust the hide on my back.

If the rest of us wanted to sneak jelly or preserves and get off without a licking, the thing to do was to get Sarah in on it. Papa might ignore the whipping-purge that Mama was organizing until he found that Sarah was mixed up in it. Then he would lay aside the county newspaper which he was given to reading, and shout at Mama, "Dat'll do! Dat'll do, Lulu! I can't stand all dat racket around de place." Of course, if Mama was really in the mood, Papa's protest would change no plans, but at times it would, and we would all escape because of Sarah. I have seen Papa actually snatch the switch out of Mama's hand when she got to Sarah. But if Mama thought that the chastisement was really in order, she would send out to the peach tree for another one and the whipping would go right on. Papa knew better than to stick his bill in when Mama was really determined. Under such circumstances, Sarah was certain to get some sort of a present on Monday when Papa came back from Sanford.

He had never struck her in his life. She never got but one from him, and that was this cruel thing at the instigation of our stepmother. Neither Papa nor Sarah ever looked at each other in the same way again, nor at the world. Nor did they look like the same people to the world who knew them. Their heads hung down and they studied the ground under their feet too much.

As for me, looking on, it made a tiger out of me. It did not matter so much to me that Sarah was Papa's favorite. I got my joys in other ways, and so, did not miss his petting. I do not think that I ever really wanted it. It made me miserable to see Sarah look like that. And six years later I paid the score off in a small way. It was on a Monday morning, six years after Sarah's heartbreak, that my stepmother threatened to beat me for my impudence, after vainly trying to get Papa to undertake the job. I guess that the memory of the time that he had struck Sarah at his wife's demand, influenced Papa and saved me. I do not think that she considered that a changed man might be in front of her. I do not think that she thought that I would resist in the presence of my father after all that had happened and shown his lack of will. I do not think that she even thought that she could whip me if I resisted. She did think, if she thought at all, that all she had to do was to start on me, and Papa would be forced to jump in and finish up the job to her satisfaction in order to stay in her good graces. Old memories of her power over him told her to assert herself, and she pitched in. She called me a sassy, impudent heifer, announced that she was going to take me down a buttonhole lower, and threw a bottle at my head. The bottle came sailing slowly through the air and missed me easily. She never should have missed.

The primeval in me leaped to life. Ha! This was the very corn I wanted to grind. Fight! Not having to put up with what she did to us through Papa! Direct action and everything up to me. I looked at her hard. And like everybody

else's enemy, her looks, her smells, her sounds were all mixed
up with her doings, and she deserved punishment for them as
well as her acts. The feelings of all those six years were pressing inside me like steam under a valve. I didn't have any
thoughts to speak of. Just the fierce instinct of flesh on
flesh—me kicking and beating on her pudgy self—those two
ugly false teeth in front—her dead on the floor—grinning
like a dead dog in the sun. Consequences be damned! If I
died, let me die with my hands soaked in her blood. I wanted
her blood, and plenty of it. That is the way I went into the
fight, and that is the way I fought it.

She had the advantage of me in weight, that was all. It did
not seem to do her a bit of good. Maybe she did not have the
guts, and certainly she underestimated mine. She gave way
before my first rush and found herself pinned against the wall,
with my fists pounding at her face without pity. She scratched
and clawed at me, but I felt nothing at all. In a few seconds,
she gave up. I could see her face when she realized that I
meant to kill her. She spat on my dress, then, and did what
she could to cover up from my renewed fury. She had given
up fighting except for trying to spit in my face, and I did not
intend for her to get away.

She yelled for Papa, but that was no good. Papa was disturbed, no doubt of it, but he wept and fiddled in the door
and asked me to stop, while her head was traveling between
my fist and the wall, and I wished that my fist had weighed a
ton. She tried to do something. She pulled my hair and
scratched at me. But I had come up fighting with boys. Hair-
pulling didn't worry me.

She screamed that she was going to get Papa's pistol and
kill me. She tried to get across the room to the dresser
drawer, but I knew I couldn't let that happen. So the fight
got hotter. A friend of hers who weighed over two hundred
pounds lived across the street. She heard the rumpus and
came running. I visualized that she would try to grab me, and
I realized that my stepmother would get her chance. So I
grabbed my stepmother by the collar and dragged her to a
hatchet against the wall and managed to get hold of it. As
Mrs. G. waddled through the living room door, I hollered to
her to get back, and let fly with that hatchet with all that my

right arm would do. It struck the wall too close to her head
to make her happy. She reeled around and rolled down those
front steps yelling that I had gone crazy. But she never came
back and the fight went on. I was so mad when I saw my
adversary sagging to the floor I didn't know what to do. I
began to scream with rage. I had not beaten more than two
years out of her yet. I made up my mind to stomp her, but at
last, Papa came to, and pulled me away.

I had a scratch on my neck and two or three on my arms,
but that was all. I was not at all pacified. She owed me four
more years. Besides there was her spit on the front of my
dress. I promised myself to pay her for the old and the new
too, the first chance I got. Years later, after I had graduated
from Barnard and I was doing research, I found out where
she was. I drove twenty miles to finish the job, only to find
out that she was a chronic invalid. She had an incurable sore
on her neck. I couldn't tackle her under such circumstances,
so I turned back, all frustrated inside. All I could do was to
wish that she had a lot more neck to rot.

That fight brought things to a head between Papa and his
wife. She said Papa had to have me arrested, but Papa said he
didn't have to do but two things—die and stay black. And
then, he would never let me sleep in jail a night. She took the
matter to the church and the people laughed. Most of them
had been praying for something like that to happen. They
were annoyed because she didn't get her head stomped. The
thing rocked on for a few months. She demanded that Papa
"handle" some of the sisters of the church who kept cracking
her about it, but he explained that there was nothing he
could do. They were old friends of my mother's and it was
natural for them to feel as they did. There were two or three
hot word battles on the church grounds, and then she left
Papa with the understanding that he could get her back when
he had made "them good-for-nothing nigger wimmens know
dat she was Mrs. Reverend." So she went on off with her lip
hung down lower than a mason's apron.

Papa went to see a lawyer and he said to send her clothes to
her if she had not come back after three weeks. And that is
just what Papa did. She "lawed" for a divorce and he let it
slide. The black Anne Boleyn had come at last to the morning

and the axe. The simile ends there. The King really had an axe. It has always seemed to me under the provocation a sad lack that preachers could not go armed like that. Perhaps it is just as well that it has been arranged so that the state has taken over the business of execution. Not every skunk in the world rates a first-class killing. Hanging is too good for some folks. They just need their behinds kicked. And that is all that woman rated. But, you understand, this was six years after I went up to Jacksonville. I put it in right here because I was thinking so hard.

But back to Jacksonville and the school. I had gotten used to the grits and gravy for breakfast, had found out how not to be bored at prayer-meeting—you could always write notes if you didn't go to sleep—and how to poke fun at acidulated disciplinarians, and how to slip through a crack in the fence and cross the street to the grocery store for ginger snaps and pickles which were forbidden between meals. I had generally made a sort of adjustment. Lessons had never worried me, though arithmetic still seemed an unnecessary evil.

Then, one day, the Second in Command sent for me to tell me that my room and board had not been paid. What was I going to do about it? I certainly didn't know. Then she gave me a free hand opinion of the Reverend John Hurston that Chief Justice Taney could not have surpassed. Every few days after that I was called in and asked what was I going to do. After a while she did not call me in, she would just yell out of the window to where I might be playing in the yard. That used to keep me shrunk up inside. I got so I wouldn't play too hard. The call might come at any time. My spirits would not have quite so far to fall.

But I stayed out the year, but not because my bills were paid. I was put to scrubbing down the stair steps every Saturday, and sent to help clean up the pantry and do what I could in the kitchen after school. Then too, the city of Jacksonville had a spelling bee in all the Negro schools and I won it for my school. I received an atlas of the world and a Bible as prizes, besides so much lemonade and cake that I told President Collier that I could feel it coming through my skin. He had such a big laugh that I made up my mind to hurry up and get grown and marry him. For his part, he didn't seem to know that he had been picked out. In fact, he seemed to be quite patient about it. Never tried to hurry my growth at all, and never mentioned the matter. He acted like he was satisfied with some stale, old, decrepit woman of twenty-five or so. It used to drive me mad. I comforted myself with the thought that he would cry his eyes out when I would suddenly appear before him, tall and beautiful and disdainful and make him beg me for a whole week before I would give in and marry him, and of course fire all of those old half-dead teachers who were hanging around him. Maybe they would drown themselves in the St. John's River. Oh, I might stop them just before they jumped in. I never did decide what to do with all my disgruntled rivals after I dragged them away from the river. They could rake up the yard, but a yard somewhere a long way from where *he* was. That would be better for everybody. A yard in Africa would be just dandy. They would naturally die of old age in a week or so.

I wrote some letters from him to me and read his tender words with tears in my eyes. I made us a secret post office behind the laundry. One day his letters to me would get written and buried, and the next day I would dig them up and read them. Then I would answer them and assure him he did not have to worry. I meant to marry him as soon as they let me put on long dresses, which I hoped would not be too far off. A month or two more ought to age me quite a bit.

This torrid love affair was conducted from a hole in the ground behind the laundry and came to an abrupt end. One of those same hateful teachers who was mean enough to get grown before I did, reported to my husband-in-reserve that it was I who had put a wet brick in her bed while she was presiding over study hour in the chapel. So much fuss over nothing! Just a brick that had been soaked overnight in a rain-barrel placed between the sheets near the foot of the bed, and they made as much fuss about it as if ice cream had been abolished.

It was true that it was a coldish spell of weather in February and all that. But what fun would a cold brick be in June? I ask you!

Oh, the perfidy, the deceit of the man to whom I had given my love and all my lovely letters in the hole behind the laundry!

He listened to this unholy female and took me into his office and closed the door. He did not fold me lovingly in his arms and say, "Darling! I understand. You did it all for me." No! The blind fool lifted up my skirt in the rear and spanked a prospective tall, beautiful lady's pants. So improper, to say the least! I made up my mind to get even. I *wouldn't* marry him now, no matter how hard he begged me. Insult me, would he? Turning up *my* dress just like I was some child! Ah, he would pine for my love and never get it. In addition to letting him starve for my love, I was going off and die in a pitiful way. Very lonely and dramatic at the same time, however.

The whole thing was so unjust. She did *not* see me put that brick in her bed. And if the duty-girl did look back over her shoulder and see me coming down the hall with the brick in my hand, what kind of a decent person is that? Going around and looking backwards at people! When I would be grown and sit up in my fine palace eating beef stew and fried chicken, that duty-girl was going to be out in my backyard gnawing door-knobs.

Time passed. Spring came up the St. John's River from down the Everglades way, and school closed in a blaze of programs, cantatas and speeches, and trunks went bumping down stairs. My brother hurried off to take a job. I was to stay there and Papa would send for me.

I kept looking out of the window so that I could see Papa when he came up the walk to the office. But nobody came for me. Weeks passed, and then a letter came. Papa said that the school could adopt me. The Second in Command sent for me and told me about it. She said that she had no place for a girl so young, and besides she was too busy to bring up any children.

It was crumbling news for me. It impressed every detail of the office and her person on my mind. I noted more clearly than ever the thick gray-black ropes of her half-Negro, half-White hair, her thin lips, and white-folks-looking nose. All in all, her yellow skin browned down by age looked like it had been dried between the leaves of a book. I had always been afraid of her sharp tongue and quick hand, but this day she seemed to speak a little softer than usual, and in half-finished sentences, as if she had her tender parts to hide. She took out her purse and handed me some money. She was going to pay my way home by the boat, and I must tell my father to send her her dollar and a half.

The boat trip was thrilling on the side-wheeler *City of Jacksonville.* The water life, the smothering foliage that draped the river banks, the miles of purple hyacinths, all thrilled me anew. The wild thing was back in the jungle.

The curtain of trees along the river shut out the world so that it seemed that the river and the chugging boat was all that there was, and that pleased me a lot. Inside, the boat was glittering with shiny brass.

White-clad waiters dashed about with trays for the first class upstairs. There was an almost ceaseless rattle of dishes. Red carpet underfoot. Big, shiny lights overhead. White men in greasy overalls popping up from down below now and then to lean on the deck rail for a breath of air. A mulatto waiter with a patch over one eye who kept bringing me slabs of pie and cake and chicken and steak sandwiches, and sent me astern to eat them. Things clattered up the gang plank, and then more things rumbled down into the hold. People on the flimsy docks waving goodbye to anybody who wanted to wave back. Wild hogs appearing now and then along the shore. 'Gators, disturbed by the wash, slipping off of palm logs into the stream. Schools of mullet breaking water now and then. Flocks of water fowl disturbed at the approach of the steamer, then settling back again to feed. Catfish as long as a man pacing the boat like porpoises for kitchen scraps. A group of turpentine hands with queer haircuts, in blue overalls with red handkerchiefs around their necks, who huddled around a tall, black man with a guitar round his neck. They ate out of shoe boxes and sang between drinks out of a common bottle. A stocking-foot woman was with them with a dirk in her garter. Her new shoes were in a basket beside her. She dipped snuff and kept missing the spittoon. The glitter of brass and the red carpet made her nervous. The captain kept passing through and pulling my hair gently and asking me to spell something, and kept being surprised when I did. He called out "separate" when I was getting off at Sanford, and I spelled it back at him as I went down the gang plank. I left him leaning on the rail and looking like he had some more words he wanted spelled. Then he threw a half dollar that fell just ahead of me and smiled goodbye.

The day after I started from Jacksonville, the boat docked at Sanford, with the town of Enterprise a shadowy suspicion across the five miles of Lake Monroe. I had to go to the railroad station to take the train for the fifteen miles to Maitland.

The conductor and the whole crew knew me from seeing me with my father so often. They remembered me for another reason, too, which embarrassed me a lot. This very train and crew had been my first experience with railroads. I had seen trains often, but never up so close as that day about four years before when Papa had decided to take me up to Sanford with him. Then I was at the station with Papa and my two oldest brothers. We heard the train blow, leaving Winter Park, three miles south. So we picked up our things and moved down from the platform to a spot beside the track. The train came thundering around Lake Lily, and snorted up to the station. I was there looking the thing dead in the face, and it was fixing its one big, mean-looking eye on me. It looked fit to gnaw me right up. It was truly a most fearsome thing!

The porter swung down and dropped his stool. The conductor in his eyeglasses stood down, changing greetings with Papa, Mr. Wescott, the station-agent, and all of the others whom he knew from long association.

"All aboard!" The train only hesitated at Maitland. It didn't really stop.

This thing was bad, but I saw a chance to save myself yet and still. It did not just have to get me if I moved fast enough.

My father swung up to the platform, and turned around. My brother Bob had me by the hand and prepared to hand me up. This was the last safe moment I had. I tore loose from Bob and dashed under the train and out again. I was going home.

Everybody yelled. The conductor louder than anybody else. "Catch her! Head her off over there!" The engineer held down his whistle. The fireman jumped off and took after me. Everybody was after me. It looked as if the whole world had turned into my enemies. I didn't have a friend to my name.

"There she goes! Hem her up! Head her off from that barbed-wire fence!" My own big brother was chasing me as hard as anybody else. My legs were getting tired and I was winded, but I was running for my life. Brother Bob headed me off from home, so I doubled back into Galloway's store and ran behind the counter. Old Harry, Galloway's son, about Bob's age, grabbed me and pulled me out. I was hauled on board kicking and screaming to the huge amusement of everybody but me. As soon as I saw the glamor of the plush and metal of the inside of that coach, I calmed down. The conductor gave the engineer the high ball and the train rolled. It didn't hurt a bit. Papa laughed and laughed. The porter passed through holding his sides. The conductor came to take Papa's ticket and kept on teasing me about hurting the train's feelings. In a little while he was back with a glass pistol filled with candy. By the time I got to Sanford, I was crazy about the train. I just wished they would quit laughing at me. The inside of that train was too pretty for words. It took years for me to get over loving it.

So when I climbed on board that morning—some four years later, I had that look of "Get away from me, porter! Don't you see I'm too big to be helped on trains"—they all smiled in memory of our first meeting, and let it go at that. The porter was a member of Papa's church in Sanford, and sat beside me when he was not busy.

So I came back to my father's house which was no longer home. The very walls were gummy with gloom. Too much went on to take the task of telling it. Papa's children were in his way, because they were too much trouble to his wife. Ragged, dirty clothes and hit-and-miss meals. The four older children were definitely gone for good. One by one, we four younger ones were shifted to the homes of Mama's friends.

Perhaps it could be no other way. Certainly no other way was open to a man who loved peace and ease the way my father did.

My stepmother was sleeping in Mama's feather bed. The one thing which Mama had brought from her father's house. She had said it must be mine. To see this interloper piled up in my mother's bed was too much for me to bear. I had to do something. The others had been miserable about it all along.

I rallied my brother Joel to my aid and we took the mattress off of the bed.

Papa had told her that it was his, so he was faced with the dilemma. I stood my ground, and the other children present backed me. She thought a good beating for me ought to settle the ownership once and for all. John took my part, he was always doing that, dear John, and physical violence, yes actual bloodshed seemed inevitable for a moment. John and Papa stood face to face, and Papa had an open knife in his hand.

Then he looked his defiant son in the eyes and dropped his hand. He just told John to leave home. However, my step-mother had lost her point. She never was pleasured to rack her bones on Mama's feather bed again. Though there were plenty of beds for her to sleep in, she hated to take any dictation at all from us, especially me.

But Papa's shoulders began to get tired. He didn't rear back and strut like he used to. His well-cut broadcloth, Stetson hats, hand-made alligator-skin shoes and walking stick had earned him the title of Big Nigger with his children. Behind his back, of course. He didn't put and take with his cane any more. He just walked along. It didn't take him near so long to put on his hat.

So my second vision picture came to be. I had seen myself homeless and uncared for. There was a chill about that picture which used to wake me up shivering. I had always thought I would be in some lone, arctic wasteland with no one under the sound of my voice. I found the cold, the desolate solitude, and earless silences, but I discovered that all that geography was within me. It only needed time to reveal it.

My vagrancy had begun in reality. I knew that. There was an end to my journey and it had happiness in it for me. It was certain and sure. But the way! Its agony was equally certain. It was before me, and no one could spare me my pilgrimage. The rod of compelment was laid to my back. I must go the way.

VIII

Back Stage and the Railroad

T HERE is something about poverty that smells like death.
Dead dreams dropping off the heart like leaves in a dry
season and rotting around the feet; impulses smothered too
long in the fetid air of underground caves. The soul lives in a
sickly air. People can be slave-ships in shoes.

This wordless feeling went with me from the time I was ten
years old until I achieved a sort of competence around
twenty. Naturally, the first five years were the worst. Things
and circumstances gave life a most depressing odor.

The five years following my leaving the school at Jacksonville were haunted. I was shifted from house to house of relatives and friends and found comfort nowhere. I was without
books to read most of the time, except where I could get
hold of them by mere chance. That left no room for selection.
I was miserable, and no doubt made others miserable around
me, because they could not see what was the matter with me,
and I had no part in what interested them.

I was in school off and on, which gave me vagrant peeps
into the light, but these intervals lacked peace because I had
no guarantee that they would last. I was growing and the
general thought was that I could bring in something. This
book-reading business was a hold-back and an unrelieved evil.
I could not do very much, but look at so-and-so. She was
nursing for some good white people. A dollar a week and
most of her clothes. People who had no parents could not
afford to sit around on school benches wearing out what
clothes they had.

One of the most serious objections to me was that having
nothing, I still did not know how to be humble. A child in
my place ought to realize I was lucky to have a roof over my
head and anything to eat at all. And from their point of view,
they were right. From mine, my stomach pains were the least
of my sufferings. I wanted what they could not conceive of. I
could not reveal myself for lack of expression, and then for

lack of hope of understanding, even if I could have found the words. I was not comfortable to have around. Strange things must have looked out of my eyes like Lazarus after his resurrection.

So I was forever shifting. I walked by my corpse. I smelt it and felt it. I smelt the corpses of those among whom I must live, though they did not. They were as much at home with theirs as death in a tomb.

Gradually, I came to the point of attempting self-support. It was a glorious feeling when it came to me. But the actual working out of the thing was not so simple as the concept. I was about fourteen then.

For one thing, I really was young for the try. Then my growth was retarded somewhat so that I looked younger than I really was. Housewives would open the door at my ring and look me over. No, they wanted some one old enough to be responsible. No, they wanted some one strong enough to do the work, and so on like that. Did my mother know I was out looking for work? Sometimes in bed at night I would ask myself that very question and wonder.

But now and then some one would like my looks and give me a try. I did very badly because I was interested in the front of the house, not the back. No matter how I resolved, I'd get tangled up with their reading matter, and lose my job. It was not that I was lazy, I just was not interested in dusting and dishwashing. But I always made friends with the children if there were any. That was not intentional. We just got together somehow. That would be fun, but going out to play did not help much on jobs.

One woman liked me for it. She had two little girls, seven and five. I was hired as an upstairs maid. For two or three days things went on very well. The president of the kitchen was a fat, black old woman who had nursed the master of the house and was a fixture. Nobody is so powerful in a southern family as one of these family fixtures. No matter who hires you, the fixture can fire you. They roam all over the house bossing everybody from the boss on down. Nobody must upset Cynthia or Rhoda or Beckey. If you can't get along with the house president you can't keep the job.

And Miz Cally was President in Full in this house. She

looked at me cut-eye first thing because the madam had hired
me without asking her about it. She went into her grumble
just as soon as I stuck my head in the kitchen door. She
looked at me for a moment with her hands on her hips and
burst out, "Lawd a'mercy! Miz Alice must done took you to
raise! She don't need no more young'uns round de place. Dis
house needs a woman to give aid and assistance."

She showed her further disapproval by vetoing every move
I made. She was to show me where to find the aprons, and
she did. Just as soon as I pulled open the drawer, she bustled
me right away from it with her hips.

"Don't you go pulling and hauling through *my* drawers! I
keeps things in they place. You take de apron I give you and
git on up dem stairs."

I didn't get mad with her. I took the apron and put it on
with quite a bit of editing by Sister Cally, and went on up the
back stairs. As I emerged on the upper floor, two pairs of
gray-blue eyes were ranged on me.

"Hello!" said the two little girls in chorus.

"Hello!" I answered back.

"You going to work for us?" the taller one asked, and fell in
beside me.

"Yeah." Maybe I cracked a smile or something, for both of
them took a hand on either side and we went on into the
room where Mrs. Alice was waiting for me to show me what
to do and how to do it.

She was a very beautiful woman in her middle twenties, and
she was combing out her magnificent hair. She looked at me
through the looking glass, and we both started to grinning
for some reason or another.

She showed me how to make beds and clean up. There
were three rooms up there, but she told me not to try to do
too much at a time. Just keep things looking sort of neat.
Then she dressed and left the house. I got things straightened
out with Helen and Genevieve acting as convoy at every step.
Things went all right till I got to the bathroom, then somehow or other we three found ourselves in a tussle. Screaming,
laughing, splashing water and tussling, when a dark shadow
filled up the door. Heinz could have wrung enough vinegar
out of Cally's look to run his pickle works.

"You going 'way from here!" she prophesied, and shook her head so vigorously that her head rag wagged. She was going to get me gone from there!

"No!" screamed Helen, the littlest girl, and held on to me.

"No! No! No!" Genevieve shrieked.

"Humph! You just wait till yo' daddy come home!" Cally gloomed. "I ain't never seen no sich caper like dis since I been borned in dis world." Then she stumped on back downstairs.

"Don't you go," Genevieve begged. "I like you."

"Me too, I like you too," Helen chorused. "If you go home, we'll go with you."

I had to wait on the table at dinner that night, with my apron too long for me. Mrs. Alice and the children were giving a glowing account of me. The boss glanced at me tolerantly a time or two. Helen would grab hold of my clothes every time I passed her chair, and play in the vegetable dishes when I offered them to her, until her father threatened to spank her hands, but he looked up at me and smiled a little. He looked to me like an aged old soul of thirty-five or so.

Cally kept on cracking the kitchen door to see how I was getting along in there, and I suspect to give the boss a view of her disapproving face.

Things rocked on for a week or two. Mrs. Alice went out more and more to bridge clubs and things like that. She didn't care whether I made up the rooms or not so long as the children were entertained. She would come in late in the afternoon and tell Cally to run upstairs and straighten up a bit.

"What's dat gal been doing?" Cally would growl. Dat gal she was talking about had been off to the park with the children, or stretched out on the floor telling stories or reading aloud from some of their story books. Their mother had been free to go about her business, and a good time was had by all — except Cally.

Before a month passed, things came to a head: Cally burst into the dining room one night and flew all over the place. The boss had to get somebody to do his cooking. She was tired of doing all the work. She just wasn't going to cook and look after things downstairs and then troop upstairs and do the work somebody else was getting paid for. She was old. Her joints hurt her so bad till she couldn't rest of nights. They really needed to get somebody to help.

Mrs. Alice sat there stark, still and quiet. The boss looked at her, then at old Cally, and then at me.

Finally, he said, "I never meant for you to work yourself down like that, Aunt Cally. You've done more than your share."

" 'Deed, Gawd knows I is!" Cally agreed belligerently, rolling her white eyeballs in my direction.

"Isn't Zora taking care of the upstairs? I thought that was what she was hired for," the boss asked, and looked at his wife.

"Taking care of what?" Cally snorted. " 'Deed, I ain't lying, Mr. Ed. I wouldn't tell a lie on nobody—"

"I know you wouldn't, Auntie," he soothed.

"Dat gal don't do a living thing round dis house but play all day long wid these young 'uns. Den I has to scuffle up dem stairs and do round, cause effen I didn't, dis here place would be like a hawg-pen. Dat's what it would. I *has* to go and do it, Mr. Ed, else it wouldn't never git done. And I'm sick and *tired*. I'm gwine 'way from here!"

"Naw, Cally, you can't do it. You been with me all my life, and I don't aim to let you go. Zora will have to go. These children are too big now to need a nurse."

What did he say that for? My public went into sound and action. Mrs. Alice was letting a tear or two slip. Otherwise she was as still as stone. But Helen scrambled out of her chair with her jaws latched back to the last notch. She stumbled up against me and swung on. Genevieve screamed "No!" in a regular chant like a cheer leader, and ran to me, too. Their mother never raised her head. The boss turned to her.

"Darling, why don't you quiet these children?" he asked gently.

"No! No! No! Zora can't go!" my cheering squad yelled, slinging tears right and left.

"Shut up!" the boss grated at the children and put his hand on the table and scuffled his feet as if he meant to rush off for the hair brush. "I'll be on you in one more minute! Hush!"

It was easy to see that his heart was not in any spanking.

His frown was not right for it. The yelling kept right on. Cally flounced on back to the kitchen, and he got up and hauled the children upstairs. In a minute he called his wife and shut the bedroom door.

I cleared off the table, and when I sat down in the kitchen to eat, Cally slammed a plate in front of me with some dried-up fried eggs left from breakfast. She put the steak away in the ice-box ostentatiously, just daring me with her eyes to cheep about it. I kept good and quiet.

In about a half hour the boss came down and talked to Cally. I was to stay on and look after the children. His wife was going to look around for a woman to take care of the upstairs and the front of the house, too. Cally would have less to do. He sort of apologized when he said the children were so attached to me that he hated to get rid of me on their account. Not once did he say a word to me. So Cally was mollified to an extent. If she had not gotten rid of me, her rank had been recognized at any rate. That was what she was fighting for anyway. He told her to go down to a certain shoe store the next day and tell them to let her have some more comfortable shoes and send the bill to him. Then he went back upstairs very quietly. Cally talked to me then, and gave me a piece of pie.

But that was not the end. I could sense that my being there was doing something to that house. There were looks between husband and wife at times. He was not satisfied, and it was not the two dollars a week I was getting. He was not mean to me, he just acted funny. His wife was as good as gold. She made me a white dress herself and bought me a Sunday hat. She would go out to her bridge clubs and things like that, but she was usually home before he got there. Sometimes she would be home before the children and I got home from our prowls. And how we did prowl! Then the boss took to coming home at odd hours and going in the kitchen and talking to Cally for a long time.

One evening he just fired me suddenly after the children had been put to bed. I hated it, because I was having all the fun in the world. He had followed me down to the foot of the stairs. While he was paying me off, Mrs. Alice came out of her room and stood at the top of the stairs.

"Ed," she began.

"Now, you go on back in your room, Alice; I'm handling this. Go on! You don't need Zora to take care of those children. She is not going to be here another day. I mean that."

He saw me out of the door, and I went off feeling sad. I didn't know what he was firing me for. The children were more than satisfied with my company. His wife seemed very glad to have me around. I couldn't see what was wrong.

Years later when I had seen more, I concluded that he was jealous of his wife. He was not one of those pretty men, and she was a beautiful thing, much younger than he was. I do not think that she ever did anything wrong, but he felt insecure. If she had to be around to keep up with the children, she had her hands full. There was much less danger of her wandering off. Cally was in his confidence. I am certain that he got full reports on his wife's goings and comings. He loved his wife dearly, and he was afraid his miracle might fade. She had told me herself that she had married at seventeen. She was certainly a lovely, soft-looking thing. She never wore the things people didn't want to look at, and she did wear things you always wanted to see, and she had an easy kind of sweet smell. A lot of men would have taken over the job of worrying with her at the drop of a hat.

Well, then, I didn't have a job any more. I didn't have money either, but I had bought a pair of shoes.

But I was lucky in a way. Somebody told the woman I was staying with about another job, so I went to see about it, and the lady took me. She was sick in the bed, and she had a little girl three years old, but this child did not shine like Helen and Genevieve. She was sort of old-looking in the face.

I didn't like that house. It frowned at me just as soon as I crossed the door-sill. It was a big house with plenty of things in it but the rooms just sat across the hall from each other and made gloomy faces back and forth.

The sick lady was named Mrs. Moncrief, and she had two older sisters who had never been married, and they gloomed. The cook was an old family relic on the female side and she was out of the habit of smiling, too.

Mr. Moncrief used to laugh, but not around the house, and it was no good laugh when he did it. The reason I knew was, about a week after I joined up, he took to waylaying me down the street a piece and walking with me. It made me feel very uncomfortable for him to do that. I didn't see what he wanted to do it for anyway. It was not long before he told me he was sick and tired of that house full of sour-looking women. He was sick of the town and everything in it. He was selling out his business and going away. He would take me to Canada with him if I wanted to go, and if I had any sense I would jump at the chance.

I kept telling him I didn't want to go. I did want to go some place else, but not with him. It sounded grand if he would just pay my way up there and he go some place else. His belly laid all over his belt, and he was so chuckle-headed that you couldn't see his collar. But he didn't seem to have but one ear, and it couldn't hear a thing but 'yes'.

So every morning, I hated to go back to that house, but I hated more to go home at night.

Finally, I got over being timid of his being the boss and just told him not to bother me. He laughed at that. Then I said that I would tell his wife, and he laughed again. The very next night he was waiting for me.

So I went in and told his wife to make him stop waylaying me. I did not tell her about Canada. I needn't worry about that. I just wanted him to stop making me feel shame by walking along with me. People might talk.

Right then I learned a lesson to carry with me through life. I'll never tell another wife. She laid there a long time and said nothing, then she tried to smile as if it were a joke that was mildly funny. Then she began to cry without moving anything in her face. It was terrible to look at, and I wanted to run out of there and hide and never let anybody see me again. But it was hard to move my feet. So I began to cry, too. She shook her head and said, "You have nothing to cry about, Zora. You haven't been lying here for three years with somebody hoping to find you dead every morning. You don't know what it means for every girl who comes in hailing distance to be mixed up in your life. You don't know what it means to give birth to a child for your husband and find that your health is gone the day the baby is born and for him not to care what becomes of the baby or you either. God! Why couldn't he leave *you* alone?"

I saw her fumbling for the glass of water on the bed-table, so I handed it to her and ran out of the house. I felt lower than sea-bottom. I ran off so that I could cry alone. I never meant to foot that house again, nor to see anybody who lived in it.

But the next day around nine o'clock he drove up to where I lived.

"So you told on me, did you?" He opened right up and I thought that he was going to kill me then and there.

"I told you if you didn't leave me alone I was going to tell," I quavered.

"Oh, that is all right, girlie. She's not my boss. She hasn't a thing to do with our business. It's you and me going to Canada, not that old maid I married by mistake. When can you be ready?"

That was too much. He was not even listening to what I had to say. I gave up and told him I could be ready on Saturday.

"That's three days off," he objected. "You can't have all that getting-ready to do. How about tomorrow night?"

"Well, all right, tomorrow night," I lied.

"Meet me at the station. You don't need your clothes. I'll buy you something decent to wear on the way. Just be there. Nope, you better stay here. I'll come get you. Don't you fool me, now. Just be there. I'm not the kind of a man that stands for no fooling. I'm not the kind of man to be worried with so much responsibilities. Never should have let myself get married in the first place. All I need is a young, full-of-feelings girl to sleep with and enjoy life. I always did keep me a colored girl. My last one moved off to Chicago and sort of left me without. I want a colored girl and I'm giving you the preference."

He went on down the steps and I ran inside to pack up my few things. In an hour I had moved. He came for me the next night, I was told, and tried to search the house to see if the landlady had tried to block him by telling a lie. He could not conceive of my not wanting to go with him.

Two weeks later it was in the papers that he had taken all of his own money that he could get his hands on and some other people's money, and had vanished. Nobody seemed to know which way he went. The Black Dispatch (Negro grapevine) reported that the colored office girl of a well-known white doctor had gone with him.

I never tried to give any information. I felt that my big mouth had worked overtime as it was. I never even went back to get my pay.

I was out of a job again. I got out of many more. Sometimes I didn't suit the people. Sometimes the people didn't suit me. Sometimes my insides tortured me so that I was restless and unstable. I just was not the type. I was doing none of the things I wanted to do. I had to do numerous uninteresting things I did not want to do, and it was tearing me to pieces.

I wanted family love and peace and a resting place. I wanted books and school. When I saw more fortunate people of my own age on their way to and from school, I would cry inside and be depressed for days, until I learned how to mash down on my feelings and numb them for a spell. I felt crowded in on, and hope was beginning to waver.

The third vision of aimless wandering was on me as I had seen it. My brother Dick had married and sent for me to come to Sanford and stay with him. I got hopeful for school again. He sent me a ticket, and I went. I didn't want to go, though. As soon as I got back to Sanford, my father ordered me to stay at his house.

It was no more than a month after I got there before my stepmother and I had our fight.

I found my father a changed person. The bounce was gone from the man. The wreck of his home and the public reaction to it was telling on him. In spite of all, I was sorry for him and that added to my resentment towards his wife.

In all fairness to her, she probably did the best she could, according to her lights. It was just tragic that her light was so poor. A little more sense would have told her that the time and manner of her marriage to my father had killed any hope of success from the start. No warning bell inside of her caused her to question the wisdom of an arrangement made over so many fundamental stumbling stones. My father certainly could not see the consequences, for he had never had to consider them too seriously. Mama had always been there to do that. Suddenly he must have realized with inward terror that Lucy was not there any more. This was not just another escapade which Mama would maul his knit for in private and smooth out publicly. It had rushed him along to where he did not want to go already and the end was not in sight. This new wife had wormed her way out of her little crack in the world to become what looked to her like a great lady, and the big river was too much for her craft. Instead of the world dipping the knee to the new-made Mrs. Reverend, they were spitting on her intentions and calling her a storm-buzzard. Certainly if my father had not built up a strong following years before, he could not have lasted three months. As it was, his foundations rotted from under him, and seven years saw him wrecked. He did not defend her and establish her. It might have been because he was not the kind of a man who could live without his friends, and his old friends, male and female, were the very ones who were leading the attack to disestablish her. Then, too, a certain amount of the prestige every wife enjoys arises out of where the man got her from and how. She lacked the comfort of these bulwarks too. She must have decided that if she could destroy his children she would be safe, but the opposite course would have been the only extenuating circumstance in the eyes of the public. The failure of the project would have been obvious in a few months or even weeks if Papa had been the kind of man to meet the conflict with courage. As it was, the misery of the situation continued for years. He was dragging around like a stepped-on worm. My brief appearance on the scene acted like a catalyzer. A few more months and the thing fell to pieces for good.

I could not bear the air for miles around. It was too personal and pressing, and humid with memories of what used to be.

So I went off to another town to find work. It was the same as at home so far as the dreariness and lack of hope and blunted impulses were concerned. But one thing did happen that lifted me up. In a pile of rubbish I found a copy of Milton's complete works. The back was gone and the book was yellowed. But it was all there. So I read *Paradise Lost* and luxuriated in Milton's syllables and rhythms without ever having heard that Milton was one of the greatest poets of the world. I read it because I liked it.

I worked through the whole volume and then I put it among my things. When I was supposed to be looking for work, I would be stretched out somewhere in the woods reading slowly so that I could understand the words. Some of them I did not. But I had read so many books that my reading vocabulary at least was not too meager.

A young woman who wanted to go off on a trip asked me to hold down her job for two months. She worked in a doctor's office and all I had to do was to answer the telephone and do around a little.

The doctor thought that I would not be suitable at first, but he had to have somebody right away so he took a deep breath and said he'd try me. We got along just very well indeed after the first day. I became so interested and useful that he said if his old girl did not come back when she promised, he was going to see to it that I was trained for a practical nurse when I was a bit older.

But just at that time I received a letter from Bob, my oldest brother. He had just graduated from Medicine and said that he wanted to help me to go to school. He was sending for me to come to him right away. His wife sent love. He knew that I was going to love his children. He had married in his Freshman year in college and had three of them.

Nothing can describe my joy. I was going to have a home again. I was going to school. I was going to be with my brother! He had remembered me at last. My five haunted years were over!

I shall never forget the exaltation of my hurried packing. When I got on the train, I said goodbye — not to anybody in particular, but to the town, to loneliness, to defeat and frustration, to shabby living, to sterile houses and numbed pangs, to the kind of people I had no wish to know; to an era. I waved it goodbye and sank back into the cushions of the seat.

It was near night. I shall never forget how the red ball of the sun hung on the horizon and raced along with the train for a short space, and then plunged below the belly-band of the earth. There have been other suns that set in significance for me, but *that* sun! It was a book-mark in the pages of a life. I remember the long, strung-out cloud that measured it for the fall.

But I was due for more frustration. There was to be no school for me right away. I was needed around the house. My brother took me for a walk and explained to me that it would cause trouble if he put me in school at once. His wife would feel that he was pampering me. Just work along and be useful around the house and he would work things out in time.

This did not make me happy at all. I wanted to get through high school. I had a way of life inside me and I wanted it with a want that was twisting me. And now, it seemed I was just as far off as before. I was not even going to get paid for working this time, and no time off. But on the other hand, I was with my beloved brother, and the children were adorable! I was soon wrapped up in them head over heels.

It was get up early in the morning and make a fire in the kitchen range. Don't make too much noise and wake up my sister-in-law. I must remember that she was a mother and needed the rest. She had borne my brother's children and deserved the best that he could do for her, and so on. It didn't sound just right. I was not the father of those children, and several months later I found out what was wrong. It came to me in a flash. She had never borne a child for me, so I did not owe her a thing. Maybe somebody did, but it certainly wasn't I. My brother was acting as if I were the father of those children, instead of himself. There was much more, but my brother is dead and I do not wish to even risk being unjust to his memory, or unkind to the living. My sister-in-law is one of the most devoted mothers in the world. She was brave and loyal to my brother when it took courage to be that way. After all she was married to him, not I.

But I made an unexpected friend. She was a white woman and poor. She had children of my own age. Her husband was an electrician. She began to take an interest in me and to put ideas in my head. I will not go so far as to say that I was poorly dressed, for that would be bragging. The best I can say is that I could not be arrested for indecent exposure. I remember wanting gloves. I had never had a pair, and one of my friends told me that I ought to have on gloves when I went anywhere. I could not have them and I was most unhappy. But then, I was not in a position to buy a handkerchief.

This friend slipped me a message one day to come to her house. We had a code. Her son would pass and whistle until I showed myself to let him know I heard. Then he would go on and as soon as I could I would follow. This particular day, she told me that she had a job for me. I was delighted beyond words.

"It's a swell job if you can get it, Zora. I think you can. I told my husband to do all he can, and he thinks he's got it hemmed up for you."

"Oooh! What is it?"

"It is a lady's maid job. She is a singer down at the theater where he is electrician. She brought a maid with her from up north, but the maid met up with a lot of colored people and looks like she's going to get married right off. She don't want the job no more. The lady asked the men around the theater to get her somebody, and my husband thought about you and I told him to tell the rest of the men he had just the right girl for a maid. It seems like she is a mighty nice person."

I was too excited to sit still. I was frightened too, because I did not know the first thing about being a lady's maid. All I hoped was that the lady would overlook that part and give me a chance to catch on.

"You got to look nice for that. So I sent Valena down to buy you a little dress." Valena was her daughter. "It's cheap, but it's neat and stylish. Go inside Valena's room and try it on."

The dress was of navy blue poplin with a box-pleated skirt and a little round, white collar. To my own self, I never did look so pretty before. I put on the dress, and Valena's dark blue felt hat with a rolled brim. She saw to it that I shined my shoes, and then gave me car-fare and sent me off with every bit of advice she could think of.

My feet mounted up the golden stairs as I entered the stage door of that theater. The sounds, the smells, the back-stage jumble of things were all things to bear me up into a sweeter atmosphere. I felt like dancing towards the dressing room when it was pointed out to me. But my friend was walking with me, coaching me how to act, and I had to be as quiet and sober as could be.

The matinee performance of *H.M.S. Pinafore* was on, so I was told to wait. In a little while a tenor and a soprano voice quit singing a duet and a beautiful blonde girl of about twenty-two came hurrying into the dressing room. I waited until she went inside and closed the door, then I knocked and was told to come in.

She looked at me and smiled so hard till she almost laughed.

"Hello, little girl," she chanted. "Where did you come from?"

"Home. I come to see you."

"Oh, you did? That's fine. What did you come to see me about?"

"I come to work for you."

"Work for me?" She threw back her head and laughed. That frightened me a great deal. Maybe it was all a joke and there was no job after all. "Doing what?" she carolled on.

"Be your lady's maid."

"You? Why, how old are you?"

"Twenty," I said, and tried to look serious as I had been told. But she laughed so hard at that, till I forgot and laughed too.

"Oh, no, you are not twenty." She laughed some more, but it was not scornful laughter. Just bubbling fun.

"Well, eighteen, then," I compromised.

"No, not eighteen, either."

"Well, then, how about sixteen?"

She laughed at that. Instead of frowning in a sedate way as I had been told, here I was laughing like a fool myself.

"I don't believe you are sixteen, but I'll let it go at that," she said.

"Next birthday. Honest."

"It's all right; you're hired. But let's don't bring this age business up again. I think I'm going to like you. What is your name?"

I told her, fearing all the time she was going to ask questions about my family; but she didn't.

"Well, Zora, I pay ten dollars a week and expenses. You think that will do?"

I almost fell over. Ten dollars each and every week! Was there that much money in the world sure enough? Compress-ti-bility!! It wouldn't take long for me to own a bank at that rate.

"Yes, ma'am!" I shouted.

"Well, change my shoes for me."

She stuck out her foot, and pointed at the pair she wanted to put on. I got them on with her tickling me in the back. She showed me a white dress she wanted to change into and I jumped to get it and hook it up. She touched up her face laughing at me in the mirror and dashed out. I was crazy about her right then. I washed out her shoelaces from a pair of white shoes and her stockings, which were on the back of a chair and wrung them out in a bath towel for quick drying, and sat down before the mirror to look at myself. It was truly wonderful!

So I had to examine all the curious cosmetics on the table. I was sort of trying them out when she came in.

That night, she let me stand in the wings and hear her sing her duet with the tenor, "Farewell, my own! Light of my life, farewell!" It was so beautiful to me that she seemed more than human. Everything was pleasing and exciting. If there was any more to Heaven than this, I didn't want to see it.

I did not go back home, that is to my brother's house, at all. I was afraid he would try to keep me. I slept on a cot in the room with Valena. She was almost as excited as I was, had come down to see me every night and had met the cast. We were important people, she and I. Her mother had to make us shut up talking and go to sleep every night.

The end of the enchanted week came and the company was to move on. Miss M—— whom I was serving asked me about my clothes and luggage. She told me not to come down to the train with an old dilapidated suitcase for that would make her ashamed. So the upshot of it was that she advanced me the money to buy one, and then paid me for the week. I paid my friend the six dollars which she had spent for my new dress. Valena gave me the hat, an extra pair of panties and stockings. I bought a comb and brush and tooth brush, paste, and two handkerchiefs. Miss M—— did not know when I came down to the station that morning that my new suitcase was stuffed with newspapers to keep my things from rattling.

The company, a Gilbert and Sullivan repertoire, had its own coach. That was another glory to dazzle my eyes. The leading man had a valet, and the contralto had an English maid, both white. I was the only Negro around. But that did not worry me in the least. I had no chance to be lonesome, because the company welcomed me like, or as, a new play-pretty. It did not strike me as curious then. I never even thought about it. Now, I can see the reason for it.

In the first place, I was a Southerner, and had the map of Dixie on my tongue. They were all northerners except the orchestra leader, who came from Pensacola. It was not that my grammar was bad, it was the idioms. They did not know of the way an average southern child, white and black, is raised on simile and invective. They know how to call names. It is an every day affair to hear somebody called a mullet-headed, mule-eared, wall-eyed, hog-nosed, gator-faced, shad-mouthed, screw-necked, goat-bellied, puzzle-gutted, camel-backed, butt-sprung, battle-hammed, knock-kneed, razor-legged, box-ankled, shovel-footed, unmated so and so! Eyes looking like skint-ginny nuts, and mouth looking like a dish-pan full of broke-up crockery! They can tell you in simile exactly how you walk and smell. They can furnish a picture gallery of your ancestors, and a notion of what your children will be like. What ought to happen to you is full of images and flavor. Since that stratum of the southern population is not given to book-reading, they take their comparisons right out of the barn yard and the woods. When they get through with you, you and your whole family look like an acre of totem-poles.

First thing, I was young and green, so the baritone started out teasing me the first day. He waylaid me down the coach aisle away from Miss M—— and told me I looked like a nice girl and he wanted to help me out. He was going to tell me just how to get along. I was very glad and thanked him. He told me to sit down by him and let him give me a few point-ers. I did and he asked me a few very ordinary questions about where I was born and so on. Very sober-faced. All of a sudden he yelled so the whole coach could hear him. "Porter! A flock of hand towels and a seven o'clock call!"

Nearly everybody burst out laughing. I couldn't see what for. I knew the joke was on me somehow, but I didn't know what it was. I sat there blank-faced and that made them laugh more. Miss M—— did not laugh. She called me and told me to sit down by her and not to listen to dirty cracks. Finally she let me know what the joke was. Then I jumped up and told that man to stop trying to run the hog over me! That set everybody off again. They teased me all the time just to hear me talk. But there was no malice in it. If I got mad and spoke my piece, they liked it even better. I was stuffed with ice cream sodas and coca-cola.

Another reason was that it was fun to them to get hold of somebody whom they could shock. I was hurt to my heart because the company manager called me into his dressing room and asked me how I liked my job. After I got through telling him how pleased I was, he rushed out with his face half-made up screaming, "Stop, oh, Zora! Please stop! Shame on you! Telling me a dirty story like that. Oh! I have never been so shocked in all my life!"

Heads popped out of dressing-rooms all over. Groans, sad head-shakings and murmurs of outrage. Sad! Sad! They were glad I had not told them such a thing. Too bad! Too bad! Not a smile in the crowd. The more I tried to explain the worse it got. Some locked their doors to shield their ears from such contamination. Finally Miss M—— broke down and laughed and told me what the gag was. For a long while nobody could get me inside a dressing room outside of Miss M——'s. But that didn't stop the teasing. They would think up more, like having one of the men contrive to walk down the aisle with me and then everybody lift shocked eyebrows, pretend to blush and wink at each other, and sigh, "Zora! Zora! What would your mother say?" I would be so upset that I wouldn't know what to do. Maybe they really believed I wasn't nice!

Another sly trick they played on my ignorance was that some of the men would call me and with a very serious face send me to some of the girls to ask about the welfare and condition of cherries and spangles. They would give me a tip and tell me to hurry back with the answer. Some of the girls would send back word that the men need not worry their heads at all. They would never know the first thing about the condition of their cherries and spangles. Some of the girls sent answers full of double talk which went over my head. The soubrette spoke her mind to the men about that practice and it stopped.

But none of this had malice in it. Just their idea of good backstage gags. By the time they stopped, it seemed that I was necessary to everybody. I was continually stuffed with sweets, nut meats, and soft-drinks. I was welcome in everybody's coach seat and the girls used to pitch pennies to see who carried me off to their hotel rooms. We played games and told stories. They often ordered beer and pretzels, but nobody offered me a drink. I heard all about their love affairs and troubles. They were all looking forward to playing or singing leads some day. Some great personage had raved about all of their performances. The dirty producers and casting directors just hadn't given them their chance. Miss M—— finally put a stop to my going off with the others as soon as she was ready for bed. I had to stay wherever she stayed after that. She had her own affairs to talk about.

She paid for a course for me in manicuring and I practiced on everybody until I became very efficient at it. That course came in handy to me later on.

With all this petting, I became as cocky as a sparrow on Fifth Avenue. I got a scrap book, and everybody gave me a picture to put in it. I pasted each one on a separate page and wrote comments under each picture. This created a great deal of interest, because some of the comments were quite pert. They egged me on to elaborate. Then I got another idea. I would comment on daily doings and post the sheets on the call-board. This took on right away. The result stayed strictly mine less than a week because members of the cast began to call me aside and tell me things to put in about others. It got to be so general that everybody was writing it. It was just my handwriting, mostly. Then it got beyond that. Most of the cast ceased to wait for me. They would take a pencil to the board and set down their own item. Answers to the wisecracks would appear promptly, and often cause uproarious laughter. They always started off with either "Zora says" or "The observant reporter of the call-board asserts"—Lord, Zora said more *things!* I was continually astonished, but always amused. There were, of course, some sly digs at sup- posedly secret love affairs at times, but no vicious thrusts. Everybody enjoyed it, even the victims. This hilarious game came to a sudden end. The company manager had been a member of the cast. One day he received a telegram offering him a fat part in a Broadway show, and of course, he left us. So a new manager was sent on from New York.

Somehow, he struck everybody wrong from the start. The baritone who was always quick on the draw said he looked like he had been soaked in greasy dish-water and had not been wiped off. Even Miss M—— who seldom "cracked"— said he reminded her of the left-overs from the stock yards. His trousers sagged at the knees, so I named him Old Bustle- Knees. His name was Smith, but he became known on the quiet as "B.K."

He was on the make, you could see that the moment he landed, and you had to give him credit for ambition. He gave Miss M—— the first chance to be his love life for the dura- tion. She snooted him as if he were actually a slaughter-house by-product. He kept on down the line until he did actually land a lady of the ensemble who had visions of becoming a lead if not actually a star. It hurt everybody, Helen's defec- tion, for she had been very popular. It must have hurt her too, because she used to come in and leave the theater at his heels with her eyes away from everybody, usually leading "B.K.'s" fox terrier on a leash. That was her symbol of office.

But having gained a heart interest did not seem to satisfy him. He took a bitter hatred of Miss M—— to his heart to nurse. He pulled every nasty, annoying trick on her that he could think of to humiliate her.

Therefore, it was decided to give him an entire issue of the call-board. The name of Smith was not in the publication but Bustle-Knees was, and no punches were pulled. It took nearly all night and half of the next day to rub it up until it glittered. Everybody had a hand in it except our lost Helen, the fox terrier and Smith. Some stage hands even put in their nickel's worth. By the time we got through, he looked like a forest full of primitive demon masks with a pacing gait.

When he read it, he was as hot as seven hells with West Hell and Ginny Gall thrown in. It was all in my handwriting, so he couldn't fire anybody. But he could and did forbid any papers to appear on the call-board again. Nothing but official notices. He told Miss M—— that I had to be fired, but she refused him flat even after he said he knew I had named him Bustle-Knees. So we knew that Helen had told him that. He had that name before she had gone over to him.

But our suffering did not last more than six weeks. He had the temerity to juggle the box-office reports to his own profit and got fired. The last I saw of him was one night after the stage was struck. There was a single bare bulb as if for rehearsal on stage and he was standing by it, his hands shoved far down in his overcoat pockets looking like first one soggy thing and then another. Helen was off side standing very still in the shadows, shifting the dog's leash from hand to hand. The next day, we were enjoying his space more than we ever had his company. Helen went to bed with a sick stomach.

Not long after that, the run came to an end. Miss M—— had a part in another show all set, but rehearsals would not start for two weeks, so she took me to her home in Boston and I found out some things which I did not want to know, particularly.

At times she had been as playful as a kitten. At others, she would be solemn and moody. She loved her mother excessively, but when she received those long, wordy letters from her, she read them with a still face, and tore them up carefully. Then she would be gloomy, and keep me beside her every minute. Sometimes she would become excessively playful. It was puzzling to see a person cry a while and then commence to romp like a puppy and keep it up for hours. Sometimes she had to have sherry before she went to bed after a hard romp with me. She invented a game for us to play in our hotel room. It was known as "Jake." She would take rouge and paint her face all over a most startling red. Then I must take eye-shadow and paint myself blue. Blue Jake and Red Jake would then chase each other into closets, across beds, into bath rooms, with our sheet-robes trailing around us and tripping us up at odd moments. We crouched and growled and ambushed each other and laughed and yelled until we were exhausted.

Then maybe next day she hardly said a word.

Of course, the members of her family had been described to me often. Her mother had been married three times. There had been four children, by the first very early marriage, but only the oldest one, John, was alive. He was a man around forty now, and never had been married. He didn't work regularly, but was very jolly and obliging. Another brother, Charlie, about twelve years younger than Johnnie, was a city fireman in Boston. He had two children. He was a son of the second marriage. Miss M—— was eight years younger than Charlie, and had a different father.

When I got to their home in the outskirts of Boston, I saw that the old lady had made improvements as she went along. Johnnie, her first born, was homely. One thing struck me forcibly; his teeth had either not come out of his gums very far, or they had been sawed off. Charlie was a big, robust Irishman who was not very handsome, but not bad at all. He would do nicely. Miss M—— was a startling blonde beauty, no less. She was doing rather well as a singer, Charlie was getting on in the Fire Department, and their older brother was just named Johnnie.

This Johnnie started in to tease me right away. His niece, Mary, Charlie's daughter, was staying with her grandmother when we arrived, and Johnnie took more pleasure in teasing Mary and me than in anything else. He just could not leave us alone. Whenever he got me separated from Mary, Miss M—— or her mother would soon show up and call me away—in a subtle way, of course, but it always happened. He could tell such funny Irish jokes that I liked to be around him.

One day he played a terrible joke on me. I washed all of my clothes and hung them out to dry, and went on back upstairs to play checkers with Mary. The house stood on a corner with a generous yard all around it. The corner was very noisy because two main street-car lines crossed there and it was a transfer point. About two hours after I had hung up my clothes, Mary and I became conscious of an unusual rumble of voices outside. We thought there had been an accident, so we rushed to the window to see.

I was petrified with horror and shame. I had three pairs of panties out on the line, and now, there was a little bunch of dandelions stuck in the clothes pins holding each pair of my panties. Men and women, but men particularly were hanging over the fence and laughing and joking. I knew right off that that was Johnnie's work. Miss M—— was gone into town on a shopping trip, so I ran downstairs crying to tell her mother about it. Being Irish, she told me not to mind Johnnie; to go out there and take them down. Unconscious of the trap, I rushed out of the kitchen door towards the line. Then the full horror struck me. In addition to the dandelions in the clothespins there was a jaunty little nosegay of them pinned on one leg of a pair! Seeing me approach the line, the crowd snickered louder. I was covered with confusion and ran back inside followed by guffaws. I told Mrs. M—— that I was not going to take down those clothes. Johnnie was sitting by the kitchen table at the window, and where he could take it all in. When I said I wouldn't take the clothes down, he got up and said, "Stop crying, Zora. I'll go take them down for you." That pacified me. He went outside and the noise turned into a riot. I looked out of the window, and Johnnie had the pair with the bouquet on it, holding it up in his hands and examining it from all angles, turning it slowly for the benefit of his audience. He felt it all over, as if somebody had them on, and kept on fooling like that until traffic was nearly tied up. I was inside throwing conniptions until his mother reminded me through her chuckles that nobody would know my panties from anybody else's. Those people out there did not know I was living. That was a good point, so I went on back upstairs, but I was mad with Johnnie for hours.

But he was so nice and jolly the next morning that I got over it. He led me into the deep corner of the yard to show me the lilacs in bloom. He talked on awhile and asked me to loan him two dollars. He had to go and see about a job for the next day, he said. He would make six dollars at it, and pay me back the next night. I ran upstairs and got the money for him. He thanked me, but told me not to tell. I promised and went back inside.

Johnnie fooled around the house for perhaps an hour and went off. Noontime came and he was not back. Miss M—— and her mother looked worried at each other but did not say too much about it. We had supper about six o'clock and he still was not back. Neither of them ate anything this time. They looked at each other and looked more than worried. They were scared. They hustled Mary and me upstairs as soon as possible. They stayed down in the kitchen and mumbled and mumbled. After another hour or so, Miss M—— called me down and asked me, with her hands trembling, if I had loaned Johnnie any money. I hesitated. I had promised not to tell. She pressed me, and seeing that there was something important about it, I told her about the two dollars. She called her mother weakly and collapsed in a chair. When her mother found out she crumpled up and had to be put to bed. The outwardly gay house had turned into a spectral place because I had loaned Johnnie two dollars. I couldn't see why. A message was hurriedly sent to Charlie and around ten o'clock, he arrived and the mumbling went on downstairs. Finally he decided to spend the night and stretched out on the couch in the living room.

About midnight, I heard a terrible scream from Mrs. M——'s room. She slept on the first floor on account of her knee. She said it was rheumatism from scrubbing too many floors.

Mary, Miss M—— and I all bolted for the head of the stairs at the same time. Another scream, "Ooh, Johnnie!" from an old, anguished throat.

Scuffling, bustling, short, angry sounds from Charlie. Running steps across the wide porch that all but surrounded the house. Down the walk to the street and away.

We rushed into Mrs. M——'s room. She was lying in bed, her face contorted in pain, and holding one shoulder with her hand. Tears were seeping from her eyes. The window onto the porch was open and Charlie was not present in the house.

"Mama! Mama!" Miss M—— screamed. "What happened?"

The old woman kept her eyes closed, and kept her hand on her shoulder. We waited, but she sobbed on with her lips pursed together.

Miss M—— began to fuss around the head of the bed to make her mother more comfortable. Finally she lifted the hand clutching the shoulder and revealed a great bluish-red bruise on the point of the shoulder, and began to cry herself.

"Oh, Mama! How did you get hurt like that? Zora, you and Mary get me some hot water and witch hazel! Oh, Mama!"

There was a trudgy scuffling on the porch, and Charlie came in the door dragging Johnnie. Charlie had a length of iron pipe in his hand and his face was something terrible to look at. Miss M—— took it all in for a long moment and without raising her voice, she asked, "Why did you do it, Johnnie? Why?"

"Why do you waste your time asking this unfortunate brute such a question?" Charlie asked Miss M——. "His crazy brain told him to do it. He's had liquor, and he went where it sent him. I have begged and begged Mama to put him back where he can't do any harm, but she won't listen to me. You heard me tonight begging her to let me call the police when he didn't come back. You begged her, but she wouldn't listen to either of us. I kept waiting for the phone to ring and say he had done something like this somewhere, but, but here—"

Johnnie stood there and never lifted his head. I felt terrible for having given him the money. But I realized too, that at that time I didn't have the faintest notion what could happen. Instead of trying to watch him so closely that it couldn't happen, they should have warned me. Charlie said as much a minute later, but his sister explained that her mother would not let her do it. Her mother had said that she would keep an eye on him.

Charlie took the clothes line and tied the passive Johnnie hand and foot in the kitchen, then came back and forced his mother to talk.

She said that she had not gone to sleep, really, lying there and worrying about her first born, when she heard the window near her bed being pushed up gently. At first, she was not sure, but as she turned over in bed, she could see the form of a man. She could see him stepping into the room. She was speechless with fright as the figure crept up to the head of the bed with the bludgeon half lifted. As the blow was about to descend, she knew from his breathing it was Johnnie. She tried to duck but the blow fell, luckily missing her head but landing on her shoulder. She screamed and Johnnie, seeing that he was not only recognized, but that the house was aroused, ran to the table at the foot of the bed and tried to pick up something there. But hearing the bustle overhead, and Charlie bursting in from the living room, he ran to the window and fled, with Charlie at his heels.

Charlie said that he had cornered him in a hedge at the other end of the block, still with the length of iron pipe in his hand. He had given up without a struggle and let himself be brought back.

It turned out that Johnnie had been after some very valuable art objects grouped on the table at the foot of the bed. They belonged to a rich Bostonian who was in Europe at the time. Mrs. M—— had once worked for her, and when she went abroad, she had left the priceless things there rather than at her house which might be burglarized. She did not dream that anyone would be tempted to burglarize the M—— home, so she had entrusted them to her former and trusted servant. No one except the family knew that they were there, and so Mrs. M—— had covered them over on the table and felt safe.

I learned that Johnnie had helped to kill a man in a robbery attempt when he was seventeen. He and his pal had done the thing but had been caught before the robbery was completed. The older boy was executed, but Johnnie's sentence was commuted to life because of his youth. He had remained in Charlestown prison for eighteen years. And no matter what the weather or the circumstances might be, his mother had never missed a visiting day, nor ever failed to take him something.

She was a widow a second time when he committed the murder. She was out in domestic service, but her love never flagged. Sometimes money was so scarce that she could not afford to pay transportation to Charlestown and take him something, too. When it got like that, she took him something and walked. Her passion was to free her son. She renewed her promise to him every time she saw him. This went on for seventeen years.

Then the man whose cook she had been for fifteen years, became governor of Massachusetts. He knew his cook's heart. So a few months after he was inaugurated, he opened the prison doors for Johnnie M——. He could not grant him a pardon because the crime had been too heinous. The best that he could do was to parole him in care of his faithful mother.

Her second son had finished high school and finally worked himself into the Fire Department; her daughter's beauty and her voice had gotten her a scholarship at the New England Conservatory of Music. They were on their way, and now, her eldest son was free again. All she had to do was to watch him and see to it that he got hold of no whiskey. Johnnie was good-natured and easy to manage as long as he was sober. But he became a savage, lusting to kill as soon as whiskey touched his brain. Kill to get more money to buy more whiskey to drive him to kill again. Those art objects represented not beauty to him, but money for whiskey and around the circle again. The fact that it was the woman who had borne him who was standing between him and the money which the treasure would bring meant nothing after he had taken a drink.

I went back upstairs that night while she still whimpered and begged Charles, "Don't call the police to take the poor, unfortunate thing back to prison. He told me time and time again that he would die if ever he was taken back, Charlie. It would be murder, Charlie. Charlie, please don't do a thing like that."

Charles pointed out that while Johnnie *was* a poor unfortunate, he was too dangerous to be at large. Even if he did not later kill his own mother, the family would be responsible if the animal killed somebody else. It was too awful to think about. Perhaps it would be the kindest thing to let him die in prison. His mother had to give up her job just to sit around and watch Johnnie. He, Charlie, had to deny his wife and children things to take care of his mother and brother. His sister, with her lovely voice had to cut her training short to make money to help support them. His mother was willing to risk the lives of innocent people and the futures of her two younger children for the sake of that inhuman wretch. And so on.

But the morning found her just as stubborn, and Charles went on back home. That afternoon a telegram came for Miss M—— to report for rehearsal in Reading, Pa., and we left that night.

I never saw the house or Johnnie again, and Miss M—— never mentioned him to me again. But from then on I knew what was haunting her face; why she had been putting off marriage with her sweetheart.

About four months later, she met a wealthy business man of Newark, and I could tell that she was sunk. It all happened very suddenly, but gloriously. She told me that now that she was going to be married and leave the stage, she did not want me to work for any one else in the business. In fact, she thought that I should not be working at all. I ought to be in school. She said she thought I had a mind, and that it would be a shame for me not to have any further training. She wished that she herself could go abroad to study, but that was definitely out of the question, now. The deep reservoir of things inside her gave off a sigh.

We were in northern Virginia then, and moving towards Baltimore. When we got there, she inquired about schools, gave me a big bearful hug, and what little money she could spare and told me to keep in touch with her. She would do whatever she could to help me out.

That was the way we parted. I had been with her for eighteen months and though neither of us realized it, I had been in school all that time. I had loosened up in every joint and expanded in every direction.

I had done some reading. Not as much as before, but more discriminate reading. The tenor was a Harvard man who had travelled on the Continent. He always had books along with him, and offered them to me more and more. The first time I asked to borrow one, he looked at me in a way that said "What for?" But when he found that I really read it and enjoyed it, he relaxed and began to hand them to me gruffly. He never acted as if he liked it, but I knew better. That was just the Harvard in him.

Then there was the music side. They broke me in to good music, that is, the classics, if you want to put it that way.

There was no conscious attempt to do this. Just from being around, I became familiar with Gilbert and Sullivan, and the best parts of the light opera field. Grand opera too, for all of the leads had backgrounds of private classical instruction as well as conservatory training. Even the bit performers and the chorus had some kind of formal training in voice, and most of them played the piano. It was not unusual for some of the principals to drop down at the piano after a matinee performance and begin to sing arias from grand opera. Sing them with a wistfulness. The arias which they would sing at the Metropolitan or La Scala as they had once hoped actively, and still hoped passively even as the hair got thinner and the hips got heavier. Others, dressed for the street, would drift over and ease into the singing. Thus I would hear solos, duets, quartets and sextets from the best known operas. They would eagerly explain to me what they were when I asked. They would go on to say how Caruso, Farrar, Mary Garden, Trentini, Schumann-Heink, Matzenauer and so forth had interpreted this or that piece, and demonstrate it by singing. Perhaps that was their trouble. They were not originators, but followers of originators. Anyway, it was perfectly glorious for me, though I am sure nobody thought of it that way. I just happened to be there while they released their inside dreams.

I can see now how capable these people were, who were taking light opera to the sticks. For instance, the opening night in Lancaster, Pa., was so riotous that the house manager came backstage and said it was certain to be held over. The company decided on the off-chance to prepare *The Chocolate Soldier* for the new week. When the curtain went up the next Monday night, a very smooth performance of the "Soldier" was unveiled to the public. They did the same thing with *The Firefly* in Bridgeport, Connecticut, later on. It was very beautiful, but tough on me. I got so sick of holding "sides" and feeding cues that I was ready to throw an acre of fits. But it did teach me the lesson that you can do what you have to do. Like that tree-climbing rabbit of Uncle Remus, who was "just 'bluged to clam dat tree." A hound was on his tail and he had to do the impossible and he did it.

More than that, I saw thirty-odd people made up of all classes and races living a communal life. There were little touches of professional jealously and a catty crack now and then, but let sickness or trouble touch any member and the whole cast rallied around to help out. It was a marvelous thing to see. There were a few there from good families and well-to-do homes who slept in shabby hotels and made meals on sandwiches without a murmur. From what they said and did, you would think they were as poor as the rest.

With all branches of Anglo-Saxon, Irish, three Jews and one Negro together in a huddle, and all friendly, there were a lot of racial gags. Everybody was so sure that nobody hesitated to pull them. It was all taken in good part. Naturally, all of the Negro gags were pulled on me. There were enough of the others to divide things up. For instance, one night, Miss M—— cut her eyes in my direction slyly, began to talk about blondes, brunettes and burnt-ettes. They gagged me so much before overture was called that it made Miss M—— go out there and cut a hog. In her long recitative in the first act of *Pinafore* where the heroine mulls over what she is leaving in her father's house and what she is going to in marrying the poor hero, she mentions dirty children crying and dingy clothes a "drying." That night she frightened herself nearly to death by chanting in full rich tones about "dingy children crying." The audience, no doubt, began to wonder what kind of a marriage it was she was contemplating. But the whole experience on that job gave me an approach to racial understanding. It was easy to keep on feeling that way. Furthermore, it discouraged any sensitiveness on my part, so that I am still not conscious of my race no matter where I may go. I found out too that you are bound to be jostled in the "crowded street of life." That in itself need not be dangerous unless you have the open razors of personal vanity in your pants pocket. The passers-by don't hurt you, but if you go around like that, they make you hurt yourself.

The experience had matured me in other ways. I had seen, I had been privileged to see folks substituting love for failure of career. I would listen to one and another pour out their feelings sitting on a stool back stage between acts and scenes. Then too, I had seen careers filling up the empty holes left by love, and covering up the wreck of things internal. Those experiences, though vicarious, made me see things and think.

And now, at last it was all over. It was not at all clear to me how I was going to do it, but I was going back to school.

One minute I felt brave and fine about it all. The wish to be back in school had never left me. But alone by myself and feeling it over, I was scared. Before this job I had been lonely; I had been bare and bony of comfort and love. Working with these people I had been sitting by a warm fire for a year and a half and gotten used to the feel of peace. Now, I was to take up my pilgrim's stick and go outside again. Maybe it would be different now. Seven of my unhappy visions had passed me and bowed. The seventh one, the house that needed paint, that had threatened me with so much suffering that I used to sit up in bed sodden with agony, had passed. I had fled from it to put on the blue poplin dress. At least that was not before me any more. I took a firm grip on the only weapon I had—hope, and set my feet. Maybe everything would be all right from now on. Maybe. Well, I put on my shoes and I started.

IX

School Again

BACK, out walking on fly-paper again. Money was what I needed to get back in school. I could have saved a lot of money if I had received it. But theatrical salaries being so uncertain, I did not get mine half the time. I had it when I had it, but when it was not paid I never worried. But now I needed it. Miss M—— was having her troubles, trying to help her folks she informed me by mail, so I never directly asked her for anything more. I had no resentment, either. It had all been very pleasant.

I tried waiting on table, and made a good waitress when my mind was on it, which was not often. I resented being patronized, more than the monotony of the job; those presumptuous cut-eye looks and supposed-to-be accidental touches on the thigh to see how I took to things. Men at the old game of "stealing a feel." People who paid for a quarter meal, left me a nickel tip, and then stood outside the door and nodded their heads for me to follow on and hear the rest of the story. But I was lacking in curiosity. I was not worrying so much about virtue. The thing just did not call me. There was neither the beauty of love, nor material advantage in it for me. After all, what is the use in having swine without pearls? Some educated men sat and talked about the things I was interested in, but if I seemed to listen, looked at me as much to say, "What would that mean to you?"

Then in the midst of other difficulties, I had to get sick. Not a sensible sickness for poor folks to have. No, I must get down with appendicitis and have to have an operation right away. So it was the free ward of the Maryland General Hospital for me.

When I was taken up to the amphitheatre for the operation I went up there placing a bet with God. I did not fear death. Nobody would miss me very much, and I had no treasures to leave behind me, so I would not go out of life looking backwards on that account. But I bet God that if I lived, I would try to find out the vague directions whispered in my ears and find the road it seemed that I must follow. How? When? Why? What? All those answers were hidden from me.

So two o'clock that day when they dressed me for surgery and took me up there in that room with the northern light and many windows, I stepped out of the chair before the nurse could interfere, walked to a window and took a good look out over Baltimore and the world as far as I could see, resigned myself to fate and unaided, climbed upon the table, and breathed deeply when the ether cone was placed over my nose.

I scared the doctor and the nurses by not waking up until nine o'clock that night, but otherwise I was all right. I was alive, so I had to win my bet with God.

Soon, I had another waitress's job, trying to save money again, but I was only jumping up and down in my own foot-tracks.

I tried several other things but always I had that feeling that you have in a dream of trying to run, and sinking to your knees at every step in soft sticky mud. And this mud not only felt obscene to my feet, it smelled filthy to my nose. How to pull out?

How then did I get back to school? I just went. I got tired of trying to get the money to go. My clothes were practically gone. Nickeling and dimering along was not getting me anywhere. So I went to the night high school in Baltimore and that did something for my soul.

There I met the man who was to give me the key to certain things. In English, I was under Dwight O. W. Holmes. There is no more dynamic teacher anywhere under any skin. He radiates newness and nerve and says to your mind, "There is something wonderful to behold just ahead. Let's go see what it is." He is a pilgrim to the horizon. Anyway, that is the way he struck me. He made the way clear. Something about his face killed the drabness and discouragement in me. I felt that the thing could be done.

I turned in written work and answered questions like everybody else, but he took no notice of me particularly until one night in the study of English poets he read *Kubla Khan* by Samuel Taylor Coleridge. You must get him to read it for you sometime. He is not a pretty man, but he has the face of a scholar, not dry and set like, but fire flashes from his deep-set eyes. His high-bridged, but sort of bent nose over his thin-lipped mouth—well the whole thing reminds you of some old Roman like Cicero, Caesar or Virgil in tan skin.

That night, he liquefied the immortal grains of Coleridge, and let the fountain flow. I do not know whether something in my attitude attracted his attention, or whether what I had done previously made him direct the stream at me. Certainly every time he lifted his eyes from the page, he looked right into my eyes. It did not make me see him particularly, but it made me see the poem. That night seemed queer, but I am so visual-minded that all the other senses induce pictures in me. Listening to Samuel Taylor Coleridge's *Kubla Khan* for the first time, I saw all that the poet had meant for me to see with him, and infinite cosmic things besides. I was not of the work-a-day world for days after Mr. Holmes's voice had ceased.

This was my world, I said to myself, and I shall be in it, and surrounded by it, if it is the last thing I do on God's green dirt-ball.

But he did something more positive than that. He stopped me after class and complimented me on my work. He did something else. He never asked me anything about myself, but he looked at me and toned his voice in such a way that I felt he knew all about me. His whole manner said, "No matter about the difficulties past and present, step on it!"

I went back to class only twice after that. I did not say a word to him about my resolve. But the next week, I went out to Morgan College to register in the high school department.

William Pickens, a negro, was the Dean there, and he fooled me too. I was prepared to be all scared of him and his kind. I had no money and no family to refer to. I just went and he talked to me. He gave me a brief examination and gave me credit for two years' work in high school and assigned me to class. He was just as understanding as Dwight Holmes in a way.

Knowing that I had no money, he evidently spoke to his wife, because she sent for me a few days later and told me enthusiastically that she had a job for me that would enable me to stay in school. Dr. Baldwin, a white clergyman, and one of the trustees of Morgan, had a wife with a broken hip. He wanted a girl to stay at the house, help her dress in the morning, undress at night and generally look after her. There was no need for anyone except in the morning and at night. He would give me a home and two dollars a week. The way Mrs. Pickens described the work to me, I could tell she knew I would be glad to accept the job and I was.

So I went to live with the Baldwins. The family consisted of the Minister, his wife and his daughter, Miss Maria, who seemed to be in her thirties and unmarried.

They had a great library, and I waded in. I acted as if the books would run away. I remember committing to memory, Gray's *Elegy in a Country Churchyard* over night, lest I never get a chance to read it again. Next I learned the *Ballad of Reading Gaol* and started on the *Rubaiyat*.

It would be dramatic in a Cinderella way if I were to say that the well-dressed students at school snubbed me and shoved me around, but that I studied hard and triumphed over them. I did study hard because I realized that I was three years behind schedule, and then again study has never been hard to me. Then too, I had hundreds of books under my skin already. Not selected reading, all of it. Some of it could be called trashy. I had been through Nick Carter, Horatio Alger, Bertha M. Clay and the whole slew of dime novelists in addition to some really constructive reading. I do not regret the trash. It has harmed me in no way. It was a help, because acquiring the reading habit early is the important thing. Taste and natural development will take care of the rest later on.

Nobody shoved me around. There were eighteen people in my class. Six of them were boys. Good-looking, well-dressed girls from Baltimore's best Negro families were class-mates of mine. Ethel Cummings, the daughter of a very successful lawyer, Bernice Naylor, whose father was a big preacher, the Hughes girls, Bernice and Gwendolyn, who were not only beautiful, but whose family is distinguished in the professions all over America. Mary Jane Watkins of New York, now a dentist, and considered the most sex-appealing thing, with her lush figure and big eyes and soft skin, and all of the girls in my class passed for pretty. It was said to be, not only the best-looking class on the campus, college or prep, but the best-looking ever to happen together. You see, Rosa Brown, who was easily the most luscious piece of gal meat in all colored Baltimore was in that class too. She had not only lovely eyes set in a cameo-like face, but shining, beautiful black curls that fell easily to her waist. She has done well by herself, too. She is now married to Tanner Moore, a prosperous lawyer of Philadelphia. Town house, cars and country place, and things like that.

Well, here was this class of pretty girls and snappy boys. The girls were in the majority, but what we had of boys were in demand in town and on campus. The class knew it caused a lot of trouble too, as the college girls were always growling about "that prep class" grabbing off the college men. They passed a rule about it, but it did not help matters. They, the college girls, just got left out of things, themselves, while the prep girls romped on.

And here I was, with my face looking like it had been chopped out of a knot of pine wood with a hatchet on somebody's off day, sitting up in the middle of all this pretty. To make things worse, I had only one dress, a change of underwear and one pair of tan oxfords.

Therefore, I did not rush up to make friends, but neither did I shrink away. My second day at school, I had to blow my nose and I had no handkerchief with me. Mary Jane Watkins was sitting next to me, so she quickly shoved her handkerchief in my hand without saying a word. We were in chapel and Dr. Spencer was up speaking. So she kept her eyes front. I nodded my thanks and so began a friendship.

Bernice Hughes, whose father, Dr. W.A.C. Hughes, was somebody really important in the Methodist Episcopal Church, and a trustee of the College, sat watching me after about a week in school. Her grey eyes were fixed on me, and her red lips were puckered in a frown. I did not know what to think. But it was in English History which I liked very much and I was not doing badly in recitation. When the period was over and the class passed on to the next room, she fell in beside me and said, "If you ain't one knowing fool! I'm naming you old Knowledge Bug." Then she laughed that kind of a laugh she has to cover up her feelings and I laughed too.

Bernice can register something that makes you look at her and like her no matter what she does.

"I'm sitting by you tomorrow, fool, and from now on. You hear me?" She went on with her catching laugh. "No use in both of us studying like a fool. You can just study for both of us."

So from then on, I was knee deep in the Hughes family. There is more looks and native ability in the Hughes clan to the square child than any I can think of off hand. If they do not always make a brilliant showing, it is not because they can't do it. Their looks and charm interfere with their brainwork, that is all. And you are not going to forget them either. If a Hughes is in town, you are going to know it in one way or another.

It soon became apparent that my lack of clothes was no drawback to my getting along. Sometimes somebody would ask me, "Zora, what do you think you'll wear to school tomorrow?" I'd humor the joke and describe what I was going to wear. But let a program or a get-together come along, and all the girls in the class would be backing me off in a corner, or writing me notes offering to lend me something to wear. I would have to take it in rotation to keep from causing hard feelings.

I got on with the boys, too. In no time I made Stanley James, a varsity football man. Then it was Douglas Camper, a senior college man. His brother was a football star at Howard University in Washington. Our class had cornered all of the college seniors so that not one college girl was escorted to the senior prom. We just couldn't see how functions like that could go on without our gang. Mary Jane had cornered Ed Wilson, the Clark Gable of the campus, for the occasion, so the marines had landed.

Whenever Miss Clarke, our English teacher, was absent, I was put in charge of the class. This happened time and time again, sometimes for a whole week at a time. With history it was the same. Once I had the history classes for nearly a month and had to be excused from my other classes. At times like that, my classmates were perfectly respectful to me until the bell rang. Then how they would poke fun at my serious face while I was teaching!

With Dean Pickens to coach me, I placed second in the school oratorical contest. Rosa Brown placed first and Bernice Hughes third, indicating that our class was determined to be head muck-de-muck in everything that went on.

My first publication was on the blackboard in the assembly hall at Morgan. I decided to write an allegory using the faculty members as characters. Most of my classmates were in the know.

I went to school extra early that morning and when the bell rang for assembly, the big board was covered with the story. Dr. Spencer, the President of Morgan, had a great shock of curly white hair. He was the kindly "Great Gray Bear" of the story. Dean Pickens was the "Ferocious Pick." Practically every faculty member was up there, to the great entertainment of the student body. Furthermore, we could see the various members of the faculty sneaking peeps at the board over their shoulders from time to time as the service went on.

When Dr. Spencer rose to read from the Bible, his face was as red as a beet under all that white hair. He ran his fingers through his hair two or three times as he kept looking back at the board.

After the short service was over, he commented on it and actually burst out laughing. Then, of course, everybody else could laugh. All except one man who was there to succeed Dean Pickens, who was going to New York to work for the N.A.A.C.P. This man clouded up and tried to rain. He was up there in the character of "Pocket Tooth" and he didn't like it. He had earned that name because his two canine teeth were extra long, but sort of square at the ends. My class decided that they looked like the pockets on my dress. So far as we were concerned, he was Pocket Tooth, and he stayed Pocket Tooth for the duration. He led devotions next morning and dared everybody to write anything like that on that board again. Dean Pickens, for all his ferocious official frown and hot temper, was full of boy. Down in his apartment, Mrs. Pickens ran things, and he played with his three children. Ruby, the youngest, seemed to have the inside track with him. I was in and out of the Pickens home every day. I actually heard him discussing with Ruby her chances of licking Harriet, her older sister. She had tried it, and failed. Dean

Pickens was full of sympathy, but he told her he was afraid Harriet was too tough for her. She had better get even with Harriet some other way. If she felt she must fight, hit Harriet one quick lick and run. That was the best advice he could give her. Mrs. Pickens put down her book and looked at her husband just as she would have at Bill, her son.

My two years at Morgan went off very happily indeed. The atmosphere made me feel right. I was at last doing the things I wanted to do. Every new thing I learned in school made me happy. The science courses were tremendously interesting to me. Perhaps it was because Professor Calloway was such an earnest teacher. I did not do well in mathematics. Why should A minus B? Who the devil was X anyway? I could not even imagine. I still do not know. I passed the courses because Professor Johnson, knowing that I did well in everything else, just made it a rule to give me a C. He probably understood that I am one of those people who have no number sense. I have been told that you can never factor A−B to the place where it comes out even. I wouldn't know because I never tried to find out.

When it came time to consider college, I planned to stay on at Morgan. But that was changed by chance. Mae Miller, daughter of the well-known Dr. Kelly Miller of Howard University, came over to Morgan to spend the weekend with her first cousins, Bernice and Gwendolyn Hughes. So we were thrown together. After a few hours of fun and capers, she said, "Zora, you are Howard material. Why don't you come to Howard?"

Now as everyone knows, Howard University is the capstone of Negro education in the world. There gather Negro money, beauty, and prestige. It is to the Negro what Harvard is to the whites. They say the same thing about a Howard man that they do about Harvard—you can tell a Howard man as far as you can see him, but you can't tell him much. He listens to the doings of other Negro schools and their graduates with bored tolerance. Not only is the scholastic rating at Howard high, but tea is poured in the manner!

I had heard all about the swank fraternities and sororities and the clothes and everything, and I knew I could never make it. I told Mae that.

"You can come and live at our house, Zora," Bernice offered. At the time, her parents were living in Washington, and Bernice and Gwendolyn were in the boarding department at Morgan. "I'll ask Mama the next time she comes over. Then you won't have any room and board to pay. We'll all get together and rustle you up a job to make your tuition."

So that summer I moved on to Washington and got a job. First, as a waitress in the exclusive Cosmos Club downtown, and later as a manicurist in the G Street shop of Mr. George Robinson. He is a Negro who has a chain of white barber shops in downtown Washington. I managed to scrape together money for my first quarter's tuition, and went up to register.

Lo and behold, there was Dwight Holmes sitting up there at Howard! He saved my spirits again. I was short of money, and Morgan did not have the class A rating that it now has. There was trouble for me and I was just about to give up and call it a day when I had a talk with Dwight Holmes. He encouraged me all he could, and so I stuck and made up all of those hours I needed.

I shall never forget my first college assembly, sitting there in the chapel of that great University. I was so exalted that I said to the spirit of Howard, "You have taken me in. I am a tiny bit of your greatness. I swear to you that I shall never make you ashamed of me."

It did not wear off. Every time I sat there as part and parcel of things, looking up there at the platform crowded with faculty members, the music, the hundreds of students about me, it would come down on me again. When on Mondays we ended the service by singing Alma Mater, I felt just as if it were the Star Spangled Banner:

> "Reared against the eastern sky
> Proudly there on hill-top high
> Up above the lake so blue
> Stands Old Howard brave and true.
> There she stands for truth and right,
> Sending forth her rays of light,
> Clad in robes of majesty
> Old Howard! We sing of thee."

My soul stood on tiptoe and stretched up to take in all that it meant. So I was careful to do my class work and be worthy to stand there under the shadow of the hovering spirit of Howard. I felt the ladder under my feet.

Mr. Robinson arranged for me to come to work at three-thirty every afternoon and work until eight-thirty. In that way, I was able to support myself. Soon, most of the customers knew I was a student, and tipped me accordingly. I averaged twelve to fifteen dollars a week.

Mr. Robinson's 1410 G Street shop was frequented by bankers, Senators, Cabinet Members, Congressmen, and Gentlemen of the Press. The National Press Club was one block down the same street, the Treasury Building was one block up the street and the Capitol not far away.

I learned things from holding the hands of men like that. The talk was of world affairs, national happenings, personalities, the latest quips from the cloak rooms of Congress and such things. I heard many things from the White House and the Senate before they appeared in print. They probably were bursting to talk to somebody, and I was safe. If I told, nobody would have believed me anyway. Besides, I was much flattered by being told and warned not to repeat what I had heard. Sometimes a Senator, a banker, a newspaper correspondent attached to the White House would all be sitting around my table at one time. While I worked on one, the others waited, and they all talked. Sometimes they concentrated on teasing me. At other times they talked about what had happened, or what they reasoned was bound to happen. Intimate stories about personalities, their secret love affairs, cloak room retorts, and the like. Soon they took me for granted and would say, "Zora knows how to keep a secret. She's all right." Now, I know that my discretion really didn't matter. They were relieving their pent-up feelings where it could do no harm.

Some of them meant more to me than others because they paid me more attention. Frederick William Wile, White House Correspondent, used to talk to me at times quite seriously about life and opportunities and things like that. He had seen three presidents come and go. He had traveled with them, to say nothing of his other traveling to and from upon the earth. He had read extensively. Sometimes he would be full of stories and cracks, such as commenting on the wife of an ex-president who had been quite the grand dame when she was First Lady. "Why, she was so glad when that man proposed to her that she fell out of bed!"

But at other times he would talk to me quite seriously about attitudes, points of view, why one man was great and another a mere facile politician, and so on.

There were other prominent members of the press who would sit and talk longer than it took me to do their hands. One of them, knowing that certain others sat around and talked, wrote out questions two or three times for me to ask and tell him what was said. Each time the questions were answered, but I was told to keep that under my hat, and so I had to turn around and lie and say the man didn't tell me. I never realized how serious it was until he offered me twenty-five dollars to ask a certain southern Congressman something and let him know as quickly as possible. He sent out and bought me a quart of French ice cream to bind the bargain. The man came in on his regular time, which was next day, and in his soft voice, began to tell me how important it was to be honorable at all times and to be trustworthy. How could I ask him then? Besides, he was an excellent Greek scholar and translated my entire lesson for me, which was from Xenophon's *Cyropædia*, and talked at length on the ancient Greeks and Persians. The news man was all right. He had to get his information the best way he could, but for me, it would have been terrible to do that nice man like that. I told the reporter how it was and he understood and never asked me again.

Mr. Johns, a pressman, big, slow, with his eternal walking stick, was always looking for a laugh. Logan, our head-porter, was his regular meat. Logan had a long head, so flat on each side that it looked like it had been pressed between two planks. His toes turned in and his answers were funny.

One day, while shining Mr. John's shoes, he told him what a fighter he was. He really was tough when he got mad, according to himself. According to Logan, Logan was mean! Just couldn't help it. He had Indian blood in him. Just mean and strong. When he straightened out his African soup-bone (arm), something was just bound to fall. If a man didn't fall when *he* hit him, he went around behind him to see what was propping him up. Yassuh! Mr. Johns listened at Logan and smiled. He egged him on to tell more of his powers. The very next day Mr. Johns came in and announced that they had a bear up at Keith's theater, and they needed somebody to wrestle with him. There was good money in it for the man who would come right forward and wrestle with that bear, and knowing that Logan needed money and that he was fearless, he had put Logan's name down. He liked Logan too well to let him get cheated out of such a swell chance to get rich and famous. All Logan needed to do was to go to the theater and tell them that Mr. Johns sent him.

"Naw sir, Mr. Johns," Logan said, "I ain't wrestling no bear. Naw sir!"

"But Logan, you told me—everybody in here heard you—that when you get mad, you go bear-hunting with your fist. You don't even have to hunt this bear. He's right up there on the corner waiting for you. You can't let me down like this. I've already told the man you would be glad to wrestle his old bear!"

"How big is dat bear, Mister Johns?"

"Oh, he is just a full grown bear, Logan. Nothing to worry about at all. He wouldn't weigh more than two hundred pounds at the outside. Soft snap for a man like you, and you weigh about that yourself, Logan."

"Naw Sir! Not no big bear like that. Naw Sir!"

"Well, Logan, what kind of a bear would you consider? You just tell me, and I'll fix it up with the man."

"Git me a little bitty baby bear, Mr. Johns, 'bout three months old. Dats de kind of bear I wants to wrestle wid. Yassuh!"

The mental picture of a big, long-armed, awkward six-footer like Logan wrestling with a tiny cub was too much for the shop. Dignity of every sort went out of the window. The bear cycle took on. Every day, important men, high in life, came in with suggestions on the wrestle. It kept up until Logan furnished them with another laugh by getting into jail over the weekend for beating his wife about a hog-head. He thought she had given a pimp the "ears offen dat head" and found out after he was in jail that it had no ears when he bought it. Mr. Johns went down and persuaded the judge to let Logan go, and then Logan in a burst of good will offered to give the judge the hog-head—still uncooked. The judge chased Logan out of the court, and that hog-head became a classic around the shop.

An incident happened that made me realize how theories go by the board when a person's livelihood is threatened. A man, a Negro, came into the shop one afternoon and sat down in Banks's chair. Banks was the manager and had the first chair by the door. It was so surprising that for a minute Banks just looked at him and never said a word. Finally, he found his tongue and asked, "What do you want?"

"Hair-cut and shave," the man said belligerently.

"But you can't get no hair-cut and shave here. Mr. Robinson has a fine shop for Negroes on U Street near Fifteenth," Banks told him.

"I know it, but I want one here. The Constitution of the United States—"

But by that time, Banks had him by the arm. Not roughly, but he was helping him out of his chair, nevertheless.

"I don't know how to cut your hair," Banks objected. "I was trained on straight hair. Nobody in here knows how."

"Oh, don't hand me that stuff!" the crusader snarled. "Don't be such an Uncle Tom."

"Run on, fellow. You can't get waited on in here."

"I'll stay right here until I do. I know my rights. Things like this have got to be broken up. I'll get waited on all right, or sue the place."

"Go ahead and sue," Banks retorted. "Go on uptown, and get your hair cut, man. Don't be so hard headed for nothing."

"I'm getting waited on right here!"

"You're next, Mr. Powell," Banks said to a waiting customer. "Sorry mister, but you better go on uptown."

"But I have a right to be waited on wherever I please," the Negro said and started towards Updyke's chair which was being emptied. Updyke whirled his chair around so that he could not sit down and stepped in front of it. "Don't you touch *my* chair!" Updyke glared. "Go on about your business."

But instead of going, he made to get into the chair by force.

"Don't argue with him! Throw him out of here!" somebody in the back cried. And in a minute, barbers, customers all lathered and with hair half cut, and porters, were all helping to throw the Negro out.

The rush carried him way out into the middle of G Street and flung him down. He tried to lie there and be a martyr, but the roar of oncoming cars made him jump up and scurry off. We never heard any more about it. I did not participate in the melee, but I wanted him thrown out, too. My business was threatened.

It was only that night in bed that I analyzed the whole thing and realized that I was giving sanction to Jim Crow, which theoretically, I was supposed to resist. But here were ten Negro barbers, three porters and two manicurists all stirred up at the threat of our living through loss of patronage. Nobody thought it out at the moment. It was an instinctive thing. That was the first time it was called to my attention that self-interest rides over all sorts of lives. I have seen the same thing happen hundreds of times since, and now I understand it. One sees it breaking over racial, national, religious and class lines. Anglo-Saxon against Anglo-Saxon, Jew against Jew, Negro against Negro, and all sorts of combinations of the three against other combinations of the three. Off-hand, you might say that we fifteen Negroes should have felt the racial thing and served him. He was one of us. Perhaps it would have been a beautiful thing if Banks had turned to the shop crowded with customers and announced that this man was going to be served like everybody else even at the risk of losing their patronage, with all of the other employees lined up in the center of the floor shouting, "So say we all!" It would have been a stirring gesture, and made the headlines for a day. Then we could all have gone home to our unpaid rents and bills and things like that. I could leave school and begin my wanderings again. The "militant" Negro who would have been the cause of it all, would have perched on the smuddled-up wreck of things and crowed. Nobody ever found out who or what he was. Perhaps he did what he did on the spur of the moment, not realizing that serving him would have ruined Mr. Robinson, another Negro who had got what he had the hard way. For not only would the G Street shop have been forced to close, but the F Street shop and all of his other six downtown shops. Wrecking George Robinson like that on a "race" angle would have been ironic tragedy. He always helped out any Negro who was trying to do anything progressive as far as he was able. He had no education himself, but he was for it. He would give any Howard University student a job in his shops if they could qualify, even if it was only a few hours a week.

So I do not know what was the ultimate right in this case. I do know how I felt at the time. There is always something fiendish and loathsome about a person who threatens to deprive you of your way of making a living. That is just human-like, I reckon.

At the University, I got on well both in class work and the matter of making friends. I could not take in but so many social affairs because I had to work, and then I had to study my lessons after work hours at night, and I was carrying a heavy program.

The teacher who most influenced me was Dr. Lorenzo Dow Turner, head of the English department. He was tall, lean, with a head of wavy black hair above his thin, aesthetic, tan-colored face. He was a Harvard man and knew his subject. His delivery was soft and restrained. The fact that he looked to be in his late twenties or early thirties at most made the girls conscious of shiny noses before they entered his classroom.

Listening to him, I decided that I must be an English teacher and lean over my desk and discourse on the 18th-Century poets, and explain the roots of the modern novel. Children just getting born were going to hear about Addison, Poe, De Quincey, Steele, Coleridge, Keats and Shelley from me, leaning nonchalantly over my desk. Defoe, Burns, Swift, Milton and Scott were going to be sympathetically, but adequately explained, with just that suspicion of a smile now and then before I returned to my notes.

The man who seemed to me to be most overpowering

was E. C. Williams, Librarian and head of the Romance Language department. He was cosmopolitan and world-traveled. His wit was instant and subtle. He was so inaccessible in a way, too. He told me once that a flirtation with a co-ed was to him like playing with a teething-ring. He liked smart, sophisticated women. He used to lunch every day with E. D. Davis, head of the Greek and German department. Davis was just the antithesis of Williams, so shy, in the Charles S. Johnson manner, in spite of his erudition. They would invite me to come along and would pay for my milk and pie. Williams did most of the talking. I put in something now and then. Davis sat and smiled. Professor Williams egged me on to kiss him. He said that Davis would throw a fit, and he wanted to be present to see it. He whispered that Davis liked to have me around, but from what he ever said, I couldn't notice. When I was sick, Professor Davis came to see me and brought me an arm load of roses, but he sat there half an hour and scarcely said a word. He just sat there and smiled now and then.

One day a pretty Washington girl visited me on the campus and joined us at lunch. She laid down a heavy barrage around E. C. Williams. He leaned back in his chair in the midst of her too obvious play and said suddenly, "Girlie, you would flirt with the Pope."

She was taken aback and turned a melting smile upon Davis and colored. "You wouldn't say that about me, would you, Professor Davis?"

"No, I'd say the only reason you wouldn't flirt with the Pope is that he is so hard to get to."

That floored us. Davis talking up like that! Then he shut up in his shell again.

All in all, I did a year and a half of work at Howard University. I would have done the two full years, but I was out on account of illness, and by the time that was over, I did not have the money for my tuition.

I joined the Zeta Phi Beta Sorority, took part in all the literary activities on the campus, and made The Stylus, the small literary society on the hill. I named the student paper *The Hill Top*. The Stylus was limited to 19 members, two of them being faculty members. Dr. Alain Leroy Locke was the presiding genius and we had very interesting meetings.

My joining The Stylus influenced my later moves. On account of a short story which I wrote for The Stylus, Charles S. Johnson, who was just then founding *Opportunity Magazine*, wrote to me for material. He explained that he was writing to all of the Negro colleges with the idea of introducing new writers and new material to the public. I sent on "Drenched in Light" and he published it. Later, he published my second story "Spunk." He wrote me a kind letter and said something about New York. So, beginning to feel the urge to write, I wanted to be in New York.

This move on the part of Dr. Johnson was the root of the so-called Negro Renaissance. It was his work, and only his hush-mouth nature has caused it to be attributed to many others. The success of *Opportunity* Award dinners was news. Later on, the best of this material was collected in a book called *The New Negro* and edited by Dr. Alain Locke, but it was the same material, for the most part, gathered and published by Dr. Charles Spurgeon Johnson, now of the Department of Social Sciences, Fisk University, Nashville, Tennessee.

Being out of school for lack of funds, and wanting to be in New York, I decided to go there and try to get back in school in that city. So the first week of January, 1925, found me in New York with $1.50, no job, no friends, and a lot of hope.

The Charles Johnsons befriended me as best they could. I could always find something to eat out at their house. Mrs. Johnson would give me carfare and encouragement. I came to worship them really, and when we had a misunderstanding, it grew out of my intense loyalty to them. A certain woman knew how I felt and persuaded me to do something to "protect" them, which she knew would hurt. Then she doubled right back and prepared them for my "perfidy." She had her own plans all worked out what to do about the schism. I saw that they believed her so I just let it go, as much as it hurt me inside. I have never ceased to regret it, nor had the sense to tell them just what happened.

So I came to New York through *Opportunity*, and through *Opportunity* to Barnard. I won a prize for a short story at the first Award dinner, May 1, 1925, and Fannie Hurst offered me a job as her secretary, and Annie Nathan Meyer offered to get me a scholarship to Barnard. My record was good enough, and I entered Barnard in the fall, graduating in 1928.

I have no lurid tales to tell of race discrimination at Barnard. I made a few friends in the first few days. Eleanor Beer, who lived on the next chair to me in Economics, was the first. She was a New York girl with a sumptuous home down in W. 71st Street, near the Hudson. She invited me down often, and her mother set out to brush me up on good manners. I learned a lot of things from them. They were well traveled and cosmopolitan. I found out about forks, who entered a room first, sat down first, and who offered to shake hands. A great deal more of material like that. These people are still lying very close to my heart. I was invited to Eleanor's wedding when she married Enzo de Chetalat, a Swiss mining engineer, but I was down in Florida at the time. So I sent her a hat-box full of orange blossoms for the occasion, so she could know how I felt.

The Social Register crowd at Barnard soon took me up, and I became Barnard's sacred black cow. If you had not had lunch with me, you had not shot from taw. I was secretary to Fannie Hurst and living at her 67th Street duplex apartment, so things were going very well with me.

Because my work was top-heavy with English, Political Science, History and Geology, my advisor at Barnard recommended Fine Arts, Economics, and Anthropology for cultural reasons. I started in under Dr. Gladys Reichard, had a term paper called to the attention of Dr. Franz Boas and thereby gave up my dream of leaning over a desk and explaining Addison and Steele to the sprouting generations.

I began to treasure up the words of Dr. Reichard, Dr. Ruth Benedict, and Dr. Boas, the King of Kings.

That man can make people work the hardest with just a look or a word, of anybody else in creation. He is idolized by everybody who takes his orders. We all call him Papa, too. One day, I burst into his office and asked for "Papa Franz" and his secretary gave me a look and told me I had better not let him hear me say that. Of course, I knew better, but at a social gathering of the Department of Anthropology at his house a few nights later, I brought it up.

"Of course, Zora is my daughter. Certainly!" he said with a smile. "Just one of my missteps, that's all." The sabre cut on his cheek, which it is said he got in a duel at Heidelberg, lifted in a smile.

Away from his office, Dr. Boas is full of youth and fun, and abhors dull, stodgy arguments. Get to the point is his idea. Don't raise a point which you cannot defend. He wants facts, not guesses, and he can pin you down so expertly that you soon lose the habit of talking all over your face. Either that, or you leave off Anthropology.

I had the same feeling at Barnard that I did at Howard, only more so. I felt that I was highly privileged and determined to make the most of it. I did not resolve to be a grind, however, to show the white folks that I had brains. I took it for granted that they knew that. Else, why was I at Barnard? Not everyone who cries, "Lord! Lord!" can enter those sacred iron gates. In her high scholastic standards, equipment, the quality of her student-body and graduates, Barnard has a right to the first line of Alma Mater. "Beside the waters of the Hudson, Our Alma Mater stands serene!" Dean Gildersleeve has that certain touch. We know there are women's colleges that are older, but not better ones.

So I set out to maintain a good average, take part in whatever went on, and just be a part of the college like everybody else. I graduated with a *B* record, and I am entirely satisfied.

Mrs. Meyer, who was the moving spirit in founding the college and who is still a trustee, did nobly by me in getting me in. No matter what I might do for her, I would still be in her debt.

Two weeks before I graduated from Barnard, Dr. Boas sent for me and told me that he had arranged a fellowship for me. I was to go south and collect Negro folk-lore. Shortly before that, I had been admitted to the American Folk-Lore Society. Later, while I was in the field, I was invited to become a member of the American Ethnological Society, and shortly after the American Anthropological Society.

Booker T. Washington said once that you must not judge a man by the heights to which he has risen, but by the depths from which he came. So to me these honors meant something, insignificant as they might appear to the world. It was a long step for the waif of Eatonville. From the depth of my inner heart I appreciated the fact that the world had not been altogether unkind to Mama's child.

While in the field, I drove to Memphis, Tennessee, and had a beautiful reconciliation with Bob, my oldest brother, and his family. We had not seen each other since I ran off to be a lady's maid. He said that it had taken him a long time to realize what I was getting at. He regretted deeply that he had not been of more service to me on the way. My father had been killed in an automobile accident during my first year at Morgan, and Bob talked to me about his last days. In reality, my father was the baby of the family. With my mother gone and nobody to guide him, life had not hurt him, but it had turned him loose to hurt himself. He had been miserable over the dispersion of his children when he came to realize that it was so. We were all so sorry for him, instead of feeling bitter as might have been expected. Old Maker had left out the steering gear when He gave Papa his talents.

In Memphis, my brother Ben was doing well as a pharmacist and owner of the East Memphis Drug Store. Between his dogs, his wife, his store, and his car, he was quite the laughing, witty person and I was glad that he was. We talked about Clifford Joel who had become, and still is, principal of the Negro High School in Decatur, Alabama, and I told him about seeing John in Jacksonville, Florida, where he was doing well with his market. I had the latest news for them on Everett, Mama's baby child, in the Post Office in Brooklyn, New York. Dick, the lovable, the irresponsible, was having a high-heel time up and down the east coast of the United States. He had never cared about school, but he had developed into a chef cook and could always take care of himself. Sarah was struggling along with a husband for whom we all wished a short sickness and a quick funeral.

It was a most happy interval for me. I drove back to New Orleans to my work in a glowing aura. I felt the warm embrace of kin and kind for the first time since the night after my mother's funeral, when we had huddled about the organ all sodden and bewildered, with the walls of our home suddenly blown down. On September 18, that house had been a hovering home. September 19, it had turned into a bleak place of desolation with unknown dangers creeping upon us from unseen quarters that made of us a whimpering huddle, though then we could not see why. But now, that was all over. We could touch each other in the spirit if not in the flesh.

X
Research

RESEARCH is formalized curiosity. It is poking and prying with a purpose. It is a seeking that he who wishes may know the cosmic secrets of the world and they that dwell therein.

Two weeks before I graduated from Barnard College, Dr. Boas had arranged a fellowship for me. I was to go south and do research in folk-lore.

I was extremely proud that Papa Franz felt like sending me. As is well known, Dr. Franz Boas of the Department of Anthropology of Columbia University, is the greatest Anthropologist alive for two reasons. The first is his insatiable hunger for knowledge and then more knowledge; and the second is his genius for pure objectivity. He has no pet wishes to prove. His instructions are to go out and find what is there. He outlines his theory, but if the facts do not agree with it, he would not warp a jot or dot of the findings to save his theory. So knowing all this, I was proud that he trusted me. I went off in a vehicle made out of Corona stuff.

My first six months were disappointing. I found out later that it was not because I had no talents for research, but because I did not have the right approach. The glamor of Barnard College was still upon me. I dwelt in marble halls. I knew where the material was all right. But, I went about asking, in carefully accented Barnardese, "Pardon me, but do you know any folk tales or folk songs?" The men and women who had whole treasuries of material just seeping through their pores, looked at me and shook their heads. No, they had never heard of anything like that around there. Maybe it was over in the next county. Why didn't I try over there? I did, and got the self-same answer. Oh, I got a few little items. But compared with what I did later, not enough to make a flea a waltzing jacket. Considering the mood of my going south, I went back to New York with my heart beneath my knees and my knees in some lonesome valley.

I stood before Papa Franz and cried salty tears. He gave me a good going over, but later I found that he was not as disappointed as he let me think. He knew I was green and feeling my oats, and that only bitter disappointment was going to purge me. It did.

What I learned from him then and later, stood me in good stead when Godmother, Mrs. R. Osgood Mason, set aside two hundred dollars a month for a two-year period for me to work.

My relations with Godmother were curious. Laugh if you will, but there was and is a psychic bond between us. She could read my mind, not only when I was in her presence, but thousands of miles away. Both Max Eastman and Richmond Barthe have told me that she could do the same with them. But, the thing that delighted her was the fact that I was her only Godchild who could read her thoughts at a distance. Her old fingers were cramped and she could not write, but in her friend Cornelia Chapin's exact script, a letter would find me in Alabama, or Florida, or in the Bahama Islands and lay me by the heels for what I was *thinking*. "You have broken the law," it would accuse sternly. "You are dissipating your powers in things that have no real meaning," and go on to lacerate me. "Keep silent. Does a child in the womb speak?"

She was just as pagan as I. She had lived for years among the Plains Indians and had collected a beautiful book of Indian lore. Often when she wished to impress upon me my garrulity, she would take this book from the shelf and read me something of Indian beauty and restraint. Sometimes, I would feel like a rabbit at a dog convention. She would invite me to dinner at her apartment, 399 Park Avenue, and then she, Cornelia Chapin, and Miss Chapin's sister, Mrs. Katherine Garrison Biddle, would all hem me up and give me what for. When they had given me a proper straightening, and they felt that I saw the light, all the sternness would vanish, and I would be wrapped in love. A present of money from Godmother, a coat from Miss Chapin, a dress from Mrs. Biddle. We had a great deal to talk about because Cornelia Chapin was a sculptor, Katherine Biddle, a poet, and Godmother, an earnest patron of the arts.

Then too, she was Godmother to Miguel Covarrubias and Langston Hughes. Sometimes all of us were there. She has several paintings by Covarrubias on her walls. She summoned us when one or the other of us returned from our labors. Miguel and I would exhibit our movies, and Godmother and the Chapin family, including brother Paul Chapin, would praise us and pan us, according as we had done. Godmother could be as tender as Mother love when she felt that you had been right spiritually. But anything, however clever, in you that felt like insincerity to her, called forth her well known "That is nothing! It has no soul in it. You have broken the law!" Her tongue was a knout, cutting off your outer pretenses, and bleeding your vanity like a rusty nail. She was merciless to a lie, spoken, acted or insinuated.

She was extremely human. There she was sitting up there at the table over capon, caviar and gleaming silver, eager to hear every word on every phase of life on a saw-mill "job." I must tell the tales, sing the songs, do the dances, and repeat the raucous sayings and doings of the Negro farthest down. She is altogether in sympathy with them, because she says truthfully, they are utterly sincere in living.

My search for knowledge of things took me into many strange places and adventures. My life was in danger several times. If I had not learned how to take care of myself in these circumstances, I could have been maimed or killed on most any day of the several years of my research work. Primitive minds are quick to sunshine and quick to anger. Some little word, look or gesture can move them either to love or to sticking a knife between your ribs. You just have to sense the delicate balance and maintain it.

In some instances, there is nothing personal in the killing. The killer wishes to establish a reputation as a killer, and you'll do as a sample. Some of them go around, making their announcements in singing:

I'm going to make me a graveyard of my own,
I'm going to make me a graveyard of my own,
Oh, carried me down on de smoky road,

> Brought me back on de coolin' board,
> But I'm going to make me a graveyard of my own.

And since the law is lax on these big saw-mill, turpentine and railroad "jobs," there is a good chance that they never will be jailed for it. All of these places have plenty of men and women who are fugitives from justice. The management asks no questions. They need help and they can't be bothered looking for a bug under every chip. In some places, the "law" is forbidden to come on the premises to hunt for malefactors who did their malefacting elsewhere. The wheels of industry must move, and if these men don't do the work, who is there to do it?

So if a man, or a woman, has been on the gang for petty-thieving and mere mayhem, and is green with jealousy of the others who did the same amount of time for a killing and had something to brag about, why not look around for an easy victim and become a hero, too? I was nominated like that once in Polk County, Florida, and the only reason that I was not elected, was because a friend got in there and staved off old club-footed Death.

> Polk County! Ah!
> Where the water tastes like cherry wine.
> Where they fell great trees with axe and muscle.

These poets of the swinging blade! The brief, but infinitely graceful, dance of body and axe-head as it lifts over the head in a fluid arc, dances in air and rushes down to bite into the tree, all in beauty. Where the logs march into the mill with its smokestacks disputing with the elements, its boiler room reddening the sky, and its great circular saw screaming arrogantly as it attacks the tree like a lion making its kill. The log on the carriage coming to the saw. A growling grumble. Then contact! Yeelld-u-u-ow! And a board is laid shining and new on a pile. All day, all night. Rumble, thunder and grumble. Yee-ee-ow! Sweating black bodies, muscled like gods, working to feed the hunger of the great tooth. Polk County!

Polk County. Black men laughing and singing. They go down in the phosphate mines and bring up the wet dust of the bones of pre-historic monsters, to make rich land in far places, so that people can eat. But, all of it is not dust. Huge ribs, twenty feet from belly to back bone. Some old-time sea monster caught in the shallows in that morning when God said, "Let's make some more dry land. Stay there, great Leviathan! Stay there as a memory and a monument to Time." Shark-teeth as wide as the hand of a working man. Joints of backbone three feet high, bearing witness to the mighty monster of the deep when the Painted Land rose up and did her first dance with the morning sun. Gazing on these relics, forty thousand years old and more, one visualizes the great surrender to chance and change when these creatures were rocked to sleep and slumber by the birth of land.

Polk County. Black men from tree to tree among the lordly pines, a swift, slanting stroke to bleed the trees for gum. Paint, explosives, marine stores, flavors, perfumes, tone for a violin bow, and many other things which the black men who bleed the trees never heard about.

Polk County. The clang of nine-pound hammers on railroad steel. The world must ride.

Hah! A rhythmic swing of the body, hammer falls, and another spike driven to the head in the tie.

> Oh, Mobile! Hank!
> Oh, Alabama! Hank!
> Oh, Fort Myers! Hank!
> Oh, in Florida! Hank!
> Oh, let's shake it! Hank!
> Oh, let's break it! Hank!
> Oh, let's shake it! Hank!
> Oh, just a hair! Hank!

The singing-liner cuts short his chant. The straw-boss relaxes with a gesture of his hand. Another rail spiked down. Another offering to the soul of civilization whose other name is travel.

Evalina! Make your dress a little longer, hark!
Oh Evalina! Make your dress a little longer, hark!
I see your thighs—
Lawd, Lawd, I see your thighs!

Oh, Angeline! Oh Angeline!
Oh, Angeline dat great, great gal of mine
And when she walks
And when she walks
And when she walks, she rocks and rolls behind!

You feel her legs
You feel her legs
You feel her legs
Then you want to feel her thighs.

Polk County. Black men scrambling up ladders into orange trees. Singing, laughing, cursing, boasting of last night's love, and looking forward to the darkness again. They do not say embrace when they mean that they slept with a woman. A behind is a behind and not a form. Nobody says anything about incompatability when they mean it does not suit. No bones are made about being fed up.

I got up this morning, and I knowed I didn't want it,
'Cause I slept last night with my hand all on it.
Yea! Polk County!
You don't know Polk County like I do
Anybody been there, tell you the same thing, too.
Eh, rider, rider!
Polk County, where the water tastes like cherry wine.

Polk County. After dark, the jooks. Songs are born out of feelings with an old beat-up piano, or a guitar for a mid-wife. Love made and unmade. Who put out dat lie, it was supposed to last forever? Love is when it is. No more here? Plenty more down the road. Take you where I'm going, woman? Hell no! Let every town furnish its own. Yeah, I'm going. Who care anything about no train fare? The railroad track is there, ain't it? I can count tires just like I been doing. I can ride de blind, can't I?

Got on de train didn't have no fare
But I rode some
Yes I rode some
Got on de train didn't have no fare
Conductor ast me what I'm doing there
But I rode some
Yes I rode some.

Well, he grabbed me by de collar and he led me
    to de door
But I rode some
Yes I rode some.
Well, he grabbed me by de collar and he led me
    to de door
He rapped me over de head with a forty-four
But I rode some
Yes I rode some.

Polk County in the jooks. Dancing the square dance. Dancing the scroush. Dancing the belly-rub. Knocking the right hat off the wrong head, and backing it up with a switchblade.

"Fan-foot, what you doing with my man's hat cocked on *your* nappy head? I know you want to see your Jesus. Who's a whore? Yeah I sleeps with my mens, but they pays me. I wouldn't be a fan-foot like you—just on de road somewhere. Runs up and down de road from job to job making pay-days and don't git a thing for but wet drawers. You kiss my black, independent, money-making ass! Fool wid me and I'll cut all your holes into one. Don't nobody hold her! Let her jump on me! She pay her way on me, and I'll pay it off. Make time in old Bartow jail for her."

Maybe somebody stops the fight before the two switchblades go together. Maybe nobody can. A short, swift dash in. A lucky jab by one opponent and the other one is dead. Maybe one gets a chill in the feet and leaps out of the door. Maybe both get cut badly and back off. Anyhow, the fun of the place goes on. More dancing and singing and buying of drinks, parched peanuts, fried rabbit. Full drummy bass from the piano with weepy, intricate right hand stuff. Singing the memories of Ella Wall, the Queen of love in the jooks of Polk County. Ella Wall, Plauchita, nothin' Liza.

Honey, let your draws hang low

It is a sad, parting song. Each verse ends up with "It's de last time, shaking in de bed with you."

> More dancing, drinks, peanuts, singing
> Roll me with your stomach, baby.
> Feed me with your tongue
> Do it a long time, baby
> Till you make me ——
> Quarters Boss! High Sheriff? Lemme git gone
>   from here!
> Cold, rainy day, some old cold, rainy day
> I'll be back, some old cold, rainy day.
>
> Oh de rocks may be my pillow, Lawd!
> De sand may be my bed
> I'll be back some old cold, rainy day.

"Who run? What you running from the man for, nigger? Me, I don't aim to run a step. I ain't going to run unless they run me. Dat white man come messing with me and I'll cut him a brand new butt-hole. I'm going to live anyhow until I die. Play me some music so I can dance! Aw, spank dat box, man!! Them white folks don't care nothing bout no nigger getting cut and kilt, nohow. They ain't coming in here. I done kilt me four and they ain't hung me yet. Beat dat box!"

"Yeah, but you ain't kilt no women, yet. They's mighty particular 'bout you killing up women."

"And I ain't killing none neither. I ain't crazy in de head. Nigger woman can kill all us men she wants to and they don't care. Leave us kill a woman and they'll run you just as long as you can find something to step on. I got good sense. I know I ain't got no show. De white mens and de nigger women is running this thing. Sing about old Georgy Buck and let's dance off of it. Hit dat box!"

> Old Georgy Buck is dead
> Last word he said
> I don't want no shortening in my bread.
> Rabbit on de log
> Ain't got no dog
> Shoot him wid my rifle, bam! bam!

And the night, the pay night rocks on with music and gambling and laughter and dancing and fights. The big pile of cross-ties burning out in front simmers down to low ashes before sun-up, so then it is time to throw up all the likker you can't keep down and go somewhere and sleep the rest off, whether your knife has blood on it or not. That is, unless some strange, low member of your own race has gone and pumped to the white folks about something getting hurt. Very few of those kind are to be found.

That is the primeval flavor of the place, and as I said before, out of this primitive approach to things, I all but lost my life.

It was in a saw-mill jook in Polk County that I almost got cut to death.

Lucy really wanted to kill me. I didn't mean any harm. All I was doing was collecting songs from Slim, who used to be her man back up in West Florida before he ran off from her. It is true that she found out where he was after nearly a year, and followed him to Polk County and he paid her some slight attention. He was knocking the pad with women, all around, and he seemed to want to sort of free-lance at it. But what he seemed to care most about was picking his guitar, and singing.

He was a valuable source of material to me, so I built him up a bit by buying him drinks and letting him ride in my car.

I figure that Lucy took a pick at me for three reasons. The first one was, her vanity was rubbed sore at not being able to hold her man. That was hard to own up to in a community where so much stress was laid on suiting. Nobody else had offered to shack up with her either. She was getting a very limited retail trade and Slim was ignoring the whole business. I had store-bought clothes, a lighter skin, and a shiny car, so she saw wherein she could use me for an alibi. So in spite of public knowledge of the situation for a year or more before I came, she was telling it around that I came and broke them up. She was going to cut everything off of me but "quit it."

Her second reason was, because of my research methods I had dug in with the male community. Most of the women liked me, too. Especially her sworn enemy, Big Sweet. She was scared of Big Sweet, but she probably reasoned that if she cut Big Sweet's protégée it would be a slam on Big Sweet and build up her own reputation. She was fighting Big Sweet through me.

Her third reason was, she had been in little scraps and been to jail off and on, but she could not swear that she had ever killed anybody. She was small potatoes and nobody was paying her any mind. I was easy. I had no gun, knife or any sort of weapon. I did not even know how to do that kind of fighting.

Lucky for me, I had friended with Big Sweet. She came to my notice within the first week that I arrived on location. I heard somebody, a woman's voice "specifying" up this line of houses from where I lived and asked who it was.

"Dat's Big Sweet," my landlady told me. "She got her foot up on somebody. Ain't she specifying?"

She was really giving the particulars. She was giving a "reading," a word borrowed from the fortune-tellers. She was giving her opponent lurid data and bringing him up to date on his ancestry, his looks, smell, gait, clothes, and his route through Hell in the hereafter. My landlady went outside where nearly everybody else of the four or five hundred people on the "job" were to listen to the reading. Big Sweet broke the news to him, in one of her mildest bulletins that his pa was a double-humpted camel and his ma was a grass-gut cow, but even so, he tore her wide open in the act of getting born, and so on and so forth. He was a bitch's baby out of a buzzard egg.

My landlady explained to me what was meant by "putting your foot up" on a person. If you are sufficiently armed— enough to stand off a panzer division—and know what to do with your weapons after you get 'em, it is all right to go to the house of your enemy, put one foot up on his steps, rest one elbow on your knee and play in the family. That is an-

other way of saying play the dozens, which is a way of saying
low-rate your enemy's ancestors and him, down to the
present moment for reference, and then go into his future as
far as your imagination leads you. But if you have no faith in
your personal courage and confidence in your arsenal, don't
try it. It is a risky pleasure. So then I had a measure of this Big
Sweet.

"Hurt who?" Mrs. Bertha snorted at my fears. "Big Sweet?
Humb! Tain't a man, woman nor child on this job going to
tackle Big Sweet. If God send her a pistol she'll send him a
man. She can handle a knife with anybody. She'll join hands
and cut a duel. Dat Cracker Quarters Boss wears two pistols
round his waist and goes for bad, but he won't break a breath
with Big Sweet lessen he got his pistol in his hand. Cause if he
start anything with her, he won't never get a chance to draw
it. She done kilt two mens on this job and they said she kilt
some before she ever come here. She ain't mean. She don't
bother nobody. She just don't stand for no foolishness, dat's
all."

Right away, I decided that Big Sweet was going to be my
friend. From what I had seen and heard in the short time I
had been there, I felt as timid as an egg without a shell. So
the next afternoon when she was pointed out to me, I waited
until she was well up the sawdust road to the Commissary,
then I got in my car and went that way as if by accident.
When I pulled up beside her and offered her a ride, she
frowned at me first, then looked puzzled, but finally broke
into a smile and got in.

By the time we got to the Commissary post office we were
getting along fine. She told everybody I was her friend. We
did not go back to the Quarters at once. She carried me
around to several places and showed me off. We made a date
to go down to Lakeland come Saturday, which we did. By the
time we sighted the Quarters on the way back from Lakeland,
she had told me, "You sho is crazy!" Which is a way of saying
I was witty. "I loves to friend with somebody like you. I aims
to look out for you, too. Do your fighting for you. Nobody
better not start nothing with you, do I'll get my switch-blade
and go round de ham-bone looking for meat."

We shook hands and I gave her one of my bracelets. After

that everything went well for me. Big Sweet helped me to collect material in a big way. She had no idea what I wanted with it, but if I wanted it, she meant to see to it that I got it. She pointed out people who knew songs and stories. She wouldn't stand for balkiness on their part. We held two lying contests, story-telling contests to you, and Big Sweet passed on who rated the prizes. In that way, there was no arguments about it.

So when the word came to Big Sweet that Lucy was threatening me, she put her foot up on Lucy in a most particular manner and warned her against the try. I suggested buying a knife for defense, but she said I would certainly be killed that way.

"You don't know how to handle no knife. You ain't got dat kind of a sense. You wouldn't even know how to hold it to de best advantage. You would draw your arm way back to stop her, and whilst you was doing all dat, Lucy would run in under your arm and be done cut you to death before you could touch her. And then again, when you sure 'nough fighting, it ain't enough to just stick 'em wid your knife. You got to ram it in to de hilt, then you pull *down*. They ain't no more trouble after dat. They's *dead*. But don't you bother 'bout no fighting. You ain't like me. You don't even sleep with no mens. I wanted to be a virgin one time, but I couldn't keep it up. I needed the money too bad. But I think it's nice for you to be like that. You just keep on writing down them lies. I'll take care of all de fighting. Dat'll make it more better, since we done made friends."

She warned me that Lucy might try to "steal" me. That is, ambush me, or otherwise attack me without warning. So I was careful. I went nowhere on foot without Big Sweet.

Several weeks went by, then I ventured to the jook alone. Big Sweet let it be known that she was not going. But later she came in and went over to the coon-can game in the corner. Thinking I was alone, Lucy waited until things were in full swing and then came in with the very man to whom Big Sweet had given the "reading." There was only one door. I was far from it. I saw no escape for me when Lucy strode in, knife in hand. I saw sudden death very near that moment. I was paralyzed with fear. Big Sweet was in a crowd over in the corner, and did not see Lucy come in. But the sudden quiet of the place made her look around as Lucy charged. My friend was large and portly, but extremely light on her feet. She sprang like a lioness and I think the very surprise of Big Sweet being there when Lucy thought she was over to another party at the Pine Mill unnerved Lucy. She stopped abruptly as Big Sweet charged. The next moment, it was too late for Lucy to start again. The man who came in with Lucy tried to help her out, but two other men joined Big Sweet in the battle. It took on amazingly. It seemed that anybody who had any fighting to do, decided to settle-up then and there. Switch-blades, ice-picks and old-fashioned razors were out. One or two razors had already been bent back and thrown across the room, but our fight was the main attraction. Big Sweet yelled to me to run. I really ran, too. I ran out of the place, ran to my room, threw my things in the car and left the place. When the sun came up I was a hundred miles up the road, headed for New Orleans.

In New Orleans, I delved into Hoodoo, or sympathetic magic. I studied with the Frizzly Rooster, and all of the other noted "doctors." I learned the routines for making and breaking marriages; driving off and punishing enemies; influencing the minds of judges and juries in favor of clients; killing by remote control and other things. In order to work with these "two-headed" doctors, I had to go through an initiation with each. The routine varied with each doctor.

In one case it was not only elaborate, it was impressive. I lay naked for three days and nights on a couch, with my navel to a rattlesnake skin which had been dressed and dedicated to the ceremony. I ate no food in all that time. Only a pitcher of water was on a little table at the head of the couch so that my soul would not wander off in search of water and be attacked by evil influences and not return to me. On the second day, I began to dream strange exalted dreams. On the third night, I had dreams that seemed real for weeks. In one, I strode across the heavens with lightning flashing from under my feet, and grumbling thunder following in my wake.

In this particular ceremony, my finger was cut and I became blood brother to the rattlesnake. We were to aid each other forever. I was to walk with the storm and hold my power, and get my answers to life and things in storms. The symbol of lightning was painted on my back. This was to be mine forever.

In another ceremony, I had to sit at the crossroads at midnight in complete darkness and meet the Devil, and make a compact. That was a long, long hour as I sat flat on the ground there alone and invited the King of Hell.

The most terrifying was going to a lonely glade in the swamp to get the black cat bone. The magic circle was made and all of the participants were inside. I was told that anything outside that circle was in deadly peril. The fire was built inside, the pot prepared and the black cat was thrown in with the proper ceremony and boiled until his bones fell apart. Strange and terrible monsters seemed to thunder up to that ring while this was going on. It took months for me to doubt it afterwards.

When I left Louisiana, I went to South Florida again, and from what I heard around Miami, I decided to go to the Bahamas. I had heard some Bahaman music and seen a Jumping Dance out in Liberty City and I was entranced.

This music of the Bahaman Negroes was more original, dynamic and African, than American Negro songs. I just had to know more. So without giving Godmother a chance to object, I sailed for Nassau.

I loved the place the moment I landed. Then, that first night as I lay in bed, listening to the rustle of a cocoanut palm just outside my window, a song accompanied by string and drum, broke out in full harmony. I got up and peeped out and saw four young men and they were singing "Bellamina," led by Ned Isaacs. I did not know him then, but I met him the next day. The song has a beautiful air, and the oddest rhythm.

> Bellamina, Bellamina!
> She come back in the harbor
> Bellamina, Bellamina
> She come back in the harbor

Put Bellamina on the dock
And paint Bellamina black! Black!
Oh, put the Bellamina on the dock
And paint Bellamina, black! Black!

I found out later that it was a song about a rum-running
boat that had been gleaming white, but after it had been captured by the United States Coast Guard and released, it was
painted black for obvious reasons.

That was my welcome to Nassau, and it was a beautiful
one. The next day I got an idea of what prolific song-makers
the Bahamans are. With that West African accent grafted on
English of the uneducated Bahaman, I was told, "you do anything, we put you in sing." I walked carefully to keep out of
"sing."

This visit to Nassau was to have far-reaching effects. I
stayed on, ran to every Jumping Dance that I heard of,
learned to "jump," collected more than a hundred tunes and
resolved to make them known to the world.

On my return to New York in 1932, after trying vainly to
interest others, I introduced Bahaman songs and dances to a
New York audience at the John Golden Theater, and both the
songs and the dances took on. The concert achieved its purpose. I aimed to show what beauty and appeal there was in
genuine Negro material, as against the Broadway concept,
and it went over.

Since then, there has been a sharp trend towards genuine
Negro material. The dances aroused a tremendous interest in
primitive Negro dancing. Hall Johnson took my group to appear with his singers at the Lewisohn Stadium that summer
and built his "Run Lil' Chillun" around them and the religious scene from my concert, "From Sun To Sun." That was
not all, the dramatized presentation of Negro work songs in
that same concert aroused interest in them and they have
been exploited by singers ever since.

I had no intention of making concert my field. I wanted to
show the wealth and beauty of the material to those who were
in the field and therefore I felt that my job was well done
when it took on.

My group was invited to perform at the New School of

Social Research; in the folk-dance carnival at the Vanderbilt Hotel in New York; at Nyack; at St. Louis; Chicago; Rollins College in Winter Park, Florida; Lake Wales; Sanford; Orlando; Constitution Hall, Washington, D.C.; and Daytona Beach, Florida.

Besides the finding of the dances and the music, two other important things happened to me in Nassau. One was, I lived through that terrible five-day hurricane of 1929. It was horrible in its intensity and duration. I saw dead people washing around on the streets when it was over. You could smell the stench from dead animals as well. More than three hundred houses were blown down in the city of Nassau alone.

Then I saw something else out there. I met Leon Walton Young. He is a grizzly, stocky black man, who is a legislator in the House. He represented the first district in the Bahamas and had done so for more than twenty years when I met him.

Leon Walton Young was either a great hero, or a black bounder, according to who was doing the talking. He was a great champion and a hero in the mouths of the lowly blacks of the islands and to a somewhat lesser degree to the native-born whites. He was a Bahaman for the Bahaman man and a stout fellow along those lines. To the English, who had been sent out to take the jobs of the natives, white and black, he was a cheeky dastard of a black colonial who needed to be put in his place. He was also too much for the mixed blood negroes of education and property, who were as prejudiced against his color as the English. What was more, Leon Walton Young had no formal education, though I found him like George Schuyler of New York to be better read than most people with college degrees. But did he, because of his lack of schooling, defer to the Negroes who had journeyed to London and Edinburgh? He most certainly did not, and what was more, he more than held his own in the hustings.

There was a much felt need for him to be put down, but those who put on the white armor of St. George to go out and slay the dragon always came back—not honorably dead on their shields—but splattered all over with mud and the seat of their pants torn and missing. A peasant mounted on a mule had unhorsed a cavalier and took his pants. The dance drums of Grantstown and Baintown would throb and his humbled opponents would be "put in sing."

He so humbled a governor, who tried to overawe Young by reminding him that he was "His Majesty's representative in these Islands" that the Governor was recalled and sent to some peaceful spot in West Africa. Young had replied to that pompous statement with, "Yes, but if you continue your tactics out here you will make me forget it."

That was one of his gentlest thumps on the Governor's pride and prestige. His Majesty's Representative accused Young of having said publicly that he, the Governor, was a bum out of the streets of London, and to his eternal rage, Young more than admitted the statement. The English appointees and the high yellows shuddered at such temerity, but the local whites and the working blacks gloried in his spunk.

A most dramatic incident came out of this struggle of the local Bahamans against the policy of the British Government of taking care of the surplus of unemployed at the expense of the Islands.

When I returned to Nassau for the fourth time in 1935, the elections for the House were on.

A Negro barrister, who is not yellow, but who liked to think he was, had thrown down the gauntlet to Young. He had informed the English that he would rid them of the troublesome Leon Walton Young. The young man whom I shall call Botts because that is not his name, got a pat on the back, and was told to go ahead.

As I said before, Young represented the First District which was the richest in the Islands. It is that end of the island of New Providence where the hotels, the homes of the wealthy foreigners and the business and Government houses are located. He had been reelected for three terms of seven years each.

A local white business man came to Young in secret and told him what was happening under cover. Young, on hearing the boasts of Botts, got busy in secret on his own. He took under his wing a young white barrister, only a year out of

Lincoln's Inn and primed him for a candidate. Botts was up for reelection, and the young white stripling was dressed to "stand" for Botts's district, which was in the outer Islands. Secret messages went to the district in the outer Islands, the political fence was looked over and put in order, and then Young launched his attack.

He stood out in the middle of Bay Street, flung wide his arms like a cross and cried out: "Send me a man to stand for First District! I am going out to Aleuthera to stand, so that this Botts, this betrayer of his country and his people, can be driven out of office. Send me a man!"

Nobody sent him a man, as he well knew they would not. His reelection was taken for granted. But he stirred the Bahamas from end to end by his gesture. People remembered things about Barrister Botts they otherwise would have forgotten. Poor people down on the waterfront remembered that, though he went for a great man now, his mother had stood down on the waterfront night after night, selling fried fish to send him to England to be educated. His father was living and prosperous. He was in business, and a member of the House, but long years ago he had divorced Botts's mother for a woman of lighter skin. But the mother had seen him through the Inner Temple. He had come back, not full of gratitude for the sacrifices she had made, but scornful of her black skin and all that she stood for. People said that he paid her ten shillings ($2.50) a week to stay away from his house. He was being accused of robbing his younger brother of funds and legal action was underway at the very moment of the election.

The election was to be on Sunday. On Friday, Botts went out in a chartered boat. He was dressed in the latest from London and quite the patrician. On the boat with him was the same white man who had given Young all the information. The man was to report on everything that went on, though Botts thought he was there out of gratitude and admiration.

On Saturday, Leon Walton Young, his protégé and his coterie of workers boarded a big black boat to go out to Aleuthera. With them was Wilbur Botts, going out to campaign against his brother. They left the old woman, mother of both of the boys on the dock. She was ragged, not too clean, and bitter. As the boat steamed out, she was muttering, "God! I wish I could go! I want to campaign against him, too!" And she shook her clenched fists in the general direction of her barrister-son's district. "God! I wish I could go!"

Before dawn on that Sunday morning, a big black boat with Leon Walton Young and his barrister protégé dropped anchor in a harbor at Aleuthera. About eight o'clock, Botts came on deck on his boat, dressed in faultless doe-skin trousers to take the air. Seeing the big black boat which had not been there the night before, he lifted his glasses and studied the boat and the people on her deck. Suddenly, he lowered his glasses and turned to the white man Leon Young had placed at his elbow, and asked, "Isn't that Young on that boat?"

The man took the glasses and pretended to find out what he already knew. "Yes, that is Walton Young."

Botts dropped heavily into a deck chair without regards to his creases. He was a sodden mess from then on through the election.

They all landed and the fight was on. The protégé of Young won without making a single speech. It was Young who dashed from place to place talking and rallying the people. By noon, Botts conceded the election to his opponent and returned to Nassau.

I was down at the wharf when the boats returned. I wanted to see the behavior of the old woman who had been divorced by her husband for being too black after he gained a certain amount of success. The same woman who had been barred from her son's home for the same reason, after she had felt no labor was too humble for her to do to put him through law school in London to come home to her a barrister. She was not there. I wondered if she was off somewhere trying to rustle up a tuppence or two, or merely that she did not want to look on his dear face when his pretentions had met his realities. She had her bitter moments, but after all, she was his mother.

Monday night the election was "in sing." Young's election

came up a few days later and as he well knew, he was returned
to his seat, but not before he had engineered the defeat of
Botts, Sr., in another district. Then the drums of Baintown
really thundered.

> Young—Dun, dun, dun, dun!
> Him a great dentist—dun, dun!
> Him pull Botts out the House!

And the common folk danced off of the feat and were very
glad. To them, life was not hopeless as long as their champion
was in the fight.

The humble Negroes of America are great song-makers,
but the Bahaman is greater. He is more prolific and his tunes
are better. Nothing is too big, or little, to be "put in sing."
They only need discovery. They are much more original than
the Calypso singers of Trinidad as will be found the moment
you put it to the proof.

I hear that now the Duke of Windsor is their great hero. To
them, he is "Our King." I would love to hear how he and his
Duchess have been put in sing.

I enjoyed collecting the folk-tales and I believe the people
from whom I collected them enjoyed the telling of them, just
as much as I did the hearing. Once they got started, the "lies"
just rolled and story-tellers fought for a chance to talk. It was
the same with the songs. The one thing to be guarded
against, in the interest of truth, was over-enthusiasm. For instance, if a song was going good, and the material ran out,
the singer was apt to interpolate pieces of other songs into it.
The only way you can know when that happens, is to know
your material so well that you can sense the violation. Even if
you do not know the song that is being used for padding, you
can tell the change in rhythm and tempo. The words do not
count. The subject matter in Negro folk songs can be anything and go from love to work, to travel, to food, to
weather, to fight, to demanding the return of a wig by a
woman who has turned unfaithful. The tune is the unity of
the thing. And you have to know what you are doing when
you begin to pass on that, because Negroes can fit in more

words and leave out more and still keep the tune than anyone I can think of.

One bit of research I did jointly for the *Journal of Negro History* and Columbia University, was in Mobile, Alabama. There I went to talk to Cudjo Lewis. That is the American version of his name. His African name was Kossola-O-Lo-Loo-Ay.

He arrived on the last load of slaves run into the United States and was the only Negro alive that came over on a slave ship. It happened in 1859 just when the fight between the South and the Abolitionists was moving toward the Civil War. He has died since I saw him.

I found him a cheerful, poetical old gentleman in his late nineties, who could tell a good story. His interpretation of the story of Jonah is marvelous.

He was a good Christian and so he pretended to have forgotten all of his African religion. He turned me off with the statement that his Nigerian religion was the same as Christianity. "We know it a God, you unner'stand, but we don't know He got a Son."

He told me in detail of the circumstances in Africa that brought about his slavery here. How the powerful Kingdom of Dahomey, finding the slave trade so profitable, had abandoned farming, hunting and all else to capture slaves to stock the barracoons on the beach at Dmydah to sell to the slavers who came from across the ocean. How quarrels were manufactured by the King of Dahomey with more peaceful agricultural nations in striking distance of Dahomey in Nigeria and Gold Coast; how they were assaulted, completely wiped off the map, their names never to appear again, except when they were named in boastful chant before the King at one of his "customs" when his glory was being sung. The able-bodied who were captured were marched to Abomey, the capital city of Dahomey and displayed to the King, then put into the barracoons to await a buyer. The too old, the too young, the injured in battle were instantly beheaded and their heads smoked and carried back to the King. He paid off on heads, dead or alive. The skulls of the slaughtered were not wasted either. The King had his famous Palace of Skulls. The Palace grounds had a massive gate of skull-heads. The wall surrounding the grounds were built of skulls. You see, the Kings of Dahomey were truly great and mighty and a lot of skulls were bound to come out of their ambitions. While it looked awesome and splendid to him and his warriors, the sight must have been most grewsome and crude to western eyes. Imagine a Palace of Hindu or Zulu skulls in London! Or Javanese skulls in The Hague!

One thing impressed me strongly from this three months of association with Cudjo Lewis. The white people had held my people in slavery here in America. They had bought us, it is true and exploited us. But the inescapable fact that stuck in my craw, was: my people had *sold* me and the white people had bought me. That did away with the folklore I had been brought up on—that the white people had gone to Africa, waved a red handkerchief at the Africans and lured them aboard ship and sailed away. I know that civilized money stirred up African greed. That wars between tribes were often stirred up by white traders to provide more slaves in the barracoons and all that. But, if the African princes had been as pure and as innocent as I would like to think, it could not have happened. No, my own people had butchered and killed, exterminated whole nations and torn families apart, for a profit before the strangers got their chance at a cut. It was a sobering thought. What is more, all that this Cudjo told me was verified from other historical sources. It impressed upon me the universal nature of greed and glory. Lack of power and opportunity passes off too often for virtue. If I were King, let us say, over the Western Hemisphere tomorrow, instead of who I am, what would I consider right and just? Would I put the cloak of Justice on my ambition and send her out a-whoring after conquests? It is something to ponder over with fear.

Cudjo's eyes were full of tears and memory of fear when he told me of the assault on his city and its capture. He said that his nation, the Takkoi, lived "three sleeps" from Dahomey. The attack came at dawn as the Takkoi were getting out of bed to go to their fields outside the city. A whooping horde of the famed Dahoman women warriors burst through the main gate, seized people as they fled from their houses and beheaded victims with one stroke of their big swords.

"Oh, oh! I runnee this way to that gate, but they there. I runnee to another one, but they there, too. All eight gates they there. Them women, they very strong. I nineteen years old, but they too strong for me. They take me and tie me. I don't know where my people at. I never see them no more."

He described the awful slaughter as the Amazons sacked the city. The clusters of human heads at their belts. The plight of those who fled through the gates to fall into the hands of the male warriors outside. How his King was finally captured and carried before the King of Dahomey, who had broken his rule and come on this expedition in person because of a grudge against the King of Takkoi, and how the vanquished monarch was led before him, bound.

"Now, that you have dared to send impudent words to me," the King of Dahomey said, "your country is conquered and you are before me in chains. I shall take you to Abomey."

"No," the King of Takkoi answered. "I am King in Takkoi. I will not go to Dahomey." He knew that he would be killed for a spectacle in Dahomey. He chose to die at home.

So two Dahoman warriors held each of his hands and an Amazon struck off his head.

Later, two representatives of a European power attended the Customs of the King at Abomey, and tell of seeing the highly polished skull of the King of Takkoi mounted in a beautiful ship-model. His name and his nation were mentioned in the chant to the glory of Dahomey. The skull was treated with the utmost respect, as the King of Dahomey would expect his to be treated in case he fell in battle. That was the custom in West Africa. For the same reason, no one of royal blood was sold into slavery. They were killed. There are no descendants of royal African blood among American Negroes for that reason. The Negroes who claim that they are descendants of royal African blood have taken a leaf out of the book of the white ancestor-hounds in America, whose folks went to England with William the Conqueror, got restless and caught the *Mayflower* for Boston, then feeling a romantic lack, rushed down the coast and descended from

Pocahontas. From the number of her children, one is forced
to the conclusion that that Pocahontas wasn't so poky, after
all.

Kossola told me of the March to Abomey after the fall of
Takkoi. How they were yoked by forked sticks and tied in a
chain. How the Dahomans halted the march the second day
in order to smoke the heads of the victims because they were
spoiling. The prisoners had to watch the heads of their friends
and relatives turning on long poles in the smoke. Abomey
and the palace of the King and then the march to the coast
and the barracoons. They were there sometime before a ship
came to trade. Many, many tribes were there, each in a separate barracoon, lest they war among themselves. The traders
could choose which tribe they wanted. When the tribe was
decided upon, he was carried into the barracoon where that
tribe was confined, the women were lined up on one side and
the men on the other. He walked down between the lines and
selected the individuals he wanted. They usually took an
equal number.

He described the embarcation and the trip across the ocean
in the *Chlotilde*, a fast sailing vessel built by the Maher
brothers of Maine, who had moved to Alabama. They were
chased by a British man-of-war on the lookout for slavers,
but the *Chlotilde* showed him her heels. Finally the cargo
arrived in Mobile. They were unloaded up the river, the boat
sunk, and the hundred-odd Africans began a four-year life of
slavery.

"We so surprised to see mule and plow. We so surprised to
see man pushee and mule pullee."

After the war, these Africans made a settlement of their
own at Plateau, Alabama, three miles up the river from Mobile. They farmed and worked in the lumber mills and bought
property. The descendants are still there.

Kossola's great sorrow in America was the death of his favorite son, David, killed by a train. He refused to believe it
was his David when he saw the body. He refused to let the
bell be tolled for him.

"If dat my boy, where his head? No, dat not my David. Dat
not my boy. My boy gone to Mobile. No. No! Don't ringee
de bell for David. Dat not him."

But, finally his wife persuaded him that the headless body on the window blind was their son. He cried hard for several minutes and then said, "Ringee de bell."

His other great sorrow was that he had lost track of his folks in Africa.

"They don't know what become of Kossola. When you go there, you tellee where I at." He begged me. He did not know that his tribe was no more upon this earth, except for those who reached the barracoon at Dmydah. None of his family was in the barracoon. He had missed seeing their heads in the smoke, no doubt. It is easy to see how few would have looked on that sight too closely.

"I lonely for my folks. They don't know. Maybe they ask everybody go there where Kossola. I know they hunt for me." There was a tragic catch in his voice like the whimper of a lost dog.

After seventy-five years, he still had that tragic sense of loss. That yearning for blood and cultural ties. That sense of mutilation. It gave me something to feel about.

Of my research in the British West Indies and Haiti, my greatest thrill was coming face to face with a Zombie and photographing her. This act had never happened before in the history of man. I mean the taking of the picture. I have said all that I know on the subject in the book *Tell My Horse*, which has been published also in England under the title *Voodoo Gods*. I have spoken over the air on "We the People" on the subject, and the matter has been so publicized that I will not go into details here. But, it was a tremendous thrill, though utterly macabre.

I went Canzo in Voodoo ceremonies in Haiti and the ceremonies were both beautiful and terrifying.

I did not find them any more invalid than any other religion. Rather, I hold that any religion that satisfies the individual urge is valid for that person. It does satisfy millions, so it is true for its believers. The Sect Rouge, also known as the Cochon Gris (gray pig) and Ving Bra-Drig (from the sound of the small drum), a cannibalistic society there, has taken cover under the name of Voodoo, but the two things are in no wise the same. What is more, if science ever gets to the bottom of Voodoo in Haiti and Africa, it will be found that some important medical secrets, still unknown to medical science, give it its power, rather than the gestures of ceremony.

XI

Books and Things

W HILE I was in the research field in 1929, the idea of
Jonah's Gourd Vine came to me. I had written a few
short stories, but the idea of attempting a book seemed so
big, that I gazed at it in the quiet of the night, but hid it away
from even myself in daylight.

For one thing, it seemed off-key. What I wanted to tell was
a story about a man, and from what I had read and heard,
Negroes were supposed to write about the Race Problem. I
was and am thoroughly sick of the subject. My interest lies in
what makes a man or a woman do such-and-so, regardless of
his color. It seemed to me that the human beings I met re-
acted pretty much the same to the same stimuli. Different
idioms, yes. Circumstances and conditions having power to
influence, yes. Inherent difference, no. But I said to myself
that that was not what was expected of me, so I was afraid to
tell a story the way I wanted, or rather the way the story told
itself to me. So I went on that way for three years.

Something else held my attention for a while. As I told you
before, I had been pitched head-foremost into the Baptist
Church when I was born. I had heard the singing, the preaching and the prayers. They were a part of me. But on the concert stage, I always heard songs called spirituals sung and
applauded as Negro music, and I wondered what would happen if a white audience ever heard a real spiritual. To me,
what the Negroes did in Macedonia Baptist Church was finer
than anything that any trained composer had done to the folk
songs.

I had collected a mass of work songs, blues and spirituals in
the course of my years of research. After offering them to two
Negro composers and having them refused on the ground
that white audiences would not listen to anything but highly
arranged spirituals, I decided to see if that was true. I
doubted it because I had seen groups of white people in my
father's church as early as I could remember. They had come

713

to hear the singing, and certainly there was no distinguished composer in Zion Hope Baptist Church. The congregation just got hold of the tune and arranged as they went along as the spirit moved them. And any musician, I don't care if he stayed at a conservatory until his teeth were gone and he smelled like old-folks, could never even approach what those untrained singers could do. LET THE PEOPLE SING, was and is my motto, and finally I resolved to see what would happen.

So on money I had borrowed, I put on a show at the John Golden Theater on January 10, 1932, and tried out my theory. The performance was well received by both the audience and the critics. Because I know that music without motion is not natural with my people, I did not have the singers stand in a stiff group and reach for the high note. I told them to just imagine that they were in Macedonia and go ahead. One critic said that he did not believe that the concert was rehearsed, it looked so natural. I had dramatized a working day on a railroad camp, from the shack-rouser waking up the camp at dawn until the primitive dance in the deep woods at night.

While I did not lose any money, I did not make much. But I am satisfied that I proved my point. I have seen the effects of that concert in all the Negro singing groups since then. Primitive Negro dancing has been given tremendous impetus. Work songs have taken on. In that performance I introduced West Indian songs and dances and they have come to take an important place in America. I am not upset by the fact that others have made something out of the things I pointed out. Rather I am glad if I have called any beauty to the attention of those who can use it.

In May, 1932, the depression did away with money for research so far as I was concerned. So I took my nerve in my hand and decided to try to write the story I had been carrying around in me. Back in my native village, I wrote first *Mules and Men*. That is, I edited the huge mass of material I had, arranged it in some sequence and laid it aside. It was published after my first novel. Mr. Robert Wunsch and Dr. John Rice were both on the faculty at Rollins College, at Winter Park, which is three miles from Eatonville. Dr. Edwin Osgood

Grover, Dr. Hamilton Holt, President of Rollins, together with Rice and Wunsch, were interested in me. I gave three folk concerts at the college under their urging.

Then I wrote a short story, "The Gilded Six-Bits," which Bob Wunsch read to his class in creative writing before he sent it off to *Story Magazine*. Thus I came to know Martha Foley and her husband, Whit Burnett, the editors of *Story*. They bought the story and it was published in the August issue, 1933. They never told me, but it is my belief that they did some missionary work among publishers in my behalf, because four publishers wrote me and asked if I had anything book-length. Mr. Bertram Lippincott, of the J. B. Lippincott Company, was among these. He wrote a gentle-like letter and so I was not afraid of him. Exposing my efforts did not seem so rash to me after reading his letter. I wrote him and said that I was writing a book. Mind you, not the first word was on paper when I wrote him that letter. But the very next week I moved up to Sanford where I was not so much at home as at Eatonville, and could concentrate more and sat down to write *Jonah's Gourd Vine*.

I rented a house with a bed and stove in it for $1.50 a week. I paid two weeks and then my money ran out. My cousin, Willie Lee Hurston, was working and making $3.50 per week, and she always gave me the fifty cents to buy groceries with. In about three months, I finished the book. The problem of getting it typed was then upon me. Municipal Judge S.A.B. Wilkinson asked his secretary, Mildred Knight, if she would not do it for me and wait on the money. I explained to her that the book might not even be taken by Lippincott. I had been working on a hope. She took the manuscript home with her and read it. Then she offered to type it for me. She said, "It is going to be accepted, all right. I'll type it. Even if the first publisher does not take it, somebody will." So between them, they bought the paper and carbon and the book was typed.

I took it down to the American Express office to mail it and found that it cost $1.83 cents to mail, and I did not have it. So I went to see Mrs. John Leonardi, a most capable woman lawyer, and wife of the County Prosecutor. She did not have the money at the moment, but she was the treasurer of the local Daughter Elks. She "borrowed" $2.00 from the treasury and gave it to me to mail my book. That was on October 3, 1933. On October 16, I had an acceptance by wire.

But it did not come so simply as that. I had been hired by the Seminole County Chamber of Commerce to entertain the business district of Sanford with my concert group for that day. I was very glad to get the work, because my landlord was pressing me for the back rent. I now owed $18. I was to receive $25 for the day, so I saw my way clear to pay up my rent, and have a little over. It was not to be that way, however. At eight o'clock of October 16, my landlord came and told me to get out. I told her that I could pay her that day, but she said she didn't believe that I would ever have that much money. No, she preferred the house. So I took my card table and my clothes up to my Uncle Isaiah's house and went off to entertain the city at eleven o'clock. The sound truck went up and down the streets and my boys sang. That afternoon while I was still on the sound truck, a Western Union messenger handed me a wire. Naturally I did not open it there. We were through at three o'clock. The Chamber of Commerce not only paid us, we were all given an order which we could take to any store we wanted and get what we chose. I needed shoes, so I took mine to a shoe store. My heart was weighing as much as cord-wood, and so I forgot the wire until I was having the shoes fitted. When I opened it and read that *Jonah's Gourd Vine* was accepted and that Lippincott was offering me $200 advance, I tore out of that place with one old shoe and one new one on and ran to the Western Union office. Lippincott had asked for an answer by wire and they got it! Terms accepted. I never expect to have a greater thrill than that wire gave me. You know the feeling when you found your first pubic hair. Greater than that. When Producer Arthur Hornblow took me to lunch at Lucey's and hired me at Paramount, it was nice — very nice. I was most elated. But I had had five books accepted then, been a Guggenheim fellow twice, spoken at three book fairs with all the literary greats of America and some from abroad, and so I was a little more used to things. So you see why Bertram Lippincott is *Colonel* Bert to me. When the Negroes in the south name a white man a colonel, it means CLASS. Something like a monarch, only bigger and better. And when the colored population in the south confer a title, the white people recognize it because the Negroes are never wrong. They may flatter an ordinary bossman by calling him "Cap'n" but when they say "Colonel," "General" and "Governor" they are recognizing something internal. It is there, and it is accepted because it can be seen.

I wrote *Their Eyes Were Watching God* in Haiti. It was dammed up in me, and I wrote it under internal pressure in seven weeks. I wish that I could write it again. In fact, I regret all of my books. It is one of the tragedies of life that one cannot have all the wisdom one is ever to possess in the beginning. Perhaps, it is just as well to be rash and foolish for a while. If writers were too wise, perhaps no books would get written at all. It might be better to ask yourself "Why?" afterwards than before. Anyway, the force from somewhere in Space which commands you to write in the first place, gives you no choice. You take up the pen when you are told, and write what is commanded. There is no agony like bearing an untold story inside you. You have all heard of the Spartan youth with the fox under his cloak.

Dust Tracks on a Road is being written in California where I did not expect to be at this time.

I did not come out here to California to write about the state. I did not come to get into the movies. I came because my good friend, Katharane Edson Mershon, invited me out here to rest and have a good time. However, I have written a book here, and gone to work in the movies. This surprises me because I did not think that I would live long enough to do anything out here but die. Friend Katharane Mershon is a mountain goat while I am a lowland turtle. I want to rock along on level ground. She can't look at a mountain without leaping on it. I think she is ashamed if she ever catches both of her feet on the same level. She cries "Excelsior!" in her sleep. Jack, her husband, told me that the reason he has that sort of smoothed-off look was because she dragged him up a mountain the next day after they got married and he has never been able to get his right shape back again. Well, 1941 was a hard year for me, too. She showed me California. Before it was over, I felt like I had spent two months walking a cross-cut saw. The minute I get to be governor of California, I mean to get me an over-sized plane and a spirit-level and fix this state so it can be looked at without rearing back. EPIC nothing! LEVEL! Level California! And I do mean L E V E L !!!!

XII

My People! My People!

"M Y PEOPLE! My people!" From the earliest rocking of my cradle days, I have heard this cry go up from Negro lips. It is forced outward by pity, scorn and hopeless resignation. It is called forth by the observations of one class of Negro on the doings of another branch of the brother in black. For instance, well-mannered Negroes groan out like that when they board a train or a bus and find other Negroes on there with their shoes off, stuffing themselves with fried fish, bananas and peanuts, and throwing the garbage on the floor. Maybe they are not only eating and drinking. The offenders may be "loud-talking" the place, and holding back nothing of their private lives, in a voice that embraces the entire coach. The well-dressed Negro shrinks back in his seat at that, shakes his head and sighs, "My people! My people!"

Now, the well-mannered Negro is embarrassed by the crude behavior of the others. They are not friends, and have never seen each other before. So why should he or she be embarrassed? It is like this: The well-bred Negro has looked around and seen America with his eyes. He or she has set himself to measure up to what he thinks of as the white standard of living. He is conscious of the fact that the Negro in America needs more respect if he expects to get any acceptance at all. Therefore, after straining every nerve to get an education, maintain an attractive home, dress decently, and otherwise conform, he is dismayed at the sight of other Negroes tearing down what he is trying to build up. It is said every day, "And that good-for-nothing, trashy Negro is the one the white people judge us all by. They think we're all just alike. My people! My people!"

What that educated Negro knows further is that he can do very little towards imposing his own viewpoint on the lowlier members of his race. Class and culture stand between. The humble Negro has a built-up antagonism to the "Big Nigger." It is a curious thing that he does not resent a white man looking down on him. But he resents any lines between himself and the wealthy and educated of his own race. "He's a nigger just like us," is the sullen rejoinder. The only answer to this is "My people! My people!"

So the quiet-spoken Negro man or woman who finds himself in the midst of one of these "broadcasts" as on the train, cannot go over and say "Don't act like that, brother. You're giving us all a black eye." He or she would know better than to try that. The performance would not only go on, it would get better with the "dickty" Negro as the butt of all the quips. The educated Negro may know all about the differential calculus and the theory of evolution, but he is fighting entirely out of his class when he tries to quip with the underprivileged. The bookless may have difficulty in reading a paragraph in a newspaper, but when they get down to "playing the dozens" they have no equal in America, and, I'd risk a sizeable bet, in the whole world. Starting off in first by calling you a seven-sided son-of-a-bitch, and pausing to name the sides, they proceed to "specify" until the tip-top branch of your family tree has been "given a reading." No profit in that to the upper class Negro, so he minds his own business and groans, "My people! My people!"

It being a traditional cry, I was bound to hear it often and under many circumstances. But it is not the only folk label that I heard. "Race Pride" — "Race Prejudice" — "Race Man" — "Race Solidarity" — "Race Consciousness" — "Race."

"Race Prejudice" I was instructed was something bad that white people used on us. It seemed that white people felt superior to black ones and would not give Negroes justice for that reason. "Race Pride" was something that, if we had it, we would feel ourselves superior to the whites. A black skin was the greatest honor that could be blessed on any man. A "Race Man" was somebody who always kept the glory and honor of his race before him. Must stand ever ready to defend the Negro race from all hurt, harm and danger. Especially if a white person said "Nigger," "You people," "Negress" or "Darkies." It was a mark of shame if somebody accused: "Why, you are not a Race Man (or woman)." People made whole careers of being "Race" men and women. They were champions of the race. "Race Consciousness" is a plea to Negroes to bear their color in mind at all times. It was just a phrase to me when I was a child. I knew it was supposed to mean something deep. By the time I got grown I saw that it was only an imposing line of syllables, for no Negro in America is apt to forget his race. "Race Solidarity" looked like something solid in my childhood, but like all other mirages, it faded as I came close enough to look. As soon as I could think, I saw that there is no such thing as Race Solidarity in America with any group. It is freely admitted that it does not exist among Negroes. Our so-called Race Leaders cry over it. Others accept it as a natural thing that Negroes should not remain an unmelting black knot in the body politic. Our interests are too varied. Personal benefits run counter to race lines too often for it to hold. If it did, we could never fit into the national pattern. Since the race line has never held any other group in America, why expect it to be effective with us? The upper class Negroes admit it in their own phrases. The lower class Negroes say it with a tale.

It seems that a Negro was asked to lead the congregation in prayer. He got down on his knees and began, "Oh, Lawd, I got something to ask You, but I know You can't do it."

"Go on, Brother Isham and ask Him."

"Lawd," Brother Isham began again, "I really want to ask You something but I just know You can't do it."

"Aw, Brother Isham, go on and tell the Lawd what you want. He's the Lawd! Ain't nothing He can't do! He can even lead a butt-headed cow by the horns. You're killing up time. Go 'head on, Brother Isham, and let the church roll on."

"Well then, Lawd, I ask You to get these Negroes together, but I know You can't do it." Then there is laughter and "My people! My people!"

Hearing things like this from my childhood, sooner or later I was bound to have some curiosity about my race of people.

What fell into my ears from time to time tended more to confuse than to clarify. One thing made a liar out of the one that went before and the thing that came after. At different times I heard opposite viewpoints expressed by the same person or persons.

For instance, come school-closing time and like formal occasions, I heard speeches which brought thunderous applause. I did not know the word for it at the time, but it did not take me long to know the material was traditional. Just as folk as the songs in church. I knew that because so many people got up and used the same, identical phrases: (a) The Negro had made the greatest progress in fifty years of any race on the face of the globe. (b) Negroes composed the most *beautiful* race on earth, being just like a flower garden with every color and kind. (c) Negroes were the bravest men on earth, facing every danger like lions, and fighting with demons. We must remember with pride that the first blood spilled for American Independence was that of the brave and daring Crispus Attucks, a Negro who had bared his black breast to the bullets of the British tyrants at Boston, and thus struck the first blow for American liberty. They had marched with Colonel Shaw during the Civil War and hurled back the forces of the iniquitous South, who sought to hold black men in bondage. It was a Negro named Simon who had been the only one with enough pity and compassion in his heart to help the Savior bear His cross upon Calvary. It was the Negro troops under Teddy Roosevelt who won the battle of San Juan Hill.

It was the genius of the Negro which had invented the steam engine, the cotton gin, the air brake, and numerous other things—but conniving white men had seen the Negro's inventions and run off and put them into practice before the Negro had a chance to do anything about it. Thus the white man got credit for what the genius of the Negro brain had produced. Were it not for the envy and greed of the white man, the Negro would hold his rightful place—the noblest and the greatest man on earth.

The people listening would cheer themselves hoarse and go home feeling good. Over the fences next day it would be agreed that it was a wonderful speech, and nothing but the God's truth. What a great people we would be if we only had our rights!

But my own pinnacle would be made to reel and rock anyway by other things I heard from the very people who always applauded "the great speech," when it was shouted to them from the school-house rostrum. For instance, let some member of the community do or say something which was considered either dumb or venial and the verdict would be "Dat's just like a nigger!" or "Nigger from nigger leave nigger"— ("Nothing from nothing leave nothing"). It was not said in either admiration or pity. Utter scorn was in the saying. "Old Cuffy just got to cut de fool, you know. Monkey see, monkey do. Nigger see de white man do something, he jump in and try to do like de white man, and make a great big old mess." "My people! My people!"

"Yeah, youse mighty right. Another monkey on de line. De white man, you understand, he was a railroad engineer, so he had a pet monkey he used to take along wid him all de time. De monkey, he set up there in de cab wid de engineer and see what he do to run de train. Way after while, figger he can run de train just as good as de engineer his own self. He was just itching to git at dat throttle and bust dat main line wide open. Well, one day de engineer jumped down at de station to git his orders and old monkey seen his chance. He just jumped up in de engineer's seat, grabbed a holt of dat throttle, and dat engine was splitting de wind down de track. So de engineer sent a message on ahead, say 'Clear de track. Monkey on de line!' Well, Brer Monk he was holding de throttle wide open and jumping up and down and laughing fit to kill. Course, he didn't know nothing about no side tracks and no switches and no schedules, so he was making a mile a minute when he hit a open switch and a string of box cars was standing on de siding. Ker-blam-er-lam-er-lam! And dat was de last of Brer Engine-driving Monk. Lovely monkey he was, but a damned poor engineer." "My people! My people!"

Everybody would laugh at that, and the laughter puzzled me some. Weren't Negroes the smartest people on earth, or something like that? Somebody ought to remind the people of what we had heard at the schoolhouse. Instead of that, there would be more monkey stories.

There was the one about the white doctor who had a pet monkey who wanted to be a doctor. Kept worrying his master to show him how, and the doctor had other troubles, too. Another man had a bulldog who used to pass the doctor's gate every day and pick a fight with the monkey. Finally, the doctor saw a way to stop the monkey from worrying him about showing him how to be a doctor. "Whip that bulldog until he evacuates, then bring me some of it, monkey. I'll take it and show you how to be a doctor, and then I'll treat it in a way so as to ruin that bulldog for life. He won't be no more trouble to you."

"Oh, I'll git it, boss. Don't you worry. I sho' wants to be a doctor, and then again, dat old bulldog sho' is worry-some."

No sooner did the bulldog reach the gate that day, than the monkey, which could not wait for the bulldog to start the fight as usual, jumped on the dog. The monkey was all over him like gravy over rice. He put all he had into it and it went on until the doctor came out and drove the dog off and gave the monkey a chance to bolt into the office with what he had been fighting for.

"Here it tis, boss. It was a tight fight, but I got it."

"Fine! Fine!" the doctor told him. "Now, gimme that bottle over there. I'll fix that bulldog so he'll never be able to sit down again. When I get through with this, he'll be ruined for life."

"Hold on there, boss! Hold on there a minute! I wish you wouldn't do dat, boss."

"How come? You want to get rid of that old bulldog, don't you?"

"Dat's right, I sho' do."

"Well, why don't you want me to fix him, then?"

"Well, boss, you see it's like dis. Dat was a tight fight, a mighty tight fight. I could have been mistaken about dat bulldog, boss, we was all tangled up together so bad. You better leave dat fixing business alone, boss. De wrong man might git hurt."

There were many other tales, equally ludicrous, in which the Negro, sometimes symbolized by the monkey, and sometimes named outright, ran off with the wrong understanding of what he had seen and heard. Several white and Negro proposals of marriage were compared, and the like. The white suitor had said his love had dove's eyes. His valet had hurried to compliment his girl by saying she had dog's eyes, and so on.

There was a general acceptance of the monkey as kinfolks. Perhaps it was some distant memory of tribal monkey reverence from Africa which had been forgotten in the main, but remembered in some vague way. Perhaps it was an acknowledgment of our talent for mimicry with the monkey as a symbol.

The classic monkey parable, which is very much alive wherever the Negroes congregate in America, is the one about "My people!"

It seems that a monkey squatted down in the middle of a highway to play. A Cadillac full of white people came along, saw the monkey at play and carefully drove around him. Then came a Buick full of more white people and did the same. The monkey kept right on playing. Way after a while a T-model Ford came along full of Negroes. But instead of driving around the monkey, the car headed straight for him. He only saved his life by a quick leap to the shoulder of the road. He sat there and watched the car rattle off in the distance and sighed "My people! My people!"

A new addition to the tale is that the monkey has quit saying "My people!" He is now saying, "Those people! Those people!"

I found the Negro, and always the blackest Negro, being made the butt of all jokes, particularly black women.

They brought bad luck for a week if they came to your house of a Monday morning. They were evil. They slept with their fists balled up ready to fight and squabble even while they were asleep. They even had evil dreams. White, yellow and brown girls dreamed about roses and perfume and kisses. Black gals dreamed about guns, razors, ice-picks, hatchets and hot lye. I heard men swear they had seen women dreaming and knew these things to be true.

"Oh, gwan!" somebody would chide, laughing. "You know dat ain't so."

"Oh, now, he ain't lying," somebody else would take up the theme. "I know for my own self. I done slept wid yaller women and I done slept wid black ones. They *is* evil. You marry a yaller or a brown woman and wake her up in de night and she will sort of stretch herself and say, "I know what I was dreaming when you woke me up. I was dreaming I had done baked you a chicken and cooked you a great big old cake, and we was at de table eating our dinner out of de same plate, and I was sitting on your lap and we was just enjoying ourselves to death!" Then she will kiss you more times than you ask her to, and go on back to sleep. But you take and wake up a black gal, now! First thing she been sleeping wid her fists balled up, and you shake her, she'll lam you five or six times before you can get her awake. Then when she do git wake she'll have off and ast you, "Nigger, what you wake me up for? Know what I was dreaming when you woke me up? I dreamt dat you shook your old rusty black fist under my nose and I split your head open wid a axe." Then she'll kick your feets away from hers, snatch de covers all over on her side, ball up her fists agin, and gwan back to sleep. You can't tell me nothing. I know." "My people!"

This always was, and is still, good for a raucous burst of laughter. I listened to this talk and became more and more confused. If it was so honorable and glorious to be black, why was it the yellow-skinned people among us had so much prestige? Even a child in the first grade could see that this was so from what happened in the classroom and on school programs. The light-skinned children were always the angels, fairies and queens of school plays. The lighter the girl, the more money and prestige she was apt to marry. So on into high school years, I was asking myself questions. Were Negroes the great heroes I heard about from the platform, or were they the ridiculous monkeys of every-day talk? Was it really honorable to be black? There was even talk that it was no use for Negro boys and girls to rub all the hair off of their heads against college walls. There was no place for them to go with it after they got all this education. Some of the older heads held that it was too much for Negroes to handle. Better leave such things for the white folks, who knew what to do with it. But there were others who were all for pushing ahead. I saw the conflict in my own home between my parents. My mother was the one to dare all. My father was satisfied.

This Negro business came home to me in incidents and ways. There was the time when Old Man Bronner was taken out and beaten. Mr. Bronner was a white man of the poor class who had settled in aristocratic Maitland. One night just after dark, we heard terrible cries back in the woods behind Park Lake. Sam Mosely, his brother Elijah, and Ike Clarke, hurried up to our gate and they were armed. The howls of pain kept up. Old fears and memories must have stirred inside of the grown folks. Many people closed and barred their doors. Papa and the men around our gate were sullen and restless as the cries churned over the woods and lake.

"Who do you reckon it is?" Sam Mosely asked.

"I don't know for sure, but some thinks it's Jim Watson. Anyhow, he ain't home yet," Clarke said, and all of them looked at each other in an asking way.

Finally Papa said, "Well, hold on a minute till I go get my rifle."

"Tain't no ifs and buts about it," Elijah Mosely said gravely. "We can't leave Jim Watson be beat to death like that."

Papa had sensed that these armed men had not come to merely stand around and talk. They had come to see if he would go with the rest. When he came out shoving the sixteen bullets into his rifle, and dropping more into his pocket, Mama made no move to stop him. "Well, we all got families," he said with an attempt at lightness. "Shoot off your gun, somebody, so de rest will know we ready."

Papa himself pointed his Winchester rifle at the sky and fired a shot. Another shot answered him from around the store and a huddle of figures came hurrying up the road in the dark.

"It's Jim Watson. Us got to go git him!" and the dozen or more men armed with double-barreled shotguns, breech-loaders, pistols and Papa's repeating Winchester hurried off on their grim mission. Perhaps not a single one of them expected to return alive. No doubt they hoped. But they went.

Mama gasped a short sentence of some sort and herded us all into the house and barred the door. Lights went out all over the village and doors were barred. Axes had been dragged in from wood piles, grass-hooks, pitch-forks and scythes were ranked up in corners behind those barred doors. If the men did not come back, or if they only came back in part, the women and children were ready to do the best they could. Mama spoke only to say she wished Hezekiah and John, the two biggest boys, had not gone to Maitland late in the afternoon. They were not back and she feared they might start home and— But she did not cry. Our seven hounds with big, ferocious Ned in the lead, barked around the house. We huddled around Mama in her room and kept quiet. There was not a human sound in all the village. Nothing had ever happened before in our vicinity to create such tension. But people had memories and told tales of what happened back there in Georgia, and Alabama and West Florida that made the skin of the young crawl with transmitted memory, and reminded the old heads that they were still flinchy.

The dark silence of the village kept up for an hour or more. The once loud cries fell and fell until our straining ears could no longer find them. Strangest of all, not a shot was fired. We huddled in the dark and waited, and died a little, and waited. The silence was ten times more punishing than the cries.

At long last, a bubble of laughing voices approached our barn from the rear. It got louder and took on other dimensions between the barn and the house. Mama hissed at us to shut up when, in fact, nobody was saying a thing.

"Hey, there Little-Bits," Papa bellowed. "Open up!"

"Strike a light, Daught," Mama told my sister, feeling around in the dark to find Sarah's hand to give her the matches which I had seen clutched in her fingers before she had put out the light. Mama had said very little, and I could not see her face in the dark; somehow she could not scratch a match now that Papa was home again.

All of the men came in behind Papa, laughing and joking, perhaps more from relief than anything else.

"Don't stand there grinning like a chessy cat, Mr. Hurston," Mama scolded. "You ain't told me a thing."

"Oh, it wasn't Jim Watson at all, Lulu. You remember 'bout a week ago Old Man Bronner wrote something in de Orlando paper about H.'s daughter and W.B.J.'s son being seen sitting around the lakes an awful lot?"

"Yeah, I heard something about it."

"Well, you know those rich white folks wasn't going to 'low nothing like dat. So some of 'em waylaid him this evening. They pulled him down off of a load of hay he was hauling and drug him off back there in de woods and tanned his hide for him."

"Did y'all see any of it?"

"Nope, we could hear him hollering for a while, though.

We never got no further than the lake. A white man, one of the J—— boys was standing in the bushes at de road. When we got ready to turn off round de lake he stepped out and spoke to us and told us it didn't concern us. They had Bronner down there tied down on his all-fours, and de men was taking turns wid dat bull whip. They must have been standing on tip-toes to do it. You could hear them licks clear out to de road."

The men all laughed. Somebody mocked Bronner's cries and moans a time or two and the crowd laughed immoderately. They had gone out to rescue a neighbor or die in the attempt, and they were back with their families. So they let loose their insides and laughed. They resurrected a joke or two and worried it like a bone and laughed some more. Then they just laughed. The men who spoke of members of their race as monkeys had gone out to die for one. The men who were always saying, "My skin-folks, but not kinfolks; my race but not my taste," had rushed forth to die for one of these same contemptibles. They shoved each other around and laughed. So I could see that what looked like ridicule was really the Negro poking a little fun at himself. At the same time, just like other people, hoping and wishing he was what the orators said he was.

My mother eased back in her chair and took a dip of snuff. Maybe she did not feel so well, for she didn't get tickled at all. After a while, she ordered us off to bed in a rough voice. Time was, and the men scattered. Mama sat right where she was until Hezekiah and John came home around ten o'clock. She gave them an awful going over with her tongue for staying out late, and then she eased to bed.

I was dredged up inside that night, so I did not think about the incident's general connection with race. Besides I had to go to sleep. But days later, it was called to my recollection again. There was a program at the Methodist Church, and Mrs. Mattie Moseley, it was announced, was to have a paper. She was also going to have a fine new dress to read it in. We all wanted to see the dress.

The time came and she had the dress on. The subject of her paper was, "What will the Negroes do with the Whites?" I do not know what she decided was to be done. It seemed equally

unimportant to the rest of the town. I remember that everybody said it was a fine subject. But the next week, the women
talked about nothing else but the new wrist watch she had
on. It was the first one ever seen in our town.

But in me, the affair stirred up more confusion. Why bring
the subject up? Something was moving around me which I
had no hooks to grasp. What was this about white and black
people that was being talked about?

Certainly nothing changed in the village. The townspeople
who were in domestic service over in Maitland or Winter Park
went to work as usual. The white people interested in Eatonville came and went as before. Mr. Irving Batchellor, the author, who had a show place in Winter Park, petted up Willie
Sewell, who was his head gardener, in the same old way.
Bishop Whipple petted Elijah Mosely, and Mrs. Mars, who
was his sister, did lots of things for Lulu Mosely, Elijah's wife.
What was all the talk about? It certainly was puzzling to me.

As time went on, the confusion grew. By the time that I
got to high school, I was conscious of a group that was neither the top nor the bottom of Negrodom. I met the type
which designates itself as "the better-thinking Negro." I was
thrown off my stride by finding that while they considered
themselves Race Champions, they wanted nothing to do with
anything frankly Negroid. They drew color lines within the
race. The Spirituals, the Blues, *any* definitely Negroid thing
was just not done. They went to the trouble at times to protest the use of them by Negro artists. Booker T. Washington
was absolutely vile for advocating industrial education. There
was no analysis, no seeking for merits. If it was old Cuffy,
down with it! "My People! My People!"

This irritated me until I got to the place where I could
analyze. The thing they were trying to do went wrong because it lacked reason. It lacked reason because they were attempting to stand equal with the best in America without
having the tools to work with. They were attempting a flight
away from Negrodom because they felt that there was so
much scorn for black skin in the nation that their only security was in flight. They lacked the happy carelessness of a class
beneath them and the understanding of the top-flight Negro
above them. Once, when they used to set their mouths in

what they thought was the Boston Crimp, and ask me about the great differences between the ordinary Negro and "the better-thinking Negro," I used to show my irritation by saying I did not know who the better-thinking Negro was. I knew who the think-they-are-better Negroes were, but who were the better-thinkers was another matter. But when I came to understand what made them make their useless motions, and saw them pacing a cage that wasn't there, I felt more sympathy than irritation. If they want to establish a sort of fur-coat peerage, let 'em! Since they can find no comfort where they happened to be born, no especial talents to lift them, and other doors are closed to them, they have to find some pleasure somewhere in life. They have to use whatever their mentality provides. "My People! My People!"

So I sensed early, that the Negro race was not one band of heavenly love. There was stress and strain inside as well as out. Being black was not enough. It took more than a community of skin color to make your love come down on you. That was the beginning of my peace.

But one thing and another kept the conflict going on inside me, off and on for years. Sometimes I was sure that the Negro race was all that the platform speakers said. Then I would hear so much self-deprecation that I would be deflated. Over and over I heard people shake their heads and explain us by the supposed prayer of a humble Negro, who got down on his knees and said: "Lawd, you know I ain't nothing. My wife, she ain't nothing. My chillun ain't nothing, and if you fool 'round us, Lawd, you won't be nothing neither."

Light came to me when I realized that I did not have to consider any racial group as a whole. God made them duck by duck and that was the only way I could see them. I learned that skins were no measure of what was inside people. So none of the Race clichés meant anything anymore. I began to laugh at both white and black who claimed special blessings on the basis of race. Therefore I saw no curse in being black, nor no extra flavor by being white. I saw no benefit in excusing my looks by claiming to be half Indian. In fact, I boast that I am the only Negro in the United States whose grandfather on the mother's side was *not* an Indian chief. Neither did I descend from George Washington, Thomas Jefferson, nor

any Governor of a Southern state. I see no need to manufac-
ture me a legend to beat the facts. I do not coyly admit to a
touch of the tarbrush to my Indian and white ancestry. You
can consider me Old Tar-Brush in person if you want to. I am
a mixed-blood, it is true, but I differ from the party line in
that I neither consider it an honor nor a shame. I neither
claim Jefferson as my grandpa, nor exclaim, "Just look how
that white man took advantage of my grandma!" It does not
matter in the first place, and then in the next place, I do not
know how it came about. Since nobody ever told me, I give
my ancestress the benefit of the doubt. She probably ran away
from him just as fast as she could. But if that white man could
run faster than my grandma, that was no fault of hers. Anyway, you must remember, he didn't have a thing to do but to
keep on running forward. She, being the pursued, had to look
back over her shoulder every now and then to see how she
was doing. And you know your ownself, how looking backwards slows people up.

In this same connection, I have been told that God meant
for all the so-called races of the world to stay just as they are,
and the people who say that may be right. But it is a well
known fact that no matter where two sets of people come
together, there are bound to be some in-betweens. It looks
like the command was given to people's heads, because the
other parts don't seem to have heard tell. When the next
batch is made up, maybe Old Maker will straighten all that
out. Maybe the men will be more tangle-footed and the
women a whole lot more faster around the feet. That will
bring about a great deal more of racial and other kinds of
purity, but a somewhat less exciting world. It might work,
but I doubt it. There will have to be something harder to get
across than an ocean to keep East and West from meeting.
But maybe Old Maker will have a remedy. Maybe even He
has given up. Perhaps in a moment of discouragement He
turned the job over to Adolf Hitler and went on about His
business of making more beetles.

I do not share the gloomy thought that Negroes in
America are doomed to be stomped out bodaciously, nor
even shackled to the bottom of things. Of course some of
them will be tromped out, and some will always be at the

bottom, keeping company with other bottom-folks. It would be against all nature for all the Negroes to be either at the bottom, top, or in between. It has never happened with anybody else, so why with us? No, we will go where the internal drive carries us like everybody else. It is up to the individual. If you haven't got it, you can't show it. If you have got it, you can't hide it. That is one of the strongest laws God ever made.

I maintain that I have been a Negro three times—a Negro baby, a Negro girl and a Negro woman. Still, if you have received no clear cut impression of what the Negro in America is like, then you are in the same place with me. There is no *The Negro* here. Our lives are so diversified, internal attitudes so varied, appearances and capabilities so different, that there is no possible classification so catholic that it will cover us all, except My people! My people!

XIII

Two Women in Particular

Two women, among the number whom I have known intimately force me to keep them well in mind. Both of them have rare talents, are drenched in human gravy, and both of them have meant a great deal to me in friendship and inward experience. One, Fanny Hurst because she is so young for her years, and Ethel Waters because she is both so old and so young for hers.

Understand me, their ages have nothing to do with their birthdays. Ethel Waters is still a young woman. Fanny Hurst is far from old.

In my undergraduate days I was secretary to Fanny Hurst. From day to day she amazed me with her moods. Immediately before and after a very serious moment you could just see her playing with her dolls. You never knew where her impishness would break out again.

One day, for instance, I caught her playing at keeping house with company coming to see her. She told me not to leave the office. If the doorbell rang, Clara, her cook, was to answer it. Then she went downstairs and told Clara that I was to answer the doorbell. Then she went on to another part of the house. Presently I heard the bell, and it just happened that I was on my way downstairs to get a drink of water. I wondered why Clara did not go to the door. What was my amazement to see Miss Hurst herself open the door and come in, greet herself graciously and invite herself to have some tea. Which she did. She went into that huge duplex studio and had toasted English muffins and played she had company with her for an hour or more. Then she came on back up to her office and went to work.

I knew that she was an only child. She did not even have cousins to play with. She was born to wealth. With the help of images, I could see that lonely child in a big house making up her own games. Being of artistic bent, I could see her making up characters to play with. Naturally she had to talk for her characters, or they would not say what she wanted them to. Most children play at that at times. I had done that extensively so I knew what she was doing when I saw her with the door half open, ringing her own doorbell and inviting herself to have some tea and muffins. When she was tired of her game, she just quit and was a grown woman again.

On another occasion, she called me up from the outside. She had been out for about two hours when she called me and told me to meet her at 67th Street and Columbus Avenue with her goloshes. She was not coming home immediately. She had to go somewhere else and she needed her goloshes. It was a gloomy day with snow and slush underfoot.

So, I grabbed up her goloshes and hurried down to the corner to wait for her to come along in a cab, as she had said. She warned me that she was at Columbus Circle and I would have to hurry, or she would be there before I was. I ran part of the way and was happy that I was there before her. I looked this a way and I looked that a way, but no Fanny Hurst peeping out of a cab. I waited from one foot to the other. The wind was searching me like the police. After a long wait I decided that something had detained her or changed her plans. Perhaps, she was trying to reach me on the phone. I hurried on back to Number 27 and went inside. Who was stretched out on the divan, all draped in a gorgeous American Beauty rose housecoat, but Fanny Hurst! Been home such a long time that she was all draped and eating candy. It was not April, but she was playing April Fool on me. She never let on to me about that trick one way or another. She was grown again by then, and looking just as solemn as if she never played.

She likes for me to drive her, and we have made several tours. Her impishness broke out once on the road. She told me to have the car all serviced and ready for next morning. We were going up to Belgrade Lakes in Maine to pay Elizabeth Marbury a visit.

So soon next day we were on the road. She was Fanny Hurst, the famous author as far as Saratoga Springs. As we drove into the heart of town, she turned to me and said, "Zora, the water here at Saratoga is marvelous. Have you ever had any of it?"

"No, Miss Hurst, I never did."

"Then we must stop and let you have a drink. It would never do for you to miss having a drink of Saratoga water."

We parked near the famous United States Hotel and got out.

"It would be nice to stop over here for the night," she said. "I'll go see about the hotel. There is a fountain over there in the park. Be sure and get yourself a drink! You can take Lummox for a run while you get your water."

I took Lummox out of the car. To say I took Lummox for a run would be merely making a speech-figure. Lummox weighed about three pounds, and with his short legs, when he thought that he was running he was just jumping up and down in the same place. But anyway, I took him along to get the water. It was so-so as far as the taste went.

When I got back to the car, she was waiting for me. It was too early in the season for the hotel to be open. Too bad! She knew I would have enjoyed it so much. Well, I really ought to have some pleasure. Had I ever seen Niagara Falls?

"No, Miss Hurst. I always wanted to see it, but I never had a chance."

"Zora! You mean to tell me that you have never seen Niagara Falls?"

"No." I felt right sheepish about it when she put it that way.

"Oh, you must see the Falls. Get in the car and let's go. You must see those Falls right now." The way she sounded, my whole life was bare up to then and wrecked for the future unless I saw Niagara Falls.

The next afternoon around five o'clock, we were at Niagara Falls. It had been a lovely trip across Northern New York State.

"Here we are, now, Zora. Hurry up and take a good look at the Falls. I brought you all the way over here so that you could see them."

She didn't need to urge me. I leaned on the rail and looked and looked. It was worth the trip, all right. It was just like watching the Atlantic Ocean jump off of Pike's Peak.

In ten minutes or so, Miss Hurst touched me and I turned around.

"Zora, have you ever been across the International Bridge? I think you ought to see the Falls from the Canadian side. Come on, so you can see it from over there. It would be too bad for you to come all the way over here to see it and not see it from the Bridge."

So we drove across the Bridge. A Canadian Customs Official tackled us immediately. The car had to be registered. How long did we intend to stay?

"You'd better register it for two weeks," Miss Hurst answered and it was done. The sun was almost down.

"Look, Zora, Hamilton is only a short distance. I know you want to see it. Come on, let's drive on, and spend the night at Hamilton."

We drove on. I was surprised to see that everything in Canada looked so much like everything in the United States. It was deep twilight when we got into Hamilton.

"They tell me Kitchener is a most interesting little place, Zora. I know it would be fun to go on there and spend the night." So on to Kitchener we went.

Here was Fanny Hurst, a great artist and globe famous, behaving like a little girl, teasing her nurse to take her to the zoo, and having a fine time at it.

Well, we spent an exciting two weeks motoring over Ontario, seeing the country-side and eating at quaint but well-appointed inns. She was like a child at a circus. She was a run-away, with no responsibilities. A man in upper New York State dangled his old cherry trees at us as we drove homeward. He didn't have any business to do it. We parked and crept over into his old orchard and ate all we could, filled up our hats and drove on. Maybe he never missed them, but if he did, Miss Hurst said that it served him right for planting trees like that to dangle at people. Teach him a lesson. We came rolling south by east laughing, eating Royal Anne cherries and spitting seeds. It was glorious! Who has not eaten stolen fruit?

Fanny Hurst, the author, and the wife of Jacques Danielson, was not with us again until we hit Westchester on the way home. Then she replaced Mrs. Hurst's little Fanny and began to discuss her next book with me and got very serious in her manner.

While Fanny Hurst brings a very level head to her dressing, she exults in her new things like any debutante. She knows exactly what goes with her very white skin, black hair and sloe eyes, and she wears it. I doubt if any woman on earth has gotten better effects than she has with black, white and red. Not only that, she knows how to parade it when she gets it on. She will never be jailed for uglying up a town.

THIS ETHEL WATERS

I am due to have this friendship with Ethel Waters, because I worked for it.

She came to me across the footlights. Not the artist alone, but the person, and I wanted to know her very much. I was too timid to go backstage and haunt her, so I wrote her letters and she just plain ignored me. But I kept right on. I sensed a great humanness and depth about her soul and I wanted to know someone like that.

Then Carl Van Vechten gave a dinner for me. A great many celebrities were there, including Sinclair Lewis, Dwight Fiske, Anna Mae Wong, Blanche Knopf, an Italian soprano, and my old friend, Jane Belo. Carl whispered to me that Ethel Waters was coming in later. He was fond of her himself and he knew I wanted to know her better, so he had persuaded her to come. Carl is given to doing nice things like that.

We got to talking, Ethel and I, and got on very well. Then I found that what I suspected, was true. Ethel Waters is a very shy person. It had not been her intention to ignore me. She had felt that I belonged to another world and had no need of her. She thought that I had been merely curious. She laughed at her error and said, "And here you were just like me all the time." She got warm and friendly, and we went on from there. When she was implored to sing, she asked me first what I wanted to hear. It was "Stormy Weather," of course, and she did it beautifully.

Then I did something for her. She told us that she was going to appear with Hall Johnson's Choir at Carnegie Hall, and planned to do some spirituals. Immediately, the Italian soprano and others present advised her not to do it. The argument was that Marian Anderson, Roland Hayes and Paul

Robeson had sung them so successfully that her audience would make comparisons and Ethel would suffer by it. I saw the hurt in Ethel's face and jumped in. I objected that Ethel was not going to do any concertized versions of spirituals. She had never rubbed any hair off of her head against any college walls and she was not going to sing that way. She was going to sing those spirituals just the way her humble mother had sung them to her.

She turned to me with a warm, grateful smile on her face, and said, "Thank you."

When she got ready to leave, she got her wraps and said, "Come on, Zora. Let's go on uptown." I went along with her, her husband, and faithful Lashley, a young woman spiritual singer from somewhere in Mississippi, whom Ethel has taken under her wing.

We kept up with each other after that, and I got to know her very well. We exchanged confidences that really mean something to both of us. I am her friend, and her tongue is in my mouth. I can speak her sentiments for her, though Ethel Waters can do very well indeed in speaking for herself. She has a homely philosophy that reaches all corners of Life, and she has words to fit when she speaks.

She is one of the strangest bundles of people that I have ever met. You can just see the different folks wrapped up in her if you associate with her long. Just like watching an open fire — the color and shape of her personality is never the same twice. She has extraordinary talents which her lack of formal education prevents her from displaying. She never had a chance to go beyond the third grade in school. A terrible fear is in me that the world will never really know her. You have seen her and heard her on the stage, but so little of her capabilities gets seen. Her struggle for adequate expression throws her into moods at times. She said to me Christmas Day of 1941, "You have the advantage of me, Zora. I can only show what is on the stage. You can write a different kind of book each time."

She is a Catholic, and deeply religious. She plays a good game of bridge, but no card-playing at her house on Sundays. No more than her mother would have had in her house. Nobody is going to dance and cut capers around her on the

Sabbath, either. What she sings about and acts out on the stage, has nothing to do with her private life.

Her background is most humble. She does not mind saying that she was born in the slums of Philadelphia in an atmosphere that smacked of the rural South. She neither drinks nor smokes and is always chasing me into a far corner of the room when I light a cigarette. She thanks God that I don't drink.

Her religious bent shows in unexpected ways. For instance, we were discussing her work in "Cabins in the Sky." She said, "When we started to rehearse the spirituals, some of those no-manners people started to swinging 'em, and get smart. I told 'em they better not play with God's music like that. I told 'em if I caught any of 'em at it, I'd knock 'em clean over into that orchestra pit." Her eyes flashed fire as she told me about it. Then she calmed down and laughed. "Of course, you know, Zora, God didn't want me to knock 'em over. That was an idea of mine."

And this fact of her background has a great deal to do with her approach to people. She is shy and you must convince her that she is really wanted before she will open up her tender parts and show you. Even in her career, I am persuaded that Ethel Waters does not know that she has arrived. For that reason, she is grateful for any show of love or appreciation. People to whom she has given her love and trust have exploited it heartlessly, like hogs under an acorn tree—guzzling and grabbing with their ears hanging over their eyes, and never looking up to see the high tree that the acorns fell off of.

She has been married twice, unhappily each time because I am certain that neither man could perceive her.

"I was thirteen when I married the first time," she confided to me. "And I was a virgin when I got married."

Now, she is in love with Archie Savage, who is a talented dancer, and formerly of the Dunham group. They met during the rehearsals for "Cabins in the Sky" and the affair is on! It looks as if they will make a wed, because they are eternally together. He has given her a taste for things outside the theater like art museums and the opera. He has sold her on the pictures, statues and paintings, but she says that this opera business sticks in her craw. She says she can't see why people fool with a thing like that that just isn't natural.

"Singing is music, Zora, but this Grand Opera is a game. The opera singers lay so much down that they can make that high note, and the audiences fades 'em the price of admission that they can't do it. Of course, all those high class folks that lay bets on high notes are good sports. If the singers haul off and win the bet, they give 'em a great big hand, and go outside for a smoke. And the only reason that opera houses don't make no more money than they do, is because so many more folks would rather bet on race horses. I don't bet on nothing because I don't think it's right. But if I did, my money would be on the horse."

Still if Sonny (our intimate name for Archie) wants to take her to the opera, she will go to please him. "He is fire and fuel to my life," she told me and played with her handkerchief like a teen-age girl.

She went on the stage at thirteen and says that she got eight dollars a week for her first salary. She was so frightened that she had to be pushed on to sing her song, and then another member of the cast had to come on with her until she could get started. Then too, they had to place a chair for her to lean on to overcome her nervousness.

At fifteen, she introduced the St. Louis Blues to the world. She saw a sheet of the music, had it played for her, then wrote to W. C. Handy for permission to use it. Handy answered on a postal card and told her to go as far as she liked, or words to that effect. If W. C. Handy had only known at that time the importance of his act!

She is gay and sombre by turns. I have listened to her telling a story and noticed her change of mood in mid-story. I have asked her to repeat something particularly pungent that she has said, and had her tell me, "I couldn't say it now. My thoughts are different. Sometime when I am thinking that same way, I'll tell it to you again."

The similes and metaphors just drip off of her lips. One day I sat in her living room on Hobart Street in Los Angeles, deep in thought. I had really forgotten that others were present. She nudged Archie Savage and pointed at me. "Salvation looking at the temple forlorn," she commented and laughed. "What you doing, Zora? Pasturing in your mind?"

"It's nice to be talking things over with you, Zora," she told me another time. "Conversation is the ceremony of companionship."

Speaking of a man we both know, she said, "The bigger lie he tells, the more guts he tells it with."

"That man's jaws are loaded with big words, but he never says a thing," she said speaking of a mutual friend. "He got his words out of a book. I got mine out of life."

"She shot him lightly and he died politely," she commented after reading in the *Los Angeles Examiner* about a woman killing her lover.

Commenting on a man who had used coarse language, she said, "I'd rather him to talk differently, but you can't hold him responsible, Zora, they are all the words he's got."

Ethel Waters has known great success and terrible personal tragedy, so she knows that no one can have everything.

"Don't care how good the music is, Zora, you can't dance on every set."

I am grateful for the friendship of Fanny Hurst and Ethel Waters. But how does one speak of honest gratitude? Who can know the outer ranges of friendship? I am tempted to say that no one can live without it. It seems to me that trying to live without friends, is like milking a bear to get cream for your morning coffee. It is a whole lot of trouble, and then not worth much after you get it.

XIV
Love

WHAT do I really know about love? I have had some experiences and feel fluent enough for my own satisfaction. Love, I find is like singing. Everybody can do enough to satisfy themselves, though it may not impress the neighbors as being very much. That is the way it is with me, but whether I know anything unusual, I couldn't say. Don't look for me to call a string of names and point out chapter and verse. Ladies do not kiss and tell any more than gentlemen do.

I have read many books where the heroine was in love for a long time without knowing it. I have talked with people and they have told me the same thing. So maybe that is the way it ought to be. That is not the way it is with me at all. I have been *out* of love with people for a long time, perhaps without finding it out. But when I fall *in*, I can feel the bump. That is a fact and I would not try to fool you. Love may be a sleepy, creeping thing with some others, but it is a mighty wakening thing with me. I feel the jar, and I know it from my head on down.

Though I started falling in love before I was seven years old, I never had a fellow until I was nearly grown. I was such a poor picker. I would have had better luck if I had stuck to boys around my own age, but that wouldn't do me. I wanted somebody with long pants on, and they acted as if they didn't know I was even born. The heartless wretches would walk right past my gate with grown women and pay me no attention at all, other than to say hello or something like that. Then I would have to look around for another future husband, only to have the same thing happen all over again.

Of course, in high school I received mushy notes and wrote them. A day or two, a week or month at most would see the end of the affair. Gone without a trace. I was in my freshman year in college when I first got excited, really.

He could stomp a piano out of this world, sing a fair baritone and dance beautifully. He noticed me, too, and I was carried away. For the first time since my mother's death, there was someone who felt really close and warm to me.

This affair went on all through my college life, with the exception of two fallings-out. We got married immediately after I finished my work at Barnard College, which should have been the happiest day of my life. St. Augustine, Florida, is a beautiful setting for such a thing.

But, it was not my happiest day. I was assailed by doubts. For the first time since I met him, I asked myself if I really were in love, or if this had been a habit. I had an uncomfortable feeling of unreality. The day and the occasion did not underscore any features of nature nor circumstance, and I wondered why. Who had cancelled the well-advertised tour of the moon? Somebody had turned a hose on the sun. What I had taken for eternity turned out to be a moment walking in its sleep.

After our last falling-out, he asked me please to forgive him, and I said that I did. But now, had I really? A wind full of memories blew out of the past and brought a chilling fog. This was not the expected bright dawn. Rather, some vagrant ray had played a trick on the night. I could not bring myself to tell him my thoughts. I just couldn't, no matter how hard I tried, but there they were crowding me from pillar to post.

Back in New York, I met Mrs. Mason and she offered me the chance to return to my research work, and I accepted it. It seemed a way out without saying anything very much. Let nature take its course. I did not tell him about the arrangement. Rather, I urged him to return to Chicago to continue his medical work. Then I stretched my shivering insides out and went back to work. I have seen him only once since then. He has married again, and I hope that he is happy.

Having made such a mess, I did not rush at any serious affair right away. I set to work and really worked in earnest. Work was to be all of me, so I said. Three years went by. I had finished that phase of research and was considering writing my first book, when I met the man who was really to lay me by the heels. I met P.M.P.

He was tall, dark brown, magnificently built, with a beautifully modelled back head. His profile was strong and good. The nose and lip were especially good front and side. But his looks only drew my eyes in the beginning. I did not fall in love with him just for that. He had a fine mind and that intrigued me. When a man keeps beating me to the draw mentally, he begins to get glamorous.

I did not just fall in love. I made a parachute jump. No matter which way I probed him, I found something more to admire. We fitted each other like a glove. His intellect got me first for I am the kind of a woman that likes to move on mentally from point to point, and I like for my man to be there way ahead of me. Then if he is strong and honest, it goes on from there. Good looks are not essential, just extra added attraction. He had all of those things and more. It seems to me that God must have put in extra time making him up. He stood on his own feet so firmly that he reared back.

To illustrate the point, I got into trouble with him for trying to loan him a quarter. It came about this way.

I lived in the Graham Court at 116th Street and Seventh Avenue. He lived down in 64th Street, Columbus Hill. He came to call one night and everything went off sweetly until he got ready to leave. At the door he told me to let him go because he was going to walk home. He had spent the only nickel he had that night to come to see me. That upset me, and I ran to get a quarter to loan him until his pay day. What did I do that for? He flew hot. In fact he was the hottest man in the five boroughs. Why did I insult him like that? The responsibility was all his. He had known that he did not have his return fare when he left home, but he had wanted to come, and so he had come. Let him take the consequences for his own acts. What kind of a coward did I take him for? How could he deserve my respect if he behaved like a cream puff? He was a *man*! No woman on earth could either lend him nor give him a cent. If a man could not do for a woman, what good was he on earth? His great desire was to do for me. *Please* let him be a *man*!

For a minute I was hurt and then I saw his point. He had done a beautiful thing and I was killing it off in my blindness. If it pleased him to walk all of that distance for my sake, it pleased him as evidence of his devotion. Then too, he wanted to do all the doing, and keep me on the receiving end. He soared in my respect from that moment on. Nor did he ever change. He meant to be the head, *so help him over the fence!*

That very manliness, sweet as it was, made us both suffer. My career balked the completeness of his ideal. I really wanted to conform, but it was impossible. To me there was no conflict. My work was one thing, and he was all of the rest. But, I could not make him see that. Nothing must be in my life but himself.

But, I am ahead of my story. I was interested in him for nearly two years before he knew it. A great deal happened between the time we met and the time we had any serious talk.

As I said, I loved, but I did not say so, because nobody asked me. I made up my mind to keep my feelings to myself since they did not seem to matter to anyone else but me.

I went South, did some more concert work and wrote *Jonah's Gourd Vine* and *Mules and Men*, then came back to New York.

He began to make shy overtures to me. I pretended not to notice for a while so that I could be sure and not be hurt. Then he gave me the extreme pleasure of telling me right out loud about it. It seems that he had been in love with me just as long as I had been with him, but he was afraid that I didn't mean him any good, as the saying goes. He had been trying to make me tell him something. He began by complimenting me on my clothes. Then one night when we had attended the Alpha Phi Alpha fraternity dance—yes, he is an Alpha man—he told me that the white dress I was wearing was beautiful, but I did not have on an evening wrap rich enough to suit him. He had in mind just the kind he wanted to see me in, and when he made the kind of money he expected to, the first thing he meant to do was to buy me a gorgeous evening wrap and everything to go with it. He wanted *his* wife to look swell. He looked at me from under his eyelashes to see how I was taking it. I smiled and so he went on.

"You know, Zora, you've got a real man on your hands. You've got somebody to do for you. I'm tired of seeing you work so hard. I wouldn't want *my* wife to do anything but look after me. Be home looking like Skookums when I got there."

He always said I reminded him of the Indian on the Skookum Apples, so I knew he meant me to understand that he wanted to be coming home to me, and with those words he endowed me with Radio City, the General Motors Corporation, the United States, Europe, Asia and some outlying continents. I had everything!

So actively began the real love affair of my life. He was then a graduate of City College, and was working for his Master's degree at Columbia. He had no money. He was born of West Indian parents in the Columbus Hill district of New York City, and had nothing to offer but what it takes—a bright soul, a fine mind in a fine body, and courage. He is so modest that I do not think that he yet knows his assets. That was to make trouble for us later on.

It was a curious situation. He was so extraordinary that I lived in terrible fear lest women camp on his doorstep in droves and take him away from me. I found out later on that he could not believe that I wanted just him. So there began an agonizing tug of war. Looking at a very serious photograph of me that Carl Van Vechten had made, he told me one night in a voice full of feeling that that was the way he wanted me to look all the time unless I was with him. I almost laughed out loud. That was just the way I felt. I hated to think of him smiling unless he was smiling at me. His grins were too precious to be wasted on ordinary mortals, especially women.

If he could only have realized what a lot he had to offer, he need not have suffered so much through doubting that he could hold me. I was hog-tied and branded, but he didn't realize it. He could make me fetch and carry, but he wouldn't believe it. So when I had to meet people on business, or went to literary parties and things like that, it would drive him into a sulk, and then he would make me unhappy. I too, failed to see how deeply he felt. I would interpret his moods as indifference and die, and die, and die.

He begged me to give up my career, marry him and live outside of New York City. I really wanted to do anything he wanted me to do, but that one thing I could not do. It was not just my contract with my publishers, it was that I had things clawing inside of me that must be said. I could not see that my work should make any difference in marriage. He was all and everything else to me but that. One did not conflict with the other in my mind. But it was different with him. He felt that he did not matter to me enough. He was the master kind. All, or nothing, for him.

The terrible thing was that we could neither leave each other alone, nor compromise. Let me seem too cordial with any male and something was going to happen. Just let him smile too broad at any woman, and no sooner did we get inside my door than the war was on! One night (I didn't decide this) something primitive inside me tore past the barriers and before I realized it, I had slapped his face. That was a mistake. He was still smoldering from an incident a week old. A fellow had met us on Seventh Avenue and kissed me on my cheek. Just one of those casual things, but it had burned up P.M.P. So I had unknowingly given him an opening he had been praying for. He paid me off then and there with interest. No broken bones, you understand, and no black eyes. I realized afterwards that my hot head could tell me to beat him, but it would cost me something. I would have to bring head to get head. I couldn't get his and leave mine locked up in the dresser-drawer.

Then I knew I was too deeply in love to be my old self. For always a blow to my body had infuriated me beyond measure. Even with my parents, that was true. But somehow, I didn't hate him at all. We sat down on the floor and each one of us tried to take all the blame. He went out and bought some pie and I made a pot of hot chocolate and we were more affectionate than ever. The next day he made me a book case that I needed and you couldn't get a pin between us.

But fate was watching us and laughing. About a month later when he was with me, the telephone rang. Would I please come down to an apartment in the Fifties and meet an out-of-town celebrity? He was in town for only two days and he wanted to meet me before he left. When I turned from the phone, P.M.P. was changed. He begged me not to go. I reminded him that I had promised, and begged him to come along. He refused and walked out. I went, but I was most unhappy.

This sort of thing kept up time after time. He would not be

reconciled to the thing. We were alternately the happiest people in the world, and the most miserable. I suddenly decided to go away to see if I could live without him. I did not even tell him that I was going. But I wired him from some town in Virginia.

Miss Barnicle of New York University asked me to join her and Alan Lomax on a short bit of research. I was to select the area and contact the subjects. Alan Lomax was joining us with a recording machine. So because I was delirious with joy and pain, I suddenly decided to leave New York and see if I could come to some decision. I knew no more at the end than I did when I went South. Six weeks later I was back in New York and just as much his slave as ever.

Really, I never had occasion to doubt his sincerity, but I used to drag my heart over hot coals by supposing. I did not know that I could suffer so. Then all of my careless words came to haunt me. For theatrical effect, I had uttered sacred words and oaths to others before him. How I hated myself for the sacrilege now! It would have seemed so wonderful never to have uttered them before.

But no matter how soaked we were in ecstasy, the telephone or the door bell would ring, and there would be my career again. A charge had been laid upon me and I must follow the call. He said once with pathos in his voice, that at times he could not feel my presence. My real self had escaped him. I could tell from both his face and his voice that it hurt him terribly. It hurt me just as much to see him hurt. He really had nothing to worry about, but I could not make him see it. So there we were. Caught in a fiendish trap. We could not leave each other alone, and we could not shield each other from hurt. Our bitterest enemies could not have contrived more exquisite torture for us.

Another phase troubled me. As soon as he took his second degree, he was in line for bigger and better jobs. I began to feel that our love was slowing down his efforts. He had brains and character. He ought to go a long way. I grew terribly afraid that later on he would feel that I had thwarted him in a way and come to resent me. That was a scorching thought. Even if I married him, what about five years from now, the way we were going?

In the midst of this, I received my Guggenheim fellowship. This was my chance to release him, and fight myself free from my obsession. He would get over me in a few months and go on to be a very big man. So I sailed off to Jamaica. But I freely admit that everywhere I set my feet down, there were tracks of blood. Blood from the very middle of my heart. I did not write because if I had written and he answered my letter, everything would have broken down.

So I pitched in to work hard on my research to smother my feelings. But the thing would not down. The plot was far from the circumstances, but I tried to embalm all the tenderness of my passion for him in *Their Eyes Were Watching God.*

When I returned to America after nearly two years in the Caribbean, I found that he had left his telephone number with my publishers. For some time, I did not use it. Not because I did not want to, but because the moment when I should hear his voice something would be in wait for me. It might be warm and eager. It might be cool and impersonal, just with overtones from the grave of things. So I went south and stayed several months before I ventured to use it. Even when I returned to New York it took me nearly two months to get up my courage. When I did make the call, I cursed myself for the delay. Here was the shy, warm man I had left.

Then we met and talked. We both were stunned by the revelation that all along we had both thought and acted desperately in exile, and all to no purpose. We were still in the toils and after all my agony, I found out that he was a sucker for me, and he found out that I was in his bag. And I had a triumph that only a woman could understand. He had not turned into a tramp in my absence, but neither had he flamed like a newborn star in his profession. He confessed that he needed my aggravating presence to push him. He had settled down to a plodding desk job and reconciled himself. He had let his waistline go a bit and that bespoke his inside feeling. That made me happy no end. No woman wants a man all finished and perfect. You have to have something to work on and prod. That waistline went down in a jiffy and he began to discuss work-plans with enthusiasm. He could see something ahead of him besides time. I was happy. If he had been crippled in both legs, it would have suited me even better.

What will be the end? That is not for me to know. Life poses questions and that two-headed spirit that rules the beginning and end of things called Death, has all the answers. And even if I did know all, I am supposed to have some private business to myself. What I do know, I have no intention of putting but so much in the public ears.

Perhaps the oath of Hercules shall always defeat me in love. Once when I was small and first coming upon the story of "The Choice of Hercules," I was so impressed that I swore an oath to leave all pleasure and take the hard road of labor. Perhaps God heard me and wrote down my words in His book. I have thought so at times. Be that as it may, I have the satisfaction of knowing that I have loved and been loved by the perfect man. If I never hear of love again, I have known the real thing.

So much for what I know about the major courses in love. However, there are some minor courses which I have not grasped so well, and would be thankful for some coaching and advice.

First is the number of men who pant in my ear on short acquaintance, "You passionate thing! I can see you are just *burning* up! Most men would be disappointing to you. It takes a man like me for you. Ahhh! I know that you will just wreck me! Your eyes and your lips tell me a lot. You are a walking furnace!" This amazes me sometimes. Often when this is whispered gustily into my ear, I am feeling no more amorous than a charter member of the Union League Club. I may be thinking of turnip greens with dumplings, or more royalty checks, and here is a man who visualizes me on a divan sending the world up in smoke. It has happened so often that I have come to expect it. There must be something about me that looks sort of couchy. Maybe it is a birth-mark. My mother could have been frightened by a bed. There is nothing to be done about it, I suppose. But, I must say about these mirages that seem to rise around me, that the timing is way off on occasion.

Number two is, a man may lose interest in me and go where his fancy leads him, and we can still meet as friends. But if I get tired and let on about it, he is certain to become an enemy of mine. That forces me to lie like the cross-ties

from New York to Key West. I have learned to frame it so that
I can claim to be deserted and devastated by him. Then he
goes off with a sort of twilight tenderness for me, wondering
what it is that he's got that brings so many women down! I
do not even have to show real tears. All I need to do is show
my stricken face and dash away from him to hide my supposed heartbreak and renunciation. He understands that I am
fleeing before his allure so that I can be firm in my resolution
to save the pieces. He knew all along that he was a hard man
to resist, so he visualized my dampened pillow. It is a good
thing that some of them have sent roses as a poultice and
stayed away. Otherwise, they might have found the poor,
heartbroken wreck of a thing all dressed to kill and gone out
for a high-heel time with the new interest, who has the new
interesting things to say and do. Now, how to break off without acting deceitful and still keep a friend?

Number three is kin to Number two, in a way. Under the
spell of moonlight, music, flowers or the cut and smell of
good tweeds, I sometimes feel the divine urge for an hour, a
day or maybe a week. Then it is gone and my interest returns
to corn pone and mustard greens, or rubbing a paragraph
with a soft cloth. Then my ex-sharer of a mood calls up in a
fevered voice and reminds me of every silly thing I said, and
eggs me on to say them all over again. It is the third presentation of turkey hash after Christmas. It is asking me to be a
seven-sided liar. Accuses me of being faithless and inconsistent if I don't. There is no inconsistency there. I was sincere
for the moment in which I said the things. It is strictly a
matter of time. It was true for the moment, but the next day
or the next week, is not that moment. No two moments are
any more alike than two snowflakes. Like snowflakes, they get
that same look from being so plentiful and falling so close
together. But examine them closely and see the multiple differences between them. Each moment has its own task and
capacity, and doesn't melt down like snow and form again. It
keeps its character forever. So the great difficulty lies in trying
to transpose last night's moment to a day which has no
knowledge of it. That look, that tender touch, was issued by
the mint of the richest of all kingdoms. That same expression
of today is utter counterfeit, or at best the wildest of inflation.

What could be more zestless than passing out cancelled checks? It is wrong to be called faithless under circumstances like that. What to do?

I have a strong suspicion, but I can't be sure that much that passes for constant love is a golded-up moment walking in its sleep. Some people know that it is the walk of the dead, but in desperation and desolation, they have staked everything on life after death and the resurrection, so they haunt the graveyard. They build an altar on the tomb and wait there like faithful Mary for the stone to roll away. So the moment has authority over all of their lives. They pray constantly for the miracle of the moment to burst its bonds and spread out over time.

But pay no attention to what I say about love, for as I said before, it may not mean a thing. It is my own bath-tub singing. Just because my mouth opens up like a prayer book, it does not just have to flap like a Bible. And then again, anybody whose mouth is cut cross-ways is given to lying, unconsciously as well as knowingly. So pay my few scattering remarks no mind as to love in general. I only know my part.

Anyway, it seems to be the unknown country from which no traveler ever returns. What seems to be a returning pilgrim is another person born in the strange country with the same-looking ears and hands. He is a stranger to the person who fared forth, and a stranger to family and old friends. He is clothed in mystery henceforth and forever. So, perhaps nobody knows, or can tell, any more than I. Maybe the old Negro folk-rhyme tells all there is to know:

> Love is a funny thing; Love is a blossom;
> If you want your finger bit, poke it at a possum.

XV

Religion

Y OU wouldn't think that a person who was born with God in the house would ever have any questions to ask on the subject.

But as early as I can remember, I was questing and seeking. It was not that I did not hear. I tumbled right into the Missionary Baptist Church when I was born. I saw the preachers and the pulpits, the people and the pews. Both at home and from the pulpit, I heard my father, known to thousands as "Reverend Jno" (an abbreviation for John) explain all about God's habits, His heaven, His ways, and Means. Everything was known and settled.

From the pews I heard a ready acceptance of all that Papa said. Feet beneath the pews beat out a rhythm as he pictured the scenery of heaven. Heads nodded with conviction in time to Papa's words. Tense snatches of tune broke out and some shouted until they fell into a trance at the recognition of what they heard from the pulpit. Come "love feast"* some of the congregation told of getting close enough to peep into God's sitting room windows. Some went further. They had been inside the place and looked all around. They spoke of sights and scenes around God's throne.

That should have been enough for me. But somehow it left a lack in my mind. They should have looked and acted differently from other people after experiences like that. But these people looked and acted like everybody else—or so it seemed to me. They ploughed, chopped wood, went possum-hunting, washed clothes, raked up back-yards and cooked collard greens like anybody else. No more ornaments and nothing. It mystified me. There were so many things they

*The "Love Feast" or "Experience Meeting" is a meeting held either the Friday night or the Sunday morning before Communion. Since no one is supposed to take Communion unless he or she is in harmony with all other members, there are great protestations of love and friendship. It is an opportunity to re-affirm faith plus anything the imagination might dictate.

neglected to look after while they were right there in the presence of All-Power. I made up my mind to do better than that if ever I made the trip.

I wanted to know, for instance, why didn't God make grown babies instead of those little measly things that messed up didies and cried all the time? What was the sense in making babies with no teeth? He knew that they had to have teeth, didn't He? So why not give babies their teeth in the beginning instead of hiding the toothless things in hollow stumps and logs for grannies and doctors to find and give to people? He could see all the trouble people had with babies, rubbing their gums and putting wood-lice around their necks to get them to cut teeth. Why did God hate for children to play on Sundays? If Christ, God's son, hated to die, and God hated for Him to die and have everybody grieving over it ever since, why did He have to do it? Why did people die anyway?

It was explained to me that Christ died to save the world from sin and then too, so that folks did not have to die anymore. That was a simple, clear-cut explanation. But then I heard my father and other preachers accusing people of sin. They went so far as to say that people were so prone to sin, that they sinned with every breath they drew. You couldn't even breathe without sinning! How could that happen if we had already been saved from it? So far as the dying part was concerned, I saw enough funerals to know that somebody was dying. It seemed to me that somebody had been fooled and I so stated to my father and two of his colleagues. When they got through with me, I knew better than to say that out loud again, but their shocked and angry tirades did nothing for my bewilderment. My head was full of misty fumes of doubt.

Neither could I understand the passionate declarations of love for a being that nobody could see. Your family, your puppy and the new bull-calf, yes. But a spirit away off who found fault with everybody all the time, that was more than I could fathom. When I was asked if I loved God, I always said yes because I knew that that was the thing I was supposed to say. It was a guilty secret with me for a long time. I did not dare ask even my chums if they meant it when they said they loved God with all their souls and minds and hearts, and would be glad to die if He wanted them to. Maybe they had found out how to do it, and I was afraid of what they might say if they found out I hadn't. Maybe they wouldn't even play with me anymore.

As I grew, the questions went to sleep in me. I just said the words, made the motions and went on. My father being a preacher, and my mother superintendent of the Sunday School, I naturally was always having to do with religious ceremonies. I even enjoyed participation at times; I was moved, not by the spirit, but by action, more or less dramatic.

I liked revival meetings particularly. During these meetings the preacher let himself go. God was called by all of His praise-giving names. The scenery of heaven was described in detail. Hallelujah Avenue and Amen Street were paved with gold so fine that you couldn't drop a pea on them but what they rang like chimes. Hallelujah Avenue ran north and south across heaven, and was tuned to sound alto and bass. Amen Street ran east and west and was tuned to "treble" and tenor. These streets crossed each other right in front of the throne and made harmony all the time. Yes, and right there on that corner was where all the loved ones who had gone on before would be waiting for those left behind.

Oh yes! They were all there in their white robes with the glittering crowns on their heads, golden girdles clasped about their waists and shoes of jewelled gold on their feet, singing the hallelujah song and waiting. And as they walked up and down the golden streets, their shoes would sing, "sol me, sol do" at every step.

Hell was described in dramatic fury. Flames of fire leaped up a thousand miles from the furnaces of Hell, and raised blisters on a sinning man's back before he hardly got started downward. Hell-hounds pursued their ever-dying souls. Everybody under the sound of the preacher's voice was warned, while yet they were on pleading terms with mercy, to take steps to be sure that they would not be a brand in that eternal burning.

Sinners lined the mourner's bench from the opening night of the revival. Before the week was over, several or all of them would be "under conviction." People, solemn of face, crept off to the woods to "praying ground" to seek religion.

Every church member worked on them hard, and there was great clamor and rejoicing when any of them "come through" religion.

The pressure on the unconverted was stepped up by music and high drama. For instance I have seen my father stop preaching suddenly and walk down to the front edge of the pulpit and breathe into a whispered song. One of his most effective ones was:

> Run! Run! Run to the City of Refuge, children!
> Run! Oh, run! Or else you'll be consumed.

The congregation working like a Greek chorus behind him, would take up the song and the mood and hold it over for a while even after he had gone back into the sermon at high altitude:

Are you ready-ee? Hah!
For that great day, hah!
When the moon shall drape her face in mourning, hah!
And the sun drip down in blood, hah!
When the stars, hah!
Shall burst forth from their diamond sockets, hah!
And the mountains shall skip like lambs, hah!
Havoc will be there, my friends, hah!
With her jaws wide open, hah!
And the sinner-man, hah!
He will run to the rocks, hah!
And cry, Oh rocks! Hah!
Hide me! Hah!
Hide me from the face of an angry God, hah!
Hide me, Ohhhhhh!
But the rocks shall cry, hah!
Git away! Sinner man git away, hah!

(Tense harmonic chant seeps over the audience.)

You run to de rocks,
CHORUS: You can't hide
SOLOIST: Oh, you run to de rocks
CHORUS: Can't hide
SOLOIST: Oh, run to de mountain, you can't hide

ALL: Can't hide sinner, you can't hide.
         Rocks cry, I'm burning too, hah!
         In the eternal burning, hah!
         Sinner man! Hah!
         Where will you stand? Hah!
         In that great gittin'-up morning? Hah!

The congregation would be right in there at the right moment bearing Papa up and heightening the effect of the fearsome picture a hundred-fold. The more susceptible would be
swept away on the tide and "come through" shouting, and
the most reluctant would begin to waver. Seldom would
there be anybody left at the mourners' bench when the revival
meeting was over. I have seen my father "bring through" as
many as seventy-five in one two-week period of revival. Then
a day would be set to begin the induction into the regular
congregation. The first thing was to hear their testimony or
Christian experience, and thus the congregation could judge
whether they had really "got religion" or whether they were
faking and needed to be sent back to "lick de calf over" again.

It was exciting to hear them tell their "visions." This was
known as admitting people to the church on "Christian experience." This was an exciting time.

These visions are traditional. I knew them by heart as did
the rest of the congregation, but still it was exciting to see
how the converts would handle them. Some of them made up
new details. Some of them would forget a part and improvise
clumsily or fill up the gap with shouting. The audience knew,
but everybody acted as if every word of it was new.

First they told of suddenly becoming conscious that they
had to die. They became conscious of their sins. They were
Godly sorry. But somehow, they could not believe. They
started to pray. They prayed and they prayed to have their sins
forgiven and their souls converted. While they laid under conviction, the hell-hounds pursued them as they ran for salvation. They hung over Hell by one strand of hair. Outside of
the meeting, any of the listeners would have laughed at the
idea of anybody with hair as close to their heads as ninety-
nine is to a hundred hanging over Hell or anywhere else by a
strand of that hair. But it was part of the vision and the con-

gregation shuddered and groaned at the picture in a fervent manner. The vision must go on. While the seeker hung there, flames of fire leaped up and all but destroyed their ever-dying souls. But they called on the name of Jesus and immediately that dilemma was over. They then found themselves walking over Hell on a foot-log so narrow that they had to put one foot right in front of the other while the howling hell-hounds pursued them relentlessly. Lord! They saw no way of rescue. But they looked on the other side and saw a little white man and he called to them to come there. So they called the name of Jesus and suddenly they were on the other side. He poured the oil of salvation into their souls and, hallelujah! They never expect to turn back. But still they wouldn't believe. So they asked God, if he had saved their souls, to give them a sign. If their sins were forgiven and their souls set free, please move that big star in the west over to the east. The star moved over. But still they wouldn't believe. If they were really saved, please move that big oak tree across the road. The tree skipped across the road and kept on growing just like it had always been there. Still they didn't believe. So they asked God for one more sign. Would He please make the sun shout so they could be sure. At that God got mad and said He had shown them all the signs He intended to. If they still didn't believe, He would send their bodies to the grave, where the worm never dies, and their souls to Hell, where the fire is never quenched. So then they cried out "I believe! I believe!" Then the dungeon shook and their chains fell off. "Glory! I know I got religion! I know I been converted and my soul set free! I never will forget that day when the morning star bust in my soul. I never expect to turn back!"

The convert shouted. Ecstatic cries, snatches of chants, old converts shouting in frenzy with the new. When the tumult finally died down, the pastor asks if the candidate is acceptable and there is unanimous consent. He or she is given the right hand of fellowship, and the next candidate takes the floor. And so on to the end.

I know now that I liked that part because it was high drama. I liked the baptisms in the lake too, and the funerals for the same reason. But of the inner thing, I was right where I was when I first began to seek answers.

Away from the church after the emotional fire had died down, there were little jokes about some of the testimony. For instance a deacon said in my hearing, "Sister Seeny ought to know better than to be worrying God about moving the sun for her. She asked Him to move de tree to convince her, and He done it. Then she took and asked Him to move a star for her and He done it. But when she kept on worrying Him about moving the sun, He took and told her, says, 'I don't mind moving that tree for you, and I don't mind moving a star just to pacify your mind, because I got plenty of *them*. I ain't got but one sun, Seeny, and I ain't going to be shoving it around to please you and nobody else. I'd like mighty much for you to believe, but if you can't believe without me moving my sun for you, you can just go right on to Hell.' "

The thing slept on in me until my college years without any real decision. I made the necessary motions and forgot to think. But when I studied both history and philosophy, the struggle began again.

When I studied the history of the great religions of the world, I saw that even in his religion, man carried himself along. His worship of strength was there. God was made to look that way too. We see the Emperor Constantine, as pagan as he could lay in his hide, having his famous vision of the cross with the injunction: "*In Hoc Signo Vinces*," and arising next day not only to win a great battle, but to start out on his missionary journey with his sword. He could not sing like Peter, and he could not preach like Paul. He probably did not even have a good straining voice like my father to win converts and influence people. But he had his good points—one of them being a sword—and a seasoned army. And the way he brought sinners to repentance was nothing short of miraculous. Whole tribes and nations fell under conviction just as soon as they heard he was on the way. They did not wait for any stars to move, nor trees to jump the road. By the time he crossed the border, they knew they had been converted. Their testimony was in on Christian experience and they were all ready for the right hand of fellowship and baptism. It seems that Reverend Brother Emperor Constantine carried the gospel up and down Europe with his revival meetings to such an extent that Christianity really took on. In Rome where Christians had been looked upon as rather indifferent lion-bait at best, and as keepers of virgins in their homes for no real good to the virgins among other things at their worst, Christianity mounted. Where before, Emperors could scarcely find enough of them to keep the spectacles going, now they were everywhere, in places high and low. The arrow had left the bow. Christianity was on its way to world power that would last. That was only the beginning. Military power was to be called in time and time again to carry forward the gospel of peace. There is not apt to be any difference of opinion between you and a dead man.

It was obvious that two men, both outsiders, had given my religion its chances of success. First the apostle Paul, who had been Saul, the erudite Pharisee, had arisen with a vision when he fell off of his horse on the way to Damascus. He not only formulated the religion, but exerted his brilliant mind to carry it to the most civilized nations of his time. Then Constantine took up with force where Paul left off with persuasion.

I saw the same thing with different details, happen in all the other great religions, and seeing these things, I went to thinking and questing again. I have achieved a certain peace within myself, but perhaps the seeking after the inner heart of truth will never cease in me. All sorts of interesting speculations arise.

Will military might determine the dominant religion of tomorrow? Who knows? Maybe Franklin Delano Roosevelt will fall on his head tomorrow and arise with a vision of Father Divine in the sky and the motto, "Peace! It's wonderful!" glowing like a rainbow above it.

Maybe our President would not even have to fall off of a horse, or a battleship, as the case might be. If Father Divine should come to control thirty million votes, the President could just skip the fall; that is, off of the horse.

Then, we might hear the former Franklin D. Roosevelt addressed as Sincere Determination. Eleanor would be Divine Eternal Commutation. Celestial Bountiful Tribulations would be Sister Frances Perkins. Harry Hopkins, Angelic Saintly Shadow. His Vocal Honor, La Guardia, would be known as Always Sounding Trumpet, and on his evident good works in his nursery, Harold Ickes would be bound to win the title of Fruitful Love Abounding.

Things getting into a fix like that, Sincere Determination, being Arch Angel in the first degree, could have the honor of handing Father Divine his first bite at every meal. Celestial B. Tribulations would be in the kitchen dividing the opinion of the cooks. Eleanor, Divine Commutation, would be a Tidings-Angel, spreading the new gospel far and wide.

The Senate Chamber would be something to see. All of the seats in the center taken out and a long table loaded down with baked hams, turkeys, cakes and pies all ready for the legislative session to begin. With Father Divine at the head and Sincere Determination at the foot, slicing ham and turkey for the saints, there might not be much peace, but the laws would be truly wonderful. The saints would not overeat, either; what with being forced to raise their hands and cry "Peace!" every time Father Divine spoke and "it's truly wonderful" every time Sincere Determination uttered a sound, their eating would be negligible.

It would be a most holy conclave around that table. Sincere Determination would naturally be Senate president, seated under a huge picture of Father Divine. There would be no more disturbing debates and wrangling. The Lord would pass the law to Sincere Determination and he would pass it on to the Senate. The Senate would pass their plates for more ham and salad.

Father Divine would confine himself to pontifical audiences and meditation. He might even get himself a shoe embroidered with a quart or two of jewels for the dowagers of Park Avenue, Beacon Street and Sutton Place to have the extreme pleasure of kissing. His foot would be in it, of course. He wouldn't belittle a lady by sending out a cold shoe for impressively devout lady-angels to kiss like that.

Naturally, Sincere Determination would be able to read the Divine mind and then pass on which ones rated crowns of empire and which didn't. It would be the privilege of our Angelic Admirals and generals, "Puissant Defenders of the Faith," to demote all infidels and correct all typographical errors, emperor to impotent, and vice versa; according as a man worships, so is he, as the saying goes.

Naturally, there would be no more private money. Father would hold it all for everybody. No more just homes. Every house a "heaven." Peace!

Our holy fighting men would have high arching wings that covered up their mouths but left their ears wide open—a splendid type of fighting saints.

Don't think this impossible because of certain natural difficulties. Father Divine's looks need not be any drawback, nor a stumbling stone to our religious faith. Just let him collect enough votes and he will be a sure-enough pretty man in this world. Men with no more personal looks than he have founded all of our great religions. After all, the cradle of a creed is no Hollywood casting office.

So, having looked at the subject from many sides, studied beliefs by word of mouth and then as they fit into great rigid forms, I find I know a great deal about form, but little or nothing about the mysteries I sought as a child. As the ancient tent-maker said, I have come out of the same door wherein I went.

But certain things have seemed to me to be true as I heard the tongues of those who had speech, and listened at the lips of books. It seems to me to be true that heavens are placed in the sky because it is the unreachable. The unreachable and therefore the unknowable always seem divine—hence, religion. People need religion because the great masses fear life and its consequences. Its responsibilities weigh heavy. Feeling a weakness in the face of great forces, men seek an alliance with omnipotence to bolster up their feeling of weakness, even though the omnipotence they rely upon is a creature of their own minds. It gives them a feeling of security. Strong, self-determining men are notorious for their lack of reverence. Constantine, having converted millions to Christianity by the sword, himself refused the consolation of Christ until his last hour. Some say not even then.

As for me, I do not pretend to read God's mind. If He has a plan of the Universe worked out to the smallest detail, it would be folly for me to presume to get down on my knees and attempt to revise it. That, to me, seems the highest form of sacrilege. So I do not pray. I accept the means at my disposal for working out my destiny. It seems to me that I have been given a mind and will-power for that very purpose. I do not expect God to single me out and grant me advantages over my fellow men. Prayer is for those who need it. Prayer seems to me a cry of weakness, and an attempt to avoid, by trickery, the rules of the game as laid down. I do not choose to admit weakness. I accept the challenge of responsibility. Life, as it is, does not frighten me, since I have made my peace with the universe as I find it, and bow to its laws. The ever-sleepless sea in its bed, crying out "how long?" to Time; million-formed and never motionless flame; the contemplation of these two aspects alone, affords me sufficient food for ten spans of my expected lifetime. It seems to me that organized creeds are collections of words around a wish. I feel no need for such. However, I would not, by word or deed, attempt to deprive another of the consolation it affords. It is simply not for me. Somebody else may have my rapturous glance at the archangels. The springing of the yellow line of morning out of the misty deep of dawn, is glory enough for me. I know that nothing is destructible; things merely change forms. When the consciousness we know as life ceases, I know that I shall still be part and parcel of the world. I was a part before the sun rolled into shape and burst forth in the glory of change. I was, when the earth was hurled out from its fiery rim. I shall return with the earth to Father Sun, and still exist in substance when the sun has lost its fire, and disintegrated in infinity to perhaps become a part of the whirling rubble in space. Why fear? The stuff of my being is matter, ever changing, ever moving, but never lost; so what need of denominations and creeds to deny myself the comfort of all my fellow men? The wide belt of the universe has no need for finger-rings. I am one with the infinite and need no other assurance.

XVI

Looking Things Over

WELL, that is the way things stand up to now. I can look back and see sharp shadows, high lights, and smudgy inbetweens. I have been in Sorrow's kitchen and licked out all the pots. Then I have stood on the peaky mountain wrappen in rainbows, with a harp and a sword in my hands.

What I had to swallow in the kitchen has not made me less glad to have lived, nor made me want to low-rate the human race, nor any whole sections of it. I take no refuge from myself in bitterness. To me, bitterness is the under-arm odor of wishful weakness. It is the graceless acknowledgment of defeat. I have no urge to make any concessions like that to the world as yet. I might be like that some day, but I doubt it. I am in the struggle with the sword in my hands, and I don't intend to run until you run me. So why give off the smell of something dead under the house while I am still in there tussling with my sword in my hand?

If tough breaks have not soured me, neither have my glory-moments caused me to build any altars to myself where I can burn incense before God's best job of work. My sense of humor will always stand in the way of my seeing myself, my family, my race or my nation as the whole intent of the universe. When I see what we really are like, I know that God is too great an artist for we folks on my side of the creek to be all of His best works. Some of His finest touches are among us, without doubt, but some more of His masterpieces are among those folks who live over the creek.

I see too, that while we all talk about justice more than any other quality on earth, there is no such thing as justice in the absolute in the world. We are too human to conceive of it. We all want the breaks, and what seems just to us is something that favors our wishes. If we did not feel that way, there would be no monuments to conquerors in our high places. It is obvious that the successful warrior is great to us because he went and took things from somebody else that we could use, and made the vanquished pay dearly for keeping it from us so long. To us, our man-of-arms is almost divine in that he seized good things from folks who could not appreciate them (well, not like we could, anyway) and brought them where they belonged. Nobody wants to hear anything about the side of the conquered. Any remarks from him is rebellion. This attitude does not arise out of studied cruelty, but out of the human bent that makes us feel that the man who wants the same thing we want, must be a crook and needs a good killing. "Look at the miserable creature!" we shout in justification. "Too weak to hold what we want!"

So looking back and forth in history and around the temporary scene, I do not visualize the moon dripping down in blood, nor the sun batting his fiery eyes and laying down in the cradle of eternity to rock himself into sleep and slumber at instances of human self-bias. I know that the sun and the moon must be used to sights like that by now. I too yearn for universal justice, but how to bring it about is another thing. It is such a complicated thing, for justice, like beauty is in the eye of the beholder. There is universal agreement of the principle, but the application brings on the fight. Oh, for some disinterested party to pass on things! Somebody will hurry to tell me that we voted God to the bench for that. But the lawyers who interpret His opinions, make His decisions sound just like they made them up themselves. Being an idealist, I too wish that the world was better than I am. Like all the rest of my fellow men, I don't want to live around people with no more principles than I have. My inner fineness is continually outraged at finding that the world is a whole family of Hurstons.

Seeing these things, I have come to the point by trying to make the day at hand a positive thing, and realizing the uselessness of gloominess.

Therefore, I see nothing but futility in looking back over my shoulder in rebuke at the grave of some white man who has been dead too long to talk about. That is just what I would be doing in trying to fix the blame for the dark days of slavery and the Reconstruction. From what I can learn, it was sad. Certainly. But my ancestors who lived and died in it are dead. The white men who profited by their labor and lives are dead also. I have no personal memory of those times, nor no responsibility for them. Neither has the grandson of the man who held my folks. So I see no need in button-holing that grandson like the Ancient Mariner did the wedding guest and calling for the High Sheriff to put him under arrest.

I am not so stupid as to think that I would be bringing this descendant of a slave-owner any news. He has heard just as much about the thing as I have. I am not so humorless as to visualize this grandson falling out on the sidewalk before me, and throwing an acre of fits in remorse because his old folks held slaves. No, indeed! If it happened to be a fine day and he had had a nice breakfast, he might stop and answer me like this:

"In the first place, I was not able to get any better view of social conditions from my grandmother's womb than you could from your grandmother's. Let us say for the sake of argument that I detest the institution of slavery and all that it implied, just as much as you do. You must admit that I was no more powerful to do anything about it in my unborn state than you were in yours. Why fix your eyes on me? I respectfully refer you to my ancestors, and bid you a good day."

If I still lingered before him, he might answer me further by asking questions like this:

"Are you so simple as to assume that the Big Surrender (Note: The South, both black and white speak of Lee's surrender to Grant as the Big Surrender) banished the concept of human slavery from the earth? What is the principle of slavery? Only the literal buying and selling of human flesh on the block? That was only an outside symbol. Real slavery is couched in the desire and the efforts of any man or community to live and advance their interests at the expense of the lives and interests of others. All of the outward signs come out of that. Do you not realize that the power, prestige and prosperity of the greatest nations on earth rests on colonies and sources of raw materials? Why else are great wars waged? If you have not thought, then why waste up time with your vapid accusations? If you have, then why single *me* out?" And like Pilate, he will light a cigar, and stroll on off without waiting for an answer.

Anticipating such an answer, I have no intention of wasting

my time beating on old graves with a club. I know that I cannot pry aloose the clutching hand of Time, so I will turn all my thoughts and energies on the present. I will settle for from now on.

And why not? For me to pretend that I am Old Black Joe and waste my time on his problems, would be just as ridiculous as for the government of Winston Churchill to bill the Duke of Normandy the first of every month, or for the Jews to hang around the pyramids trying to picket Old Pharaoh. While I have a handkerchief over my eyes crying over the landing of the first slaves in 1619, I might miss something swell that is going on in 1942. Furthermore, if somebody were to consider my grandmother's ungranted wishes, and give *me* what *she* wanted, I would be too put out for words.

What do I want, then? I will tell you in a parable. A Negro deacon was down on his knees praying at a wake held for a sister who had died that day. He had his eyes closed and was going great guns, when he noticed that he was not getting anymore "amens" from the rest. He opened his eyes and saw that everybody else was gone except himself and the dead woman. Then he saw the reason. The supposedly dead woman was trying to sit up. He bolted for the door himself, but it slammed shut so quickly that it caught his flying coattails and held him sort of static. "Oh, no, Gabriel!" the deacon shouted, "dat ain't no way for you to do. I can do my own running, but you got to 'low me the same chance as the rest."

I don't know any more about the future than you do. I hope that it will be full of work, because I have come to know by experience that work is the nearest thing to happiness that I can find. No matter what else I have among the things that humans want, I go to pieces in a short while if I do not work. What all my work shall be, I don't know that either, every hour being a stranger to you until you live it. I want a busy life, a just mind and a timely death.

But if I should live to be very old, I have laid plans for that so that it will not be too tiresome. So far, I have never used coffee, liquor, nor any form of stimulant. When I get old, and my joints and bones tell me about it, I can sit around and write for myself, if for nobody else, and read slowly and carefully the mysticism of the East, and re-read Spinoza with love and care. All the while my days can be a succession of coffee cups. Then when the sleeplessness of old age attacks me, I can have a likker bottle snug in my pantry and sip away and sleep. Get mellow and think kindly of the world. I think I can be like that because I have known the joy and pain of deep friendship. I have served and been served. I have made some good enemies for which I am not a bit sorry. I have loved unselfishly, and I have fondled hatred with the red-hot tongs of Hell. That's living.

I have no race prejudice of any kind. My kinfolks, and my "skinfolks" are dearly loved. My own circumference of everyday life is there. But I see their same virtues and vices everywhere I look. So I give you all my right hand of fellowship and love, and hope for the same from you. In my eyesight, you lose nothing by not looking just like me. I will remember you all in my good thoughts, and I ask you kindly to do the same for me. Not only just me. You who play the zig-zag lightning of power over the world, with the grumbling thunder in your wake, think kindly of those who walk in the dust. And you who walk in humble places, think kindly too, of others. There has been no proof in the world so far that you would be less arrogant if you held the lever of power in your hands. Let us all be kissing-friends. Consider that with tolerance and patience, we godly demons may breed a noble world in a few hundred generations or so. Maybe all of us who do not have the good fortune to meet or meet again, in this world, will meet at a barbecue.

APPENDIX
TO
DUST TRACKS ON A ROAD

"My People, My People!"

M Y PEOPLE, MY PEOPLE!" This very minute, nations of people are moaning it and shaking their heads with a sigh. Thousands and millions of people are uttering it in different parts of the globe. Differences of geography and language make differences in sound, that's all. The sentiment is the same. Yet and still it is a private wail, sacred to my people.

Not that the expression is hard to hear. It is being thrown around with freedom. It is the interpretation that is difficult. No doubt hundreds of outsiders standing around have heard it often enough, but only those who have friended with us like Carl Van Vechten know what it means.

Which ever way you go to describe it—the cry, the sigh, the wail, the groaning grin or grinning groan of "My People, My People!" bursts from us when we see sights that bring on despair.

Say that a brown young woman, fresh from the classic halls of Barnard College and escorted by a black boy from Yale, enters the subway at 50th street. They are well-dressed, well-mannered and good to look at. The eyes of the entire coach agree on that. They are returning from a concert by Marian Anderson and are still vibrating from her glowing tones. They are saying happy things about the tribute the huge white audience paid her genius and her arts. Oh yes, they say, "the Race is going to amount to something after all. Definitely! Look at George W. Carver and Ernest Just and Abram Harris, and Barthe is getting on right well with his sculpture and E. Simms Campbell is holding his own on *Esquire* and oh yes, Charles S. Johnson isn't doing so badly either. Paul Robeson, E. Franklin Frazier, Roland Hayes, well you just take them for granted. There is hope indeed for the Race."

By that time the train pulls into 72nd street. Two scabby-looking Negroes come scrambling into the coach. The coach is not full. There are plenty of seats, but no matter how many vacant seats there are, no other place will do, except side by side with the Yale-Barnard couple. No, indeed! Being dirty and smelly, do they keep quiet otherwise? A thousand times, No! They woof, bookoo, broadcast and otherwise distriminate from one end of the coach to the other. They consider it a golden opportunity to put on a show. Everybody in the coach being new to them, they naturally have not heard about the way one of the pair beat his woman on Lenox Avenue. Therefore they must be told in great detail what led up to the fracas, how many teeth he knocked out during the fight, and what happened after. His partner is right there, isn't he? Well, all right now. He's in the conversation too, so he must talk out of his mouth and let the coach know just how he fixed *his* woman up when she tried that same on *him*.

Barnard and Yale sit there and dwindle and dwindle. They do not look around the coach to see what is in the faces of the white passengers. They know too well what is there. Some are grinning from the heel up and some are stonily quiet. But both kinds are thinking "That's just like a Negro." Not just like *some* Negroes, mind you, No, like all. Only difference is some Negroes are better dressed. Feeling all of this like rock-salt under the skin, Yale and Barnard shake their heads and moan "My People, My People!"

Maybe at the other end of the coach another couple are saying the same thing but with a different emotion. They say it with a chuckle. They have enjoyed the show, and they are saying in the same tone of voice that a proud father uses when he boasts to others about that bad little boy of his at home. "Mischievous, into everything, beats up all the kids in the neighborhood. Don't know what I'm going to do with the little rascal." That's the way some folks say the thing.

Certain of My People have come to dread railway day coaches for this same reason. They dread such scenes more than they do the dirty upholstery and other inconveniences of a Jim Crow coach. They detest the forced grouping. The railroad company feels "you are all colored aren't you? So why not all together? If you are not all alike, *that's your own fault.* Once upon a time you were all alike. You had no business to change. If you are not that way, then it's just too bad. You're supposed to be like that." So when sensitive souls are forced to travel that way they sit there numb and when some free soul takes off his shoes and socks, they mutter "My race but not My taste." When somebody else eats fried fish, bananas and a mess of peanuts and throws all the leavings on the floor, they gasp "My skinfolks but not my kinfolks." And sadly over all, they keep sighing "My People, My People!"

Who are My People? I would say all those hosts spoken of as Negroes, Colored folks, Aunt Hagar's chillun, the brother in black, Race men and women, and My People. They range in color from Walter White, white through high yaller, yaller, Punkin color, high brown, vaseline brown, seal brown, black, smooth black, dusty black, rusty black, coal black, lam black and damn black. My people there in the south of the world, the east of the world, in the west and even some few in the north. Still and all, you can't just point out my people by skin color.

White people have come running to me with a deep wrinkle between the eyes asking me things. They have heard talk going around about this passing, so they are trying to get some information so they can know. So since I have been asked, that gives me leave to talk right out of my mouth.

In the first place, this passing business works both ways. All the passing is not passing for white. We have white folks among us passing for colored. They just happened to be born with a tinge of brown in the skin and took up being colored as a profession. Take James Weldon Johnson for instance.

There's a man white enough to suit Hitler and he's been passing for colored for years.

Now, don't get the idea that he is not welcome among us. He certainly is. He has more than paid his way. But he just is not a Negro. You take a look at him and ask why I talk like that. But you know, I told you back there not to depend too much on skin. You'll certainly get mis-put on your road if you put too much weight on that. Look at James Weldon Johnson from head to foot, but don't let that skin color and that oskobolic hair fool you. Watch him! Does he parade when he walks? No, James Weldon Johnson proceeds. Did anybody ever, *ever* see him grin? No, he smiles. He couldn't give a grin if he tried. He can't even Uncle Tom. Not that I complain of "Tomming" if it's done right.

"Tomming" is not an aggressive act, it is true, but it has its uses like feinting in the prize ring. But James Weldon Johnson can't Tom. He has been seen trying it, but it was sad. Let him look around at some of the other large Negroes and hand over the dice.

No, I never expect to see James Weldon Johnson a success in the strictly Negro Arts, but I would not be at all surprised to see him crowned. The man is just full of that old monarch material. If some day I looked out of my window on Seventh Avenue and saw him in an ermine robe and a great procession going to the Cathedral of St. John the Divine to be crowned I wouldn't be a bit surprised. Maybe he'd make a mighty fine king at that. He's tried all he knew how to pass for colored, but he just hasn't made it. His own brother is scared in his presence. He bows and scrapes and calls him The Duke.

So now you say "Well, if you can't tell who My People are by skin color, how are you going to know?" There's more ways than one of telling, and I'm going to point them out right now.

A

Wait until you see a congregation of more than two dark com-plected people. If they can't agree on a single, solitary thing, then you can go off satisfied. Those are My People. It's just against nature for us to agree with each other. We not only refuse to agree, we'll get mad and fight about it. *But only each other!* Anybody else can cool us off right now. We fly hot quick, but we are easily cooled when we find out the person who made us mad is not another Negro.

There is the folk-tale of the white man who hired five men to take hold of a rope to pull up a cement block. They caught hold and gave a yank and the little stone flew way up to the pulley the first time. The men looked at one 'nother in surprise and so one of them said to the bossman: "Boss, how come you hire all of us to pull up that one little piece of rock? One man could do that by hisself." "Yeah, I know it," the bossman told him, "but I just wanted to see five Negroes pulling together once."

Then there is the story of the man who was called on to pray. He got down and he said "Oh Lord, I want to ask something, but I know you can't do it. I just *know* you can't do it." Then he took a long pause.

Somebody got restless and said "Go ahead and ask Him. That's God you talking to. He can do anything."

The man who was praying said "I know He is supposed to do all things, but this what I wants to ask. . . ."

"Aw go on and ask Him. God A'Mighty can do anything. Go on, brother, and ask Him and finish up your prayer."

"Well, alright, I'll ask Him. O Lord, I'm asking you because they tell me to go ahead. I'm asking you something, but I just know you can't do it. I just *know* you can't do it but I'll just ask you. Lord, I'm asking you to bring my people together, but I *know* you can't do it, Lord. Amen."

Maybe the Lord *can* do it, but he hasn't done it yet.

It do say in the Bible that the Lord started the disturbance himself. It was the sons of Ham who built the first big city and started the tower of Babel. They were singing and building their way to heaven when the Lord came down and confused their tongues. We haven't built no more towers and things like that but we still got the confusion. The other part about the building and what not may be just a folk-tale, but we've got proof about the tongue power.

So when you find a set of folks who won't agree on a thing, those are My People.

B

If you have your doubts, go and listen to the man. If he hunts for six big words where one little one would do, that's My People. If he can't find that big word he's feeling for, he is going to make a new one. But somehow or other that new-made word fits the thing it was made for. Sounds good, too. Take for instance the time when the man needed the word *slander* and he didn't know it. He just made the word distriminate and anybody that heard the word would know what he meant. "Don't distriminate de woman." Somebody didn't know the word total nor entire so they made bodacious. Then there's asterperious, and so on. When you find a man chewing up the dictionary and spitting out language, that's My People.

C

If you still have doubts, study the man and watch his ways. See if all of him fits into today. If he has no memory of yesterday, nor no concept of tomorrow, then he is My People. There is no tomorrow in the man. He mentions the word plentiful and often. But there is no real belief in a day that is not here and present. For him to believe in a tomorrow would mean an obligation to consequences. There is no sense of consequences. Else he is not My People.

D

If you are still not satisfied, put down two piles of money. Do not leave less than a thousand dollars in one pile and do not leave more than a dollar and a quarter in the other. Expose these two sums where they are equally easy to take. If he takes the thousand dollars he is not My People. That is settled. My People never steal more than a dollar and a quarter. This test is one of the strongest.

E

But the proof positive is the recognition of the monkey as our brother. No matter where you find the brother in black he is telling a story about his brother the monkey. Different languages and geography, but that same tenderness. There is recognition everywhere of the monkey as a brother. Whenever we want to poke a little fun at ourselves, we throw the cloak of our short-comings over the monkey. This is the American classic:

The monkey was playing in the road one day and a big new Cadillac come down the road full of white people. The driver saw the monkey and drove sort of to one side and went on. Several more cars came by and never troubled the monkey at all. Way after while here come long a Ford car full of Colored folks. The driver was showing off, washing his foot in the gas tank. The car could do 60 and he was doing 70 (he had the accelerator down to the floor). Instead of slowing up when he saw the monkey, he got faster and tried to run over him. The monkey just barely escaped by jumping way to one side. The Negro hollered at him and said, "Why de hell don't you git out of de way? You see me washing my feet in the gas tank! I ought to kill you." By that time they went on down the road. The monkey sat there and shook his head and said "My People, My People!" However, Georgette Harvey, that superb actress, said that she had spoken with our brother the monkey recently and he does not say "My People" any more. She says the last monkey she talked with was saying "Those People, Those People!" Maybe he done quit the Race. Walked out cold on the family.

F

If you look at a man and mistrust your eyes, do something and see if he will imitate you right away. If he does, that's My People. We love to imitate. We would rather do a good imitation than any amount of something original. Nothing is half so good as something that is just like something else. And no title is so coveted as the "black this or that." Roland Hayes is right white folksy that way. He has pointedly refused the title of "The Black Caruso." It's got to be Roland Hayes or nothing. But he is exceptional that way. We have Black Patti, Black Yankees, Black Giants. Rose McClendon was referred to time and again as the Black Barrymore. Why we even had a Black Dillinger! He was the Negro that Dillinger carried out of Crown Point when he made his famous wooden gun escape. Of course he didn't last but a day or two after he got back to Detroit or Buffalo, or where ever he was before the police gave him a black-out. He could have kept quiet and lived a long time perhaps, but he would rather risk dying than to miss wearing his title. As far as he was able, he was old Dillinger himself. Julian, the parachute jumper, risked his life by falling in the East River pretending he knew how to run an aeroplane like Lindbergh to gain his title of Black Eagle. Lindbergh landed in Paris and Julian landed in New-York harbor, but, anyhow, he flew some.

What did Haiti ever do to make the world glad it happened? Well, they held a black revolution right behind the white one in France. And now their Senators and Deputies go around looking like cartoons of French Ministers and Senators in spade whiskers and other goatee forms. They wave their hands and arms and explain about their latin temperaments, but it is not impressive. If you didn't hear them talk, in a bunch, they could be Adam Powell's Abbysinia Baptist Church turning out and nobody would know the difference.

In Jamaica, the various degrees of Negroes put on some outward show to impress you that no matter what your eyes tell you, that they are really white folks— *white* English folks inside. The moment you meet a mulatto there he makes an opportunity to tell you who his father was. You are bound to hear a lot about that Englishman or that Scot. But never a word about the black mama. It is as if she didn't exist. Had never existed at all. You get the impression that Jamaica is the place where roosters lay eggs. That these Englishmen come there and without benefit of females they just scratch out a nest and lay an egg that hatches out a Jamaican.

As badly as the Ethiopians hated to part with Haile Selassie and freedom, it must be some comfort to have Mussolini for a model. By now, all the Rasses and other big shots are tootching out their lips ferociously, gritting their teeth and otherwise making faces like Il Duce. And I'll bet you a fat man against sweet back that all the little boy Ethiopians are doing a mean pouter pigeon strut around Addis Ababa.

And right here in these United States, we don't miss doing a thing that the white folks do, possible or impossible. Education, Sports, keeping up with the Joneses and the whole shebang. The unanswerable retort to criticism is "The white folks do it, don't they?" In Mobile, Alabama, I saw the Millionaires' ball. A man who roomed in the same house with me got me a ticket and carried me to a seat in the balcony. He warned me not to come down on the dance floor until the first dance was over. The Millionaires and their lady friends would want the floor all to themselves for that dance. It was very special. I was duly impressed, I tell you.

The ball opened with music. A fairly good dance orchestra was on the job. That first dance, exclusively for the Millionaires, was announced and each Millionaire and his lady friend were announced by name as they took the floor.

"John D. Rockefeller, dancing with Miss Selma Jones!" I looked down and out walked Mr. Rockefeller in a pair of white wool pants with a black pin stripe, pink silk shirt without a coat because it was summer time. Ordinarily, Mr. Rockefeller delivered hats for a millinery shop, but not tonight.

Commodore Vanderbilt was announced and took the floor. The Commodore was so thin in his ice-cream pants that he just had no behind at all. Mr. Ford pranced out with his lady doing a hot cutout. J. P. Morgan entered doing a mean black-bottom, and so on. Also each Millionaire presented his lady friend with a five-dollar gold piece after the dance. It was reasoned the Millionaires would have done the same for the same pleasure.

G

Last but not least, My People love a show. We love to act more than we love to see acting done. We love to look at them and we love to put them on, and we love audiences when we get to specifying.

That's why some of us take advantage of trains and other public places like dance halls and picnics. We just love to dramatize.

Now you've been told, so you ought to know. But maybe, after all the Negro doesn't really exist. What we think is a race is detached moods and phases of other people walking around. What we have been talking about might not exist at all. Could be the shade patterns of something else thrown on the ground—other folks, seen in shadow. And even if we do exist it's all an accident anyway. God made everybody else's color. We took ours by mistake. The way the old folks tell it, it was like this, you see.

God didn't make people all of a sudden. He made folks by degrees. First he stomped out the clay and then he cut out the patterns and propped 'em against the fence to dry. Then after they was dry, He took and blowed the breath of life into 'em and sent 'em on off. Next day He told everybody to come up and get toe-nails. So everybody come and got their toe-nails and finger-nails and went on off. Another time He said for everybody to come get their Nose and Mouth because He was giving 'em out that day. So everybody come got noses and mouths and went on off. Kept on like that till folks had everything but their color. So one day God called everybody up and said, "Now I want everybody around the throne at seven o'clock sharp tomorrow morning. I'm going to give out color tomorrow morning and I want everybody here on time. I got a lot more creating to do and I want to give out this color and be through with that."

Seven o'clock next morning God was sitting on His throne with His great crown on His head. He looked North, He looked East, He looked West and He looked Australia and blazing worlds was falling off of His teeth. After a while He looked down from His high towers of elevation and considered the Multitudes in front of Him. He looked to His left and said, "Youse red people!" so they all turned red and said "Thank you, God" and they went on off. He looked at the next host and said, "Youse yellow people!" and they got yellow and said "Thank you, God" and they went on off. Then He looked at the next multitude and said, "Youse white people" and they got white and told Him, "Thank you, God" and they went on off. God looked on His other hand and said, "Gabriel, look like I miss some hosts." Gabriel looked all around and said, "Yes, sir, several multitudes ain't here." "Well," God told him, "you go hunt 'em up and tell 'em I say they better come quick if they want any color. Fool with me and I won't give out no more." So Gabriel went round everywhere hunting till way after while he found the lost multitudes down by the Sea of Life asleep under a tree. So he told them they better hurry if they wanted any color. God wasn't going to wait on them much longer. So everybody jumped up and went running up to the throne. When the first ones got there they couldn't stop because the ones behind kept on pushing and shoving. They kept on until the throne was careening way over to one side. So God hollered at 'em "Get back! Get back!!" But they thought He said "Git black!" So they got black and just kept the thing agoing.

So according to that, we are no race. We are just a collection of people who overslept our time and got caught in the draft.

ZORA NEALE HURSTON
July 2, 1937
Port-au-Prince, Haiti.

Seeing the World As It Is

T HING lies forever in her birthing-bed and glories. But hungry Time squats beside her couch and waits. His frame was made out of emptiness, and his mouth set wide for prey. Mystery is his oldest son, and power is his portion.

That brings me before the unlived hour, that first mystery of the Universe with its unknown face and reflecting back. For it was said on the day of first sayings that Time should speak backward over his shoulder, and none should see his face, so scornful is he of the creatures of Thing.

What the faceless years will do to me, I do not know. I see Time's footprints, and I gaze into his reflections. My knees have dragged the basement of Hell and I have been in Sorrow's Kitchen, and it has seemed to me that I have licked out all the pots. The winters have been and my soul-stuff has lain mute like a plain while the herds of happenings thundered across my breast. In these times there were deep chasms in me which had forgotten their memory of the sun.

But time has his beneficent moods. He has commanded some servant-moments to transport me to high towers of elevation so that I might look out on the breadth of things. This is a privilege granted to a servant of many hours, but a master of few, from the master of a trillion billion hours and the servant of none.

In those moments I have seen that it is futile for me to seek the face of, and fear, an accusing God withdrawn somewhere beyond the stars in space. I myself live upon a star, and I can be satisfied with the millions of assurances of deity about me. If I have not felt the divinity of man in his cults, I have found it in his works. When I lift my eyes to the towering structures of Manhattan, and look upon the mighty tunnels and bridges of the world, I know that my search is over, and that I can depart in peace. For my soul tells me, "Truly this is the son of God. The rocks and the winds, the tides and the hills are his servants. If he talks in finger-rings, he works in horizons which dwarf the equator. His works are as noble as his words are foolish."

I found that I had no need of either class or race prejudice, those scourges of humanity. The solace of easy generalization was taken from me, but I received the richer gift of individualism. When I have been made to suffer or when I have been made happy by others, I have known that individuals were responsible for that, and not races. All clumps of people turn out to be individuals on close inspection.

This has called for a huge cutting of dead wood on my part. From my earliest remembrance, I heard the phrases, "Race Problem," "Race Pride," "Race Man or Woman," "Race Solidarity," "Race Consciousness," "Race Leader," and the like. It was a point of pride to be pointed out as a "Race Man." And to say to one, "Why, you are not a race man," was low-rating a person. Of course these phrases were merely sounding syllables to me as a child. Then the time came when I thought they meant something. I cannot say that they ever really came clear in my mind, but they probably were as clear to me as they were to the great multitude who uttered them. Now, they mean nothing to me again. At least nothing that I want to feel.

There could be something wrong with me because I see Negroes neither better nor worse than any other race. Race pride is a luxury I cannot afford. There are too many implications behind the term. Now, suppose a Negro does something really magnificent, and I glory, not in the benefit to mankind, but in the fact that the doer was a Negro. Must I not also go hang my head in shame when a member of my race does something execrable? If I glory, then the obligation is laid upon me to blush also. I *do* glory when a Negro does something fine, I gloat because he or she has done a fine thing, but not because he was a Negro. That is incidental and accidental. It is the human achievement which I honor. I execrate a foul act of a Negro but again not on the grounds that the doer was a Negro, but because it was foul. A member of my race just happened to be the fouler of humanity. In other words, I know that I cannot accept responsibility for thirteen million people. Every tub must sit on its own bottom regardless. So "Race Pride" in me had to go. And anyway, why should I be proud to be a Negro? Why should anybody be proud to be white? Or yellow? Or red? After all, the word "race" is a loose classification of physical characteristics. It tells nothing about the insides of people. Pointing at achievements tells nothing either. Races have never done anything. What seems race achievement is the work of individuals. The white race did not go into a laboratory and invent incandescent light. That was Edison. The Jews did not work out Relativity. That was Einstein. The Negroes did not find out the inner secrets of peanuts and sweet potatoes, nor the secret of the development of the egg. That was Carver and Just. If you are under the impression that every white man is an Edison, just look around a bit. If you have the idea that every Negro is a Carver, you had better take off plenty of time to do your searching.

No, instead of Race Pride being a virtue, it is a sapping vice. It has caused more suffering in the world than religious opinion, and that is saying a lot.

"Race Conscious" is about the same as Race Pride in meaning. But, granting the shade of difference, all you say for it is, "Be continually conscious of what race you belong to so you can be proud." That is the effect of the thing. But what use is that? I don't care which race you belong to. If you are only one quarter honest in your judgment, you can seldom be proud. Why waste time keeping conscious of your physical aspects? What the world is crying and dying for at this moment is less race consciousness. The human race would blot itself out entirely if it had any more. It is a deadly explosive on the tongues of men. I choose to forget it.

This Race Problem business, now. I have asked many well-educated people of both races to tell me what the problem is. They look startled at first. Then I can see them scratching around inside themselves hunting for the meaning of the words which they have used with so much glibness and unction. I have never had an answer that was an answer, so I have had to make up my own. Since there is no fundamental conflict, since there is no solid reason why the blacks and the whites cannot live in one nation in perfect harmony, the only thing in the way of it is Race Pride and Race Consciousness on both sides. A bear has been grabbed by the tail. The captor and the captured are walking around a tree snarling at each other. The man is scared to turn the bear loose, and his hand-hold is slipping. The bear wants to go on about his business, but he feels that something must be done about that tail-hold. So they just keep on following each other around the tree.

So Race Pride and Race Consciousness seem to me to be not only fallacious, but a thing to be abhorred. It is the root of misunderstanding and hence misery and injustice. I cannot, with logic cry against it in others and wallow in it myself. The only satisfaction to be gained from it anyway is, "I ain't nothing, my folks ain't nothing, but that makes no difference at all. I belong to such-and-such a race." Poor nourishment according to my notion. Mighty little to chew on. You have to season it awfully high with egotism to make it tasty.

Priding yourself on your physical make up, something over which you have no control, is just another sign that the human cuss is determined not to be grateful. He gives himself a big hand on the way he looks and lets on that he arranged it all himself. God got suspicious that he was going to be like that before He made him, and that is why Old Maker caught up on all of His creating before He made Man. He knew that if Man had seen how He did it, just as soon as a woman came along to listen to him, Man would have been saying, "See that old striped tiger over there? *I* made him. Turned him out one morning before breakfast." And so on until there would not have been a thing in Heaven or earth that he didn't take credit for. So God did the only thing he could to narrow down the field for boasting. He made him late and kept him dumb.

And how can Race Solidarity be possible in a nation made up of as many elements as these United States? It could result in nothing short of chaos. The fate of each and every group is bound up with the others. Individual ability in any group must function for all the rest. National disaster touches us all. There is no escape in grouping. And in practice there can be no sharp lines drawn, because the interest of every individual in any racial group is not identical with the others. Section, locality, self-interest, special fitness, and the like set one group of Anglo-Saxons, Jews, and Negroes against another set of Anglo-Saxons, Jews, and Negroes. We are influenced by a pain in the pocket just like everybody else. During the Civil War Negroes fought in the Confederate Army because many Negroes were themselves slave-owners, and were just as mad at Lincoln as anybody else in the South. Anybody who goes before a body and purports to plead for what "The Negro" wants, is a liar and knows it. Negroes want a variety of things and many of them diametrically opposed. There is no single Negro nor no single organization which can carry the thirteen million in any direction. Even Joe Louis can't do it, but he comes nearer to it than anyone else at present.

And why should Negroes be united? Nobody else in America is. If it were true, then one of two other things would be true. One, that they were united on what the white people are united on, and it would take a God to tell what that is; and be moving towards complete and immediate assimilation. Or we would be united on something specially Negroid, and that would lead towards a hard black knot in the body politic which would be impossible of place in the nation. All of the upper class Negroes certainly want political and economic equality. That is the most universal thing I can pin down.

Negroes are just like anybody else. Some soar. Some plod ahead. Some just make a mess and step back in it—like the rest of America and the world. So Racial Solidarity is a fiction and always will be. Therefore, I have lifted the word out of my mouth.

A Race Man is somebody, not necessarily able, who places his race before all else. He says he will buy everything from a Negro merchant as far as possible, support all "race" institutions and movements and so on. The only thing that keeps this from working is that it is impossible to form a nation within a nation. He makes spurts and jerks at it, but every day he is forced away from it by necessity. He finds that he can neither make money nor spend money in a restricted orbit. He is part of the national economy. But he can give the idea plenty of talk. He springs to arms over such things as the title of Carl Van Vechten's book, *Nigger Heaven*, or Will Rogers saying over the radio that most of the cowboy songs were nothing more than adaptations of "nigger tunes." He does this because he feels that he is defending his race. Sometimes the causes are just, and sometimes they are ridiculous. His zeal is honest enough; it is merely a lack of analysis that leads him into error.

As I said before, the Race Leader is a fiction that is good only at the political trough. But it is not nearly so good as it used to be. The white political leaders have found out more or less that they cannot deliver wholesale. Many of them are successful in a way, but not in any great, big, plushy way. The politician may try ever so hard, but, if people won't follow, he just can't lead. Being an American, I am just like the rest of the Yankees, the Westerners, the Southerners, the Negroes, the Irish, the Indians, and the Jews. I don't lead well either. Don't just tell me what to do. Tell me what is being contemplated and let me help figure on the bill. That is my idea, and I am going to stick to it. Negroes are so much like the rest of America that they not only question what is put before them, but they have got so they order something else besides gin at the bars, which is certainly a sign of something. So I have thrown over the idea of Race Leadership, too.

I know that there is race prejudice, not only in America, but also wherever two races meet together in numbers. I have met it in the flesh, and I have found out that it is never all on one side, either. I do not give it heart room because it seems to me to be the last refuge of the weak. From what little I have been able to learn, I know that goodness, ability, vice, and dumbness know nothing about race lives or geography. I do not wish to close the frontiers of life upon my own self. I do not wish to deny myself the expansion of seeking into individual capabilities and depths by living in a space whose boundaries are race and nation. Lord, give my poor stammering tongue at least one taste of the whole round world, if you please, Sir.

And then I know so well that the people who make a boast of racial, class, or national prejudices do so out of a sense of incapability to which they refuse to give a voice. Instead they try to be ingenious by limiting competition. They are racial card-sharks trying to rig the game so that they cannot lose. Trying to stack the deck. If I choose to call these card-palmers poor sports, then the burden of proof is on them. I give the matter the corner of my eye and smile at the backhand compliment, for I know that if I had been born where *they* were born, and they had been born where *I* was born, it is hardly likely that we ever would have met. So I smile and not bitterly, either. For I know that Equality is as you do it and not as you talk it.

If you are better than I, you can tell me about it if you want to, but then again, show me so I can know. It is always good to be learning something. But if you never make me know it, I'll keep on questioning. I love to be in the presence of my superiors. If I don't catch on right away, crumble it up fine so I can handle it. And then again, if you can't *show* me your superiority, don't bother to bring the mess up, lest I merely rate you as a bully.

Since I wash myself of race pride and repudiate race solidarity, by the same token I turn my back upon the past. I see no reason to keep my eyes fixed on the dark years of slavery and the Reconstruction. I am three generations removed from it, and therefore have no experience of the thing. From what I can learn, it was sad. No doubt America would have been better off if it never had been. But it was and there is no use in beating around the bush. Still, there seems to me to be nothing but futility in gazing backward over my shoulder and buking the grave of some white man who has been dead too long to talk about. Neither do I see any use in button-holing his grandson about it. The old man probably did cut some capers back there, and I'll bet you anything my old folks didn't like it. But the old man is dead. My old folks are dead. Let them wrestle all over Hell about it if they want to. That is their business. The present is upon me and that white man's grandchildren as well. I have business with the grandson as of today. I want to get on with the business in hand. Since I cannot pry loose the clutching hand of time, I will settle for some influence on the present. It is ridiculous for me to make out that I'm Old Black Joe and waste my time rehashing his problems. That would be just as ridiculous as it would be for the Jews to hang around the pyramids trying to get a word with Old Cheops. Or for the English to be billing the Duke of Normandy the first of every month.

I am all for starting something brand new in co-operation with the present incumbent. If I don't get any co-operation, I am going to start something anyway. The world is not just going to stand still looking like a fool at a funeral if I can help it. Let's bring up right now and lay a hearing on it.

Standing on the watch-wall and looking, I no longer expect the millennium. It would be wishful thinking to be searching for justice in the absolute. People are not made so it will happen, because from all I can see, the world is a whole family of Hurstons. It has always been a family of Hurstons, so it is foolish to expect any justice untwisted by the selfish hand. Look into the Book of Books and it is not even there. The Old Testament is devoted to what was right and just from the viewpoint of the Ancient Hebrews. All of their enemies were twenty-two carat evil. They, the Hebrews, were never aggressors. The Lord wanted His children to have a country full of big grapes and tall corn. Incidentally while they were getting it, they might as well get rid of some trashy tribes that He never did think much of, anyway. With all of its figs and things, Canaan was their destiny. God sent somebody especially to tell them about it. If the conquest looked like bloody rape to the Canaanites, that was because their evil ways would not let them see a point which was right under their nose. So you had to drive it in under the ribs. King David, who invented the "protection" racket in those days before he was saved by being made king, was a great hero. He only killed and pillaged to help out his own folks. He was a man after God's own heart, and was quite serviceable in helping God get rid of no-count rascals who were cluttering up the place.

The New Testament is not quite so frank but it is equally biased. Paul and the disciples set up a New Order in Palestine after the death of Jesus, but the Jews gave it nothing but their shoulder-blades. So now, the Orthodox Jew became a manifest enemy of right. To this day, the names of Pharisee and Sadducee are synonymous with hypocrite and crook to ninety-nine and a half percent of the Christian world. While in fact, the Pharisee was an order small in number, highly educated, well born, and clean living men whose mission was to guard the purity of the creed. The Sadducees were almost as lofty. Naturally in the turmoil of the times, they got embroiled in politics in the very nature of the form of their government, but so have both branches of Christianity.

Then there is the slaughter of the innocents by Herod. One thing strikes me curious about that slaughter. The unconverted Jews never seemed to have missed their babies. So Herod must have carefully selected babies from families who forty years later were going to turn Christian. He probably did not realize what a bad example he was setting for the new religionists. He could not have known that centuries later Christians would themselves slaughter more innocents in one night than his soldiers ever saw.

Those Jews who would not accept Christianity look very bad in the New Testament. And two thousand years have gone by and all the Western World uses the sign of the Cross, but it is evident that the Jews are not the only ones who do not accept it. The Occident has never been christianized and never will be. It is an oriental concept which the sons of hammer-throwing Thor have no enzymes to digest. It calls for meekness, and the West is just not made meek. Instead of being proud to turn the other cheek, our boast is beating the other fellow to the punch.

We have even turned the Gospel of peace into a wrestle, we club each other over the head to prove who is the best missionary. Nature asserts itself. We can neither give up our platitudes nor our profits. The platitudes sound beautiful, but the profits feel like silk.

Popes and Prelates, Bishops and Elders have halted sermons on peace at the sound of battle and rushed out of their pulpits brandishing swords and screaming for blood in Jesus' name. The pews followed the pulpit in glee. So it is obvious that the Prince of Peace is nothing more than a symbol. He has been drafted into every army in the Occident. He must have a delegate behind every cannon. We have tangled with the soft and yielding thing for twenty long centuries without any more progress than letting the words take up around the house. We are moral enough, just not Christians. If we love meekness as we say, then Napoleon should be pictured in a nun's robe, Bismarck in a cassock and George Washington in a Gandhi diaper. The pedestals should read "These stones do honor to our meekest men. Their piety laid millions low. Praise the Lord!" The actual representation would reveal the confusion in our minds. According to our worship, Joe Louis rates a Cardinal's hat.

But back to Mahatma Gandhi. His application of Christian principles is causing us great distress. We want the people to hear about it from Greenland's icy mountains, to India's coral strand, but we do wish that they would not lose their heads and carry the thing too far, like Gandhi does for instance. It is a bad thing for business.

No, actual justice is somewhere away off. We only see its flickering image here. Everybody has it on his tongue and nobody has it at heart. Take, for instance, the matter of conquest.

The Kings of Dahomey once marched up and down West Africa, butchering the aged and the helpless of the surrounding tribes and nations, and selling the able off into Western slavery. The Dahomans would have been outraged if anybody had said they were unjust. What could be more just? The profits were enormous. But they did feel that there was no more justice in the world when the French came in and conquered them. The French would have shrugged down the Pyramids if they had been told that they were not just. What could be fairer? The Germans have now conquered the French and the French wonder how those Germans can be so lacking in soul. But the Germans open their blue eyes in amazement. Why, nothing could be more reasonable and just. If the world cannot find pure justice among the Germans, they will never find it anywhere. If the French want to be unfair enough to begrudge them their little profit on the deal, it shows how narrow and mean-minded a Frenchman really can be.

There is no diffused light on anything international so that a comparatively whole scene may be observed. Light is sharply directed on one spot, leaving not only the greater part in darkness but also denying by implication that the great unlighted field exists. It is no longer profitable, with few exceptions, to ask people what they think, for you will be told what they wish, instead. Perhaps at no other period in the history of the world have people lived in such a dreamy state. People even waste time denouncing their enemies in open warfare for shooting back too hard, or too accurately. There is no attempt to be accurate as to truth, however. The whole idea is to be complimentary to one's self and keep alive the dream. The other man's side commits gross butcheries. One's own side wins smashing victories.

Being human and a part of humanity, I like to think that my own nation is more just than any other in spite of the facts on hand. It makes me feel prouder and bigger to think that way. But now and then the embroidered hangings blow aside, and I am less exalted. I see that the high principles enunciated so throatedly are like the flowers in spring—they have nothing to do with the case. If my conclusions are in error, then the orators and copy-books were wrong to start off with. I should have been told in the very beginning that those were words to copy, but not to go by. But they didn't tell me that. They swore by jeepers and by joe that there were certain unshakable truths that no man nor nation could make out without.

There was the dignity of man. His inalienable rights were sacred. Man, noble man, had risen in his might and glory and had stamped out the vile institution of slavery. That is just what they said. But I know that the principle of human bondage has not yet vanished from the earth. I know that great nations are standing on it. I would not go so far as to deny that there has been no progress toward the concept of liberty. Already it has been agreed that the name of slavery is very bad. No civilized nation will use such a term anymore. Neither will they keep the business around the home. Life will be on a loftier level by operating at a distance and calling it acquiring sources of raw material, and keeping the market open. It has been decided also, that it is not cricket to enslave one's own kind. That is unspeakable tyranny.

But must a nation suffer from lack of prosperity and expansion by lofty concepts? Not at all! If a ruler can find a place way off where the people do not look like him, kill enough of them to convince the rest that they ought to support him with their lives and labor, that ruler is hailed as a great conqueror, and people build monuments to him. The very weapons he used are also honored. They picture him in unforgetting stone with the sacred tool of his conquest in his hand. Democracy, like religion, never was designed to make our profits less.

Now, for instance, if the English people were to quarter troops in

France, and force the French to work for them for forty-eight cents a week while they took more than a billion dollars a year out of France, the English would be Occidentally execrated. But actually, the British Government does just that in India, to the glory of the democratic way. They are hailed as not only great Empire builders, the English are extolled as leaders of civilization. And the very people who claim that it is a noble thing to die for freedom and democracy cry out in horror when they hear tell of a "revolt" in India. They even wax frothy if anyone points out the inconsistency of their morals. So this life as we know it is a great thing. It would have to be, to justify certain things.

I do not mean to single England out as something strange and different in the world. We, too, have our Marines in China. We, too, consider machine gun bullets good laxatives for heathens who get constipated with toxic ideas about a country of their own. If the patient dies from the treatment, it was not because the medicine was not good. We are positive of that. We have seen it work on other patients twice before it killed them and three times after. Then, too, no matter what the outcome, you have to give the doctor credit for trying.

The United States being the giant of the Western World, we have our responsibilities. The little Latin brother south of the border has been a trifle trying at times. Nobody doubts that he means to be a good neighbor. We know that his intentions are the best. It is only that he is so gay and fiesta-minded that he is liable to make arrangements that benefit nobody but himself. Not a selfish bone in his body, you know. Just too full of rumba. So it is our big brotherly duty to teach him right from wrong. He must be taught to share with big brother before big brother comes down and kicks his teeth in. A big *good* neighbor is a lovely thing to have. We are far too moral a people to allow poor Latin judgment to hinder good works.

But there is a geographical boundary to our principles. They are not to leave the United States unless we take them ourselves. Japan's application of our principles to Asia is never to be sufficiently deplored. We are like the southern planter's bride when he kissed her the first time.

"Darling," she fretted, "do niggers hug and kiss like this?"

"Why, I reckon they do, honey. Fact is, I'm sure of it. Why do you ask?"

"You go right out and kill the last one of 'em tomorrow morning. Things like this is much too good for niggers."

Our indignation is more than justified. We Westerners composed that piece about trading in China with gunboats and cannons long decades ago. Japan is now plagiarizing in the most flagrant manner.

We also wrote that song about keeping a whole hemisphere under your wing. Now the Nipponese are singing our song all over Asia. They are full of stuff and need a good working out. The only holdback to the thing is that they have copied our medicine chest. They are stocked up with the same steel pills and cannon plasters that Doctor Occident prescribes.

Mexico, the dear little papoose, has been on the sick list, too. Gangrene had set in in the upper limbs, so to speak, and amputation was the only thing which could save the patient. Even so, the patient malingered for a long time, and internal dosage had to be resorted to on occasion. The doctor is not sure that all of the germs have been eradicated from the system as yet, but, when the patient breaks out of the hospital, what can the doctor do?

In great and far-sighted magnanimity, no cases have been overlooked. The African tribesmen were saved from the stuffiness of overweening pride and property just in the nick of time.

Looking at all these things, I am driven to the conclusion that democracy is a wonderful thing, but too powerful to be trusted in any but purely occidental hands. Asia and Africa should know about it. They should die for it in defense of its originators, but they must not use it themselves.

All around me, bitter tears are being shed over the fate of Holland, Belgium, France, and England. I must confess to being a little dry around the eyes. I hear people shaking with shudders at the thought of Germany collecting taxes in Holland. I have not heard a word against Holland collecting one twelfth of poor people's wages in Asia. That makes the ruling families in Holland very rich, as they should be. What happens to the poor Javanese and Balinese is unimportant; Hitler's crime is that he is actually doing a thing like that to his own kind. That is international cannibalism and should be stopped. He is a bandit. That is true, but that is not what is held against him. He is muscling in on well-established mobs. Give him credit. He cased some joints away off in Africa and Asia, but the big mobs already had them paying protection money and warned him to stay away. The only way he can climb out of the punk class is to high-jack the load and that is just what he is doing. President Roosevelt could extend his four freedoms to some people right here in America before he takes it all aboard, and, no doubt, he would do it too, if it would bring in the same amount of glory. I am not bitter, but I see what I see. He can call names across an ocean, but he evidently has not the courage to speak even softly at home. Take away the ocean and he simmers right down. I wish that I could say differently, but I cannot. I will fight for my country, but I will not lie for her. Our country is so busy playing "fence" to the mobsters that the cost in human suffering cannot be considered yet. We can take that up in the next depression.

As I see it, the doctrines of democracy deal with the aspirations of men's souls, but the application deals with things. One hand in somebody else's pocket and one on your gun, and you are highly civilized. Your heart is where it belongs—in your pocket-book. Put it in your bosom and you are backward. Desire enough for your own use only, and you are a heathen. Civilized people have things to show to the neighbors.

This is not to say, however, that the darker races are visiting angels, just touristing around here below. They have acted the same way when they had a chance and will act that way again, comes the break. I just think it would be a good thing for the Anglo-Saxon to get the idea out of his head that everybody else owes him something just for being blonde. I am forced to the conclusion that two-thirds of them do hold that view. The idea of human slavery is so deeply ground in that the pink-toes can't get it out of their system. It has just been decided to move the slave quarters farther away from the house. It would be a fine thing if on leaving office, the blond brother could point with pride to the fact that his administration had done away with group-profit at the expense of others. I know well that it has never happened before, but it could happen, couldn't it?

To mention the hundred years of the Anglo-Saxon in China alone is proof enough of the evils of this view point. The millions of Chinese who have died for our prestige and profit! They are still dying for it. Justify it with all the proud and pretty phrases you please, but if we think our policy is right, you just let the Chinese move a gunboat in the Hudson to drum up trade with us. The scream of outrage would wake up saints in the backrooms of Heaven. And what is worse, we go on as if the so-called inferior people are not thinking; or if they do, it does not matter. As if no day could ever come when that which went over the Devil's back will buckle under his belly. People may not be well-armed at present, but you can't stop them from thinking.

I do not brood, however, over the wide gaps between ideals and practices. The world is too full of inconsistencies for that. I recognize that men are given to handling words long before those words have any internal meaning for them. It is as if we were children playing in a field and found something round and hard to play with. It may be full of beauty and pleasure, and then again it may be full of death.

And now to another matter. Many people have pointed out to me that I am a Negro, and that I am poor. Why then have I not joined a party of protest? I will tell you why. I see many good points in, let us say, the Communist Party. Anyone would be a liar and a fool to claim that there was no good in it. But I am so put together that I do not have much of a herd instinct. Or if I must be connected with the flock, let *me* be the shepherd my ownself. That is just the way I am made.

You cannot arouse any enthusiasm in me to join in a protest for the boss to provide me with a better hoe to chop his cotton with. Why must I chop cotton at all? Why fix a class of cotton-choppers? I will join in no protests for the boss to put a little more stuffing in my bunk. I don't even want the bunk. I want the boss's bed. It seems to me that the people who are enunciating these principles are so saturated with European ideas that they miss the whole point of America. The people who founded this country, and the immigrants who came later, came here to get away from class distinctions and to keep their unborn children from knowing about them. I am all for the idea of free vertical movement, nothing horizontal. Let him who can, go up, and him who cannot stay there, mount down to the level his capabilities rate. It works out that way anyhow, hence the saying from shirt-sleeves to shirt-sleeves in three generations. The able at the bottom always snatch the ladder from under the weak on the top rung. That is the way it should be. A dead grandfather's back has proven to be a poor prop time and time again. If they have gone up there and stayed, they had something more than a lucky ancestor. So I can get no lift out of nominating myself to be a peasant and celebrating any feasts back stairs. I want the front of the house and I am going to keep on trying even if I never satisfy my plan.

Then, too, it seems to me that if I say a whole system must be upset for me to win, I am saying that I cannot sit in the game, and that safer rules must be made to give me a chance. I repudiate that. If others are in there, deal me a hand and let me see what I can make of it, even though I know some in there are dealing from the bottom and cheating like hell in other ways. If I can win anything in a game like that, I know I'll end up with the pot if the sharks can be eliminated. As the Negroes say down south, "You can't beat me and my prayers," and they are not talking about supplications either when they talk like that. I don't want to bother with any boring from within. If the leaders on the left feel that only violence can right things, I see no need of finger-nail warfare. Why not take a stronger position? Shoot in the hearse, don't care how sad the funeral is. Get the feeling of the bantam hen jumping on the mule. Kill dead and go to jail. I am not bloodthirsty and have no yearning for strife, but if what they say is true, that there must be this upset, why not make it cosmic? A lot of people would join in for the drama of it, who would not be moved by guile.

I do not say that my conclusions about anything are true for the Universe, but I have lived in many ways, sweet and bitter, and they feel right for me. I have seen and heard. I have sat in judgment upon the ways of others, and in the voiceless quiet of the night I have also called myself to judgment. I cannot have the joy of knowing that I found always a shining reflection of honor and wisdom in the mirror of my soul on those occasions. I have given myself more harrowing pain than anyone else has ever been capable of giving me. No one else can inflict the hurt of faith unkept. I have had the corroding insight at times of recognizing that I am a bundle of sham and tinsel, honest metal and sincerity that cannot be untangled. My dross has given my other parts great sorrow.

But, on the other hand, I have given myself the pleasure of sunrises blooming out of oceans, and sunsets drenching heaped-up clouds. I have walked in storms with a crown of clouds about my head and the zig zag lightning playing through my fingers. The gods of the upper air have uncovered their faces to my eyes. I have made friends with trees and vales. I have found out that my real home is in the water, that the earth is only my step-mother. My old man, the Sun, sired me out of the sea.

Like all mortals, I have been shaped by the chisel in the hand of Chance—bulged out here by a sense of victory, shrunken there by the press of failure and the knowledge of unworthiness. But it has been given to me to strive with life, and to conquer the fear of death. I have been correlated to the world so that I know the indifference of the sun to human emotions. I know that destruction and construction are but two faces of Dame Nature, and that it is nothing to her if I choose to make personal tragedy out of her unbreakable laws.

So I ask of her few things. May I never do good consciously, nor evil unconsciously. Let my evil be known to me in advance of my acts, and my good when Nature wills. May I be granted a just mind and a timely death.

While I am still far below the allotted span of time, and notwithstanding, I feel that I have lived. I have the joy and pain of strong friendships. I have served and been served. I have made enemies of which I am not ashamed. I have been faithless, and then I have been faithful and steadfast until the blood ran down into my shoes. I have loved unselfishly with all the ardor of a strong heart, and I have hated with all the power of my soul. What waits for me in the future? I do not know. I cannot even imagine, and I am glad for that. But already, I have touched the four corners of the horizon, for from hard searching it seems to me that tears and laughter, love and hate, make up the sum of life.

The Inside Light—Being a
Salute to Friendship

Now take friendship for instance. It is a wonderful trade, a noble thing for anyone to work at. God made the world out of tough things, so it could last, and then He made some juice out of the most interior and best things that He had and poured it around for flavor.

You see lonesome-looking old red hills who do not even have clothes to cover their backs just lying there looking useless. Looking just like Old Maker had a junk pile like everybody else. But go back and look at them late in the day and see the herd of friendly shadows browsing happily around the feet of those hills. Then gaze up at the top and surprise the departing sun, all colored-up with its feelings, saying a sweet good night to those lonesome hills, and making them a promise that he will never forget them. So much tender beauty in a parting must mean a friendship. "I will visit you with my love," says the sun. That is why the hills endure.

Personally, I know what it means. I have never been as good a friend as I meant to be. I keep seeing new heights and depths of possibilities which ought to be reached, only to be frustrated by the press of life which is no friend to grace. I have my loyalties and my unselfish acts to my credit, but I feel the lack of perfection in them, and it leaves a hunger in me.

But I have received unaccountable friendship that is satisfying. Such as I am, I am a precious gift, as the unlettered Negro would say it. Stripped to my skin, that is just what I am. Without the juice of friendship, I would not be even what I seem to be. So many people have stretched out their hands and helped me along my wander. With the eye of faith, some have beheld me at Hell's dark door, with no rudder in my hand, and no light in my heart, and steered me to a peace within. Some others have flown into that awful place west and south of old original Hell and, with great compassion, lifted me off of the blistering coals and showed me trees and flowers. All these are the powers and privileges of friendship.

So many evidences of friendship have been revealed to me, that time and paper would not bear the load. Friendships of a moment, an hour or a day, that were nevertheless important, by humble folk whose names have become dusted over, while the feeling of the touch remained, friendly expression having ways like musk. It can throw light back on a day that was so dark, that even the sun refused to take responsibility for it.

It was decreed in the beginning of things that I should meet Mrs. R. Osgood Mason. She had been in the last of my prophetic visions from the first coming of them. I could not know that until I met her. But the moment I walked into the room, I knew that this was the end. There were the two women just as I had always seen them, but always in my dream the faces were misty. Miss Cornelia Chapin was arranging a huge bowl of Calla lilies as I entered the room. There were the strange flowers I had always seen. Her posture was as I had seen it hundreds of times. Mrs. Mason was seated in a chair and everything about her was as I knew it. Only now I could see her face. Born so widely apart in every way, the key to certain phases of my life had been placed in her hand. I had been sent to her to get it. I owe her and owe her and owe her! Not only for material help, but for spiritual guidance.

With the exception of Godmother, Carl Van Vechten has bawled me out more times than anyone else I know. He has not been one of those white "friends of the Negro" who seeks to earn it cheaply by being eternally complimentary. If he is your friend, he will point out your failings as well as your good points in the most direct manner. Take it or leave it. If you can't stand him that way, you need not bother. If he is not interested in you one way or another, he will tell you that, too, in the most off-hand manner, but he is as true as the equator if he is for you. I offer him and his wife Fania Marinoff my humble and sincere thanks.

Both as her secretary and as a friend, Fanny Hurst has picked on me to my profit. She is a curious mixture of little girl and very sophisticated woman. You have to stop and look at her closely to tell which she is from moment to moment. Her transitions are quick as lightning and just as mysterious. I have watched her under all kinds of conditions, and she never ceases to amaze me. Behold her phoning to a swanky hotel for reservations for herself and the Princess Zora, *and* parading me in there all dressed up as an Asiatic person of royal blood and keeping a straight face while the attendants goggled at me and bowed low! Like a little girl, I have known her in the joy of a compelling new gown to take me to tea in some exclusive spot in New York. I would be the press agent for her dress, for everybody was sure to look if *they* saw somebody like me strolling into the Astor or the Biltmore. She can wear clothes and who knows it is her? On the spur of the moment she has taken me galloping over thousands of miles of this North American continent in my Chevrolet for a lark, and then just as suddenly decided to return and go to work. In one moment after figuratively playing with her dolls, she is deep in some social problem. She has been my good friend for many years, and I love her.

To the James Huberts, of Urban League fame, I offer something precious from the best of my treasures. If ever I came to feel that they no longer cared, I would be truly miserable. They elected me to be a Hubert and I mean to hold them to it.

To the Beers, Eleanor Beer de Chetelat, and her mother, Mrs. George W. Beer, twenty-one guns!

I am indebted to Amy Spingarn in a most profound manner. She knows what I mean by that.

Harry T. Burleigh, composer of "Deep River" and other great tunes, worked on me while I was a student to give me perspective and poise. He kept on saying that Negroes did not aim high enough as a rule. They mistook talent for art. One must work. Art was more than inspiration. Besides, he used to take me out to eat in good places to get me used to things. He looks like Otto Kahn in brown-skin *and* behaves like a maharajah, with which I do not quarrel.

Of the people who have served me, Bob Wunsch is a man who has no superiors and few equals. Where the man gets all of his soul meat from, I really would like to know. All the greed and grime of the world passes him and never touches him, somehow. I wish that I could make him into a powder and season up the human dough so something could be made out of it. He has enough flavoring in him to do it.

The way I can say how I feel about Dr. Henry Allen Moe is to say that he is twin brother to Bob Wunsch. You cannot talk to the man without feeling that you could have done better in the past and rushing out to improve up from where you are. He has something glinty inside of him that he can't hide. If you have seen him, you have been helped.

I have said that I am grateful to the Charles S. Johnsons and I mean it. Not one iota of their kindness to me has been forgotten.

I fell in love with Jane Belo because she is not what she is supposed to be. She has brains and talent and uses them when she was born rich and pretty, and could have gotten along without any sense. She spent years in Bali studying native custom. She returned to America and went down into the deep South to make comparative studies, with me along. Often as we rode down lonesome roads in South Carolina, I wondered about her tremendous mental energy, and my admiration grew and grew. I also wondered at times why she liked me so much. Certainly it was not from want of friends. Being born of a rich Texas family, familiar with the drawing rooms of America and the continent, she certainly is not starved for company. Yet she thinks that I am a desirable friend to have, and acts like it.

Now, she is married to Dr. Frank Tannenbaum, Department of History, Columbia University, and they have a farm up the state and actually milk cows. She draws and paints well enough to make a living at it if she had to, has written things in Anthropology that Dr. Margaret Mead approves of, milks cows and sets her little hat over her nose. How can you place a person like that? I give up. She can just keep on being my friend, and I'll let somebody else explain her.

I value Miguel and Rose Covarrubias for old time's sake. Long before they were married, we polished off many a fried chicken together. Along with Harry Block, we fried "hand chicken" (jointed fried chicken to be eaten with the hand) and settled the affairs of the world over the bones. We did many amusing but senseless things, and kept up our brain power by eating more chicken. Maybe that is why Miguel is such a fine artist. He has hewed to the line, and never let his success induce him to take to trashy foods on fancy plates.

James Weldon Johnson and his wife Grace did much to make my early years in New York pleasant and profitable. I have never seen any other two people who could be right so often, and charming about it at the same time.

Walter White and his glamorous Gladys used to have me over and feed me on good fried chicken in my student days for no other reason than that they just wanted to. They have lent me some pleasant hours. I mean to pay them back sometime.

There are so many others, Colonel and Mrs. Bert Lippincott, Frank Frazier, Paul and Eslanda Robeson, Lawrence Brown, Calvin J. Ferguson, Dr. Edwin Osgood Grover, Dr. Hamilton Holt, H. P. Davis, J. P. McEvoy, Edna St. Vincent Millay, Dr. and Mrs. Simeon L. Carson of Washington, D.C., along with Betram Barker. As I said in the beginning of this, that I was a precious gift, what there is of me. I could not find space for all of the donors on paper, though there is plenty of room in my heart. I am just sort of assembled up together out of friendship and put together by time.

Josephine Van Doltzen Pease, that sprout of an old Philadelphia family who writes such charming stories for children, and our mutual friend, Edith Darling Thompson, are right inside the most inside part of my heart. They are both sacred figures on my altar when I deck it to offer something to love.

How could I ever think I could make out without that remarkable couple Whit Burnett and Martha Foley? I just happened to put his name down first. Either way you take that family, it's got a head to it. One head with whiskers to it, and one plain, but both real heads. Even little David, their son, has got his mind made up. Being little, he gets over-ruled at times, but he knows what he wants to do and puts a lot of vim into the thing. It is not his fault if Whit and Martha have ideas of censorship. I have no idea what he will pick out to do by the time he gets grown, but, whatever it is, you won't find any bewildered David Foley-Burnett wandering around. I'll bet you a fat man on that. Two fat men to your skinny one.

Another California crowd that got me liking them and grateful too, is that Herbert Childs, with his cherub-looking wife.

Katharane Edson Mershon has been a good friend to me. She is a person of immense understanding. It makes me sit and ponder. I do not know whether her ready sympathy grows out of her own experiences, or whether it was always there and only expanded by having struggled herself. I suppose it is both.

She was born of Katherine Philips Edson, the woman who put the minimum wage law for women on the statute books of California. It was no fault of hers that dirty politics later rubbed it out. She did many other things for the good of California, like fighting for the preservation of the Redwood forests. She sat, a lone woman, in the Washington Disarmament Conference, and, after forty, sent her two sons through good colleges by the sweat of her brow.

So Katharane Edson Mershon probably inherited some feelings. Anyway, she took life in her hands and hied herself away from home at sixteen and went forth to dance for inside expression. She did important things in the now famous Play House of Pasadena, conducted a school of dance and was a director for the famous school of Ruth St. Denis. After she married, she spent nine years in Bali, conducting a clinic at her own expense. More than that, she did not do it by proxy. She was there every day, giving medicine for fever, washing sores and sitting by the dying. Dancing was her way of doing things but she was impelled by mercy into this other field. Her husband was with her in this. His main passion is making gardens, but he threw himself into the clinic with enthusiasm.

For me, she gave me back my health and my hope, and I have her to thank for the sparing of my unprofitable life.

Jack Mershon, husband of Katharane's heart, is the son of William B. Mershon of Saginaw, Michigan. This William B. went into the Michigan forests and hacked him out a fortune. Tough as whit leather, with a passion for hunting and fishing, he nevertheless is one of the best informed men in the world on Americana, with especial emphasis on the Northwest. He has endowed parks, settlements, replanted whole forests of millions of trees in Michigan, and done things to make Saginaw a fine city, which the younger generation knows little about, because he himself says nothing.

Jack like his wife ran off from home and supported himself on the stage. He is soft in manner, but now and then you can see some of the gruff old stuff of William B. Mershon oozing through his hide. That same kind of mule-headedness on one side and generosity on the other. He will probably never be a hard-cussing, hard-driving empire builder like his old man, but what he aims to do, he does.

Mrs. Mershon invited me out to California, and a story starts from that. Being trustful and full of faith, I hurried out there. She fed me well, called in the doctors and cleared the malaria out of my marrow, took me to I. Magnin's and dressed me up. I was just burning up with gratitude and still did not suspect a thing.

Then I began to notice a leer in her eye! This woman had designs on me. I could tell that from her look, but I could not tell what it was. I should have known! I should have been suspicious, but I was dumb to the fact and did not suspect a thing until I was ambushed.

One day she said to me off-hand, "You ought to see a bit of California while you are out here."

"Oh, that would be fine!" I crackled and gleamed at the idea. So I saw California! At first, I thought it was just to give *me* some pleasure, but I soon found out it was the gleeful malice of a Californiac taking revenge upon a poor defenseless Florida Fiend.

She fried me in the deserts, looking at poppies, succulents (cactus, to you and everybody else except Californiacs), Joshua trees, kiln dried lizards and lupin bushes. Just look at those wild lilacs! Observe that chaparrel! Don't miss that juniper. Don't say you haven't seen our cottonwood. Regard those nobles (California oaks).

Next thing I know, we would be loping up some rough-back mountain and every hump and hollow would be pointed out to me. No need for me to murmur that I had to watch the road while driving. Just look at that peak! Now! You can look down over that rim. When I took refuge in watching the road, she switched technique on me. Her husband, Jack Mershon, was pressed into service, so all I had to do was to sit in the back seat of the Buick while Katharane twisted my head from side to side and pointed out the sights.

From San Diego up, we looked at every wave on the Pacific, lizards, bushes, prune and orange groves, date palms, eucalyptus, gullies with and without water that these Californiacs call rivers, asphalt pits where the remains of prehistoric animals had been found, the prehistoric bones in person, saber-tooth tigers, short-faced bears (bears, before bears saw Californiacs and pulled long faces), old fashioned elephants that ran mostly to teeth, saurians and what not. Then there was barracuda and shark meat, abalones, beaches full of people in dark sun glasses, Hollywood, and slacks with hips in them all swearing to God and other responsible characters that they sure look pretty, and most of them lying and unrepentant. Man! I saw Southern California, and thought I had done something. Me, being from Florida, I had held my peace, and only murmured now and then a hint or two about our own climate and trees and things like that. Nothing offensive, you understand. I wouldn't really say how good it was, because I wanted to be polite. So I drew a long breath when we had prospected over Southern California, and I had kept from exploding.

"Now, I shall take you to see Northern California—the best part of the state," my fiendish friend gloated. "Ah, the mountains!"

"But, I don't care too much about mountains," I murmured through the alkali in my mouth.

"You are going to see it just the same. You are not going back east and pretend you saw none of the beauty of my state. You are going to see California, and like it—you Florida Fiend. Just because your Florida mud-turtles have been used to bogging down in swamps and those Everglades, whatever they are—and they don't sound like much to me, is no reason for you to ignore the beauties of California mountains. Let's go!"

So we went north. We drove over rocky ridges and stopped on ledges miles up in the air and gazed upon the Pacific. Redwood forests, Golden Gates, cable cars, missions, gaps, gullies, San Simeon-with-William Randolph Hearst, Monterey-with-history, Carmel-with-artists and atmosphere, Big Sur and Santa Barbara, Bay Bridges and Giant Sequoia, Alcatraz, wharves, Capitol buildings, mountains that didn't have sense enough to know it was summer and time to take off their winter clothes, seals, seal-rocks, and then seals on seal-rocks, pelicans and pelican rocks and then that [   ] Pacific!

Finally, back at Carmel, I struck. A person has just so many places to bump falling down rocky cliffs. But did I escape? No, indeed! I was standing on a big pile of bony rocks on Point Lobos, when I announced that I thought I (sort of) had the idea of California and knew what it was about.

"Oh, no!" Katharane grated maliciously. "Seen California! Why, this is the second largest state in the Union! You haven't half seen it, but you are going to. I've got you out here and I mean to rub your nose in California. You are going to see it, I'm here to tell you." So on we went. I saw, and I saw and I *saw*! Man! I tell you that I saw California. For instance, I saw the hats in San Francisco! Finally, I came to the conclusion that in Los Angeles the women get hats imposed upon them. In San Francisco, they go out in the woods and shoot 'em.

Then after I had galloped from one end of the state to the other and from edge to ocean and back again, Katharane Mershon up and tells me, "All I wanted you to see was the redwoods!"

I mean to write to the Florida Chamber of Commerce and get them to trick a gang of Californiacs to Florida and let me be the guide. It is going to be good, and I wouldn't fool you. From Key West to the Perdido river they are going to see every orange tree, rattlesnake, gopher, coudar, palm tree, sand pile, beach mango tree, sapodilla, kumquat, alligator, tourist trap, celery patch, bean field, strawberry, lake, jook, gulf, ocean and river in between, and if their constitutions sort of wear away, it will be unfortunate, but one of the hazards of war.

But California is nice. *Buen* nice! Of course they lie about the California climate a little more than we do about ours, but you don't hold that against them. They have to, to rank up with us. But at that this California is a swell state, especially from Santa Barbara on north. Of course, coming from Florida, I feel like the man when he saw a hunch back for the first time—it seems that California does wear its hips a bit high. I mean all those mountains. Too much of the state is standing up on edge. To my notion, land is supposed to lie down and be walked on—not rearing up, staring you in the face. It is too biggity and imposing. But on the whole, California will do for a lovely state until God can make up something better. So I forgive Katharane Mershon for showing me the place. Another score for friendship.

Therefore, I can say that I have had friends. Friendship is a mysterious and ocean-bottom thing. Who can know the outer ranges of it? Perhaps no human being has ever explored its limits. Anyway, God must have thought well of it when He made it. Make the attempt if you want to, but you will find that trying to go through life without friendship, is like milking a bear to get cream for your morning coffee. It is a whole lot of trouble, and then not worth much after you get it.

11:00 A.M. July 20, 1941
1392 Hull Lane
Altadena, California

Concert

A<small>ND NOW</small>, I must mention something, not because it means so much to me, but because it did mean something to others.

On January 10, 1932, I presented a Negro Folk Concert at the John Golden Theater in New York.

I am not a singer, a dancer, nor even a musician. I was, therefore, seeking no reputation in either field. I did the concert because I knew that nowhere had the general public ever heard Negro music as done by Negroes. There had been numerous concerts of Negro spirituals by famous Negro singers, but none as it was done by, let us say, Macedonia Baptist Church. They had been tampered with by musicians, and had their faces lifted to the degree that when real Negroes heard them, they sat back and listened just like white audiences did. It was just as strange to them as to the Swedes, for example. Beautiful songs and arrangements but going under the wrong titles.

Here was the difference. When I was coming up, I had heard songs and singing. People made the tunes and sang them because they were pretty and satisfied something. Then I got away from home and learned about "holler singing." Holler singing or classic, if you want to call it that, is not done for the sake of agreeable sound. It is a sporting proposition. The singer, after years of training, puts out a brag that he or she can perform certain tricks with the voice, and the audience comes and bets him the admission price that he can't do it. They lean back in the seats and wait eagerly for the shake, the high jump or the low dive. If the performer makes it, he rakes in the pot. If not, he can go back and yell "Whoa! Har! Gee!" to some mule.

I saw that Negro music and musicians were getting lost in the betting ring. I did not hope to stop the ones who were ambitious to qualify as holler experts. That was all right in its place. I just wanted people to know what real Negro music sounded like. There were the two things.

Of course, I had known this all along, but my years of research accented this situation inside of me and troubled me. Was the real voice of my people never to be heard? This ersatz Negro music was getting on. It was like the story from Hans Christian Andersen where the shadow became the man. That would not have been important if the arrangements had been better music than the originals, but they were not. They conformed more to Conservatory rules of music but that is not saying much. They were highly flavored with Bach and Brahms, and Gregorian chants, but why drag them in? It seemed to me a determined effort to squeeze all of the rich black juice out of the songs and present a sort of musical octoroon to the public. Like some more "passing for white."

Now in collecting tales and hoodoo rituals, I had taken time out to collect a mass of Negro songs of all descriptions. I was not supposed to do that, but I could not resist it. Sitting around in saw-mill quarters, turpentine camps, prison camps, railroad camps and jooks, I soaked them in as I went. My people are not going to do but so much of anything before they sing something. I always encouraged it because I loved it and could not be different. I brought this mass home, seeing all the possibilities for some Negro musicians to do something fine with it.

Being a friend of Hall Johnson's, I turned it over to him to use as he wished with his concert group. He kept it for nearly a year. I called him up about it two or three times and finally he told me that he saw no use for it. The public only wanted to hear spirituals, and spirituals that had been well arranged. I knew that he was mistaken, for white people used to crowd Zion Hope Baptist Church, where my father was pastor to hear the singing, and there certainly were no trained musicians around there. I had seen it in various Negro churches where the congregations just grabbed hold of a tune and everybody worked on it in his or her own way to magnificent harmonic effect. I knew that they liked the work songs, for I had seen them park their cars by a gang of workers just to listen to what happened. So in spite of what he said, I kept to my own convictions.

When he gave me back the songs, I talked about a real Negro concert for a while, to anybody who would listen, and then decided to do it. But I felt that I did not know enough to do it alone.

Not only did I want the singing very natural, I wanted to display West Indian folk dancing. I had been out in the Bahama Islands collecting material and had witnessed the dynamic Fire Dance which had three parts; the Jumping Dance, The Ring Play and the Congo. It was so stirring and magnificent that I had to admit to myself that we had nothing in America to equal it. I went to the dancing every chance I got, and took pains to learn them. I could just see an American audience being thrilled.

So the first step I took was to assemble a troup of sixteen Bahamans who could dance. Then I went back to Hall Johnson with the proposition that we combine his singers and my dancers for a dramatic concert. I had the script all written. It was a dramatization of a working day on a Florida railroad camp with the Fire Dance for a climax. Hall Johnson looked it over and agreed to the thing.

But his mind must have changed, because I took my dancers up to his studio four times, but the rehearsals never came off. Twice he was not even there. Once he said he had a rehearsal of his own group which could not be put off, and once there was no explanation. Besides, something unfortunate happened. While my dancers sat around me and waited, two or three of the singers talked in stage whispers about "monkey chasers dancing." They ridiculed the whole idea. Who wanted to be mixed up with anything like that?

The American Negroes have the unfortunate habit of speaking of West Indians as "monkey-chasers," pretending to believe that the West Indians catch monkeys and stew them with rice.

I heard what was being said very distinctly, but I hoped that my group did not. But they did and began to show hurt in their faces. I could not let them feel that I shared the foolish prejudice, which I do not, so I had to make a move. I showed my resentment, gathered my folks, and we all went down to my place in 66th Street. It looked as if I were licked. I had spoken to a man in Judson's Bureau in Steinway Hall about booking us, and now it all looked hopeless. So I went down next day to call it all off.

He said I ought to go ahead. It sounded fine to him. But go ahead on my own. He happened to know that Gaston, Hall Johnson's manager, wanted me headed off. He saw in my idea a threat to Hall Johnson's group. "You are being strung along on this rehearsal gag to throw you off. Go ahead on your own."

So I went ahead. We rehearsed at my house, here and there, and anywhere. The secretary to John Golden liked the idea after seeing a rehearsal and got me the theater. She undertook to handle the press for me, so I just turned over the money to her and she did well by me.

I had talked Godmother, Mrs. R. Osgood Mason, into helping me. Dr. Locke, her main Negro confidant, had opposed it at first, but he was finally won over. You see, he had been born in Philadelphia, educated at Harvard and Oxford and had never known the common run of Negroes. He was not at all sympathetic to our expression. To his credit, he has changed his viewpoint.

Then came that Sunday night of the tenth. We had a good house, mostly white shirt fronts and ermine. Godmother was out there sitting close enough for me to see her and encourage me. Locke was there, too, in faultless tails. He came back stage to give me a pat of encouragement and went back out front. I needed it. I was as nervous as I could be, and if I had known then as much as I know now, I would have been even more nervous. Fools rush in where angels fear to tread.

From the lifting of the curtain on the dawn scene where the shack rouser awakens the camp to the end of the first half, it was evident that the audience was with us. The male chorus "lined track" and "spiked" to tremendous applause. The curtain had to be lifted and lowered and then again. I was standing there in the wings still shivering, when Lee Whipper, who had played the part of the itinerant preacher in a beautiful manner, gave me a shove and I found myself out on the stage. A tremendous burst of applause met me, and so I had to say something.

I explained why I had done it. That music without motion was unnatural with Negroes, and what I had tried to do was to present Negro singing in a natural way—with action. I don't know what else I said, but the audience was kind and I walked off to an applauding house.

Right here, let me set something straight. Godmother had meant for me to call Dr. Locke to the stage to make any explanations, but she had not told me. Neither had Locke told me. I was stupid. When he told me where he would be sitting, he evidently thought that would be enough. But I had not thought of any speech in all my troubles of rehearsals, making costumes and keeping things going. It just had not occurred to me. I would not have been out there myself if Lee Whipper had not shoved me. I found out later that I had seemed to ignore Dr. Locke, for which I am very sorry. I would have much rather had him make a thought-out speech than my improvising. It just did not occur to me in all my excitement. It may be too late, but I ask him please to pardon me. He had been helpful and I meant him good.

The second half of the program went off even better than the first. As soon as the curtain went up on the Fire Dancers, their costuming got a hand. It broke out time and again during the dancing and thundered as Caroline Rich and Strawn executed the last movement with the group as a back-ground. It was good it was the last thing, for nothing could have followed it.

Hall Johnson did a generous thing. I had sent tickets and he and his manager came back stage and Hall said, "You proved your point all right. When you talked to me about it, it sounded like a crazy mess. I really came to see you do a flop, but it was swell!" I thought that was fine of Hall.

The New School of Social Research presented us six weeks later and we danced at the Vanderbilt, Nyack, and various places. But I was worn out with back stage arguments, eternal demands for money, a disturbance in my dance group because one of the men, who was incidentally the poorest dancer of all, preached that I was an American exploiting them and they ought to go ahead under his guidance. Stew-Beef, Lias Strawn and Motor-Boat pointed out to him that they had never dreamed of dancing in public until I had picked them up. I had rehearsed them for months, fed them and routined them into something. Why had *he* never thought of it before I did. He had discouraged the others from joining me until it began to look successful. So they meant to stick with me, American or no American. But two of the women joined the trouble maker and I fired all three of them. The whole thing was beginning to wear me down. When some other things began to annoy me, I decided to go home to Florida and try to write the book I had in mind, which was *Jonah's Gourd Vine*. Before it was hardly started, I heard that Hall Johnson had raided my group and was using it in his "Run Little Chillun." I never saw the production, but I was told that the religious scene was the spitting image of the one from my concert also. As I said, I never saw it so I wouldn't know.

But this I do know, that people became very much alive to West Indian dancing and work songs. I have heard myself over the air dozens of times and felt the influence of that concert running through what has been done since. My name is never mentioned, of course, because that is not the way theater people do things, but that concert and the rave notices I got from the critics shoved the viewpoint over towards the natural Negro.

Theater Arts Magazine photographed us and presented us in its April issue following the concert at the John Golden. The Folk Dance Society presented us at the Vanderbilt. We appeared at the first National Folk Festival in St. Louis in 1934, at Chicago in 1934, and at Constitution Hall in Washington, D.C. In Chicago, I had only ten days to try to prepare a full length program and it was not smooth considering that I had only very raw material to work with in so short a time, but at that the dancers and a dramatic bit went over splendidly and got good notices. Katherine Dunham loaned us her studio for rehearsal twice, which was kind of her. Anyway, West Indian dancing had gone west and created interest just as it had done in the east. When I got to Jamaica on my first Guggenheim fellowship in 1936, I found that Katherine Dunham had been there a few months before collecting dances, and had gone on to Haiti.

I made no real money out of my concert work. I might have done so if I had taken it up as a life work. But I am satisfied in knowing that I established a trend and pointed Negro expression back towards the saner ground of our own unbelievable originality.

SELECTED ARTICLES

Contents

The Eatonville Anthology

I

THE PLEADING WOMAN

MRS. TONY ROBERTS is the pleading woman. She just loves to ask for things. Her husband gives her all he can rake and scrape, which is considerably more than most wives get for their housekeeping, but she goes from door to door begging for things.

She starts at the store. "Mist' Clarke," she sing-songs in a high keening voice, "gimme lil' piece uh meat tuh boil a pot uh greens wid. Lawd knows me an' mah chillen is SO hongry! Hits uh SHAME! Tony don't fee-ee-eee-ed me!"

Mr. Clarke knows that she has money and that her larder is well stocked, for Tony Roberts is the best provider on his list. But her keening annoys him and he arises heavily. The pleader at this shows all the joy of a starving man being seated at a feast.

"Thass right Mist' Clarke. De Lawd loveth de cheerful giver. Gimme jes' a lil' piece 'bout dis big (indicating the width of her hand) an' de Lawd'll bless yuh."

She follows this angel-on-earth to his meat tub and superintends the cutting, crying out in pain when he refuses to move the knife over just a teeny bit mo'.

Finally, meat in hand, she departs, remarking on the meanness of some people who give a piece of salt meat only two-fingers wide when they were plainly asked for a hand-wide piece. Clarke puts it down to Tony's account and resumes his reading.

With the slab of salt pork as a foundation, she visits various homes until she has collected all she wants for the day. At the Piersons, for instance: "Sister Pierson, plee-ee-ease gimme uh han'ful uh collard greens fuh me an' mah po' chillen! 'Deed, me an' mah chillen is SO hongry. Tony doan' fee-ee-eed me!"

Mrs. Pierson picks a bunch of greens for her, but she springs away from them as if they were poison. "Lawd a mussy, Mis' Pierson, you ain't gonna gimme dat lil' eye-full uh greens fuh me an' mah chillen, is you? Don't be so graspin': Gawd won't bless yuh. Gimme uh han'full mo'. Lawd, some folks is got everything, an' theys jes' as gripin' an' stingy!"

Mrs. Pierson raises the ante, and the pleading woman moves on to the next place, and on and on. The next day, it commences all over.

II

TURPENTINE LOVE

Jim Merchant is always in good humor—even with his wife. He says he fell in love with her at first sight. That was some years ago. She has had all her teeth pulled out, but they still get along splendidly.

He says the first time he called on her he found out that she was subject to fits. This didn't cool his love, however. She had several in his presence.

One Sunday, while he was there, she had one, and her mother tried to give her a dose of turpentine to stop it. Accidently, she spilled it in her eye and it cured her. She never had another fit, so they got married and have kept each other in good humor ever since.

III

Becky Moore has eleven children of assorted colors and sizes. She has never been married, but that is not her fault. She has never stopped any of the fathers of her children from proposing, so if she has no father for her children it's not her fault. The men round about are entirely to blame.

The other mothers of the town are afraid that it is catching. They won't let their children play with hers.

IV

TIPPY

Sykes Jones' family all shoot craps. The most interesting member of the family—also fond of bones, but of another kind—is Tippy, the Jones' dog.

He is so thin, that it amazes one that he lives at all. He

sneaks into village kitchens if the housewives are careless about the doors and steals meats, even off the stoves. He also sucks eggs.

For these offenses he has been sentenced to death dozens of times, and the sentences executed upon him, only they didn't work. He has been fed bluestone, strychnine, nux vomica, even an entire Peruna bottle beaten up. It didn't fatten him, but it didn't kill him. So Eatonville has resigned itself to the plague of Tippy, reflecting that it has erred in certain matters and is being chastened.

In spite of all the attempts upon his life, Tippy is still willing to be friendly with anyone who will let him.

V

The Way of a Man with a Train

Old Man Anderson lived seven or eight miles out in the country from Eatonville. Over by Lake Apopka. He raised feed-corn and cassava and went to market with it two or three times a year. He bought all of his victuals wholesale so he wouldn't have to come to town for several months more.

He was different from us citybred folks. He had never seen a train. Everybody laughed at him for even the smallest child in Eatonville had either been to Maitland or Orlando and watched a train go by. On Sunday afternoons all of the young people of the village would go over to Maitland, a mile away, to see Number 35 whizz southward on its way to Tampa and wave at the passengers. So we looked down on him a little. Even we children felt superior in the presence of a person so lacking in worldly knowledge.

The grown-ups kept telling him he ought to go see a train. He always said he didn't have time to wait so long. Only two trains a day passed through Maitland. But patronage and ridicule finally had its effect and Old Man Anderson drove in one morning early. Number 78 went north to Jacksonville at 10:20. He drove his light wagon over in the woods beside the railroad below Maitland, and sat down to wait. He began to fear that his horse would get frightened and run away with the wagon. So he took him out and led him deeper into the grove and tied him securely Then he returned to his wagon

and waited some more. Then he remembered that some of
the train-wise villagers had said the engine belched fire and
smoke. He had better move his wagon out of danger. It
might catch afire. He climbed down from the seat and placed
himself between the shafts to draw it away. Just then 78 came
thundering over the trestle spouting smoke, and suddenly began blowing for Maitland. Old Man Anderson became so
frightened he ran away with the wagon through the woods
and tore it up worse than the horse ever could have done. He
doesn't know yet what a train looks like, and says he doesn't
care.

VI

COON TAYLOR

Coon Taylor never did any real stealing. Of course, if he
saw a chicken or a watermelon or muskmelon or anything like
that that he wanted he'd take it. The people used to get mad
but they never could catch him. He took so many melons
from Joe Clarke that he set up in the melon patch one night
with his shotgun loaded with rock salt. He was going to fix
Coon. But he was tired. It is hard work being a mayor,
postmaster, storekeeper and everything. He dropped asleep
sitting on a stump in the middle of the patch. So he didn't see
Coon when he came. Coon didn't see him either, that is, not at
first. He knew the stump was there, however. He had opened
many of Clarke's juicy Florida Favorite on it. He selected his
fruit, walked over to the stump and burst the melon on it. That
is, he thought it was the stump until it fell over with a yell.
Then he knew it was no stump and departed hastily from those
parts. He had cleared the fence when Clarke came to, as it
were. So the charge of rock-salt was wasted on the desert air.

During the sugar-cane season, he found he couldn't resist
Clarke's soft green cane, but Clarke did not go to sleep this
time. So after he had cut six or eight stalks by the moonlight,
Clarke rose up out of the cane strippings with his shotgun
and made Coon sit right down and chew up the last one of
them on the spot. And the next day he made Coon leave his
town for three months.

VII

VILLAGE FICTION

Joe Lindsay is said by Lum Boger to be the largest manufacturer of prevarications in Eatonville; Brazzle (late owner of the world's leanest and meanest mule) contends that his business is the largest in the state and his wife holds that he is the biggest liar in the world.

Exhibit A—He claims that while he was in Orlando one day he saw a doctor cut open a woman, remove everything—liver, lights and heart included—clean each of them separately; the doctor then washed out the empty woman, dried her out neatly with a towel and replaced the organs so expertly that she was up and about her work in a couple of weeks.

VIII

Sewell is a man who lives all to himself. He moves a great deal. So often, that 'Lige Moseley says his chickens are so used to moving that every time he comes out into his backyard the chickens lie down and cross their legs, ready to be tied up again.

He is baldheaded; but he says he doesn't mind that, because he wants as little as possible between him and God.

IX

Mrs. Clarke is Joe Clarke's wife. She is a soft-looking, middle-aged woman, whose bust and stomach are always holding a get-together.

She waits on the store sometimes and cries every time he yells at her which he does every time she makes a mistake, which is quite often. She calls her husband "Jody." They say he used to beat her in the store when he was a young man, but he is not so impatient now. He can wait until he goes home.

She shouts in Church every Sunday and shakes the hand of fellowship with everybody in the Church with her eyes closed, but somehow always misses her husband.

X

Mrs. McDuffy goes to Church every Sunday and always shouts and tells her "determination." Her husband always sits in the back row and beats her as soon as they get home. He says there's no sense in her shouting, as big a devil as she is. She just does it to slur him. Elijah Moseley asked her why she didn't stop shouting, seeing she always got a beating about it. She says she can't "squinch the sperrit." Then Elijah asked Mr. McDuffy to stop beating her, seeing that she was going to shout anyway. He answered that she just did it for spite and that his fist was just as hard as her head. He could last just as long as she. So the village let the matter rest.

XI

DOUBLE-SHUFFLE

Back in the good old days before the World War, things were very simple in Eatonville. People didn't fox-trot. When the town wanted to put on its Sunday clothes and wash behind the ears, it put on a "breakdown." The daring younger set would two-step and waltz, but the good church members and the elders stuck to the grand march. By rural canons dancing is wicked, but one is not held to have danced until the feet have been crossed. Feet don't get crossed when one grand marches.

At elaborate affairs the organ from the Methodist church was moved up to the hall and Lizzimore, the blind man presided. When informal gatherings were held, he merely played his guitar assisted by any volunteer with mouth organs or accordians.

Among white people the march is as mild as if it had been passed on by Volstead. But it still has a kick in Eatonville. Everybody happy, shining eyes, gleaming teeth. Feet dragged 'shhlap, shhlap! to beat out the time. No orchestra needed. Round and round! Back again, parse-me-la! shlap! shlap! Strut! Strut! Seaboard! Shlap! Shlap! Tiddy bumm! Mr. Clarke in the lead with Mrs. Moseley.

It's too much for some of the young folks. Double shuffling commences. Buck and wing. Lizzimore about to break his guitar. Accordion doing contortions. People fall back against the walls, and let the soloist have it, shouting as they clap the old, old double shuffle songs.

> 'Me an' mah honey got two mo' days
> Two mo' days tuh do de buck'

Sweating bodies, laughing mouths, grotesque faces, feet drumming fiercely. Deacons clapping as hard as the rest.

> "Great big nigger, black as tar
> Trying tuh git tuh hebben on uh 'lectric car."

> "Some love cabbage, some love kale
> but I love a gal wid a short skirt tail."

> Long tall angel—steppin' down,
> Long white robe an' starry crown.

> 'Ah would not marry uh black gal (bumm bumm!)
> Tell yuh de reason why
> Every time she comb her hair
> She make de goo-goo eye.

> Would not marry a yaller gal (bumm bumm!)
> Tell yuh de reason why
> Her neck so long an' stringy
> Ahm 'fraid she'd never die.

> Would not marry uh preacher
> Tell yuh de reason why
> Every time he comes tuh town
> He makes de chicken fly.

When the buck dance was over, the boys would give the floor to the girls and they would parse-me-la with a slye eye out of the corner to see if anybody was looking who might "have them up in church" on conference night. Then there would be more dancing. Then Mr. Clarke would call for everybody's best attention and announce that *'freshments was served! Every gent'man would please take his lady by the arm and scorch her right up to de table fur a treat!*

Then the men would stick their arms out with a flourish and ask their ladies: "You lak chicken? Well, then, take a wing."

And the ladies would take the proffered "wings" and parade up to the long table and be served. Of course most of them had brought baskets in which were heaps of jointed and fried chicken, two or three kinds of pies, cakes, potato pone and chicken purlo. The hall would separate into happy groups about the baskets until time for more dancing.

But the boys and girls got scattered about during the war, and now they dance the fox-trot by a brand new piano. They do waltz and two-step still, but no one now considers it good form to lock his chin over his partner's shoulder and stick out behind. One night just for fun and to humor the old folks, they danced, that is, they grand marched, but everyone picked up their feet. *Bah!!*

XII

THE HEAD OF THE NAIL

Daisy Taylor was the town vamp. Not that she was pretty. But sirens were all but non-existent in the town. Perhaps she was forced to it by circumstances. She was quite dark, with little brushy patches of hair squatting over her head. These were held down by shingle-nails often. No one knows whether she did this for artistic effect or for lack of hair-pins, but there they were shining in the little patches of hair when she got all dressed for the afternoon and came up to Clarke's store to see if there was any mail for her.

It was seldom that anyone wrote to Daisy, but she knew that the men of the town would be assembled there by five o'clock, and some one could usually be induced to buy her some soda water or peanuts.

Daisy flirted with married men. There were only two single men in town. Lum Boger, who was engaged to the assistant school-teacher, and Hiram Lester, who had been off to school at Tuskegee and wouldn't look at a person like Daisy. In addition to other drawbacks, she was pigeon-toed and her petticoat was always showing so perhaps he was justified. There was nothing else to do except flirt with married men.

This went on for a long time. First one wife then another complained of her, or drove her from the preserves by threat.

But the affair with Crooms was the most prolonged and

serious. He was even known to have bought her a pair of shoes.

Mrs. Laura Crooms was a meek little woman who took all of her troubles crying and talked a great deal of leaving things in the hands of God.

The affair came to a head one night in orange picking time. Crooms was over at Oneido picking oranges. Many fruit pickers move from one town to the other during the season.

The *town* was collected at the store-postoffice as is customary on Saturday nights. The *town* has had its bath and with its week's pay in pocket fares forth to be merry. The men tell stories and treat the ladies to soda-water, peanuts and peppermint candy.

Daisy was trying to get treats, but the porch was cold to her that night.

"Ah don't keer if you don't treat me. What's a dirty lil nickel?" She flung this at Walter Thomas. "The ever-loving Mister Crooms will gimme anything atall Ah wants."

"You better shet up yo' mouf talking 'bout Albert Crooms. Heah his wife comes right now."

Daisy went akimbo. "Who? Me! Ah don't keer whut Laura Crooms think. If she ain't a heavy hip-ted Mama enough to keep him, she don't need to come crying to me."

She stood making goo-goo eyes as Mrs. Crooms walked upon the porch. Daisy laughed loud, made several references to Albert Crooms, and when she saw the mail-bag come in from Maitland she said, "Ah better go in an' see if Ah ain't got a letter from Oneido."

The more Daisy played the game of getting Mrs. Crooms' goat, the better she liked it. She ran in and out of the store laughing until she could scarcely stand. Some of the people present began to talk to Mrs. Crooms—to egg her on to halt Daisy's boasting, but she was for leaving it all in the hands of God. Walter Thomas kept on after Mrs. Crooms until she stiffened and resolved to fight. Daisy was inside when she came to this resolve and never dreamed anything of the kind could happen. She had gotten hold of an envelope and came laughing and shouting, "Oh, Ah can't stand to see Oneido lose!"

There was a box of ax-handles on display on the porch,

propped up against the door jamb. As Daisy stepped upon the porch, Mrs. Crooms leaned the heavy end of one of those handles heavily upon her head. She staggered from the porch to the ground and the timid Laura, fearful of a counter-attack, struck again and Daisy toppled into the town ditch. There was not enough water in there to do more than muss her up. Every time she tried to rise, down would come that ax-handle again. Laura was fighting a scared fight. With Daisy thoroughly licked, she retired to the store porch and left her fallen enemy in the ditch. None of the men helped Daisy—even to get out of the ditch. But Elijah Moseley, who was some distance down the street when the trouble began arrived as the victor was withdrawing. He rushed up and picked Daisy out of the mud and began feeling her head.

"Is she hurt much?" Joe Clarke asked from the doorway.

"I don't know," Elijah answered. "I was just looking to see if Laura had been lucky enough to hit one of those nails on the head and drive it in."

Before a week was up, Daisy moved to Orlando. There in a wider sphere, perhaps, her talents as a vamp were appreciated.

XIII

Pants and Cal'line

Sister Cal'line Potts was a silent woman. Did all of her laughing down inside, but did the thing that kept the town in an uproar of laughter. It was the general opinion of the village that Cal'line would do anything she had a mind to. And she had a mind to do several things.

Mitchell Potts, her husband, had a weakness for women. No one ever believed that she was jealous. She did things to the women, surely. But most any townsman would have said that she did them because she liked the novel situation and the queer things she could bring out of it.

Once he took up with Delphine—called Mis' Pheeny by the town. She lived on the outskirts on the edge of the piney woods. The town winked and talked. People don't make secrets of such things in villages. Cal'line went about her business with her thin black lips pursed tight as ever, and her shiny black eyes unchanged.

"Dat devil of a Cal'line's got somethin' up her sleeve!" The town smiled in anticipation.

"Delphine is too big a cigar for her to smoke. She ain't crazy," said some as the weeks went on and nothing happened. Even Pheeny herself would give an extra flirt to her over-starched petticoats as she rustled into church past her of Sundays.

Mitch Potts said furthermore, that he was tired of Cal'line's foolishness. She had to stay where he put her. His African soup-bone (arm) was too strong to let a woman run over him. 'Nough was 'nough. And he did some fancy cussing, and he was the fanciest cusser in the county.

So the town waited and the longer it waited, the odds changed slowly from the wife to the husband.

One Saturday, Mitch knocked off work at two o'clock and went over to Maitland. He came back with a rectangular box under his arm and kept straight on out to the barn and put it away. He ducked around the corner of the house quickly but even so, his wife glimpsed the package. Very much like a shoe-box. So!

He put on the kettle and took a bath. She stood in her bare feet at the ironing board and kept on ironing. He dressed. It was about five o'clock but still very light. He fiddled around outside. She kept on with her ironing. As soon as the sun got red, he sauntered out to the barn, got the parcel and walked away down the road, past the store and out into the piney woods. As soon as he left the house, Cal'line slipped on her shoes without taking time to don stockings, put on one of her husband's old Stetsons, worn and floppy, slung the axe over her shoulder and followed in his wake. He was hailed cheerily as he passed the sitters on the store porch and answered smiling sheepishly and passed on. Two minutes later passed his wife, silently, unsmilingly, and set the porch to giggling and betting.

An hour passed perhaps. It was dark. Clarke had long ago lighted the swinging kerosene lamp inside.

*   *   *   *   *

Once 'way back yonder before the stars fell all the animals used to talk just like people. In them days dogs and rabbits was the best of friends—even tho both of them was stuck on the same gal—which was Miss Nancy Coon. She had the sweetest smile and the prettiest striped and bushy tail to be found anywhere.

They both run their legs nigh off trying to win her for themselves—fetching nice ripe persimmons and such. But she never give one or the other no satisfaction.

Finally one night Mr. Dog popped the question right out. "Miss Coon," he says, "Ma'am, also Ma'am which would you ruther be—a lark flyin' or a dove a settin'?"

Course Miss Nancy she blushed and laughed a little and hid her face behind her bushy tail for a spell. Then she said sorter shy like, "I does love yo' sweet voice, brother dawg—but—but I ain't jes' exactly set in my mind yit."

Her and Mr. Dog set on a spell, when up comes hopping Mr. Rabbit wid his tail fresh washed and his whiskers shining. He got right down to business and asked Miss Coon to marry him, too.

"Oh, Miss Nancy," he says, "Ma'am, also Ma'am, if you'd see me settin' straddle of a mud-cat leadin' a minnow, what would you think? Ma'am also Ma'am?" Which is a out and out proposal as everybody knows.

"Youse awful nice, Brother Rabbit and a beautiful dancer, but you cannot sing like Brother Dog. Both you uns come back next week to gimme time for to decide."

They both left arm-in-arm. Finally Mr. Rabbit says to Mr. Dog, "Taint no use in me going back—she ain't gwinter have me. So I mought as well give up. She loves singing, and I ain't got nothing but a squeak."

"Oh, don't talk that a' way," says Mr. Dog, tho' he is glad Mr. Rabbit can't sing none.

"Thass all right, Brer Dog. But if I had a sweet voice like you got, I'd have it worked on and make it sweeter."

"How! How! How!" Mr. Dog cried, jumping up and down.

"Lemme fix it for you, like I do for Sister Lark and Sister Mocking-bird."

"When? Where?" asked Mr. Dog, all excited. He was figuring that if he could sing just a little better Miss Coon would be bound to have him.

"Just you meet me t'morrer in de huckleberry patch," says the rabbit and off they both goes to bed.

The dog is there on time next day and after a while the rabbit comes loping up.

"Mawnin', Brer Dawg," he says kinder chippy like. "Ready to git yo' voice sweetened?"

"Sholy, sholy, Brer Rabbit. Let's we all hurry about it. I wants tuh serenade Miss Nancy from de piney woods tuh night."

"Well, den, open yo' mouf and poke out yo' tongue," says the rabbit.

No sooner did Mr. Dog poke out his tongue than Mr. Rabbit split it with a knife and ran for all he was worth to a hollow stump and hid hisself.

The dog has been mad at the rabbit ever since.

Anybody who don't believe it happened, just look at the dog's tongue and he can see for himself where the rabbit slit it right up the middle.

Stepped on a tin, mah story ends.

The Messenger, September–November 1926

How It Feels To Be Colored Me

I AM colored but I offer nothing in the way of extenuating circumstances except the fact that I am the only Negro in the United States whose grandfather on the mother's side was *not* an Indian chief.

I remember the very day that I became colored. Up to my thirteenth year I lived in the little Negro town of Eatonville, Florida. It is exclusively a colored town. The only white people I knew passed through the town going to or coming from Orlando. The native whites rode dusty horses, the Northern tourists chugged down the sandy village road in automobiles. The town knew the Southerners and never stopped cane chewing when they passed. But the Northerners were something else again. They were peered at cautiously from behind curtains by the timid. The more venturesome would come out on the porch to watch them go past and got just as much pleasure out of the tourists as the tourists got out of the village.

The front porch might seem a daring place for the rest of the town, but it was a gallery seat to me. My favorite place was atop the gate-post. Proscenium box for a born first-nighter. Not only did I enjoy the show, but I didn't mind the actors knowing that I liked it. I actually spoke to them in passing. I'd wave at them and when they returned my salute, I would say something like this: "Howdy-do-well-I-thank-you-where-you-goin'?" Usually automobile or the horse paused at this, and after a queer exchange of compliments, I would probably "go a piece of the way" with them, as we say in farthest Florida. If one of my family happened to come to the front in time to see me, of course negotiations would be rudely broken off. But even so, it is clear that I was the first "welcome-to-our-state" Floridian, and I hope the Miami Chamber of Commerce will please take notice.

During this period, white people differed from colored to me only in that they rode through town and never lived there. They liked to hear me "speak pieces" and sing and wanted to see me dance the parse-me-la, and gave me generously of their small silver for doing these things, which seemed strange to me for I wanted to do them so much that I needed bribing to stop. Only they didn't know it. The colored people gave no dimes. They deplored any joyful tendencies in me, but I was their Zora nevertheless. I belonged to them, to the nearby hotels, to the county—everybody's Zora.

But changes came in the family when I was thirteen, and I was sent to school in Jacksonville. I left Eatonville, the town of the oleanders, as Zora. When I disembarked from the riverboat at Jacksonville, she was no more. It seemed that I had suffered a sea change. I was not Zora of Orange County any more, I was now a little colored girl. I found it out in certain ways. In my heart as well as in the mirror, I became a fast brown—warranted not to rub nor run.

But I am not tragically colored. There is no great sorrow dammed up in my soul, nor lurking behind my eyes. I do not mind at all. I do not belong to the sobbing school of Negrohood who hold that nature somehow has given them a lowdown dirty deal and whose feelings are all hurt about it. Even in the helter-skelter skirmish that is my life, I have seen that the world is to the strong regardless of a little pigmentation more or less. No, I do not weep at the world—I am too busy sharpening my oyster knife.

Someone is always at my elbow reminding me that I am the grand-daughter of slaves. It fails to register depression with me. Slavery is sixty years in the past. The operation was successful and the patient is doing well, thank you. The terrible struggle that made me an American out of a potential slave said "On the line!" The Reconstruction said "Get set!"; and the generation before said "Go!" I am off to a flying start and I must not halt in the stretch to look behind and weep. Slavery is the price I paid for civilization, and the choice was not with me. It is a bully adventure and worth all that I have paid through my ancestors for it. No one on earth ever had a greater chance for glory. The world to be won and nothing to be lost. It is thrilling to think—to know that for any act of mine, I shall get twice as much praise or twice as much blame. It is quite exciting to hold the center of the national stage, with the spectators not knowing whether to laugh or to weep.

The position of my white neighbor is much more difficult.

No brown specter pulls up a chair beside me when I sit down to eat. No dark ghost thrusts its leg against mine in bed. The game of keeping what one has is never so exciting as the game of getting.

I do not always feel colored. Even now I often achieve the unconscious Zora of Eatonville before the Hegira. I feel most colored when I am thrown against a sharp white background.

For instance at Barnard. "Beside the waters of the Hudson" I feel my race. Among the thousand white persons, I am a dark rock surged upon, overswept by a creamy sea. I am surged upon and overswept, but through it all, I remain myself. When covered by the waters, I am; and the ebb but reveals me again.

Sometimes it is the other way around. A white person is set down in our midst, but the contrast is just as sharp for me. For instance, when I sit in the drafty basement that is The New World Cabaret with a white person, my color comes. We enter chatting about any little nothing that we have in common and are seated by the jazz waiters. In the abrupt way that jazz orchestras have, this one plunges into a number. It loses no time in circumlocutions, but gets right down to business. It constricts the thorax and splits the heart with its tempo and narcotic harmonies. This orchestra grows rambunctious, rears on its hind legs and attacks the tonal veil with primitive fury, rending it, clawing it until it breaks through to the jungle beyond. I follow those heathen—follow them exultingly. I dance wildly inside myself; I yell within, I whoop; I shake my assegai above my head, I hurl it true to the mark *yeeeeooww!* I am in the jungle and living in the jungle way. My face is painted red and yellow, and my body is painted blue. My pulse is throbbing like a war drum. I want to slaughter something—give pain, give death to what, I do not know. But the piece ends. The men of the orchestra wipe their lips and rest their fingers. I creep back slowly to the veneer we call civilization with the last tone and find the white friend sitting motionless in his seat, smoking calmly.

"Good music they have here," he remarks, drumming the table with his fingertips.

Music! The great blobs of purple and red emotion have not touched him. He has only heard what I felt. He is far away and I see him but dimly across the ocean and the continent that have fallen between us. He is so pale with his whiteness then and I am *so* colored.

At certain times I have no race, I am *me*. When I set my hat at a certain angle and saunter down Seventh Avenue, Harlem City, feeling as snooty as the lions in front of the Forty-Second Street Library, for instance. So far as my feelings are concerned, Peggy Hopkins Joyce on the Boule Mich with her gorgeous raiment, stately carriage, knees knocking together in a most aristocratic manner, has nothing on me. The cosmic Zora emerges. I belong to no race nor time, I am the eternal feminine with its string of beads.

I have no separate feeling about being an American citizen and colored. I am merely a fragment of the Great Soul that surges within the boundaries. My country, right or wrong.

Sometimes, I feel discriminated against, but it does not make me angry. It merely astonishes me. How *can* any deny themselves the pleasure of my company! It's beyond me.

But in the main, I feel like a brown bag of miscellany propped against a wall. Against a wall in company with other bags, white, red and yellow. Pour out the contents, and there is discovered a jumble of small things priceless and worthless. A first-water diamond, an empty spool, bits of broken glass, lengths of string, a key to a door long since crumbled away, a rusty knife-blade, old shoes saved for a road that never was and never will be, a nail bent under the weight of things too heavy for any nail, a dried flower or two, still a little fragrant. In your hand is the brown bag. On the ground before you is the jumble it held—so much like the jumble in the bags, could they be emptied, that all might be dumped in a single heap and the bags refilled without altering the content of any greatly. A bit of colored glass more or less would not matter. Perhaps that is how the Great Stuffer of Bags filled them in the first place—who knows?

The World Tomorrow, May 1928

from *Negro: An Anthology*

CHARACTERISTICS OF NEGRO EXPRESSION

DRAMA

THE Negro's universal mimicry is not so much a thing in itself as an evidence of something that permeates his entire self. And that thing is drama.

His very words are action words. His interpretation of the English language is in terms of pictures. One act described in terms of another. Hence the rich metaphor and simile.

The metaphor is of course very primitive. It is easier to illustrate than it is to explain because action came before speech. Let us make a parallel. Language is like money. In primitive communities actual goods, however bulky, are bartered for what one wants. This finally evolves into coin, the coin being not real wealth but a symbol of wealth. Still later even coin is abandoned for legal tender, and still later for cheques in certain usages.

Every phase of Negro life is highly dramatised. No matter how joyful or how sad the case there is sufficient poise for drama. Everything is acted out. Unconsciously for the most part of course. There is an impromptu ceremony always ready for every hour of life. No little moment passes unadorned.

Now the people with highly developed languages have words for detached ideas. That is legal tender. "That-which-we-squat-on" has become "chair." "Groan-causer" has evolved into "spear," and so on. Some individuals even conceive of the equivalent of cheque words, like "ideation" and "pleonastic." Perhaps we might say that *Paradise Lost* and *Sartor Resartus* are written in cheque words.

The primitive man exchanges descriptive words. His terms are all close fitting. Frequently the Negro, even with detached words in his vocabulary—not evolved in him but transplanted on his tongue by contact—must add action to it to make it do. So we have "chop-axe," "sitting-chair," "cook-pot" and the like because the speaker has in his mind the picture of the object in use. Action. Everything illustrated. So we can say the white man thinks in a written language and the Negro thinks in hieroglyphics.

A bit of Negro drama familiar to all is the frequent meeting of two opponents who threaten to do atrocious murder one upon the other.

Who has not observed a robust young Negro chap posing upon a street corner, possessed of nothing but his clothing, his strength and his youth? Does he bear himself like a pauper? No, Louis XIV could be no more insolent in his assurance. His eyes say plainly "Female, halt!" His posture exults "Ah, female, I am the eternal male, the giver of life. Behold in my hot flesh all the delights of this world. Salute me, I am strength." All this with a languid posture, there is no mistaking his meaning.

A Negro girl strolls past the corner lounger. Her whole body panging* and posing. A slight shoulder movement that calls attention to her bust, that is all of a dare. A hippy undulation below the waist that is a sheaf of promises tied with conscious power. She is acting out "I'm a darned sweet woman and you know it."

These little plays by strolling players are acted out daily in a dozen streets in a thousand cities, and no one ever mistakes the meaning.

WILL TO ADORN

The will to adorn is the second most notable characteristic in Negro expression. Perhaps his idea of ornament does not attempt to meet conventional standards, but it satisfies the soul of its creator.

In this respect the American Negro has done wonders to the English language. It has often been stated by etymologists that the Negro has introduced no African words to the language. This is true, but it is equally true that he has made over a great part of the tongue to his liking and has had his revision accepted by the ruling class. No one listening to a Southern white man talk could deny this. Not only has he softened and toned down strongly consonanted words like "aren't" to "aint" and the like, he has made new force words out of old feeble elements. Examples of this are "ham-

*From "pang."

shanked," "battle-hammed," "double-teen," "bodaciously," "muffle-jawed."

But the Negro's greatest contribution to the language is: (1) the use of metaphor and simile; (2) the use of the double descriptive; (3) the use of verbal nouns.

1. METAPHOR AND SIMILE

One at a time, like lawyers going to heaven.
You sho is propaganda.
Sobbing hearted.
I'll beat you till: (*a*) rope like okra, (*b*) slack like lime, (*c*) smell like onions.
Fatal for naked.
Kyting along.
That's a lynch.
That's a rope.
Cloakers — deceivers.
Regular as pig-tracks.
Mule blood — black molasses.
Syndicating — gossiping.
Flambeaux — cheap café (lighted by flambeaux).
To put yo'self on de ladder.

2. THE DOUBLE DESCRIPTIVE

High-tall.
Little-tee-ninchy (tiny).
Low-down.
Top-superior.
Sham-polish.
Lady-people.
Kill-dead.
Hot-boiling.
Chop-axe.
Sitting-chairs.
De watch wall.
Speedy-hurry.
More great and more better.

3. VERBAL NOUNS

She features somebody I know.
Funeralize.

Sense me into it.
Puts the shamery on him.
'Taint everybody you kin confidence.
I wouldn't friend with her.
Jooking—playing piano or guitar as it is done in Jook-
    houses (houses of ill-fame).
Uglying away.
I wouldn't scorn my name all up on you.
Bookooing (beaucoup) around—showing off.

NOUNS FROM VERBS
Won't stand a broke.
She won't take a listen.
He won't stand straightening.
That is such a compelment.
That's a lynch.

The stark, trimmed phrases of the Occident seem too bare
for the voluptuous child of the sun, hence the adornment. It
arises out of the same impulse as the wearing of jewelry and
the making of sculpture—the urge to adorn.

On the walls of the homes of the average Negro one always
finds a glut of gaudy calendars, wall pockets and advertising
lithographs. The sophisticated white man or Negro would
tolerate none of these, even if they bore a likeness to the
Mona Lisa. No commercial art for decoration. Nor the calendar nor the advertisement spoils the picture for this lowly
man. He sees the beauty in spite of the declaration of the
Portland Cement Works or the butcher's announcement. I
saw in Mobile a room in which there was an over-stuffed
mohair living-room suite, an imitation mahogany bed and
chifferobe, a console victrola. The walls were gaily papered
with Sunday supplements of the *Mobile Register*. There were
seven calendars and three wall pockets. One of them was
decorated with a lace doily. The mantel-shelf was covered
with a scarf of deep home-made lace, looped up with a huge
bow of pink crêpe paper. Over the door was a huge litho-
graph showing the Treaty of Versailles being signed with a
Waterman fountain pen.

It was grotesque, yes. But it indicated the desire for beauty.

And decorating a decoration, as in the case of the doily on the gaudy wall pocket, did not seem out of place to the hostess. The feeling back of such an act is that there can never be enough of beauty, let alone too much. Perhaps she is right. We each have our standards of art, and thus are we all interested parties and so unfit to pass judgment upon the art concepts of others.

Whatever the Negro does of his own volition he embellishes. His religious service is for the greater part excellent prose poetry. Both prayers and sermons are tooled and polished until they are true works of art. The supplication is forgotten in the frenzy of creation. The prayer of the white man is considered humorous in its bleakness. The beauty of the Old Testament does not exceed that of a Negro prayer.

ANGULARITY

After adornment the next most striking manifestation of the Negro is Angularity. Everything that he touches becomes angular. In all African sculpture and doctrine of any sort we find the same thing.

Anyone watching Negro dancers will be struck by the same phenomenon. Every posture is another angle. Pleasing, yes. But an effect achieved by the very means which an European strives to avoid.

The pictures on the walls are hung at deep angles. Furniture is always set at an angle. I have instances of a piece of furniture in the *middle* of a wall being set with one end nearer the wall than the other to avoid the simple straight line.

ASYMMETRY

Asymmetry is a definite feature of Negro art. I have no samples of true Negro painting unless we count the African shields, but the sculpture and carvings are full of this beauty and lack of symmetry.

It is present in the literature, both prose and verse. I offer an example of this quality in verse from Langston Hughes:

I aint gonna mistreat ma good gal any more,
I'm just gonna kill her next time she makes me sore.

. . . .

I treats her kind but she don't do me right,
She fights and quarrels most ever' night.

. . . .

I can't have no woman's got such low-down ways
Cause de blue gum woman aint de style now'days.

. . . .

I brought her from the South and she's goin on back,
Else I'll use her head for a carpet tack.

It is the lack of symmetry which makes Negro dancing so difficult for white dancers to learn. The abrupt and unexpected changes. The frequent change of key and time are evidences of this quality in music. (Note the St. Louis Blues.)

The dancing of the justly famous Bo-Jangles and Snake Hips are excellent examples.

The presence of rhythm and lack of symmetry are paradoxical, but there they are. Both are present to a marked degree. There is always rhythm, but it is the rhythm of segments. Each unit has a rhythm of its own, but when the whole is assembled it is lacking in symmetry. But easily workable to a Negro who is accustomed to the break in going from one part to another, so that he adjusts himself to the new tempo.

DANCING

Negro dancing is dynamic suggestion. No matter how violent it may appear to the beholder, every posture gives the impression that the dancer will do much more. For example, the performer flexes one knee sharply, assumes a ferocious face mask, thrusts the upper part of the body forward with clenched fists, elbows taut as in hard running or grasping a thrusting blade. That is all. But the spectator himself adds the picture of ferocious assault, hears the drums and finds himself keeping time with the music and tensing himself for the struggle. It is compelling insinuation. That is the very reason the spectator is held so rapt. He is participating in the performance himself— carrying out the suggestions of the performer.

The difference in the two arts is: the white dancer attempts to express fully; the Negro is restrained, but succeeds in gripping the beholder by forcing him to finish the action the performer suggests. Since no art ever can express all the variations conceivable, the Negro must be considered the greater artist, his dancing is realistic suggestion, and that is about all a great artist can do.

Negro Folklore

Negro folklore is not a thing of the past. It is still in the making. Its great variety shows the adaptability of the black man: nothing is too old or too new, domestic or foreign, high or low, for his use. God and the Devil are paired, and are treated no more reverently than Rockefeller and Ford. Both of these men are prominent in folklore, Ford being particularly strong, and they talk and act like good-natured stevedores or mill-hands. Ole Massa is sometimes a smart man and often a fool. The automobile is ranged alongside of the ox-cart. The angels and the apostles walk and talk like section hands. And through it all walks Jack, the greatest culture hero of the South; Jack beats them all—even the Devil, who is often smarter than God.

Culture Heroes

The Devil is next after Jack as a culture hero. He can outsmart everyone but Jack. God is absolutely no match for him. He is good-natured and full of humour. The sort of person one may count on to help out in any difficulty.

Peter the Apostle is the third in importance. One need not look far for the explanation. The Negro is not a Christian really. The primitive gods are not deities of too subtle inner reflection; they are hard-working bodies who serve their devotees just as laboriously as the suppliant serves them. Gods of physical violence, stopping at nothing to serve their followers. Now of all the apostles Peter is the most active. When the other ten fell back trembling in the garden, Peter wielded the blade on the posse. Peter first and foremost in all action. The gods of no peoples have been philosophic until the people themselves have approached that state.

The rabbit, the bear, the lion, the buzzard, the fox are

culture heroes from the animal world. The rabbit is far in the lead of all the others and is blood brother to Jack. In short, the trickster-hero of West Africa has been transplanted to America.

John Henry is a culture hero in song, but no more so than Stacker Lee, Smokey Joe or Bad Lazarus. There are many, many Negroes who have never heard of any of the song heroes, but none who do not know John (Jack) and the rabbit.

Examples of Folklore and the Modern Culture Hero:

WHY DE PORPOISE'S TAIL IS ON CROSSWISE

Now, I want to tell you 'bout de porpoise. God had done made de world and everything. He set de moon and de stars in de sky. He got de fishes of de sea, and de fowls of de air completed.

He made de sun and hung it up. Then He made a nice gold track for it to run on. Then He said, "Now, Sun, I got everything made but Time. That's up to you. I want you to start out and go round de world on dis track just as fast as you kin make it. And de time it takes you to go and come, I'm going to call day and night." De Sun went zoonin' on cross de elements. Now, de porpoise was hanging round there and heard God what he tole de Sun, so he decided he'd take dat trip round de world hisself. He looked up and saw de Sun kytin' along, so he lit out too, him and dat Sun!

So de porpoise beat de Sun round de world by one hour and three minutes. So God said, "Aw naw, this aint gointer do! I didn't mean for nothin' to be faster than de Sun!" So God run dat porpoise for three days before he run him down and caught him, and took his tail off and put it on crossways to slow him up. Still he's de fastest thing in de water.

And dat's why de porpoise got his tail on crossways.

ROCKEFELLER AND FORD

Once John D. Rockefeller and Henry Ford was woofing at each other. Rockefeller told Henry Ford he could build a solid gold road round the world. Henry Ford told him if he would he would look at it and see if he liked it, and if he did he would buy it and put one of his tin lizzies on it.

ORIGINALITY

It has been said so often that the Negro is lacking in originality that it has almost become a gospel. Outward signs seem to bear this out. But if one looks closely its falsity is immediately evident.

It is obvious that to get back to original sources is much too difficult for any group to claim very much as a certainty. What we really mean by originality is the modification of ideas. The most ardent admirer of the great Shakespeare cannot claim first source even for him. It is his treatment of the borrowed material.

So if we look at it squarely, the Negro is a very original being. While he lives and moves in the midst of a white civilisation, everything that he touches is re-interpreted for his own use. He has modified the language, mode of food preparation, practice of medicine, and most certainly the religion of his new country, just as he adapted to suit himself the Sheik hair-cut made famous by Rudolph Valentino.

Everyone is familiar with the Negro's modification of the whites' musical instruments, so that his interpretation has been adopted by the white man himself and then re-interpreted. In so many words, Paul Whiteman is giving an imitation of a Negro orchestra making use of white-invented musical instruments in a Negro way. Thus has arisen a new art in the civilised world, and thus has our so-called civilisation come. The exchange and re-exchange of ideas between groups.

IMITATION

The Negro, the world over, is famous as a mimic. But this in no way damages his standing as an original. Mimicry is an art in itself. If it is not, then all art must fall by the same blow that strikes it down. When sculpture, painting, acting, dancing, literature neither reflect nor suggest anything in nature or human experience we turn away with a dull wonder in our hearts at why the thing was done. Moreover, the contention that the Negro imitates from a feeling of inferiority is incorrect. He mimics for the love of it. The group of Negroes who slavishly imitate is small. The average Negro glories in his ways. The highly educated Negro the same. The self-despisement lies in a middle class who scorns to do or be anything Negro. "That's just like a Nigger" is the most terrible rebuke one can lay upon this kind. He wears drab clothing, sits through a boresome church service, pretends to have no interest in the community, holds beauty contests, and otherwise apes all the mediocrities of the white brother. The truly cultured Negro scorns him, and the Negro "farthest down" is too busy "spreading his junk" in his own way to see or care. He likes his own things best. Even the group who are not Negroes but belong to the "sixth race," buy such records as "Shake dat thing" and "Tight lak dat." They really enjoy hearing a good bible-beater preach, but wild horses could drag no such admission from them. Their ready-made expression is: "We done got away from all that now." Some refuse to countenance Negro music on the grounds that it is niggerism, and for that reason should be done away with. Roland Hayes was thoroughly denounced for singing spirituals until he was accepted by white audiences. Langston Hughes is not considered a poet by this group because he writes of the man in the ditch, who is more numerous and real among us than any other.

But, this group aside, let us say that the art of mimicry is better developed in the Negro than in other racial groups. He does it as the mocking-bird does it, for the love of it, and not because he wishes to be like the one imitated. I saw a group of small Negro boys imitating a cat defecating and the subsequent toilet of the cat. It was very realistic, and they enjoyed it as much as if they had been imitating a coronation ceremony. The dances are full of imitations of various animals. The buzzard lope, walking the dog, the pig's hind legs, holding the mule, elephant squat, pigeon's wing, falling off the log, seabord (imitation of an engine starting), and the like.

ABSENCE OF THE CONCEPT OF PRIVACY

It is said that Negroes keep nothing secret, that they have no reserve. This ought not to seem strange when one considers that we are an outdoor people accustomed to communal life. Add this to all-permeating drama and you have the explanation.

There is no privacy in an African village. Loves, fights, possessions are, to misquote Woodrow Wilson, "Open disagreements openly arrived at." The community is given the benefit of a good fight as well as a good wedding. An audience is a necessary part of any drama. We merely go with nature rather than against it.

Discord is more natural than accord. If we accept the doctrine of the survival of the fittest there are more fighting honors than there are honors for other achievements. Humanity places premiums on all things necessary to its well-being, and a valiant and good fighter is valuable in any community. So why hide the light under a bushel? Moreover, intimidation is a recognised part of warfare the world over, and threats certainly must be listed under that head. So that a great threatener must certainly be considered an aid to the fighting machine. So then if a man or woman is a facile hurler of threats, why should he or she not show their wares to the community? Hence the holding of all quarrels and fights in the open. One relieves one's pent-up anger and at the same time earns laurels in intimidation. Besides, one does the community a service. There is nothing so exhilarating as watching well-matched opponents go into action. The entire world likes action, for that matter. Hence prize-fighters become millionaires.

Likewise love-making is a biological necessity the world over and an art among Negroes. So that a man or woman who is proficient sees no reason why the fact should not be moot. He swaggers. She struts hippily about. Songs are built on the power to charm beneath the bed-clothes. Here again we have individuals striving to excel in what the community considers an art. Then if all of his world is seeking a great lover, why should he not speak right out loud?

It is all in a view-point. Love-making and fighting in all their branches are high arts, other things are arts among other groups where they brag about their proficiency just as brazenly as we do about these things that others consider matters for conversation behind closed doors. At any rate, the white man is despised by Negroes as a very poor fighter individually, and a very poor lover. One Negro, speaking of white men, said, "White folks is alright when dey gits in de bank and on de law bench, but dey sho' kin lie about wimmen folks."

I pressed him to explain. "Well you see, white mens makes out they marries wimmen to look at they eyes, and they know they gits em for just what us gits em for. 'Nother thing, white mens say they goes clear round de world and wins all de wim-men folks way from they men folks. Dat's a lie too. They don't win nothin, they buys em. Now de way I figgers it, if a woman don't want me enough to be wid me, 'thout I got to pay her, she kin rock right on, but these here white men don't know what to do wid a woman when they gits her— dat's how come they gives they wimmen so much. They got to. Us wimmen works jus as hard as us does an come home an sleep wid us every night. They own wouldn't do it and it's de mens fault. Dese white men done fooled theyself bout dese wimmen.

"Now me, I keeps me some wimmens all de time. Dat's whut dey wuz put here for—us mens to use. Dat's right now, Miss. Y'all wuz put here so us mens could have some plea-sure. Course I don't run round like heap uh men folks. But if my ole lady go way from me and stay more'n two weeks, I got to git me somebody, aint I?"

THE JOOK

Jook is the word for a Negro pleasure house. It may mean a bawdy house. It may mean the house set apart on public works where the men and women dance, drink and gamble. Often it is a combination of all these.

In past generations the music was furnished by "boxes," another word for guitars. One guitar was enough for a dance; to have two was considered excellent. Where two were play-ing one man played the lead and the other seconded him. The first player was "picking" and the second was "fram-ming," that is, playing chords while the lead carried the melody by dexterous finger work. Sometimes a third player was added, and he played a tom-tom effect on the low strings. Believe it or not, this is excellent dance music.

Pianos soon came to take the place of the boxes, and now player-pianos and victrolas are in all of the Jooks.

Musically speaking, the Jook is the most important place in America. For in its smelly, shoddy confines has been born the secular music known as blues, and on blues has been founded jazz. The singing and playing in the true Negro style is called "jooking."

The songs grow by incremental repetition as they travel

from mouth to mouth and from Jook to Jook for years before they reach outside ears. Hence the great variety of subject-matter in each song.

The Negro dances circulated over the world were also conceived inside the Jooks. They too make the round of Jooks and public works before going into the outside world.

In this respect it is interesting to mention the Black Bottom. I have read several false accounts of its origin and name. One writer claimed that it got its name from the black sticky mud on the bottom of the Mississippi river. Other equally absurd statements gummed the press. Now the dance really originated in the Jook section of Nashville, Tennessee, around Fourth Avenue. This is a tough neighbourhood known as Black Bottom—hence the name.

The Charleston is perhaps forty years old, and was danced up and down the Atlantic seaboard from North Carolina to Key West, Florida.

The Negro social dance is slow and sensuous. The idea in the Jook is to gain sensation, and not so much exercise. So that just enough foot movement is added to keep the dancers on the floor. A tremendous sex stimulation is gained from this. But who is trying to avoid it? The man, the woman, the time and the place have met. Rather, little intimate names are indulged in to heap fire on fire.

These too have spread to all the world.

The Negro theatre, as built up by the Negro, is based on Jook situations, with women, gambling, fighting, drinking. Shows like "Dixie to Broadway" are only Negro in cast, and could just as well have come from pre-Soviet Russia.

Another interesting thing—Negro shows before being tampered with did not specialise in octoroon chorus girls. The girl who could hoist a Jook song from her belly and lam it against the front door of the theatre was the lead, even if she were as black as the hinges of hell. The question was "Can she jook?" She must also have a good belly wobble, and her hips must, to quote a popular work song, "Shake like jelly all over and be so broad, Lawd, Lawd, and be so broad." So that the bleached chorus is the result of a white demand and not the Negro's.

The woman in the Jook may be nappy headed and black, but if she is a good lover she gets there just the same. A favorite Jook song of the past has this to say:

Singer: It aint good looks dat takes you through dis world.
Audience: What is it, good mama?
Singer: Elgin* movements in your hips
       Twenty years guarantee.

And it always brought down the house too.

> Oh de white gal rides in a Cadillac,
> De yaller gal rides de same,
> Black gal rides in a rusty Ford
> But she gits dere just de same.

The sort of woman her men idealise is the type that is put forth in the theatre. The art-creating Negro prefers a not too thin woman who can shake like jelly all over as she dances and sings, and that is the type he put forth on the stage. She has been banished by the white producer and the Negro who takes his cue from the white.

Of course a black woman is never the wife of the upper class Negro in the North. This state of affairs does not obtain in the South, however. I have noted numerous cases where the wife was considerably darker than the husband. People of some substance, too.

This scornful attitude towards black women receives mouth sanction by the mud-sills.

Even on the works and in the Jooks the black man sings disparaging of black women. They say that she is evil. That she sleeps with her fists doubled up and ready for action. All over they are making a little drama of waking up a yaller† wife and a black one.

A man is lying beside his yaller wife and wakes her up. She says to him, "Darling, do you know what I was dreaming when you woke me up?" He says, "No honey, what was you dreaming?" She says, "I dreamt I had done cooked you a big, fine dinner and we was setting down to eat out de same plate

*Elegant (?).
†Yaller (yellow), light mulatto.

and I was setting on yo' lap jus huggin you and kissin you and you was so sweet."

Wake up a black woman, and before you kin git any sense into her she be done up and lammed you over the head four or five times. When you git her quiet she'll say, "Nigger, know whut I was dreamin when you woke me up?"

You say, "No honey, what was you dreamin?" She says, "I dreamt you shook yo' rusty fist under my nose and I split yo' head open wid a axe."

But in spite of disparaging fictitious drama, in real life the black girl is drawing on his account at the commissary. Down in the Cypress Swamp as he swings his axe he chants:

> Dat ole black gal, she keep on grumblin,
> New pair shoes, new pair shoes,
> I'm goint to buy her shoes and stockings
> Slippers too, slippers too.

Then adds aside: "Blacker de berry, sweeter de juice."

To be sure the black gal is still in power, men are still cutting and shooting their way to her pillow. To the queen of the Jook!

Speaking of the influence of the Jook, I noted that Mae West in "Sex" had much more flavor of the turpentine quarters than she did of the white bawd. I know that the piece she played on the piano is a very old Jook composition. "Honey let yo' drawers hang low" had been played and sung in every Jook in the South for at least thirty-five years. It has always puzzled me why she thought it likely to be played in a Canadian bawdy house.

Speaking of the use of Negro material by white performers, it is astonishing that so many are trying it, and I have never seen one yet entirely realistic. They often have all the elements of the song, dance, or expression, but they are misplaced or distorted by the accent falling on the wrong element. Every one seems to think that the Negro is easily imitated when nothing is further from the truth. Without exception I wonder why the black-face comedians *are* blackface; it is a puzzle — good comedians, but darn poor niggers. Gershwin and the other "Negro" rhapsodists come under this same axe. Just about as Negro as caviar or Ann Pennington's athletic Black Bottom. When the Negroes who knew the

Black Bottom in its cradle saw the Broadway version they asked each other, "Is you learnt dat *new* Black Bottom yet?" Proof that it was not *their* dance.

And God only knows what the world has suffered from the white damsels who try to sing Blues.

The Negroes themselves have sinned also in this respect. In spite of the goings up and down on the earth, from the original Fisk Jubilee Singers down to the present, there has been no genuine presentation of Negro songs to white audiences. The spirituals that have been sung around the world are Negroid to be sure, but so full of musicians' tricks that Negro congregations are highly entertained when they hear their old songs so changed. They never use the new style songs, and these are never heard unless perchance some daughter or son has been off to college and returns with one of the old songs with its face lifted, so to speak.

I am of the opinion that this trick style of delivery was originated by the Fisk Singers; Tuskeegee and Hampton followed suit and have helped spread this misconception of Negro spirituals. This Glee Club style has gone on so long and become so fixed among concert singers that it is considered quite authentic. But I say again, that not one concert singer in the world is singing the songs as the Negro songmakers sing them.

If anyone wishes to prove the truth of this let him step into some unfashionable Negro church and hear for himself.

To those who want to institute the Negro theatre, let me say it is already established. It is lacking in wealth, so it is not seen in the high places. A creature with a white head and Negro feet struts the Metropolitan boards. The real Negro theatre is in the Jooks and the cabarets. Self-conscious individuals may turn away the eye and say, "Let us search elsewhere for our dramatic art." Let 'em search. They certainly won't find it. Butter Beans and Susie, Bo-Jangles and Snake Hips are the only performers of the real Negro school it has ever been my pleasure to behold in New York.

DIALECT

If we are to believe the majority of writers of Negro dialect and the burnt-cork artists, Negro speech is a weird thing, full of "ams" and "Ises." Fortunately we don't have to believe them. We may go directly to the Negro and let him speak for himself.

I know that I run the risk of being damned as an infidel for declaring that nowhere can be found the Negro who asks "am it?" nor yet his brother who announces "Ise uh gwinter." He exists only for a certain type of writers and performers.

Very few Negroes, educated or not, use a clear clipped "I." It verges more or less upon "Ah." I think the lip form is responsible for this to a great extent. By experiment the reader will find that a sharp "I" is very much easier with a thin taut lip than with a full soft lip. Like tightening violin strings.

If one listens closely one will note too that a word is slurred in one position in the sentence but clearly pronounced in another. This is particularly true of the pronouns. A pronoun as a subject is likely to be clearly enunciated, but slurred as an object. For example: "You better not let me ketch yuh."

There is a tendency in some localities to add the "h" to "it" and pronounce it "hit." Probably a vestige of old English. In some localities "if" is "ef."

In story telling "so" is universally the connective. It is used even as an introductory word, at the very beginning of a story. In religious expression "and" is used. The trend in stories is to state conclusions; in religion, to enumerate.

I am mentioning only the most general rules in dialect because there are so many quirks that belong only to certain localities that nothing less than a volume would be adequate.

CONVERSIONS AND VISIONS

The vision is a very definite part of Negro religion. It almost always accompanies conversion. It always accompanies the call to preach.

In the conversion the vision is sought. The individual goes forth into waste places and by fasting and prayer induces the vision. The place of retirement chosen is one most likely to have some emotional effect upon the seeker. The cemetery, to a people who fear the dead, is a most suggestive place to gain visions. The dense swamps with the possibility of bodily mishaps is another favorite.

Three days is the traditional period for seeking the vision. Usually the seeker is successful, but now and then he fails. Most seekers "come through religion" during revival meetings, but a number come after the meeting has closed.

Certain conversion visions have become traditional, but all sorts of variations are interpolated in the general framework of the convention, from the exceedingly frivolous to the most solemn. One may go to a dismal swamp, the other to the privy house. The imagination of one may carry him to the last judgment and the rimbones of nothing, the vision of another may hobble him at washing collard greens. But in each case there is an unwillingness to believe—to accept the great good fortune too quickly. So God is asked for proof. One man told me that he refused to believe that he had truly been saved and said: "Now, Lord, if you have really saved my soul, I ask you to move a certain star from left to right." And the star shot across the heavens from the left hand to the right. But still he wouldn't believe. So he asked for the sun to shout and the sun shouted. He still didn't believe. So he asked for one more sign. But God had grown impatient with his doubtings and told him sharply that if he didn't believe without further proof that He'd send his soul to hell. So he ran forth from his hiding and proclaimed a new-found savior.

In another case, a woman asked that a tree be moved and it stepped over ten feet, and then she asked for the star and God told her He had given her one sign and if she couldn't believe and trust Him for the balance He'd send her soul to torment.

Another woman asked for a windstorm and it came. She asked for the star to move and it did. She asked for the sun to shout and God grew angry and rebuked her like the others.

Still another woman fell under conviction in a cow lot and asked for a sign. " 'Now, Lord, if you done converted my soul, let dat cow low three times and I'll believe.' A cow said, 'Mooo—oo, moo—oo—oo, moo—ooo—ooo'—and I knowed I had been converted and my soul set free."

Three is the holy number and the call to preach always comes three times. It is never answered until the third time. The man flees from the call, but is finally brought to accept it.

God punishes him by every kind of misfortune until he finally acknowledges himself beaten and makes known the call. Some preachers say the spirit whipped them from their heads to their heels. They have been too sore to get out of bed because they refused the call. This never ceased until the surrender. Sometimes God sends others to tell them they are chosen. But in every case the ministers refuse to believe the words of even these.

We see that in conversion the sinner is first made conscious of his guilt. This is followed by a period called "lyin' under conviction" which lasts for three days. After which Jesus converts the supplicant, and the supplicant refuses to believe without proof, and only gives in under threat of eternal damnation. He flees from this to open acknowledgment of God and salvation. First from the outside comes the accusation of sin. Then from within the man comes the consciousness of guilt, and the sufferer seeks relief from Heaven. When it is granted, it is at first doubted, but later accepted. We have a mixture of external and internal struggles.

The call to preach is altogether external. The vision seeks the man. Punishment follows if he does not heed the call, or until he answers.

In conversion, then, we have the cultural pattern of the person seeking the vision and inducing it by isolation and fasting. In the call to preach we have the involuntary vision—the call seeking the man.

Coming Through Religion

I went out to pray in my back yard. I had done prayed and prayed but didn't know how to pray. I had done seen vision on top of vision, but still I wouldn't believe. Then I said: "Lord, let my head be a footstool for you." He says: "I plant my feet in the sea, follow after me. Your sins are forgiven and your soul set free. Go and tell the world what a kind Saviour you have found." I broke out the privy and went running and the voice kept following: "I set your feet on the rock of eternal ages; and the wind may blow and the storm may rise, but nothing shall frighten you from the shore."

I carried them messages.

"Jesus." "I am Jesus." "Father!" "I am the Father, and the Father is in me." It just continued and He sent me to the unconverted. I had some more visions. In one of them I laid down and a white man come to me all dressed in white and he had me stretched out on de table and clipped my breath three times and the third time I rose and went to a church door and there was a weeping willow. There was a four-cornered garden and three more knelt with me in the four corners. And I had to pray, to send up a prayer.

The next vision I had a white woman says: "I am going home with you." I didn't want her to go. My house was not in order. Somebody stopped her. When I got home, a tall white man was standing at my door with a palmetto hat. I noticed he was pale-like. He was looking down on my steps. They was washed with redding.* He says: "I have cleaned your house. How do you like it?" I looked down on it and after he was gone I said: "I don't like that. It looks too much like blood." After I was converted it come to me about the blood and I knew it was Jesus, and my heart was struck with sorrow that to think I had been walking upon His precious blood all this time and didn't believe.

(Mrs. SUSANNA SPRINGER.)

I was a lad of a boy when I found Jesus sweet to my ever-dying soul. They was running p'tracted meetin and all my friends was gettin religion and joinin de church; but I never paid it no mind. I was hard. But I dont keer how hard you is, God kin reach you when He gits ready for you. One day, bout noon, it was de 9th day of June, 1886, when I was walkin in my sins, wallerin in my sins, dat He tetched me wid de tip of His finger and I fell right where I was and laid there for three long days and nights. I layed there racked in pain under sentence of death for my sins. And I walked over hell on a narrer foot log so I had to put one foot right in front de other, one foot right in front de other wid hell gapped wide open beneath my sin-loaded and slippery feet. And de hell hounds was barkin on my tracks and jus before dey rushed me into hell and judgement I cried: "Lawd, have mercy," and I crossed over safe. But still I wouldn't believe. Then I saw myself hangin over hell by one strand of hair and de flames of fire leapin up a thousand miles to swaller my soul and I cried: "Jesus, save my soul and I'll believe, I'll believe." Then I found myself on solid ground and a tall white man beckoned for me to come to him and I went, wrapped in my guilt, and he 'nointed me wid de oil of salvation and healed all my wounds. Then I found myself layin on de ground under a scrub oak and I cried: "I believe,

---

*Brick dust is used in New Orleans to seam steps. It leaves them reddish.

I believe." Then Christ spoke peace to my soul and de dungeon shook and my chains fell off, and I went shoutin in His name and praising Him. I put on de whole armor of faith and I speck to stay in de fiel till I die.

(Deacon ERNEST HUFFMAN.)

First thing started me—it come to me dat I had to die. And worried me so I got talkin wid an old Christ man—about seventy years old. I wasn't but twentyone. And I started out from his instruction and I heered people say in my time dat de speerit would command you to de graveyard (to pray). And I ast de Lawd not to send me dere cause I wuz skeered uh de graveyard. But every answer I got commanded me to the graveyard.

One cold night, March de twentieth, 1867, at night, de speerit command me to de graveyard and I didn't go. And de Lawd sent Death after me and when I knowed anything I was on my way to de graveyard. And when I got dere I fell. I fell right between two graves and I saw Him when He laid me upon a table in my vision. I was naked and He split me open. And there was two men there—one on each side of de table. I could hear de knives clicking in me, inside. And after dey got through wid me, they smothed they hand over de wound and I wuz healed. And when I found myself I wuz standin naked beside de table and there was three lights burnin on de table. De one in de middle wuz de brightest. I wuzn't between de two graves no more. When I got up from between de two graves, I tracked my guide by de drops of blood. I could hear de blood dripping from Him before me. It said as it dropped: "Follow me." And I looked at de three lights and dey tole me to reach forth wid my right hand and grasp de brightest one and I did. It wuz shining like de Venus star. And they tole me it wuz to be my guidin star. I found myself before I left de table wid five white balls in each hand. "Them is the ten tablets I give you." And I put my hands to my breast and I put the balls inside me. Then He slapped something on my breast and said: "Now, you are breastplated and shielded." He pointed: "Go to yonder white house. You will find there one who will welcome you." And when I got to de steps I thowed my foot on de first step and de house rang and a lady come out and welcomed me in. And when I got inside, as far as mortal eye could behold, the robes was hanging level and touched my head as I passed under. Then I found myself robed in the color of gold. Then I commenced shouting. And when I commenced shouting I found myself leaving the graveyard. And He told me that was my robe for me bye and bye. In dat swamp where dat graveyard was there was catamounts and panters and wild beasts but not a one of 'em touched me and I laid there all night.

Now He tole me, He said: "You got the three witnesses. One is water, one is spirit, and one is blood. And these three correspond with the three in heben—Father, Son and Holy Ghost."

Now I ast Him about this lyin in sin and He give me a handful of seeds and He tole me to sow 'em in a bed and He tole me: "I want you to watch them seeds." The seeds come up about in places and He said: "Those seeds that come up, they died in the heart of the earth and quickened and come up and brought forth fruit. But those seeds that didn't come up, they died in the heart of the earth and rottened.

"And a soul that dies and quickens through my spirit they will live forever, but those that dont never pray, they are lost forever."

(Rev. JESSIE JEFFERSON.)

SHOUTING

There can be little doubt that shouting is a survival of the African "possession" by the gods. In Africa it is sacred to the priesthood or acolytes, in America it has become generalised. The implication is the same, however. It is a sign of special favor from the spirit that it chooses to drive out the individual consciousness temporarily and use the body for its expression.

In every case the person claims ignorance of his actions during the possession.

Broadly speaking, shouting is an emotional explosion, responsive to rhythm. It is called forth by (1) sung rhythm; (2) spoken rhythm; (3) humming rhythm; (4) the foot-patting or hand-clapping that imitates very closely the tom-tom.

The more familiar the expression, the more likely to evoke response. For instance, "I am a soldier of the cross, a follower of the meek and lowly lamb. I want you all to know I am fighting under the blood-stained banner of King Jesus" is more likely to be amen-ed than any flourish a speaker might get off. Perhaps the reason for this is that the hearers can follow the flow of syllables without stirring the brain to grasp the sense. Perhaps it is the same urge that makes a child beg for the same story even though he knows it so well that he can correct his parents if a word is left out.

Shouting is a community thing. It thrives in concert. It is

the first shout that is difficult for the preacher to arouse. After that one they are likely to sweep like fire over the church. This is easily understood, for the rhythm is increasing with each shouter who communicates his fervor to someone else.

It is absolutely individualistic. While there are general types of shouting, the shouter may mix the different styles to his liking, or he may express himself in some fashion never seen before.

Women shout more frequently than men. This is not surprising since it is generally conceded that women are more emotional than men.

The shouter always receives attention from the church. Members rush to the shouter and force him into a seat or support him as the case might be. Sometimes it is necessary to restrain him to prevent injury to either the shouter or the persons sitting nearest, or both. Sometimes the arms are swung with such violence that others are knocked down. Sometimes in the ecstasy the shouter climbs upon the pew and kicks violently away at all; sometimes in catalepsis he falls heavily upon the floor and might injure himself if not supported, or fall upon others and wound. Often the person injured takes offense, believing that the shouter was paying off a grudge. Unfortunately this is the case at times, but it is not usual.

There are two main types of shouters: (1) Silent; (2) Vocal. There is a sort of intermediary type where one stage is silent and the other vocal.

The silent type take with violent retching and twitching motions. Sometimes they remain seated, sometimes they jump up and down and fling the body about with great violence. Lips tightly pursed, eyes closed. The seizure ends by collapse.

The vocal type is the more frequent. There are all gradations from quiet weeping while seated, to the unrestrained screaming while leaping pews and running up and down the aisle. Some, unless restrained, run up into the pulpit and embrace the preacher. Some are taken with hysterical laughing spells.

The cases will illustrate the variations.

(1) During sermon. Cried "well, well," six times. Violent

action for forty seconds. Collapsed and restored to her seat by members.

(2) During chant. Cried "Holy, holy! Great God A'mighty!" Arose and fell in cataleptic fit backwards over pew. Flinging of arms with clenched fists, gradually subsiding to quiet collapse. Total time: two minutes.

(3) During pre-prayer humming chant. Short screams. Violent throwing of arms. Incoherent speech. Total time: one minute thirty seconds.

(4) During sermon. One violent shout as she stood erect: two seconds. Voiceless gestures for twenty-nine seconds. She suddenly resumed her seat and her attention to the words of the preacher.

(5) During sermon. One single loud scream: one and one-half seconds.

(6) During singing. Violent jumping up and down without voice. Pocket book cast away. Time: one minute forty seconds.

(7) During prayer. Screaming: one second. Violent shoulder-shaking, hat discarded: nineteen seconds.

(8) During sermon. Cataleptic. Stiffly back over the pew. Violent but voiceless for twenty seconds. Then arms stiff and outstretched, palms open stark and up. Collapse. Time: three minutes.

(9) During sermon. Young girl. Running up and down the aisle: thirty seconds. Then silence and rush to the pulpit: fourteen seconds; prevented at the altar rail by deacon. Collapse in the deacon's arms and returned to seat. Total time: one minute fifteen seconds.

(10) During chant after prayer. Violent screams: twelve seconds. Scrambles upon pew and steps upon the back of pew still screaming: five seconds. Voiceless struggle with set teeth as three men attempt to restore her to seat. She is lifted horizontal but continues struggle: one minute forty-eight seconds. Decreasing violence, making ferocious faces: two minutes. Calm with heavy breathing: twenty-one seconds.

(11) During sermon. Man quietly weeping: nineteen seconds. Cried "Lawd! My soul is burning with hallow-ed fire!" Rises and turns round and round six times. Carried outside by the deacons.

(12) During sermon. Man jumping wildly up and down flat-footed crying "Hallelujah!": twenty-two seconds. Pulled back into his seat. Muscular twitching: one minute thirty-five seconds. Quiet weeping: one minute. Perfect calm.

MOTHER CATHERINE

One must go straight out St. Claude below the Industrial Canal and turn south on Flood Street and go almost to the Florida Walk. Looking to the right one sees a large enclosure walled round with a high board fence. A half-dozen flags fly bravely from eminences. A Greek cross tops the chapel. A large American flag flies from the huge tent.

A marsh lies between Flood Street and that flag-flying enclosure, and one must walk. As one approaches, the personality of the place comes out to meet one. No ordinary person created this thing.

At the gate there is a rusty wire sticking out through a hole. That is the bell. But a painted notice on the gate itself reads: "Mother Seal is a holy spirit and must not be disturbed."

One does not go straight into the tent, into the presence of Mother Catherine (Mother Seal). One is conducted into the chapel to pray until the spirit tells her to send for you. A place of barbaric splendor, of banners, of embroideries, of images bought and images created by Mother Catherine herself; of an altar glittering with polished brass and kerosene lamps. There are 356 lamps in this building, but not all are upon the main altar.

The walls and ceilings are decorated throughout in red, white and blue. The ceiling and floor in the room of the Sacred Heart are striped in three colors and the walls are panelled. The panels contain a snake design. This is not due to Hoodoo influence but to African background. I note that the African loves to depict the grace of reptiles.

On a placard: *Speak so you can speak again.*

It would take a volume to describe in detail all of the things in and about this chapel under its Greek cross. But we are summoned by a white-robed saint to the presence.

Mother Catherine holds court in the huge tent. On a raised platform is her bed, a piano, instruments for a ten-piece orchestra, a huge coffee urn, a wood stove, a heater, chairs and rockers and tables. Backless benches fill the tent.

Catherine of Russia could not have been more impressive upon her throne than was this black Catherine sitting upon an ordinary chair at the edge of the platform within the entrance to the tent. Her face and manner are impressive. There is nothing cheap and theatrical about her. She does things and arranges her dwelling as no occidental would. But it is not for effect. It is for feeling. She might have been the matriarchal ruler of some nomad tribe as she sat there with the blue band about her head like a coronet; a white robe and a gorgeous red cape falling away from her broad shoulders, and the box of shaker salt in her hand like a rod of office. I know this reads incongruous, but it did not look so. It seemed perfectly natural for me to go to my knees upon the gravel floor, and when she signalled to me to extend my right hand, palm up for the dab of blessed salt, I hurried to obey because she made me feel that way.

She laid her hand upon my head.

"Daughter, why have you come here?"

"Mother, I come seeking knowledge."

"Thank God. Do y'all hear her? She come here lookin for wisdom. Eat de salt, daughter, and get yo mind with God and me. You shall know what you come to find out. I feel you. I felt you while you was sittin in de chapel. Bring her a veil."

The veil was brought and with a fervent prayer placed upon my head. I did not tell Mother then that I wanted to write about her. That came much later, after many visits. When I did speak of it she was very gracious and let me photograph her and everything behind the walls of her manger.

I spent two weeks with her, and attended nightly and Sunday services continuously at her tent. Nothing was usual about these meetings. She invariably feeds the gathering. Good, substantial food too. At the Sunday service the big coffee urn was humming, and at a certain point she blessed bread and broke it, and sprinkled on a bit of salt. This she gave to everyone present. To the adults she also gave a cup of coffee. Every cup was personally drawn, sweetened and tasted by her and handed to the communicants as they passed before the platform. At one point she would command everyone to file past the painted barrel and take a glass of water. These things had no inner meaning to an agnostic, but it did drive the dull monotony of the usual Christian service away. It was something, too, to watch the faith it aroused in her followers.

All during her sermons two parrots were crying from their cages. A white cockatoo would scream when the shouting grew loud. Three canary birds were singing and chirping happily all through the service. Four mongrel dogs strolled about. A donkey, a mother goat with her kid, numbers of hens, a sheep—all wandered in and out of the service without seeming out of place. A Methodist or Baptist church —or one of any denomination whatever—would have been demoralised by any one of these animals. Two dogs fought for a place beside the heater. Three children under three years of age played on the platform in the rear without distracting the speaker or the audience. The blue and red robed saint stood immobile in her place directly behind the speaker and the world moved on.

Unlike most religious dictators Mother Catherine does not crush the individual. She encourages originality. There is an air of gaiety about the enclosure. All of the animals are treated with tenderness.

No money is ever solicited within the enclosure of the Manger. If you feel to give, you may. Mother wears a pouch suspended from her girdle. You may approach the platform at any time and drop your contribution in. But you will be just as welcome if you have nothing. All of the persons who live at the Manger are there at Mother Catherine's expense. She encourages music and sees that her juveniles get off to school on time.

There is a catholic flavor about the place, but it is certainly not catholic. She has taken from all the religions she knows anything about any feature that pleases her.

Hear Mother Seal: "Good evening, Veils and Banners!

"God tells me to tell you (*invariable opening*) that He holds the world in the middle of His hand.

"There is no hell beneath this earth. God wouldn't build a hell to burn His breath.

"There is no heaven beyond dat blue globe. There is a between-world between this brown earth and the blue above. So says the beautiful spirit.

"When we die, where does the breath go? Into trees and grass and animals. Your flesh goes back to mortal earth to fertilise it. So says the beautiful spirit.

"Our brains is trying to make something out of us. Everybody can be something good.

"It is right that a woman should lead. A womb was what God made in the beginning, and out of that womb was born Time, and all that fills up space. So says the beautiful spirit.

"Some are weak to do wisdom things, but strong to do wicked things.

"He could have been born in the biggest White House in the world. But the reason He didn't is that He knowed a falling race was coming what couldn't get to no great White House, so He got born so my people could all reach.

"God is just as satisfied with the damnation of men as He is with their salvation. So says the beautiful spirit.

"It is not for people to know the whence.

"Don't teach what the apostles and the prophets say. Go to the tree and get the pure sap and find out whether they were right.

"No man has seen spirit—men can see what spirit does, but no man can see spirit."

As she was ready to grant blessings an evil thought reached her and she sat suddenly on a chair and covered her face with her hands, explaining why she did so. When it passed she rose, "Now I will teach you again."

Here the food was offered up but not distributed until the call came from the spirit.

St. Prompt Succor brought the basin and towel at a signal. She washed her hands and face.

It is evident that Mother Seal takes her stand as an equal with Christ.

No nailing or building is done on Friday. A carpenter may saw or measure, but no nailing or joining.

She heals by the laying on of hands, by suggestion and copious doses of castor oil and Epsom salts. She heals in the tent and at great distances. She has blessed water in the barrel for her followers, but she feels her divinity to such an extent that she blesses the water in the hydrants at the homes of her followers without moving out of her tent.

No one may cross his legs within the Manger. That is an insult to the spirit.

Mother Catherine's conception of the divinity of Christ is that Joseph was his foster father as all men are foster fathers, in that all children are of God and all fathers are merely the means.

All of her followers wear her insignia. The women wear a veil of unbleached muslin; the men, an arm-band. All bear the crescent and M.C.S. (Mother Catherine's Saints). They must be worn everywhere.

In late February and early March it rained heavily and many feared a flood. Mother Seal exhorted all of her followers to pin their faith in her. All they need do is believe in her and come to her and eat the blessed fish she cooked for them and there would be no flood. "God," she said, "put oars in the fishes' hands. Eat this fish and you needn't fear the flood no more than a fish would."

All sympathetic magic. Chicken, beef, lamb are animals of pleasing blood. They are used abundantly as food and often in healing. A freshly killed chicken was split open and bound to a sore leg.

All of her followers, white and colored, are her children. She has as many of one race as the other.

"I got all kinds of children, but I am they mother. Some of 'em are saints; some of 'em are conzempts (convicts) and jail-birds; some of 'em kills babies in their bodies; some of 'em walks the streets at night—but they's all my children. God got all kinds, how come I cain't love all of mine? So says the beautiful spirit.

"Now y'all go home in faith. I'm going to appear to you all in three days. Don't doubt me. Go home in faith and pray."

There is a period in the service given over to experiences.

One woman had a vision. She saw a flash of lightning on the wall. It wrote, "Go to Mother Seal." She came with pus on the kidneys and was healed.

A girl of fourteen had a vision of a field of spinach that turned to lilies with one large lily in the middle. The field was her church and the large lily was Mother Catherine.

Most of the testimony has to do with acknowledging that they have been healed by Mother's power, or relating how the wishes they made on Mother came true.

Mother Catherine's religion is matriarchal. Only God and the mother count. Childbirth is the most important element in the creed. Her compound is called the Manger, and is dedicated to the birth of children in or out of wedlock.

Over and over she lauds the bringing forth. *There is no sinful birth*. And the woman who avoids it by abortion is called a "damnable extrate."

Mother Catherine was not converted by anyone. Like Christ, Mohammed, Buddha, the call just came. No one stands between her and God.

After the call she consecrated her body by refraining from the sex relation, and by fasting and prayer.

She was married at the time. Her husband prayed two weeks before he was converted to her faith. Whereupon she baptised him in a tub in the backyard. They lived together six months as a holy man and woman before the call of the flesh made him elope with one of her followers.

She held her meetings first on Jackson Avenue, but the crowds that swarmed about her made the authorities harry her. So some of her wealthy followers bought the tract of land below the Industrial Canal where the Manger now is.

God sent her into the Manger over a twelve-foot board fence—not through a gate. She must set no time for her going but when the spirit gave the word. After her descent through the roof of the chapel she has never left the grounds but once, and that was not intentional. She was learning to drive a car within the enclosure. It got out of control and tore a hole through the fence before it stopped. She called to her followers to "Come git me!" (She must not set her foot on the unhallowed ground outside the Manger.) They came and reverently lifted her and bore her back inside. The spot in the yard upon which she was set down became sacred, for a voice spoke as her feet touched the ground and said, "Put down here the Pool of Gethsemane so that the believers may have holy water to drink." The well is under construction at this writing.

UNCLE MONDAY

People talk a whole lot about Uncle Monday, but they take good pains not to let him hear none of it. Uncle Monday is an out-and-out conjure doctor. That in itself is enough to make the people handle him carefully, but there is something about him that goes past hoodoo. Nobody knows anything about him, and that's a serious matter in a village of less than three hundred souls, especially when a person has lived there for forty years and more.

Nobody knows where he came from nor who his folks might be. Nobody knows for certain just when he did come to town. He was just there one morning when the town awoke. Joe Lindsay was the first to see him. He had some turtle lines set down on Lake Belle. It is a hard lake to fish because it is entirely surrounded by a sooky marsh that is full of leeches and moccasins. There is plenty of deep water once you pole a boat out beyond the line of cypress pines, but there are so many alligators out there that most people don't think the trout are worth the risk. But Joe had baited some turtle lines and thrown them as far as he could without wading into the marsh. So next morning he went as early as he could see light to look after his lines. There was a turtle head on every line, and he pulled them up cursing the 'gators for robbing his hooks. He says he started on back home, but when he was a few yards from where his lines had been set something made him look back, and he nearly fell dead. For there was an old man walking out of the lake between two cypress knees. The water there was too deep for any wading, and besides, he says the man was not wading, he was walking vigorously as if he were on dry land.

Lindsay says he was too scared to stand there and let the man catch up with him, and he was too scared to move his feet; so he just stood there and saw the man cross the marshy strip and come down the path behind him. He says he felt the hair rise on his head as the man got closer to him, and somehow he thought about an alligator slipping up on him. But he says that alligators were in the front of his mind that morning because first, he had heard bull 'gators fighting and bellowing all night long down in this lake, and then his turtle lines had been robbed. Besides, everybody knows that the father of all 'gators lives in Belle Lake.

The old man was coming straight on, taking short quick steps as if his legs were not long enough for his body, and working his arms in unison. Lindsay says it was all he could do to stand his ground and not let the man see how scared he was, but he managed to stand still anyway. The man came up to him and passed him without looking at him seemingly. After he had passed, Lindsay noticed that his clothes were perfectly dry, so he decided that his own eyes had fooled him. The old man must have come up to the cypress knees in a boat and then crossed the marsh by stepping from root to root. But when he went to look, he found no convenient roots for anybody to step on. Moreover, there was no boat on the lake either.

The old man looked queer to everybody, but still no one would believe Lindsay's story. They said that he had seen no more than several others—that is, that the old man had been seen coming from the direction of the lake. That was the first that the village saw of him, way back in the late 'eighties, and so far, nobody knows any more about his past than that. And that worries the town.

Another thing that struck everybody unpleasantly was the fact that he never asked a name nor a direction. Just seemed to know who everybody was, and called each and every one by their right name. Knew where everybody lived too. Didn't earn a living by any of the village methods. He didn't garden, hunt, fish, nor work for the white folks. Stayed so close in the little shack that he had built for himself that sometimes three weeks would pass before the town saw him from one appearance to another.

Joe Clarke was the one who found out his name was Monday. No other name. So the town soon was calling him Uncle Monday. Nobody can say exactly how it came to be known that he was a hoodoo man. But it turned out that that was what he was. People said he was a good one too. As much as they feared him, he had plenty of trade. Didn't take him long to take all the important cases away from Ant Judy, who had had a monopoly for years.

He looked very old when he came to the town. Very old, but firm and strong. Never complained of illness.

But once, Emma Lou Pittman went over to his shack early in the morning to see him on business, and ran back with a fearsome tale. She said that she noticed a heavy trail up to his door and across the steps, as if a heavy, bloody body had been dragged inside. The door was cracked a little and she could hear a great growling and snapping of mighty jaws. It wasn't exactly a growling either, it was more a subdued howl in a bass tone. She shoved the door a little and peeped inside to see if some varmint was in there attacking Uncle Monday. She figured he might have gone to sleep with the door ajar and a catamount, or a panther, or a bob-cat might have gotten in. He lived near enough to Blue Sink Lake for a 'gator to have come in the house, but she didn't remember ever hearing of them tracking anything but dogs.

But no; no varmint was inside there. The noise she heard was being made by Uncle Monday. He was lying on a pallet of pine-straw in such agony that his eyes were glazed over. His right arm was horribly mangled. In fact, it was all but torn away from right below the elbow. The side of his face was terribly torn too. She called him, but he didn't seem to hear her. So she hurried back for some men to come and do something for him. The men came as fast as their legs would bring them, but the house was locked from the outside and there was no answer to their knocking. Mrs. Pittman would have been made out an awful liar if it were not for the trail of blood. So they concluded that Uncle Monday had gotten hurt somehow and had dragged himself home, or had been dragged by a friend. But who could the friend have been?

Nobody saw Uncle Monday for a month after that. Every day or so, someone would drop by to see if hide or hair could be found of him. A full month passed before there was any news. The town had about decided that he had gone away as mysteriously as he had come.

But one evening around dusk-dark Sam Merchant and Jim Gooden were on their way home from a squirrel hunt around

Lake Belle. They swore that, as they rounded the lake and approached the footpath that leads towards the village, they saw what they thought was the great 'gator that lives in the lake crawl out of the marsh. Merchant wanted to take a shot at him for his hide and teeth, but Gooden reminded him that they were loaded with bird shot, which would not even penetrate a 'gator's hide, let alone kill it. They say the thing they took for the 'gator then struggled awhile, pulling off something that looked like a long black glove. Then he scraped a hole in the soft ground with his paws and carefully buried the glove which had come from his right paw. Then without looking either right or left, he stood upright and walked on towards the village. Everybody saw Uncle Monday come thru the town, but still Merchant's tale was hard to swallow. But, by degrees, people came to believe that Uncle Monday could shed any injured member of his body and grow a new one in its place. At any rate, when he reappeared his right hand and arm bore no scars.

The village is even sceptical about his dying. Once Joe Clarke said to Uncle Monday, "I'god, Uncle Monday, aint you skeered to stay way off by yo'self, old as you is?"

Uncle Monday asked, "Why would I be skeered?"

"Well, you liable to take sick in de night sometime, and you'd be dead befo' anybody would know you was even sick."

Uncle Monday got up off the nail keg and said in a voice so low that only the men right close to him could hear what he said, "I have been dead for many a year. I have come back from where you are going." Then he walked away with his quick short steps, and his arms bent at the elbow, keeping time with his feet.

It is believed that he has the singing stone, which is the greatest charm, the most powerful "hand" in the world. It is a diamond and comes from the mouth of a serpent (which is thought of as something different from an ordinary snake) and is the diamond of diamonds. It not only lights your home without the help of any other light, but it also warns its owner of approach.

The serpents who produce these stones live in the deep waters of Lake Maitland. There is a small island in this lake and a rare plant grows there, which is the only food of this serpent. She only comes to nourish herself in the height of a violent thunderstorm, when she is fairly certain that no human will be present.

It is impossible to kill or capture her unless nine healthy people have gone before to prepare the way with THE OLD ONES, and then more will die in the attempt to conquer her. But it is not necessary to kill or take her to get the stone. She has two. One is embedded in her head, and the other she carries in her mouth. The first one cannot be had without killing the serpent, but the second one may be won from her by trickery.

Since she carries this stone in her mouth, she cannot eat until she has put it down. It is her pilot, that warns her of danger. So when she comes upon the island to feed, she always vomits the stone and covers it with earth before she goes to the other side of the island to dine.

To get this diamond, dress yourself all over in black velvet. Your assistant must be dressed in the same way. Have a velvet-covered bowl along. Be on the island before the storm reaches its height, but leave your helper in the boat and warn him to be ready to pick you up and flee at a moment's notice.

Climb a tall tree and wait for the coming of the snake. When she comes out of the water, she will look all about her on the ground to see if anyone is about. When she is satisfied that she is alone, she will vomit the stone, cover it with dirt and proceed to her feeding ground. Then, as soon as you feel certain that she is busy eating, climb down the tree as swiftly as possible, cover the mound hiding the stone with the velvet-lined bowl and flee for your life to the boat. The boatman must fly from the island with all possible speed. For as soon as you approach the stone it will ring like chiming bells, and the serpent will hear it. Then she will run to defend it. She will return to the spot, but the velvet-lined bowl will make it invisible to her. In her wrath she will knock down grown trees and lash the island like a hurricane. Wait till a calm fair day to return for the stone. She never comes up from the bottom of the lake in fair weather. Furthermore, a serpent who has lost her mouth-stone cannot come to feed alone after that. She must bring her mate. The mouth-stone is their guardian, and when they lose it they remain in constant danger unless accompanied by one who has the singing stone.

They say that Uncle Monday has a singing stone, and that is why he knows everything without being told.

Whether he has the stone or not, nobody thinks of doubting his power as a hoodoo man. He is feared, but sought when life becomes too powerful for the powerless. Mary Ella Shaw backed out on Joe-Nathan Moss the day before the wedding was to have come off. Joe-Nathan had even furnished the house and bought rations. His people, her people, everybody tried to make her marry the boy. He loved her so, and besides he had put out so much of his little cash to fix for the marriage. But Mary Ella just wouldn't. She had seen Caddie Brewton, and she was one of the kind who couldn't keep her heart still after her eye had wandered.

So Joe-Nathan's mama went to see Uncle Monday. He said, "Since she is the kind of woman that lets her mind follow her eye, we'll have to let the snake-bite cure itself. You go on home. Never no man will keep her. She kin grab the world full of men, but she'll never keep one any longer than from one full moon to the other."

Fifteen years have passed. Mary Ella has been married four times. She was a very pretty girl, and men just kept coming, but not one man has ever stayed with her longer than the twenty-eight days. Besides her four husbands, no telling how many men she has shacked up with for a few weeks at a time. She has eight children by as many different men, but still no husband.

John Wesley Hogan was another driver of sharp bargains in love. By his own testimony and experience, all women from eight to eighty were his meat, but the woman who was sharp enough to make him marry her wasn't born and her mama was dead. They couldn't frame him and they couldn't scare him.

Mrs. Bradley came to him nevertheless about her Dinkie. She called him out from his work-place and said, "John Wesley, you know I'm a widder-woman and I aint got no husband to go to de front for me, so I reckon I got to do de talkin' for me and my chile. I come in de humblest way I know how to ast you to go 'head and marry my chile befo' her name is painted on de signposts of scorn."

If it had not made John Wesley so mad, it would have been funny to him. So he asked her scornfully, " 'Oman, whut you take me for? You better git outa my face wid dat mess! How you reckon *I* know who Dinkie been foolin roun wid? Don't try to come dat mess over *me*. I been all over de North. I aint none of yo' fool. You must think I'm Big Boy. They kilt Big Boy shootin after Fat Sam so there aint no mo' fools in de world. Ha, ha! All de wimmen *I* done seen! I'll tell you like de monkey tole de elephant—don't bull me, big boy! If you want Dinkie to git married off so bad, go grab one of dese country clowns. I aint yo' man. Taint no use you goin runnin to de high-sheriff neither. I got witness to prove Dinkie knowed more'n I do."

Mrs. Bradley didn't bother with the sheriff. All he could do was to make John Wesley marry Dinkie; but by the time the interview was over that wasn't what the stricken mother wanted. So she waited till dark, and went on over to Uncle Monday.

Everybody says you don't have to explain things to Uncle Monday. Just go there, and you will find that he is ready for you when you arrive. So he set Mrs. Bradley down at a table, facing a huge mirror hung against the wall. She says he had a loaded pistol and a huge dirk lying on the table before her. She looked at both of the weapons, but she could not decide which one she wanted to use. Without a word, he handed her a gourd full of water and she took a swallow. As soon as the water passed over her tongue she seized the gun. He pointed towards the looking-glass. Slowly the form of John Wesley formed in the glass and finally stood as vivid as life before her. She took careful aim and fired. She was amazed that the mirror did not shatter. But there was a loud report, a cloud of bluish smoke and the figure vanished.

On the way home, Brazzle told her that John Wesley had dropped dead, and Mr. Watson had promised to drive over to Orlando in the morning to get a coffin for him.

Ant Judy Bickerstaff

Uncle Monday wasn't the only hoodoo doctor around there. There was Ant Judy Bickerstaff. She was there before the coming of Uncle Monday. Of course it didn't take long for professional jealousy to arise. Uncle Monday didn't seem to mind Ant Judy, but she resented him, and she couldn't hide her feelings.

This was natural when you consider that before his coming she used to make all the "hands" around there, but he soon drew off the greater part of the trade.

Year after year this feeling kept up. Every now and then some little incident would accentuate the rivalry. Monday was sitting on top of the heap, but Judy was not without her triumphs.

Finally she began to say that she could reverse anything that he put down. She said she could not only reverse it, she could throw it back on *him*, let alone his client. Nobody talked to him about her boasts. People never talked to him except on business anyway. Perhaps Judy felt safe in her boasting for this reason.

Then one day she took it in her head to go fishing. Her children and grandchildren tried to discourage her. They argued with her about her great age and her stiff joints. But she had her grandson to fix her a trout pole and a bait pole and set out for Blue Sink, a lake said to be bottomless by the villagers. Furthermore, she didn't set out till near sundown. She didn't want any company. It was no use talking, she felt that she just must go fishing in Blue Sink.

She didn't come home when dark came, and her family worried a little. But they reasoned she had probably stopped at one of her friend's houses to rest and gossip, so they didn't go to hunt her right away. But when the night wore on and she didn't return, the children were sent out to locate her.

She was not in the village. A party was organised to search Blue Sink for her. It was after nine o'clock at night when the party found her. She was in the lake. Lying in shallow water and keeping her old head above the water by supporting it on her elbow. Her son Ned said that he saw a huge alligator dive away as he shined the torch upon his mother's head.

They bore Ant Judy home and did everything they could for her. Her legs were limp and useless and she never spoke a word, not a coherent word, for three days. It was more than a week before she could tell how she came to be in the lake.

She said that she hadn't really wanted to go fishing. The

family and the village could witness that she never had fooled round the lakes. But that afternoon she *had* to go. She couldn't say why, but she knew she must go. She baited her hooks and stood waiting for a bite. She was afraid to sit down on the damp ground on account of her rheumatism. She got no bites. When she saw the sun setting she wanted to come home, but somehow she just couldn't leave the spot. She was afraid, terribly afraid down there on the lake, but she couldn't leave.

When the sun was finally gone and it got dark, she says she felt a threatening, powerful evil all around her. She was fixed to the spot. A small but powerful whirlwind arose right under her feet. Something terrific struck her and she fell into the water. She tried to climb out, but found that she could not use her legs. She thought of 'gators and otters, and leeches and gar-fish, and began to scream, thinking maybe somebody would hear her and come to her aid.

Suddenly a bar of red light fell across the lake from one side to the other. It looked like a fiery sword. Then she saw Uncle Monday walking across the lake to her along this flaming path. On either side of the red road swam thousands of alligators, like an army behind its general.

The light itself was awful. It was red, but she never had seen any red like it before. It jumped and moved all the time, but always it pointed straight across the lake to where she lay helpless in the water. The lake is nearly a mile wide, but Ant Judy says Uncle Monday crossed it in less than a minute and stood over her. She closed her eyes from fright, but she saw him right on thru her lids.

After a brief second she screamed again. Then he growled and leaped at her. "Shut up!" he snarled. "Part your lips just one more time and it will be your last breath! Your bragging tongue has brought you here and you are going to stay here until you acknowledge my power. So you can throw back my work, eh? I put you in this lake; show your power and get out. You will not die, and you will not leave this spot until you give consent in your heart that I am your master. Help will come the minute you knuckle under."

She fought against him. She felt that once she was before her own altar she could show him something. He glowered down upon her for a spell and then turned and went back across the lake the way he had come. The light vanished behind his feet. Then a huge alligator slid up beside her where she lay trembling and all her strength went out of her. She lost all confidence in her powers. She began to feel if only she might either die or escape from the horror, she would never touch another charm again. If only she could escape the maw of the monster beside her! Any other death but that. She wished that Uncle Monday would come back so that she might plead with him for deliverance. She opened her mouth to call, but found that speech had left her. But she saw a light approaching by land. It was the rescue party.

Ant Judy never did regain the full use of her legs, but she got to the place where she could hobble about the house and yard. After relating her adventure on Lake Blue Sink she never called the name of Uncle Monday again.

The rest of the village, always careful in that respect, grew almost as careful as she. But sometimes when they would hear the great bull 'gator, that everybody knows lives in Lake Belle, bellowing on cloudy nights, some will point the thumb in the general direction of Uncle Monday's house and whisper, "The Old Boy is visiting the home folks tonight."

SPIRITUALS AND NEO-SPIRITUALS

The real spirituals are not really just songs. They are unceasing variations around a theme.

Contrary to popular belief their creation is not confined to the slavery period. Like the folk-tales the spirituals are being made and forgotten every day. There is this difference: the makers of the song of the present go about from town to town and church to church singing their songs. Some are printed and called ballads, and offered for sale after the services at ten and fifteen cents each. Others just go about singing them in competition with other religious minstrels. The lifting of the collection is the time for the song battles. Quite a bit of rivalry develops.

These songs, even the printed ones, do not remain long in their original form. Every congregation that takes it up alters it considerably. For instance, *The Dying Bed Maker*, which is easily the most popular of the recent compositions, has been changed to *He's a Mind Regulator* by a Baptist church in New Orleans.

The idea that the whole body of spirituals are "sorrow songs" is ridiculous. They cover a wide range of subjects from a peeve at gossipers to Death and Judgment.

The nearest thing to a description one can reach is that they are Negro religious songs, sung by a group, and a group bent on expression of feelings and not on sound effects.

There never has been a presentation of genuine Negro spirituals to any audience anywhere. What is being sung by the concert artists and glee clubs are the works of Negro composers or adaptors *based* on the spirituals. Under this head come the works of Harry T. Burleigh, Rosamond Johnson, Lawrence Brown, Nathaniel Dett, Hall Johnson and Work. All good work and beautiful, but *not* the spirituals. These neo-spirituals are the outgrowth of the glee clubs. Fisk University boasts perhaps the oldest and certainly the most famous of these. They have spread their interpretation over America and Europe. Hampton and Tuskegee have not been unheard. But with all the glee clubs and soloists, there has not been one genuine spiritual presented.

To begin with, Negro spirituals are not solo or quartette material. The jagged harmony is what makes it, and it ceases to be what it was when this is absent. Neither can any group be trained to reproduce it. Its truth dies under training like flowers under hot water. The harmony of the true spiritual is not regular. The dissonances are important and not to be ironed out by the trained musician. The various parts break in at any old time. Falsetto often takes the place of regular voices for short periods. Keys change. Moreover, each singing of the piece is a new creation. The congregation is bound by no rules. No two times singing is alike, so that we must consider the rendition of a song not as a final thing, but as a mood. It won't be the same thing next Sunday.

Negro songs to be heard truly must be sung by a group, and a group bent on expression of feelings and not on sound effects.

Glee clubs and concert singers put on their tuxedoes,* bow

*Evening dress.

prettily to the audience, get the pitch and burst into magnificent song—but not *Negro* song. The real Negro singer cares nothing about pitch. The first notes just burst out and the rest of the church join in—fired by the same inner urge. Every man trying to express himself through song. Every man for himself. Hence the harmony and disharmony, the shifting keys and broken time that make up the spiritual.

I have noticed that whenever an untampered-with congregation attempts the renovated spirituals, the people grow self-conscious. They sing sheepishly in unison. None of the glorious individualistic flights that make up their own songs. Perhaps they feel on strange ground. Like the unlettered parent before his child just home from college. At any rate they are not very popular.

This is no condemnation of the neo-spirituals. They are a valuable contribution to the music and literature of the world. But let no one imagine that they are the songs of the people, as sung by them.

The lack of dialect in the religious expression—particularly in the prayers—will seem irregular.

The truth is, that the religious service is a conscious art expression. The artist is consciously creating—carefully choosing every syllable and every breath. The dialect breaks through only when the speaker has reached the emotional pitch where he loses self-consciousness.

In the mouth of the Negro the English language loses its stiffness, yet conveys its meaning accurately. "The booming bounderries of this whirling world" conveys just as accurate a picture as mere "boundaries," and a little music is gained besides. "The rim bones of nothing" is just as truthful as "limitless space."

Negro singing and formal speech are breathy. The audible breathing is part of the performance and various devices are resorted to to adorn the breath taking. Even the lack of breath is embellished with syllables. This is, of course, the very antithesis of white vocal art. European singing is considered good when each syllable floats out on a column of air, seeming not to have any mechanics at all. Breathing must be hidden. Negro song ornaments both the song and the mechanics. It is said of a popular preacher, "He's got a good straining voice." I will make a parable to illustrate the difference between Negro and European.

A white man built a house. So he got it built and he told the man: "Plaster it good so that nobody can see the beams and uprights." So he did. Then he had it papered with beautiful paper, and painted the outside. And a Negro built him a house. So when he got the beams and all in, he carved beautiful grotesques over all the sills and stanchions, and beams and rafters. So both went to live in their houses and were happy.

The well-known "ha!" of the Negro preacher is a breathing device. It is the tail end of the expulsion just before inhalation. Instead of permitting the breath to drain out, when the wind gets too low for words, the remnant is expelled violently. Example: (inhalation) "And oh!"; (full breath) "my Father and my wonder-working God"; (explosive exhalation) "ha!"

Chants and hums are not used indiscriminately as it would appear to a casual listener. They have a definite place and time. They are used to "bear up" the speaker. As Mama Jane of Second Zion Baptist Church, New Orleans, explained to me: "What point they come out on, you bear 'em up."

For instance, if the preacher should say: "Jesus will lead us," the congregation would bear him up with: "I'm got my ha-hands in my Jesus' hands." If in prayer or sermon, the mention is made of nailing Christ to the cross: "Didn't Calvary tremble when they nailed Him down."

There is no definite post-prayer chant. One may follow, however, because of intense emotion. A song immediately follows prayer. There is a pre-prayer hum which depends for its material upon the song just sung. It is usually a pianissimo continuation of the song without words. If some of the people use the words it is done so indistinctly that they would be hard to catch by a person unfamiliar with the song.

As indefinite as hums sound, they also are formal and can be found unchanged all over the South. The Negroised white hymns are not exactly sung. They are converted into a barbaric chant that is not a chant. It is a sort of liquefying of words. These songs are always used at funerals and on any solemn occasion. The Negro has created no songs for death and burials, in spite of the sombre subject matter contained in some of the spirituals. Negro songs are one and all based on a dance-possible rhythm. The heavy interpretations have been added by the more cultured singers. So for funerals fitting white hymns are used.

Beneath the seeming informality of religious worship there is a set formality. Sermons, prayers, moans and testimonies have their definite forms. The individual may hang as many new ornaments upon the traditional form as he likes, but the audience would be disagreeably surprised if the form were abandoned. Any new and original elaboration is welcomed, however, and this brings out the fact that all religious expression among Negroes is regarded as art, and ability is recognised as definitely as in any other art. The beautiful prayer receives the accolade as well as the beautiful song. It is merely a form of expression which people generally are not accustomed to think of as art. Nothing outside of the Old Testament is as rich in figure as a Negro prayer. Some instances are unsurpassed anywhere in literature.

There is a lively rivalry in the technical artistry of all of these fields. It is a special honor to be called upon to pray over the covered communion table, for the greatest prayer-artist present is chosen by the pastor for this, a lively something spreads over the church as he kneels, and the "bearing up" hum precedes him. It continues sometimes through the introduction, but ceases as he makes the complimentary salutation to the deity. This consists in giving to God all the titles that form allows.

The introduction to the prayer usually consists of one or two verses of some well-known hymn. "O, that I knew a secret place" seems to be the favorite. There is a definite pause after this, then follows an elaboration of all or parts of the Lord's Prayer. Follows after that what I call the setting, that is, the artist calling attention to the physical situation of himself and the church. After the dramatic setting, the action begins.

There are certain rhythmic breaks throughout the prayer, and the church "bears him up" at every one of these. There is in the body of the prayer an accelerando passage where the audience takes no part. It would be like applauding in the middle of a solo at the Metropolitan. It is here that the artist comes forth. He adorns the prayer with every sparkle of earth, water and sky, and nobody wants to miss a syllable. He comes down from this height to a slower tempo and is borne up again. The last few sentences are unaccompanied, for here again one listens to the individual's closing peroration. Several may join in the final amen. The best figure that I can think of is that the prayer is an obligato over and above the harmony of the assembly.

Negro: An Anthology, Nancy Cunard, ed., 1934

Works-in-Progress for
The Florida Negro

FOLKLORE AND MUSIC

FOLKLORE is the boiled-down juice of human living. It does not belong to any special time, place, nor people. No country is so primitive that it has no lore, and no country has yet become so civilized that no folklore is being made within its boundaries.

Folklore in Florida is still in the making. Folk tunes, tales, and characters are still emerging from the lush glades of primitive imagination before they can be finally drained by formal education and mechanical inventions.

A new folk hero has come to be in the Florida prison camps, and his name is Daddy Mention. It is evident that he is another incarnation of Big John de Conquer or, that hero of the slavery days who could out-smart Ole Massa, God, and the Devil. He is the wish-fulfilment projection. The wily Big John compensated for the helplessness of the slave in the hands of the master, and Daddy Mention does the same for the convict in the prison camp.

In folklore, as in everything else that people create, the world is a great, big, old serving-platter, and all the local places are like eating-plates. Whatever is on the plate must come out of the platter, but each plate has a flavor of its own because the people take the universal stuff and season it to suit themselves on the plate. And this local flavor is what is known as originality. So when we speak of Florida folklore, we are talking about that Florida flavor that the story- and song-makers have given to the great mass of material that has accumulated in this sort of culture delta. And Florida *is* lush in material because the State attracts such a variety of workers to its industries.

Thinking of the beginnings of things in a general way, it could be said that folklore is the first thing that man makes out of the natural laws that he finds around him—beyond the necessity of making a living. After all, culture and discovery are forced marches on the near and the obvious. The group mind uses up a great part of its life-span trying to ask infinity some questions about what is going on around its doorsteps. And the more that the group knows about its own doorstep, the more it can bend and control what it sees there, the more civilized we say it is. For what we call civilization is an accumulation of recognitions and regulations of the commonplace. How many natural laws of things have been recognized, classified, and utilized by these people? That is the question that is being asked in reality when the "progress" of a locality is being studied. Every generation or so some individual with extra keen perception grasps something of the obvious about us and hitches the human race forward slightly by a new "law." For instance, millions of things had been falling on and about men for thousands of years before the falling apple hit Newton on the head and made him see the attraction of the earth for all unsupported objects heavier than air. So we have the law of gravity.

In the same way, art is a discovery in itself. Seen in detail it is a series of discoveries, perhaps intended in the first instance to stave off boredom. In a long range view, art is the setting up of monuments to the ordinary things about us, in a moment and in time. Examples are the great number of representations of men and women in wood and stone at the moment of the kill or at the bath; or a still moment of a man or beast in the prime of strength, or a woman at the blow of her beauty. Perhaps the monument is made in word and tune, but anyway, such is the urge of art. Folklore is the arts of the people before they find out that there is any such thing as art, and they make it out of whatever they find at hand.

Way back there when Hell wasn't no bigger than Maitland, man found out something about the laws of sound. He had found out something before he even stood erect to think. He found out that sounds could be assembled and manipulated and that such a collection of sound forms could become as definite and concrete as a war-axe or a food-tool. So he had language and song. Perhaps by some happy accident he found out about percussion sounds and spacing the intervals for tempo and rhythm. Anyway, it is evident that the sound-arts were the first inventions and that music and literature grew from the same root. Somewhere songs for sound-singing branched off from songs for story-telling until we arrive at prose.

The singing grew like this: First a singing word or syllable repeated over and over like frogs in a pond; then followed sung phrases and chanted sentences as more and more words were needed to portray the action of the battle, the chase, or the dance. Then man began to sing of his feelings or moods, as well as his actions, and it was found that the simple lyre was adequate to walk with the words expressing moods. The Negro blues songs, of which Florida has many fine examples, belong in the lyric class; that is, feelings set to strings. The oldest and most typical form of Negro blues is a line stating the mood of the singer repeated three times. The stress and variation is carried by the tune and the whole thing walks with rhythm.

Look at the "East Coast Blues" and see how:

Love ain't nothing but the *easy-going* heart disease;
Love ain't nothing but the easy-going heart *disease*;
Oh, *love* ain't *nothing* but the *easy-going heart disease.*

The next step going up is still a three-line stanza. The second line is a repetition of the first so far as the words go, but the third line is a "flip" line that rhymes with the others. The sample that follows is from a widespread blues song that originated in Palm Beach:

When you see me coming h'ist your window high;
When you see me coming h'ist your window high;
Done got blood-thirsty, don't care how I die.

Incidentally, this is the best known form as far as the commercial blues is concerned because in the early days of the commercial blues, Porter Grainger, who wrote most of these songs, followed this pattern exclusively.

The blues song, "Halimuhfack," is still more complicated as to word-pattern. The title is a corruption of Halifax. The extra syllables are added for the sake of rhythm:

You may leave and go to Halimuhfack,
But my slow drag will-uh bring you back;
Well, you may go, but this will bring you back.

Literary progress in construction is even more evident in "Angeline." Here is seen a pattern of a stanza of a rhymed couplet which also rhymes with the succeeding couplet. In addition, it carries out connected thought.

> Oh, Angeline! Oh, Angeline!
> Oh, Angeline that great, great gal of mine!
>
> And when she walk, and when she walk,
> And when she walk, she rocks and reels behind;
>
> You feel her legs, you feel her legs,
> You feel her legs, and you want to feel her thighs;
>
> You feel her thighs, you feel her thighs,
> You feel her thighs, then you want to go on high;
>
> You go on high, you go on high,
> You go on high, then you fade away and die;
>
> Oh, Angeline! Oh, Angeline!
> Oh, Angeline that great, great gal of mine!

"Uncle Bud," that best loved of Negro working songs is a rhymed couplet with a swinging refrain:

> Uncle Bud is a man, a man in full;
> His back is strong like a Jersey bull.
> *Refrain:*
> Uncle Bud, Uncle Bud, Uncle Bud, Uncle Bud,
>   Uncle Bud.
>
> 'Tain't no use in you raising sand,
> You got to take that crap off of grandpa's land.
> *Refrain:*
>
> Uncle Bud's got cotton ain't got no squares;
> Uncle Bud's got gal ain't got no hairs.

Folk song making has become rather well developed when it arrives at the stage of the ballad. "Delia," from around Fernandina, and "John Henry," from who knows where, are good examples:

Delia

Coonie told Delia on a Christmas eve night,
If you tell me 'bout my mama I'm sho going to take your life,
She's dead, she's dead and gone.

(Coonie shoots Delia to death during the course of several
    verses)

Coonie in the jail-house drinking out a silver cup
Poor Delia in the graveyard don't care if she never wake up
She's dead, she's dead and gone

(Coonie justifies his killing of Delia)

Mama, Oh mama, how could I stand
When all round my bedside was full of married men
So she's dead, she's dead and gone

John Henry

John Henry driving on the right hand side,
Steam drill driving on the left,
Says before I'll let your steam drill beat me down,
I'll hammer my fool self to death, lawd!
Hammer my fool self to death.

John Henry told his captain,
Says when you go to town,
Please bring me back a nine-pound hammer,
And I'll drive your steel on down, Lawd!
Drive your steel on down.

John Henry went upon the mountain
Just to whip a little steel,
But the rocks so tall, John Henry so small,
He laid down his hammer and he cried, lawd!
He laid down his hammer and he cried.

John Henry had a little woman,
The dress she wore was red,
Says I'm going down the track and she never looked back
I'm going where John Henry fell dead, lawd!
Going where John Henry fell dead.

A ballad catches the interest of everybody in that it is more or less a story that is sung. The power of the group to create and transmit a story is increased. Before, there was music mostly for music's sake. But in the ballad the storyteller is merely using the vehicle of music to carry a tale. The interest of the listener has shifted from sound and rhythm to characterization and action. The music has become the servant of the words. Looping back to the more primitive forms, it is evident that the often meaningless words are mere excuses for repeating the haunting tune. But in the ballad the words make the tune. Take "John Henry," for example, and it is plain that the words and the music are one and the same thing. Read the words aloud and you have the tune. The stresses and lack of stresses all come where they would naturally be if the story were told without music. In other words, the ballad is the prelude to prose.

The ballad is, however, not the only road to prose. Among the other progressions are the folk-rhymes. In biology it is generally accepted that the evolution of an organism is reviewed in the embryo. In folk literature it is the same. Anyone who has been around children knows that they pass through various phases from the mere repeating of pleasing single notes to the phase of rhyme-making. This usually occurs when they are between six and eight years old. These verses seldom make sense. They are made for the sake of sound. The child is discovering sound laws for himself. The adult primitive does the same thing on his way to prose. So, rhyme for the sake of sound, furnishes evidence of the youth of literature. The second step is a combination of sound and sense. Every nation and race has a large body of observations on life coupled with rhyme for the sake of sound. Here are some samples from the Florida area:

1.

Love is a funny thing, love is a blossom;
If you want your finger bit, poke it at a possum.

2.

Count from your little finger back to your thumb;
If you start anything I got you some.

3.

Nought is a nought, figger's a figger;
All for the white man, none for the nigger.

4.

Some love collards, some love kale;
I love a girl with a short shirt tail.

5.

The wind may blow, the door may slam;
That what you shooting ain't worth a damn.

In each of these rhymes there is a sense line and a sound
line. The speaker might easily have said what was necessary
without the rhyme, but it was felt that the couplet was more
forceful and beautiful than the simple statement, but the real
significance of these rhymes is that there is no thought of
vocal or instrumental accompaniment—just a talking sentence. So that brings it right next door to prose.

FOLK TALES

The age of prose in every locality and among all races over-
laps the twilight of poetry. Like song, prose grows from the
short and often pointless tale to the long and complicated
story with a smashing climax. All this is quite evident in the
folk tales of the Negro-American. A single incident, or even a
vivid description, is often offered as a story. Here are some
samples of this from various parts of Florida:

1.

Once there was a man and he was so little that he had to
climb up on a box to look over a grain of sand.

2.

It was a man and he was so big and fat till he went to whip
his little boy for something. The little boy run up under his
papa's belly and hid up under there for six months.

3.

(A common way of telling a story is to dramatize it)

Story-teller: What is the ugliest man you ever seen?

Helper: Oh, I seen a man so ugly that he could set up behind a jimpson weed and hatch monkeys.

Another Helper: Oh, that man wasn't so ugly! I knowed a man that could set up behind a tombstone and hatch hants.

Story-teller: Aw, them wasn't no ugly men you all is talking about! Fact is, them is pretty mens. I knowed a man and he was so ugly that you could throw him in the Mississippi River and skim ugly for six months.

4.

(Explanation of the hurricane of 1928)

So the storm met the hurricane in Palm Beach and they set down and ate breakfast together. Then the hurricane said to the storm, "Let's go down to Miami and shake that thing!"

5.

They have strong winds on the Florida west coast, too. One day the wind blowed so hard till it blowed a well up out of the ground. Then one day it blowed so hard till it blowed a crooked road straight. Another time it blowed and blowed and scattered the days of the week so bad till Sunday didn't come until late Tuesday evening.

6.

It gets pretty hot around Tampa, too. Two mens got on the train at Jacksonville to go to Tampa and they were wearing blue serge suits. The weather got so hot till when the train got to Tampa just two blue suits stepped down off the train. The mens had done melted out of the suits.

7.

They raises big vegetables down around the Everglades, too. Yes sir! That's rich land around down there. Take for instance, my old man planted sweet potatoes one year and when it come time to dig them potatoes, one of them had done got so big till they had to make a saw-mill job out of it. Well, they built a saw-mill and put whole crews of mens to work cutting up that big old sweet potato. And so that year everybody in Florida had houses made out of sweet potato slabs. And what you reckon everybody ate that year? Well, they lived off of potato pone, made out of the sawdust from that great big old tater my old man raised.

8.

Round Ocala you can find some land that is sort of poor for raising things. My old man bought some land over round there and it was so poor till he give it to a congregation to build a church. Well, they called a preacher and built the church, and they all met there to open it up. But that land was so poor till they had to telegraph to Jacksonville for ten sacks of commercional (fertilizer) and spread it all over the ground before they could raise a tune.

9.

My old man was late planting his corn that year. Everybody else had corn knee-high. So one morning my old man took and told us we better plant some corn. So my brother John was opening the furrows and I was dropping corn and my baby brother was coming long behind me hilling it up. So I looked back over my shoulder and seen that the corn was coming up right behind me as fast as I was dropping it and it was growing so fast till I knowed that it wasn't going to make nothing but fodder. So I hollered to my baby brother Joel to sit down on some of them hills of corn to stunt the corn so it would make corn instead of fodder. Well, my brother Joel done like I told him and the next day he dropped us back a note and said, "Passed through heaven yesterday at twelve o'clock selling roasting ears to the angels."

10.

Sis Snail took sick in the bed, you know, and she didn't get no better so afterwhile she hollered for her husband and she told him say, "Honey, I reckon you better go get the doctor for me. I'm *so* sick and don't look like I'm on the mend." Brer Snail told her, "All right, I'll go get the doctor for you. Give me time to go get my hat." So Sis Snail rolled from pillar to post in the bed. After seven years she heard a noise at the door and she said, "I know that's my husband with the doctor, and I am so glad! Lord knows I'm so sick. Honey, is that you with the doctor?" Brer Snail hollered back and told her, "Don't try to rush me! I ain't gone yet." It had took him seven years to get to the door.

II.

It was close to Christmas time, so God was going to Palatka. The Devil was walking the same road and he seen God and jumped behind a stump to keep God from seeing him. He done that for two reasons. In the first place he wanted to catch God Christmas gift and get a present out of God and then again he didn't want to give God nothing, so that's how come he jumped behind the stump. God was sort of busy in His mind counting over His new angels so He wasn't paying no attention to stumps. When He got right long there beside the Devil, he jumped out from behind the stump and hollered, "Christmas gift!" at God. God seen what the Devil had done but He kept right on walking. He just looked back over His shoulder and said, "Take the East Coast." And that is why people have so many storms and mosquitoes on the East Coast because it is the Devil's property.

12.

(Big John De Conquer is the culture hero of the American Negro folk tales. He is the Jason, or Ulysses, of the Greeks; Baldur of the Norse tales; Jack-the-Giant-Killer of European mythology. He is the success story that all weak people create to compensate for their weakness. He is a projection of the poor and humble into the realms of the mighty. By cunning or by brute might he overcomes the ruling class and utterly confounds its strength. He is among men what Brer Rabbit is among the animals. In the Ole Massa tales he compensates the slave for his futility. He even outwits the Devil, who in Negro mythology is smarter than God.)

Ole Massa had a nigger named John, you know. Ole Massa lakted (liked) John because he learned everything Ole Massa tried to teach him and he never forgot nothing you told him. Ole Big John used to go and stand in the chimney corner every night at the big house and listen to see what Ole Massa talked about. Then he would go back and tell the other niggers in the quarters that he could tell fortunes. If he hear Ole Massa tell Ole Miss that he was going to kill hogs next day, John would come back and tell them, "Well, Ole Massa is going to kill hogs tomorrow." Them others would ask, "What make you say that, John?" "I'm a fortune teller and nothing ain't hid from me." So sure enough when Ole Massa come out next morning he would tell everybody to get ready for the big hog killing. It kept on like that until they all believed John when he said anything.

The way he fooled Ole Massa and Ole Miss was he was hanging round the back door when he seen the water throwed out that Ole Miss had done bathed in and he seen her diamond ring get throwed out in the water. John seen a turkey gobler grab up that ring and swallow it down. So when Ole Miss looked for her ring and couldn't find it she started to cry and say that somebody had done stole her diamond ring that Ole Massa give her for a birthday present. John he come tole Ole Massa that he could find the ring for Ole Miss. So Massa told him to find it if he could and he would give John a fine shoat. So John told him to kill that certain turkey gobler and he would find the ring. Ole Massa told him not to fool him into killing his prize turkey rooster, do he aimed to kill ole John. When he killed the gobler there was the ring sure enough, so then Ole Massa believed everything John told him.

One day when Ole Massa was talking with some more betting white folks he told them, "I got a nigger that can tell fortunes." One man told him, "No, he can't tell no fortunes, neither!" Massa told him, "I'll bet you forty acres of bottom land that Big John can tell fortunes." The man told Ole Massa, "Why don't you back your judgment with your money? Bet me something! I'll bet you my whole plantation that nigger can't tell no fortunes. I'll bet you every inch of land I own."

Ole Massa had him where he wanted him, so he reared back and said, "I didn't know you was going to make a betting thing out my statement, but since I see you do, let's make it worth my time. I'm a fighting dog, you know, and my hide is worth money. I bet you my whole plantation against yours, and every horse and every mule and every hog and every nigger on the place that my nigger John *can* tell fortunes." So they took paper and signed up the bet. They made arrangements to prove the thing out a week from that day. Massa come home and told John what he done done, and he told John, too, "John I done bet everything I got in the world on you and you better not make me lose everything I got, do I sure will kill you."

The day of the bet come and Ole Massa told John the night before to be ready bright and soon to go to the betting ground with him to prove out the thing. Ole Massa used to ride a fine prancing horse, and John used to ride a fat mule right along with Massa everywhere he went. He used to be up every morning and have Massa's saddle horse at the door before Massa get out of bed. But this morning Massa was up and had done saddled his own horse and had to go wake John up. John was so scared because he knowed he couldn't tell no fortunes and he knowed that he was going to make Ole Massa lose everything he had and then Massa was going to shoot him. So he hung way back behind Massa on the way to where they was holding the bet.

When they got to the place, why, everybody was there from all over the world because they had done heard about this big bet. John and Ole Massa got there and Ole Massa lit down from his horse real spry, but John just sort of slid off of that mule and stood there. The man that was betting against Ole Massa had the privilege to fix the proof, so John was carried off a little piece and when he come back he seen a great big old iron washpot turned down over something and the man told John to tell them what was under that washpot. Ole Massa told him he better think good 'cause he sure meant to kill him if he didn't tell it right and make him lose his place. It was very still because all of them had seen what was under the pot except John, and they was all waiting to see what he had to say. John looked at the pot and he walked all around it three or four times but he couldn't get the least inkling of what was under that pot. He begin to sweat and to scratch his head and Ole Massa looked at John and he begin to sweat, too. Finally John decided he might just as well give up and let Ole Massa kill him and be done with it. So he said, "Well, you got the old 'coon at last." When he said that, Ole Massa throwed his hat up in the air and let out a whoop. Everybody whooped except the man that was betting against Massa, because that was what was under the pot, a big old 'coon (raccoon). So none of them never did know that John didn't know what was under that pot. Massa give John his freedom and a hundred dollars, and Massa went off to Philadelphia to celebrate and left John in charge of everything.

13.

When Massa went off to celebrate his bet, he left John in charge of everything. So soon as him and Ole Miss got on the train to go, John sent word round to all the plantations to ask his friends to a big eating and drinking. "Massa is gone to Philly-mah-York (corruption of New York and Philadelphia) and won't be back in three weeks. He done left everything in my charge. Come on over for a big time." He sent word round to all the niggers on all the plantations like that. While some of them was gone to carry out the invitations, he told some more to go into Massa's lot and kill hogs until you could walk on them.

So that night everybody come to eat and to drink and John really had done spread a table. Everybody that could get hold of the white folks clothes had them on that night. John, he opened up the whole house and took Ole Massa's big rocking chair and put it up on Massa's big bed and then he got up in it to sit down so he could be sitting high when he called the figures for the dance. He was sitting up in his high seat with a box of Massa's fine cigars under his arm and one in his mouth: "Ladies right! First couple to the floor! Sashay all!" When he seen a couple of poor-looking white folks come in. John looked at them and said, "Take them poor folks out of here and carry them back to the kitchen where they belong. Give them plenty to eat, but don't allow them back up front again. Nothing but quality up here."

You see, John didn't know that was Ole Massa and Ole Miss done slipped back to see what he would do in their absence. So they ate some of the good meat first and then they washed the dirt off their faces and come back into the room where John was sitting up in the rocking chair in the bed.

"John," Massa told him, "now you done smoked up my

fine cigars and killed up my hogs and got all these niggers in my house carrying on like they crazy when I trusted you with my place. Now I am going to take you out to that big persimmon tree and kill you. You needs a good hanging and that is just what you are going to get."

John asked him, "Massa, will you grant me one little favor before you kill me?" Massa told him yes, but hurry up because he was anxious to hang a man who would cut the capers that John had cut. John called his friend Ike to one side and told him, "Ike, Ole Massa is going to take me out to the pessimmon tree to hang me. I want you to get up in that tree with a box of matches and every time I ask God for a sign, you strike a match. That is the only way to save my life." So Ike run ahead and got up in the tree with the box of matches. After while here come Massa with John and a rope to hang him. He throwed the rope over a high limb and tied one end around John's neck. At that time John said, "Massa, will you let me pray before you kill me?" Massa told him to go ahead and pray but he better pray fast because he was tired of waiting to hang him. So John got down and said, "O Lord, if you mean to stop Massa from hanging me, give me a sign." When he said that, Ike struck a match and when Massa see that light up the tree, he begin to get scared. John made out he didn't see Massa flinch and he kept right on praying. "O Lord, if you mean to kill Ole Massa tonight, give me another sign." Ike struck another match. Ole Massa said, "That's all right, John, don't pray no more." John kept right on praying. "O Lord, if you mean to put Massa to death tonight with his wife and all his chillun, give me another sign." Ike struck a whole heap of matches at that and Old Massa lit out from there, running just as fast as he could. And after that he give John and everybody else they freedom and that is how Negroes got their freedom — because John fooled Ole Massa so bad.

Big John Today.

There are numerous other stories of John's doings with Ole Massa, of his tricking strong men out of contests, of his visits to heaven and hell, and his victories over the Devil. Casual listeners have confused John de Conquer with John Henry, but this is far from correct. John Henry is celebrated for one single act of bravery and strength, in the manner of Casey Jones. While John de Conquer is a hero cycle yet unfinished. The strongest herb used in hoodoo is called Big John de Conquer root. Nothing is supposed to stand against it. There have been no stories of John's death, except the ones told in order to show him carrying on in heaven. He is up to his old tricks there also.

Daddy Mention.

Just when or where Daddy Mention came into being, none of the guests at the Duval County (Florida) Blue-Jay (prison farm) seem to know. Only one thing is certain about this wonder-working prisoner: Every other prisoner claims to have known him.

Not that any of his former friends can describe Daddy Mention to you, or even tell you very many close details about him. They agree, however, that he has been an inmate of various and sundry Florida jails, prison camps, and road farms for years.

In fact, it is this unusual power of omnipresence that first arouses the suspicions of the listeners: was Daddy Mention perhaps a legendary figure? Prisoners will insist that he was in the Bartow jail on a 90-day sentence, "straight up," when they were doing time there. Then another will contradict and say it must have been some other time, because that was the period when Daddy was in Marion County, "making a bit in the road gang." The vehemence with which both sides argue would seem to prove that Daddy was in neither place, and that very likely he was nowhere.

Legendary though Daddy Mention may be, however, the tales of his exploits are vividly told by the prisoners. All the imagination, the color, and the action of the "John" stories of other sections are duplicated in Daddy's activities; it is peculiar that the exploits, far-fetched though they may seem, seldom fall on unbelieving ears. A selection of the Daddy Mention tales appear in *Florida: A Guide to the Southernmost State.*

On the west coast, from Key West to Tampa, there is a tremendous addition of Cuban music, tales and folk ways. On the east coast, from Fort Pierce to Key West, there is an even stronger element seeping into Negro folk ways. This is something brought into the United States by the flood of Negro

workers from the Bahamas. The Negro music is more dynamic and compelling than that of the American Negro, and
the dance movements are more arresting; perhaps because the
Bahaman offerings are more savage. The Bahaman, and the
West Indian Negro generally, has had much less contact with
the white man than the American Negro. As a result, speech,
music, dancing, and other modes of expression are definitely
nearer the African. Thus the seeker finds valuable elements
long lost to the American Negro. This is because the Negro
slave on the continent of North America, unlike the island
slave, was never allowed to remain in tribal groups. This is
both to prevent uprisings and to speed up his Americaniza-
tion. Also on American soil the slave came into direct contact
with the master and the master's family almost daily, whereas
the system of absentee ownership was prevalent in the West
Indies, and the slave owner might not visit his plantations
once in ten years. There might be three hundred slaves under
the care of one white overseer, who could not concern himself with the personal contact that most masters relish with
their own property.

Bahaman drum rhythms are truly magnificent. The songs
are nearly all dance songs and the words are mere excuses to
introduce the tunes. A rhythmic phrase is repeated until the
fire-tuned drum grows cold and slack in the head and must
be tuned and tightened by fire again. Then another tune is
introduced.

Of the dance tunes, there are two main types: the jumping
dance and the ring dance. The jumping dance tune is short
and repetitious. As soon as a dancer chooses a partner, it begins all over again. The length varies. There are "one move"
rhythms, two moves, and so on. For instance, in a three-move
dance, the dancer "cuts pork": enters the circle and does a
solo dance; chooses a partner and retires.

"Lime, Oh, Lime"

Lime, Oh, lime, (cutting pork, a preliminary movement)
Juice and all;
Lime, Oh, lime, Dessa hold your back (Leaps into ring);
Oh, Dessa! (one move) Oh Dessa! (two moves) Oh
    Dessa!, etc.

The ring play is more elaborate and florid, though it is actually less difficult to do. The dancer chosen enters the ring at the first syllable of the verse and moves around the ring in search of a partner. All dancers in the ring clap their hands loudly throughout the movement. The selected partner steps out of the ring when a rhythmic moment arrives.

"Bone Fish"

Good morning, Father Fisher; good morning Father Brown;
Have you any sea-crabs, sell me one or two.
Bone fish is biting, have no bait to catch him;
Every married man got his own bone fish.

(The circling ceases and the dancer faces his choice.)

Eh, eh, looy loo! (The two dance out to the center of the
    ring)
Eh, eh, lolly loo, eh, eh, lolly loo! (This continues until
    the original dancer leaves the ring so that the other
    may in turn choose a partner. Then, the verse begins
    all over again.)

One is astonished to find that all of the Bahaman tunes have an African tribal origin. Let the dancers but hear an air and they can instantly tell you to which tribe it belongs. This is a Nago, that an Ibo, another a Congo, another a Yoruba (the proudest and most arrogant of all the Negro tribes in the West Indies). One hears such screams of outrage, "What! A Congo man stands in the face of a Yoruba and talks such! Don't you cheek me, Congo!"

Nightly in Palm Beach, Fort Pierce, Miami, Key West and other cities of the Florida east coast, the hot drum heads throb and the African-Bahaman folk arts seep into the soil of America.

Also in Florida are the Cuban-African and the Bahaman-African folk tales. It is interesting to note that the same Brer Rabbit tales of the American Negro are told by these islanders. One also finds the identical tales in Haiti and the British West Indies. Since it is not possible for these same stories to have arisen in America and become so widely distributed through the western world wherever the Negro exists, the wide distribution denotes a common origin in West Africa. It has been noted by Carita Doggett Corse that these same tales are told by the Florida Indians. But this does not mean that they are purely Indian tales as those recorded by John R. Swanson (*Myths and Tales of the Southeastern Indians*, Bulletin 88, Bureau of Am. Eth. Smithsonian Inst.). On the contrary, it merely accentuates the amount of contact which the Negroes have had with Southeastern Indians in the past. Since it is well known that runaway slaves fled to the Indian communities of southern Georgia and Florida in great numbers, the explanation of the Brer Rabbit tales among the Indians is obvious.

One fact stands out as one examines the Negro folk tales which have come to Florida from various sources. There is no such thing as a Negro tale which lacks point. Each tale brims over with humor. The Negro is determined to laugh even if he has to laugh at his own expense. By the same token, he spares nobody else. His world is dissolved in laughter. His "bossman," his woman, his preacher, his jailer, his God, and himself, all must be baptized in the stream of laughter. A case in point is the explanation of why Negroes are black.

"You know God didn't make people all of a sudden. He made them by degrees when He had some spare time from the creating He was doing. First start off He took a great big hunk of clay and stomped it all out until it was nice and smooth. Then He cut out all the human shapes and stood them up against His long gold fence to dry. Then when they was all dried, He blowed the breath of life into them and they walked on off. That had took God two or three working days to do that. Then one day He told everybody to come up and get their eyes. So they all come up and got eyes. Another day when He had some spare time He called everybody to come up and get their noses and mouths, and they all come got them. Then one day He give out toe-nails and so on till people was almost finished. The last thing He called everybody and told them, 'Tomorrow morning at seven o'clock I am going to give out color. I want everybody here on time because I got plenty creating to do tomorrow and I don't want to lose no time.'

"Next morning at seven o'clock God was sitting on his throne with His high gold crown on. He looked north, He looked west, He looked east, and He looked Australia; and blazing worlds was falling off His teeth. There was the great multitude standing there before Him. He begin to give out color right away. He looked at a great big multitude over at His left hand and said, 'Youse yellow folks.' They said 'Thank you, Massa,' and walked off. He looked at another squaddle and told them 'Youse red people.' They thanked Him and went on off. He told the next crowd say, 'Youse white people.' They said, 'Thank you, Jesus,' and they went on off. God looked around on his other hand and told Gabriel, 'Look like I miss some multitudes.' Gabriel looked all around the throne and said, 'Yes sir, it is some multitudes missing. I reckon they will be along after while.' So God set there a whole hour and a half without doing a thing. After that He said, 'Look here, Gabriel, you go and find them multitudes that ain't got their color yet and you tell them I say they better come on here and get their color because when I get up from here today I am never to give out no more color. And if they don't hurry and come on here pretty soon they won't get none now.'

"Gabriel went off and way after while he found great multitudes that didn't have no color. Gabriel told them they better come on up there and get their color before God changed His mind. He was getting mighty tired of waiting. So they all jumped up from where they was and went running on up to the throne hollering about, 'Give us our color! We want our color! We got just as much right to have some color as anybody else.'

"The first one that got to the throne couldn't stop because those behind kept on pushing and shoving until the throne was careening way over one side and God got vexed and hollered, 'Get back! Get back!' But they misunderstood Him and thought He said 'get black,' so they just got black, and we been keeping the thing up ever since."

This will to humor and building to a climax which is so universal in the American Negro tales is sadly lacking in Negro tales elsewhere. This proves that what has always been thought of as native Negro humor is in fact something native to American soil. But anyway, if the other elements that go to fill up the Florida plate of Negro folklore do not possess the humor of the native American Negro, still their contributions certainly are important in other ways, so that Florida has the most tempting, the most highly flavored Negro plate around the American platter.

> Biddy, biddy bend, my story is end.
> Turn loose the rooster and hold the hen.

NEGRO MYTHICAL PLACES

Negroes like all other ethnological groups have their mythical cities and places. Those mentioned here are well-known in Florida as well as other states where the folk-negro exists.

Diddy-Wah-Diddy*

This is the largest and best known of the Negro mythical places. Its geography is that it is "way off somewhere." It is reached by a road that curves so much that a mule pulling a wagonload of fodder can eat off the back of the wagon as he goes. It is a place of no-work and no worry for man and beast. A very restful place where even the curbstones are good sitting-chairs. The food is even already cooked. If a traveller gets hungry all he needs to do is to sit down on the curbstone and wait and soon he will hear something hollering "Eat me! Eat me! Eat me!" and a big baked chicken will come along with a knife and fork stuck in its sides. He can eat all he wants and let the chicken go and it will go on to the next one that needs something to eat. By that time a big deep sweet potato pie is pushing and shoving to get in front of the traveller with a knife all stuck up in the middle of it so he just cuts a piece off of that and so on until he finishes his snack. Nobody can ever eat it all up. No matter how much you eat it grows just that much faster. It is said "Everybody would live in Diddy-Wah-Diddy if it wasn't so hard to find and so hard to get to

*On Route #17 north of Jacksonville the white owner of a large barbecue stand has named his place Diddy-Wah-Diddy. He said he did it because he was always hearing the Negroes around there talking about this mythical place of good things to eat, especially the barbecue. So he thought that it would prove a good title.

after you even know the way." Everything is on a large scale there. Even the dogs can stand flat-footed and lick crumbs off of heaven's tables. The biggest man there is known as Moon-Regulator because he reaches up and stops and starts it at his convenience. That is why there are some dark nights when the moon does not shine at all. He did not feel like putting it out that night.

Zar

This is the farthest known point of the imagination. It is away on the other side of Far. Little is known about the doings of the people of Zar because only one or two travellers have ever found their way back.

Beluthahatchie (Beh-loo-tha-hatchie)

This is the country where all unpleasant doings and sayings are forgotten. It is a sort of land of forgiveness. When a woman throws up to her man something that happened in the past (some act that he has perpetrated against happiness), he may merely reply, "I thought that was in Beluthahatchie." (I thought that was forgiven and forgotten long ago.) Under other circumstances one person may say to another, "Oh, that's in Beluthahatchie." (That is already forgotten. Don't mention it. I hold nothing against you.) This place is "The sea of forgetfulness where nothing may rise to accuse me in this world, nor condemn me in the judgment."

West Hell

West Hell is the hottest and toughest part of that warm territory. The most desperate malefactors are the only ones condemned to West Hell, which is some miles west of Regular Hell. These souls are changed to rubber coffins so that they go bouncing through Regular Hell and on to their destination without having to be carried by attendants as the Devil does not like to send his imps into West Hell oftener than is absolutely necessary. This suburb of Hell is celebrated as the spot where the Devil and Big John De Conqueror had their famous fight. Big John De Conqueror had flown to Hell on the back of an eagle, had met the Devil's daughters and fallen in love with the baby girl child. She agreed to elope with him and they had stolen the Devil's famous pair of horses that went by the name of Hallowed-Be-Thy-Name, and Thy-Kingdom-Come. When the Devil found out about it he hitched up his equally famous jumping bull and went in pursuit. He overtook the fleeing lovers in West Hell and they fought all over the place, so good a man, so good a devil! But way after while John tore off one of the Devil's arms and beat him, and married the Devil's daughter. But before he left Hell he passed out ice water to everybody in there. If you don't believe he done it, just go down to Hell and ask any body there and they will tell you all about it. He even turned the damper down in some parts of Hell so it's a whole lot cooler there now than it used to be. They even have to make a fire in the fireplace in the parlor now on cool nights in the wintertime. John did that because he says him and his wife expect to go home to see her folks some time and he don't like the house kept so hot like the Devil been keeping it. And if he go back there and find that that damper has been moved up again he means to tear up the whole job and turn West Hell into an ice-house.

Heaven

In this city there is the celebrated Sea of Glass where the angels go out to glide every afternoon for their pleasure. There are many golden streets, but the two main arteries of travel are Amen Street, running north and south, which is intersected right in front of the Throne by Hallelujah Avenue running from the east side of Heaven to the west. All of the streets are a pleasure to walk on, but Hallelujah Avenue and Amen streets are "tuned" streets. They play tunes when they are walked upon. They do not play any particular or set tunes. They play whatever tunes the feet of the walker plays as he struts. All of the shoes have songs in them too. Everybody's shoes sing sol me, sol do, sol me, sol do as they walk up and down in Heaven. The rumor is that there are no more Negroes in Heaven. God used to let them go there in great numbers, but one Negro came there who could not wait until Old Gabriel showed him how to fly. He was so eager to use his new wings that he took off over Heaven and got so cocky he tried to fly across God's nose. He fell and tore down a lot of God's big gold and jewelled hanging-lamps and knocked over several of those big golded up vases that are standing all over Heaven. When he got through falling down and breaking up, God just gave him a look and Gabriel knew just what to do. He went to the Negro and ripped off his wings. He told the destruction-maker says, "And it will be a long, long, time before you get any more wings too." The Negro told Gabriel, "I don't care if I never get no more. I sure was a flying fool when I had 'em." So since that time they have been mighty careful up there and some folks say that no more Negroes have qualified as yet.

In addition to Zar, Be-loo-tha-hatchie, Diddy-Wah-Diddy, and West Hell, there is also Ginny-Gall, where they eat cow belly skin and all. It is a place of tremendous want where folks learn to make any sort of shift. It is a place of take whatever you can get.

> "I'd just soon to be in Ginny-Gall
> Where the folks eat cowbelly skin and all."

THE OCOEE RIOT

This happened on election day, November 2, 1920. Though the catastrophe took place in Ocoee, and it is always spoken of as the Ocoee Riot, witnesses both white and Negro state that it was not the regular population of Ocoee which participated in the affair. It is said that the majority of whites of the community deplored it at the time and have refused to accept full responsibility for it since.

According to witnesses, the racial disorder began in Winter Garden, a citrus town about three miles from Ocoee. There had been very lively electioneering during the Harding campaign, and the Negroes who were traditional Republicans were turning out in mass at the polls. Some of the poor whites who are traditional Democrats resented this under the heading that the Negroes were voting jobs away from the local people. It was decided with a great deal of heat to prevent the blacks from voting, which was done. Over in Ocoee, the blacks and the whites were turning out to the polls with great enthusiasm and no trouble was contemplated. In the afternoon, however, many of the whites of Winter Garden came on over to Ocoee celebrating election day. Seeing the Ocoee Negroes swarming to the polls, they began to urge the Ocoee whites to stop them, citing the evil happenings of the Reconstruction. Finally the Negroes were being pushed and shoved at the polls. Then they were ordered away, but some of them persisted.

The first act of physical violence occurred when Mose Norman came up to the polls to vote in defiance of the warning for Negroes to keep away. He was struck and driven off. But he did not let the matter drop so easily. He got into his automobile and drove to Orlando, the County seat to see one Mr. Cheney, a well-known lawyer there and told him what was happening. He advised Mose Norman that the men who were interfering with the voting were doing so illegally and that it was a very serious matter indeed. He instructed Mose to return to Ocoee and to take the names of all the Negroes who had been denied their constitutional right to vote, and some say he advised Norman to also take the names of the whites who were violating the polls. Mose Norman returned to Ocoee and parked his car on the main street of the town near the place of polling and got out. While he was away from the car, some of the disorderly whites from Winter Garden went to the car and searched it and found a shotgun under the seat. When he returned to the car, he was set upon and driven off. His speedy foot work was the only thing that saved him from serious injury. When this got around, the Negroes generally stayed away from the polling place and began to leave town for the day. Two or three more were hustled and beaten however during the afternoon. Then the white mobs began to parade up and down the streets and grew more disorderly and unmanageable. Towards sundown, it was suggested that they go over to Mose Norman's house and give him a good beating for his officiousness and for being a smart-aleck. But some one going around the lake had seen him visiting July Perry, a very prosperous Negro farmer and contractor and they decided, come nightfall, they would go to the home of Perry and drag Mose out and chastise him.

In the meantime, The Black Dispatch (grapevine) had published all that was happening and most of the Negroes had left town or hidden out in the orange groves. July Perry armed himself and prepared to defend himself and his home. His friends all took to the woods and groves and left him to his courage. Even his sons hid out with the rest. His wife and daughter alone remained in the house with him. Perhaps they were afraid to leave the shelter of the house. Terrible rumors were about. Two of the three churches had been burned. The whole Negro settlement was being assaulted. It was cried that Langmaid, a Negro carpenter had been beaten and castrated. But one thing was certain, Mose Norman, who had been the match to touch off the explosion could not be found. He had thoroughly absented himself from the vicinity. When asked by some of the Negroes why he had had the gun under the seat of his car, he explained that he was doing some clearing out at Tildenville for Mr. Saddler, and always had his gun handy for a little hunting. At any rate, no Negro except July Perry had maintained his former address. So night dusted down on Ocoee, with the mobs seeking blood and ashes and July Perry standing his lone watch over his rights to life and property.

The night color gave courage to many men who had been diffident during the day hours. Fire was set to whole rows of Negro houses and the wretches who had thought to hide by crawling under these building were shot or shot at as they fled from the flames. In that way Maggie Genlack and her daughter were killed and their bodies left and partially burned by the flames that consumed their former home. The daughter was far advanced in pregnancy and so felt unequal to flight since there was no conveyance that she could get. Her mother would not leave her alone as all the others vanished out of the quarters. They took counsel together and the old woman and her pregnant daughter crept under the house to escape the notice of the mob. Roosevelt Barton died of fire and gunshot wounds when the barn of July Perry was put to flames. He had thought that that would be a good hiding place, but when the fury of the crowd swept over the Perry place, the barn was fired and when Roosevelt tried to rush out he was driven back by a bullet to die in the fire. But this only happened after a pitched battle had been fought at Perry's house, with July Perry against the mob.

He loaded his high powered rifle and waited, at the same time unwilling to believe that the white people with whom he had worked and associated so long would permit the irresponsibles from Winter Garden to harm him or his things. Nevertheless he waited ready to do that which becomes a man. He could not know that the mob was not seeking him at all, that they had come there because they thought that Mose Norman was hiding about the place. Perhaps if the mob had not been so sure that Mose was there that it was unnecessary to ask, all might have been different. They might have called out to him and he might have assured them by word of mouth or invited them in to see for themselves. They did not know that Norman had only spent a few minutes at the Perry home and then fled away to the groves. So they there outside began the assault upon the front of the house to gain entrance and Perry defended his door with all that he could command. He was effective. The mob was forced to retreat, and considered what was best to do. It was decided that while some kept up the harassment at the front, others would force an entrance through the back. Never had any of the mob suspected that Perry was alone in the house. They thought from the steady fire that several Negroes were at bay in there. It was Sam Salsbury who took a running start and kicked the back door open. Perry had not expected this, but he whirled at once and began to shoot at the gaping mouth of the door. His daughter terrified at this new danger tried to run out of the door and was shot in the shoulder by her father who had not expected her to run into the line of fire. But the next bullet struck Sam Salsbury in the arm and the rear attackers retreated. But not before Elmer McDonald and a man named Overberry had lost their lives. The council decided that reinforcements were necessary to take the place so the whole fighting force withdrew. Some phoned to Orlando to friends to come and help. Some phoned to Apopka and to other points. Some went in cars to bring help. So there was a lull in the fighting for two or three hours.

July Perry had not gone unhurt. A bullet or two had hit him. So in the lull his wife persuaded him to leave. He was weak from his hurts so she lent her strength to get him away from the house and far down into the cane patch where they felt he would not be found. When the re-inforced mob came back the doors were open and the searchers found only Perry's wounded daughter there. They did nothing to harm her but began an intensive hunt for Perry. It was around dawn when they found him weak and helpless in his hiding place and he was removed to the jail in Orlando. It was after sun-up when the mob stormed the jail and dragged him out and tied him to the back of a car and killed him and left his body swinging to a telephone post beside the highway.

That was the end of what happened in Ocoee on election day, 1920.

THE SANCTIFIED CHURCH

The rise of the various groups of "Saints" in America in the last twenty years is not the appearance of a new religion as has been reported. It is, in fact, the older forms of Negro religious expression asserting themselves against the new.

Frequently they are confused with the white "protest protestantism" known as Holy-Rollers. There are Negro Holy-Rollers, but they are very sparse compared to the other forms of sanctification. The two branches of the Sanctified Church are (a) Church of God in Christ, (b) Saints of God in Christ. There is very little difference between the two except for the matter of administration.

The sanctified church is a protest against the highbrow tendency in Negro Protestant congregations as the Negroes gain more education and wealth. It is understandable that they take on the religious attitudes of the white man which is a rule so staid and restricted that it seems unbearably dull to the more primitive Negro who associates the rhythm of sound and motion with religion. In fact, the Negro has not been Christianized as extensively as is generally believed. The great masses are still standing before their pagan altars and calling old gods by a new name. As evidence of this, note the drumlike rhythm of *all* Negro spirituals. All Negro-made church music is dance possible. The mode and the mood of the concert artists who do Negro spirituals is absolutely foreign to the Negro churches. It is a conservatory concept that has nothing to do with the actual rendition in the congregations who make the songs. They are twisted in concert from their barbaric rhythms into Gregorian chants and apocryphal appendages to Bach and Brahms. But go into the church and see the priest before the altar chanting his barbaric thunder-poem before the altar with the audience behaving something like a Greek chorus in that they "pick him up" on every telling point and emphasize it. That is called "bearing him up" and it is not done just any old way. The chant that breaks out from time to time must grow out of what has been said and done. "Whatever point he come out on, honey, you bear him up on it," Mama Jane told the writer. So that the service is really drama with music. And since music without motion is unnatural among Negroes there is always something that approaches dancing—in fact IS dancing—in such a ceremony. So the congregation is restored to its primitive altars under the new name of Christ. Then there is the expression known as "shouting" which is nothing more than a continuation of the African "Possession" by the gods. The gods possess the body of the worshipper and he or she is supposed to know nothing of their actions until the god decamps. This is still prevalent in most Negro protestant churches and is universal in the Sanctified churches. They protest against the more highbrow churches' efforts to stop it. It must also be noted that the sermon in these churches is not the set thing that it is in the other protestant churches. It is loose and formless and is in reality merely a framework upon which to hang more songs. Every opportunity to introduce a new rhythm is eagerly seized upon. *The whole movement of the Sanctified church is a rebirth of song-making! It has brought in a new era of spiritual-making.*

These songs by their very beauty cross over from the little storefronts and the like occupied by the "Saints" to the larger and more fashionable congregations and from there to the great world. These more conscious church-goers, despising these humble tune-makers as they do always resist these songs as long as possible, but finally succumb to their charm. So that it is ridiculous to say that the spirituals are the Negro's "sorrow songs." For just as many are being made in this post-slavery period as ever were made in slavery as far as anyone can find. At any rate the people who are now making spirituals are the same as those who made them in the past and not the self-conscious propagandist that our latter-day pity men would have us believe. They sang sorrowful phrases then as they do now because they sounded well, and not because of the thought-content.

Examples of new spirituals that have become widely known:

1. *He Is a Lion of the House of David*
2. *Stand By Me*
3. *This Little Light I Got*
4. *I Want Two Wings*
5. *I'm Going Home on the Morning Train*
6. *I'm Your Child*

There are some crude anthems made also among these singers.

O Lord, O Lord

1. O Lord, O Lord, let the words of my mouth, O Lord
   Let the words of my mouth, meditations of my heart
   Be accepted in Thy sight, O Lord.

(From the   Psalm, "Let the words of my mouth and the meditation of my heart be accepted in thy sight, O Lord.")

2. Beloved, beloved, Now are we the sons of God
   And it doth not yet appear what we shall be
   But we know, but we know, but we know, but we know
   When He shall appear, when He shall appear
   When He shall appear, when He shall appear
   We shall be like Him, we shall be like Him
   We shall see Him as He is.

(St. Paul: Beloved, now are we the sons of God but it doth not yet appear what we shall be. But we know that when He shall appear we shall be like Him and see Him as He is.)

The Saints, or the Sanctified Church is a revitalizing element in Negro music and religion. It is putting back into Negro religion those elements which were brought over from Africa and grafted onto Christianity as soon as the Negro came in contact with it, but which are being rooted out as the American Negro approaches white concepts. The people who make up the sanctified groups, while admiring the white brother in many ways think him ridiculous in church. They feel that the white man is too cut and dried and business-like to be of much use in a service. There is a well-distributed folk-tale depicting a white man praying in church that never fails to bring roars of laughter when it is told. The writer first found the story in Polk county but later found it all over the south.

THE WHITE MAN'S PRAYER

It had been a long dry spell and every body had done worried about the crops so they thought they better hold a prayer meeting about it and ask God for some rain. So they asked Brother John to send up the prayer because everybody said that he was really a good man if there was one in the county. So brother John got down on his knees in the meeting and begin to pray, and this is how he prayed:

"O Lahd (this pronunciation is always stressed and always brings a laugh). The first thing I want you to understand is that this is a white man talking to you. This ain't no nigger whooping and hollering for something and then don't know what to do with it after he gits it.

"This is a white man talking to you and I want you to pay me some attention. Now in the first place, Lahd, we would like a little rain. It's been powerful dry round here and we needs rain mighty bad. But don't come in no storm like you did last year. Come cam (calm) and gentle and water our crops. And now another thing, Lahd, don't let these niggers be as sassy this coming year as they have in the past. That's all, Lahd, AMEN."

The real, singing Negro derides the Negro who adopts the white man's religious ways in the same manner. They say of that type of preacher, "Why he don't preach at all. He just lectures." And the way they say the word "lecture" makes it sound like horse-stealing. "Why, he sound like a white man preaching." There is great respect for the white man as a law-giver, banker, builder and the like, but the folk Negro do not crave his religion at all. They are not angry about it, they merely pity him because it is generally held that he just can't do any better that way. But the Negro who imitates the whites comes in for spitting scorn. So they let him have his big solemn church all to himself while they go on making their songs and music and dance motions to go along with it, and shooting new life into American music. I say American music because it has long been established that the tunes from the street and the church change places often. So they go on unknowingly influencing American music and enjoying themselves hugely while doing so, in spite of the derision from the outside.

It is to be noted the strong sympathy between the white "saints" and the Negro ones. They attend each others' meetings frequently, and it is interesting to see the white saint attempting the same rhythms and movements. Often the preacher preaches the sermon (in the Negro manner) and the Negroes carry on the singing. Even the definite African "possession" attitudes of dancing mostly on one foot and stumbling about to a loose rhythm is attempted. These same steps can be seen in Haiti when a man or a woman is "mounted" by a loa, or spirit.

ART AND SUCH

When the scope of American art is viewed as a whole, the contributions of the Negro are found to be small, if we exclude the anonymous folk creations of music tales and dances. One immediately takes into consideration that only three generations separate the Negro from the muteness of slavery, and recognizes that creation is in its stumbling infancy.

Taking things as time goes we have first the long mute period of slavery during which many undreamed-of geniuses must have lived and died. Folk tales and music tell us this much. Then the hurly-burly of the Reconstruction and what followed when the black mouth became vocal. But nothing creative came out of this period because this new man, this first talking black man, was necessarily concerned with his newness. The old world he used to know had been turned upside down and so made new for him, naturally engaged his wonder and attention. Therefore and, in consequence, he had to spend some time, a generation or two, talking out his thoughts and feelings he had during centuries of silence.

He rejoiced with the realization of old dreams and he cried new cries for wounds that had become scars. It was the age of cries. If it seems monotonous one remembers the ex-slave had the pitying ear of the world. He had the encouragement of Northern sympathizers.

In spite of the fact that no creative artist who means anything to the Arts of Florida, the United States nor the world came out of this period, those first twenty-five years are of tremendous importance no matter which way you look at it. What went on inside the Negro was of more importance than the turbulent doings going on external of him. This post-war generation time was a matrix from which certain ideas came that have seriously affected art creation as well as every other form of Negro expression, including the economic.

Out of this period of sound and emotion came the Race Man and Race Woman; that great horde of individuals known as "Race Champions." The great Frederick Douglass was the original pattern, no doubt, for these people who went up and down the land making speeches so fixed in type as to become a folk pattern. But Douglass had the combination of a great cause and the propitious moment as a setting for his talents and he became a famous man. These others had the wish to be heard and a set of phrases so they became "Race" Men or Women as the case might be. It was the era of tongue and lung. The "leaders" loved to speak and the new-freed field hands loved gatherings and brave words, so the tribe increased.

It was so easy to become a Race Leader in those days. So few Negroes knew how to read and write that any black man who was proficient in these arts was something to be wondered at. What had been looked upon as something that only the brains of the master-kind could cope with was done by a black person! Astonishing! He must be exceptional to do all that! He was a leader, and went north to his life work of talking the race problem. He could and did teach school like white folks. If he was not "called to preach" he most certainly was made a teacher and either of these positions made him a local leader. The idea grew and traveled. When the first Negroes entered northern colleges even the northern whites were tremendously impressed. It was apparent that while setting the slaves free they had declared the equality of men, they did not actually believe any such thing except as voting power. To see a Negro enter Yale to attempt to master the same courses as the whites was something to marvel over. To see one actually take a degree at Harvard, let us say, was a miracle. The phenomenon was made over and pampered. He was told so often that his mentality stood him alone among his kind and that it was a tragic accident that made him a Negro that he came to believe it himself and struck the tragic pose. Naturally he became a leader. Any Negro who graduated from a white school automatically became a national leader and as such could give opinions on anything at all in which the word Negro occurred. But it had to be sad. Any Negro who had all that brains to be taking a degree at a white college was bound to know every thought and feeling of every other Negro in America, however remote from him, and he was bound to feel sad. It was assumed that no Negro brain could ever grasp the curriculum of a white college, so the black man who did had come by some white folk's brain by accident and there was bound to be conflict between his dark body and his white mind. Hence the stultifying doctrine that has not altogether been laughed out of existence at the present. In spite of the thousands and thousands of Negro graduates of good colleges, in spite of hundreds of graduates of New England and Western Colleges, there are gray-haired graduates of New England colleges still clutching at the vapors of uniqueness. Despite the fact that Negroes have distinguished themselves in every major field of activity in the nation some of the left-overs still grab at the mantle of "Race Leader." Just let them hear that white people have curiosity about some activity among Negroes, and these "leaders" will not let their shirt-tails touch them (i.e. sit down) until they have rushed forward and offered themselves as an authority on the subject whether they have ever heard of it before or not. In the very face of a situation as different from the 1880s as chalk is from cheese, they stand around and mouth the same trite phrases, and try their practised-best to look sad. They call spirituals "Our Sorrow Songs" and other such tom-foolery in an effort to get into the spotlight if possible without having ever done anything to improve education, industry, invention, art and never having uttered a quotable line. Though he is being jostled about these days and paid scant attention, the Race Man is still with us—he and his Reconstruction pulings. His job today is to rush around seeking for something he can "resent."

How has this Race attitude affected the Arts in Florida? In Florida as elsewhere in America this background has worked the mind of the creator. Can the black poet sing a song to the morning? Upsprings the song to his lips but it is fought back. He says to himself, "Ah this is a beautiful song inside me. I feel the morning star in my throat. I will sing of the star and the morning." Then his background thrusts itself between his lips and the star and he mutters, "Ought I not to be singing of our sorrows? That is what is expected of me and I shall be considered forgetful of our past and present. If I do not some will even call me a coward. The one subject for a Negro is the Race and its sufferings and so the song of the morning must be choked back. I will write of a lynching instead." So the same old theme, the same old phrases get done again to the detriment of art. To him no Negro exists as an individual—he exists only as another tragic unit of the Race. This in spite of the obvious fact that Negroes love and hate and fight and play and strive and travel and have a thousand and one interests in life like other humans. When his baby cuts a new tooth he brags as shamelessly as anyone else without once weeping over the prospect of some Klansman knocking it out when and if the child ever gets grown. The Negro artist knows all this but he conceives that a Negro can do nothing but weave something in his particular art form about the Race problem. The writer thinks that he has been brave in following in the groove of the Race champions, when the truth is, it is the line of least resistance and least originality—certain to be approved of by the "champions" who want to hear the same thing over and over again even though they already know it by heart, and certain to be unread by everybody else. It is the

same thing as waving the American flag in a poorly constructed play. Anyway, the effect of the whole period has been
to fix activities in a mold that precluded originality and denied
creation in the arts.

Results:

In painting one artist, O. Richard Reid of Fernandina
who at one time created a stir in New York Art Circles with
his portraits of Fannie Hurst, John Barrymore and H. L.
Mencken. Of his recent works we hear nothing.

In sculpture, Augusta Savage of Green Cove Springs is
making greater and greater contributions to what is significant in American Art. Her subjects are Negroid for the most
part but any sort of preachment is absent from her art. She
seems striving to reach out to the rimbones of nothing and in
so doing she touches a responsive chord in the universe and
grows in stature.

The world of music has been enriched by the talents of J.
Rosamond Johnson, a Jacksonville Negro. His range has been
from light and frivolous tunes of musical comedy designed to
merely entertain to some beautiful arrangements of spirituals
which have been sung all over the world in concert halls. His
truly great composition is the air which accompanies the
words of the so-called "Negro National Anthem." The bitter-
sweet poem is by his brother James Weldon Johnson.

Though it is not widely known, there is a house in Fernandina, Florida whose interior is beautifully decorated in
original wood-carving. It is the work of the late Brooks
Thompson who was born a slave. Without ever having known
anything about African Art, he has achieved something very
close to African concepts on the walls, doors and ceilings of
three rooms. His doors are things of wondrous beauty. The
greater part of the work was done after he was in his seven-
ties. "The feeling just came and I did it," is his explanation of
how the carpenter turned wood-carver in his old age.

In literature Florida has two names: James Weldon Johnson, of many talents and Zora Neale Hurston. As a poet
Johnson wrote scattered bits of verse, and he wrote lyrics for
the music of his brother Rosamond. Then he wrote the
campaign song for Theodore Roosevelt's campaign, "You're
Alright Teddy" which swept the nation. After Theodore

Roosevelt was safe in the White House he appointed the poet as Consul to Venezuela. The time came when Johnson published volumes of verse and collected a volume of Negro sermons which he published under the title of *God's Trombones.* Among his most noted prose works are "The Autobiography of an Ex-Colored Man," *Black Manhattan* and his story of his own life, *Along This Way.*

Zora Neale Hurston won critical acclaim for two new things in Negro fiction. The first was an objective point of view. The subjective view was so universal that it had come to be taken for granted. When her first book, *Jonah's Gourd Vine,* a novel, appeared in 1934, the critics announced across the nation, "Here at last is a Negro story without bias. The characters live and move. The story is about Negroes but it could be anybody. It is the first time that a Negro story has been offered without special pleading. The characters in the story are seen in relation to themselves and not in relation to the whites as has been the rule. To watch these people one would conclude that there were no white people in the world. The author is an artist that will go far."

The second element that attracted attention was the telling of the story in the idiom—not the dialect—of the Negro. The Negro's poetical flow of language, his thinking in images and figures was called to the attention of the outside world. It gave verisimilitude to the narrative by stewing the subject in its own juice.

Zora Hurston is the author of three other books, "Mules and Men," "Their Eyes Were Watching God" (published also in England; translated into the Italian by Ada Prospero and published in Rome), and "Tell My Horse."

It is not to be concluded from these meager offerings in the arts that Negro talent is lacking. There has been a cruel waste of genius during the long generations of slavery. There has been a squandering of genius during the three generations since Surrender on Race. So the Negro begins feeling with his fingers to find himself in the plastic arts. He is well established in music, but still a long way to go to overtake his possibilities. In literature the first writings have been little more than the putting into writing the sayings of the Race Men and

Women and champions of "Race Consciousness." So that what was produced was a self-conscious document lacking in drama, analysis, characterization and the universal oneness necessary to literature. But the idea was not to produce literature—it was to "champion the Race." The Fourteenth and Fifteenth Amendments got some pretty hard wear and that sentence "You have made the *greatest* progress in so and so many years" was all the art in the literature in the purpose and period.

But one finds on all hands the weakening of race consciousness, impatience with Race Champions and a growing taste for literature as such. The wedge has entered the great inert mass and one may expect some noble things from the Florida Negro in Art in the next decade.

Written for the Florida Federal Writers' Project,
The Florida Negro (unpublished), 1938

Stories of Conflict

UNCLE TOM'S CHILDREN. By Richard Wright. New York: Harper & Bros. (The Story Press.) 1938. $2.50.

THIS IS a book about hatreds. Mr. Wright serves notice by his title that he speaks of people in revolt, and his stories are so grim that the Dismal Swamp of race hatred must be where they live. Not one act of understanding and sympathy comes to pass in the entire work.

But some bright new lines to remember come flashing from the author's pen. Some of his sentences have the shocking-power of a forty-four. That means that he knows his way around among words. With his facility, one wonders what he would have done had he dealt with plots that touched the broader and more fundamental phases of Negro life instead of confining himself to the spectacular. For, though he has handled himself well, numerous Negro writers, published and unpublished, have written of this same kind of incident. It is the favorite Negro theme just as how the stenographer or some other poor girl won the boss or the boss's son is the favorite white theme. What is new in the four novelettes included in Mr. Wright's book is the wish-fulfillment theme. In each story the hero suffers but he gets his man.

In the first story, "Big Boy Leaves Home," the hero, Big Boy, takes the gun away from a white soldier after he has shot two of his chums and kills the white man. His chum is lynched, but Big Boy gets away. In the second story there is a flood on the Mississippi and in a fracas over a stolen rowboat, the hero gets the white owner of the boat and is later shot to death himself. He is a stupid, blundering character, but full of pathos. But then all the characters in this book are elemental and brutish. In the third story, the hero gets the white man most Negro men rail against—the white man who possesses a Negro woman. He gets several of them while he is about the business of choosing to die in a hurricane of bullets and fire because his woman has had a white man. There is lavish killing here, perhaps enough to satisfy all male black readers. In the fourth story neither the hero nor his adversary is killed, but the white foe bites the dust just the same. And in this story is summed up the conclusions that the other three stories have been moving towards.

In the other three stories the reader sees the picture of the South that the communists have been passing around of late. A dismal, hopeless section ruled by brutish hatred and nothing else. Mr. Wright's author's solution, is the solution of the PARTY—state responsibility for everything and individual responsibility for nothing, not even feeding one's self. And march!

Since the author himself is a Negro, his dialect is a puzzling thing. One wonders how he arrived at it. Certainly he does not write by ear unless he is tone-deaf. But aside from the broken speech of his characters, the book contains some beautiful writing. One hopes that Mr. Wright will find in Negro life a vehicle for his talents.

The Saturday Review, April 2, 1938

The "Pet Negro" System

Brothers and Sisters, I take my text this morning from the Book of Dixie. I take my text and I take my time.

Now it says here, "And every white man shall be allowed to pet himself a Negro. Yea, he shall take a black man unto himself to pet and to cherish, and this same Negro shall be perfect in his sight. Nor shall hatred among the races of men, nor conditions of strife in the walled cities, cause his pride and pleasure in his own Negro to wane."

Now, belov-ed Brothers and Sisters, I see you have all woke up and you can't wait till the service is over to ask me how come? So I will read you further from the sacred word which says here:

"Thus spake the Prophet of Dixie when slavery was yet a young thing, for he saw the yearning in the hearts of men. And the dwellers in the bleak North, they who pass old-made phrases through their mouths, shall cry out and say, 'What are these strange utterances? Is it not written that the hand of every white man in the South is raised against his black brother? Do not the sons of Japheth drive the Hammites before them like beasts? Do they not lodge them in shacks and hovels and force them to share the crops? Is not the condition of black men in the South most horrible? Then how doth this scribe named Hurston speak of pet Negroes? Perchance she hath drunk of new wine, and it has stung her like an adder?' "

Now, my belov-ed, before you explode in fury you might look to see if you know your facts or if you merely know your phrases. It happens that there are more angles to this race-adjustment business than are ever pointed out to the public, white, black or in-between. Well-meaning outsiders make plans that look perfect from where they sit, possibly in some New York office. But these plans get wrecked on hidden snags. John Brown at Harpers Ferry is a notable instance. The simple race-agin-race pattern of those articles and speeches on the subject is not that simple at all. The actual conditions do not jibe with the fulminations of the so-called spokesmen of the white South, nor with the rhetoric of the champions of the Negro cause either.

II

Big men like Bilbo, Heflin and Tillman bellow threats which they know they couldn't carry out even in their own districts. The orators at both extremes may glint and glitter in generalities, but the South lives and thinks in individuals. The North has no interest in the particular Negro, but talks of justice for the whole. The South has no interest, and pretends none, in the mass of Negroes but is very much concerned about the individual. So that brings us to the pet Negro, because to me at least it symbolizes the web of feelings and mutual dependencies spun by generations and generations of living together and natural adjustment. It isn't half as pretty as the ideal adjustment of theorizers, but it's a lot more real and durable, and a lot of black folk, I'm afraid, find it mighty cosy.

The pet Negro, belov-ed, is someone whom a particular white person or persons wants to have and to do all the things forbidden to other Negroes. It can be Aunt Sue, Uncle Stump, or the black man at the head of some Negro organization. Let us call him John Harper. John is the pet of Colonel Cary and his lady, and Colonel Cary swings a lot of weight in his community.

The Colonel will tell you that he opposes higher education for Negroes. It makes them mean and cunning. Bad stuff for Negroes. He is against having lovely, simple blacks turned into rascals by too much schooling. But there are exceptions. Take John, for instance. Worked hard, saved up his money and went up there to Howard University and got his degree in education. Smart as a whip! Seeing that John had such a fine head, of course he helped John out when necessary. Not that he would do such a thing for the average darky, no sir! He is no nigger lover. Strictly unconstructed Southerner, willing to battle for white supremacy! But his John is different.

So naturally when John finished college and came home, Colonel Cary knew he was the very man to be principal of the Negro high school, and John got the post even though some-

one else had to be eased out. And making a fine job of it.
Decent, self-respecting fellow. Built himself a nice home and
bought himself a nice car. John's wife is county nurse; the
Colonel spoke to a few people about it and she got the job.
John's children are smart and have good manners. If all the
Negroes were like them he wouldn't mind what advancement
they made. But the rest of them, of course, lie like the cross-
ties from New York to Key West. They steal things and get
drunk. Too bad, but Negroes are like that.

Now there are some prominent white folk who don't see
eye to eye with Colonel Cary about this John Harper. They
each have a Negro in mind who is far superior to John. They
listen to eulogies about John only because they wish to be
listened to about their own pets. They pull strings for the
Colonel's favorites knowing that they will get the same thing
done for theirs.

Now, how can the Colonel make his attitude towards John
Harper jibe with his general attitude towards Negros? Easy
enough. He got his general attitude by tradition, and he has
no quarrel with it. But he found John truthful and honest,
clean, reliable and a faithful friend. He *likes* John and so considers him as white inside as anyone else. The treatment made
and provided for Negroes generally is suspended, restrained
and done away with. He knows that John is able to learn what
white people of similar opportunities learn. Colonel Cary's
affection and respect for John, however, in no way extend to
black folk in general.

When you understand that, you see why it is so difficult to
change certain things in the South. His particular Negroes are
not suffering from the strictures, and the rest are no concern
of the Colonel's. Let their own white friends do for them. If
they are worth the powder and lead it would take to kill
them, they have white friends; if not, then they belong in the
"stray nigger" class and nobody gives a damn about them. If
John should happen to get arrested for anything except assault and murder upon the person of a white man, or rape,
the Colonel is going to stand by him and get him out. It
would be a hard-up Negro who would work for a man who
couldn't get his black friends out of jail.

And mind you, the Negroes have their pet whites, so to

speak. It works both ways. Class-consciousness of Negroes is an angle to be reckoned with in the South. They love to be associated with "the quality" and consequently are ashamed to admit that they are working for "strainers." It is amusing to see a Negro servant chasing the madam or the boss back on his or her pedestal when they behave in an unbecoming manner. Thereby he is to a certain extent preserving his own prestige, derived from association with that family.

If ever it came to the kind of violent showdown the orators hint at, you could count on all the Colonel Carys tipping off and protecting their John Harpers; and you could count on all the John Harpers and Aunt Sues to exempt their special white folk. And that means that pretty nearly everybody on both sides would be exempt, except the "pore white trash" and the "stray niggers," and not all of them.

III

An outsider driving through a street of well-off Negro homes, seeing the great number of high-priced cars, will wonder why he has never heard of this side of Negro life in the South. He has heard about the shacks and the sharecroppers. He has had them before him in literature and editorials and crusading journals. But the other side isn't talked about by the champions of white supremacy, because it makes their stand, and their stated reasons for keeping the Negro down, look a bit foolish. The Negro crusaders and their white adherents can't talk about it because it is obviously bad strategy. The worst aspects must be kept before the public to force action.

It has been so generally accepted that all Negroes in the South are living under horrible conditions that many friends of the Negro up North actually take offense if you don't tell them a tale of horror and suffering. They stroll up to you, cocktail glass in hand, and say, "I am a friend of the Negro, you know, and feel awful about the terrible conditions down there." That's your cue to launch into atrocities amidst murmurs of sympathy. If, on the other hand, just to find out if they really have done some research down there, you ask, "What conditions do you refer to?" you get an injured, and sometimes a malicious, look. Why ask foolish questions? Why drag in the many Negroes of opulence and education? Yet these comfortable, contented Negroes are as real as the share-croppers.

There is, in normal times, a regular stream of high-powered cars driven by Negroes headed North each summer for a few weeks' vacation. These people go, have their fling, and hurry back home. Doctors, teachers, lawyers, businessmen, they are living and working in the South because that is where they want to be. And why not? Economically, they are at ease and more. The professional men do not suffer from the competition of their white colleagues to anything like they do up North. Personal vanity, too, is served. The South makes a sharp distinction between the upper-class and lower-class Negro. Businessmen cater to him. His word is *good* downtown. There is some Mr. Big in the background who is interested in him and will back his fall. All the plums that a Negro can get are dropped in his mouth. He wants no part of the cold, impersonal North. He notes that there is segregation and discrimination up there, too, with none of the human touches of the South.

As I have said, belov-ed, these Negroes who are petted by white friends think just as much of their friends across the line. There is a personal attachment that will ride over practically anything that is liable to happen to either. They have their fingers crossed, too, when they say they don't like white people. "White people" does not mean their particular friends, any more than niggers means John Harper to the Colonel. This is important. For anyone, or any group, counting on a solid black South, or a solid white South in opposition to each other will run into a hornet's nest if he discounts these personal relations. Both sides admit the general principle of opposition, but when it comes to putting it into practice, behold what happens. There is a quibbling, a stalling, a backing and filling that nullifies all the purple oratory.

So well is this underground hook-up established, that it is not possible to keep a secret from either side. Nearly everybody spills the beans to his favorite on the other side of the color line—in strictest confidence, of course. That's how the "petting system" works in the South.

Is it a good thing or a bad thing? Who am I to pass judgment? I am not defending the system, belov-ed, but trying to explain it. The lowdown fact is that it weaves a kind of basic fabric that tends to stabilize relations and give something to work from in adjustments. It works to prevent hasty explosions. There are some people in every community who can always talk things over. It may be the proof that this race situation in America is not entirely hopeless and may even be worked out eventually.

There are dangers in the system. Too much depends on the integrity of the Negro so trusted. It cannot be denied that this trust has been abused at times. What was meant for the whole community has been turned to personal profit by the pet. Negroes have long groaned because of this frequent diversion of general favors into the channels of private benefits. Why do we not go to Mr. Big and expose the Negro in question? Sometimes it is because we do not like to let white people know that we have folks of that ilk. Sometimes we make a bad face and console ourselves, "At least one Negro has gotten himself a sinecure not usually dealt out to us." We curse him for a yellow-bellied sea-buzzard, a ground-mole and a woods-pussy, call him a white-folkses nigger, an Uncle Tom, and a handkerchief-head and let it go at that. In all fairness, it must be said that these terms are often flung around out of jealousy: somebody else would like the very cinch that the accused has grabbed himself.

But when everything is discounted, it still remains true that white people North and South have promoted Negroes—usually in the capacity of "representing the Negro"—with little thought of the ability of the person promoted but in line with the "pet system." In the South it can be pointed to scornfully as a residue of feudalism; in the North no one says *what* it is. And that, too, is part of the illogical, indefensible but somehow useful "pet system."

IV

The most powerful reason why Negroes do not do more about false "representation" by pets is that they know from experience that the thing is too deep-rooted to be budged.

The appointer has his reasons, personal or political. He can always point to the beneficiary and say, "Look, Negroes, you have been taken care of. Didn't I give a member of your group a big job?" White officials assume that the Negro element is satisfied and they do not know what to make of it when later they find that so large a body of Negroes charge indifference and double-dealing. The white friend of the Negroes mumbles about ingratitude and decides that you simply can't understand Negroes . . . just like children.

A case in point is Dr. James E. Shepard, President of the North Carolina State College for Negroes. He has a degree in pharmacy, and no other. For years he ran a one-horse religious school of his own at Durham, North Carolina. But he has always been in politics and has some good friends in power at Raleigh. So the funds for the State College for Negroes were turned over to him, and his little church school became the Negro college so far as that State is concerned. A fine set of new buildings has been erected. With a host of Negro men highly trained as educators within the State, not to mention others who could be brought in, a pharmacist heads up higher education for Negroes in North Carolina. North Carolina can't grasp why Negroes aren't perfectly happy and grateful.

In every community there is some Negro strong man or woman whose word is going to go. In Jacksonville, Florida, for instance, there is Eartha White. You better see Eartha if you want anything from the white powers-that-be. She happens to be tremendously interested in helping the unfortunates of her city and she does get many things for them from the whites.

I have white friends with whom I would, and do, stand when they have need of me, race counting for nothing at all. Just friendship. All the well-known Negroes could honestly make the same statement. I mean that they all have strong attachments across the line whether they intended them in the beginning or not. Carl Van Vechten and Henry Allen Moe could ask little of me that would be refused. Walter White, the best known race champion of our time, is hand and glove with Supreme Court Justice Black, a native of Alabama and an ex-Klansman. So you see how this friendship business makes a sorry mess of all the rules made and provided. James Weldon Johnson, the crusader for Negro rights, was bogged to his neck in white friends whom he loved and who loved him. Dr. William E. Burkhardt DuBois, the bitterest opponent of the white race that America has ever known, loved Joel Spingarn and was certainly loved in turn by him. The thing doesn't make sense. It just makes beauty.

Friendship, however it comes about, is a beautiful thing. The Negro who loves a white friend is shy in admitting it because he dreads the epithet "white folks' nigger!" The white man is wary of showing too much warmth for his black friends for fear of being called "nigger-lover," so he explains his attachment by extolling the extraordinary merits of his black friend to gain tolerance for it.

This is the inside picture of things, as I see it. Whether you like it or not, is no concern of mine. But it is an important thing to know if you have any plans for racial manipulations in Dixie. You cannot batter in doors down there, and you can save time and trouble, and I do mean trouble, by hunting up the community keys.

In a way, it is a great and heartening tribute to human nature. It will be bound by nothing. The South frankly acknowledged this long ago in its laws against marriage between blacks and whites. If the Southern law-makers were so sure that racial antipathy would take care of racial purity, there would have been no need for the laws.

"And no man shall seek to deprive a man of his Pet Negro. It shall be unwritten-lawful for any to seek to prevent him in his pleasure thereof. Thus spoke the Prophet of Dixie." *Selah.*

The American Mercury, May 1943

High John de Conquer

MAYBE, now, we used-to-be black African folks can be of some help to our brothers and sisters who have always been white. You will take another look at us and say that we are still black and, ethnologically speaking, you will be right. But nationally and culturally, we are as white as the next one. We have put our labor and our blood into the common causes for a long time. We have given the rest of the nation song and laughter. Maybe now, in this terrible struggle, we can give something else — the source and soul of our laughter and song. We offer you our hope-bringer, High John de Conquer.

High John de Conquer came to be a man, and a mighty man at that. But he was not a natural man in the beginning. First off, he was a whisper, a will to hope, a wish to find something worthy of laughter and song. Then the whisper put on flesh. His footsteps sounded across the world in a low but musical rhythm as if the world he walked on was a singing-drum. The black folks had an irresistible impulse to laugh. High John de Conquer was a man in full, and had come to live and work on the plantations, and all the slave folks knew him in the flesh.

The sign of this man was a laugh, and his singing-symbol was a drum-beat. No parading drum-shout like soldiers out for show. It did not call to the feet of those who were fixed to hear it. It was an inside thing to live by. It was sure to be heard when and where the work was the hardest, and the lot the most cruel. It helped the slaves endure. They knew that something better was coming. So they laughed in the face of things and sang, "I'm so glad! Trouble don't last always." And the white people who heard them were struck dumb that they could laugh. In an outside way, this was Old Massa's fun, so what was Old Cuffy laughing for?

Old Massa couldn't know, of course, but High John de Conquer was there walking his plantation like a natural man. He was treading the sweat-flavored clods of the plantation, crushing out his drum tunes, and giving out secret laughter.

He walked on the winds and moved fast. Maybe he was in Texas when the lash fell on a slave in Alabama, but before the blood was dry on the back he was there. A faint pulsing of a drum like a goatskin stretched over a heart, that came nearer and closer, then somebody in the saddened quarters would feel like laughing, and say, "Now, High John de Conquer, Old Massa couldn't get the best of *him*. That old John was a case!" Then everybody sat up and began to smile. Yes, yes, that was right. Old John, High John could beat the unbeatable. He was top-superior to the whole mess of sorrow. He could beat it all, and what made it so cool, finish it off with a laugh. So they pulled the covers up over their souls and kept them from all hurt, harm and danger and made them a laugh and a song. Night time was a joke, because daybreak was on the way. Distance and the impossible had no power over High John de Conquer.

He had come from Africa. He came walking on the waves of sound. Then he took on flesh after he got here. The sea captains of ships knew that they brought slaves in their ships. They knew about those black bodies huddled down there in the middle passage, being hauled across the waters to helplessness. John de Conquer was walking the very winds that filled the sails of the ships. He followed over them like the albatross.

It is no accident that High John de Conquer has evaded the ears of white people. They were not supposed to know. You can't know what folks won't tell you. If they, the white people, heard some scraps, they could not understand because they had nothing to hear things like that with. They were not looking for any hope in those days, and it was not much of a strain for them to find something to laugh over. Old John would have been out of place for them.

Old Massa met our hope-bringer all right, but when Old Massa met him, he was not going by his right name. He was traveling, and touristing around the plantations as the laugh-provoking Brer Rabbit. So Old Massa and Old Miss and their young ones laughed with and at Brer Rabbit and wished him well. And all the time, there was High John de Conquer playing his tricks of making a way out of no-way. Hitting a straight lick with a crooked stick. Winning the jack pot with no other stake but a laugh. Fighting a mighty battle without outside-showing force, and winning his war from within. Really winning in a permanent way, for he was winning with the soul of the black man whole and free. So he could use it afterwards. For what shall it profit a man if he gain the whole world, and lose his own soul? You would have nothing but a cruel, vengeful, grasping monster come to power. John de Conquer was a bottom-fish. He was deep. He had the wisdom tooth of the East in his head. Way over there, where the sun rises a day ahead of time, they say that Heaven arms with love and laughter those it does not wish to see destroyed. He who carries his heart in his sword must perish. So says the ultimate law. High John de Conquer knew a lot of things like that. He who wins from within is in the "Be" class. *Be* here when the ruthless man comes, and *be* here when he is gone.

Moreover, John knew that it is written where it cannot be erased, that nothing shall live on human flesh and prosper. Old Maker said that before He made any more sayings. Even a man-eating tiger and lion can teach a person that much. His flabby muscles and mangy hide can teach an emperor right from wrong. If the emperor would only listen.

II

There is no established picture of what sort of looking-man this John de Conquer was. To some, he was a big, physical-looking man like John Henry. To others, he was a little, hammered-down, low-built man like the Devil's doll-baby. Some said that they never heard what he looked like. Nobody told them, but he lived on the plantation where their old folks were slaves. He is not so well known to the present generation of colored people in the same way that he was in slavery time. Like King Arthur of England, he has served his people, and gone back into mystery again. And, like King Arthur, he is not dead. He waits to return when his people shall call again. Symbolic of English power, Arthur came out of the water, and with Excalibur, went back into the water again. High John de Conquer went back to Africa, but he left his power here, and placed his American dwelling in the root of a certain plant. Only possess that root, and he can be summoned at any time.

"Of course, High John de Conquer got plenty power!" Aunt Shady Anne Sutton bristled at me when I asked her about him. She took her pipe out of her mouth and stared at me out of her deeply wrinkled face. "I hope you ain't one of these here smart colored folks that done got so they don't believe nothing, and come here questionizing me so you can have something to poke fun at. Done got shamed of the things that brought us through. Make out 'tain't no such thing no more."

When I assured her that that was not the case, she went on.

"Sho John de Conquer means power. That's bound to be so. He come to teach and tell us. God don't leave nobody ignorant, you child. Don't care where He drops you down, He puts you on a notice. He don't want folks taken advantage of because they don't know. Now, back there in slavery time, us didn't have no power of protection, and God knowed it, and put us under watch-care. Rattlesnakes never bit no colored folks until four years after freedom was declared That was to give us time to learn and to know. 'Course, I don't know nothing about slavery personal like. I wasn't born till two years after the Big Surrender. Then I wasn't nothing but a infant baby when I was born, so I couldn't know nothing but what they told me. My mama told me, and I know that she wouldn't mislead me, how High John de Conquer helped us out. He had done teached the black folks so they knowed a hundred years ahead of time that freedom was coming. Long before the white folks knowed anything about it at all.

"These young Negroes reads they books and talk about the war freeing the Negroes, but Aye, Lord! A heap sees, but a few knows. 'Course, the war was a lot of help, but how come the war took place? They think they knows, but they don't. John de Conquer had done put it into the white folks to give us our freedom, that's what. Old Massa fought against it, but us could have told him that it wasn't no use. Freedom just *had* to come. The time set aside for it was there. That war was just a sign and a symbol of the thing. That's the truth! If I tell the truth about everything as good as I do about that, I can go straight to Heaven without a prayer."

Aunt Shady Anne was giving the inside feeling and meaning to the outside laughs around John de Conquer. He romps, he clowns, and looks ridiculous, but if you will, you can read something deeper behind it all. He is loping on off from the Tar Baby with a laugh.

Take, for instance, those words he had with Old Massa about stealing pigs.

Old John was working in Old Massa's house that time, serving around the eating table. Old Massa loved roasted young pigs, and had them often for dinner. Old John loved them too, but Massa never allowed the slaves to eat any at all. Even put aside the left-over and ate it next time. John de Conquer got tired of that. He took to stopping by the pig pen when he had a strong taste for pig-meat, and getting himself one, and taking it on down to his cabin and cooking it.

Massa began to miss his pigs, and made up his mind to squat for who was taking them and give whoever it was a good hiding. So John kept on taking pigs, and one night Massa walked him down. He stood out there in the dark and saw John kill the pig and went on back to the "big house" and waited till he figured John had it dressed and cooking. Then he went on down to the quarters and knocked on John's door.

"Who dat?" John called out big and bold, because he never dreamed that it was Massa rapping.

"It's me, John," Massa told him. "I want to come in."

"What you want, Massa? I'm coming right out."

"You needn't do that, John. I want to come in."

"Naw, naw, Massa. You don't want to come into no old slave cabin. Youse too fine a man for that. It would hurt my feelings to see you in a place like this here one."

"I tell you I want to come in, John!"

So John had to open the door and let Massa in. John had seasoned that pig *down*, and it was stinking pretty! John knowed Old Massa couldn't help but smell it. Massa talked on about the crops and hound dogs and one thing and another, and the pot with the pig in it was hanging over the fire in the chimney and kicking up. The smell got better and better.

Way after while, when that pig had done simbled down to a low gravy, Massa said, "John, what's that you cooking in that pot?"

"Nothing but a little old weasly possum, Massa. Sickliest little old possum I ever did see. But I thought I'd cook him anyhow."

"Get a plate and give me some of it, John. I'm hungry."

"Aw, naw, Massa, you ain't hongry."

"Now, John, I don't mean to argue with you another minute. You give me some of that in the pot, or I mean to have the hide off of your back tomorrow morning. Give it to me!"

So John got up and went and got a plate and a fork and went to the pot. He lifted the lid and looked at Massa and told him, "Well, Massa, I put this thing in here a possum, but if it comes out a pig, it ain't no fault of mine."

Old Massa didn't want to laugh, but he did before he caught himself. He took the plate of brownded-down pig and ate it up. He never said nothing, but he gave John and all the other house servants roast pig at the big house after that.

III

John had numerous scrapes and tight squeezes, but he usually came out like Brer Rabbit. Pretty occasionally, though, Old Massa won the hand. The curious thing about this is, that there are no bitter tragic tales at all. When Old Massa won, the thing ended up in a laugh just the same. Laughter at the expense of the slave, but laughter right on. A sort of recognition that life is not one-sided. A sense of humor that said, "We are just as ridiculous as anybody else. We can be wrong, too."

There are many tales, and variants of each, of how the Negro got his freedom through High John de Conquer. The best one deals with a plantation where the work was hard, and Old Massa mean. Even Old Miss used to pull her maids' ears with hot firetongs when they got her riled. So, naturally, Old John de Conquer was around that plantation a lot.

"What we need is a song," he told the people after he had

figured the whole thing out. "It ain't here, and it ain't no place I knows of as yet. Us better go hunt around. This has got to be a particular piece of singing."

But the slaves were scared to leave. They knew what Old Massa did for any slave caught running off.

"Oh, Old Massa don't need to know you gone from here. How? Just leave your old work-tired bodies around for him to look at, and he'll never realize youse way off somewhere, going about your business."

At first they wouldn't hear to John, that is, some of them. But, finally, the weak gave in to the strong, and John told them to get ready to go while he went off to get something for them to ride on. They were all gathered up under a big hickory nut tree. It was noon time and they were knocked off from chopping cotton to eat their dinner. And then that tree was right where Old Massa and Old Miss could see from the cool veranda of the big house. And both of them were sitting out there to watch.

"Wait a minute, John. Where we going to get something to wear off like that. We can't go nowhere like you talking about dressed like we is."

"Oh, you got plenty things to wear. Just reach inside your-selves and get out all those fine raiments you been toting around with you for the last longest. They is in there, all right. I know. Get 'em out, and put 'em on."

So the people began to dress. And then John hollered back for them to get out their musical instruments so they could play music on the way. They were right inside where they got their fine raiments from. So they began to get them out. No-body remembered that Massa and Miss were setting up there on the veranda looking things over. So John went off for a minute. After that they all heard a big sing of wings. It was John come back, riding on a great black crow. The crow was so big that one wing rested on the morning, while the other dusted off the evening star.

John lighted down and helped them, so they all mounted on, and the bird took out straight across the deep blue sea. But it was a pearly blue, like ten squillion big pearl jewels dissolved in running gold. The shore around it was all grainy gold itself.

Like Jason in search of the golden fleece, John and his party went to many places, and had numerous adventures. They stopped off in Hell where John, under the name of Jack, married the Devil's youngest daughter and became a popular character. So much so, that when he and the Devil had some words because John turned the dampers down in old Original Hell and put some of the Devil's hogs to barbecue over the coals, John ran for High Chief Devil and won the election. The rest of his party was overjoyed at the possession of power and wanted to stay there. But John said no. He reminded them that they had come in search of a song. A song that would whip Old Massa's earlaps down. The song was not in Hell. They must go on.

The party escaped out of Hell behind the Devil's two fast horses. One of them was named Hallowed-Be-Thy-Name, and the other, Thy-Kingdom-Come. They made it to the mountain. Somebody told them that the Golden Stairs went up from there. John decided that since they were in the vicinity, they might as well visit Heaven.

They got there a little weary and timid. But the gates swung wide for them, and they went in. They were bathed, robed, and given new and shining instruments to play on. Guitars of gold, and drums, and cymbals and wind-singing instruments. They walked up Amen Avenue, and down Hallelujah Street, and found with delight that Amen Avenue was tuned to sing bass and alto. The west end was deep bass, and the east end alto. Hallelujah Street was tuned for tenor and soprano, and the two promenades met right in front of the throne and made harmony by themselves. You could make any tune you wanted to by the way you walked. John and his party had a very good time at that and other things. Finally, by the way they acted and did, Old Maker called them up before His great workbench, and made them a tune and put it in their mouths. It had no words. It was a tune that you could bend and shape in most any way you wanted to fit the words and feelings that you had. They learned it and began to sing.

Just about that time a loud rough voice hollered, "You Tunk! You July! You Aunt Diskie!" Then Heaven went black before their eyes and they couldn't see a thing until they saw the hickory nut tree over their heads again. There was everything just like they had left it, with Old Massa and Old Miss sitting on the veranda, and Massa was doing the hollering.

"You all are taking a mighty long time for dinner," Massa said. "Get up from there and get on back to the field. I mean for you to finish chopping that cotton today if it takes all night long. I got something else, harder than that, for you to do tomorrow. Get a move on you!"

They heard what Massa said, and they felt bad right off. But John de Conquer took and told them, saying, "Don't pay what he say no mind. You know where you got something finer than this plantation and anything it's got on it, put away. Ain't that funny? Us got all that, and he don't know nothing at all about it. Don't tell him nothing. Nobody don't have to know where us gets our pleasure from. Come on. Pick up your hoes and let's go."

They all began to laugh and grabbed up their hoes and started out.

"Ain't that funny?" Aunt Diskie laughed and hugged herself with secret laughter. "Us got all the advantage, and Old Massa think he got us tied!"

The crowd broke out singing as they went off to work. The day didn't seem hot like it had before. Their gift song came back into their memories in pieces, and they sang about glittering new robes and harps, and the work flew.

IV

So after a while, freedom came. Therefore High John de Conquer has not walked the winds of America for seventy-five years now. His people had their freedom, their laugh and their song. They have traded it to the other Americans for things they could use like education and property, and acceptance. High John knew that that was the way it would be, so he could retire with his secret smile into the soil of the South and wait.

The thousands upon thousands of humble people who still believe in him, that is, in the power of love and laughter to win by their subtle power, do John reverence by getting the root of the plant in which he has taken up his secret dwelling, and "dressing" it with perfume, and keeping it on their person, or in their houses in a secret place. It is there to help them overcome things they feel that they could not beat otherwise, and to bring them the laugh of the day. John will never forsake the weak and the helpless, nor fail to bring hope to the hopeless. That is what they believe, and so they do not worry. They go on and laugh and sing. Things are bound to come out right tomorrow. That is the secret of Negro song and laughter.

So the brother in black offers to these United States the source of courage that endures, and laughter. High John de Conquer. If the news from overseas reads bad, and the nation inside seems like it is stuck in the Tar Baby, listen hard, and you will hear John de Conquer treading on his singing-drum. You will know then, that no matter how bad things look now, it will be worse for those who seek to oppress us. Even if your hair comes yellow, and your eyes are blue, John de Conquer will be working for you just the same. From his secret place, he is working for all America now. We are all his kinfolks. Just be sure our cause is right, and then you can lean back and say, "John de Conquer would know what to do in a case like this, and then he would finish it off with a laugh."

White America, take a laugh out of our black mouths, and win! We give you High John de Conquer.

The American Mercury, October 1943

Negroes Without Self-Pity

I MAY be wrong, but it seems to me that what happened at a Negro meeting in Florida the other day is important— important not only for Negroes and not only for Florida. I think that it strikes a new, wholesome note in the black man's relation to his native America.

It was a meeting of the Statewide Negro Defense Committee. C. D. Rogers, President of the Central Life Insurance Company of Tampa, got up and said: "I will answer that question of whether we will be allowed to take part in civic, state and national affairs. The answer is—yes!" Then he explained why and how he had come to take part in the affairs of his city.

"The truth is," he said, "that I am not always asked. Certainly in the beginning I was not. As a citizen, I saw no reason why I should wait for an invitation to interest myself in things that concerned me just as much as they did other residents of Tampa. I went and I asked what I could do. Knowing that I was interested and willing to do my part, the authorities began to notify me ahead of proposed meetings, and invited me to participate. I see no point in hanging back, and then complaining that I have been excluded from civic affairs.

"I know that citizenship implies duties as well as privileges. It is time that we Negroes learn that you can't get something for nothing. Negroes, merely by being Negroes, are not exempted from the natural laws of existence. If we expect to be treated as citizens, and considered in community affairs, we must come forward as citizens and shoulder our part of the load. The only citizens who count are those who give time, effort and money to the support and growth of the community. *Share the burden where you live!*"

And then J. Leonard Lewis, attorney for the Afro-American Life Insurance, had something to say. First he pointed to the growing tension between the races throughout the country. Then he, too, broke tradition. The upper-class Negro, he said, must take the responsibility for the Negro part in these disturbances.

"It is not enough," he said, "for us to sit by and say 'We didn't do it. Those irresponsible, uneducated Negroes bring on all this trouble.' We must not only do nothing to whip up the passions among them, we must go much further. We must abandon our attitude of aloofness to the less educated. We must get in touch with them *and head off these incidents before they happen.*

"How can we do that? There is always some man among them who has great prestige with them. He can do what we cannot do, because he is of them and understands them. If he says fight, they fight. If he says, 'Now put away that gun and be quiet,' they are quiet. We must confer with these people, and cooperate with them to prevent these awful outbreaks that can do no one any good and everybody some harm. Let us give up our attitude of isolation from the less fortunate among us, and do what we can for peace and good-will between the races."

Not anything world-shaking in such speeches, you will say. Yet something profound has happened, of which these speeches are symptoms and proofs. Look back over your shoulder for a minute. Count the years. If you take in the twenty-odd years of intense Abolitionist speaking and writing that preceded the Civil War, the four war years, the Reconstruction period and recent Negro rights agitations, you have at least a hundred years of indoctrination of the Negro that he is an object of pity. Becoming articulate, this was in him and he said it. "We were brought here against our will. We were held as slaves for two hundred and forty-six years. We are in no way responsible for anything. We are dependents. We are due something from the labor of our ancestors. Look upon us with pity and give!" The whole expression was one of self-pity without a sense of belonging to America and what went on here.

Put that against the statements of Rogers and Lewis, and you get the drama of the meeting. The audience agreed and applauded. Tradition was tossed overboard without a sigh. Dr. J. R. E. Lee, president of Florida A and M College for Negroes, got up and elaborated upon the statements: *"Go forward with the nation. We are citizens and have our duties as such."* Nobody mentioned slavery, Reconstruction, nor any such matter. It was a new and strange kind of Negro meeting—without tears of self-pity. It was a sign and symbol of something in the offing.

My Most Humiliating Jim Crow Experience

M Y MOST humiliating Jim Crow experience came in New York instead of the South as one would have expected. It was in 1931 when Mrs. R. Osgood Mason was financing my researches in anthropology. I returned to New York from the Bahama Islands ill with some disturbances of the digestive tract.

Godmother (Mrs. Mason liked for me to call her Godmother) became concerned about my condition and suggested a certain white specialist at her expense. His office was in Brooklyn.

Mr. Paul Chapin called up and made the appointment for me. The doctor told the wealthy and prominent Paul Chapin that I would get the best of care.

So two days later I journeyed to Brooklyn to submit myself to the care of the great specialist.

His reception room was more than swanky, with a magnificent hammered copper door and other decor on the same plane as the door.

But his receptionist was obviously embarrassed when I showed up. I mentioned the appointment and got inside the door. She went into the private office and stayed a few minutes, then the doctor appeared in the door all in white, looking very important, and also very unhappy from behind his round stomach.

He did not approach me at all, but told one of his nurses to take me into a private examination room.

The room was private all right, but I would not rate it highly as an examination room. Under any other circumstances, I would have sworn it was a closet where the soiled towels and uniforms were tossed until called for by the laundry. But I will say this for it, there was a chair in there wedged in between the wall and the pile of soiled linen.

The nurse took me in there, closed the door quickly and disappeared. The doctor came in immediately and began in a desultory manner to ask me about symptoms. It was evident he meant to get me off the premises as quickly as possible.

935

Being the sort of objective person I am, I did not get up and sweep out angrily as I was first disposed to do. I stayed to see just what would happen, and further to torture him more. He went through some motions, stuck a tube down my throat to extract some bile from my gall bladder, wrote a prescription and asked for twenty dollars as a fee.

I got up, set my hat at a reckless angle and walked out, telling him that I would send him a check, which I never did. I went away feeling the pathos of Anglo-Saxon civilization.

And I still mean pathos, for I know that anything with such a false foundation cannot last. Whom the gods would destroy, they first make mad.

Negro Digest, June 1944

The Rise of the Begging Joints

PEOPLE have been telling me to clap hands, crack jokes, and generally cut Big Jim by the acre. I ought to look and see. Great joy was around me.

When I turned around and asked why I should jump Juba and burn red fire without ceasing, they told me, "Look! No more slavery days, and even the Reconstruction is past and gone. Aunt Hagar's chillun are eating high on the hog."

Now, there is nothing I favor more than clapping hands in drumtime, and dancing all night long, unless it is having something to clap hands and dance over. But I didn't see too clear; so I said, "Pick up your points. Tell me, and then make see, so I can dance it off."

So they told me again and often. Sometimes they said it with arm-gestures. Same thing all over again: the Reconstruction is over. Everything is fresh and new.

But I am not cutting my capers yet awhile, because I don't know for certain.

I do see a great many Negroes with college degrees, fur coats, big houses and long cars. That is just fine, and I like it. That looks really up-to-time. On the other hand, I see some things that look too much like 1875 in the lap of 1944, and they worry me.

Those Begging Joints, for instance. That is not the name they go by, of course. Some folks with their mouths full of flattery call them normal schools, colleges, and even universities. I'm sort of tie-tongued and short-patienced, so I call them a functional name and let it go at that.

The "puhfessahs," principals, presidents and potentates who run these institutions seem to like them mighty fine. They will tell you without your even asking that these are "great works." Further, that they themselves are latter-day martyrs, electing to "carry on this great work for our people, so that our girls and boys may get some sort of an education." They tootch out the mouth to say this so that it oozes out in an unctuous tone of voice. There is also a ceremonial face-making, with eye-gleams, to go along with the sound. If you don't make some fast time away from there, you are going to hear all about how they were born in a log cabin. Think of that! And now, look! They have builded this g-r-e-a-t institution! The mouth-spread would take in the mighty expanse of Columbia University, but you look around and see something that would have been a miracle in 1875, but nothing to speak of in this day and year of our Lord.

The next thing you know, the talk has gotten around to funds. It always gets around to funds. Money is needed to carry on the g-r-e-a-t work. If you don't know any better, you will soon be shaking with apprehension at the prospect of this institution's closing its doors, and never another Negro girl or boy learning her or his ABC's. If you know anything about Negro education, you come out of your spasm quickly when you remember that there are such Class A seats of learning as Howard University, Fisk University, Morgan State College, Atlanta University and affiliates, Tuskegee, Morehouse, Talladega, Hampton, Florida A. and M., Southern, Bennett, Virginia State and Lincoln U. In addition, there are most all the Northern white colleges except Princeton with Negro graduates and students. For those with ambition but less funds, there are the state-supported colleges for Negroes in every Southern state. Quite a number of colored folk have even earned degrees at the leading universities of Europe, from Scandinavia to Spain.

But in spite of this, you are asked to shake and shiver over the prospective fate of some puny place without a single gifted person in its meager faculty, with only token laboratories or none, and very little else besides its FOUNDER. The Founder is the thing! And the Founder exists to raise funds.

II

Where can one of these Begging Joints be found? There are two or more left in every state in the South.

With so many good colleges available to Negroes, why do these Begging Joints keep on existing? Because there are so many poor Negroes, and so many rich white people, who don't know very much. They not only do not know, but they are very incurious.

The colored families from which the Begging Joints draw their students know nothing about the importance of curricula for accrediting. They think that just finishing, "schooling out," is all that is necessary. Just so it is a school. Forty years ago, that would have been all right.

But, not only has the responsibility of the Negro population shifted, the concept of education has changed. Competition is keen, and every chick and child has to pull his weight in efficiency or get trampled in the rush. And that is the tragedy of promoting 1880 in 1944.

These institutions have two things to sell to the folks who are still living in the just-after-slavery aura. One of these is "Off" and the other is the equivalent of the medieval virtue belt. And both of these things take us back to the nineteenth century.

In those days, any kind of school education was something for a Negro to have and threw glitter all around the owner, even to distant cousins. To send your son or daughter *Off* to school marked you as a Big Negro, getting more like the white folks every day. So *Off* became the thing to strive for. It then brought the exalted job of teaching school, plus social preference in everything, including marriage.

Off has lost its glamor for the upper-class Negroes, but it still has some attraction for the lower class. Almost never will an upper-class Negro send his children away until after high school, if a fairly good school is at hand. When he does so, it is either because the local secondary school is not accredited, and will hamper the entrance to some good college, or because of some family reason. It is not because of any prestige of *Off*. But there are still those to whom *Off* is a putting-of-the-family-foot on the ladder, an offsetting of the necessity of labor over the washtub and the cookstove.

The virtue belt factor comes in like this. During slavery, there was no encouragement to continence on the plantations. Quite the contrary. So when freedom came, it is too much to expect that it would have been acquired immediately. There was little immorality really, just a lack of concept about the thing. So in the first generation or so after Emancipation, a mighty lot of girls got "ruint." Hence the first boarding schools that got started were more like reformatories with instruction on the side. You sent your daughter *Off*, if you could afford it, more to keep her from getting "ruint" than to get her educated. Naturally, even those ugly-faced, chilly, warden-like matrons were no more capable of thwarting a boy-crazy girl than her parents were. Daughter often brought her "diploma" home in her arms. Love will find a way.

The instances of this are fewer these days, but the idea is still being sold to parents—"We are not like that Howard University and Fisk. We don't allow our girls to go walking across the campus with boys. And no dancing together. No, indeed! Of course we are not so big as those places. But the students at those schools don't learn a thing! All they do is socialize."

It is true that schools like Howard and Fisk place no ban on ordinary social contacts. It is true that there is some dancing. But what the Begging Joint Puhfessahs neglect to mention is that such colleges as Fisk and Howard run small chance of getting any under-privileged, unrestrained girls among the students. They have the pick of the nation. The instances in them of the kinds of troubles the Puhfessahs suggest fearsomely are negligible.

But the simple woman toiling over a washtub or cookstove does not understand that. So she sends her daughter *Off* to get her virtue guarded, at the instigation of the Puhfessah. It may be a locking of the stable after the horse is stolen, but that is not important to the Puhfessah. If daughter is an indifferent student, that is not important either. The "Great Work" needs students.

No students, no school. No school, no excuse to seek funds. No funds, the principal is faced with a major change in his or her way of living. A terrible loss of prestige, plus going to work with the hands. No more of giving his life and life's blood to the "doing of something for my people." The Puhfessah is in no position to pick and choose among prospective students. He must take what he can get or fold. And God forbid the folding!

So the doer of good works begs a good living for himself in the name of his people. And that is all right for him. But what about the poor black men and women bowed down over mops or standing over the white folks' cookstoves to send daughter or son to the Begging Joint to dress the stage for the educational Fagin? And what of the students?

After two to four years, the janitor's or cook's son or daughter has a piece of paper tied up with a snatch of ribbon. He has had several years of considering himself above the commonality of Negro existence. He thinks sweat and overalls are not for him. But after many trials he finds that he can get no better employment than the boy he used to know next door. He is Jim Jones again, instead of Mr. James Jones, prospective principal of a school. He cannot meet the requirements of the state board of education. He may have learned a smattering of some trade at his school, but not enough to help him much when skilled labor is demanded. Time and money have been wasted, and in addition, he feels a bitter loss of face.

Some, pressed by necessity, adjust themselves and do what must be done. Others, just as pressed, never do. They cannot fit in where they think they belong, but will not adjust themselves to the level of their fitness. They go through life scornful of those who work with their hands, and resentful of the better-prepared Negroes. I know one man of this type who will not wear overalls, no matter how dirty the job that he has to do, because to him overalls are the symbol of the common Negro, and he fears to be so classified. The highest "position" that he has ever held since he left college more than twenty years ago has been a minor one in a 5- and 10-cent store, but he clings to his delusion of grandeur still.

But the Begging Joint does a greater disservice still to the individual, the race and the nation. That is its perpetuation of the double standard in education. Even Southern legislators have come to realize that there must be only one, and the requirements of the Negro state and county schools are being sharply raised year by year. Beginning about 1930, the State of Florida began displacing its old-fashioned Negro teachers with more highly trained ones, preferably from the big Northern colleges. Other states have similar policies. But the little private schools are out of the jurisdiction of the state boards of education. All the state boards can do is to refuse to accredit the backward institution.

The raising of the Negro educational standard is an obvious necessity, since the inefficient are a drag on all. The city, the state and the nation need all their useful people, regardless of race and kind. There is no longer any place for the black man who "does very well for a Negro." He has got to be good these days, and I said *good*. But the Begging Joints are still doing nothing but trying to put exclamation points behind what was considered good away back in 1880 when the majority of white people thought that all Negroes were something less than human.

III

As for the white donors to these Begging Joints, they need their heads examined. I am going to give them full credit for being friends of the Negro. But even so, why can't they be intelligent about it? If they want to do something for Negro education, why not look into things and give where it will do some good?

Mind you, I am not seeking funds. I am not a Founder— and not consequently, a member of the Order of Higher Mendicants, as George Schuyler so aptly puts it. You were the one who said that you wanted to do something for Negro education. All I say is, if you really mean what you say, come out of the backwoods of your mind and do some figuring up. You must know that this is the greatest industrial nation on earth, and that during the last two generations the colleges have followed the trend of the nation's needs. Industry calls for scientists. They must be trained in laboratories, so colleges of any account must have these. Not only must they have them, but they must be able to make the constant replacements necessary to keep up with the latest developments. What would have equipped a whole college fifty years ago is required now for a comprehensive laboratory in chemistry, physics or biology.

Now, why give five thousand dollars a year to Chitterling Switch "college" in the backwoods of Mississippi, let us say, when it is some one-cylinder outfit with perhaps two hundred students? Five thousand is not going to be any help, not in the fix it is in. Five million is more like what it would take to bring it up to our time. Five thousand will just about pay for prexy's new Cadillac, with possibly enough over to put some chairs in a classroom.

Since you really want to do something for Negro education, give to one of the colleges which already has something to build on. You might, for instance, give to Howard University's great medical school. It is turning out doctors and dentists who compare favorably with the best in the nation. The money could be used for laboratory replacements, or to sponsor some serious young medico who yearns to make further research.

Or if you are inclined toward literature, give to the library fund of Morgan State College, at Baltimore. It has a fine library, and aims to make it the finest possible. Or give to the school of Social Sciences at Fisk which, under Dr. Charles S. Johnson, has increased the sum total of knowledge in that field considerably in the last decade. Or send the check to Atlanta University. Its department of sociology is getting grand results.

I wouldn't put it past some of you to tell me that it is your own money, and you can do with it as you please. You are free, white and twenty-one. But you see, I'm free, black and twenty-one; and if you tell me that, I will know and understand that you have no genuine interest in Negro education. Or if you think you have, you haven't taken a sounding in the last forty years. You are way behind the times.

I have made it my business to talk with patrons of the Chitterling Switch kind of a school in the last three years, and I have been astonished at the number of persons giving money to a school without even inquiring into the curriculum or looking into the training of the faculty. They were under the delusion that the school to which they gave was at the top of Negro education. Indeed, the majority had the idea that there was no other kind for Negroes to go to. Some did not even know that there were colleges provided by the state. They fluttered about raising little sums impelled by the fear that if the little place were not kept in condition to keep on crippling young black folks, there would be no other chance for Negroes to get hamstrung for life.

Instead of being a help, many donors have been giving aid and assistance to the defeat of those who need a chance more than anyone else in America.

What is the general history behind these little knowledge-traps? First, there were those little piney-woods schools opened by the Abolitionist church groups immediately after the Civil War. Fired by the Cause, hundreds, perhaps thousands, of pious Northerners came South and gave themselves to teach the freemen how to read and write. But the greatest emphasis was on the Bible. Those who were first taught, were urged to go forth and spread what they had learned to others.

Then the "do something for my people" era came in on the trailing clouds of Booker T. Washington. He was responsible, but he didn't mean any harm. Tuskegee was a success, with tycoons of industry and finance rolling down in their private cars to see and be awed. They saw Booker T. Washington as the Moses of his race. They donated millions to give body to the idea of Booker T. So in the black world, the man was magical. He sat with Presidents. He went abroad and stood with kings. This school-founding thing was something!

Without the genius of his idea and the surprise of its newness, hundreds of other Negroes deserted pulpits, plows, washtubs and cookpots and went out founding schools. The outer offices of financiers began to be haunted by people "doing something for my people." There remained only one Tuskegee. But then, there was only one Booker T. Washington.

These Begging Joints were a natural part of the times when they were started and in a way they were all right for then. But they are unburied corpses in 1944. We can bury the carcasses any time we will or may. All it takes is a made-up mind.

The American Mercury, March 1945

Crazy for This Democracy

THEY tell me this democracy form of government is a wonderful thing. It has freedom, equality, justice, in short, everything! Since 1937 nobody has talked about anything else.

The late Franklin D. Roosevelt sort of re-decorated it, and called these United States the boastful name of "The Arsenal of Democracy."

The radio, the newspapers, and the columnists inside the newspapers, have said how lovely it was.

All this talk and praise-giving has got me in the notion to try some of the stuff. All I want to do is to get hold of a sample of the thing, and I declare, I sure will try it. I don't know for myself, but I have been told that it is really wonderful.

Like the late Will Rogers, all I know is what I see by the papers. It seems like now, I do not know geography as well as I ought to, or I would not get the wrong idea about so many things. I heard so much about "global" "world-freedom" and things like that, that I must have gotten mixed up about oceans.

I thought that when they said Atlantic Charter, that meant me and everybody in Africa and Asia and everywhere. But it seems like the Atlantic is an ocean that does not touch anywhere but North America and Europe.

Just the other day, seeing how things were going in Asia, I went out and bought myself an atlas and found out how narrow this Atlantic ocean was. No wonder that those Four Freedoms couldn't get no further than they did! Why, that poor little ocean can't even wash up some things right here in America, let alone places like India, Burma, Indo-China, and the Netherlands East Indies. We need two more whole oceans for that.

Maybe, I need to go out and buy me a dictionary, too. Or perhaps a spelling-book would help me out a lot. Or it could be that I just mistook the words. Maybe I mistook a British pronunciation for a plain American word. Did F.D.R., aristo-

crat from Groton and Harvard, using the British language say
"arse-and-all" of Democracy when I thought he said plain
arsenal? Maybe he did, and I have been mistaken all this time.
From what is going on, I think that is what he must have said.

That must be what he said, for from what is happening
over on that other, unmentioned ocean, we look like the Ass-
and-All of Democracy. Our weapons, money, and the blood
of millions of our men have been used to carry the English,
French and Dutch and lead them back on the millions of unwilling Asiatics. The Ass-and-all-he-has has been very useful.

The Indo-Chinese are fighting the French now in Indo-
China to keep the freedom that they have enjoyed for five or
six years now. The Indonesians are trying to stay free from the
Dutch, and the Burmese and Malayans from the British.

But American soldiers and sailors are fighting along with
the French, Dutch and English to rivet these chains back on
their former slaves. How can we so admire the fire and determination of Toussaint Louverture to resist the orders of Napoleon to "Rip the gold braids off those Haitian slaves and
put them back to work" after four years of freedom, and be
indifferent to these Asiatics for the same feelings under the
same circumstances?

Have we not noted that not one word has been uttered
about the freedom of the Africans? On the contrary, there
have been mutterings in undertones about being fair and giving different nations sources of raw materials there? The Ass-
and-All of Democracy has shouldered the load of subjugating
the dark world completely.

The only Asiatic power able to offer any effective resistance
has been double-teened by the combined powers of the Occident and rendered incapable of offering or encouraging resistance, and likewise removed as an example to the dark people
of the world.

The inference is, that God has restated the superiority of
the West. God always does like that when a thousand white
people surround one dark one. Dark people are always "bad"
when they do not admit the Divine Plan like that. A certain
Javanese man who sticks up for Indonesian Independence is
very lowdown by the papers, and suspected of being a Japanese puppet. Wanting the Dutch to go back to Holland and

go to work for themselves! The very idea! A very, very bad man, that Javanese.

As for me, I am just as sceptical as this contrary Javanese. I accept this idea of Democracy. I am all for trying it out. It must be a good thing if everybody praises it like that. If our government has been willing to go to war and to sacrifice billions of dollars and millions of men for the idea, I think that I ought to give the thing a trial.

The only thing that keeps me from pitching headlong into the thing is the presence of numerous Jim Crow laws on the statute books of the nation. I am crazy about the idea of this Democracy. I want to see how it feels. Therefore, I am all for the repeal of every Jim Crow law in the nation here and now. Not in another generation or so. The Hurstons have already been waiting eighty years for that. I want it here and now.

And why not? A lot of people in these United States have been saying all this time that things ought to be equal. Numerous instances of inequality have been pointed out, and fought over in the courts and in the newspapers. That seems like a waste of time to me.

The patient has the small-pox. Segregation and things like that are the bumps and blisters on the skin, and not the disease, but evidence and symptoms of the sickness. The doctors around the bedside of the patient, are desperately picking bumps. Some assume that the opening of one blister will cure the case. Some strangely assert that a change of climate is all that is needed to kill the virus in the blood!

But why this sentimental oversimplification in diagnosis? Do the doctors not know anything about the widespread occurrence of this disease? It is NOT peculiar to the South. Canada, once the refuge of escaping slaves, has now its denomination of second-class citizens, and they are the Japanese and other non-Caucasians. The war cannot explain it, because enemy Germans are not put in that second class.

Jim Crow is the rule in South Africa, and is even more extensive than in America. More rigid and grinding. No East Indian may ride first-class in the trains of British-held India. Jim Crow is common in all colonial Africa, Asia and the Netherlands East Indies. There, too, a Javanese male is punished for flirting back at a white female. So why this stupid assumption that "moving North" will do away with social smallpox? Events in the northern cities do not bear out this juvenile contention.

So why the waste of good time and energy, and further delay the recovery of the patient by picking him over bump by bump and blister to blister? Why not the shot of serum that will kill the thing in the blood? The bumps are symptoms. The symptoms cannot disappear until the cause is cured.

These Jim Crow laws have been put on the books for a purpose, and that purpose is psychological. It has two edges to the thing. By physical evidence, back seats in trains, backdoors of houses, exclusion from certain places and activities, to promote in the mind of the smallest white child the conviction of First by Birth, eternal and irrevocable like the place assigned to the Levites by Moses over the other tribes of the Hebrews. Talent, capabilities, nothing has anything to do with the case. Just FIRST BY BIRTH.

No one of darker skin can ever be considered an equal. Seeing the daily humiliations of the darker people confirm the child in its superiority, so that it comes to feel it the arrangement of God. By the same means, the smallest dark child is to be convinced of its inferiority, so that it is to be convinced that competition is out of the question, and against all nature and God.

All physical and emotional things flow from this premise. It perpetuates itself. The unnatural exaltation of one ego, and the equally unnatural grinding down of the other. The business of some whites to help pick a bump or so is even part of the pattern. Not a human right, but a concession from the throne has been made. Otherwise why do they not take the attitude of Robert Ingersoll that all of it is wrong? Why the necessity for the little concession? Why not go for the under-skin injection? Is it a bargaining with a detail to save the whole intact? It is something to think about.

As for me, I am committed to the hypodermic and the serum. I see no point in the picking of a bump. Others can erupt too easily. That same one can burst out again. Witness the easy scrapping of FEPC. No, I give my hand, my heart and my head to the total struggle. I am for complete repeal of

All Jim Crow Laws in the United States once and for all, and right now. For the benefit of this nation and as a precedent to the world.

I have been made to believe in this democracy thing, and I am all for tasting this democracy out. The flavor must be good. If the Occident is so intent in keeping the taste out of darker mouths that it spends all those billions and expends all those millions of lives, colored ones too, to keep it among themselves, then it must be something good. I crave to sample this gorgeous thing. So I cannot say anything different from repeal of all Jim Crow laws! Not in some future generation, but repeal *now* and forever!!

Negro Digest, December 1945

What White Publishers Won't Print

I HAVE been amazed by the Anglo-Saxon's lack of curiosity about the internal lives and emotions of the Negroes, and for that matter, any non-Anglo-Saxon peoples within our borders, above the class of unskilled labor.

This lack of interest is much more important than it seems at first glance. It is even more important at this time than it was in the past. The internal affairs of the nation have bearings on the international stress and strain, and this gap in the national literature now has tremendous weight in world affairs. National coherence and solidarity is implicit in a thorough understanding of the various groups within a nation, and this lack of knowledge about the internal emotions and behavior of the minorities cannot fail to bar out understanding. Man, like all the other animals fears and is repelled by that which he does not understand, and mere difference is apt to connote something malign.

The fact that there is no demand for incisive and full-dress stories around Negroes above the servant class is indicative of something of vast importance to this nation. This blank is NOT filled by the fiction built around upper-class Negroes exploiting the race problem. Rather, it tends to point it up. A college-bred Negro still is not a person like other folks, but an interesting problem, more or less. It calls to mind a story of slavery time. In this story, a master with more intellectual curiosity than usual, set out to see how much he could teach a particularly bright slave of his. When he had gotten him up to higher mathematics and to be a fluent reader of Latin, he called in a neighbor to show off his brilliant slave, and to argue that Negroes had brains just like the slave-owners had, and given the same opportunities, would turn out the same.

The visiting master of slaves looked and listened, tried to trap the literate slave in Algebra and Latin, and failing to do so in both, turned to his neighbor and said:

"Yes, he certainly knows his higher mathematics, and he can read Latin better than many white men I know, but I cannot bring myself to believe that he understands a thing that he is doing. It is all an aping of our culture. All on the outside. You are crazy if you think that it has changed him inside in the least. Turn him loose, and he will revert at once to the jungle. He is still a savage, and no amount of translating Virgil and Ovid is going to change him. In fact, all you have done is to turn a useful savage into a dangerous beast."

That was in slavery time, yes, and we have come a long, long way since then, but the troubling thing is that there are still too many who refuse to believe in the ingestion and digestion of western culture as yet. Hence the lack of literature about the higher emotions and love life of upper-class Negroes and the minorities in general.

Publishers and producers are cool to the idea. Now, do not leap to the conclusion that editors and producers constitute a special class of un-believers. That is far from true. Publishing houses and theatrical promoters are in business to make money. They will sponsor anything that they believe will sell. They shy away from romantic stories about Negroes and Jews because they feel that they know the public indifference to such works, unless the story or play involves racial tension. It can then be offered as a study in Sociology, with the romantic side subdued. They know the scepticism in general about the complicated emotions in the minorities. The average American just cannot conceive of it, and would be apt to reject the notion, and publishers and producers take the stand that they are not in business to educate, but to make money. Sympathetic as they might be, they cannot afford to be crusaders.

In proof of this, you can note various publishers and producers edging forward a little, and ready to go even further when the trial balloons show that the public is ready for it. This public lack of interest is the nut of the matter.

The question naturally arises as to the why of this indifference, not to say scepticism, to the internal life of educated minorities.

The answer lies in what we may call THE AMERICAN MUSEUM OF UNNATURAL HISTORY. This is an intangible built on folk belief. It is assumed that all non-Anglo-Saxons are uncomplicated stereotypes. Everybody knows all about them. They are lay figures mounted in the museum where all may take them in at a glance. They are made of bent wires without insides at all. So how could anybody write a book about the non-existent?

The American Indian is a contraption of copper wires in an eternal war-bonnet, with no equipment for laughter, expressionless face and that says "How" when spoken to. His only activity is treachery leading to massacres. Who is so dumb as not to know all about Indians, even if they have never seen one, nor talked with anyone who ever knew one?

The American Negro exhibit is a group of two. Both of these mechanical toys are built so that their feet eternally shuffle, and their eyes pop and roll. Shuffling feet and those popping, rolling eyes denote the Negro, and no characterization is genuine without this monotony. One is seated on a stump picking away on his banjo and singing and laughing. The other is a most amoral character before a share-cropper's shack mumbling about injustice. Doing this makes him out to be a Negro "intellectual." It is as simple as all that.

The whole museum is dedicated to the convenient "typical." In there is the "typical" Oriental, Jew, Yankee, Westerner, Southerner, Latin, and even out-of-favor Nordics like the German. The Englishman "I say old chappie," and the gesticulating Frenchman. The least observant American can know them all at a glance. However, the public willingly accepts the untypical in Nordics, but feels cheated if the untypical is portrayed in others. The author of *Scarlet Sister Mary* complained to me that her neighbors objected to her book on the grounds that she had the characters thinking, "and everybody know that Nigras don't think."

But for the national welfare, it is urgent to realize that the minorities do think, and think about something other than the race problem. That they are very human and internally, according to natural endowment, are just like everybody else. So long as this is not conceived, there must remain that feeling of unsurmountable difference, and difference to the average man means something bad. If people were made right, they would be just like him.

The trouble with the purely problem arguments is that they leave too much unknown. Argue all you will or may about injustice, but as long as the majority cannot conceive of a Negro or a Jew feeling and reacting inside just as they do, the majority will keep right on believing that people who do not look like them cannot possibly feel as they do, and conform to the established pattern. It is well known that there must be a body of waived matter, let us say, things accepted and taken for granted by all in a community before there can be that commonality of feeling. The usual phrase is having things in common. Until this is thoroughly established in respect to Negroes in America, as well as of other minorities, it will remain impossible for the majority to conceive of a Negro experiencing a deep and abiding love and not just the passion of sex. That a great mass of Negroes can be stirred by the pageants of Spring and Fall; the extravaganza of summer, and the majesty of winter. That they can and do experience discovery of the numerous subtle faces as a foundation for a great and selfless love, and the diverse nuances that go to destroy that love as with others. As it is now, this capacity, this evidence of high and complicated emotions, is ruled out. Hence the lack of interest in a romance uncomplicated by the race struggle has so little appeal.

This insistence on defeat in a story where upperclass Negroes are portrayed, perhaps says something from the subconscious of the majority. Involved in western culture, the hero or the heroine, or both, must appear frustrated and go down to defeat, somehow. Our literature reeks with it. Is it the same as saying, "You can translate Virgil, and fumble with the differential calculus, but can you really comprehend it? Can you cope with our subtleties?"

That brings us to the folklore of "reversion to type." This curious doctrine has such wide acceptance that it is tragic. One has only to examine the huge literature on it to be convinced. No matter how high we may *seem* to climb, put us under strain and we revert to type, that is, to the bush. Under a superficial layer of western culture, the jungle drums throb in our veins.

This ridiculous notion makes it possible for that majority who accept it to conceive of even a man like the suave and scholarly Dr. Charles S. Johnson to hide a black cat's bone on his person, and indulge in a midnight voodoo ceremony, complete with leopard skin and drums if threatened with the loss of the presidency of Fisk University, or the love of his wife. "Under the skin . . . better to deal with them in business, etc., but otherwise keep them at a safe distance and under control. I tell you, Carl Van Vechten, think as you like, but they are just not like us."

The extent and extravagance of this notion reaches the ultimate in nonsense in the widespread belief that the Chinese have bizarre genitals, because of that eye-fold that makes their eyes seem to slant. In spite of the fact that no biology has ever mentioned any such difference in reproductive organs makes no matter. Millions of people believe it. "Did you know that a Chinese has . . ." Consequently, their quiet contemplative manner is interpreted as a sign of slyness and a treacherous inclination.

But the opening wedge for better understanding has been thrust into the crack. Though many Negroes denounced Carl Van Vechten's *Nigger Heaven* because of the title, and without ever reading it, the book, written in the deepest sincerity, revealed Negroes of wealth and culture to the white public. It created curiosity even when it aroused scepticism. It made folks want to know. Worth Tuttle Hedden's *The Other Room* has definitely widened the opening. Neither of these well-written works take a romance of upper-class Negro life as the central theme, but the atmosphere and the background is there. These works should be followed up by some incisive and intimate stories from the inside.

The realistic story around a Negro insurance official, dentist, general practitioner, undertaker and the like would be most revealing. Thinly disguised fiction around the well known Negro names is not the answer, either. The "exceptional" as well as the Ol' Man Rivers has been exploited all out of context already. Everybody is already resigned to the "exceptional" Negro, and willing to be entertained by the "quaint." To grasp the penetration of western civilization in a minority, it is necessary to know how the average behaves and lives. Books that deal with people like in Sinclair Lewis' *Main Street* is the neccessary metier. For various reasons, the average, struggling, non-morbid Negro is the best-kept secret in America. His revelation to the public is the thing needed to do away with that feeling of difference which inspires fear, and which ever expresses itself in dislike.

It is inevitable that this knowledge will destroy many illusions and romantic traditions which America probably likes to have around. But then, we have no record of anybody sinking into a lingering death on finding out that there was no Santa Claus. The old world will take it in its stride. The realization that Negroes are no better nor no worse, and at times just as boring as everybody else, will hardly kill off the population of the nation.

Outside of racial attitudes, there is still another reason why this literature should exist. Literature and other arts are supposed to hold up the mirror to nature. With only the fractional "exceptional" and the "quaint" portrayed, a true picture of Negro life in America cannot be. A great principle of national art has been violated.

These are the things that publishers and producers, as the accredited representatives of the American people, have not as yet taken into consideration sufficiently. Let there be light!

Negro Digest, April 1950

Court Order Can't Make Races Mix

EDITOR: I promised God and some other responsible characters, including a bench of bishops, that I was not going to part my lips concerning the U.S. Supreme Court decision on ending segregation in the public schools of the South. But since a lot of time has passed and no one seems to touch on what to me appears to be the most important point in the hassle, I break my silence just this once. Consider me as just thinking out loud.

The whole matter revolves around the self-respect of my people. How much satisfaction can I get from a court order for somebody to associate with me who does not wish me near them? The American Indian has never been spoken of as a minority and chiefly because there is no whine in the Indian. Certainly he fought, and valiantly for his lands, and rightfully so, but it is inconceivable of an Indian to seek forcible association with anyone. His well known pride and self-respect would save him from that. I take the Indian position.

Now a great clamor will arise in certain quarters that I seek to deny the Negro children of the South their rights, and therefore I am one of those "handkerchief-head niggers" who bow low before the white man and sell out my own people out of cowardice. However an analytical glance will show that that is not the case.

If there are not adequate Negro schools in Florida, and there is some residual, some inherent and unchangeable quality in white schools, impossible to duplicate anywhere else, then I am the first to insist that Negro children of Florida be allowed to share this boon. But if there are adequate Negro schools and prepared instructors and instructions, then there is nothing different except the presence of white people.

For this reason, I regard the ruling of the U.S. Supreme Court as insulting rather than honoring my race. Since the days of the never-to-be-sufficiently-deplored Reconstruction, there has been current the belief that there is no greater delight to Negroes than physical association with whites. The doctrine of the white mare. Those familiar with the habits of mules are aware that any mule, if not restrained, will auto-matically follow a white mare. Dishonest mule-traders made money out of this knowledge in the old days.

Lead a white mare along a country road and slyly open the gate and the mules in the lot would run out and follow this mare. This ruling being conceived and brought forth in a sly political medium with eyes on '56, and brought forth in the same spirit and for the same purpose, it is clear that they have taken the old notion to heart and acted upon it. It is a cun-ning opening of the barnyard gate with the white mare am-bling past. We are expected to hasten pell-mell after her.

It is most astonishing that this should be tried just when the nation is exerting itself to shake off the evils of Commu-nist penetration. It is to be recalled that Moscow, being made aware of this folk belief, made it the main plank in their cam-paign to win the American Negro from the 1920s on. It was the come-on stuff. Join the party and get yourself a white wife or husband. To supply the expected demand, the party had scraped up this-and-that off of park benches and skid rows and held them in stock for us. The highest types of Negroes were held to be just panting to get hold of one of these ob-jects. Seeing how flat that program fell, it is astonishing that it would be so soon revived. Politics does indeed make strange bedfellows.

But the South had better beware in another direction. While it is being frantic over the segregation ruling, it had better keep its eyes open for more important things. One in-stance of Govt by fiat has been rammed down its throat. It is possible that the end of segregation is not here and never meant to be here at present, but the attention of the South directed on what was calculated to keep us busy while more ominous things were brought to pass. The stubborn South and the Midwest kept this nation from being dragged farther to the left than it was during the New Deal.

But what if it is contemplated to do away with the two-party system and arrive at Govt by administrative decree? No questions allowed and no information given out from the ad-ministrative dept? We could get more rulings on the same subject and more far-reaching any day. It pays to weigh every saving and action, however trivial as indicating a trend.

In the ruling on segregation, the unsuspecting nation might have witnessed a trial-balloon. A relatively safe one, since it is sectional and on a matter not likely to arouse other sections of the nation to the support of the South. If it goes off fairly well, a precedent has been established. Govt by fiat can replace the Constitution. You don't have to credit me with too much intelligence and penetration, just so you watch carefully and think.

Meanwhile, personally, I am not delighted. I am not persuaded and elevated by the white mare technique. Negro schools in the state are in very good shape and on the improve. We are fortunate in having Dr. D. E. Williams as head and driving force of Negro instruction. Dr. Williams is relentless in his drive to improve both physical equipment and teacher-quality. He has accomplished wonders in the 20 years past and it is to be expected that he will double that in the future.

It is well known that I have no sympathy nor respect for the "tragedy of color" school of thought among us, whose fountain-head is the pressure group concerned in this court ruling. I can see no tragedy in being too dark to be invited to a white school social affair. The Supreme Court would have pleased me more if they had concerned themselves about enforcing the compulsory education provisions for Negroes in the South as is done for white children. The next 10 years would be better spent in appointing truant officers and looking after conditions in the homes from which the children come. Use to the limit what we already have.

Thems my sentiments and I am sticking by them. Growth from within. Ethical and cultural desegregation. It is a contradiction in terms to scream race pride and equality while at the same time spurning Negro teachers and self-association. That old white mare business can go racking on down the road for all I care.

Eau Gallie   ZORA NEALE HURSTON

Orlando Sentinel, August 11, 1955

CHRONOLOGY

NOTE ON THE TEXTS

NOTES

Chronology

1891   Born Zora Lee Hurston January 7 in Notasulga, Macon County, Alabama, fifth child of Lucy Ann Potts, born December 1865, and John Hurston, born January 1861, a Baptist preacher, farmer, and carpenter. (Parents are both from Notasulga. Mother's father, Richard Potts, became a landowner after the Civil War. Father's family worked on cotton plantations. Both grandfathers were born in Georgia; both grandmothers are from Alabama.) Siblings are Hezekiah Robert (Bob), born November 1882, John Cornelius, born January 1885, Richard William, born January 1887, and Sarah Emmeline, born December 1889.

1893   Brother Joel (later known as "Clifford Joel") born March 4.

1894   Family moves to Eatonville, Florida, a small town five miles north of Orlando that was incorporated in 1886 (Hurston later describes it as the first incorporated black community in America; in 1900 its population is 125). Most men work as day laborers; women find domestic jobs in nearby towns of Maitland and Winter Park, both of which are popular with northern tourists. (Parents will eventually own five acres of land and eight-room house; father becomes pastor of the Zion Hope Baptist Church and the Macedonia Baptist Church, and will serve as moderator of the South Florida Baptist Association.)

1895   Brother Benjamin Franklin born December 7.

1897   Father is elected mayor of Eatonville (will serve three terms).

1898   Brother Edward Everett born October 26.

1900   Hurston attends Hungerford School in Eatonville, founded by Mary and Russell Calhoun, former students of Booker T. Washington at Tuskegee Institute. Helped in studies by mother, a former country school teacher and superintendent of the Sunday school. Loves verbal playfulness and the "lies" (stories) adults tell on the porch of Joe Clarke's store ("the heart and spring of the town").

961

1901   Impresses two visiting northern white women with her
            ability to read; they give her books, including the
            Grimms' and Andersen's fairy tales, Greek and Roman
            myths, Norse legends, *Gulliver's Travels*, and works by
            Rudyard Kipling and Robert Louis Stevenson.

1904   Mother dies on September 18. Hurston is sent in October
            to school in Jacksonville where Sarah is a student; Bob
            attends the Florida Baptist Academy in Jacksonville (later
            Florida Memorial College at St. Augustine).

1905   Hurston continues in school in Jacksonville; when her
            school bill is not paid she scrubs stairs on Saturdays and
            cleans kitchens after school. Wins spelling competition
            held among all the Negro schools in Jacksonville. Learns
            from Sarah that father has remarried. Sarah marries and
            moves to Palmetto, Florida, taking Everett with her.
            School officials pay for Hurston's return home several
            weeks after end of term when father fails to send for her.

1906–11   After brothers John and Richard leave home, Hurston
            and her younger siblings are sent to live with friends and
            relatives of their mother. Hurston dislikes her stepmother
            intensely and blames her for the dispersion of the family.
            Moves from one house to another and attends school in-
            termittently. Works as a domestic.

1912   Lives with brother Dick and his wife in Sanford, Florida,
            until her father tells her to come home. Has physical
            fight with her stepmother. Hurston leaves to find work
            in another town.

1914–15   Moves into home of brother Bob, now a doctor in Mem-
            phis, who promises to send her to school; is disappointed
            when he tells her that she must first help his wife take care
            of their three children and the home.

1915–16   Travels with a Gilbert & Sullivan troupe as maid to the
            lead singer. Falls ill in Baltimore and is unable to continue
            touring; has appendix removed in free ward of Maryland
            General Hospital.

1917–18   Works as waitress in Baltimore. Attends night high school
            (tells school officials year of her birth is 1901). Inspired by

teacher Dwight O. W. Holmes. Father dies in automobile accident on August 10. Enters Morgan Academy (high school division of what is now Morgan State University) in September 1917, and is aided by Dean William Pickens, who finds her domestic work in exchange for room and board in home of one of the white trustees of the school. Graduates in June 1918 and moves to Washington, partly at the suggestion of May Miller, daughter of mathematician and essayist Kelly Miller, dean of the College of Arts and Sciences at Howard University. Works during summer as waitress at the Cosmos Club, and then as manicurist in a black-owned barber shop that serves whites only. Enters the preparatory school at Howard University in September.

1919–20   Begins courses in the college department at Howard; receives an associate degree in 1920 (will attend Howard intermittently through 1924 but does not receive B.A.). Majors in English; studies with pioneering black linguist Lorenzo Dow Turner (later author of *Africanisms in the Gullah Dialect*) and Dwight O. W. Holmes, who has since moved to Howard. Joins Zeta Phi Beta sorority. Meets Herbert Sheen, a student from Decatur, Illinois.

1921   Joins literary club sponsored by philosophy professor Alain Locke and Montgomery Gregory, professor of English and drama. Publishes her first story, "John Redding Goes to Sea" (set in Eatonville), and a poem, "O Night," in the May number of club magazine *Stylus*. Regularly attends literary salon held by poet Georgia Douglas Johnson, which attracts local and visiting writers such as Locke, Bruce Nugent, Jean Toomer, W.E.B. Du Bois, essayist and fiction writer Marita Bonner, journalist and poet Alice Dunbar-Nelson, novelist and poet Jessie Fauset (literary editor of NAACP magazine *The Crisis*), poet Angelina Grimké, and Hurston's friend May Miller (who later becomes an educator, playwright, and poet).

1922   Publishes poems "Night," "Journey's End," and "Passion" in *Negro World*, the official newspaper of Marcus Garvey's Universal Negro Improvement Association.

1924   Publishes short story "Drenched in Light" in *Opportu-*
        nity, literary journal sponsored by the Urban League. Be-
        gins correspondence with journal's editor, Charles S.
        Johnson.

1925   With Johnson's encouragement, moves to New York City
        in January. Submits two stories, "Black Death" and
        "Spunk," and a play, *Color Struck*, to literary contest
        sponsored by *Opportunity*. Wins two second-place prizes
        and attends the magazine's awards dinner, where she
        meets poets Langston Hughes and Countee Cullen and
        novelists Carl Van Vechten, Annie Nathan Meyer, and
        Fannie Hurst. Accepts job with Hurst as personal secre-
        tary, but does not have adequate clerical skills and works
        instead as a chauffeur and companion (continues job until
        the end of 1926; friendship with Hurst continues for de-
        cades). Begins working occasionally as a domestic for
        Meyer, who secures her a scholarship to Barnard College
        for the fall (Meyer is one of the college's founders). Pub-
        lishes story "Spunk" in the June number of *Opportunity*
        (it is reprinted later in the year in the signal anthology of
        the Harlem Renaissance, *The New Negro*, edited by Alain
        Locke). Enters Barnard in September as its only African-
        American student; studies anthropology with Franz Boas
        (anthropology faculty also includes Ruth Benedict and
        Gladys Reichard). Publishes article "The Hue and Cry
        about Howard University," criticizing students' negative
        attitude toward Negro spirituals, in the September num-
        ber of *The Messenger*, Harlem journal co-founded by labor
        leader A. Philip Randolph.

1926   Begins field work for Boas in Harlem, measuring the
        skulls of passersby to disprove theories of racial inferiority.
        Moves to apartment at 43 West 66th Street, not far from
        Fannie Hurst; it is furnished with donations from friends.
        Submits story "Muttsy" and comic play *The First One*,
        based on the biblical legend of Ham, to the *Opportunity*
        contest ("Muttsy" wins second-place award and is pub-
        lished in August). In the summer begins meeting with
        Langston Hughes, poet Gwendolyn Bennett, painter
        Aaron Douglas, bohemian writer and artist Bruce
        Nugent, and novelist Wallace Thurman to plan *Fire!!*, a
        quarterly "devoted to the younger Negro artists." First
        and only number is published in November; Hurston

contributes "Sweat" and play *Color Struck*. In September folktale "Possum or Pig" is published in *Forum* and the first installment of "The Eatonville Anthology" appears in *The Messenger*.

1927   Publishes *The First One* in *Ebony and Topaz*, edited by Charles S. Johnson. With Boas' help, receives $1,400 research fellowship from the Association for the Study of Negro Life and History, founded and directed by African-American historian Carter G. Woodson. Leaves New York in February to collect folklore in the South. After a visit to Eatonville goes to Jacksonville to begin work. Visits brother John and buys used car for $300, which she names "Sassy Susie." Marries Herbert Sheen, now a medical student, in St. Augustine, Florida, on May 19. Visits brothers Bob and Ben, a pharmacist and owner of a drugstore, in Memphis (brother Dick is a traveling chef on the East Coast; Joel is the principal of the Negro high school in Decatur, Alabama; Everett is working in the post office in Brooklyn, N.Y; Sarah is married to a man the family does not like). Sheen returns in August to Rush Medical School in Chicago. Hurston accidently meets Langston Hughes in Mobile, Alabama. Drives him to New York, stopping in Tuskegee, Alabama, where they visit the grave of Booker T. Washington with Jessie Fauset, and in Macon, Georgia, where they see blues singer Bessie Smith perform and visit her in her hotel room. Hurston drives along southern back roads, and tells Hughes, who has never been South before, about her research in black folkways. Seeking financial help to create opera based on southern black folk material, Hurston meets Charlotte Mason (Mrs. Rufus Osgood Mason) in September through Alain Locke. (Mason, born Charlotte van der Veer Quick in Princeton, New Jersey, in 1854, had previously lived among the Plains Indians while sponsoring the field work of Natalie Curtis. At Locke's urging, she offered financial assistance to black artists, including Hughes, Claude McKay, sculptor Richmond Barthe, painter Aaron Douglas, and choirmaster Hall Johnson. Hurston later wrote that a "psychic bond" existed between her and "Godmother" who "was just as pagan as I.") Publishes two articles in *Journal of Negro History* in October: "Communication," transcriptions from archives in St. Augustine, Florida, about Fort

Moosa, a 17th-century black settlement, and "Cudjo's
Own Story of the Last African Slaver," based partly on
interviews with Cudjo Lewis, reputed to be sole survivor
of the last slave ship to land in the United States, but
heavily supplemented by passages taken from *Historic
Sketches of the Old South* by Emma Langdon Roche (pla-
giarism is not detected until 1972). Returns to interview
Lewis several times in December and completes book-
length manuscript inspired by his life. Signs contract with
Mason on December 8; under its terms, Mason employs
Hurston as an independent agent to compile and collect
information concerning "the music, poetry, folk-lore, literature, hoodoo, conjure, manifestations of art and kin-
dred subjects relating to and existing among the North
American negroes . . ." Contract gives ownership of collected material to Mason and forbids Hurston to make
material known to anyone not designated in writing by
Mason; for her services, Hurston receives stipend of $200
per month (contract is eventually extended through
March 1931).

1928   Relationship with Sheen ends in January (they are divorced
on July 7, 1931). Resumes collecting folklore and in March
goes to sawmill camp operated by Everglades Cypress
Lumber Company near Loughman, Polk County, Florida,
that draws workers from across the South. Finds camp a
rich source of material, including folktales, work songs,
proverbs, sermons, children's rhymes, and blues. Meets
"Big Sweet," who becomes a central figure in *Mules and
Men* and *Dust Tracks on a Road.* Travels throughout
Florida, staying in and near the towns of Mulberry, Pierce,
and Lakeland (carries a pearl-handled revolver while traveling alone). Publishes "How It Feels To Be Colored Me" in
the May number of *World Tomorrow*; declares that she is
not "tragically colored." Fee goes to pay creditors for
Fire!!. Writes but does not publish essay "The Emperor
Effaces Himself," satirizing Marcus Garvey. Receives B.A.
degree from Barnard College in May. Rests in Eatonville,
then travels through Alabama; plans a volume of work
songs with music for piano and guitar. Arrives in New
Orleans in August to begin investigation of hoodoo.
Makes friends with the community of believers and followers of legendary priestess Marie Leveau (died c. 1875).
Remains in Louisiana through the winter.

1929   Stays with brother John in Jacksonville in April while organizing field notes (has by then collected more than 95,000 words of stories, games, and material on conjure and religion, along with numerous photographs). Rents a small house in Eau Gallie, hamlet north of Melbourne, Florida. Transcribes sermon preached by the Reverend C. C. Lovelace on May 3 (it will become part of first novel, *Jonah's Gourd Vine*). Falls ill with a liver ailment and is hospitalized in St. Augustine. Moves to Miami and has second and third drafts of folklore manuscript typed. Writes Hughes with ideas for a play on which they will collaborate, proposing they call it "Jook." Travels to Nassau, Bahamas, in October to collect more material, convinced by encounters with Bahamians in Florida that links exist between African-American and African-Caribbean folklore. In Nassau discovers strong African elements in Bahamian culture, including knowledge that some Bahamians had about where their ancestors came from in Africa. Experiences powerful five-day hurricane during stay. Returns to Miami after two weeks because of lack of money. Leaves for New Orleans on October 23 to continue research, as well as to help Boas' Columbia University colleague Otto Klineberg collect material (Mason has forbidden her to do so); remains in New Orleans until December. Finds that Mason's demands complicate relationship with Boas, particularly requirement that Mason's identity not be revealed.

1930   Spends January and February in the Bahamas. Writes "Dance Songs and Tales from the Bahamas" (published in July–September *Journal of American Folklore*). Lives in a rooming house in Westfield, New Jersey, from March to June; works clandestinely on play *Mule Bone: A Comedy of Negro Life* with Hughes, dictating to typist Louise Thompson, who is also receiving money from Mason. (Based on folktale "The Bone of Contention," which Hurston had collected and set in Eatonville, *Mule Bone* presents a series of oral and musical performances.) Hurston works on dialogue while Hughes concentrates on play construction and plot revisions. Returns to Florida in June, promising to complete the second act. In October, files for copyright as the sole author.

1931   Moves back to 43 West 66th Street; continues to organize field notes for folklore manuscript. Engages Elizabeth Marbury as literary agent. Takes part in bitter dispute with Hughes over rights to *Mule Bone*. Despite sporadic efforts at continued collaboration and reconciliation, the play is not produced and their friendship ends. Employment by Mason ends officially in March, but Hurston continues to receive $100 monthly stipend. Sends folklore manuscript (which will become *Mules and Men*) to friend and editor Harry Block, who likes the material but advises that it will need to be shaped into a sustained narrative for a general audience. Tries to place the monograph on Cudjo Lewis (variously titled "Kossula" and "Barracoon"). After it is rejected by Harper Brothers and Covici-Friede, withdraws it from Viking "for extensive revisions." Writes for theatrical revue *Fast and Furious*, featuring music by composers J. Rosamund Johnson and Porter Grainger and performances by black vaudevillians Jackie (Moms) Mabley and Tim Moore (who later plays "Kingfish" on television show *Amos and Andy*). Revue opens on September 15 and closes within a week; begins work on another show, *Jungle Scandals*, also with music by Grainger; the show never opens. Begins to work on *The Great Day*, a folk concert loosely structured around a single day in the life of a railroad camp; the show features much of the material later published in *Mules and Men* (Mason has refused permission to include conjure material). Gathers a group of performers and dancers and begins rehearsals. "Hoodoo in America" appears in December *Journal of American Folklore*.

1932   Special performance of *The Great Day* presented on January 10 at the John Golden Theatre on Broadway. Hurston sells her car to pay theater rental deposit and her radio to pay for performers' carfare, and borrows $530 from Mason, promising her entire box-office receipts in return. Program notes, written by Locke, emphasize the material's authenticity. Though reviews are favorable, no Broadway producer offers to take the show. Borrows more money from Mason, who has a legal document drawn itemizing material Hurston can use for "theatrical purposes." Excerpts from the show are presented at the New School for Social Research in New York on March 29, and at a cabaret at the Hotel Vanderbilt, sponsored by the Folk Dance Society, on

April 22. Too few engagements force the disbanding of the troupe. Exhausted and suffering from intestinal illness, Hurston persuades Mason to pay her fare home and leaves for Eatonville on April 28. Meets Hamilton Holt, president of whites-only Rollins College in Winter Park, and Edwin O. Grover, a Rollins professor, who invite her to visit the campus. Mason ends support permanently. Works with Robert Wunsch of Rollins English department on production of the show, now called *From Sun to Sun*, recruiting most cast members from friends and relatives in Eatonville.

1933 Suffers severe intestinal pain and conducts rehearsals on an automobile cushion. Writes one-act play, "The Fiery Chariot," for inclusion in the show. First performance is given in small experimental theater in January and then in main auditorium at Rollins in February. Schedules shows in other Florida cities; performances are given to segregated audiences. Special performance is held in Eatonville later in February. Hopes that with resources from Rollins she will realize dream of building a Negro theater. Learns that Charlotte Mason had entered New York Hospital on February 22 (she will remain there until her death on April 15, 1946). Writes "The Gilded Six-Bits," which Wunsch submits to *Story*; it appears in August. When publisher Bertram Lippincott, impressed with her story, writes to her, Hurston replies that she is working on a novel. Moves to nearby Sanford, rents house with bed and stove for $1.50 a week and, with 50 cents a week for food, given by cousin, begins to write *Jonah's Gourd Vine*. Mails the completed manuscript on October 3. Receives telegram on October 16 from Lippincott accepting it with offer of a $200 advance.

1934 Publishes essays "Characteristics of Negro Expression," "Spirituals and Neo-Spirituals," "Conversions and Visions," "Shouting," "Mother Catherine," and "Uncle Monday" in anthology *Negro*, edited by Nancy Cunard. Joins the faculty of Bethune-Cookman College in Daytona Beach, Florida, in January, expecting to establish a school of dramatic arts "based on pure Negro expression." Finds herself in disagreement with the school's president, Mary McLeod Bethune (soon to be founder of the National Council of Negro Women and an adviser to

President Roosevelt). Hurston resents the college's social obligations and low pay. After producing another version of *From Sun to Sun*, Hurston leaves the faculty. Takes group of performers to St. Louis to participate in National Folk Festival, April 29–May 2. Corresponds regularly with James Weldon Johnson, Locke, and Van Vechten. *Jonah's Gourd Vine* published in May. Lippincott agrees to publish *Mules and Men*. Spends the summer revising the manuscript while living in a cabin near the sawmill camp in Loughman, Florida, where she had collected much of her material. In September "The Fire and the Cloud," short story based on the biblical Moses, is published in *Challenge*, black literary journal edited by Dorothy West. Continues to produce folklore concerts, including one at Fisk University; Fisk's president, Thomas Jones, invites Hurston to apply for position as a drama professor, with the suggestion that she enroll for a year at Yale, at Fisk's expense, to study dramatic arts. Publishes review of *God Shakes Creation*, by David M. Cohn, in *New York Herald Tribune Books*, November 3. *Singing Steel*, a version of *Great Day*, is performed in Chicago in late November with cast made up of students Hurston met while staying at the Chicago South Parkway YWCA. Officials of the Julius Rosenwald Foundation see the performance and invite Hurston to apply for fellowship to pursue Ph.D. in anthropology at Columbia. Writes in her application that "it is almost useless to collect material to lie upon the shelves of scientific societies. . . . The Negro material is eminently suited to drama and music. In fact it *is* drama and music and the world and America in particular needs what this folk material holds." The Foundation offers Hurston $3,000 over two years, and she goes to New York to enroll for spring semester. Publishes article "Race Cannot Become Great Until It Recognizes Its Talent," a plea to blacks to recognize the value of African-American folklore, in the *Washington Tribune* on December 29.

1935   Proposes to study general ethnology and then prepare for field work in Haiti. Although plan is endorsed by Boas, the Rosenwald Foundation disapproves of her doing fieldwork and withdraws its original support, instead offering Hurston $100 a month for total fellowship of $700. Hurston enrolls in Columbia, but does not attend class. Begins writing novel and submits draft to Lippin-cott in the late spring. Gives interviews discussing *Jonah's Gourd Vine* and the forthcoming *Mules and Men*. Joins folklorists Alan Lomax and Mary Elizabeth Barnicle in June and travels with them through the South recording material for the Music Division of the Library of Congress. Gains access to rural black communities; Lomax credits her with being "almost entirely responsible for the success" of the first part of the expedition. Returns to New York in August. Takes job as a dramatic coach for the Works Progress Administration Federal Theatre Project in Harlem. *Mules and Men* is published in October to good reviews.

1936   Awarded a Guggenheim Fellowship in March to study Obeah practices in the West Indies. Arrives in Kingston, Jamaica, on April 14, after making a brief stopover in Haiti. Travels throughout the island, visiting all of its parishes; spends much time with a community of Maroons, descendants of people legendary for their resistance to slavery. Researches surviving African elements in Jamaican religious practices. Departs for Haiti on September 22 to continue her research. Finds a surfeit of material in Haiti and learns Creole. Begins novel *Their Eyes Were Watching God* and completes it on December 19.

1937   Returns to the United States in March. After receiving fellowship renewal from Guggenheim, goes back to Haiti in May. Suffers "violent gastric disturbance" in late June; frightened, believes it is related to studies of voodoo. Spends two weeks in bed, then continues to travel through Haiti while recuperating, but does not resume intensive research. Suggests that the Guggenheim Foundation fund a college of African-American music, with lectures by Duke Ellington, Fats Waller, Louis Armstrong, singer Ethel Waters, and tap dancer Bill Robinson. Returns to Florida in September, then travels to New York for the publication of *Their Eyes Were Watching God* on September 18. Novel is well received by most reviewers, although Richard Wright in *New Masses* on October 5 faults it for its lack of ideas and use of "minstrel technique." Hurston publishes a profile of Fannie Hurst in *The Saturday Review* October 9, and a review of *The Hurricane's Chil-*

dren by Carl Carmer in *New York Herald Tribune Books*,
December 26.

1938   Reacts angrily to Locke's commentary on *Their Eyes* in
            January *Opportunity*, in which he asked when she would
            begin writing "social document fiction"; writes "The
            Chick With One Hen" in response, which *Opportunity*
            declines to publish. Returns to Florida in February. Com-
            pletes manuscript based on her Caribbean research in
            Maitland in mid-March. Reviews Wright's *Uncle Tom's
            Children* in *Saturday Review*, April 2, criticizing it for its
            rendering of black southern speech and its violent repre-
            sentations of black life. Joins the Federal Writers' Project
            in Jacksonville, Florida, in April as an editor for the
            Florida volume in the American Guide series. Becomes
            involved in another Project book, "The Florida Negro"
            (never completed), patterned on Federal Writers' Project
            volume *The Negro in Virginia*. Becomes supervisor of the
            Negro unit of the Florida Federal Writers' Project. Travels
            to Washington to argue for salary increases and equip-
            ment. Leads choir sponsored by the Rollins College Folk-
            lore Group at the National Folk Festival in Washington.
            Visits black communities in the Everglades with a record-
            ing machine in July. Often takes time off to work on
            novel, *Moses, Man of the Mountain*, telling no one where
            she is. Caribbean book, *Tell My Horse*, is published in Oc-
            tober to disappointing reviews.

1939   Writes essay "Now Take Noses," caricaturing biological
            rationalizations of racial differences (later published in
            Cordially Yours, volume of essays written by participants
            in the 1939 Boston Book Fair). Receives an honorary
            Doctor of Letters degree from Morgan State College in
            June. Returns to Florida, where she records 18 songs, sto-
            ries, and explanations for the Library of Congress and the
            Folk Arts Committee of the WPA on June 18. Marries
            Albert Price III, a 23-year-old WPA playground worker,
            on June 27, in Fernandina, Nassau County, Florida (gives
            her year of birth as 1910). Leaves Price in Florida to join
            faculty of North Carolina College for Negroes in Durham
            (later North Carolina Ce....al University). Intends to start
            a drama program but becomes dissatisfied with conditions
            at the college and quarrels with the school's founder
            and president, James Edward Shepard, a leading black

educator (remains for the academic year but does not stage any plays). Lectures to white drama group in Chapel Hill on black drama and meets Paul Green, Pulitzer Prize–winning playwright and professor of drama at the University of North Carolina. Attends Green's weekly seminar and makes plans to collaborate with him on a play. In October *Tell My Horse* is published in England as *Voodoo Gods: an Inquiry into Native Myths and Magic in Jamaica and Haiti*; sales earn back $500 advance within a week. *Moses, Man of the Mountain* is published in November to mixed reviews.

1940   Files for divorce from Price in February, but they briefly reconcile and travel together to Beaufort, South Carolina, in summer, where Hurston does research on religious trances in "sanctified" churches and other topics, and helps produce a film as part of project led by anthropologist Jane Belo. (Film from expedition is deposited at the Museum of Natural History in New York.) Contracts malaria. Writes essay "Ritualistic Expression from the Lips of the Communicants of the Seventh Day Church of God, Beaufort, South Carolina" (unpublished). Returns to New York in late summer. Lectures, renews old friendships, and considers book projects; publisher Bertram Lippincott suggests she write an autobiography.

1941   Moves in late spring to Los Angeles at the invitation of Katharine Mershon, a wealthy friend; works on autobiography, *Dust Tracks on a Road*. Unsuccessfully tries to arrange for singer and actress Ethel Waters to give a benefit concert for the Hungerford School in Eatonville. Publishes short story "Cock Robin, Beale Street" in the *Southern Literary Messenger* in July. Begins work in October as story consultant at Paramount Pictures (continues until January 1942). Works on revisions of autobiography; removes critique of American imperialism after Japanese attack on Pearl Harbor on December 7.

1942   Lectures at black colleges throughout the South. Moves to St. Augustine to complete revisions of *Dust Tracks*. Spends summer collecting folklore in Florida. Publishes "Story in Harlem Slang" in July *American Mercury*. Profiles Lawrence Silas, an African-American cattleman in Florida, in *The Saturday Evening Post*, September 5

("Negro" is printed under her by-line). Returns to St. Augustine; teaches creative writing part-time at Florida Normal, a local black college, and collects data on the Seminole Indians. Begins friendship with author Marjorie Kinnan Rawlings. *Dust Tracks* is published in November to generally good reviews. Hurston is profiled in *Who's Who in America*, *Current Biography*, and *Twentieth Century Authors*, where she lists her favorite authors as Anatole France, Gorky, Shaw, Hugo, Mark Twain, Dickens, Robert Nathan, Cather, Irvin Cobb, Anne Morrow Lindbergh, and Sinclair Lewis.

1943   Moves to Daytona Beach, Florida. Purchases the *Wanago*, a 32-foot houseboat with 44 horsepower engine (will live on houseboats for the next four years). Joins Florida Negro Defense Committee, local civil rights group that Hurston favors because it does not see blacks as victims. Gives talks to segregated audiences of GIs as part of Recreation in War program, sponsored by Florida governor's wife, Mary Holland. *Dust Tracks* is awarded the $1,000 Anisfield-Wolf Book Award for the best book on race relations and Hurston is featured on the cover of *Saturday Review*, sponsor of the award, on February 20. Quoted in the *New York World Telegram* on February 1 as asserting that blacks are much better off in the South than in the North: "In other words the Jim Crow system works." After Roy Wilkins, assistant executive secretary of the NAACP, attacks her in the New York *Amsterdam News* on February 27 for talking "arrant and even vicious nonsense" for the purpose of selling her book, Hurston claims that she was misquoted. Travels to Washington in March to receive the annual Distinguished Alumni Award from Howard University and speaks to a meeting of Zeta Phi Beta. Publishes three articles in *American Mercury*: "The 'Pet Negro' System" in May, "High John de Conquer" in October, and "Negroes Without Self-Pity" in November. Divorce from Price granted November 9.

1944   Engagement to James Howell Pitts of Cleveland is announced in New York *Amsterdam News* on February 5, but marriage never takes place. Publishes "The Last Slave Ship" in *American Mercury* in March. Stays at Harlem's Hotel Theresa in the spring. Collaborates on a musical comedy with Dorothy Waring, a white writer whose husband, Stephen Kelen d'Oxylion, is a theatrical producer. Tentatively titled "Polk County," the play is to use material from "High John de Conquer," *Mules and Men*, and *Mule Bone*. Finishes play despite differences in artistic viewpoint with Waring. Contributes to the ongoing series "My Most Humiliating Jim Crow Experience" in June number of *Negro Digest*, recounting her treatment by expensive Brooklyn medical specialist who examined her in a laundry closet rather than his office. Returns to Florida, then sails back to New York on the *Wanago*. Arrives in November hoping to secure backing for production of "Polk County." After Reginald Brett, English adventurer and gold miner, tells her of unexplored Mayan ruins on the Patuca River in Honduras, Hurston applies unsuccessfully to the Guggenheim Foundation and the Library of Congress for support to do ethnographic fieldwork there.

1945   Returns to Daytona Beach and purchases new houseboat, *Sun Tan*. Publishes "The Rise of the Begging Joints," attacking "inferior" black colleges and secondary schools, in *American Mercury* in March. Makes plans to go to Honduras on schooner of Miami adventurer and friend Fred Irvine, but postpones trip to work on novel. Suffers severe intestinal pains. Writes *Mrs. Doctor*, novel about upper-class blacks, which is rejected by Lippincott in September. Finishes novel set in Eatonville, incorporating elements of myth and legend, but it is also rejected. Publishes "Crazy For This Democracy," attacking failure of the United States to extend freedom to blacks at home and to people of color abroad, in the *Negro Digest* in December.

1946   After efforts to raise money for Honduras trip fail, goes to New York to work on unsuccessful political campaign of Grant Reynolds, Republican who is running for Congress in Harlem against Democrat Adam Clayton Powell, Jr. Stays in New York after campaign, living in a rented room on 124th Street. Organizes "block mothers plan," community self-help program offering child care to Harlem women. Feeling depressed, does not look up old acquaintances; considers New York generally to be "a basement to hell," due to the impact of national, class, and race hatreds. Reviews *How God Fix Jonah* by Lorenz Graham on November 24, and *Shining Trumpets* by Rudi Blesh on December 22, for the *New York Herald Tribune Weekly Book Review*.

1947   Reviews *Journey to Accompong* by Katherine Dunham on January 12 and *Trinidad Village* by Melville and Frances Herskovits on March 9 for the *New York Herald Tribune Weekly Book Review*. Through Rawlings' introduction, Hurston signs contract with Scribner's and receives $500 advance; Maxwell Perkins is to be her editor, but he dies in June. Sails for Honduras on May 4. Stays at the Hotel Cosenza in Puerto Cortés, travels along the coast, admires its widely contrasting scenery, and regrets lack of money to do fieldwork in the interior. Receives a second advance from Scribner's and remains in Puerto Cortés, writing *Seraph on the Suwanee* (earlier titles are "Good Morning Sun" and "Sign of the Sun"). Mails draft to New York in September, then continues making revisions through December. *Caribbean Melodies for Chorus of Mixed Voices*, with arrangements by William Grant Still, is published by Oliver Ditson in Philadelphia. Negatively reviews Robert Tallant's *Voodoo in New Orleans* in the October–December *Journal of American Folklore*.

1948   Leaves Honduras on February 20 for editorial meeting with Scribner's. Completes final manuscript on March 17. Spends the summer at Constance Seabrook's home in Rhinebeck, New York. Takes a room at 140 West 112th Street in Harlem. After being falsely accused of molesting a ten-year-old boy, the son of the landlady who had rented her the room on 124th Street in 1946, Hurston is arrested on September 13. Moves to an apartment in the Bronx, leaving no forwarding address. Assisted with legal representation by Scribner's and her editor, Burroughs Mitchell. Devastated by her indictment in early October, based on charges supported solely by the word of young accuser. Story is printed in the press in mid-October as the result of tip from a black court employee. Hurston denies charges, presenting passport to prove she was in Honduras when the alleged crime occurred; wonders whether racism is responsible for court's acceptance of the child's accusations, and vows "to fight this horrible thing to the finish and clear my reputation." *Seraph* is published on October 11 to generally favorable reviews. Feels completely betrayed by her country and race when the Baltimore *Afro-American*, a nationally distributed newspaper, publishes story on October 23 headlined "Boys, 10, Accuse Zora," with subheading "Novelist Arrested on Morals Charge. Reviewer of Author's Latest Book Notes Character Is 'Hungry for Love' " (story falsely claims there are three boys involved). Hurston writes Van Vechten that she has "resolved to die."

1949   Case against Hurston is dismissed in March after investigation by Manhattan District Attorney's office shows that the boy is "disturbed" (Hurston had earlier advised his mother to have him tested at Bellevue Hospital). Reviews *New Day* by Victor Stafford Reid in the *New York Herald Tribune Weekly Book Review* on March 20. Returns to Florida. Sails with Fred Irvine on a cruise to the Bahamas. Lives on Irvine's boat in Miami and makes plans to return to Honduras. Despair subsides. Begins a new novel. Writes story "Conscience of the Court," about the trial of a black woman accused of assaulting a white man in an effort to protect her white female employer.

1950   Takes a job as a maid on Rivo Island, an affluent Miami neighborhood. When "Conscience of the Court" is published in *The Saturday Evening Post*, employer discovers Hurston is author and on March 27 article appears in the *Miami Herald* headlined "Famous Negro Author Working as Maid Here Just 'to Live a Little.' " National wire services pick up the story, which quotes Hurston as saying that she is "written out" and has taken job to do research with intention of starting a magazine "for and by domestics." Continues to work on new novel, "The Lives of Barney Turk," about the adventures of a white Floridian who travels to Central America and Hollywood (novel later rejected by Scribner's). In April *Negro Digest* publishes "What White Publishers Won't Print," attacking policies that allow only "exceptional" or "quaint" blacks to be portrayed. Leaves Rivo Island to work for conservative George Smathers, who is running against liberal Claude Pepper in the Democratic Senate primary (Smathers wins). "I Saw Negro Votes Peddled," published in November *American Legion Magazine*, offends many blacks, including moderate civil-rights leaders such as Lester Granger of the Urban League. Moves in with

friends in Belle Glade, Florida. Buys used car to explore
the Everglades.

1951   Works on novel "The Golden Bench of God," based on
the life of Madame C. J. Walker (1867–1919; born Sarah
Breedlove), who invented and manufactured products for
straightening black women's hair and became the first
black woman millionaire. Writes her literary agent, Jean
Parker Waterbury, that she plans to make it a "truly indig-
enous Negro novel," written from inside the black American world. Publishes "Mourner's Bench, Communist
Line: Why the Negro Won't Buy Communism" in the
June *American Legion Magazine,* arguing that blacks resent and reject the patronizing appeals of the Communist
Party. Moves to Eau Gallie in mid-June, renting for $5 a
week the same one-room cabin she had lived in when
finishing *Mules and Men* (will live there for five years).
Works happily repairing house and planting vegetable and
flower gardens. Learns that Scribner's has rejected "The
Golden Bench of God." Publishes "A Negro Voter Sizes
Up Taft" in *The Saturday Evening Post,* December 8, favorable profile of Ohio Senator Robert Taft, a leading candidate for the 1952 Republican presidential nomination.

1952   Lives contentedly in Eau Gallie, where her beautiful gardens attract sightseers. Begins sequel (never finished) to
Dust Tracks, writes stories about her pet dog Spot, adapts
biblical tales, researches articles on Florida cattle and co-
lonialism in Southeast Asia, and considers writing about
career women returning to work in the home. Has increasing difficulty selling work. Gives five folk concerts in
six weeks to earn money. Declines invitation to speak at
Taft *vs.* Eisenhower forum in Boston in March because
she has no winter coat. Increasingly plagued by health
problems, including a tropical virus contracted from
drinking impure water in Honduras, gall bladder infec-
tion, irritated colon, and the effects of obesity. Hired by
the *Pittsburgh Courier* to cover the trial of Ruby Mc-
Collum, a black woman charged with the murder of a
prominent white doctor who had been her lover. Unable
to gain permission to interview McCollum, Hurston
asks William Bradford Huie, a journalist and one of the
South's best-known white anti-segregationists, to intercede. Hurston's stories defending McCollum appear in

the *Courier* from October 11, 1952, to May 2, 1953. (Mc-Collum was sentenced to death; after the sentence was overturned on appeal, she was declared mentally incompetent and committed to a state hospital where she remained for 20 years; Huie published a book on the case in 1956, *Ruby McCollum: Woman in the Suwanee Jail*, which included Hurston's reporting.)

1953   Works on biography of Herod the Great, project she has contemplated for many years. Reads about Herod in works of Flavius Josephus, Livy, Eusebius, Strabo, and Nicolas of Damascus. Perceives Herod to have been a great soldier, statesman, and lover and hopes that dramatic treatment of his life will interest Cecil B. DeMille, Hollywood producer and director of biblical epics.

1954   Continues to work on Herod the Great, which she acknowledges has become her "great obsession"; invites Winston Churchill to write the book's introduction and commentary.

1955   Writes letter to the Orlando *Sentinel* in August condemning the 1954 Supreme Court decision in *Brown* v. *Board of Education*, which ruled segregated schools unconstitutional; Hurston criticizes the Court's implication that black children could learn only when they went to school with whites. Letter is widely reprinted in southern newspapers and produces a sensation that surprises Hurston and angers civil-rights leaders. Scribner's rejects the Herod manuscript, which has grown to encompass Jewish history and the origins of a "movement" which produced Christianity and Western civilization. Despite the rejection, Hurston continues to work on the book.

1956   Engages a "book hunting agency" to find copies of *Dust Tracks* and *Their Eyes Were Watching God* to send to Dutch translator Margrit Sablonière. Receives eviction notice in March from landlord, who is selling the house. Moves out in mid-May. Receives award for "education and human relations" at the Bethune-Cookman College commencement in late May. Takes job in June as library clerk at Patrick Air Force Base in Cocoa Beach, Florida, and is paid $1.88 an hour for filing technical literature. Hates job.

1957   Fired from job in May (supervisor explains that she is
            "too well educated"). Receives unemployment insurance.
            Moves to Merritt Island and lives in a house trailer and
            drives an old station wagon. Suffers from stomach ulcer,
            but continues to work on "Herod." After C. E. Bolen,
            publisher of the *Fort Pierce Chronicle*, a local black news-
            paper, invites her to write for his publication in Decem-
            ber, Hurston moves to Fort Pierce and for the next two
            years writes articles on various subjects and contributes a
            column on "Hoodoo and Black Magic."

1958   Works as substitute teacher at Lincoln Park Academy, the
            segregated public school for blacks in Fort Pierce. Rents
            small cinder-block house at 1734 School Court. Plants
            azaleas, gardenias, morning glories, collard greens, and
            tomatoes. Works on "Herod" and tries to find another
            publisher. Becomes good friends with her landlord and
            physician, Dr. C. C. Benton, who visits often and occa-
            sionally buys her groceries. Health deteriorates: suffers
            from high blood pressure, as well as intestinal pains.

1959   Suffers stroke and is left weak and mentally distracted.
            Applies to the county welfare office in May for money to
            pay for medicine; begins receiving food vouchers in June.
            Writes occasionally for the *Chronicle*. Condition contin-
            ues to deteriorate and on October 29 Hurston enters the
            Saint Lucie County Welfare Home. Refuses to contact
            members of family; has long been out of touch with
            friends and acquaintances from earlier years of her life.

1960   Dies January 28 in the Saint Lucie County Welfare Home
            from "hypertensive heart disease." Following funeral on
            February 7 paid for by collection from local friends and
            acquaintances, Hurston is buried in an unmarked grave in
            the Garden of Heavenly Rest, a segregated cemetery in
            Fort Pierce.

Note on the Texts

This volume presents the texts of *Mules and Men* and *Tell My Horse*, Zora Neale Hurston's two books on folklore; a new, restored text of her autobiography, *Dust Tracks on a Road*; and a selection of 22 articles, some that were published in periodicals and books and others (not published during her lifetime) that were written for the Federal Writers' Project in Florida.

Hurston made several trips through the South in 1927–29 to collect folklore and then began to organize her extensive field notes into a manuscript. Shaping the book was difficult, and Hurston wrote several drafts before discovering the structure she wanted to use. The book was completed in Eatonville, Florida, in late summer 1932, but Hurston was unable to find a publisher until Bertram Lippincott, who had published her novel *Jonah's Gourd Vine,* accepted it in 1934. Lippincott urged Hurston to make the book less technical and to add the material on hoodoo that had appeared in *The Journal of American Folklore* (October–December 1931). Hurston agreed and spent the summer of 1934 making revisions. *Mules and Men,* with an introduction by Franz Boas and illustrations by Miguel Covarrubias, was published by J. B. Lippincott, Inc., in October 1935. Hurston made no further revisions in the book. The text printed here, including the introduction and illustrations, is that of the first and only edition published during her lifetime.

Tell My Horse is the result of Hurston's fieldwork in Jamaica and Haiti during the years 1936 and 1937. The book was completed in March 1938 and published by Lippincott in October 1938. Hurston made no further revisions in the book, and the text and photographs printed here are those of the first edition. The Creole passages in the book, especially those in the Appendix, present a particular problem because it is clear that Hurston and her editors did not carefully proofread them. Since the orthography of Haitian Creole was not established until 1979, many variations in spelling and in the use of apostrophes and accents were common in the 1930s; these variations are accepted in this volume. However, the 1938 edition contained many careless settings, such as "u" repeatedly printed "n," single words made into two, and two words made into one. All these errors have been corrected in this volume and recorded in the list of typographical errors at the end of this note. One error occurring consistently throughout the book—the spelling of the musical instrument "ascon" without a cedilla—has been corrected to the more usual

Creole spelling of "asson," but has not been listed. The Creole text printed above the music in the appendix has been similarly corrected, but no emendation has been made within the musical notation.

Hurston began writing her autobiography *Dust Tracks on a Road* early in 1941 at the urging of her publisher Bertram Lippincott. She probably completed an early draft by late July or early August 1941, since the manuscript of a concluding chapter not used in the first edition, "Seeing the World as It Is," is dated July 5, 1941, and the manuscript of another unused chapter, "The Inside Light—Being a Salute to Friendship," is dated July 20, 1941. Examination of the setting copy and other related materials, however, reveals that before the book was published by J. B. Lippincott in November 1942 it had gone through many changes.

The typed setting copy of *Dust Tracks* and other associated papers, donated by Hurston to the James Weldon Johnson Collection in the Beinecke Library at Yale University, are in Box I, Folders 10–15, of the Hurston Papers. Folder 10 contains holograph manuscripts of six chapters, only two of which, "School Again" and "Love," became part of the completed book. The other four manuscripts are early draft versions of chapters titled "The Inside Light—Being a Salute to Friendship"; "Concert"; "My People, My People" (a text different from the book version); and "Seeing the World as It Is." Folder 11 contains four typed chapters: "My People, My People" (dated Port-au-Prince, Haiti, July 2, 1937, and different from the book and holograph versions of that chapter); "Seeing the World as It Is"; and two copies, ribbon and carbon, of "Chapter Eleven" (an unused intermediary version of a concluding chapter). Folders 12–15 contain the marked typescript used as setting copy for the book, including a typed title page dated Los Angeles, California, January 14, 1942, indicating the date of another completed draft. Hurston's handwritten and signed note on the title page reads: "To The James Weldon Johnson Memorial Collection of Negro Arts and Letters at Yale University through the efforts of Carl Van Vechten to enrich it." At the bottom of the page she wrote: "Parts of this manuscript were not used in the final composition of the book for publisher's reasons."

Since the Lippincott editorial files have not been located, it is not possible to determine all the stages of composition the book went through before it was completed, but an examination of the existing materials does give some idea of the process of revision. For instance, when Hurston (perhaps on the advice of an editor) revised chapter XII, "My People, My People," she retained some of the original holograph chapter, moved another part to chapter II, "My Folks," and omitted the last section of the holograph version (later used in an article, "The 'Pet Negro' System"). The final version of chapter XII also uses some material from the rejected concluding chapter, "Seeing the World as It Is" (dated July 5, 1941). A small portion of "Seeing the World as It Is" was used in chapter XVI, "Looking Things Over," which became the concluding chapter used in the published version. Parts of the holograph chapter "Concert" were incorporated into chapters X and XI of the completed book, and parts of the holograph chapter "The Inside Light—Being a Salute to Friendship" (dated July 20, 1941) were incorporated into chapters IX, X, and XI. The two unused concluding chapter typescripts ("Seeing the World as It Is" and "Chapter Eleven") and the marked setting copy also show many intermediary stages of composition. Changes in pagination and chapter numbers indicate that the book at one time had as few as eleven chapters and at another time as many as eighteen. Some chapters were obviously written later than others, such as chapter XIV, "Love"; some were revised and expanded, such as chapter II, "My Folks"; some were shifted from one position to another, such as chapter XV, "Religion." A close examination of the pagination seems to indicate that the 11-chapter draft consisted of chapters I, II, V, VI, VII, VIII, IX, XV, XII, XIII (according to the final chapter numbers presented in this volume), plus the unused concluding "Chapter Eleven."

Although the surviving materials give some idea of the kinds of revision Hurston made while working with her editors, they do not make it possible to recreate the text she originally intended. They do, however, show her final intention, in the form of the typescript she prepared for use as setting copy. This typescript was cut by her editors by almost 10 percent before the book was published in November 1942. The deletions fall into three basic categories: possibly libelous material, political opinion, and sexually explicit passages. Most of the deletions in the first half of the book were made in the typescript, and most of the deletions in the second half were made after the book had been set in galleys. The typescript contains some holograph corrections and additions made by Hurston, as well as a few editorial alterations of style and corrections of typographical errors. Because the cuts were not initiated by Hurston but were made "for publisher's reasons," the text of *Dust Tracks on a Road* printed here is that of Hurston's complete final typescript, including her holograph revisions and additions; typographical errors have been corrected. Therefore, this is the first publication of the restored and unexpurgated text of *Dust Tracks on a Road*. Special thanks are due to Henry Louis Gates, Jr., for consultation on this new text. The deletions made by Hurston's editors in the first edition are indicated in the notes to this volume.

This volume also includes an appendix of four chapters related to the autobiography. The version of "My People, My People" that Hurston wrote in Haiti in 1937, before she had thought of doing an autobiography, was used only slightly when she was composing *Dust Tracks on a Road.* The text printed here is that of the typed copy in Folder 11. "Seeing the World as It Is" was Hurston's earlier concluding chapter (at that time the fourteenth). It bears editors' marks, queries, disagreements, misunderstandings about Hurston's use of the word "Orient," and numerous deletion marks against paragraphs, as well as this concluding comment: "Suggest eliminating international opinions as irrelevant to autobiography." The text printed here is that of the typed copy in Folder 11. For the two other pieces, "The Inside Light—Being a Salute to Friendship" and "Concert," the texts printed here are those of the holograph manuscripts in Folder 10.

Hurston never collected her articles in book form. Of the 22 articles selected for inclusion here, all but five were published during her lifetime in magazines and books but were not reprinted while she was alive. The other five were not published during her lifetime. The specific texts of the articles used in this volume are listed below.

"The Eatonville Anthology" was published in *The Messenger* in three parts: parts 1–11 appeared in September 1926, parts 12–13 in October 1926, and the final unnumbered piece in November 1926. It was not reprinted during Hurston's lifetime. The story in part 13 was left incomplete in the periodical (see note 823.36 in this volume).

"How It Feels To Be Colored Me" was published in *The World Tomorrow* in May 1928 and was not reprinted during Hurston's lifetime.

"Characteristics of Negro Expression," "Conversions and Visions," "Shouting," "Mother Catherine," "Uncle Monday," and "Spirituals and Neo-Spirituals" were all published in *Negro: An Anthology,* edited by Nancy Cunard and published in an edition of 1,000 by Wishart & Company in London, England, on February 15, 1934. They were not reprinted during Hurston's lifetime.

"Folklore and Music," "Negro Mythical Places," "The Sanctified Church," and "The Ocoee Riot" were all written for "The Florida Negro," a project that was never completed, during the time Hurston worked for the Federal Writers' Project in Florida in 1938. The texts printed here are from the typescripts in the Florida Historical

Society Papers in the University of South Florida Library, Tampa, Florida. The text of "Art and Such," written for the Federal Writers' Project and not published during Hurston's lifetime, is from *Reading Black, Reading Feminist: A Critical Anthology,* edited by Henry Louis Gates, Jr., published in New York by Meridian Press, 1990.

"Stories of Conflict," a review of Richard Wright's *Uncle Tom's Children,* was published in *The Saturday Review,* April 2, 1938.

"The 'Pet Negro' System," based on material originally written by Hurston as part of her autobiography, was published in *The American Mercury,* March 1943. A revised and condensed version was published in *Negro Digest* in June 1943. The text printed here is that of *The American Mercury.*

"High John de Conquer" was published in *The American Mercury,* October 1943.

"Negroes Without Self-Pity" was published in *The American Mercury,* November 1943.

"My Most Humiliating Jim Crow Experience" was published as part of a series under that title in *Negro Digest,* June 1944.

"The Rise of the Begging Joints" was published in *The American Mercury,* March 1945. A condensed version entitled "Beware the Begging Joints" was published in *Negro Digest* in May 1945. The text printed here is that of *The American Mercury.*

"Crazy for this Democracy" was published in *Negro Digest,* December 1945.

"What White Publishers Won't Print" was published in *Negro Digest,* April 1950.

"Court Order Can't Make Races Mix," appeared as a letter to the editor in the *Orlando Sentinel* on August 11, 1955.

This volume presents the texts of the original holographs, typescripts, and printings chosen for inclusion here; it does not attempt to reproduce features of the typographic design of the printed texts, such as display capitalization of chapter openings. The texts are printed without change, except for the correction of typographical errors. Spelling, punctuation, and capitalization are often expressive features, and they are not altered, even when inconsistent or irregular. The following is a list of typographical errors corrected, cited by page and line number: 17.29, already."; 17.36, please.; 24.26, coat an; 32.34–35, "Ah . . . you!"; 35.36, its; 37.6, that; 44.36, Charlies; 45.22, Massa' bout; 46.16, Yo,; 56.3, "Jack; 60.30, Ella, Wall; 62.4–5, County. [line break followed by paragraph indentation] How; 73.36, his; 79.21, 'im.; 82.34, fortunes.; 84.5–6, train bid; 86.12, Lennie; 86.28, put in; 88.8, Pinkney.; 88.13, Pinkney.; 88.20, it.; 89.24, seegar."; 101.13, Oliver,; 112.19, tired.; 119.26, place.; 120.16, Yelled;

123.11, breath."; 123.18, Talkin'; 124.7, "My . . . people,"; 124.8, "You; 125.28, him,; 129.14, Aint; 131.4, years; 132.10, Gran'pa"; 133.39, such; 134.14, go' head; 134.28, "Dat; 135.24, Willie."; 135.35, Allen's; 136.35, 2:21); 140.16, game",; 144.33, dere.'; 148.37, her,; 154.32, begin'; 155.27, Gal.'"; 166.16, Somewhere." Said; 194.39, See glossary; 211.37, So.; 215.18, harm.; 225.31, as of; 244.2, Rythm; 256.15, times; 277.12, Liebowitz; 278.36, instrument and of; 288.21, must; 297.11, "penner."; 298.27, weed." He; 302.20, do go; 314.25, even is; 324.1, The flung; 332.15, fellows,; 334.36–335.2, "fire . . . is." "But; 335.10, Sam." Someone; 336.7, bertayed; 346.27, Christophe; 348.24, The editor; 349.27, says; 356.6, Andre'; 358.2, Sejourne'; 365.9, capitol; 386.17, passes.; 388.35, mouter; 390.6, ninim; 390.15, Mirorize; 390.16, Movin; 390.25, Docu, Doca; 390.31, Moun; 390.31, mouti'; 400.30, 'Ogoun; 401.22, said; 415.20, capitol; 418.17, Eternal; 418.20, Gabriel Raphael; 418.35, Erzulie,; 424.17, l'our; 429.5, onape'; 429.30, Anhe'; 430.25, rabi; 443.17, Moudong; 443.38, head; 444.28, tonelle; 444.33, the the; 447.30, Moudong; 448.38, gown,; 451.16, quit; 451.31, features; 456.5, remenant; 456.21, woman; 456.34, to openly; 457.12, souless; 461.16, langarge; 461.26, one more; 461.32, baggage; 461.33, duange' on; 461.36, me."; 461.37, ca on; 461.37, connasis; 461.37, Mais, on; 463.17, horses; 497.16, originator's; 501.28, Faitre; 501.29, Maide'; 508.24, Dore'; 514.34, Kussula; 515.38, Abomeh; 519.23, tattoed; 521.29, He . . . calling,; 521.38, yes."; 524.7, besides; 525.27, varigated; 528.13, and be; 533.6, ro seé; 533.8, Ersu lie; 534.3, laquain; 534.3, rétem songéogoun Fé raille; 534.3, conso lé; 534.4, prendconrail; 534.5, ron sima lade; 534.5, non yé; 534.6, nonyé; 534.6, con so le; 534.7, con rail; 535.3, Aanago; 535.4, Ana go Cotéma; 535.9, timoun; 535.10, yoma; 535.10, man dé; 535.11, yéma; 535.11, man dé on; 535.12, pa pa; 535.5, poté; 536.12, mi sè; 536.13, pon; 537.7, Dan; 537.8, qui té; 537.8, tom bé; 537.9, Dan; 537.10, tom bé; 538.2, Sa lut; 538.3, sé vi; 538.5, sé vi; 539.3, çonça; 539.3, I bo; 539.4, danté; 539.5, çam danté I bo; 539.5, An an Iyan man; 539.12, gindémoin; 539.13, gindé moins; 540.2, wè do; 540.3, Wè do Fiolĕ; 540.4, Dam ba la; 540.9, tra vail; 540.10, tra vail; 540.11, dor mi; 540.11, sou per; 541.2, Pim ba; 541.7, rè lè; 541.8, rè lè; 541.8, Sa longgo; 541.9, Tousa Tou sa rè lè; 541.9, Sa longgo; 542.5, Ello Loco Ma Lo.; 543.3, Mam bo; 543.4, pra lé quáléfré; 543.4, m'pra lé; 543.5, yo Mam bo; 543.5, ron; 543.5, I san; 543.6, céron; 543.6, ron; 544.3, cá conclèv oh! lèv oh!; 545.2, pon; 545.3, chan té; 545.3, oud ronan hounfort ou; 545.4, on mon tre criole than son ni vo Pi Vo on criole; 545.5, ga té mo yen; 545.6, ni vo pon; 545.7, chan télnan houn for; 545.7, Pi ga; 545.7, mon tré; 545.7, chan son; 546.2, man yanga dé; 546.3, ga dé houn for; 546.3, ma yan; 546.3–4, be! Gué Man; 546.4, guí; 546.4, Man yanga dé houn for;

546.5, Ga dé houn for; 546.5, So bo; 546.5, Man yan; 546.12, conle; 546.12, man de; 546.13, Sane; 546.13, conlé; 546.13, man dé dra po; 546.13, O goun; 549.2, D. L. DUROSEAU; 813.12, Me!; 813.33, me!; 818.35, Mosely; 822.16, I don't; 835.8, track; 841.9, its; 858.32, spirit."; 912.21, fullfilment; 920.10, Sheppard; 957.13, of.

Notes

In the notes below, reference numbers denote page and line of this volume (the line count includes chapter headings). No note is made for material included in standard desk-reference books such as Webster's *Collegiate, Biographical,* and *Geographical* dictionaries. Footnotes in the text and the glossary on pages 229–31 are Hurston's own. Biblical references are keyed to the King James Version. Translations of Haitian Creole are by Dr. Régine A. Latortue, chair of the department of Africana studies at Brooklyn College. For further background than is contained in the Notes and the Chronology, see Robert E. Hemenway, *Zora Neale Hurston: A Literary Biography* (Urbana: University of Illinois Press, 1977); Karla Holloway, *The Character of the Word: The Texts of Zora Neale Hurston* (Westport: Greenwood Press, 1987); Lillie Pearl Howard, *Zora Neale Hurston* (Boston: Twayne Publishers, 1980); and N. Y. Nathiri, *Zora! Zora Neale Hurston: A Woman and Her Community* (Orlando: Sentinel Communications Co., 1991).

MULES AND MEN

39.13   trace chains] Harness chains.

58.7   "Chirck, . . . crow."] Singing game in which the predatory "craney crow" tries to catch the "chicks" while the "hen" tries to protect them.

66.4   Ah fade yuh] Crapshooting slang for taking one's bet, covering one's offered bet.

66.7   hard heads] Black persons.

81.9   'vaperator] Evaporators are receptacles used either to boil down sugar cane or maple sap or to generate steam for a still.

157.35–36   Seaboard . . . A.C.L.] The Seaboard Air Line and Atlantic Coast Line railroads.

180.35–36   fanfootin'] Running around, seeking sexual relations.

184.22   tignon] Traditional head kerchief.

211.29   kotch] Or cotch, a card game.

TELL MY HORSE

The translations of Haitian Creole in the notes below are by Dr. Régine A. Latortue.

277.9–10   Norman W. Manley] A leader of the Jamaican bar, Manley (1893–1969) was appointed King's Counsel in 1932; he founded the People's National Party, Jamaica's first political party, in 1938, and was Jamaican chief minister, 1952–59, and prime minister, 1959–62.

277.12   Leibowitz] Samuel Leibowitz (1893–1978), New York criminal defense attorney who helped defend the Scottsboro boys.

280.19   "Of Thee I Sing"] Musical comedy (1931), book by George S. Kaufman, Morrie Ryskind, Ira Gershwin, music by George Gershwin.

283.16   Mrs. Norman W. Manley] Edna Swithenbank Manley.

294.15–16   some one . . . dances] Dancer, choreographer, and writer Katherine Dunham (b. 1910) received a Rosenwald Foundation fellowship to study dance in the Caribbean while a student of anthropology at the University of Chicago; she later created dance forms using African and Caribbean movements and formed the Katherine Dunham Dance Company. She described her stay in Accompong in *Journey to Accompong* (1945).

294.29   Afro-Karamante'] Persons brought from the Gold Coast as slaves were known as Coromantee in Jamaica; spelled Karamante, the name came to refer to the "secret" language of the Maroons.

307.17   hasslets] Or haslets, edible inner organs.

314.12   coolie] A reference to East Indians.

332.12   Cacos] A term for peasants from the northern hills who fought for various political leaders and against the American occupation of Haiti.

333.26   Theodore] Davilmar Theodore became president in November 1914 and fled into exile on a Dutch steamer on February 22, 1915, the day before Sam's revolutionary army entered Port-au-Prince. Sam was elected president by the national assembly on March 4, 1915.

333.27   General Bobo] Rosalvo Bobo, minister of the interior under Theodore, began fomenting a revolution in the north shortly after Sam became president; his Caco forces began threatening Cap Haitien in June 1915.

334.4   Champ de Mars] Chief square in Port-au-Prince and the location of the president's palace.

335.6   Polynice] A general with a history of distinguished service.

342.12   Dr. Dorsainville] Physician J. C. Dorsainvil, author of books on Haitian history, voodoo, and psychology.

345.32   patriots of 1804] Jean Jacques Dessalines (1758–1806), Henri Christophe (1767–1820; as Henri I, king of northern Haiti from 1807), and Alexandre Pétion (1770–1818; president of an independent republic in southern Haiti from 1807) were among the army leaders who on January 1, 1804, abjured allegiance to France, established the name of Haiti for the former colony of St.-Domingue, and wrote a declaration of independence in which Dessalines was proclaimed governor-general of Haiti for life with the authority to choose his successor. After Dessalines was crowned emperor in October, a new constitution declared Haiti an independent free and sovereign state, abolished slavery, and forbade the acquisition of property by whites of any nationality.

349.8   Gros Negre] A person of wealth or position, or one who has held a political office or a high military position.

351.7   Vincent] Sténio Vincent was president of Haiti, 1930–41.

355.8   Quentin Reynolds] An American journalist.

358.6–8   Creole . . . religion.] Haitian Creole was established as a written language in 1979. Before then transcribers used various spellings and forms of apostrophes and accents. Some words used in rituals, songs, or as passwords are not translatable. Creole was recognized as an official language of the state, and voodoo as a legitimate religion, in the constitution adopted in 1987. Faine was the author of *Philologie Creole* (1937).

367.19   Ah Bo Bo!] A ritual acclamation similar to "so be it," used somewhat like "Amen."

374.2–3   David . . . Absalom.] 2 Samuel 18:33.

374.5   Damon . . . Jonathan.] In classical legend, Damon offered himself as a hostage so that his friend Pythias, condemned to death by Dionysius of Syracuse, could go home to settle his affairs. When Pythias returned just in time to prevent Damon's execution in his stead, the tyrant was so moved that he released both men. For David and Jonathan, see 2 Samuel 1:26.

382.31   Damballah . . . ou.] Damballah Ouedo, you are the wise man in your temple.

382.35–383.3   Damballah . . . yo.] Ah Damballah, good day, good day, good day, Damballah Ouedo! / Then to ask, Damballah, how are you, oh, oh, oh yes I am fine, Damballah / Ouido, I am fine, I am with you.

388.33–36   "Erzulie . . . Maitresse."] "Erzulie Tocan Freida Dahomey, You are the one we need, you are the best / Mistress [i.e., Goddess] Erzulie Freida Tocan, my spirit is yours / You are the true Mistress [Goddess]."

390.6–7   "Erzulie, . . . yagaza."] "Godmother [i.e., Goddess] Erzulie, oh! hey! Godmother [Goddess] Erzulie, oh! hey! / Your spirit rises within me; it is I, yagaza."

390.9–16   "General . . . yagaza."] "General Jean-Baptiste, oh little [i.e., dear, dear little] godfather / You have entered the temple, yes godfather / All the ladies are on their knees, their rosary in hand / Praying to you about their tribulations / The children are on their knees, rosary in hand / God-

mother [i.e., Goddess] Erzulie oh, Hey, grandmother Erzulie Freida / Dague, Tocan, Miroize, godmother [goddess] oh, hey / Your spirit rises within
me; it is I, yagaza."

390.19–27   "Oh Aziblo . . . yo.]   "Oh Aziblo, who says, who says this is
bo yo / Ba houn bloco ita ona yo, Damballah Ouedo / Tocan, Syhrinise o
Agoue', Ouedo, Pap Ogoun oh, / Dambala, O Legba Hypolite, Oh / Ah
Brozacaine, Azaca, Neque, nago, nago, breaks their hearts / Oh Loco, co
loco, bel loco Ouedo, African Loco / Ta Manibo, Doçu, Doça, D agoué
myself / Negue, candilica calicassague, ata, couine des / Oh mogue', Cle-
mezie, Clemeille, tie them all, papa."

390.29–31   "Erzulie, . . . Hey!"]   "Erzulie, Godmother [i.e., Goddess]
oh, hey grandmother Erzulie / Freida dague, Tocan Miroize, mother, godmother [goddess] oh, hey! / Your spirit rises within me; it is I yagaza, Hey!"

394.3–6   "Papa Legba, . . . moin."]   "Papa Legba, open the gate for me,
agoe / Papa Legba, open the gate for me / Attibon Legba, open the gate so
I may enter / So I may truly enter [the temple], so that my *loa* [god] may
enter; then I can thank my *loa*."

397.9   Va, . . . Valadi.]   Go, Loco, Loco Valadi' . . .

398.32–34   The White . . . Wirkus.]   In *The White King of La Gonave*
(1931), which he wrote with Taney Dudley, Wirkus claims that as a U.S. marine assigned to the island in 1925 he was crowned king by the supreme queen
of Congo societies of La Gonave, and reigned until he was transferred to the
constabulary at Port-au-Prince in 1929.

404.19–20   "Har'au . . . morts]   "Har'au Va Erique Dan, Sobo Dis You
who are [exist] / It is God who is the Master, [God of] Africa Guinea, all the
dead . . . "

417.29–30   "Papa . . . passer."]   See page 394.3–6 and note.

418.14–17   Ela Grand-Pere . . . sain'en.]   Ela Eternal Great-Father [i.e.,
Almighty God], / Us: Ela Eternal Great-Father, sin dior e' / Ela Eternal
Great-Father, Sin dior docor Ague' / Ela Eternal Great-Father Sime nan-min
bon O sain'en.

423.35–36   "Afrique-Guinin . . . nous."]   "God of Africa Atibon Legba,
open the gate for us."

424.5–8   "Au nom . . . Defait."]   "In the name of the Great Master
[i.e., Almighty God; the God of gods, the Christian Catholic God], Tocan
Frieda Dahomey, Marassas, Dossou, Dossa, all the Spirits, Atibon, Ogoun,
Locos, Africans who do, Africans who undo."

424.16–17   "Ce Letbah, . . . l'ouvri."]   "It is Legba who is coming, it is
papa Legba, let the gate be open."

424.35–36   "Ouanga . . . Croix."]   "Accept this offering papa Legba,

Legba Touton, Legba Atibon—" . . . "All houncis make the sign of the cross."

429.5–6   "Aisan, hey! . . . Gis."]   "Aisan, hey! You are letting it flow / Aisan, hey! Oua te' Corone' Gis."

429.29–32   "Loco Anbe'! . . . he'!"]   "Loco Anbe'! It is Loco . . . Loco he'!"

430.24–25   "Vivant . . . rainmin."]   "The disciples do not love the *loa*, they hate voodoo, it is only the spells that they like."

447.3–6   "Wah, . . . Pas Tombé."]   "Wah, wah, wah, wah, wah, O bay . . . / Do not fall."

447.15–18   Bah day . . . eee.]   These lines are not translatable.

477.30–31   Pas capab']   They are not capable; they cannot.

485.39   *Tome Premier]   *Description topographique, physique, civile, politique et historique de la partie française de l'île de Saint-Domingue,* (2 vols., 1797), Vol. I.

487.6–8   Carrefour tingindingue . . . bas]   Crossroad, tingindingue, half-high, half-low / Crossroad, tingindingue, half-high, half-low /Let us go, tingindingue, half-high, half-low . . .

488.13   "Sortie . . . malingue']   Exiting from the cemetery, my entire body feels dis-eased . . .

492.28–29   "Si lili . . . haut."]   "Si lili te' houmba, min dia, half high."

533.7–8   MAITRESSE . . . gaza.]   MISTRESS ERSULIE / Godmother [i.e., Goddess] Ersulie, oh! Godmother [Goddess] Ersulie, oh! Ersulie ya gaga gaaza / The dew is abundant until the sun rises. / The dew is abundant until the sun rises. / Godmother [Goddess] Ersulie oh! Godmother [Goddess] Ersulie oh! Ersulie ya gaza.

534.2–8   Féraille . . . sura.]   Féraille oh! in whose hands shall I leave things [i.e., who will be the protector of my temple?] / Whenever I think of you, Ogoun Féraille / I have some consolation and gain more courage oh! / But what happens if I become ill? oh / What happens if my body drowns? oh! what will happen then? / Yet I have some consolation and gain more courage oh! / so bé guim as sura.

535.2–4   Coté . . . Anago . . .]   Where shall I go [i.e., where goes my life] Where shall I go Médi oh! / Anago Where shall I go Where shall I go Médi oh! / Anago . . .

535.9–13   Bonjour . . . Bon.]   Good morning papa Legba good morning my children / Good morning papa Legba good morning my children / I am asking you how you are doing / I am asking you how you are doing / good morning papa Legba good morning my children Good.

536.2–6   Adia . . . félé.] Adia give me the pole that is all broken / Adia give me the pole that is all broken / Adia give me the one that is marked broken / Adia give me the one that is marked broken / Adia give me the pole that is all broken.

536.12–15   Adi . . . moins.] Good lord what would I say if I am last oh! / look at the misery heaped upon my shoulders / good lord what would I say if I am last oh! / look at the misery heaped upon my shoulders.

537.2–3   St. Jacques . . . moin.] St. Jacques is not there St. Jacques is not there St. Jacques is not there / I am the one who is there St Jacques is not there oh! the dog bit me.

537.7–10   Nous . . . oh!] We want to see Don Petro We want to see oh! / We want to see if they'll let the house fall down / We want to see Don Petro We want to see oh! / We want to see oh! If they'll let the house fall down oh!

538.2–5   Salut . . . moins Salut.] Greetings to me oh! Greetings to me oh! Greetings to me / We serve in your house oh! Greetings to me. / oh dear lord greetings to me oh Greetings to me oh Greetings to me / we serve in your house oh! Greetings to me Greetings.

539.2–5   Ibo . . . man.] Ibo Lélé Ibo Lélé Iyanman / what's wrong with you Ibo Lélé / that is how I dance Ibo Iyanman oh! Anan Iyanman / That's how I dance Ibo Iyanman oh! Anan Iyanman.

539.11–13   Ibo . . . moins.] Ibo I am alone oh! Ibo I am alone oh! / Ibo I am alone oh! I have no mother to guide me / Grand Ibo I am alone oh! I have no mother to guide me.

540.2–4   Fiolé . . . Dambala.] Fiolé for Dambalá Dambala Wèdo / Fiolé oh! Dambala Wèdo Fiolé for Dambala/ Dambala Wèdo Fiolé for Dambala.

540.9–12   Ogoun . . . souper.] Ogoun works oh! Ogoun for food / Ogoun works oh! Ogoun for food / Ogoun works all night long so that Ogoun can eat / last night Ogoun went to sleep without supper.

541.2   Zin . . . Pimba] Apparently untranslatable.

541.7   Tousa . . . Salonggo.] All, All of this is called also Salonggo . . .

542.2–5   Loco . . . Ello. . .] Loco Mabia Ebon Azacan Loco Mabia Ello oh! / Loco Mabia Ello Azagan Loco Mabia Ello oh! / Jean valou I am Jean valou / I am Loco Loco Mabia Ello . . .

543.2–6   Mambo . . . oh!] Mambo Isan I am leaving Oh! I am leaving for Africa/ I'm leaving to go look for my family Mambo Isan I am leaving / Oh! I am leaving for Africa I'm leaving to go look for my family / Mambo Isan oh! you are the one holding me back Mambo Isan oh! / you are the one holding me back you are the [only] one who can release me oh!

544.2–3   Filé . . . oh!] Crawling we crawl behind the wife of Dambala Wèdo / Crawling we crawl behind Dambala Wèdo who is the snake oh! . . .

545.2–9   Aroquè . . . nivo.] Aroquè if you have a new song to sing / you'll sing it in your temple only in your temple / Don't you dare sing your new song in Creole / Creole will spoil your chances with Agoë ta royo, / the Black from the blue well, the Black from salty waters, the black with golden shells. / If you have a new song to sing / You'll sing it in your temple Don't you dare sing your new song in Creole.

546.2–5   Gué . . . bé!] Gué Manyan manyan guard the temple / you must guard the temple Sobo gué manyan be! / O gué Manyan Manyan / guard the temple Sobo / Guard the temple Sobo Gué Manyan bé!

546.12–14   Alou . . . baba.] Alou man dia hé! Ogoun oh! ohsans yo oh! aho! / Alou man O the blood of whoever asks for the flag will spill / The blood of whoever asks for the flag will spill unless Ogoun stops it.

547.3–5   Carrefour . . . bas] See note 487.6–8.

547.14   Sortie . . . malingue] See note 488.13.

548.2–4   Héla . . . yen.] Hail eternal father saint Joseph / Hail eternal father saint Josephdo co agué / Hail eternal father, all is in the hands of God the Almighty.

549.1   LA MYSTÉRIEUSE, MÉRINGUE] "The Mysterious Woman, Meringue." A meringue is a dance.

549.3   ETONNEMENT, . . . CARACTÉRISTIQUE] "Wonder [or Astonishment, or Amazement], Characteristic Meringue."

550.1–2   —BONNE . . . à] "Good Mood/Haitian Meringue/to . . ."

551.1   OLGA . . . PAR] "Olga, Meringue by."

552.2   CHANSON DE CALICOT] "Calicot Song."

553.1   LA DOUCEUR] "Softness [or Sweetness]."

DUST TRACKS ON A ROAD

562.15   Clinch] Brigadier General Duncan Lamont Clinch (1787–1849) fought against the Seminole at the battles of the Withlacoochee River, December 1835 and January 1836.

562.17   Miccanopy, Billy Bow-legs] Chiefs of the Seminole during the Second Seminole War (1835–42).

570.37–571.2   There was . . . morals.] Cut from the typescript and omitted in the Lippincott and later editions.

572.14   chick-mah-chick] See note 58.7.

574.5   trace-chain] See note 39.13.

576.18–22   It was . . . paper.] Cut in galleys and omitted in the Lippin-cott and later editions.

577.32   hasslits] See note 307.17.

586.27   doubleteened] Variant of "double-teamed," ganged up on.

598.13–14   columns . . . McIntyre] The syndicated column "New York Day by Day" by McIntyre (1884–1938) ran in about 300 newspapers from 1912 to 1938.

600.31–32   She'd have . . . for her!] Cut from the typescript and omit-ted in the Lippincott and later editions.

600.33–601.28   The other . . . married.] Cut from the typescript and omitted in the Lippincott and later editions.

606.6–17   It is like . . . go back.] Cut from the typescript and omitted in the Lippincott and later editions.

621.40   hoo-raw's nest.] Jumbled mess (a hoorah is an imaginary bird of untidy habits).

640.5–641.23   I cleared . . . hat.] Cut from the typescript and omitted in the Lippincott and later editions.

641.35–644.9   The sick . . . pay.] Cut from the typescript and omitted in the Lippincott and later editions.

651.35–652.9   He waylaid . . . joke was. Then] Cut from the typescript and omitted in the Lippincott and later editions.

654.7–655.21   This hilarious . . . after that,] Cut from the typescript and omitted in the Lippincott and later editions.

656.5–662.8   Of course, . . . sweetheart.] Cut in galleys and omitted in the Lippincott and later editions.

663.17–18   Farrar, . . . Matzenauer] American dramatic soprano Geral-dine Farrar (1882–1967), Austrian-American contralto Ernestine Schumann-Heink (1861–1936), also known for singing German lieder, and Hungarian mezzo-soprano Margarete Matzenauer (1881–1963) were with the Metropoli-tan Opera. Scottish-born soprano Mary Garden (1874?–1967) was with the Chicago Opera, and Emma Trentini (1881?–1959), Italian star of the Manhat-tan Opera, 1906–10, was then appearing in Broadway operettas and vaude-ville.

663.25–664.35   I can see . . . yourself.] Cut from the typescript and omitted in the Lippincott and later editions.

663.29–33   *The Chocolate. . . Firefly*] Oscar Straus's *Der tapfere Soldat*

(1908; titled *The Chocolate Soldier*, New York, 1909), based on George Bernard Shaw's *Arms and the Man*, and *The Firefly* (1912), romantic comic operetta written for Emma Trentini, music by Rudolf Friml and words by Otto Harbach.

673.23   Kelly Miller] At Howard University from 1890 to 1934, Miller (1863–1939) served as professor of mathematics and sociology; as dean of the College of Arts and Sciences, 1907–19, he oversaw the modernization of the curriculum and a substantial increase in enrollment. He was also known for his writings and lectures on education and race.

676.2–5   such as commenting . . . bed!"] Cut in galleys and omitted in the Lippincott and later editions.

677.33–678.6   The mental . . . shop.] Cut in galleys and omitted in the Lippincott and later editions.

681.21–32   One day . . . shell again.] Cut from the typescript and omitted in the Lippincott and later editions.

682.29–37   and when we . . . happened.] Cut from the typescript and omitted in the Lippincott and later editions.

688.13–14   Richmond Barthe] African-American sculptor (1901–89) known for his black figures. Barthé won Rosenwald (1928–29) and Guggenheim (1940–41) fellowships and his work was displayed in major galleries and museums in New York City and at the 1939 World's Fair.

692.1–13   Evalina! . . . thighs.] Cut in galleys and omitted in the Lippincott and later editions.

692.22   'Cause . . . on it.] Cut from the typescript and omitted in the Lippincott and later editions.

693.26–28   and don't git . . . into one.] Partially cut in the typescript and in galleys and omitted in the Lippincott and later editions.

694.3   Honey, . . . low] Cut in galleys and omitted in the Lippincott and later editions.

694.4–10   "It's de . . . make me ——] Cut in galleys and omitted in the Lippincott and later editions.

694.20–21   Dat white . . . butt-hole.] Cut in galleys and omitted in the Lippincott and later editions.

697.16–17   She done kilt . . . here.] Cut in galleys and omitted in the Lippincott and later editions.

699.27   "two-headed"] In *Mules and Men*, defined as doctors of conjure, so-called because they had "twice as much sense."

702.30   George Schuyler] Schuyler (1895–1977) was an African-American journalist, satirist, columnist for the Pittsburgh *Courier* (from 1924) and author of *Black No More* (1931) and *Slaves Today* (1932). In later life he was known for his political conservatism.

703.18–706.10   A most dramatic . . . fight.]   Cut in galleys and omitted in the Lippincott and later editions.

708.6–8   Imagine . . . Hague!]   Cut in galleys and omitted in the Lippincott and later editions.

711.30   I went Canzo]   See page 448.6–452.22 in this volume.

717.20–21   Spartan . . . cloak.]   In Plutarch's life of Lycurgus, Spartan stoicism is illustrated by a youth who maintains his composure while a stolen fox cub, hidden under his cloak, gnaws at his vitals.

722.20–21   Negro . . . Hill.]   The Ninth and Tenth Cavalry, African-American units, and Roosevelt's Rough Riders (First Volunteer Cavalry) were among the units that took Kettle Hill during the American attack on the San Juan heights overlooking Santiago de Cuba, July 1, 1898, in an important battle of the Spanish-American War.

731.15–28   So I . . . nothing neither."]   These paragraphs were transposed in typescript and in the Lippincott and later editions.

735.7–30   On another . . . played.]   Cut in galleys and omitted in the Lippincott and later editions.

735.34–35   Elizabeth Marbury]   An author's representative, writer, and French translator; Marbury (1856–1933) became Hurston's literary agent in 1931.

737.26–35   A man . . . fruit?]   Cut in galleys and omitted in the Lippincott and later editions.

738.19   Wong . . . Knopf,]   Wong (1908–81) was an American actress. Blanche Wolf Knopf (d. 1966) worked with her husband, publisher Alfred A. Knopf.

740.10–35   "Cabins . . . Dunham group]   The Broadway musical *Cabin in the Sky* starring Waters and featuring Dunham (see note 294.15–16) and her company opened in October 1940; choreography was by Dunham, book by Lynn Root, lyrics by John Latouche, music by Vernon Duke.They were also principals in the 1943 film version.

740.30–741.18   She has been . . . teen-age girl.]   Cut in galleys and omitted in the Lippincott and later editions.

744.37   P.M.P.]   Changed to "A.W.P." in the Lippincott and later editions.

761.26–763.13   Will military . . . casting office.]   Cut in galleys and omitted in the Lippincott and later editions.

765.29–766.11   I see too, . . . we want!"]   Cut in galleys and omitted in the Lippincott and later editions.

773.24–26   Just . . . Campbell]   Just (1883–1941), a research scientist and zoologist at Howard University, visiting researcher in Germany, Italy, and France, and editor of leading scientific journals, initiated studies of marine eggs and formulated new concepts of cell life and metabolism; Harris (1899–1963), an economist, author, and supporter of an integrated labor movement, was head of the economics department at Howard University, 1936–45, and professor at the University of Chicago, 1946–63; Campbell (1906–71), a painter and cartoonist whose work would continue to appear in major magazines, also created the syndicated cartoon "Cuties." For Barthé, see note 688.13–14.

777.5   asterperious]   Haughty (a combination of "Astor" and "imperious").

778.3   Georgette Harvey]   Harvey (1884?–1952) starred in Broadway comedies and dramas.

778.17   Black Patti]   Operatic soprano Sissieretta Jones (1868–1933) was dubbed by the press the "Black Patti" after Italian opera star Adelina Patti (1843–1919), a term her manager used, although Jones found it condescending. She made concert tours of the West Indies and Europe, sang at the White House and the 1892 Pittsburgh Exposition, but was barred from singing at the Metropolitan Opera because of her race; she concluded her career touring the nation as the star of *Black Patti's Troubadours,* 1893–1916.

778.17–18   Rose McClendon . . . Barrymore]   McClendon (1884 or 1885–1936), an outstanding stage actress of the 1920s and 1930s, also starred in the "John Henry, Black River Giant" radio series and was an organizer of the Negro People's Theater. Ethel Barrymore (1879–1959) is said to have remarked in 1926 that McClendon could "teach all of them [actresses] distinction."

778.25–27   Julian . . . Eagle]   Pilot, adventurer, lecturer, and Harlem celebrity Hubert Fauntleroy Julian (b. 1897) was dubbed "the Black Eagle" by the press in 1923 for his exploits as a stunt parachutist. On July 4, 1924, three years before Lindbergh's solo transatlantic flight, Julian launched the hydroplane *Ethiopia I* from the Harlem River, planning to be the first person to fly solo to Africa. Shortly after takeoff the aircraft was pulled off balance by a damaged pontoon and crashed into Flushing Bay. Julian survived the crash.

790.14–15   the flowers . . . case.]   Cf. Gilbert and Sullivan, *The Mikado* (1885), Act 2: "The flowers that bloom in the spring, tra la, / Have nothing to do with the case."

792.37   four freedoms]   In a message to Congress, January 6, 1941, Franklin Roosevelt said "we look forward to a world founded on four basic human freedoms": freedom of speech and expression, freedom of worship, freedom from want, and freedom from fear.

802.25 [   ]] Brackets indicate an illegible word in the holograph manuscript.

807.5 Whipper] Actor and writer Leigh Whipper (1876?–1975) was featured in New York plays including *In Abraham's Bosom* (1926), *Porgy* (1927), *Of Mice and Men* (1937; and film, 1939), and *Stevedore* (1939); he appeared in other films including *The Ox-Bow Incident* (1943); with Billy Mills he wrote the Broadway show *Yeah Man* (1932).

808.30 Katherine Dunham] See note 294.15–16; in the 1940s Dunham and her company toured the United States, and after the war, Europe.

SELECTED ARTICLES

823.36 inside.] No more of the "Pants and Cal'line" incident appeared in *The Messenger*; for a related story, see pages 573.37–575.11 in this volume.

824.12 a lark . . . settin'?] In the traditional African-American courting riddle, a flying lark is a woman in search of a mate, while a setting dove is a woman who has found one.

824.22 mud-cat] The flathead catfish.

829.8 Peggy . . . Mich] Joyce (1893?–1957) was an American showgirl; the Boulevard St. Michel in Paris is called the Boul'Mich.

830.29 *Sartor Resartus*] By Thomas Carlyle.

835.13–14 Bo-Jangles and Snake Hips] Bill "Bojangles" Robinson, considered the originator of modern tap-dancing, and Earl "Snake-Hips" Tucker, a nightclub and Broadway star known for his acrobatic and "shimmy" dancing and "barrelhousing" hip movements.

839.8 "Shake . . . lak dat."] Blues standards that were originally folk songs. "Shake That Thing" was featured by Ethel Waters in 1921 and recorded by her and Charlie Jackson in 1925.

839.37–38 "Open . . . arrived at."] "Open covenants of peace, openly arrived at" was one of the Fourteen Points Woodrow Wilson presented in his message to Congress on January 18, 1918, outlining American terms for ending World War I.

844.38–39 Ann . . . Bottom.] Pennington "introduced" the dance in George White's *Scandals* in 1926.

845.8 Fisk Jubilee Singers] Organized in 1867 by George L. White, treasurer of Fisk University, the group gained fame performing Negro spirituals in concert tours of the United States and Europe.

845.34   Butter Beans and Susie] Jodie "Butterbeans" and Susie Haw-
thorne Edwards, vaudeville performers who toured the country as "Butterbeans and Susie" after their on-stage marriage in 1917. Besides performing
comedy sketches, he danced (specializing in the "Heebie Jeebies") and she
sang the blues; the act concluded with an old-fashioned cakewalk.

879.24   Drive . . . down.] This line, inadvertently omitted in the typescript, is taken from an earlier version.

884.35–888.33   Ole Massa . . . so bad.] For another version, cf. page
82.24–85.40 in this volume.

892.2   Carita Doggett Corse] Corse was state director of the Federal
Writers' Project in Florida and author of *Dr. Andrew Turnbull and the New
Smyrna Colony* (1919).

892.22–893.36   "You know God . . . since."] For another version, cf.
page 603.17–604.38 in this volume.

903.21   the   Psalm] Psalm 19:14 (Hurston left a blank space in the
manuscript).

903.30–32   Beloved . . . is).] 1 John 3:2.

909.10   Augusta Savage] Hurston noted her intention to add a list of
Savage's work, but failed to include it. A leading artist of the Harlem Renaissance, Savage (1892–1962) was born in Florida. Her works, variously executed
in plaster, marble, and wood, include *Lift Every Voice and Sing,* a harp-shaped
group sculpture exhibited at the 1939 New York World's Fare; *Martiniquaise;
Envy; Gamin,* a figure of an African-American city youth; *After the Glory,* a
condemnation of war, and sculptures of W.E.B. Du Bois and Marcus Garvey,
among others. She was a supervisor of the Works Progress Administration
Arts Projects and the first director of the Harlem Community Art Center.

909.23   "Negro . . . Anthem"] "Lift Every Voice and Sing" (1899).

915.4   Bilbo, . . . Tillman] U.S. senators Theodore Gilman Bilbo
(1877–1947) of Mississippi, James Thomas Heflin (1869–1951) of Alabama,
and Benjamin Ryan Tillman (1847–1918) of South Carolina were leading
spokesmen for white supremacy.

920.36   Henry Allen Moe] Moe (b. 1894) was secretary of the John
Simon Guggenheim Memorial Foundation and lecturer at Columbia University School of Law.

931.12   Tar Baby.] An effigy set up to trap a curious trickster in various
Negro folk-tales.

942.23   George S. Schuyler] See note 702.30.

945.7–8   "The Arsenal of Democracy."] In a fireside chat, December 29,
1940, President Roosevelt argued that aid to Great Britain was essential to

American national defense, and said: "We must be the great arsenal of democracy."

945.22   Atlantic Charter]   Name for a declaration of principles issued August 14, 1941, by Roosevelt and Prime Minister Churchill following their shipboard conference off Newfoundland. It outlined in eight points policies which they hoped would shape the postwar world, including "the right of all peoples to choose the form of government under which they will live."

945.28–29   Four Freedoms]   See note 792.37.

946.30   double-teened]   See note 586.27.

946.38   Javanese man]   Indonesian nationalist leader Sukarno (1901–70), who had collabaorated with the Japanese during their occupation of the Dutch East Indies, 1942–45. In August 1945 Sukarno and other nationalists declared independence from the Netherlands. Indonesia became a sovereign republic in 1949.

948.39   scrapping of FEPC]   The federal Fair Employment Practices Commission was established in 1941 by an executive order forbidding discrimination in the employment of workers in government and defense industries. Congress failed to act on a proposal to create a permanent peacetime FEPC and denied the commission funding in 1945; it was terminated in 1946.

952.25   author . . . *Sister Mary*]   South Carolina novelist Julia Peterkin (1880–1961).

956.4–5   U.S. . . . schools]   In *Brown* v. *Board of Education,* decided May 17, 1954, the Supreme Court unanimously ruled that segregation in public schools violated the equal protection clause of the Fourteenth Amendment and that the "separate but equal" doctrine established in the *Plessy* v. *Ferguson* decision (1896) had no place in public education because separate educational facilities were "inherently unequal."

CATALOGING INFORMATION

Hurston, Zora Neale.
  [Selections. 1995]
  Folklore, memoirs, and other writings / Zora Neale Hurston.
  Edited by Cheryl A. Wall.
      p.   cm. — (The Library of America ; 75)
  Contents: Mules and men—Tell my horse—Dust tracks on a road—
Selected articles.
  1. Folklorists—United States—Biography.   2. Afro-American novelists—
20th century—Biography.   3. Afro-Americans—Folklore.   I. Title.
II. Mules and men.   III. Tell my horse.   IV. Dust tracks on a road.
V. Series.
GR55.H86A3   1995   94-21384
398'.092—dc20
ISBN 0-940450-84-4

THE LIBRARY OF AMERICA SERIES

This book is set in 10 point Linotron Galliard,
a face designed for photocomposition by Matthew Carter
and based on the sixteenth-century face Granjon. The paper is
acid-free Ecusta Nyalite and meets the requirements for permanence
of the American National Standards Institute. The binding
material is Brillianta, a woven rayon cloth made by
Van Heek-Scholco Textielfabrieken, Holland.
The composition is by The Clarinda
Company. Printing and binding by
R. R. Donnelley & Sons Company.
Designed by Bruce Campbell.

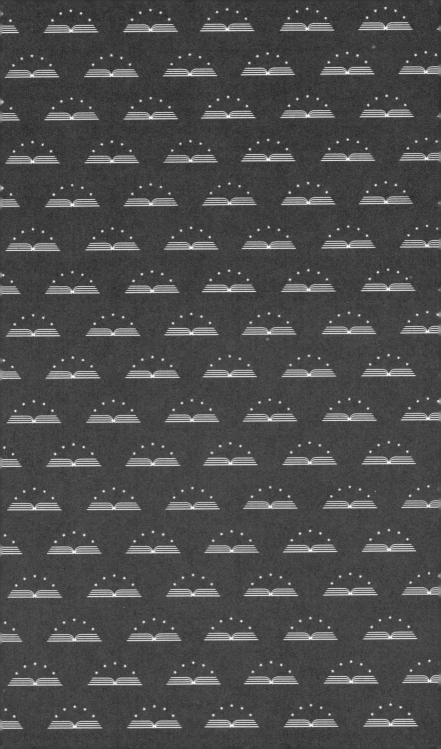